Manchester College Library.

163
———
W2

NO. 83

Lincoln Literary Fraternity
LIBRARY.

Presented by

J. C. Murray

Date 1896

No book to be taken from the Hall without the permission of the librarian.

FRONTISPIECE.—"STORY OF THE BIBLE ANIMALS."

THE ANIMALS ENTER THE ARK.

Story of the Bible Animals

A Description of the
Habits and Uses of every living
Creature mentioned in the Scriptures,

WITH

EXPLANATION OF PASSAGES IN THE OLD AND NEW TESTAMENTS IN
WHICH REFERENCE IS MADE TO THEM.

BY

J. G. WOOD,

AUTHOR OF "HOMES WITHOUT HANDS,"
"THE ILLUSTRATED NATURAL HISTORY," ETC.

---

300 ILLUSTRATIONS.

PUBLISHED BY THE
CHARLES FOSTER PUBLISHING CO.,
No. 716 Sansom Street,
PHILADELPHIA, PA.

WAR-HORSES AND ANCIENT EGYPTIAN CHARIOT.

See page 307.

PREFACE.

Owing to the different conditions of time, language, country, and race under which the various books of the Holy Scriptures were written, it is impossible that they should be rightly understood at the present day without some study of the customs and manners of Eastern peoples, as well as of the countries in which they lived.

The Oriental character of the scriptural writings causes them to abound with metaphors and symbols taken from the common life of the time.

They contain allusions to the trees, flowers, and herbage, the creeping things of the earth, the fishes of the sea, the birds of the air, and the beasts which abode with man or dwelt in the deserts and forests.

Unless, therefore, we understand these writings as those understood them for whom they were written, it is evident that we shall misinterpret instead of rightly comprehending them.

The field which is laid open to us is so large that only one department of Natural History—namely, Zoology—can be treated in this work, although it is illustrated by many references to other branches of Natural History, to the physical geography of Palestine, Egypt, and Syria, the race-character of the inhabitants, and historical parallels.

The importance of understanding the nature, habits, and uses of the animals which are constantly mentioned in the Bible, cannot be overrated as a means of elucidating the Scriptures, and without this knowledge we shall not only miss the point of innumerable passages of the Old and New Testaments, but the words of our Lord Himself will often be totally misinterpreted, or at least lose part of their significance.

The object of the present work is therefore, to take in its proper succession, every creature whose name is given in the Scriptures, and to supply so much of its history as will enable the reader to understand all the passages in which it is mentioned.

SHEPHERD LEADING SHEEP AND GOATS TO THEIR FOLD IN THE ROCK.
See page 191.

THE AUTHOR.

The Rev. J. G. Wood is a native of London, England. He was educated at Oxford University, and has long been known, both in England and America, as not only a learned and accurate writer on Natural History, but a popular one as well, having the happy faculty of making the results of scientific study and painstaking observation, interesting and instructive to all classes of readers.

He has published a number of works on the most familiar departments of the history of animals, designed to awaken popular interest in the study. Their titles are "Sketches and Anecdotes of Animal Life;" "Common Objects of the Seashore and Country;" "My Feathered Friends;" "Homes Without Hands"—being a description of the habitations of animals,—and the "Illustrated Natural History," a book which is widely known both in England and America as a standard work of great value. It has given the author celebrity, and has caused him to be considered an eminent authority on the subject which it treats.

It is evident, from these facts, that it would be difficult to find a man better qualified than Mr. Wood, to write a book describing the animals mentioned in the Bible.

Profoundly impressed with the ignorance which prevails towards so important a feature of the Scriptural Narrative, he has devoted his ripe powers and special knowledge to the work of dissipating it, and in this volume, not only fully describes the nature and habits of all the animals mentioned in the Scriptures, but tells the story of their relations to mankind.

Mr. Wood is a clergyman of the Church of England, and was for a time connected with Christ Church, Oxford. He has devoted himself mainly, however, to authorship in the field which he has chosen, and in which he has become so well known. In his works he usually employs a popular style of writing, and does not make scientific terms prominent. This is especially true of the "Story of the Bible Animals," which from its easy and interesting character is adapted to the comprehension of young and old.

viii

ANY of the pictures in this book are taken from the living animals, or from photographs and sketches by Eastern travellers. Others represent imaginary scenes, or ancient historical events, and have been designed by skillful artists after careful study of the subjects.

LIST OF ILLUSTRATIONS.

[A complete Index of Subjects will be found at the end of this Volume.]

NO.		PAGE
1.	THE ANIMALS ENTER THE ARK	2
2.	WAR-HORSES AND ANCIENT EGYPTIAN CHARIOT	4
3.	SHEPHERD LEADING SHEEP AND GOATS TO THEIR FOLD IN THE ROCK	6
4.	A DESERT-SCENE	8
5.	THE GARDEN OF EDEN	19
6.	LION DRINKING AT A POOL	21
7.	A LION KILLS THE PROPHET FROM JUDAH	22
8.	LION AND TIGER	23
9.	THE LION REPLIES TO THE THUNDER	25
10.	LIONESS AND YOUNG	27
11.	LION CARRYING HOME SUPPLIES	31
12.	AFRICAN LIONS	32
13.	THE LION ATTACKS THE HERD	34
14.	THE LAIR OF THE LION	35
15.	THE LION LISTENS TO THE APPROACH OF THE HUNTER	39
16.	THE LEOPARD	43
17.	LEOPARD ATTACKING A HERD OF DEER	45
18.	THE LEOPARD LEAPS UPON HIS PREY	47
19.	WAITING	49
20.	LEOPARD	51
21.	CAT AND KITTENS	52
22.	CAT	54
23.	DOGS IN AN EASTERN CITY AT NIGHT	57
24.	SHIMEI EXULTING OVER KING DAVID	59
25.	LAZARUS LYING AT THE RICH MAN'S DOOR	62
26.	THE DEATH OF JEZEBEL	63

STORY OF THE BIBLE ANIMALS.

NO.		PAGE
27.	Syrian Dog	64
28.	Eastern Water-Seller	68
29.	Wolves Attacking a Flock of Sheep	70
30.	Wolves Chasing Deer	72
31.	The Wolf	73
32.	Wolves Attacking Wild Goats	75
33.	The Jackal	76
34.	Foxes or Jackals Devouring the Carcase of a Goat	77
35.	A Feast in Prospect	79
36.	A Feast Secured	81
37.	A Trespasser	83
38.	Leopard Robbed of its Prey by Hyænas	87
39.	Hyænas Devouring Bones	89
40.	Weasels	93
41.	The Bitter Bit	95
42.	Badgers	99
43.	Supposed Form and Arrangement of the Tabernacle	101
44.	Bears Descending the Mountains	105
45.	On the Watch	107
46.	Seeking an Outlook	109
47.	A Family Party	111
48.	Bear	112
49.	Porcupine	113
50.	The Mole-Rat	115
51.	The Mouse	119
52.	Dagon Fallen Down before the Ark	120
53.	Mouse and Nest	121
54.	Jerboa or Leaping-Mouse	122
55.	The Field-Mouse	123
56.	The Syrian Hare	127
57.	A Timid Group	129
58.	Altar of Burnt-Offering	133
59.	The Prodigal Son Returns	134
60.	Abraham Offers Food to the Three Strangers	135
61.	Oxen Treading Out Grain	139
62.	Eastern Ox-Cart	140

LIST OF ILLUSTRATIONS.

NO.		PAGE
63.	The Ark of the Covenant being Drawn by Cows	141
64.	Ploughing with Oxen	143
65.	Mummy of a Sacred Bull taken from an Egyptian Tomb	146
66.	Animals being Sold for Sacrifice in the Porch of the Temple	147
67.	Jeroboam Sets up a Golden Calf at Bethel	148
68.	The Buffalo	149
69.	The Bhainsa, or Domestic Buffalo, and Camel Drawing the Plough	151
70.	Wild Bull or Oryx	155
71.	The Oryx	157
72.	The Unicorn	158
73.	The Bison	160
74.	Bison Killing Wolf	161
75.	The Gazelle or Roe of Scripture	163
76.	Gazelles	164
77.	The Falcon Used in Our Hunt	168
78.	The Arab is Delighted at the Success of the Hunt	169
79.	The Gazelle	170
80.	The Addax	172
81.	The Bubale or Fallow Deer of Scripture	175
82.	Sheep	176
83.	Arabs Journeying to Fresh Pastures	178
84.	View of the Pyramids	179
85.	Jacob Meets Rachel at the Well	182
86.	Eastern Shepherd Watching his Flock	183
87.	David Gathers Stones from the Brook to Cast at Goliath	185
88.	An Eastern Shepherd	186
89.	Sheep Following their Shepherd	187
90.	Ancient Sheep-Pen	190
91.	The Poor Man's Lamb	193
92.	The Rich Man's Feast	193
93.	Flocks of Sheep being taken into Jerusalem	195
94.	Sounding the Trumpets in the Year of Jubilee	202
95.	Ram's Horn Trumpet	203

NO.		PAGE
96.	A Lamb upon the Altar of Burnt Offering	204
97.	The Place of Sacrifice	206
98.	The Chamois	211
99.	Chamois Defending its Young	213
100.	Chasing the Aoudad	214
101.	The Mouflon	216
102.	Jacob Deceives his Father and Takes Esau's Blessing	218
103.	The Angel Appears to Gideon	219
104.	Eastern Water-Carriers with Bottles made of Goat-Skin	224
105.	Goats on the March	228
106.	Herd of Goats Attacked by a Lion	231
107.	Arabian Ibex, the Wild Goat of Scripture	236
108.	The Deer	238
109.	Red Deer	239
110.	Fallow Deer or Hind of Scripture	240
111.	A Quiet Spot	241
112.	Red Deer and Fawn	243
113.	The Leader of the Herd	245
114.	The Watchful Doe	247
115.	A Kneeling Camel	248
116.	Jacob Leaves Laban and Returns to Canaan	249
117.	A Camp in the Desert	250
118.	A Grateful Shade	253
119.	Camels Laden with Boughs	257
120.	Morning in the Desert: Starting of the Caravan	258
121.	The Camel Post	261
122.	A Runaway	263
123.	An Arab Sheik Mounted Upon his Camel	264
124.	Aaron's Rod Bears Almonds	266
125.	Camel Riding	267
126.	The Deloul, or Swift Camel	268
127.	Another Mode of Riding the Camel	270
128.	Passing a Camel in a Narrow Street of an Eastern City	277
129.	Moses at the Burning Bush	278

LIST OF ILLUSTRATIONS.

NO.		PAGE
130.	An Arab Encampment	279
131.	On the March	281
132.	Hair of the Camel	283
133.	Camel Going through a "Needle's Eye"	285
134.	A Rest in the Desert	287
135.	Bactrian Camels Drawing Cart	289
136.	Trial of Arab Horses	292
137.	An Arab Horse of the Kochlani Breed	293
138.	The War-Horse	295
139.	Arab Horses	297
140.	Buying an Arab Horse	299
141.	The Arab's Favorite Steeds	301
142.	Pharaoh Pursues the Israelites with Chariots and Horses, and the Sea covers them	302
143.	Elijah is Carried Up	304
144.	The Israelites, led by Joshua, take Jericho	308
145.	Ancient Battlefield	309
146.	Chariot of State	311
147.	Ancient Egyptian Sculpture Representing a Victorious King in his Chariot Slaying his Enemies	313
148.	Mummy of an Egyptian King over Three Thousand Years Old	314
149.	Ass and Driver	315
150.	Entering Jerusalem	317
151.	Syrian Asses	319
152.	A Street in Cairo, Egypt	322
153.	Beggar in the Streets of Cairo	324
154.	Night-Watch in Cairo	325
155.	Hunting Wild Asses	331
156.	Mules of the East	334
157.	Absalom is Caught in the Boughs of an Oak Tree	335
158.	Daniel Refuses to Eat the King's Meat	337
159.	The Prodigal Son	340
160.	Eleazar Refuses to Eat Swine's Flesh	341
161.	A Mother and her Seven Sons Tortured for Refusing to Eat Swine's Flesh	342

STORY OF THE BIBLE ANIMALS

NO.		PAGE
162.	The Evil Spirits enter a Herd of Swine	343
163.	Wild Boars Devouring the Carcase of a Deer	344
164.	Wild Boars	345
165.	Wild Boars Destroying a Vineyard	347
166.	Indian Elephant	349
167.	King Solomon, Seated upon his Throne, Receives the Queen of Sheba	350
168.	Indian Elephants	351
169.	The War-Elephant	355
170.	African Elephants	359
171.	Elephants' Watering-Place	361
172.	Tiger	363
173.	Tiger in the Reeds	364
174.	Head of Tiger	365
175.	The Hyrax	367
176.	Hippopotamus	372
177.	Hippopotamus Pool	375
178.	The Great Jaws of the Hippopotamus	376
179.	Hippopotamus Emerging from the River	377
180.	Hippopotamus Eating Grass	379
181.	A Hippopotamus-Hunt in Egypt	381
182.	Hippopotamus and Trap	384
183.	The Baboon	387
184.	The Rhesus Monkey	389
185.	Feeding the Monkeys in India	390
186.	Troublesome Neighbors	391
187.	Monkeys Entering a Plantation	392
188.	Slothful Monkeys	393
189.	A Privileged Race	394
190.	The Wanderoo	396
191.	The Enemy Discovered	397
192.	Bonnet Monkeys	399
193.	The Bat	401
194.	Bats' Resting-Place	403
195.	Great Fox-Headed Bat, or Flying Fox	405
196.	Cave near the Site of Ancient Jericho	406

LIST OF ILLUSTRATIONS.

NO.		PAGE
197.	Night in the Tropics	407
198.	Leopards	408
199.	The Home of the Vulture	411
200.	The Lammergeier	412
201.	A Successful Defence	415
202.	Struck from a Dizzy Height	417
203.	The Vulture's Nest	418
204.	The Egyptian Vulture, or Gier Eagle	420
205.	Vultures	425
206.	The Eagle and the Hare	430
207.	Eagles	432
208.	Eagle Returning to the Nest with her Prey	435
209.	The Osprey Searching for Fish	437
210.	Snatched from the Deep: The Osprey Rises with his Prey	439
211.	The Kite, or Vulture of Scripture	441
212.	The Peregrine Falcon, or Glede	444
213.	The Lanner Falcon	446
214.	The Hawk	447
215.	Kestrel Hovering Over a Field in Search of Prey	449
216.	The Windhover, or Kestrel	450
217.	The Barn Owl	454
218.	The Little Owl	456
219.	Caught Napping	457
220.	Raven.—Barn Owl.—Eagle Owl	459
221.	A Family Council	460
222.	The Night Hawk on the Wing	462
223.	The Night Hawk	463
224.	The Swallow	466
225.	Lost from the Flock	469
226.	The Swallow and Swift	471
227.	View of the Sea of Galilee	472
228.	The Swallow's Favorite Haunt	473
229.	Swallows at Home	475
230.	The Hoopoe	478
231.	Eastern Housetops	479

NO.		PAGE
232.	READING THE LAW TO THE PEOPLE AFTER THE RETURN FROM CAPTIVITY	482
233.	THE BLUE THRUSH, OR SPARROW OF SCRIPTURE	483
234.	THE TREE SPARROW	485
235.	SPARROWS	486
236.	A FOREST SCENE	487
237.	THE GREAT SPOTTED CUCKOO	488
238.	NOAH RECEIVES THE DOVE	489
239.	JESUS DRIVES OUT OF THE TEMPLE THE MONEYCHANGERS AND THOSE WHO SOLD DOVES	493
240.	THE ROCK DOVE	494
241.	BLUE ROCK PIGEONS	495
242.	THE TURTLE DOVE	497
243.	THE HEN AND HER BROOD	498
244.	THE DOMESTIC FOWL	499
245.	POULTRY	500
246.	THE PEACOCK	501
247.	PEAFOWL	503
248.	FEATHERS OF THE PEACOCK	504
249.	PARTRIDGES	505
250.	THE GREEK PARTRIDGE	507
251.	PARTRIDGE AND THEIR YOUNG	508
252.	EASTERN QUAIL	509
253.	THE QUAIL	510
254.	FLIGHT OF QUAIL	515
255.	THE RAVEN	517
256.	ELIJAH FED BY RAVENS	518
257.	RAVENS' ROOSTING-PLACE	521
258.	RAVENS' NEST	522
259.	OSTRICH AND NEST	527
260.	ARABS HUNTING THE OSTRICH	533
261.	THE BITTERN	537
262.	BITTERN AND CORMORANT	539
263.	THE HOME OF THE BITTERN	541
264.	THE HERON	543
265.	THE HOME OF THE HERON	545

LIST OF ILLUSTRATIONS.

NO.		PAGE
266.	The Papyrus Plant	548
267.	The Home of the Crane	549
268.	The Crane	550
269.	The Stork	553
270.	Storks and their Nests	555
271.	A Nest of the White Stork	559
272.	Ibis and Gallinule	561
273.	The Pelican	568
274.	Lizards	575
275.	Tortoises	577
276.	The Dhubb and the Tortoise	578
277.	Water Tortoise	579
278.	Crocodile Attacking Horses	587
279.	A Crocodile Pool of Ancient Egypt	590
280.	Crocodiles of the Upper Nile	591
281.	Ichneumon Devouring the Eggs of the Crocodile	597
282.	A Crocodile Trap	599
283.	A Fight for Life	601
284.	The Cyprius, or Lizard	602
285.	The Chameleon	605
286.	Gecko and Chameleon	606
287.	The Gecko	609
288.	Serpents	611
289.	Boa Constrictor and Tiger	613
290.	Cobra and Cerastes	615
291.	The Israelites are Bitten by Serpents in the Wilderness, and Moses Lifts Up the Serpent of Brass	616
292.	The Serpent-Charmer	619
293.	The Viper	621
294.	Teaching Cobras to Dance	623
295.	Horned Viper	625
296.	The Viper, or Epheh	627
297.	The Toxicoa	628
298.	The Frog	630
299.	Fishes	633
300.	A River Scene	635

NO.		PAGE
301.	Peter Catches the Fish	636
302.	Muræna, Long-Headed Barbel, and Sheat Fish	638
303.	Sucking Fish, Tunny, and Coryphene	640
304.	Fishing Scene on the Sea of Galilee	642
305.	Mode of Dragging the Seine Net	645
306.	Nile Perch, Surmullet, and Stargazer	647
307.	The Pearl Oyster	653
308.	Insects	655
309.	A Swarm of Locusts	659
310.	The Locust	663
311.	The Bee	665
312.	The Hornet and its Nest	669
313.	Ants on the March	671
314.	Ant of Palestine	675
315.	The Crimson Worm	677
316.	Mordecai is Led through the City upon the King's Horse	679
317.	Butterflies of Palestine	682
318.	Noxious Flies of Palestine	685
319.	The Scorpion	690
320.	Coral	694

STORY OF THE BIBLE ANIMALS.

THE LION.

Frequent mention of the Lion in the Scriptures—The Lion employed as an emblem in the Bible—Similarity of the African and Asiatic species—The chief characteristics of the Lion—its strength, activity, and mode of seizing its prey—The Lion hunt.

Of all the undomesticated animals of Palestine, none is mentioned so frequently as the Lion. This may appear the more remarkable, because for many years the Lion has been extinct in Palestine. The leopard, the wolf, the jackal, and the hyæna, still retain their place in the land, although their numbers are comparatively few; but the Lion has vanished completely out of the land. The reason for this disappearance is twofold, first, the thicker population; and second, the introduction of firearms.

No animal is less tolerant of human society than the Lion. In the first place, it dreads the very face of man, and as a rule, whenever it sees a man will slink away and hide itself. There are, of course, exceptional cases to this rule. Sometimes a Lion becomes so old and stiff, his teeth are so worn, and his endurance so slight, that he is unable to chase his usual prey, and is obliged to seek for other means of subsistence. In an unpopulated district, he would simply be starved to death, but when his lot is cast in the neighbourhood of human beings, he is perforce obliged to become a " man-eater." Even in that case, a Lion will seldom attack a man, unless he should be able to do so unseen, but will hang about the villages, pouncing on the women as they come to the wells for water, or upon the little children as they stray from their parents, and continually shifting his quarters lest he should be assailed during his sleep. The Lion requires a very large tract of country for his maintenance, and the consequence is, that in proportion as the land is populated does the number of Lions decrease.

Firearms are the special dread of the Lion. In the first place, the Lion, like all wild beasts, cannot endure fire, and the flash of the gun terrifies him greatly. Then, there is the report, surpassing even his roar in resonance; and lastly, there is the unseen bullet, which seldom kills him at once, but mostly drives him to furious anger by the pain of his wound, yet which he does not dread nearly so much as the harmless flash and report. There is another cause of the Lion's banishment from the Holy Land. It is well known that to attract any wild beast or bird to some definite spot, all that is required is to provide them with a suitable and undisturbed home, and a certainty of food. Consequently, the surest method of driving them away is to deprive them of both these essentials. Then the Lion used to live in forests, which formerly stretched over large tracts of ground, but which have long since been cut down, thus depriving the Lion of its home, while the thick population and the general use of firearms have deprived him of his food. In fact, the Lion has been driven out of Palestine, just as the wolf has been extirpated from England.

But, in the olden times, Lions must have been very plentiful. There is scarcely a book in the Bible, whether of the Old or New Testaments, whether historical or prophetical, that does not contain some mention of this terrible animal; sometimes describing the actions of individual Lions, but mostly using the

THE LION. 21

LION DRINKING AT A POOL.

word as an emblem of strength and force, whether used for a good purpose or abused for a bad one.

There are several varieties of Lion, which may be reduced to two, namely, the African and the Asiatic Lion. It is almost certain, however, that these animals really are one and the same species, and that the trifling differences which exist between an African and an Asiatic Lion, are not sufficient to justify a naturalist in considering them to be distinct species. The habits of both are identical, modified, as is sure to be the case, by the difference of locality; but then, such variations in habit are con-

A LION KILLS THE PROPHET FROM JUDAH.

tinually seen in animals confessedly of the same species, which happen to be placed in different conditions of climate and locality.

That it was once exceedingly plentiful in Palestine is evident, from a very cursory knowledge of the Holy Scriptures. It is every where mentioned as a well-known animal, equally familiar and dreaded. When the disobedient prophet was killed by the Lion near Bethel, the fact seemed not to have caused any surprise in the neighbourhood. When the people came out to rescue the body of the prophet, they wondered much because the

Lion was standing by the fallen man, but had not torn him, and had left the ass unhurt. But that a Lion should have killed a man seems to have been an event which was not sufficiently rare to be surprising.

We will now proceed to those characteristics of the Lion which bear especial reference to the Scriptures.

In the first place, size for size, the Lion is one of the strongest of beasts.

LION AND TIGER.

Moreover, the strength of the Lion is equally distributed over the body and limbs, giving to the animal an easy grace of movement which is rare except with such a structure. A full-grown Lion cannot only knock down and kill, but can carry away in its mouth, an ordinary ox; and one of these terrible animals has been known to pick up a heifer in its mouth, and to leap over a wide ditch still carrying its burden. Another Lion carried a two-year old heifer, and was chased for five hours by mounted farmers, so that it must have traversed a very considerable distance. Yet, in the whole of this long journey, the legs of the heifer had only two or three times touched the ground.

It kills man, and comparatively small animals, such as deer and antelopes, with a blow of its terrible paw ; and often needs to give no second blow to cause the death of its victim. The sharp talons are not needed to cause death, for the weight of the blow is sufficient for that purpose.

When the hunter pursues it with dogs, after the usual fashion, there is often a great slaughter among them, especially among those that are inexperienced in the chase of the Lion. Urged by their instinctive antipathy, the dogs rush forward to the spot where the Lion awaits them, and old hounds bay at him from a safe distance, while the young and inexperienced among them are apt to convert the sham attack into a real one. Their valour meets with a poor reward, for a few blows from the Lion's terrible paws send his assailants flying in all directions, their bodies streaming with blood, and in most cases a fatal damage inflicted, while more than one unfortunate dog lies fairly crushed by the weight of a paw laid with apparent carelessness upon its body. There is before me a Lion's skin, a spoil of one of these animals shot by the celebrated sportsman, Gordon Cumming. Although the skin lies flat upon the floor, and the paws are nothing but the skin and talons, the weight of each paw is very considerable, and always surprises those who hear it fall on the floor.

There are several Hebrew words which are used for the Lion, but that which signifies the animal in its adult state is derived from an Arabic word signifying strength ; and therefore the Lion is called the Strong-one, just as the Bat is called the Night-flier. No epithet could be better deserved, for the Lion seems to be a very incarnation of strength, and, even when dead, gives as vivid an idea of concentrated power as when it was living. And, when the skin is stripped from the body, the tremendous muscular development never fails to create a sensation of awe. The muscles of the limbs, themselves so hard as to blunt the keen-edged knives employed by a dissecter, are enveloped in their glittering sheaths, playing upon each other like well-oiled machinery, and terminating in tendons seemingly strong as steel, and nearly as impervious to the knife. Not until the skin is removed can any one form a conception of the enormously powerful muscles of the neck, which enable the Lion to lift the

THE LION REPLIES TO THE THUNDER.

weighty prey which it kills, and to convey it to a place of security.

Although usually unwilling to attack an armed man, it is one of the most courageous animals in existence when it is driven to fight, and if its anger is excited, it cares little for the number of its foes, or the weapons with which they are armed. Even the dreaded firearms lose their terrors to an angry Lion, while a Lioness, who fears for the safety of her young, is simply the most terrible animal in existence. We know how even a hen will fight for her chickens, and how she has been known to beat off the fox and the hawk by the reckless fury of her attack. It may be easily imagined, therefore, that a Lioness actuated by equal courage, and possessed of the terrible weapons given to her by her Creator, would be an animal almost too formidable for the conception of those who have not actually witnessed the scene of a Lioness defending her little ones.

The roar of the Lion is another of the characteristics for which it is celebrated. There is no beast that can produce a sound that could for a moment be mistaken for the roar of the Lion. The Lion has a habit of stooping his head towards the ground when he roars, so that the terrible sound rolls along like thunder, and reverberates in many an echo in the far distance. Owing to this curious habit, the roar can be heard at a very great distance, but its locality is rendered uncertain, and it is often difficult to be quite sure whether the Lion is to the right or the left of the hearer.

There are few sounds which strike more awe than the Lion's roar. Even at the Zoological Gardens, where the hearer knows that he is in perfect safety, and where the Lion is enclosed in a small cage faced with strong iron bars, the sound of the terrible roar always has a curious effect upon the nerves. It is not exactly fear, because the hearer knows that he is safe; but it is somewhat akin to the feeling of mixed awe and admiration with which one listens to the crashing thunder after the lightning has sped its course. If such be the case when the Lion is safely housed in a cage, and is moreover so tame that even if he did escape, he would be led back by the keeper without doing any harm, the effect of the roar must indeed be terrific when the Lion is at liberty, when he is in his own country, and when the shades of evening prevent him from being seen even at a short distance.

LIONESS AND YOUNG.

In the dark, there is no animal so invisible as a Lion. Almost every hunter has told a similar story—of the Lion's approach at night, of the terror displayed by dogs and cattle as he drew near, and of the utter inability to see him, though he was so close that they could hear his breathing. Sometimes, when he has crept near an encampment, or close to a cattle inclosure, he does not proceed any farther lest he should venture within the radius illumined by the rays of the fire. So he crouches closely to the ground, and, in the semi-darkness, looks so like a large stone, or a little hillock, that any one might pass close to it without perceiving its real nature. This gives the opportunity for which the Lion has been watching, and in a moment he strikes down the careless straggler, and carries off his prey to the den. Sometimes, when very much excited, he accompanies the charge with a roar, but, as a general fact, he secures his prey in silence.

The roar of the Lion is very peculiar. It is not a mere outburst of sound, but a curiously graduated performance. No description of the Lion's roar is so vivid, so true, and so graphic as that of Gordon Cumming: "One of the most striking things connected with the Lion is his voice, which is extremely grand and peculiarly striking. It consists at times of a low, deep moaning, repeated five or six times, ending in faintly audible sighs. At other times he startles the forest with loud, deep-toned, solemn roars, repeated five or six times in quick succession, each increasing in loudness to the third or fourth, when his voice dies away in five or six low, muffled sounds, very much resembling distant thunder. As a general rule, Lions roar during the night, their sighing moans commencing as the shades of evening envelop the forest, and continuing at intervals throughout the night. In distant and secluded regions, however, I have constantly heard them roaring loudly as late as nine or ten o'clock on a bright sunny morning. In hazy and rainy weather they are to be heard at every hour in the day, but their roar is subdued."

Lastly, we come to the dwelling-place of the Lion. This animal always fixes its residence in the depths of some forest, through which it threads its stealthy way with admirable certainty. No fox knows every hedgerow, ditch, drain, and covert better than the Lion knows the whole country around his den.

Each Lion seems to have his peculiar district, in which only himself and his family will be found. These animals seem to parcel out the neighbourhood among themselves by a tacit law like that which the dogs of eastern countries have imposed upon themselves, and which forbids them to go out of the district in which they were born. During the night he traverses his dominions; and, as a rule, he retires to his den as soon as the sun is fairly above the horizon. Sometimes he will be in wait for prey in the broadest daylight, but his ordinary habits are nocturnal, and in the daytime he is usually asleep in his secret dwelling-place.

We will now glance at a few of the passages in which the Lion is mentioned in the Holy Scriptures, selecting those which treat of its various characteristics.

The terrible strength of the Lion is the subject of repeated reference. In the magnificent series of prophecies uttered by Jacob on his deathbed, the power of the princely tribe of Judah is predicted under the metaphor of a Lion—the beginning of its power as a Lion's whelp, the fulness of its strength as an adult Lion, and its matured establishment in power as the old Lion that couches himself and none dares to disturb him. Then Solomon, in the Proverbs, speaks of the Lion as the "strongest among beasts, and that turneth not away for any."

Solomon also alludes to its courage in the same book, Prov. xxviii. 1, in the well-known passage, "The wicked fleeth when no man pursueth: but the righteous are bold as a lion." And, in 2 Sam. xxiii. 20, the courage of Benaiah, one of the mighty three of David's army, is specially honoured, because he fought and killed a Lion single-handed, and because he conquered "two lion-like men of Moab." David, their leader, had also distinguished himself, when a mere keeper of cattle, by pursuing and killing a Lion that had come to plunder his herd. In the same book of Samuel which has just been quoted (xvii. 10), the valiant men are metaphorically described as having the hearts of Lions.

The ferocity of this terrible beast of prey is repeatedly mentioned, and the Psalms are full of such allusions, the fury and anger of enemies being compared to the attacks of the Lion.

Many passages refer to the Lion's roar, and it is remarkable that the Hebrew language contains several words by which the different kind of roar is described. One word, for example, represents the low, deep, thunder-like roar of the Lion seeking its prey, and which has already been mentioned. This is the word which is used in Amos iii. 4, "Will a lion roar in the forest when he hath no prey?" and in this passage the word which is translated as Lion signifies the animal when full grown and in the prime of life. Another word is used to signify the sudden exulting cry of the Lion as it leaps upon its victim. A third is used for the angry growl with which a Lion resents any endeavour to deprive it of its prey, a sound with which we are all familiar, on a miniature scale, when we hear a cat growling over a mouse which she has just caught. The fourth term signifies the peculiar roar uttered by the young Lion after it has ceased to be a cub and before it has attained maturity. This last term is employed in Jer. li. 38, "They shall *roar* together like lions; they shall *yell* as lions' whelps," in which passage two distinct words are used, one signifying the roar of the Lion when searching after prey, and the other the cry of the young Lions.

The prophet Amos, who in his capacity of herdsman was familiar with the wild beasts, from which he had to guard his cattle, makes frequent mention of the Lion, and does so with a force and vigour that betoken practical experience. How powerful is this imagery, "The lion hath roared; who will not fear? The Lord God hath spoken; who can but prophesy?" Here we have the picture of the man himself, the herdsman and prophet, who had trembled many a night, as the Lions drew nearer and nearer; and who heard the voice of the Lord, and his lips poured out prophecy. Nothing can be more complete than the parallel which he has drawn. It breathes the very spirit of piety, and may bear comparison even with the prophecies of Isaiah for its simple grandeur.

It is remarkable how the sacred writers have entered into the spirit of the world around them, and how closely they observed the minutest details even in the lives of the brute beasts. There is a powerful passage in the book of Job, iv. 11, "The old lion perisheth for lack of prey," in which the writer betrays his thorough knowledge of the habits of the animal, and is aware that the usual mode of a Lion's death is through hunger, in consequence of his increasing inability to catch prey.

The nocturnal habits of the Lion and its custom of lying in

THE LION.

wait for prey are often mentioned in the Scriptures. The former habit is spoken of in that familiar and beautiful passage in the Psalms (civ. 20), "Thou makest darkness, and it is night; wherein all the beasts of the forest do creep forth. The young Lions roar after their prey; and seek their meat from God. The sun ariseth, they gather themselves together, and lay them down in their dens."

LION CARRYING HOME SUPPLIES.

An animal so destructive among the flocks and herds could not be allowed to carry out its depredations unchecked, and as we have already seen, the warfare waged against it has been so successful, that the Lions have long ago been fairly extirpated in Palestine. The usual method of capturing or killing the Lion was by pitfalls or nets, to both of which there are many references in the Scriptures.

The mode of hunting the Lion with nets was identical with that which is practised in India at the present time. The precise locality of the Lion's dwelling-place having been discovered, a circular wall of net is arranged round it, or if only a few nets can be obtained, they are set in a curved form, the concave side being towards the Lion. They then send dogs into the thicket, hurl stones and sticks at the den, shoot arrows into it, fling

32 STORY OF THE BIBLE ANIMALS.

AFRICAN LIONS.

burning torches at it, and so irritate and alarm the animal that it rushes against the net, which is so made that it falls down and envelopes the animal in its folds. If the nets be few, the drivers go to the opposite side of the den, and induce the Lion to escape in the direction where he sees no foes, but where he is sure to run against the treacherous net. Other large and dangerous animals were also captured by the same means.

Another and more common, because an easier and a cheaper method was, by digging a deep pit, covering the mouth with a slight covering of sticks and earth, and driving the animal upon the treacherous covering. It is an easier method than the net, because after the pit is once dug, the only trouble lies in throwing the covering over its mouth. But, it is not so well adapted for taking beasts alive, as they are likely to be damaged, either by the fall into the pit, or by the means used in getting them out again. Animals, therefore, that are caught in pits are generally, though not always, killed before they are taken out. The net, however, envelops the animal so perfectly, and renders it so helpless, that it can be easily bound and taken away. The hunting net is very expensive, and requires a large staff of men to work it, so that none but a rich man could use it in hunting.

The passages in which allusion is made to the use of the pitfall in hunting are too numerous to be quoted, and it will be sufficient to mention one or two passages, such as those wherein the Psalmist laments that his enemies have hidden for him their net in a pit, and that the proud have digged pits for him.

Lions that were taken in nets seem to have been kept alive in dens, either as mere curiosities, or as instruments of royal vengeance. Such seems to have been the object of the Lions which were kept by Darius, into whose den Daniel was thrown, by royal command, and which afterwards killed his accusers when thrown into the same den. It is plain that the Lions kept by Darius must have been exceedingly numerous, because they killed at once the accusers of Daniel, who were many in number, together with their wives and children, who, in accordance with the cruel custom of that age and country, were partakers of the same punishment with the real culprits. The whole of the first part of Ezek. xix. alludes to the custom of taking Lions alive and keeping them in durance afterwards.

Sometimes the Lion was hunted as a sport, but this amusement seems to have been restricted to the great men, on account of its expensive nature. Such hunting scenes are graphically depicted in the famous Nineveh sculptures, which represent the hunters pursuing their mighty game in chariots, and destroying them with arrows. Rude, and even conventional as are these sculptures, they have a spirit, a force, and a truthfulness, that prove them to have been designed by artists to whom the scene was a familiar one.

THE LION ATTACKS THE HERD.

Upon the African Continent the Lion reigns supreme, monarch of the feline race.

Whatever may be said of the distinction between the Asiatic and African Lion, there seems to be scarcely sufficient grounds for considering the very slight differences a sufficient warrant for constituting separate species. From all accounts, it seems that the

HEAD OF AN AFRICAN LION.

habits of all Lions are very similar, and that a Lion acts like a Lion whether found in Africa or Asia.

An old Boer, as the Dutch settlers of Southern Africa are called, gave me a most interesting account of an adventure with a Lion.

The man was a well-known hunter, and lived principally by the sale of ivory and skins. He was accustomed each year to make a trip into the game country, and traded with the Kaffirs, or native blacks, under very favorable auspices. His stock in trade consisted of guns and ammunition, several spans of fine oxen, some horses, and about a dozen dogs.

A Lion which appeared to have been roaming about the country happened to pass near this hunter's camp, and scenting the horses and oxen, evidently thought that the location would suit him for a short period. A dense wood situated about a mile from the camp afforded shelter, and this spot the Lion selected as a favorable position for his headquarters.

The hunter had not to wait for more than a day, before the suspicions which had been aroused by some broad footmarks, which he saw imprinted in the soil, were confirmed into a certainty that a large Lion was concealed near his residence.

It now became a question of policy whether the Boer should attack the Lion, or wait for the Lion to attack him. He thought it possible that the savage beast, having been warned off by the dogs, whose barking had been continued and furious during the night on which the Lion was supposed to have passed, might think discretion the better part of valor, and consequently would move farther on, in search of a less carefully guarded locality upon which to quarter himself. He determined, therefore, to wait, but to use every precaution against a night-surprise.

The Lion, however, was more than a match for the man; for during the second night a strong ox from his best span was quietly carried off, and, although there was some commotion among the dogs and cattle, it was then thought that the alarm had scared the Lion away.

The morning light, however, showed that the beast had leaped the fence which surrounded the camp, and, having killed the ox, had evidently endeavored to scramble over it again with the ox in his possession. The weight of the Lion and the ox had caused the stakes to give way, and the Lion had easily carried off his prey through the aperture.

The track of the Lion was immediately followed by the Boer, who took with him a negro and half a dozen of his best dogs. The tracks were easily seen, and the hunter had no difficulty in deciding that the Lion was in the wood previously mentioned. But this in itself was no great advance, for the place was overgrown with a dense thicket of thorn-bushes, creepers, and long grass, forming a jungle so thick and impenetrable that for a man to enter seemed almost impossible.

It was therefore agreed that the Boer should station himself on one side, while the negro went to the other side of the jungle, the dogs meanwhile being sent into the thicket.

This arrangement, it was hoped, would enable either the hunter or the negro to obtain a shot; for they concluded that the dogs, which were very courageous animals, would drive the Lion out of the bushes.

The excited barking of the dogs soon indicated that they had discovered the Lion, but they appeared to be unable to drive him from his stronghold; for, although they would scamper away every now and then, as though the enraged monster was chasing them, still they returned to bark at the same spot.

Both of the hunters fired several shots, with the hope that a stray bullet might find its way through the underwood to the heart of the savage beast, but a great quantity of ammunition was expended and no result achieved.

At length, as the dogs had almost ceased to bark, it was considered advisable to call them off. But all the whistling and shouting failed to recall more than two out of the six, and one of these was fearfully wounded. The others, it was afterwards found, had been killed by the Lion: a blow from his paw had sufficed to break the back or smash the skull of all which had come within his reach.

Thus the first attempt on the Lion was a total failure, and the hunter returned home lamenting the loss of his dogs, and during the night watched beside his enclosure; but the Lion did not pay him a second visit.

Early on the following evening, accompanied by the negro, he started afresh for the wood; and, having marked the spot from which the Lion had on the former occasion quitted the dense thorny jungle, the two hunters ascended a tree and watched during the whole night in the hope of obtaining a shot at the hated marauder. But while they were paying the residence of the Lion a visit *he* favored the camp with a call, and this time, by way of variety, carried away a very valuable horse, which he conveyed to the wood, being wise enough to walk out and to return by a different path from that he had previously used, consequently avoiding the ambush prepared for him.

When the hunter returned to his camp, he was furious at this new loss, and determined upon a plan which, though dangerous, still appeared the most likely to insure the destruction of the ravenous monster.

This plan was to enter the wood alone, without attendant or dogs, and with noiseless, stealthy movements creep near enough to the Lion to obtain a shot.

Now, when we consider the difficulty of moving through thick bushes without making a noise, and remember the watchful habits of every member of the cat tribe, we may be certain that to surprise the Lion was a matter of extreme difficulty, and that the probability was that the hunter would meet with disaster.

At about ten o'clock on the morning after the horse-slaughter, the hunter started for the wood armed with a double-barrelled smooth-bore gun, and prepared to put forth his utmost skill in stalking his dangerous enemy.

Now, it is the nature of the Lion, when gorged, to sleep during the day; and if the animal has carried off any prey, it usually conceals itself near the remnants of its feast, to watch them until ready for another meal.

The hunter was aware of this, and laid his plans very judiciously. He approached the wood slowly and silently, found the track of the Lion, and began tracing it to find the spot where the remains of the horse could be seen.

He moved forward very slowly and with great caution, being soon surrounded by the thick bushes, the brightness of the plain also being succeeded by the deep gloom of the wood. Being an experienced hand at bush-craft, he was able to walk or crawl without causing either a dried stick to crack or a leaf to rustle, and he was aware that his progress was without noise; for the small birds. usually so watchful and alert, flew away only when he approached close to them, thus showing that their eyes, and not their ears, had made them conscious of the presence of man.

Birds and monkeys are the great obstacles in the bush to the

THE LION. 39

THE LION LISTENS TO THE APPROACH OF THE HUNTER.

success of a surprise, for the birds fly from tree to tree and whistle or twitter, whilst the monkeys chatter and grimace, expressing by all sorts of actions that a strange creature is approaching. When, therefore, the bushranger finds that birds and monkeys are unconscious of his presence until they see him, he may be satisfied that he has traversed the bush with tolerable silence, and has vanquished such dangerous betrayers of his presence as dried sticks and dead leaves.

The hunter had not proceeded thus more than fifty yards into the jungle, before he found indications that he was close upon the lair of the Lion: a strong leonine scent was noticeable, and part of the carcase of his horse was visible between the bushes. Instead, therefore, of advancing farther, as an incautious or inexperienced bushranger would have done, he crouched down behind a bush and remained motionless.

All animals are aware of the advantages of a surprise, and the cat tribe especially practise the ambuscading system. The hunter, therefore, determined, if possible, to turn the tables on the Lion, and to surprise, rather than to be surprised.

He concluded that the Lion, even when gorged with horseflesh, would not be so neglectful of his safety as to sleep with more than one eye closed, and that, although he had crept with great care through the bush, he had probably, from some slight sound, caused the Lion to be on the alert; if, therefore, he should approach the carcase of the horse, he might be pounced upon at once.

After remaining silent and watchful for several minutes, the hunter at length saw that an indistinctly-outlined object was moving behind some large broad-leafed plants at about twenty paces from him.

This object was the Lion. It was crouched behind some shrubs, attentively watching the bushes where the hunter was concealed. Its head only was clearly visible, the body being hidden by the foliage.

It was evident that the Lion was suspicious of something, but was not certain that anything had approached.

The hunter, knowing that this was a critical period for him, remained perfectly quiet. He did not like to risk a shot at the forehead of the Lion, for it would require a very sure aim to insure a death-wound, and the number of twigs and branches would be almost certain to deflect the bullet.

The Lion, after a careful inspection, appeared to be satisfied, and laid down behind the shrubs. The hunter then cocked both barrels of his heavy gun and turned the muzzle slowly around, so that he covered the spot on which the Lion lay, and shifted his position so as to be well placed for a shot.

The slight noise he made in moving, attracted the attention of the Lion, who immediately rose to his feet. A broadside shot, which was the most sure, could not be obtained, so the hunter fired at the head of the animal, aiming for a spot between the eyes. The ball struck high, as is usually the case when the distance is short, and the charge of powder heavy, but the Lion fell over on its back, rising, however, almost immediately and uttering a terrific roar.

In regaining its feet it turned its side to the hunter, giving him the opportunity he had so anxiously waited for. Aiming at a spot behind the shoulder, he fired again, and had the satisfaction of seeing the savage beast, maddened by the pain of a mortal wound, tearing up the ground in its fury within a very few paces of his hiding-place.

By degrees its fierce roars subsided into angry growls, and the growls into heavy moans, until the terrible voice was hushed and silence reigned throughout the wood.

The hunter immediately started off home, and brought his negroes and dogs to the spot, where they found stretched dead upon the ground a Lion of the largest size.

Before sunset that evening its skin was pegged down at the hunter's camp, and all were filled with delight, knowing that they would be no more disturbed by the fierce marauder.

THE LEOPARD.

The Leopard not often mentioned in the Scriptures—its attributes exactly described—Probability that several animals were classed under the name—How the Leopard takes its prey—Craft of the Leopard—its ravages among the flocks—The empire of man over the beast—The Leopard at Bay—Localities wherein the Leopard lives—The skin of the Leopard—Various passages of Scripture explained.

OF the LEOPARD but little is said in the Holy Scriptures.

In the New Testament this animal is only mentioned once, and then in a metaphorical rather than a literal sense. In the Old Testament it is casually mentioned seven times, and only in two places is the word Leopard used in the strictly literal sense. Yet, in those brief passages of Holy Writ, the various attributes of the animal are delineated with such fidelity, that no one could doubt that the Leopard was familiarly known in Palestine. Its colour, its swiftness, its craft, its ferocity, and the nature of its dwelling-place, are all touched upon in a few short sentences scattered throughout the Old Testament, and even its peculiar habits are alluded to in a manner that proves it to have been well known at the time when the words were written.

It is my purpose in the following pages to give a brief account of the Leopard of the Scriptures, laying most stress on the qualities to which allusion is made, and then to explain the passages in which the name of the animal occurs.

In the first place, it is probable that under the word Leopard are comprehended three animals, two of which, at least, were thought to be one species until the time of Cuvier. These three animals are the LEOPARD proper (*Leopardus varius*), the OUNCE (*Leopardus uncia*), and the CHETAH, or HUNTING LEOPARD (*Gueparda jubata*). All these three species belong to the same family of animals; all are spotted and similar in colour, all are nearly alike in shape, and all are inhabitants of Asia, while two of them, the Leopard and the Chetah, are also found in Africa.

THE LEOPARD.

It is scarcely necessary to mention that the Leopard is a beast of prey belonging to the cat tribe, that its colour is tawny, variegated with rich black spots, and that it is a fierce and voracious animal, almost equally dreaded by man and beast. It inhabits many parts of Africa and Asia, and in those portions of the country which are untenanted by mankind, it derives all its sustenance from the herb-eating animals of the same tracts.

THE LEOPARD.

To deer and antelopes it is a terrible enemy, and in spite of their active limbs, seldom fails in obtaining its prey. Swift as is the Leopard, for a short distance, and wonderful as its spring, it has not the enduring speed of the deer or antelope, animals which are specially formed for running, and which, if a limb is shattered, can run nearly as fast and quite as far on three legs as they can when all four limbs are uninjured. Instinctively knowing its inferiority in the race, the Leopard supplies by cunning the want of enduring speed.

It conceals itself in some spot whence it can see far around without being seen, and thence surveys the country. A tree is the usual spot selected for this purpose, and the Leopard, after climbing the trunk by means of its curved talons, settles itself in the fork of the branches, so that its body is hidden by the boughs, and only its head is shown between them. With such scrupulous care does it conceal itself, that none but a practised hunter can discover it, while any one who is unaccustomed to the woods cannot see the animal even when the tree is pointed out to him.

As soon as the Leopard sees the deer feeding at a distance, he slips down the tree and stealthily glides off in their direction. He has many difficulties to overcome, because the deer are among the most watchful of animals, and if the Leopard were to approach to the windward, they would scent him while he was yet a mile away from them. If he were to show himself but for one moment in the open ground he would be seen, and if he were but to shake a branch or snap a dry twig he would be heard. So, he is obliged to approach them against the wind, to keep himself under cover, and yet to glide so carefully along that the heavy foliage of the underwood shall not be shaken, and the dry sticks and leaves which strew the ground shall not be broken. He has also to escape the observation of certain birds and beasts which inhabit the woods, and which would certainly set up their alarm-cry as soon as they saw him, and so give warning to the wary deer, which can perfectly understand a cry of alarm, from whatever animal it may happen to proceed.

Still, he proceeds steadily on his course, gliding from one covert to another, and often expending several hours before he can proceed for a mile. By degrees he contrives to come tolerably close to them, and generally manages to conceal himself in some spot towards which the deer are gradually feeding their way. As soon as they are near enough, he collects himself for a spring, just as a cat does when she leaps on a bird, and dashes towards the deer in a series of mighty bounds. For a moment or two they are startled and paralysed with fear at the sudden

LEOPARD ATTACKING A HERD OF DEER.

appearance of their enemy, and thus give him time to get among them. Singling out some particular animal, he leaps upon it, strikes it down with one blow of his paw, and then, couching on the fallen animal, he tears open its throat, and laps the flowing blood.

In this manner does it obtain its prey when it lives in the desert, but when it happens to be in the neighbourhood of human habitations, it acts in a different manner. Whenever man settles himself in any place, his presence is a signal for the beasts of the desert and forest to fly. The more timid, such as the deer and antelope, are afraid of him, and betake themselves as far away as possible. The more savage inhabitants of the land, such as the lion, leopard, and other animals, wage an unequal war against him for a time, but are continually driven farther and farther away, until at last they are completely expelled from the country. The predaceous beasts are, however, loth to retire, and do so by very slow degrees. They can no longer support themselves on the deer and antelopes, but find a simple substitute for them in the flocks and herds which man introduces, and in the seizing of which there is as much craft required as in the catching of the fleeter and wilder animals. Sheep and goats cannot run away like the antelopes, but they are penned so carefully within inclosures, and guarded so watchfully by herdsmen and dogs, that the Leopard is obliged to exert no small amount of cunning before it can obtain a meal.

Sometimes it creeps quietly to the fold, and escapes the notice of the dogs, seizes upon a sheep, and makes off with it before the alarm is given. Sometimes it hides by the wayside, and as the flock pass by it dashes into the midst of them, snatches up a sheep, and disappears among the underwood on the opposite side of the road. Sometimes it is crafty enough to deprive the fold of its watchful guardian. Dogs which are used to Leopard-hunting never attack the animal, though they are rendered furious by the sound of its voice. They dash at it as if they meant to devour it, but take very good care to keep out of reach of its terrible paws. By continually keeping the animal at bay, they give time for their master to come up, and generally contrive to drive it into a tree, where it can be shot.

But instances have been known where the Leopard has taken advantage of the dogs, and carried them off in a very cunning

THE LEOPARD LEAPS UPON HIS PREY.

manner. It hides itself tolerably near the fold, and then begins to growl in a low voice. The dogs think that they hear a Leopard at a distance, and dash towards the sound with furious barks and yells. In so doing, they are sure to pass by the hiding-place of the Leopard, which springs upon them unawares, knocks one of them over, and bounds away to its den in the woods. It does not content itself with taking sheep or goats from the fold, but is also a terrible despoiler of the hen-roosts, destroying great numbers in a single night when once it contrives to find its way into the house.

As an instance of the cunning which seems innate in the Leopard, I may mention that whenever it takes up its abode near a village, it does not meddle with the flocks and herds of its neighbours, but prefers to go to some other village at a distance for food, thus remaining unsuspected almost at the very doors of the houses.

In general, it does not willingly attack mankind, and at all events seems rather to fear the presence of a full-grown man. But, when wounded or irritated, all sense of fear is lost in an overpowering rush of fury, and it then becomes as terrible a foe as the lion himself. It is not so large nor so strong, but it is more agile and quicker in its movements; and when it is seized with one of these paroxysms of anger, the eye can scarcely follow it as it darts here and there, striking with lightning rapidity, and dashing at any foe within reach. Its whole shape seems to be transformed, and absolutely to swell with anger; its eyes flash with fiery lustre, its ears are thrown back on the head, and it continually utters alternate snarls and yells of rage. It is hardly possible to recognise the graceful, lithe glossy creature, whose walk is so noiseless, and whose every movement is so easy, in the furious passion-swollen animal that flies at every foe with blind fury, and pours out sounds so fierce and menacing that few men, however well armed, will care to face it.

As is the case with most of the cat tribe, the Leopard is an excellent climber, and can ascend trees and traverse their boughs without the least difficulty. It is so fond of trees, that it is seldom to be seen except in a well-wooded district. Its favourite residence is a forest where there is plenty of underwood, at least six or seven feet in height, among which trees are sparingly interspersed. When crouched in this cover it is prac-

WAITING.

tically invisible, even though its body may be within arm's length of a passenger. The spotted body harmonizes so perfectly with the broken lights and deep shadows of the foliage that even a practised hunter will not enter a covert in search of a Leopard unless he is accompanied by dogs. The instinct which teaches the Leopard to choose such localities is truly wonderful, and may be compared with that of the tiger, which cares little for underwood, but haunts the grass jungles, where the long, narrow blades harmonize with the stripes which decorate its body.

The skin of the Leopard has always been highly valued on account of its beauty, and in Africa, at the present day, a robe made of its spotted skin is as much an adjunct of royalty as is the ermine the emblem of judicial dignity in England. In more ancient times, a leopard skin was the official costume of a priest, the skin being sometimes shaped into a garment, and sometimes thrown over the shoulders and the paws crossed over the breast.

Such is a general history of the Leopard. We will now proceed to the various passages in which it is mentioned, beginning with its outward aspect.

In the first place, the Hebrew word Namer signifies "spotted," and is given to the animal in allusion to its colours. The reader will now see how forcible is the lament of Jeremiah, "Can the Ethiopian change his skin, or the Leopard his spots?" Literally, "Can the Ethiopian change his skin, or the spotted one his spots?"

The agility and swiftness of the Leopard are alluded to in the prediction by the prophet Habakkuk of the vengeance that would come upon Israel through the Chaldeans. In chap. i. 5, we read: "I will work a work in your days, which ye will not believe though it be told you. For, lo, I raise up the Chaldeans, that bitter and hasty nation, which shall march through the breadth of the land, to possess the dwelling-places that are not theirs. They are terrible and dreadful; their judgment and their dignity shall proceed of themselves. Their horses also are swifter than the Leopards, and are more fierce than the evening wolves."

The craftiness of the Leopard, and the manner in which it lies in wait for its prey, are alluded to in more than one passage of Holy Writ. Hosea the prophet alludes to the Leopard, in a few simple words which display an intimate acquaintance with the habits of this formidable animal, and in this part of his prophecies he displays that peculiar local tone which distinguishes his writings. Speaking of the Israelites under the metaphor of a flock, or a herd, he proceeds to say: "According to their pasture so were they filled; they were filled, and their heart was exalted; therefore have they forgotten me. Therefore I will be unto them as a lion, as a Leopard by the way will I observe them." The reader will note the peculiar force of this sentence, whereby God signifies that He will destroy them openly, as a lion rushes on its prey, and that he will chastise them unexpectedly, as if it were a Leopard crouching by the wayside, and watching for the flock to pass, that it may spring on its prey unexpectedly. The same habit of the Leopard is also alluded to by Jeremiah, who employs precisely the same imagery as is used by Habakkuk. See Jer. v. 5, 6, "These have altogether broken the yoke, and burst the bonds. Wherefore a lion out of the forest shall slay them, and a wolf of the evenings shall spoil them, a leopard shall watch over their cities." It is evident from the employment of this image by two prophets, the one being nearly a hundred years before the other, that the crafty, insidious habits of the Leopard were well known in Palestine, and that the metaphor would tell with full force among those to whom it was addressed.

THE CAT.

The Cat never mentioned by name in the canonical Scriptures, and only once in the Apocrypha—The Cat domesticated among the Egyptians, and trained in bird-catching—Neglected capabilities of the Cat—Anecdote of an English Cat that caught fish for her master—Presumed reason why the Scriptures are silent about the Cat—The Cat mentioned by Baruch.

IT is a very remarkable circumstance that the word CAT is not once mentioned in the whole of the canonical Scriptures, and only once in the Apocrypha.

The Egyptians, as is well known, kept Cats domesticated in their houses, a fact which is mentioned by Herodotus, in his second book, and the 66th and 67th chapters. After describing the various animals which were kept and fed by this nation, he proceeds to narrate the habits of the Cat, and writes as follows: "When a fire takes place, a supernatural impulse seizes the cats. For the Egyptians, standing at a distance, take care of the cats and neglect to quench the fire; but the cats make their escape, and leaping over the men, cast themselves into the fire, and when this occurs, great lamentations are made among the Egyptians. In whatever house a cat dies of a natural death, all the family shave their eyebrows. All cats that die are carried to certain sacred houses, where, after being embalmed, they are buried in the city of Bubastis."

Now, as many of those cat-mummies have been discovered in good preservation, the species has been identified with the Egytian Cat of the present day, which is scientifically termed *Felis maniculatus*. Not only did the Egyptians keep Cats at their houses, but, as is shown by certain sculptures, took the animals with them when they went bird-catching, and employed them in securing their prey. Some persons have doubted this statement, saying, that in the first place, the Cat is not possessed of sufficient intelligence for the purpose; and that in the second place, as the hunter is represented as catching wild fowl, the Cat would not be able to assist him, because it would not enter the water. Neither objection is valid, nor would have been made by a naturalist.

There are no grounds whatever for assuming that the Cat has not sufficient intelligence to aid its master in hunting. On the contrary, there are many familiar instances where the animal has been trained, even in this country, to catch birds and other game, and bring its prey home. By nature the Cat is an accomplished hunter, and, like other animals of the same disposition, can be taught to use its powers for mankind. We all know that the chetah, a member of the same tribe, is in constant use at the present day, and we learn from ancient sculptures that the lion was employed for the same purpose. Passing from land to water, mankind has succeeded in teaching the seal and the otter to plunge into the water, catch their finny prey, and deliver it to their owners. Among predaceous birds, we have trained the eagle, the falcon, and various hawks, to assist us in hunting the finned and feathered tribes, while we have succeeded in teaching the cormorant to catch fish for its master, and not for itself. Why, then, should the Cat be excepted from a rule so general?

The fact is, the Cat has been, although domesticated for so many centuries, a comparatively neglected animal; and it is the fashion to heap upon it the contumacious epithets of sullen, treacherous, selfish, spiteful, and intractable, just as we take as our emblems of stupidity the ass and the goose, which are really among the most cunning of the lower animals. We have never tried to teach the Cat the art of hunting for her owners, but that is no reason for asserting that the animal could not be taught.

As to entering the water, every one who is familiar with the habits of the Cat knows perfectly well that the Cat will voluntarily enter water in chase of prey. A Cat does not like to wet her feet, and will not enter the water without a very powerful reason, but when that motive is supplied, she has no hesitation about it. A curious and valuable confirmation of this fact appeared some time ago in "The Field" newspaper, in which was recorded the history of an old fisherman, whose Cat invariably went to sea with him, and as invariably used to leap overboard, seize fish in her mouth, and bring them to the side of the boat, where her kindly owner could lift her out, together with the captured fish.

The Cat, then, having been the favoured companion of the Egyptians, among whom the Israelites lived while they multiplied from a family into a nation, it does seem very remarkable that the sacred writers should not even mention it. There is no prohibition of the animal, even indirectly, in the Mosaic law; but it may be the case that the Israelites repudiated the Cat simply because it was so favoured by their former masters.

THE DOG.

Antipathy displayed by Orientals towards the Dog, and manifested throughout the Scriptures—Contrast between European and Oriental Dogs—Habits of the Dogs of Palestine—The City Dogs and their singular organization—The herdsman's Dog—Various passages of Scripture—Dogs and the crumbs—their numbers—Signor Pierotti's experience of the Dogs—Possibility of their perfect domestication—The peculiar humiliation of Lazarus—Voracity of the Wild Dogs—The fate of Ahab and Jezebel—Anecdote of a volunteer Watch-dog—Innate affection of the Dog towards mankind—Peculiar local Instinct of the Oriental Dog—Albert Smith's account of the Dogs at Constantinople—The Dervish and his Dogs—The Greyhound—Uncertainty of the word.

SCARCELY changed by the lapse of centuries, the Oriental of the present day retains most of the peculiarities which distinguished him throughout the long series of years during which the books of sacred Scripture were given to the world. In many of these characteristics he differs essentially from Europeans of the present day, and exhibits a tone of mind which seems to be not merely owing to education, but to be innate and inherent in the race.

One of these remarkable characteristics is the strange loathing with which he regards the Dog. In all other parts of the world, the Dog is one of the most cherished and valued of animals, but among those people whom we popularly class under the name of Orientals, the Dog is detested and despised. As the sacred books were given to the world through the mediumship of Orientals, we find that this feeling towards the Dog is manifested whenever the animal is mentioned; and whether we turn to the books of the Law, the splendid poetry of the Psalms and the book of Job, the prophetical or the historical portions of the Old Testament, we find the name of the Dog repeatedly mentioned; and in every case in connexion with some repulsive idea. If we turn from the Old to the New Testament, we find the same idea manifested, whether in the Gospels, the Epistles, or the Revelation.

To the mind of the true Oriental the very name of the Dog carries with it an idea of something utterly repugnant to his nature, and he does not particularly like even the thought of the animal coming across his mind. And this is the more extraordinary, because at the commencement and termination of their history the Dog was esteemed by their masters. The Egyptians, under whose rule they grew to be a nation, knew the value of the Dog, and showed their appreciation in the many works of art which have survived to our time. Then the Romans, under whose iron grasp the last vestiges of nationality crumbled away, honoured and respected the Dog, made it their companion, and introduced its portrait into their houses. But, true to their early traditions, the Jews of the East have ever held the Dog in the same abhorrence as is manifested by their present masters, the followers of Mahommed.

Owing to the prevalence of this feeling, the Dogs of Oriental towns are so unlike their more fortunate European relatives, that they can hardly be recognised as belonging to the same species. In those lands the traveller finds that there is none of the wonderful variety which so distinguishes the Dog of Europe. There he will never see the bluff, sturdy, surly, faithful mastiff, the slight gazelle-like greyhound, the sharp, intelligent terrier, the silent, courageous bulldog, the deep-voiced, tawny bloodhound, the noble Newfoundland, the clever, vivacious poodle, or the gentle, silken-haired spaniel.

As he traverses the streets, he finds that all the dogs are alike, and that all are gaunt, hungry, half starved, savage, and cowardly, more like wolves than dogs, and quite as ready as wolves to attack when they fancy they can do so with safety. They prowl about the streets in great numbers, living, as they best can, on any scraps of food that they may happen to find. They have no particular masters, and no particular homes. Charitable persons will sometimes feed them, but will never make companions of them, feeling that the very contact of a dog would be a pollution. They are certainly useful animals, because they act as scavengers, and will eat almost any animal substance that comes in their way.

The strangest part of their character is the organization which prevails among them. By some extraordinary means they divide the town into districts, and not one dog ever ventures out of

DOGS IN AN EASTERN CITY AT NIGHT.

that particular district to which it is attached. The boundaries, although invisible, are as effectual as the loftiest walls, and not even the daintiest morsel will tempt a dog to pass the mysterious line which forms the boundary of his district. Generally, these bands of dogs are so savage that any one who is obliged to walk in a district where the dogs do not know him is forced to carry a stout stick for his protection. Like their European relatives, they have great dislike towards persons who are dressed after a fashion to which they are unaccustomed, and therefore are sure to harass any one who comes from Europe and wears the costume of his own country. As is customary among animals which unite themselves in troops, each band is under the command of a single leader, whose position is recognised and his authority acknowledged by all the members.

These peculiarities are to be seen almost exclusively in the dogs which run wild about the towns, because there is abundant evidence in the Scriptures that the animal was used in a partially domesticated state, certainly for the protection of their herds, and possibly for the guardianship of their houses. That the Dog was employed for the first of these purposes is shown in Job xxx. i: "But now they that are younger than I have me in derision, whose fathers I would have disdained to have set with the dogs of my flock." And that the animal was used for the protection of houses is thought by some commentators to be shown by the well-known passage in Is. lvi. 10 : "His watchmen are blind : they are all ignorant, they are all dumb dogs, they cannot bark; sleeping, lying down, loving to slumber." Still, it is very probable that in this passage the reference is not made to houses, but to the flocks and herds which these watchmen ought to have guarded.

The rooted dislike and contempt felt by the Israelites towards the Dog is seen in numerous passages. Even in that sentence from Job which has just been quoted, wherein the writer passionately deplores the low condition into which he has fallen, and contrasts it with his former high estate, he complains that he is despised by those whose fathers he held even in less esteem than the dogs which guarded his herds. There are several references to the Dog in the books of Samuel, in all of which the name of the animal is mentioned contemptuously. For example, when David accepted the challenge of Goliath, and went to meet his gigantic enemy without the ordinary protection of mail, and armed only with a sling and his shepherd's staff, Goliath said to him, "Am I a dog, that thou comest to me with staves?" (1 Sam. xvii. 43.) And in the same book, chapter xxiv. 14, David remonstrates with Saul for pursuing so insignificant a person as himself, and said, "After whom is the King of Israel come out? after a dead dog, after a flea."

The same metaphor is recorded in the second book of the same writer. Once it was employed by Mephibosheth, the lame son of Jonathan, when extolling the generosity of David, then King of Israel in the place of his grandfather Saul: "And he bowed himself, and said, 'What is thy servant, that thou shouldest look upon such a dead dog as I am?'" (2 Sam. ix. 8.)

SHIMEI EXULTING OVER KING DAVID.

In the same book, chapter xvi. 9, Abishai applies this contemptuous epithet to Shimei, who was exulting over the troubled monarch with all the insolence of a cowardly nature, "Why should this dead dog curse my lord the king?" Abner also makes use of a similar expression, "Am I a dog's head?" And we may also refer to the familiar passage in 2 Kings viii. 13.

Elisha had prophesied to Hazael that he would become king on the death of Ben-hadad, and that he would work terrible mischief in the land. Horrified at these predictions, or at all events pretending to be so, he replied, "But what, is thy servant a dog, that he should do this great thing?"

If we turn from the Old to the New Testament, we find the same contemptuous feeling displayed towards the Dog. It is mentioned as an intolerable aggravation of the sufferings endured by Lazarus the beggar as he lay at the rich man's gate, that the dogs came and licked his sores. In several passages, the word Dog is employed as a metaphor for scoffers, or unclean persons, or sometimes for those who did not belong to the Church, whether Jewish or Christian. In the Sermon on the Mount our Lord himself uses this image, "Give not that which is holy unto dogs" (Matt. vii. 6.) In the same book, chapter xv. 26, Jesus employs the same metaphor when speaking to the Canaanitish woman who had come to ask him to heal her daughter: "It is not meet to take the children's bread and cast it to dogs." And that she understood the meaning of the words is evident from her answer, in which faith and humility are so admirably blended. Both St. Paul and St. John employ the word Dog in the same sense. In his epistle to the Philippians, chapter iii. 2, St. Paul writes, "Beware of dogs, beware of evil workers." And in the Revelation, chapter xxii. 14, these words occur: "Blessed are they that do his commandments, that they may have right to the tree of life, and may enter in through the gates to the city; for without are dogs, and sorcerers, ... and murderers, and idolaters, and whomsoever loveth and maketh a lie."

That the dogs of ancient times formed themselves into bands just as they do at present is evident from many passages of Scripture, among which may be mentioned those sentences from the Psalms, wherein David is comparing the assaults of his enemies to the attacks of the dogs which infested the city. "Thou hast brought me into the dust of death; for dogs have compassed me, the assembly of the wicked have enclosed me." This passage will be better appreciated when the reader has perused the following extract from a recent work by Signor Pierotti. After giving a general account of the Dogs of Palestine and their customs, he proceeds as follows:—

"In Jerusalem, and in the other towns, the dogs havê an organization of their own. They are divided into families and districts, especially in the night time, and no one of them ventures to quit his proper quarter; for if he does, he is immediately attacked by all the denizens of that into which he intrudes, and is driven back, with several bites as a reminder. Therefore, when an European is walking through Jerusalem by night, he is always followed by a number of canine attendants, and greeted at every step with growls and howls. These tokens of dislike, however, are not intended for him, but for his followers, who are availing themselves of his escort to pass unmolested from one quarter to another.

"During a very hard winter, I fed many of the dogs who frequented the road which I traversed almost every evening, and afterwards, each time that I passed, I received the homage not only of the individuals, but of the whole band to which they belonged, for they accompanied me to the limits of their respective jurisdictions and were ready to follow me to my own house, if I did but give them a sign of encouragement, coming at my beck from any distance. They even recollected the signal two years afterwards, though it was but little that I had given them."

The account which this experienced writer gives of the animal presents a singular mixture of repulsive and pleasing traits, the latter being attributable to the true nature of the Dog, and the former to the utter neglect with which it is treated. He remarks that the dogs which run wild in the cities of Palestine are ill-favoured, ill-scented, and ill-conditioned beasts, more like jackals or wolves than dogs, and covered with scars, which betoken their quarrelsome nature. Yet, the same animals lose their wild, savage disposition, as soon as any human being endeavours to establish that relationship which was evidently intended to exist between man and the dog. How readily even these despised and neglected animals respond to the slightest advance, has been already shown by Sig. Pierotti's experience, and there is no doubt that these tawny, short-haired, wolf-like animals, could be trained as perfectly as their more favoured brethren of the western world.

As in the olden times, so at the present day, the dogs lie about in the streets, dependent for their livelihood upon the offal that is flung into the roads, or upon the chance morsels that may be thrown to them. An allusion to this custom is made in the well-known passage in Matt. xv. The reader will remember the circumstance that a woman of Canaan, and therefore not an Israelite, came to Jesus, and begged him to heal her daughter, who was vexed with a devil. Then, to try her faith, He said, "It

LAZARUS LYING AT THE RICH MAN'S DOOR.

is not meet to take the children's bread, and to cast it to dogs." And she said, "Truth, Lord: yet the dogs eat of the crumbs which fall from their master's table." Now, the "crumbs" which are here mentioned are the broken pieces of bread which were used at table, much as bread is sometimes used in eating fish.

The form of the "loaves" being flat, and much like that of the oat-cake of this country, adapted them well to the purpose. The same use of broken bread is alluded to in the parable of Lazarus, who desired to be fed with the crumbs that fell from the rich man's table, *i. e.* to partake of the same food as the dogs which swarmed round him and licked his sores.

THE DEATH OF JEZEBEL.

The "crumbs," however liberally distributed, would not nearly suffice for the subsistence of the canine armies, and their chief support consists of the offal, which is rather too plentifully flung into the streets. If the body of any animal, not excluding their own kind, be found lying in the streets, the dogs will assemble round it, and tear it to pieces, and they have no scruples even in devouring a human body. Of course, owing to the peculiar feeling entertained by the Orientals towards the Dog, no fate can be imagined more repulsive to the feelings of humanity than to be eaten by dogs; and therein lies the terror of the fate which was prophesied of Ahab and Jezebel. Moreover, the blood, even of the lower animals, was held in great sanctity, and it was in those days hardly possible to invoke a more dreadful fate upon any one than that his blood should be lapped by dogs.

We lose much of the real force of the Scriptures, if we do not possess some notion of the manners and customs of Palestine and the neighbouring countries, as well as of the tone of mind prevalent among the inhabitants. In our own country, that any one should be eaten by dogs would be a fate so contrary to usage, that we can hardly conceive its possibility, and such a fate would be out of the ordinary course of events. But, if such a fate should happen to befall any one, we should have no stronger feeling of pity than the natural regret that the dead person was not buried with Christian rites.

But, with the inhabitants of Palestine, such an event was by no means unlikely. It was, and is still, the custom to bury the corpse almost as soon as life has departed, and such would ordinarily have been the case with the dead body of Jezebel. But, through fear of the merciless Jehu, by whose command she had been flung from the window of her own palace, no one dared to remove her mangled body. The dogs, therefore, seized upon their prey; and, even before Jehu had risen from the banquet with which he celebrated his deed, nothing was left of the body but the skull, the feet, and the hands.

SYRIAN DOG.

In Mr. Tristram's work, the author has recognised the true dog nature, though concealed behind an uninviting form: "Our watch-dog, Beirût, attached himself instinctively to Wilhelm, though his canine instinct soon taught him to recognise every one of our party of fourteen, and to cling to the tents, **whether** in motion or at rest, as his home. Poor Beirût! though the veriest pariah in appearance, thy plebeian form encased as noble a dog-heart as ever beat at the sound of a stealthy step."

The same author records a very remarkable example of the sagacity of the native Dog, and the fidelity with which it will keep guard over the property of its master. "The guard-house provided us, unasked, with an invaluable and vigilant sentry, who was never relieved, nor ever quitted the post of duty. The poor Turkish conscript, like every other soldier in the world, is fond of pets, and in front of the grim turret that served for a guard-house was a collection of old orange-boxes and crates, thickly peopled with a garrison of dogs of low degree, whose attachment to the spot was certainly not purchased by the loaves and fishes which fell to their lot.

"One of the family must indeed have had hard times, for she had a family of no less than five dependent on her exertions, and on the superfluities of the sentries' mess. With a sagacity almost more than canine, the poor gaunt creature had scarcely seen our tents pitched before she came over with all her litter and deposited them in front of our tent. At once she scanned the features of every member of the encampment, and introduced herself to our notice. During the week of our stay, she never quitted her post, or attempted any depredation on our kitchen-tent, which might have led to her banishment. Night and day she proved a faithful and vigilant sentry, permitting no stranger, human or canine, European or Oriental, to approach the tents without permission, but keeping on the most familiar terms with ourselves and our servants.

"On the morning of our departure, no sooner had she seen our camp struck, than she conveyed her puppies back to their old quarters in the orange-box, and no entreaties or bribes could induce her to accompany us. On three subsequent visits to Jerusalem, the same dog acted in a similar way, though no longer embarrassed by family cares, and would on no account permit any strange dog, nor even her companions at the guard-house, to approach within the tent ropes."

After perusing this account of the Dog of Palestine, two points strike the reader. The first is the manner in which the Dog, in spite of all the social disadvantages under which it labours, displays one of the chief characteristics of canine nature, namely, the yearning after human society. The animal in question had already attached herself to the guard-house, where she could meet with some sort of human converse, though the inborn prejudices of the Moslem would prevent the soldiers from inviting her to associate with them, as would certainly have been done by European soldiers. She nestled undisturbed in the orange-box, and, safe under the protection of the guard, brought up her young family in their immediate neighbourhood. But, as soon as Europeans arrived, her instinct told her that they would be closer associates than the Turkish soldiers who were quartered in the guard-house, and accordingly she removed herself and her family to the shelter of their tents.

Herein she carried out the leading principle of a dog's nature. A dog *must* have a master, or at all events a mistress, and just in proportion as he is free from human control, does he become less dog-like and more wolf-like. In fact, familiar intercourse with mankind is an essential part of a dog's true character, and the animal seems to be so well aware of this fact, that he will always contrive to find a master of some sort, and will endure a life of cruel treatment at the hands of a brutal owner rather than have no master at all.

The second point in this account is the singular local instinct which characterises the Dogs of Palestine and other eastern countries, and which is as much inbred in them as the faculty of marking game in the pointer, the combative nature in the bulldog, the exquisite scent in the bloodhound, and the love of water in the Newfoundland dog. In this country, we fancy that the love of locality belongs especially to the cat, and that the Dog cares little for place, and much for man. But, in this case, we find that the local instinct overpowered the yearning for human society. Fond as was this dog of her newly-found friends, and faithful as she was in her self-imposed service, she would not follow them away from the spot where she had been born, and where she had produced her own young.

This curious love for locality has evidently been derived from the traditional custom of successive generations, which has passed from the realm of reason into that of instinct. The reader will remember that Sig. Pierotti mentions an instance where the dogs which he had been accustomed to feed would follow him as far as the limits of their particular district, but would go no farther. The late Albert Smith, in his "Month at Constantinople," gives a similar example of this characteristic. He first describes the general habits of the dogs.

On the first night of his arrival, he could not sleep, and went to the window to look out in the night. "The noise I heard then I shall never forget. To say that if all the sheep-dogs, in going to Smithfield on a market-day, had been kept on the constant bark, and pitted against the yelping curs upon all the carts in London, they could have given any idea of the canine uproar that now first astonished me, would be to make the feeblest of images. The whole city rang with one vast riot. Down below me, at Tophané—over-about Stamboul—far away at Scutari—the whole sixty thousand dogs that are said to overrun Constantinople appeared engaged in the most active extermination of each other, without a moment's cessation. The yelping, howling, barking, growling, and snarling, were all merged into one uniform and continuous even sound, as the noise of frogs becomes when heard at a distance. For hours there was no lull. I went to sleep, and woke again, and still, with my windows open, I heard the same tumult going on; nor was it until daybreak that anything like tranquillity was restored.

"Going out in the daytime, it is not difficult to find traces of the fights of the night about the limbs of all the street dogs. There is not one, among their vast number, in the possession of a perfect skin. Some have their ears gnawed away or pulled off; others have their eyes taken out; from the backs and haunches of others perfect steaks of flesh had been torn away; and all bear the scars of desperate combats.

"Wild and desperate as is their nature, these poor animals are susceptible of kindness. If a scrap of bread is thrown to one of them now and then, he does not forget it; for they have, at times, a hard matter to live—not the dogs amongst the shops of Galata or Stamboul, but those whose 'parish' lies in the large burying-grounds and desert places without the city; for each keeps, or rather is kept, to his district, and if he chanced to venture into a strange one, the odds against his return would be very large. One battered old animal, to whom I used occasionally to toss a scrap of food, always followed me from the hotel to the cross street in Pera, where the two soldiers stood on guard, but would never come beyond this point. He knew the fate that awaited him had he done so; and therefore, when I left him, he would lie down in the road, and go to sleep until I came back.

"When a horse or camel dies, and is left about the roads near the city, the bones are soon picked very clean by these dogs, and they will carry the skulls or pelves to great distances. I was told that they will eat their dead fellows—a curious fact, I believe, in canine economy. They are always troublesome, not to say dangerous, at night; and are especially irritated by Europeans, whom they will single out amongst a crowd of Levantines."

In the same work there is a short description of a solitary dervish, who had made his home in the hollow of a large plane-tree, in front of which he sat, surrounded by a small fence of stakes only a foot or so in height. Around him, but not venturing within the fence, were a number of gaunt, half-starved dogs, who prowled about him in hopes of having an occasional morsel of food thrown to them. Solitary as he was, and scanty as must have been the nourishment which he could afford to them, the innate trustfulness of the dog-nature induced them to attach themselves to human society of some sort, though their master was one, and they were many—he was poor, and they were hungry.

EASTERN WATER-SELLER.

THE WOLF.

Identity of the animal indisputable—its numbers, past and present—The Wolf never mentioned directly—its general habits—References in Scripture—its mingled ferocity and cowardice—its association into packs—The Wolf's bite—How it takes its prey—its ravages among the flocks—Allusions to this habit—The shepherd and his nightly enemies—Mr. Tristram and the Wolf—A semi tamed Wolf at Marsaba.

THERE is no doubt that the Hebrew word *Zeëb*, which occurs in a few passages of the Old Testament, is rightly translated as WOLF, and signifies the same animal as is frequently mentioned in the New Testament.

This fierce and dangerous animal was formerly very plentiful in Palestine, but is now much less common, owing to the same causes which have extirpated the lion from the country. It is a rather remarkable fact, that in no passage of Holy Writ is the Wolf directly mentioned. Its name is used as a symbol of a fierce and treacherous enemy, but neither in the Old nor New Testament does any sacred writer mention any act as performed by the Wolf. We have already heard of the lion which attacked Samson and was killed by him, of the lion which slew the disobedient prophet, and of the lions which spared Daniel when thrown into their den. We also read of the dogs which licked Ahab's blood, and ate the body of Jezebel, also of the bears which tore the mocking children.

But in no case is the Wolf mentioned, except in a metaphorical sense ; and this fact is the more remarkable, because the animals were so numerous that they were very likely to have exercised some influence on a history extending over such a lengthened range of years, and limited to so small a portion of the earth. Yet we never hear of the Wolf attacking any of the personages mentioned in Scripture ; and although we are told of the exploit of David, who pursued a lion and a bear that had taken a lamb out of his fold, we are never told of any similar deed in connexion with the Wolf.

This animal was then what it is now. Seldom seen by day, it lies hidden in its covert as long as the light lasts, and steals out in search of prey in the evening. This custom of the Wolf is mentioned in several passages of Holy Scripture, such as that in Jer. v. 5, 6: "These have altogether broken the yoke, and burst the bonds. Wherefore a lion out of the forest shall slay them, and a wolf of the evenings shall spoil them." In this passage the reader will see that the rebellious Israelites are

WOLVES ATTACKING A FLOCK OF SHEEP.

compared to restive draught cattle which have broken away from their harness and run loose, so that they are deprived of the protection of their owners, and exposed to the fury of wild beasts. A similar reference is made in Hab. i. 8: "Their horses also are swifter than the leopards, and are more fierce than the evening wolves." The same habit of the Wolf is alluded to in

Zeph. iii. 3 : "Her princes within her are roaring lions; her judges are evening wolves."

Individually, the Wolf is rather a timid animal. It will avoid a man rather than meet him. It prefers to steal upon its prey and take it unawares, rather than to seize it openly and boldly. It is ever suspicious of treachery, and is always imagining that a trap is laid for it. Even the shallow device of a few yards of rope trailing from any object, or a strip of cloth fluttering in the breeze, is quite sufficient to keep the Wolf at bay for a considerable time. This fact is well known to hunters, who are accustomed to secure the body of a slain deer by simply tying a strip of cloth to its horn. If taken in a trap of any kind, or even if it fancies itself in an enclosure from which it can find no egress, it loses all courage, and will submit to be killed without offering the least resistance. It will occasionally endeavour to effect its escape by feigning death, and has more than once been known to succeed in this device.

But, collectively, the Wolf is one of the most dangerous animals that can be found. Herding together in droves when pressed by hunger, the wolves will openly hunt prey, performing this task as perfectly as a pack of trained hounds. Full of wiles themselves, they are craftily wise in anticipating the wiles of the animals which they pursue ; and even in full chase, while the body of the pack is following on the footsteps of the flying animal, one or two are detached on the flanks, so as to cut it off if it should attempt to escape by doubling on its pursuers.

There is no animal which a herd of wolves will not attack, and very few which they will not ultimately secure. Strength avails nothing against the numbers of these savage foes, which give no moment of rest, but incessantly assail their antagonist, dashing by instinct at those parts of the body which can be least protected, and lacerating with their peculiar short, snapping bite. Should several of their number be killed or disabled, it makes no difference to the wolves, except that a minute or two are wasted in devouring their slain or wounded brethren, and they only return to the attack the more excited by the taste of blood. Swiftness of foot avails nothing against the tireless perseverance of the wolves, who press on in their peculiar, long, slinging gallop, and in the end are sure to tire out the swifter footed but less enduring animal that flees before them. The stately buffalo is conquered by the ceaseless assaults of the wolves; the bear has been forced to succumb to them, and the fleet-footed stag finds his swift limbs powerless to escape the pursuing band, and his branching horns unable to resist their furious onset when once they overtake him.

WOLVES CHASING DEER.

That the Wolf is a special enemy to the sheep-fold is shown in many parts of the Scriptures, both in the Old and New Testaments, especially in the latter. In John x. 1–16, Jesus compares himself to a good shepherd, who watches over the fold, and, if the wolves should come to take the sheep, would rather give up His life than they should succeed. But the false teachers are compared to bad shepherds, hired for money, but having no interest in the sheep, and who therefore will not expose themselves to danger in defence of their charge.

This metaphor was far more effective in Palestine, and at that time, than it is in this country and at the present day. In this

THE WOLF.

THE WOLF.

land, the shepherd has no anxiety about the inroads of wild beasts, but in Palestine one of his chief cares was to keep watch at night lest the wolves should attack the fold, and to drive them away himself in case they should do so. Therefore the shepherd's life was one which involved no small danger as well as anxiety, and the metaphor used by our Lord gains additional force from the knowledge of this fact.

A similar metaphor is used when Jesus wished to express in forcible terms the dangers to which the chosen seventy would oft be subjected, and the impossibility that they should be able to overcome the many perils with which they would be surrounded. "Go your ways: behold, I send you forth as lambs among wolves" (Luke x. 3).

Mr. Tristram several times met wolves while he was engaged in his travels, and mostly saw solitary specimens. One such encounter took place in the wilderness of Judah: "On my way back, I met a fine solitary wolf, who watched me very coolly, at the distance of sixty yards, while I drew my charge and dropped a bullet down the barrel. Though I sent the ball into a rock between his legs as he stood looking at me in the wady, he was not sufficiently alarmed to do more than move on a little more quickly, ever and anon turning to look at me, while gradually increasing his distance. Darkness compelled me to desist from the chase, when he quietly turned and followed me at a respectful distance. He was a magnificent animal, larger than any European wolf, and of a much lighter colour."

Those who are acquainted with the character of the animal will appreciate the truthfulness of this description. The cautious prowl at a distance, the slow trot away when he fancied he might be attacked, the reverted look, and the final turning back and following at a respectful distance, are all characteristic traits of the Wolf, no matter to what species it may belong, nor what country it may inhabit.

On another occasion, while riding in the open plain of Gennesaret, the horse leaped over the bank of a little ditch, barely three feet in depth. After the horse had passed, and not until then, a Wolf started out of the ditch, literally from under the horse's hoofs, and ran off. The animal had been crouching under the little bank, evidently watching for some cows and calves which were grazing at a short distance, under the charge of a

WOLVES ATTACKING WILD GOATS.

Bedouin boy. The same author mentions that one of the monks belonging to the monastery at Marsaba had contrived to render a Wolf almost tame. Every evening at six o'clock the Wolf came regularly across the ravine, ate a piece of bread, and then went back again. With the peculiar jealousy of all tamed animals, the Wolf would not suffer any of his companions to partake of his good fortune. Several of them would sometimes accompany him, but as soon as they came under the wall of the monastery he always drove them away.

The inhabitants of Palestine say that the Wolves of that country hunt singly, or at most in little packs of few in number. Still they dread the animal exceedingly on account of the damage it inflicts upon their flocks of sheep and goats.

THE JACKAL.

THE FOX OR JACKAL.

The two animals comprehended under one name—The Jackal—its numbers in ancient and modern Palestine—General habits of the Jackal—Localities where the Jackal is found—Samson, and the three hundred "foxes"—Popular objections to the narrative—The required number easily obtained—Signor Pierotti's remarks upon the Jackal—An unpleasant position—How the fields were set on fire—The dread of fire inherent in wild beasts—The truth of the narrative proved—The Fox and Jackal destructive among grapes

THERE are several passages in the Old Testament in which the word FOX occurs, and it is almost certain that the Hebrew word *Shuâl,* which is rendered in our translation as Fox, is used rather loosely, and refers in some places to the Jackal, and in others to the Fox. We will first take those passages in which the former rendering of the word is evidently the right one, and will begin by examining those characteristics of the animal which afford grounds for such an assertion.

Even at the present time, the Jackal is extremely plentiful in Palestine; and as the numbers of wild beasts have much decreased in modern days, the animals must have been even more numerous than they are at present. It is an essentially nocturnal and gregarious animal. During the whole of the day the Jackals lie concealed in their holes or hiding-places, which are usually cavities in the rocks, in tombs, or among ruins. At nightfall they issue from their dens, and form themselves into packs, often consisting of several hundred individuals, and prowl about in search of food. Carrion of various kinds forms their

THE FOX OR JACKAL.   77

FOX AND YOUNG.

chief subsistence, and they perform in the country much the same task as is fulfilled by the dogs in the cities.

If any animal should be killed, or even severely wounded, the Jackals are sure to find it out and to devour it before the daybreak. They will scent out the track of the hunter, and feed upon the offal of the beasts which he has slain. If the body of a human being were to be left on the ground, the Jackals would certainly leave but little traces of it; and in the olden times of warfare, they must have held high revelry in the battle-field after the armies had retired. It is to this propensity of the Jackal that David refers—himself a man of war, who had fought on many a battle-field, and must have seen the carcases of the slain mangled by these nocturnal prowlers : " Those that seek my soul, to destroy it, shall go into the lower parts of the earth. They shall fall by the sword; they shall be a portion for foxes " (Ps. lxiii. 9, 10). Being wild beasts, afraid of man, and too cowardly to attack him even when rendered furious by hunger, and powerful by force of numbers, they keep aloof from towns and cities, and live in the uninhabited parts of the country. Therefore the prophet Jeremiah, in his Book of Lamentations, makes use of the following forcible image, when deploring the pitiful state into which Judæa had fallen : " For this our heart is faint; for these things our eyes are dim : because of the mountain of Zion, which is desolate, the foxes walk upon it" (Lam. v. 17). And Ezekiel makes use of a similar image : " O Israel, thy prophets are like foxes in the desert."

But, by far the most important passage in which the Fox is mentioned, is that wherein is recorded the grotesque vengeance of Samson upon the Philistines: " And Samson went and caught three hundred foxes, and took firebrands, and turned tail to tail, and put a firebrand in the midst between two tails. And when he had set the brands on fire, he let them go into the standing corn of the Philistines, and burnt up both the shocks and also the standing corn, with the vineyards and olives" (Judges xv. 4, 5). Now, as this is one of the passages of Holy Writ to which great objections have been taken, it will be as well to examine these objections, and see whether they have any real force. The first of these objections is, that the number of foxes is far too great to have been caught at one time, and to this objection two answers have been given. The first answer is, that

A FEAST IN PROSPECT.

they need not have been caught at once, but by degrees, and kept until wanted. But the general tenor of the narrative is undoubtedly in favour of the supposition that this act of Samson was unpremeditated, and that it was carried into operation at once, before his anger had cooled. The second answer is, that the requisite number of Foxes might have been miraculously sent to Samson for this special purpose. This theory is really so foolish and utterly untenable, that I only mention it because it has been put forward. It fails on two grounds: the first being that a miracle would hardly have been wrought to enable Samson to revenge himself in so cruel and unjustifiable a manner; and the second, that there was not the least necessity for any miracle at all.

If we put out of our minds the idea of the English Fox, an animal comparatively scarce in this country, and solitary in its habits, and substitute the extremely plentiful and gregarious Jackal, wandering in troops by night, and easily decoyed by hunger into a trap, we shall see that double the number might have been taken, if needful. Moreover, it is not to be imagined that Samson caught them all with his own hand. He was at the head of his people, and had many subordinates at his command, so that a large number of hunters might have been employed simultaneously in the capture. In corroboration of this point, I insert an extremely valuable extract from Signor Pierotti's work, in which he makes reference to this very portion of the sacred history:—

"It is still very abundant near Gaza, Askalon, Ashdod, Ekron, and Ramleh. I have frequently met with it during my wanderings by night, and on one occasion had an excellent opportunity of appreciating their number and their noise.

"One evening in the month of January, while it was raining a perfect deluge, I was obliged, owing to the dangerous illness of a friend, to return from Jerusalem to Jaffa. The depth of snow on the road over a great part of the mountain, the clayey mud in the plain, and the darkness of the night, prevented my advancing quickly; so that about half-past three in the morning I arrived on the bank of a small torrent, about half an hour's journey to the east of Ramleh. I wished to cross: my horse at first refused, but, on my spurring it, advanced and at once sank up to the breast, followed of course by

A FEAST SECURED.

my legs, thus teaching me to respect the instinct of an Arab horse for the future.

"There I stuck, without the possibility of escape, and consoled my horse and myself with some provisions that I had in my saddle-bags, shouting and singing at intervals, in the hope of obtaining succour, and of preventing accidents, as I knew that the year before a mule in the same position had been mistaken for a wild beast, and killed. The darkness was profound, and the wind very high; but, happily, it was not cold; for the only things attracted by my calls were numbers of jackals, who remained at a certain distance from me, and responded to my cries, especially when I tried to imitate them, as though they took me for their music-master.

"About five o'clock, one of the guards of the English consulate at Jerusalem came from Ramleh and discovered my state. He charitably returned thither, and brought some men, who extricated me and my horse from our unpleasant bath, which, as may be supposed, was not beneficial to our legs.

"During this most uncomfortable night, I had good opportunity of ascertaining that, if another Samson had wished to burn again the crops in the country of the Philistines, he would have had no difficulty in finding more than three hundred jackals, and catching as many as he wanted in springs, traps, or pitfalls. (See Ps. cxl. 5.)"

The reader will now see that there was not the least difficulty in procuring the requisite number of animals, and that consequently the first objection to the truth of the story is disposed of.

We will now proceed to the second objection, which is, that if the animals were tied tail to tail, they would remain on or near the same spot, because they would pull in different directions, and that, rather than run about, they would turn round and fight each other. Now, in the first place, we are nowhere told that the tails of the foxes, or jackals, were placed in contact with each other, and it is probable that some little space was left between them. That animals so tied would not run in a straight line is evident enough, and this was exactly the effect which Samson wished to produce. Had they been at liberty, and the fiery brand fastened to their tails, they would have run straight to their dens, and produced but little effect. But their captor,

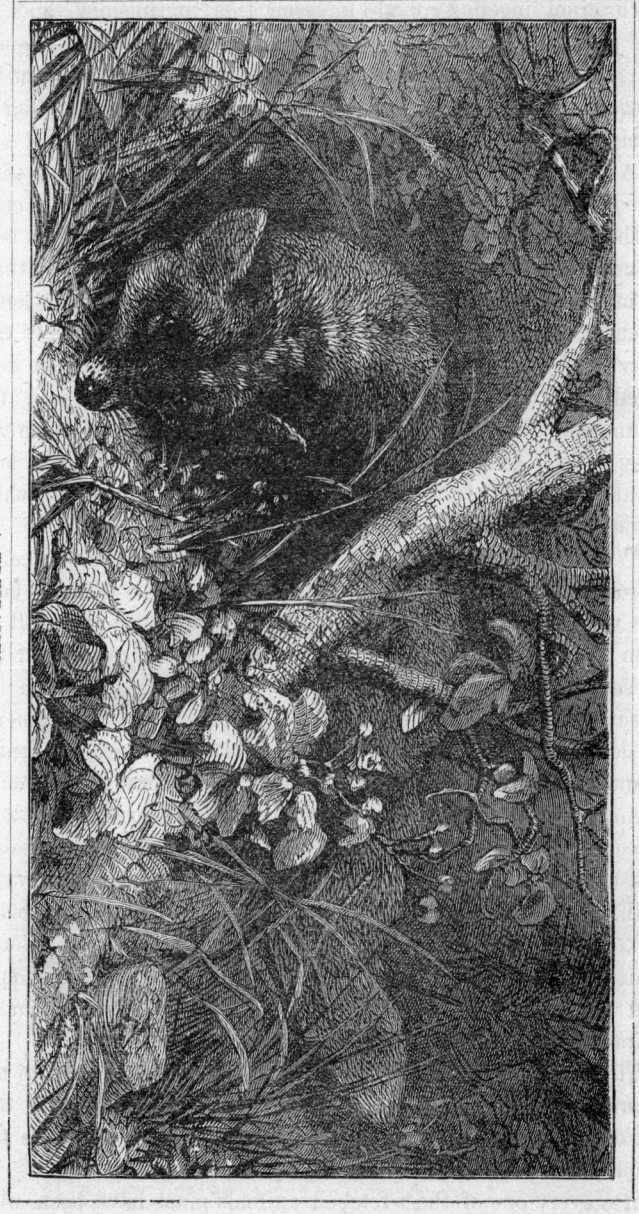

A TRESPASSER.

with cruel ingenuity, had foreseen this contingency, and, by the method of securing them which he adopted, forced them to pursue a devious course, each animal trying to escape from the dreaded firebrand, and struggling in vain endeavours to drag its companion towards its own particular den.

All wild animals have an instinctive dread of fire; and there is none, not even the fierce and courageous lion, that dares enter within the glare of the bivouac fire. A lion has even been struck in the face with a burning brand, and has not ventured to attack the man that wielded so dreadful a weapon. Consequently it may be imagined that the unfortunate animals that were used by Samson for his vindictive purpose, must have been filled with terror at the burning brands which they dragged after them, and the blaze of the fire which was kindled wherever they went. They would have no leisure to fight, and would only think of escaping from the dread and unintelligible enemy which pursued them.

When a prairie takes fire, all the wild inhabitants flee in terror, and never think of attacking each other, so that the bear, the wolf, the cougar, the deer, and the wild swine, may all be seen huddled together, their natural antagonism quelled in the presence of a common foe. So it must have been with the miserable animals which were made the unconscious instruments of destruction. That they would stand still when a burning brand was between them, and when flames sprang up around them, is absurd. That they would pull in exactly opposite directions with precisely balanced force is equally improbable, and it is therefore evident that they would pursue a devious path, the stronger of the two dragging the weaker, but being jerked out of a straight course and impeded by the resistance which it would offer. That they would stand on the same spot and fight has been shown to be contrary to the custom of animals under similar circumstances.

Thus it will be seen that every objection not only falls to the ground, but carries its own refutation, thus vindicating this episode in sacred history, and showing, that not only were the circumstances possible, but that they were highly probable. Of course every one of the wretched animals must have been ultimately burned to death, after suffering a prolonged torture from the firebrand that was attached to it. Such a consideration would, however, have had no effect for deterring Samson from employing them. The Orientals are never sparing of pain, even when inflicted upon human beings, and in too many cases they seem utterly unable even to comprehend the cruelty of which they are guilty. And Samson was by no means a favourable specimen of his countrymen. He was the very incarnation of strength, but was as morally weak as he was corporeally powerful; and to that weakness he owed his fall. Neither does he seem to possess the least trace of forbearance any more than of self-control, but he yields to his own undisciplined nature, places himself, and through him the whole Israelitish nation, in jeopardy, and then, with a grim humour, scatters destruction on every side in revenge for the troubles which he has brought upon himself by his own acts.

THE HYÆNA.

The Hyæna not mentioned by name, but evidently alluded to—Signification of the word Zabua—Translated in the Septuagint as Hyæna—A scene described by the prophet Isaiah—The Hyæna plentiful in Palestine at the present day—its well-known cowardice and fear of man—The uses of the Hyæna and the services which it renders—The particular species of Hyæna—The Hyæna in the burial-grounds—Hunting the Hyæna - Curious superstition respecting the talismanic properties of its skin—Precautions adopted in flaying it—Popular legends of the Hyæna and its magical powers—The cavern home of the Hyæna—The valley of Zeboim.

ALTHOUGH in our version of the Scriptures the Hyæna is not mentioned by that name, there are two passages in the Old Testament which evidently refer to that animal, and therefore it is described in these pages. If the reader will refer to the prophet Jeremiah, xii. 7–9, he will find these words: " I have forsaken mine house, I have left mine heritage; I have given the dearly beloved of my soul into the hand of her enemies. Mine heritage is unto me as a lion in the forest; it crieth out against me: therefore have I hated it. Mine heritage is unto me as a speckled bird; the birds round about are against her: come ye, assemble all the beasts of the field, come to devour." Now, the word *zabua* signifies something that is streaked, and in the Authorized Version it is rendered as a speckled bird. But in the Septuagint it is rendered as Hyæna, and this translation is thought by many critical writers to be the true one. It is certain that the word *zabua* is one of the four names by which the Talmudical writers mention the Hyæna, when treating of its character; and it is equally certain that such a rendering makes the passage more forcible, and is in perfect accordance with the habits of predacious animals.

The whole scene which the Prophet thus describes was evidently familiar to him. First, we have the image of a deserted country, allowed to be overrun with wild beasts. Then we have the lion, which has struck down its prey, roaring with exultation, and defying any adversary to take it from him. Then, the lion having eaten his fill and gone away, we have the Hyænas, vultures, and other carrion-eating creatures, assembling around the carcase, and hastening to devour it. This is a scene which has been witnessed by many hunters who have pursued their sport in lands where lions, hyænas, and vultures are found; and all these creatures were inhabitants of Palestine at the time when Jeremiah wrote.

At the present day, the Hyæna is still plentiful in Palestine, though in the course of the last few years its numbers have sensibly diminished. The solitary traveller, when passing by night from one town to another, often falls in with the Hyæna, but need suffer no fear, as it will not attack a human being, and prefers to slink out of his way. But dead, and dying, or wounded animals are the objects for which it searches; and when it finds them, it devours the whole of its prey. The lion will strike down an antelope, an ox, or a goat—will tear off its flesh with its long fangs, and lick the bones with its rough tongue until they are quite cleaned. The wolves and jackals will follow the lion, and eat every soft portion of the dead animal, while the vultures will fight with them for the coveted morsels. But the Hyæna is a more accomplished scavenger than lion, wolf, jackal, or vulture; for it will eat the very bones themselves, its tremendously-powerful jaws and firmly-set teeth enabling it to crush even the leg-bone of an ox, and its unparalleled digestive powers enabling it to assimilate the sharp and hard fragments which would kill any creature not constituted like itself.

In a wild, or even a partially-inhabited country, the **Hyæna**

LEOPARD ROBBED OF ITS PREY BY HYÆNAS.

is, therefore, a most useful animal. It may occasionally kill a crippled or weakly ox, and sometimes carry off a sheep; but, even in that case, no very great harm is done, for it does not meddle with any animal that can resist. But these few delinquencies are more than compensated by the great services which it renders as scavenger, consuming those substances which even the lion cannot eat, and thus acting as a scavenger in removing objects which would be offensive to sight and injurious to health.

The species which is mentioned in the Scriptures is the Striped Hyæna (*Hyæna striata*); but the habits of all the species are almost exactly similar. We are told by travellers of certain towns in different parts of Africa which would be unendurable but for the Hyænas. With the disregard for human life which prevails throughout all savage portions of that country, the rulers of these towns order executions almost daily, the bodies of the victims being allowed to lie where they happened to fall. No one chooses to touch them, lest they should also be added to the list of victims, and the decomposing bodies would soon cause a pestilence but for the Hyænas, who assemble at night round the bodies, and by the next morning have left scarcely a trace of the murdered men.

Even in Palestine, and in the present day, the Hyæna will endeavour to rifle the grave, and to drag out the interred corpse. The bodies of the rich are buried in rocky caves, whose entrances are closed with heavy stones, which the Hyæna cannot move; but those of the poor, which are buried in the ground, must be defended by stones heaped over them. Even when this precaution is taken, the Hyæna will sometimes find out a weak spot, drag out the body, and devour it.

In consequence of this propensity, the inhabitants have an utter detestation of the animal. They catch it whenever they can, in pitfalls or snares, using precisely the same means as were employed two thousand years ago; or they hunt it to its den, and then kill it, stripping off the hide, and carrying it about still wet, receiving a small sum of money from those to whom they show it. Afterwards the skin is dressed, by rubbing it with lime and salt, and steeping it in the waters of the Dead Sea. It is then made into sandals and leggings, which are thought to be powerful charms, and to defend the wearer from the Hyæna's bite.

THE HYÆNA.

They always observe certain superstitious precautions in flaying the dead animal. Believing that the scent of the flesh would corrupt the air, they invariably take the carcase to the leeward of the tents before they strip off the skin. Even in the animal which has been kept for years in a cage, and has eaten nothing but fresh meat, the odour is too powerful to be agreeable,

HYÆNAS DEVOURING BONES.

as I can testify from practical experience when dissecting a Hyæna that had died in the Zoological Gardens; and it is evident that the scent of an animal that has lived all its life on carrion must be almost unbearable. The skin being removed, the carcase is burnt, because the hunters think that by this process the other Hyænas are prevented from finding the body of their comrade, and either avenging its death or taking warning by its fate.

Superstitions seem to be singularly prevalent concerning the Hyæna. In Palestine, there is a prevalent idea that if a Hyæna meets a solitary man at night, it can enchant him in such a manner as to make him follow it through thickets and over rocks, until he is quite exhausted, and falls an unresisting prey; but that over two persons he has no such influence, and therefore a solitary traveller is gravely advised to call for help as soon as he sees a Hyæna, because the fascination of the beast would be neutralized by the presence of a second person. So firmly is this idea rooted in the minds of the inhabitants, that they will never travel by night, unless they can find at least one companion in their journey.

In Northern Africa there are many strange superstitions connected with this animal, one of the most curious of which is founded on its well-known cowardice. The Arabs fancy that any weapon which has killed a Hyæna, whether it be gun, sword, spear, or dagger, is thenceforth unfit to be used in warfare. "Throw away that sword," said an Arab to a French officer, who had killed a Hyæna, "it has slain the Hyæna, and it will be treacherous to you."

At the present day, its numbers are not nearly so great in Palestine as they used to be, and are decreasing annually. The cause of this diminution lies, according to Signor Pierotti, more in the destruction of forests than in the increase of population and the use of fire-arms, though the two latter causes have undoubtedly considerable influence.

There is a very interesting account by Mr. Tristram of the haunt of these animals. While exploring the deserted quarries of Es Sumrah, between Beth-arabah and Bethel, he came upon a wonderful mass of hyænine relics. The quarries in which were lying the half-hewn blocks, scored with the marks of wedges, had evidently formed the resort of Hyænas for a long series of years. "Vast heaps of bones of camels, oxen, and sheep had been collected by these animals, in some places to the depth of two or three feet, and on one spot I counted the skulls of seven camels. There were no traces whatever of any human remains. We had here a beautiful recent illustration of the mode of foundation of the old bone caverns, so valuable to the geologist. These bones must all have been brought in by the Hyænas, as no camel or sheep could possibly have entered the caverns alive, nor could any floods have washed them in. Near the entrance where the water percolates, they were already forming a soft breccia."

The second allusion to the Hyæna is made in 1 Sam. xiii. 18, " Another company turned to the way of the border that looketh to the Valley of Zeboim towards the wilderness," *i.e.* to the Valley of Hyænas.

The colour of the Striped Hyæna varies according to its age. When young, as is the case with many creatures, birds as well as mammals, the stripes from which it derives its name are much more strongly marked than in the adult specimen. The general hue of the fur is a pale grey-brown, over which are drawn a number of dark stripes, extending along the ribs and across the limbs.

In the young animal these stripes are nearly twice as dark and twice as wide as in the adult, and they likewise appear on the face and on other parts of the body, whence they afterwards vanish. The fur is always rough; and along the spine, and especially over the neck and shoulders, it is developed into a kind of mane, which gives a very fierce aspect to the animal. The illustration shows a group of Hyænas coming to feed on the relics of a dead animal. The jackals and vultures have eaten as much of the flesh as they can manage, and the vultures are sitting, gorged, round the stripped bones. The Hyænas are now coming up to play their part as scavengers, and have already begun to break up the bones in their crushing-mills of jaws.

THE WEASEL.

Difficulty of identifying the Weasel of Scripture—The Weasel of Palestine—Suggested identity with the Ichneumon.

THE word Weasel occurs once in the Holy Scriptures, and therefore it is necessary that the animal should be mentioned. There is a great controversy respecting the identification of the animal, inasmuch as there is nothing in the context which gives the slightest indication of its appearance or habits.

The passage in question is that which prohibits the Weasel and the mouse as unclean animals (see Lev. xi. 29). Now the word which is here translated Weasel is *Choled*, or *Chol'd*; and, I believe, never occurs again in the whole of the Old Testament. Mr. W. Houghton conjectures that the Hebrew word Choled is identical with the Arabic *Chuld* and the Syriac *Chuldo*, both words signifying a mole; and therefore infers that the unclean animal in question is not a Weasel, but a kind of mole.

The Weasel does exist in Palestine, and seems to be as plentiful there as in our own country. Indeed, the whole tribe of Weasels is well represented, and the polecat is seen there as well as the Weasel.

There is hardly any animal which, for its size, is so much dreaded by the creatures on it which it preys as the common Weasel.

Although its small proportions render a single Weasel an insignificant opponent to man or dog, yet it can wage a sharp battle even with such powerful foes, and refuses to yield except at the last necessity.

The proportions of the Weasel are extremely small, a full-grown male not exceeding ten inches in length. The color of its fur is bright reddish-brown on the upper parts of the body, and the under-portions are pure white. The audacity and courage of this little animal are really remarkable. It seems to hold every being except itself in the most sovereign contempt, and, to all appearances, is as ready to match itself against a man as against a mouse.

It is a terrible foe to many of the smaller animals, such as rats

WEASELS.

and mice, and performs a really good service to the farmer in destroying many of these farmyard pests. The Weasel is specially dreaded by rats and mice, because there is no hole through which they can pass that will not also admit the passage of their enemy; and, as the Weasel is most persevering and determined in pursuit, it seldom happens that rats or mice escape when their little foe has set itself fairly on their track.

Not only does the Weasel pursue its prey through the windings of the burrows, but it will even cross water in the chase. When it has at last reached its victim, it leaps upon the devoted creature and endeavours to fix its teeth in the back of the neck, where it retains its deadly hold in spite of every struggle on the part of the wounded animal. If the attack be rightly made and the animal a small one, the Weasel can drive its teeth into the brain and cause instantaneous death.

The Weasel is very fond of eggs, and young birds of all kinds. It is said that an egg that has been broken by a Weasel, can always be recognized, by the peculiar mode which the little creature employs for the purpose.

Instead of breaking the egg to pieces or biting a large hole in the shell, the Weasel contents itself with making quite a small aperture at one end, through which it abstracts the liquid contents.

A curious example of the courage of the Weasel, is related by a gentleman who while crossing a field at dusk, saw an owl pounce upon some object on the ground, and carry it in the air.

In a short time the bird showed signs of distress, trying to free itself from some annoying object by means of its talons, and flapping about in a very bewildered manner.

Soon afterwards the owl fell dead to the earth; and when the spectator of the aërial combat approached, a weasel ran away from the dead body of the bird, itself being apparently uninjured. On examination of the owl's body, it was found that the Weasel, which had been marked out for the owl's repast, had in its turn become the assailant, and had attacked the unprotected parts which lie beneath the wings. A considerable wound had been made in that spot, and the large blood-vessels torn through.

THE BITER BIT.

THE BADGER.

Difficulty in identifying the Tachash *of Scripture—References to "Badgers' skins"—The Dugong thought to be the Badger—The Bedouin sandals—Nature of the materials for the Tabernacle - Habits of the Badger—The species found in Palestine—Uses of the Badgers' skins—Looseness of zoological terms.*

UNTIL very lately, there was much difficulty in ascertaining whether the word *Tachash* has been rightly translated as Badger. It occurs in several parts of the Scriptures, and almost invariably is used in relation to a skin or fur of some sort. We will first examine the passages in which the Badger is mentioned, and then proceed to identify the animal.

Nearly all the references to the Badger occur in the book of Exodus, and form part of the directions for constructing the Tabernacle and its contents. The first notice of the word occurs in Exodus xxv. 5, where the people of Israel are ordered to bring their offerings for the sanctuary, among which offerings are gold, silver, and brass, blue, purple, and scarlet, fine linen, goats' hair, rams' skins dyed red, badgers' skins, and shittim wood—all these to be used in the construction of the Tabernacle. Then a little farther on, in chapter xxvi. 14, we find one of the special uses to which the badgers' skins were to be put, namely, to make the outer covering or roof of the tabernacle. Another use for the badgers' skins was to form an outer covering for the ark, table

THE BADGER.

of shewbread, and other furniture of the Tabernacle, when the people were on the march.

In all these cases the badger-skin is used as a covering to defend a building or costly furniture, but there is one example where it is employed for a different purpose. This passage occurs in the book of Ezekiel, chapter xvi. 10. The prophet is speaking of Jerusalem under the image of a woman, and uses these words, " I anointed thee with oil; I clothed thee also with broidered work, and shod thee with badger's skin, and I girded thee about with fine linen, and I covered thee with silk. I decked thee also with ornaments, and I put bracelets upon thy hands, and a chain upon thy neck, and I put a jewel on thy forehead, and earrings in thine ears, and a beautiful crown upon thine head."

So we have here the fact, that the same material which was used for the covering of the Tabernacle, and of the sacred furniture, could also be used for the manufacture of shoes. This passage is the more valuable because of an inference which may be drawn from it. The reader will see that the badger-skin, whatever it may have been, must have been something of considerable value, and therefore, in all probability, something of much rarity.

In the present instance, it is classed with the most luxurious robes that were known in those days, and it is worthy of special mention among the bracelet, earrings, necklace, and coronal with which the symbolized city was adorned. If the reader will now refer to the passage in which the children of Israel were commanded to bring their offerings, he will see that in those cases also the badger-skins were ranked with the costliest articles of apparel that could be found, and had evidently been brought from Egypt, the peculiar home of all the arts ; together with the vast quantity of gold and jewels which were used for the same sacred purpose.

Now we find that the badger-skins in question must possess three qualities : they must be costly, they must be capable of forming a defence against the weather, and they must be strong enough to be employed in the manufacture of shoes. If we accept the word Tachash as signifying a Badger, we shall find that these conditions have been fulfilled.

But many commentators have thought that badger-skins could

not have been procured in sufficient numbers for the purpose, and have therefore conjectured that some other animal must be signified by the word Tachash.

A species of dugong (*Halicore hemprichii*) is the animal that has been selected as the Badger of the Scriptures. It is one of the marine mammalia, and always lives near the shore, where it can find the various algæ on which it feeds. It is a gregarious animal, and, as it frequently ascends rivers for some distance, it may be captured in sufficient numbers to make both its flesh and skin useful. Moreover, it is of considerable size, fourteen or fifteen feet in length being its usual dimensions, so that a comparatively small number of the skins would be required for the covering of the Tabernacle.

That shoes can be made of it is evident from the fact that at the present day shoes, or rather sandals, are made from its hide, and are commonly used by the Bedouins. But the very qualities and peculiarities which render it a fit material for the sandal of a half-naked Bedouin Arab, who has to walk continually over hard, hot, sandy, and rough ground, would surely make it unsuitable for the delicate shoes worn by a woman of rank who spends her time in the house, and the rest of whose clothing is of fine linen and silk, embroidered with gold and jewels. In our own country, the hobnailed shoes of the ploughman and the slight shoe of a lady are made of very different materials, and it is reasonable to conjecture that such was the case when the passage in question was written.

Then Dr. Robinson, who admits that the hide of the dugong could hardly have been used as the material for a lady's shoe, thinks that it would have answered very well for the roof of the Tabernacle, because it was large, clumsy, and coarse. It seems strange that he did not also perceive that the two latter qualities would completely disqualify such skins for that service. Everything clumsy and coarse was studiously prohibited, and nothing but the very best was considered fit for the Tabernacle of the Lord. By special revelation, Moses was instructed to procure, not merely the ordinary timber of the country for the framework—not only the fabrics which would keep out rain and wind—not simply the metals in common use, from which to make the lamps and other furniture—not the ordinary oils for supplying the lamps; but, on the contrary, the finest

BADGERS.

linen, the most elaborate embroidery, the rarest woods, the purest gold, the costliest gems, were demanded, and nothing common or inferior was accepted. The commonest material that was permitted was the long, soft fleece of rams' wool; but, even in that case, the wool had to be dyed of the regal scarlet—a dye so rare and so costly that none but the wealthiest rulers could use it. Even the very oil that burned in the lamps must be the purest olive-oil, prepared expressly for that purpose.

The very fact, therefore, that any article was plentiful and could easily be obtained, would be a proof that such article was not used for so sacred a purpose; while it is impossible that anything coarse and clumsy could have been accepted for the construction of that Tabernacle within which the Shekinah ever burned over the Mercy-seat—over which the cloud rested by day, and the fire shone by night, visible external proofs of the Divine glory within.

We therefore dismiss from our minds the possibility of accepting any material for it which was not exceptionably valuable, and which would be employed in the uses of ordinary life. The great object of the minutely-elaborate directions which were given through Moses to the Israelites was evidently to keep continually before their eyes the great truth that they owed all to God, and that their costliest offerings were but acknowledgments of their dependence.

We will now presume that the Tachash of the Pentateuch and Ezekiel is really the animal which we know by the name of Badger. It exists throughout the whole of the district traversed by the Israelites, though it is not very plentiful, nor is it easily taken. Had such been the case, its fur would not have been employed in the service of the sanctuary.

It is nocturnal in its habits, and very seldom is seen during the hours of daylight, so that it cannot be captured by chase. It is not gregarious, so that it cannot be taken in great numbers, as is the case with certain wild animals which have been thought to be the Tachash of Scripture. It is not a careless animal, so that it cannot be captured or killed without the exercise of considerable ingenuity, and the expenditure of much time and trouble. It is one of the burrowing animals, digging for itself a deep subterranean home, and always ready whenever it is

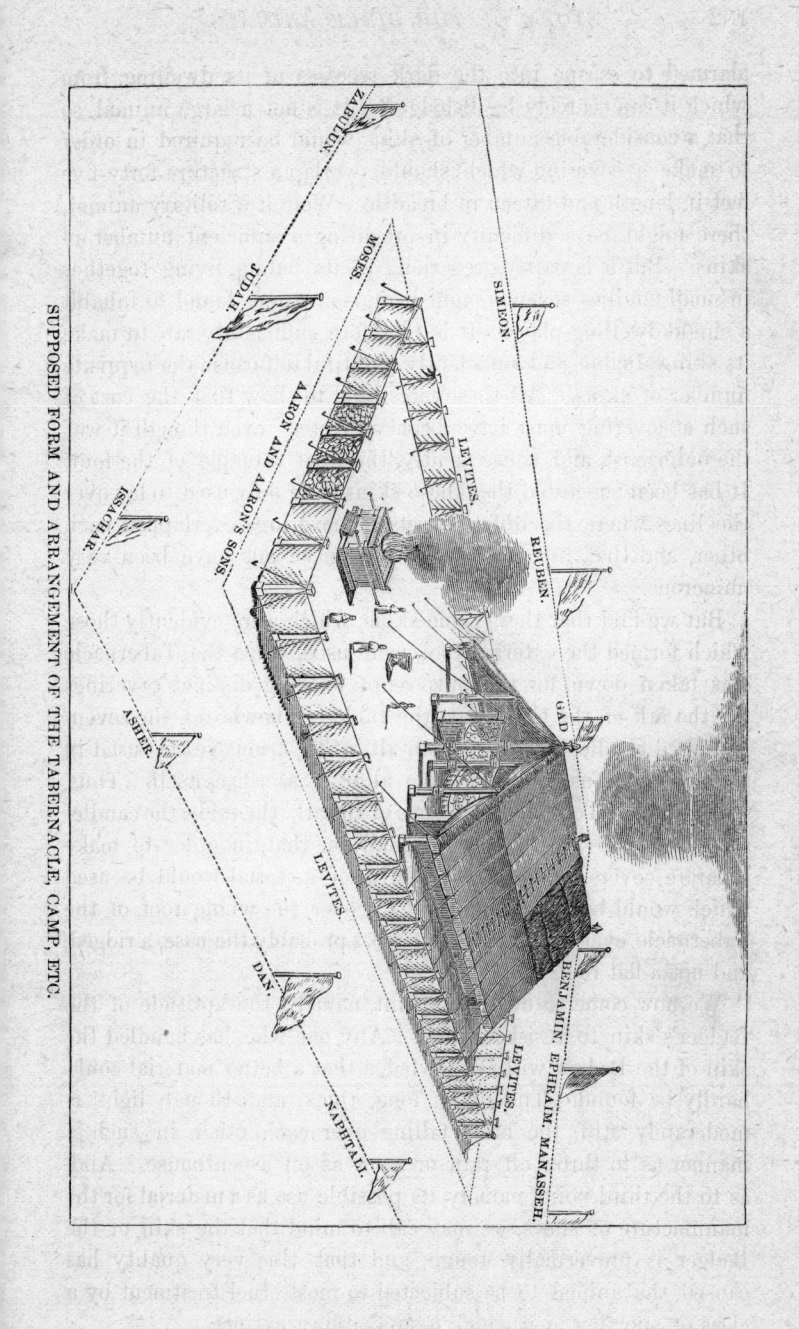

SUPPOSED FORM AND ARRANGEMENT OF THE TABERNACLE, CAMP, ETC.

alarmed to escape into the dark recesses of its dwelling, from which it can scarcely be dislodged. It is not a large animal, so that a considerable number of skins would be required in order to make a covering which should overlap a structure forty-five feet in length and fifteen in breadth. Were it a solitary animal, there might be a difficulty in procuring a sufficient number of skins. But it is partly gregarious in its habits, living together in small families, seven or eight being sometimes found to inhabit a single dwelling-place. It is, therefore, sufficiently rare to make its skin valuable, and sufficiently plentiful to furnish the requisite number of skins. All these facts tend to show that the cost of such a covering must have been very great, even though it was the outermost, and, consequently, the least valuable of the four. It has been suggested that these skins were only used to lay over the lines where the different sets of coverings overlapped each other, and that, in consequence, they need not have been very numerous.

But we find that these same skins, which were evidently those which formed the external roof, were used, when the Tabernacle was taken down, for the purpose of forming distinct coverings for the ark of the testimony, the table of shewbread, the seven-branched candlestick, the golden altar, the various vessels used in the ministrations, and lastly, the altar of sacrifice itself. Thus, when we recollect the dimensions of the ark, the table, the candlestick, and the two altars, we shall see that, in order to make separate covers for them, a quantity of material would be used which would be amply sufficient to cover the whole roof of the Tabernacle, even if it had, as was most probably the case, a ridged, and not a flat roof.

We now come to our next point, namely, the aptitude of the Badger's skin to resist weather. Any one who has handled the skin of the Badger will acknowledge that a better material could hardly be found. The fur is long, thick, and, though light, is moderately stiff, the hairs falling over each other in such a manner as to throw off rain or snow as off a penthouse. And, as to the third point, namely, its possible use as a material for the manufacture of shoes, we may call to mind that the skin of the Badger is proverbially tough, and that this very quality has caused the animal to be subjected to most cruel treatment by a class of sporting men which is now almost extinct.

The Septuagint gives little assistance in determining the precise nature of the Tachash, and rather seems to consider the word as expressive of the colour with which the fur was dyed than that of the animal from which it was taken. Still, it must be remembered that not only are zoological terms used very loosely in the Scriptures, but that in Hebrew, as in all other languages, the same combination of letters often expresses two different ideas, so that the word Tachash may equally signify a colour and an animal. Moreover, it has been well pointed out that the repeated use of the word in the plural number shows that it cannot refer to colour; while its almost invariable combination with the Hebrew word that signifies a skin implies that it does not refer to colour, but to an animal.

What that animal may be, is, as I have already mentioned, conjectural. But, as the authorized translation renders the word as Badger, and as this reading fulfils the conditions necessary to its identification, and as no other reading does fulfil them, we cannot be very far wrong if we accept that translation as the correct one, and assume the Tachash of the Scriptures to be the animal which we call by the name of Badger.

THE BEAR.

The Syrian Bear—Identity of the Hebrew and Arabic titles—Its colour variable according to age—Bears once numerous in Palestine, and now only occasionally seen—Reason for their diminution—Present localities of the Bear, and its favourite haunts—Food of the Bear—Its general habits - Its ravages among the flocks—The Bear dangerous to mankind—The Bear robbed of her whelps—Illustrative passages—Its mode of fighting—Various references to the Bear, from the time of Samuel to that of St. John.

WHATEVER doubt may exist as to the precise identity of various animals mentioned in the Scriptures, there is none whatever as to the creature which is frequently alluded to under the name of Bear.

The Hebrew word is *Dôb*, and it is a remarkable fact that the name of this animal in the Arabic language is almost identical with the Hebrew term, namely, *Dubh*. The peculiar species of Bear which inhabits Palestine is the Syrian Bear (*Ursus Isabellinus*), and, though it has been variously described by different eye-witnesses, there is no doubt that the same species was seen by them all. As is the case with many animals, the Syrian Bear changes its colour as it grows older. When a cub, it is of a darkish brown, which becomes a light brown as it approaches maturity. But, when it has attained its full growth, it becomes cream-coloured, and each succeeding year seems to lighten its coat, so that a very old Bear is nearly as white as its relative of the Arctic regions. Travellers, therefore, who have met the younger specimens, have described them as brown in hue, while those who have seen more aged individuals have stated that the colour of the Syrian Bear is white.

Owing to the destruction of forests, the Bear, which is essentially a lover of the woods, has decreased considerably in number. Yet, even at the present time, specimens may be seen by the watchful traveller, mostly about the range of Lebanon, but sometimes at a considerable distance from that locality. Mr. Tristram, for example, saw it close to the Lake of Gennesaret. "We never met with so many wild animals as on one of those days. First of all, a wild boar got out of some scrub close to us, as we were ascending the valley. Then a deer was started below, ran up the cliff, and wound along the ledge, passing close to us. Then a large ichneumon almost crossed my feet and ran into a cleft; and, while endeavouring to trace him, I was amazed to see a brown Syrian Bear clumsily but rapidly clamber down the rocks and cross the ravine. He was, however, far too cautious to get within hailing distance of any of the riflemen."

The same author mentions that some of the chief strongholds of this Bear are certain clefts in the face of a precipitous chasm through which the river Leontes flows. This river runs into the sea a few miles northward of Tyre, and assists in carrying off the melted snows from the Lebanon range of mountains. His description is so picturesque, that it must be given in his own words. "The channel, though a thousand feet deep, was so narrow that the opposite ridge was within gunshot. Looking down the giddy abyss, we could see the cliff on our side partially

BEARS DESCENDING THE MOUNTAINS.

covered with myrtle, bay, and caper hanging from the fissures, while the opposite side was perforated with many shallow caves, the inaccessible eyries of vultures, eagles, and lanner falcons, which were sailing in multitudes around. The lower part had many ledges clad with shrubs, the strongholds of the Syrian Bear, though inaccessible even to goats. Far beneath dashed the milk-white river, a silver line in a ruby setting of oleanders, roaring doubtless fiercely, but too distant to be heard at the height on which we stood. This *cleft* of the Leontes was the only true Alpine scenery we had met with in Palestine, and in any country, and amidst any mountains, it would attract admiration."

On those elevated spots the Bear loves to dwell, and throughout the summer-time generally remains in such localities. For the Bear is one of the omnivorous animals, and is able to feed on vegetable as well as animal substances, preferring the former when they can be found. There is nothing that a Bear likes better than strawberries and similar fruits, among which it will revel throughout the whole fruit season, daintily picking the ripest berries, and becoming wonderfully fat by the constant banquet. Sometimes, when the fruits fail, it makes incursions among the cultivated grounds, and is noted for the ravages which it makes among a sort of vetch which is much grown in the Holy Land.

But during the colder months of the year the Bear changes its diet, and becomes carnivorous. Sometimes it contents itself with the various wild animals which it can secure, but sometimes it descends to the lower plains, and seizes upon the goats and sheep in their pastures. This habit is referred to by David, in his well-known speech to Saul, when the king was trying to dissuade him from matching himself against the gigantic Philistine. "And Saul said to David, Thou art not able to go against this Philistine to fight with him : for thou art but a youth, and he a man of war from his youth. . . . . Thy servant kept his father's sheep, and there came a lion and a bear, and took a lamb out of the flock : and I went out after him, and smote him, and delivered it out of his hand ; and when he arose against me, I caught him by the beard, and smote him, and slew him. Thy servant slew both the lion and the bear : and this uncircumcised Philistine shall be as one of them, seeing he hath defied the armies of the living God."—1 Sam. xvii. 33—36.

ON THE WATCH.

Though not generally apt to attack mankind, it will do so if first attacked, and then becomes a most dangerous enemy. See, for example, that most graphic passage in the book of the prophet Amos, whose business as a herdsman must have made him conversant with the habits, not only of the flocks and herds which he kept, but of the wild beasts which might devour them:—" Woe unto you that desire the day of the Lord! to what end is it for you? the day of the Lord is darkness, and not light. As if a man did flee from a lion, and a bear met him; or went into a house, and leaned his hand on the wall, and a serpent bit him." (v. 19.)

Another reference to the dangerous character of the Bear is made in 2 Kings ii. 23, 24, in which is recorded that two she-bears came out of the wood near Bethel, and killed forty-two of the children that mocked at Elisha.

As the Bear is not swift of foot, but rather clumsy in its movements, it cannot hope to take the nimbler animals in open chase. It prefers to lie in wait for them in the bushes, and to strike them down with a sudden blow of its paw, a terrible weapon, which it can wield as effectively as the lion uses its claws. An allusion to this habit is made in the Lamentations of Jeremiah (iii. 10), "He was unto me as a bear lying in wait, and as a lion in secret places."

Harmless to man as it generally is, there are occasions on which it becomes a terrible and relentless foe, not seeking to avoid his presence, but even searching for him, and attacking him as soon as seen. In the proper season of the year, hunters, or those who are travelling through those parts of the country infested by the Bear, will sometimes find the cubs, generally two in number, their mother having left them in the den while she has gone to search for food. Although they would not venture to take the initiative in an attack upon either of the parents, they are glad of an opportunity which enables them to destroy one or two Bears without danger to themselves. The young Bears are easily killed or carried off, because at a very early age they are as confident as they are weak, and do not try to escape when they see the hunters approaching.

The only danger lies in the possibility that their deed may be discovered by the mother before they can escape from the locality, and, if she should happen to return while the robbers

SEEKING AN OUTLOOK.

are still in the neighbourhood, a severe conflict is sure to follow. At any time an angry Bear is a terrible antagonist, especially if it be wounded with sufficient severity to cause pain, and not severely enough to cripple its movements. But, when to this easily-roused ferocity is added the fury of maternal feelings, it may be imagined that the hunters have good reason to fear its attack.

To all animals that rear their young is given a sublime and almost supernatural courage in defending their offspring, and from the lioness, that charges a host of armed men when her cubs are in danger, to the hen, which defies the soaring kite or prowling fox, or to the spider, that will give up her life rather than abandon her yet unhatched brood, the same self-sacrificing spirit actuates them all. Most terrible therefore is the wrath of a creature which possesses, as is the case of the Bear, the strongest maternal affections, added to great size, tremendous weapons, and gigantic strength. That the sight of a Bear bereaved of her young was well known to both writers and contemporary readers of the Old Testament, is evident from the fact that it is mentioned by several writers, and always as a familiar illustration of furious anger. See for example 2 Sam. xvii. 8, when Hushai is dissuading Absalom from following the cautious counsel of Ahithophel, "For thou knowest thy father and his men, that they be mighty men of war, and they be chafed in their minds as a bear robbed of her whelps in the field." Solomon also, in the Proverbs (xvii. 12), uses the same image, "Let a bear robbed of her whelps meet a man, rather than a fool in his folly."

When the Bear fights, it delivers rapid strokes with its armed paw, tearing and rending away everything that it strikes. A blow from a bear's paw has been several times known to strip the entire skin, together with the hair, from a man's head, and, when fighting with dogs, to tear its enemies open as if each claw were a chisel.

Bears are capable of erecting themselves on their hinder limbs, and of supporting themselves in an upright position with the greatest ease. When attacked in close combat, they have a habit of rearing themselves upon their hinder feet—a position which enables them to deliver with the greatest effect the terrific blows with their fore paws, upon which they chiefly rely in defending themselves.

With fearful ingenuity, the Bear, when engaged with a human foe, directs its attack upon the head of its antagonist, and, as previously stated, has been known to strike off the entire scalp with a single blow.

A FAMILY-PARTY.

A hunter who had the misfortune to be struck down by a Bear—and the singular good fortune to afterwards escape from it—says, that when he was lying on the ground at the mercy of the angry beast, the animal, after biting him upon the arms and legs, deliberately settled itself upon his head and began to scarify it in the fiercest manner, leaving wounds eight and nine inches in length.

Bears are the more terrible antagonists from their extreme tenacity of life, and the fearful energy which they compress into the last moment of existence, when they are suffering from a mortal wound. Unless struck in the heart or brain, the mortally-wounded Bear is more to be feared than if it had received no injury whatever, and contrives to wreak more harm in the few minutes that immediately precede its death, than it had achieved while still uninjured.

Many a hunter has received mortal hurts by incautiously approaching a Bear, which lay apparently dead, but was in reality only stunned.

THE PORCUPINE.

Presumed identity of the Kippôd with the Porcupine—Habits of the Porcupine—the common Porcupine found plentifully in Palestine.

ALTHOUGH, like the hedgehog, the Porcupine is not mentioned by name in the Scriptures, many commentators think that the word Kippôd signifies both the hedgehog and Porcupine.

That the two animals should be thought to be merely two varieties of one species is not astonishing, when we remember the character of the people among whom the Porcupine lives. Not having the least idea of scientific geology, they look only to the most conspicuous characteristics, and because the Porcupine and hedgehog are both covered with an armature of quills, and the quills are far more conspicuous than the teeth, the inhabitants of Palestine naturally class the two animals together. In reality, they belong to two very different orders, the hedgehog being classed with the shrew-mice and moles, while the Porcupine is a rodent animal, and is classed with the rats, rabbits, beavers, marmots, and other rodents.

It is quite as common in Palestine as the hedgehog, a fact which increases the probability that the two animals may have been mentioned under a common title. Being a nocturnal animal, it retires during the day-time to some crevice in a rock or burrow in the ground, and there lies sleeping until the sunset awakens it and calls it to action. And as the hedgehog is also a nocturnal animal, the similarity of habit serves to strengthen the mutual resemblance.

The Porcupine is peculiarly fitted for living in dry and unwatered spots, as, like many other animals, of which our common rabbit is a familiar example, it can exist without water, obtaining the needful moisture from the succulent roots on which it feeds.

The sharply pointed quills with which its body is covered are solid, and strengthened in a most beautiful manner by internal ribs, that run longitudinally through them, exactly like those of the hollow iron masts, which are now coming so much into use. As they are, in fact, greatly developed hairs, they are continually shed and replaced, and when they are about to fall are so loosely attached that they fall off if pulled slightly, or even if the animal shakes itself. Consequently the shed quills that lie about the localities inhabited by the Porcupine indicate its whereabouts, and so plentiful are these quills in some places, that quite a bundle can be collected in a short time.

There are many species of Porcupines which inhabit different parts of the world, but that which has been mentioned is the common Porcupine of Europe, Asia, and Africa.

THE MOLE.

The two Hebrew words which are translated as Mole — Obscurity of the former name—A parallel case in our own language—The second name — The Moles and the Rats, why associated together—The real Mole of Scripture, its different names, and its place in zoology—Description of the Mole-rat and its general habits—Curious superstition—Discovery of the species by Mr. Tristram—Scripture and science—How the Mole-rat finds its food—Distinction between the Mole and the present animal.

There are two words which are translated as Mole in our authorized version of the Bible. One of them is so obscure that there seems no possibility of deciding the creature that is represented by it. We cannot even tell to what class of the animal kingdom it refers, because in more than one place it is mentioned as one of the unclean birds that might not be eaten (translated as *swan* in our version), whereas, in another place, it is enumerated among the unclean creeping things.

We may conjecture that the same word might be used to designate two distinct animals, though we have no clue to their identification. It is rather a strange coincidence, in corroboration of this theory, that our word Mole signifies three distinct objects—firstly, an animal; secondly, a cutaneous growth; and thirdly, a bank of earth. Now, supposing English to be a dead

THE MOLE-RAT.

language, like the Hebrew, it may well be imagined that a translator of an English book would feel extremely perplexed when he saw the word Mole used in such widely different senses.

The best Hebraists can do no more than offer a conjecture founded on the structure of the word *Tinshemeth*, which is thought by some to be the chameleon. Some think that it is the Mole, some the ibis, some the salamander, while others consider it to be the centipede; and in neither case have any decisive arguments been adduced.

We will therefore leave the former of these two names, and proceed to the second, *Chephor-peroth*.

This word occurs in that passage of Isaiah which has already been quoted when treating of the bat. "In that day a man shall cast his idols of silver and his idols of gold, which they made each one to himself to worship, to the moles and to the bats; to go into the clefts of the rocks and into the tops of the ragged rocks, for fear of the Lord and for the glory of his majesty, when he ariseth to shake terribly the earth."

It is highly probable that the animal in question is the Mole of Palestine, which is not the same as our European species, but is much larger in size, and belongs to a different order of mammalia. The true Mole is one of the insectivorous and carnivorous animals, and is allied to the shrews and the hedgehogs; whereas the Mole of Palestine (*Spalax typhlus*) is one of the rodents, and allied to the rabbits, mice, marmots, and jerboas. A better term for it is the Mole-rat, by which name it is familiar to zoologists. It is also known by the names of Slepez and Nenni.

In length it is about eight inches, and its colour is a pale slate. As is the case with the true Moles, the eyes are of very minute dimensions, and are not visible through the thick soft fur with which the whole head and body are covered. Neither are there any visible external ears, although the ear is really very large, and extremely sensitive to sound. This apparent privation of both ears and eyes gives to the animal a most singular and featureless appearance, its head being hardly recognisable as such but for the mouth, and the enormous projecting teeth, which not only look formidable, but really are so. There is a curious superstition in the Ukraine, that if a man will dare to grasp a Mole-rat in his bare hand, allow it to bite him, and then squeeze it to death, the hand that did the deed will ever afterwards possess the virtue of healing goitre or scrofula.

This animal is spread over a very large tract of country, and is very common in Palestine. Mr. Tristram gives an interesting account of its discovery. "We had long tried in vain to capture the Mole of Palestine. Its mines and its mounds we had seen everywhere, and reproached ourselves with having omitted the mole-trap among the items of our outfit. From the size of the mounds and the shallowness of the subterranean passages, we felt satisfied it could not be the European species, and our hopes of solving the question were raised when we found that one of them had taken up its quarters close to our camp. After several vain attempts to trap it, an Arab one night brought a live Mole in a jar to the tent. It was no Mole properly so called, but the Mole-rat, which takes its place throughout Western Asia. The man, having observed our anxiety to possess a specimen, refused to part with it for less than a hundred piastres, and scornfully rejected the twenty piastres I offered. Ultimately, Dr. Chaplin purchased it for five piastres after our departure, and I kept it alive for some time in a box, feeding it on sliced onions."

The same gentleman afterwards caught many of the Mole-rats, and kept them in earthen vessels, as they soon gnawed their way through wood. They fed chiefly on bulbs, but also ate sopped bread. Like many other animals, they reposed during the day, and were active throughout the night.

The author then proceeds to remark on the peculiarly appropriate character of the prophecy that the idols should be cast to the Moles and the bats. Had the European Mole been the animal to which reference was made, there would have been comparatively little significance in the connexion of the two names, because, although both animals are lovers of darkness, they do not inhabit similar localities. But the Mole-rat is fond of frequenting deserted ruins and burial-places, so that the Moles and the bats are really companions, and as such are associated together in the sacred narrative. Here, as in many other instances, we find that closer study of the Scriptures united to more extended knowledge are by no means the enemies of religion, as some well-meaning, but narrow-minded persons think. On the contrary, the Scriptures were never so well understood, and their truth and force so well recognised, as at the present day; and science has proved to be, not the destroyer of the Bible, but its interpreter. We shall soon cease to hear of "Science *versus* the Bible," and shall substitute "Science and the Bible *versus* Ignorance and Prejudice."

The Mole-rat needs not to dig such deep tunnels as the true Moles, because its food does not lie so deep. The Moles live chiefly upon earthworms, and are obliged to procure them in the varying depths to which they burrow. But the Mole-rat lives mostly upon roots, preferring those of a bulbous nature. Now bulbous roots are, as a rule, situated near the surface of the ground, and, therefore, any animal which feeds upon them must be careful not to burrow too deeply, lest it should pass beneath them. The shallowness of the burrows is thus accounted for Gardens are often damaged by this animal, the root-crops, such as carrots and onions, affording plenty of food without needing much exertion.

The Mole-rat does not keep itself quite so jealously secluded as does our common Mole, but occasionally will come out of the burrow and lie on the ground, enjoying the warm sunshine. Still it is not easily to be approached; for though its eyes are almost useless, the ears are so sharp, and the animal is so wary, that at the sound of a footstep it instantly seeks the protection of its burrow, where it may bid defiance to its foes.

How it obtains its food is a mystery. There seems to be absolutely no method of guiding itself to the precise spot where a bulb may be growing. It is not difficult to conjecture the method by which the Mole discovers its prey. Its sensitive ears may direct it to the spot where a worm is driving its way through the earth, and should it come upon its prey, the very touch of the worm, writhing in terror at the approach of its enemy, would be sufficient to act as a guide. I have kept several Moles, and always noticed that, though they would pass close to a worm without seeming to detect its presence, either by sight or scent, at the slightest touch they would spring round, dart on the worm, and in a moment seize it between their jaws. But with the Mole-rat the case is different. The root can utter no sound, and can make no movement, nor is it likely that the odour of the bulb should penetrate through the earth to a very great distance.

THE MOUSE.

The Mice which marred the land—The Field-mouse—Its destructive habits and prolific nature—The Hamster, and its habits—The Jerboa, its activity and destructiveness—Various species of Dormice and Sand-rats.

THAT the Mouse mentioned in the Old Testament was some species of rodent animal is tolerably clear, though it is impossible to state any particular species as being signified by the Hebrew word *Akbar*. The probable derivation of this name is from two words which signify " destruction of corn," and it is therefore evident that allusion is made to some animal which devours the produce of the fields, and which exists in sufficient numbers to make its voracity formidable.

Some commentators on the Old Testament translate the word Akbar as jerboa. Now, although the jerboa is common in Syria, it is not nearly so plentiful as other rodent animals, and would scarcely be selected as the means by which a terrible disaster is made to befall a whole country. The student of Scripture is well aware that, in those exceptional occurrences which are called miracles, a needless development of the wonder-working power is never employed. We are not to suppose, for example, that the clouds of locusts that devoured the harvests of the Egyptians were created for this express purpose, but that their already existing hosts were concentrated upon a limited area, instead of being spread over a large surface. Nor need we fancy that the frogs which rendered their habitations unclean, and contaminated their food, were brought into existence simply to inflict a severe punishment on the fastidious and superstitious Egyptians.

Of course, had such an exercise of creative power been needed, it would have been used, but we can all see that a needless miracle is never worked. He who would not suffer even a crumb of the miraculously multiplied bread to be wasted, is not likely to waste that power by which the miracle was wrought.

DAGON FALLEN DOWN BEFORE THE ARK.

If we refer to the early history of the Israelitish nation, as told in 1 Sam. iv.—vi., we shall find that the Israelites made an unwarrantable use of the ark, by taking it into battle, and that it was captured and carried off into the country of the Philistines. Then various signs were sent to warn the captors to send the ark back to its rightful possessors. Dagon, their great god, was prostrated before it, painful diseases attacked them, so that many died, and scarcely any seem to have escaped, while their harvests were ravaged by numbers of "mice that marred the land."

The question is now simple enough. If the ordinary translation is accepted, and the word Akbar rendered as Mouse, would the necessary conditions be fulfilled, *i.e.* would the creature be

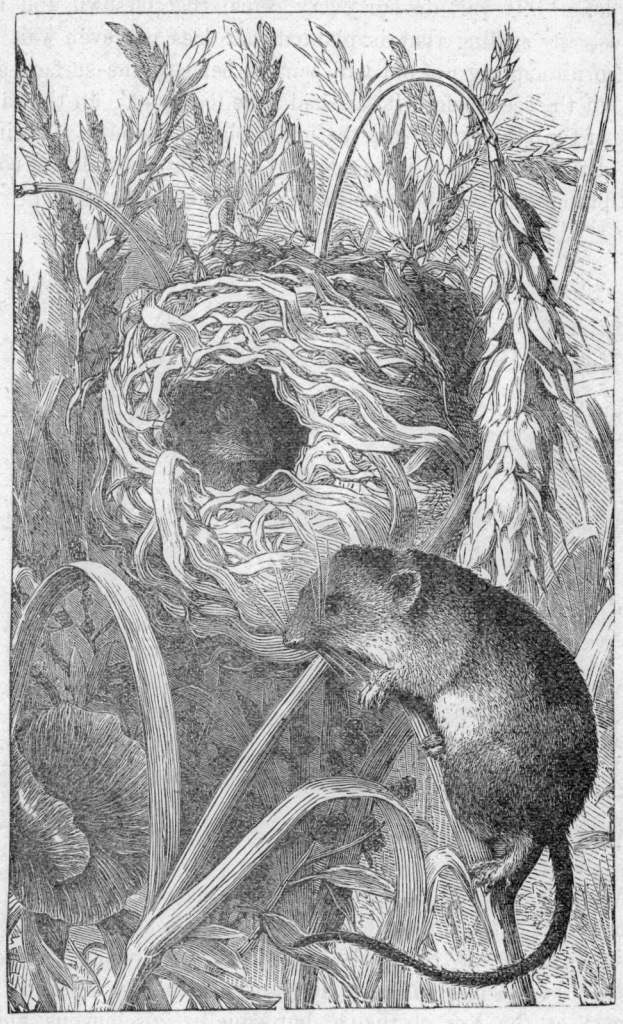

MOUSE AND NEST.

destructive, and would it exist in very great numbers? Now we shall find that both these conditions are fulfilled by the common Field-mouse.

This little creature is, in proportion to its size, one of the most destructive animals in the world. Let its numbers be increased from any cause whatever, and it will most effectually "mar the land." It will devour every cereal that is sown, and kill almost any sapling that is planted. It does not even wait for the corn to spring up, but will burrow beneath the surface, and dig out the seed before it has had time to sprout. In the early part of the year, it will eat the green blade as soon as it springs out of the ground, and is an adept at climbing the stalks of corn, and plundering the ripe ears in the autumn.

JERBOA, OR LEAPING MOUSE.

When stacked or laid up in barns, the harvest is by no means safe, for the Mice will penetrate into any ordinary barn, and find their way into any carelessly-built stack, from which they can scarcely be ejected. The rat itself is not so dire a foe to the farmer, as the less obtrusive, but equally mischievous Field-mouse. The ferret will drive the rats out of their holes, and if they have taken possession of a wheat-stack they can be ejected by depriving them of access to water. But the burrows of the Field-mouse are so small that a ferret cannot make its way through them, and the nightly dew that falls on the stack affords an ample supply of water.

When the Field-mouse is deprived of the food which it loves best, it finds a subsistence among the trees. Whenever mice can discover a newly-planted sapling, they hold great revel upon it, eating away the tender young bark as high as they can reach, and consequently destroying the tree as effectually as if it were

THE FIELD-MOUSE.

cut down. Even when the young trees fail them, and no tender bark is to be had, the Field-mice can still exert their destructive powers. They will then betake themselves to the earth, burrow beneath its surface, and devour the young rootlets of the forest trees. All botanists know that a healthy tree is continually pushing forward fresh roots below the ground, in order to gain sufficient nourishment to supply the increasing growth above. If, therefore, these young roots are destroyed, the least harm that can happen to the tree is that its further growth is arrested; while, in many cases, the tree, which cannot repair the injuries it has received, droops gradually, and finally dies. Even in this country, the Field-mouse has proved itself a terrible enemy to the agriculturist, and has devastated considerable tracts of land.

So much for the destructive powers of the Field-mouse, and the next point to be considered is its abundance.

Nearly all the rats and mice are singularly prolific animals, producing a considerable number at a brood, and having several broods in a season. The Field-mouse is by no means an exception to the general rule, but produces as many young in a season as any of the Mice.

Not only is it formidable from its numbers, but from the insidious nature of its attacks. Any one can see a rabbit, a hare, or even a rat; but to see a Field-mouse is not easy, even when the little creatures are present in thousands. A Field-mouse never shows itself except from necessity, its instinct teaching it to escape the observation of its many furred and feathered enemies. Short-legged and soft-furred, it threads its noiseless way among the herbage with such gentle suppleness that scarcely a grass-blade is stirred, while, if it should be forced to pass over a spot of bare ground, the red-brown hue of its fur prevents it from being detected by an inexperienced eye. Generally the Field-mouse is safe from human foes, and has only to dread the piercing eye and swift wings of the hawk, or the silent flight and sharp talons of the owl.

Although there can be no doubt that the Field-mouse is one of the animals to which the name of Akbar is given, it is probable that many species were grouped under this one name. Small rodents of various kinds are very plentiful in Palestine, and there are several species closely allied to the Field-mouse itself.

Among them is the Hamster (*Cricetus frumentarius*), so widely known for the ravages which it makes among the crops. This terribly destructive animal not only steals the crops for immediate subsistence, but lays up a large stock of provisions for the winter, seeming to be actuated by a sort of miserly passion for collecting and storing away. There seems to be no bounds to the quantity of food which a Hamster will carry into its subterranean store-house, from seventy to one hundred pounds' weight being sometimes taken out of the burrow of a single animal. The fact of the existence of these large stores shows that the animal must need them, and accordingly we find that the Hamster is only a partial hibernator, as it is awake during a considerable portion of the winter months, and is consequently obliged to live on the stores which it has collected.

It is an exceedingly prolific animal, each pair producing on an average twenty-five young in the course of a year. The families are unsociable, and, as soon as they are strong enough to feed themselves, the young Hamsters leave their home, and make separate burrows for themselves. Thus we see that the Hamster, as well as the Field-mouse, fulfils the conditions which are needed in order to class it under the general title of Akbar.

I have already stated that some translators of the Bible use the word Jerboa as a rendering of the Hebrew Akbar. As the Jerboa certainly is found in Palestine, there is some foundation for this idea, and we may safely conjecture that it also is one of the smaller rodents which are grouped together under the appellation of Mouse.

The Common Jerboa (*Dipus Ægyptiacus*) is plentiful in Palestine, and several other species inhabit the same country, known at once by their long and slender legs, which give them so curious a resemblance to the kangaroos of Australia. The Jerboas pass over the ground with astonishing rapidity. Instead of creeping stealthily among the grass-blades, like the short-limbed field-mouse, the Jerboa flies along with a succession of wonderful leaps, darting here and there with such rapidity that the eye can scarcely follow its wayward movements. When quiet and undisturbed, it hops along gently enough, but as soon as it takes alarm, it darts off in its peculiar manner, which is to the ordinary walk of quadrupeds what the devious course of a frightened snipe is to the steady flight of birds in general.

It prefers hot and dry situations, its feet being defended by a thick coating of stiff hairs, which serve the double purpose of protecting it from the heat, and giving it a firm hold on the ground. It is rather a destructive animal, its sharp and powerful teeth enabling it to bite its way through obstacles which would effectually stop an ordinary Mouse. That the Jerboa may be one of the Akbarim is rendered likely by the prohibition in Lev. xi. 29, forbidding the Mouse to be eaten. It would be scarcely probable that such a command need have been issued against eating the common Mouse, whereas the Jerboa, a much larger and palatable animal, is always eaten by the Arabs. The Hamster is at the present day eaten in Northern Syria.

Beside these creatures there are the Dormice, several species of which animal inhabit Palestine at the present day. There are also the Sand-rats, one species of which is larger than our ordinary rats. The Sand-rats live more in the deserts than the cultivated lands, making their burrows at the foot of hills, and among the roots of bushes.

THE HARE.

The prohibitions of the Mosaic law—The chewing of the cud, and division of the hoof—Identity of the Hare of Scripture—Rumination described—The Hare a rodent and not a ruminant—Cowper and his Hares—Structure of the rodent tooth—The Mosaic law accommodated to its recipients—The Hares of Palestine and their habits.

AMONG the many provisions of the Mosaic law are several which refer to the diet of the Israelites, and which prohibit certain kinds of food. Special stress is laid upon the flesh of animals, and the list of those which may be lawfully eaten is a singularly restricted one, all being excluded except those which "divide the hoof and chew the cud." And, lest there should be any mistake about the matter, examples are given both of those animals which may and those which may not be eaten.

The ox, sheep, goat, and antelopes generally are permitted as lawful food, because they fulfil both conditions; whereas there is a special prohibition of the swine, because it divides the hoof but does not chew the cud, and of the camel, coney, and hare because they chew the cud, but do not divide the hoof. Our business at present is with the last of these animals.

Considerable discussion has been raised concerning this animal, because, as is well known to naturalists, the Hare is not one of the ruminant animals, but belongs to the same order as the rat, rabbit, beaver, and other rodents. Neither its teeth nor its stomach are constructed for the purpose of enabling it to ruminate, *i.e.* to return into the mouth the partially-digested food, and then to masticate it afresh; and therefore it has been thought that either there is some mistake in the sacred narrative or that the Hebrew word has been mistranslated.

THE SYRIAN HARE.

Taking the latter point first, as being the simplest of the two, we find that the Hebrew word which is rendered as Hare is Arnebeth, and that it is rendered in the Septuagint as Dasypus, or the Hare,—a rendering which the Jewish Bible adopts. That the Arnebeth is really the Hare may also be conjectured from the fact that the Arabic name for that animal is Arneb. In consequence of the rather wide sense to which the Greek word Dasypus (*i.e.* hairy-foot) is used, some commentators have suggested that the rabbit may have been included in the same title. This, however, is not at all likely, inasmuch as the Hare is very plentiful in Palestine, and the rabbit is believed not to be indigenous to that part of the world. And, even if the two animals had been classed under the same title, the physiological difficulty would not be removed.

Before proceeding further, it will be as well to give a brief description of the curious act called rumination, or "chewing the cud."

There are certain animals, such as the oxen, antelopes, deer, sheep, goats, camels, &c. which have teeth unfitted for the rapid mastication of food, and which therefore are supplied with a remarkable apparatus by which the food can be returned into the mouth when the animal has leisure, and be re-masticated before it passes into the true digestive organs.

For this purpose they are furnished with four stomachs, which are arranged in the following order. First comes the paunch or "rumen" (whence the word "ruminating"), into which passes the food in a very rough state, just as it is torn, rather than bitten, from the herbage, and which is analogous to the crop in birds. It thence passes into the second stomach, or "honeycomb," the walls of which are covered with small angular cells. Into those cells the food is received from the first stomach, and compressed into little balls, which can be voluntarily returned into the mouth for mastication.

After the second mastication has been completed, the food passes at once into the third stomach, and thence into the fourth, which is the true digesting cavity. By a peculiar structure of these organs, the animal is able to convey its food either into the first or third stomach, at will, *i.e.* into the first when the grass is eaten, and into the third after rumination. Thus it will be seen that an animal which chews the cud must have teeth of a certain character, and be possessed of the fourfold stomach which has just been described.

Two points are conceded which seem to be utterly irreconcilable with each other. The first is that the Mosaic law distinctly states that the Hare chews the cud; the second is, that in point of fact the Hare is not, and cannot be, a ruminating animal, possessing neither the teeth nor the digestive organs which are indispensable for that process. Yet, totally opposed as these statements appear to be, they are in fact, not so irreconcilable as they seem.

A TIMID GROUP.

Why the flesh of certain animals was prohibited, we do not at the present time know. That the flesh of swine should be forbidden food is likely enough, considering the effects which the habitual eating of swine's flesh is said to produce in hot countries. But it does seem very strange that the Israelites should have been forbidden to eat the flesh of the camel, the coney (or hyrax), and the Hare, and that these animals should have been specified is a proof that the eating or refraining from their flesh was not a mere sanitary regulation, but was a matter of importance. The flesh of all these three animals is quite as good and nutritious as that of the oxen, or goats, which are eaten in Palestine, and that of the Hare is far superior to them. Therefore, the people of Israel, who were always apt to take liberties with the restrictive laws, and were crafty enough to evade them on so many occasions, would have been likely to pronounce that the flesh of the Hare was lawful meat, because the animal chewed the cud, or appeared to do so, and they would discreetly have omitted the passage which alluded to the division of the hoof.

To a non-scientific observer the Hare really does appear to chew the cud. When it is reposing at its ease, it continually moves its jaws about as if eating something, an action which may readily be mistaken for true rumination. Even Cowper, the poet, who kept some hares for several years, and had them always before his eyes, was deceived by this mumbling movement of the jaws. Speaking of his favourite hare, "Puss," he proceeds as follows: "Finding him exceedingly tractable, I made it my custom to carry him always after breakfast into the garden, where he hid himself generally under the leaves of a cucumber vine, sleeping, *or chewing the cud*, till evening."

The real object of this continual grinding or mumbling movement is simple enough. The chisel-like incisor teeth of the rodent animals need to be rubbed against each other, in order to preserve their edge and shape, and if perchance such friction should be wanting to a tooth, as, for example, by the breaking of the opposite tooth, it becomes greatly elongated, and sometimes grows to such a length as to prevent the animal from eating. Instinctively, therefore, the Hare, as well as the rabbit and other rodents, always likes to be nibbling at something, as any one knows who has kept rabbits in wooden hutches, the object of this nibbling not being to eat the wood, but to keep the teeth in order.

But we may naturally ask ourselves, why the Mosaic law, an emanation from heaven, should mention an animal as being a ruminant, when its very structure shows that such an act was utterly imposible? The answer is clear enough. The law was suited to the capacity of those for whom it was intended, and was never meant to be a handbook of science, as well as a code of religious duties and maxims. The Jews, like other Orientals, were indifferent to that branch of knowledge which we designate by the name of physical science, and it was necessary that the language in which the law was conveyed to them should be accommodated to their capabilities of receiving it.

It would have been worse than useless to have interrupted the solemn revelation of Divine will with a lesson in comparative anatomy; the object of the passage in question being, not to teach the Jews the distinctive characteristics of a rodent and a ruminant, but to guard against their mistaking the Hare for one of the ruminants which were permitted as food. That they would in all probability have fallen into that mistake is evident from the fact that the Arabs are exceedingly fond of the flesh of the Hare, and accept it, as well as the camel, as lawful food, because it chews the cud, the division of the hoof not being considered by them as an essential.

Hares are very plentiful in Palestine, and at least two species are found in that country. One of them, which inhabits the more northern and hilly portion of Palestine, closely resembles our own species, but has not ears quite so long in proportion, while the head is broader. The second species, which lives in the south, and in the valley of the Jordan, is very small, is of a light dun colour, and has very long ears. In their general habits, these Hares resemble the Hare of England.

CATTLE.

The cattle of Palestine, and their decadence at the present day—Ox-flesh not used for food in modern times—Oxen of the stall, and oxen of the pasture—The use of the ox in agriculture—The yoke and its structure—The plough and the goad—The latter capable of being used as a weapon—Treading out the corn—The cart and its wheels—The ox used as a beast of burden—Cattle turned loose to graze—The bulls of Bashan—Curiosity of the ox-tribe—A season of drought—Branding the cattle—An Egyptian field scene—Cattle-keeping an honourable post—The ox as used for sacrifice—Ox-worship—The bull Apis, and his history—Persistency of the bull-worship—Jeroboam's sin—Various names of cattle—The Indian buffalo.

UNDER this head we shall treat of the domesticated oxen of Scripture, whether mentioned as Bull, Cow, Ox, Calf, Heifer, &c.

Two distinct species of cattle are found in Palestine, namely, the ordinary domesticated ox, and the Indian buffalo, which lives in the low-lying and marshy valley of the Jordan. Of this species we shall treat presently.

The domesticated cattle are very much like our own, but there is not among them that diversity of breed for which this country is famous; nor is there even any distinction of long and short horned cattle. There are some places where the animals are larger than in others, but this difference is occasioned simply by the better quality and greater quantity of the food.

As is the case in most parts of the world where civilization has made any progress, Domesticated Cattle were, and still are, plentiful in Palestine. Even at the present time the cattle are in common use, though it is evident, from many passages of Holy Writ, that in the days of Judæa's prosperity cattle were far more numerous than they are now, and were treated in a better fashion.

To take their most sacred use first, a constant supply of cattle was needed for the sacrifices, and, as it was necessary that every animal which was brought to the altar should be absolutely perfect, it is evident that great care was required in order that the breed should not deteriorate, a skill which has long been rendered useless by the abandonment of the sacrifices.

ALTAR OF BURNT-OFFERING.

Another reason for their better nurture in the times of old is that in those days the ox was largely fed and fatted for the table, just as is done with ourselves. At the present day, the of the cattle is practically unused as food, that of the sheep or goat being always employed, even when a man gives a feast to his friends. But, in the old times, stalled oxen, *i. e.* oxen kept asunder from those which were used for agricultural purposes, and expressly fatted for the table, were in constant use. See for example the well-known passage in the Prov. xv. 17, "Better is a dinner of herbs where love is, than a stalled ox and hatred therewith." Again, the Prophet Jeremiah makes use of a curious simile, "Egypt is like a very fair heifer, but destruction cometh; it cometh out of the north. Also her hired men are in the midst of her like fatted bullocks [or, bullocks of the stall], for they also are turned back, and are fled away together." (Jer. xlvi. 20.) And in 1 Kings iv. 22, 23, when describing the glories of Solomon's household, the sacred writer draws a distinction between the oxen which were especially fattened for the table of the king and the superior officers, and those which were consumed by the lower orders of his household: " And Solomon's provision for one day was thirty measures of fine flour, and three-score measures of meal, ten fat oxen, and twenty oxen out of the pastures, and an hundred sheep, beside harts, and roebucks, and fallow-deer, and fatted fowl."

THE PRODIGAL SON RETURNS, AND THE FATTED CALF IS KILLED.

Calves—mostly, if not always, bull-calves—were largely used for food in Palestine, and in the households of the wealthy were fatted for the table. See, for example, the familiar parable of the prodigal son, in which the rejoicing father is mentioned as preparing a great feast in honour of his son's return, and ordering the fatted calf to be killed—the calf in question being evidently one of the animals that were kept in good condition against any festive occasion. And, even in the earliest history of the Bible, the custom of keeping a fatted calf evidently prevailed, as is shown by the conduct of Abraham, who, when he was visited by

ABRAHAM OFFERS FOOD TO THE THREE STRANGERS.

the three heavenly guests, "ran unto the herd, and fetched a calf, tender and good," and had it killed and dressed at once, after the still existing fashion of the East.

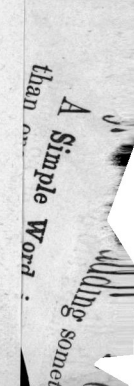

But, even in the times of Israel's greatest prosperity, the chief use of the ox was as an agricultural labourer, thus reversing the custom of this country, where the horse has taken the place of the ox as a beast of draught, and where cattle are principally fed for food. Ploughing was, and is, always performed by oxen, and allusions to this office are scattered plentifully through the Old and New Testaments.

When understood in this sense, oxen are almost always spoken of in connexion with the word "yoke," and as each yoke comprised two oxen, it is evident that the word is used as we employ the term "brace," or pair. The yoke, which is the chief part of the harness, is a very simple affair. A tolerably stout beam of wood is cut of a sufficient length to rest upon the necks of the oxen standing side by side, and a couple of hollows are scooped out to receive the crest of the neck. In order to hold it in its place, two flexible sticks are bent under their necks, and the ends fixed into the beam of the yoke. In the middle of this yoke is fastened the pole of the plough or cart, and this is all the harness that is used, not even traces being required.

It will be seen that so rude an implement as this would be very likely to gall the necks of the animals, unless the hollows were carefully smoothed, and the heavy beam adapted to the necks of the animals. This galling nature of the yoke, so familiar to the Israelites, is used repeatedly as a metaphor in many passages of the Old and New Testaments. These passages are too numerous to be quoted, but I will give one or two of the most conspicuous among them. The earliest mention of the yoke in the Scriptures is a metaphor.

After Jacob had deceived his father, in procuring for himself the blessing which was intended for his elder brother, Isaac comforts Esau by the prophecy that, although he must serve his brother, yet "it shall come to pass when thou shalt have the dominion, that thou shalt break his yoke from off thy neck." Again, in the next passage where the yoke is mentioned, namely, Lev. xxvi. 13, the word is employed in the metaphorical sense. "I am the Lord your God, which brought you forth out of the land of Egypt, that ye should not be their bondmen, and I have broken the bands of your yoke, and made you go upright."

The plough was equally simple, and consisted essentially of a bent branch, one end of which was armed with an iron point by way of a share, while the other formed the pole or beam, and was fastened to the middle of the yoke. It was guided by a handle, which was usually a smaller branch that grew from the principal one. A nearly similar instrument is used in Asia Minor to the present day, and is a curious relic of the most ancient times of history, for we find on the Egyptian monuments figures of the various agricultural processes, in which the plough is made after this simple manner.

Of course such an instrument is a very ineffective one, and can but scratch, rather than plough the ground, the warmth of the climate and fertility of the land rendering needless the deep ploughing of our own country, where the object is to turn up the earth to the greatest possible depth. One yoke of oxen was generally sufficient to draw a plough, but occasionally a much greater number were required. We read, for example, of Elisha, who, when he received his call from Elijah, was ploughing with twelve yoke of oxen, *i. e.* twenty-four. It has been suggested, that the twelve yoke of oxen were not all attached to the same plough, but that there were twelve ploughs, each with its single yoke of oxen. This was most probably the case.

The instrument with which the cattle were driven was not a whip, but a goad. This goad was a long and stout stick, armed with a spike at one end, and having a kind of spud at the other, with which the earth could be scraped off the share when it became clogged. Such an instrument might readily be used as a weapon, and, in the hands of a powerful man, might be made even more formidable than a spear. As a weapon, it often was used, as we see from many passages of the Scriptures. For example, it is said in Judges iii. 31, " that Shamgar the son of Anath killed six hundred Philistines with an ox-goad."

Afterwards, in the beginning of Saul's reign, when the Israelites fairly measured themselves against the Philistines, it was found that only Saul and Jonathan were even tolerably armed. Fearful of the numbers and spirit of the Israelites, the Philistines had disarmed them, and were so cautious that they did not even allow them to possess forges wherewith to make or sharpen the various agricultural instruments which they possessed, lest they should surreptitiously provide themselves with weapons. The only smith's tool which they were allowed to retain was a file with which each man might trim the edges of the ploughshares, mattocks, axes, and sharpen the points of the goad.

The only weapons which they could muster were made of their agricultural implements, and among the most formidable of them was the goad.

How the goad came into use in Palestine may easily be seen. The Egyptians, from among whom the people of Israel passed into the Promised Land, did not use the goad in ploughing, but the whip, which, from the representations on the Egyptian monuments, was identical with the koorbash, or "cow-hide" whip, which is now in use in the same country. But this terrible whip, which is capable, when wielded by a skilful hand, of cutting deep grooves through the tough hide of the ox, could not be obtained by the Jews, because the hippopotamus, of whose hide it was made, did not live in or near Palestine. They therefore were forced to use some other instrument wherewith to urge on the oxen, and the goad was clearly the simplest and most effective implement for this purpose.

After the land was ploughed and sown, and the harvest was ripened, the labours of the oxen were again called into requisition, first for threshing out the corn, and next for carrying or drawing the grain to the storehouses.

In the earlier days, the process of threshing was very simple. A circular piece of ground was levelled, and beaten very hard and flat, its diameter being from fifty to a hundred feet. On this ground the corn was thrown, and a number of oxen were driven here and there on it, so that the constant trampling of their feet shook the ripe grain out of the ears. The corn was gathered together in the middle of the floor, and as fast as it was scattered by the feet of the oxen, it was thrown back towards the centre.

Afterwards, an improvement was introduced in the form of a rough sledge, called "moreg," to which the oxen were harnessed by a yoke, and on which the driver stood as he guided his team round the threshing-floor. This instrument is mentioned in Isa. xli. 15 : "Behold, I will make thee a new and sharp threshing instrument having teeth [or mouths] : thou shalt thresh the mountains, and beat them small, and shalt make the hills as chaff." Mention is also made of the same implement in 2 Sam. xxiv. 22, where it is related that Araunah the Jebusite offered to give David the oxen for a burnt-sacrifice, and the moregs and other implements as wood with which they could be burned.

The work of treading out the corn was a hard and trying one for the oxen, and it was probably on this account that the kindly edict was made, that the oxen who trod out the corn should not be muzzled. As a rule, the cattle were not fed nearly as carefully as is done with us, and so the labours of the threshing-floor would find a compensation in the temporary abundance of which the animals might take their fill.

OXEN TREADING OUT GRAIN.

After the corn was threshed, or rather trodden out, the oxen had to draw it home in carts. These were but slight improvements on the threshing-sledge, and were simply trays or shallow boxes on a pair of wheels. As the wheels were merely slices cut from the trunk of a tree, and were not furnished with iron tires, they were not remarkable for roundness, and indeed, after a little time, were worn into rather irregular ovals, so that the task of dragging a cart over the rough roads was by no means an easy one. And, as the axle was simply a stout pole fastened to the bottom of the cart, and having its rounded ends thrust through holes in the middle of the wheels, the friction was enormous. As, moreover, oil and grease were far too precious

EASTERN OX-CART.

luxuries to be wasted in lubricating the axles, the creaking and groaning of the wheels was a singularly disagreeable and ear-piercing sound.

The common hackery of India is a good example of the carts mentioned in the Scriptures. As with the plough, the cart was drawn by a couple of oxen, connected by the yoke. The two kinds of cart, namely, the tray and the box, are clearly indicated in the Scriptures. The new cart on which the Ark was placed when it was sent back by the Philistines (see 1 Sam. vi. 7) was evidently one of the former kind, and so was that which was made twenty years afterwards, for the purpose of conveying the Ark to Jerusalem.

Although the cattle were evidently better tended in the olden times than at present, those animals which were used for agriculture seem to have passed rather a rough life, especially in the winter time. It is rather curious that the Jews should have had no idea of preserving the grass by making it into hay, as is done in Europe. Consequently the chief food of the cattle was the straw and chaff which remained on the threshing-floor after the grain had been separated.

THE ARK OF THE COVENANT BEING DRAWN BY COWS.

This, indeed, was the only use to which the straw could be put, for it was so crushed and broken by the feet of the oxen and the threshing-sledge that it was rendered useless.

The want of winter forage is the chief reason why cattle are so irregularly disposed over Palestine, many parts of that country being entirely without them, and only those districts containing them in which fresh forage may be found throughout the year.

Except a few yoke of oxen, which are kept in order to draw carts, and act as beasts of burden, the cattle are turned loose for a considerable portion of the year, and run about in herds from one pasturage to another. Thus they regain many of the characteristics of wild animals, and it is to this habit of theirs that many of the Scriptural allusions can be traced.

For example, see Ps. xxii. 12, "Many bulls have compassed me, strong bulls of Bashan have beset me round. They gaped on me with their mouths [or, their mouths opened against me] as a ravening and a roaring lion." This passage alludes to the curiosity inherent in cattle, which have a habit of following objects which they do not understand or dislike, and surrounding it with looks of grave wonderment. Even in their domesticated state this habit prevails. When I was a boy, I sometimes amused myself with going into a field where a number of cows and oxen were grazing, and lying down in the middle of it. The cattle would soon become uneasy, toss their heads about, and gradually draw near on every side, until at last they would be pressed together closely in a circle, with their heads just above the object of their astonishment. Their curious, earnest looks have always been present to my mind when reading the above quoted passage.

The Psalmist does not necessarily mean that the bulls in question were dangerous animals. On the contrary, the bulls of Palestine are gentle in comparison with our own animals, which are too often made savage by confinement and the harsh treatment to which they are subjected by rough and ignorant labourers. In Palestine a pair of bulls may constantly be seen attached to the same yoke, a thing that never would be seen in this country.

The custom of turning the herds of cattle loose to find pasture for themselves is alluded to in Joel i. 18, "How do the beasts groan! the herds of cattle are perplexed because they have no pasture." We can easily imagine to ourselves the terrible time to which the prophet refers, "when the rivers of waters are dried up, and the fire hath devoured the pastures of the wilderness," as it is wont to do when a spark falls upon grass dried up and withered, by reason of the sun's heat and the lack of water. Over such a country, first withered by drought, and then desolated by fire, would the cattle wander, vainly searching on the dusty and blackened surface for the tender young blades which always spring up on a burnt pasture as soon as the first rains fall. Moaning and bellowing with

PLOUGHING WITH OXEN.

thirst and disappointment, they would vainly seek for food or water in places where the seed lies still under the clods where it was sown (v. 17), where the vines are dried up, and the fig, the pomegranate and the palm (v. 12) are all withered for want of moisture.

Such scenes are still to be witnessed in several parts of the world. Southern Africa is sometimes sadly conspicuous for them, an exceptional season of drought keeping back the fresh grass after the old pastures have been burned (the ordinary mode of cultivating pasture land). Then the vast herds of cattle, whose milk forms the staff of life to the inhabitants, wander to and fro, gathering in masses round any spot where a spring still yields a little water, and bellowing and moaning with thirst as they press their way towards the spot where their owners are doling out to each a small measure of the priceless fluid.

The cattle are branded with the mark of their owners, so that in these large herds there might be no difficulty in distinguishing them when they were re-captured for the plough and the cart. On one of the Egyptian monuments there is a very interesting group, which has furnished the idea for the plate which illustrates this article. It occurs in the tombs of the kings at Thebes, and represents a ploughing scene. The simple two-handled plough is being dragged by a pair of cows, who have the yoke fastened across the horns instead of lying on the neck, and a sower is following behind, scattering the grain out of a basket into the newly-made furrows. In front of the cows is a young calf, which has run to meet its mother, and is leaping for joy before her as she steadily plods along her course.

The action of both animals is admirably represented; the steady and firm gait of the mother contrasting with the light, gambolling step and arched tail of her offspring.

In the olden times of the Israelitish race, herd-keeping was considered as an honourable occupation, in which men of the highest rank might engage without any derogation to their dignity. We find, for instance, that Saul himself, even after he had been appointed king, was acting as herdsman when the people saw the mistake they had made in rejecting him as their monarch, and came to fetch their divinely-appointed leader from his retirement. (See 1 Sam. xi. 5.) Doeg, too, the faithful companion of Saul, was made the chief herdsman of his master's cattle, so that for Saul to confer such an office, and Doeg to accept it, shows that the post was one of much honour. And afterwards, when David was in the zenith of his power, he completed the organization of his kingdom, portioning out not only his army into battalions, and assigning a commanding officer to each battalion, but also appointing a ruler to each tribe, and setting officers over his treasury, over the vineyards, over the olive-trees, over the storehouses, and over the cattle. And these offices were so important that the names of their holders are given at length in 1 Chron. xxvii. those of the various herdsmen being thought as worthy of mention as those of the treasurers, the military commanders, or the headmen of the tribes.

Before concluding this necessarily short account of the domesticated oxen of Palestine, it will be needful to give a few lines to the animal viewed in a religious aspect. Here we have, in bold contrast to each other, the divine appointment of certain cattle to be slain as sacrifices, and the reprobation of worship paid to those very cattle as living emblems of divinity. This false worship was learned by the Israelites during their long residence in Egypt, and so deeply had the customs of the Egyptian religion sunk into their hearts, that they were not eradicated after the lapse of centuries. It may easily be imagined that such a superstition, surrounded as it was with every external circumstance which could make it more imposing, would take a powerful hold of the Jewish mind.

Chief among the multitude of idols or symbols was the god Apis, represented by a bull. Many other animals, specially the cat and the ibis, were deeply honoured among the ancient Egyptians, as we learn from their own monuments and from the works of the old historians. All these creatures were symbols as well as idols, symbols to the educated and idols to the ignorant.

None of them was held in such universal honour as the bull Apis. The particular animal which represented the deity, and which was lodged with great state and honour in his temple at Memphis, was thought to be divinely selected for the purpose, and to be impressed with certain marks. His colour must be black, except a square spot on the forehead, a crescent-shaped white spot on the right side, and the figure of an eagle on his back. Under the tongue must be a knob shaped like the sacred scarabæus, and the hairs of his tail must be double.

This representative animal was only allowed to live for a certain time, and when he had reached this allotted period, he was taken in solemn procession to the Nile, and drowned in

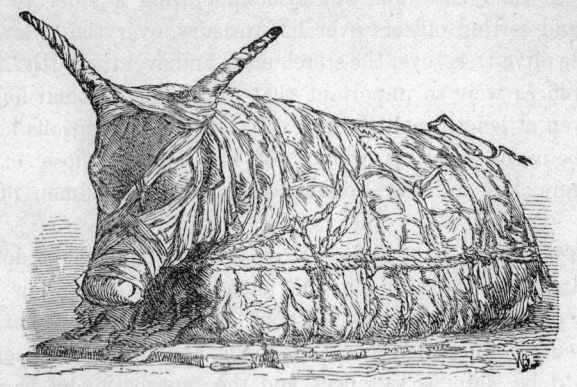

MUMMY OF A SACRED BULL TAKEN FROM AN EGYPTIAN TOMB.

its sacred waters. His body was then embalmed, and placed with great state in the tombs at Memphis.

After his death, whether natural or not, the whole nation went into mourning, and exhibited all the conventional signs of sorrow, until the priests found another bull which possessed the distinctive marks. The people then threw off their mourning robes, and appeared in their best attire, and the sacred bull was exhibited in state for forty days before he was taken to his temple at Memphis. The reader will here remember the analogous case of the Indian cattle, some of which are held to be little less than incarnations of divinity.

Even at the very beginning of the exodus, when their minds must have been filled with the many miracles that had been wrought in their behalf, and with the cloud and fire of Sinai actually before their eyes, Aaron himself made an image of a calf in gold, and set it up as a symbol of the Lord. That the idol in question was intended as a symbol by Aaron is evident from the words which he used when summoning the people to worship, "To-morrow is a feast of the Lord" (Gen. xxxii. 5). The people, however, clearly lacked the power of discriminating between the

ANIMALS BEING SOLD FOR SACRIFICE IN THE PORCH OF THE TEMPLE.

symbol and that which it represented, and worshipped the image just as any other idol might be worshipped. And, in spite of the terrible and swift punishment that followed, and which showed the profanity of the act, the idea of ox-worship still remained among the people.

Five hundred years afterwards we find a familiar example of it in the conduct of Jeroboam, "who made Israel to sin," the peculiar crime being the open resuscitation of ox-worship. "The king made two calves of gold and said unto them, It is too much for you to go up to Jerusalem: behold thy gods, O Israel, which

JEROBOAM SETS UP A GOLDEN CALF AT BETHEL.

brought thee up out of the land of Egypt. And he set the one in Bethel, and the other put he in Dan. . . . And he made an house of high places, and made priests of the lowest of the people, which were not of the tribe of Levi. And Jeroboam ordained a feast. . . . like unto the feast in Judah, and he offered upon the altar. So did he in Bethel, sacrificing unto the calves that he had made."

Here we have a singular instance of a king of Israel repeating, after a lapse of five hundred years, the very acts which had drawn down on the people so severe a punishment, and which were so contrary to the law that they had incited Moses to fling down and break the sacred tables on which the commandments had been divinely inscribed.

ANOTHER species of the ox-tribe now inhabits Palestine, though commentators rather doubt whether it is not a comparatively late importation. This is the true BUFFALO (*Bubalus buffelus*, Gray), which is spread over a very large portion of the earth, and is very plentiful in India. In that country there are two distinct breeds of the Buffalo, namely, the Arnee, a wild

THE BUFFALO.

variety, and the Bhainsa, a tamed variety. The former animal is much larger than the latter, being sometimes more than ten feet in length from the nose to the root of the tail, and measuring between six and seven feet in height at the shoulder. Its horns are of enormous length, the tail is very short, and tufts of hair grow on the forehead and horns. The tamed variety is at least one-third smaller, and, unlike the Arnee, never seems to get into high condition. It is an ugly, ungainly kind of beast, and is rendered very unprepossessing to the eye by the bald patches which are mostly found upon its hide.

Being a water-loving animal, the Buffalo always inhabits the low-lying districts, and is fond of wallowing in the oozy marshes in which it remains for hours, submerged all but its head, and tranquilly chewing the cud while enjoying its mud-bath. While thus engaged the animal depresses its horns so that they are scarcely visible, barely allowing more than its eyes, ears, and nostrils to remain above the surface, so that the motionless heads are scarcely distinguishable from the grass and reed tufts which stud the marshes. Nothing is more startling to an inexperienced traveller than to pass by a silent and tranquil pool where the muddy surface is unbroken except by a number of black lumps and rushy tufts, and then to see these tufts suddenly transformed into twenty or thirty huge beasts rising out of the still water as if by magic. Generally, the disturber of their peace had better make the best of his way out of their reach, as the Buffalo, whether wild or tame, is of a tetchy and irritable nature, and resents being startled out of its state of dreamy repose.

In the Jordan valley the Buffalo is found, and is used for agriculture, being of the Bhainsa, or domesticated variety. Being much larger and stronger than the ordinary cattle, it is useful in drawing the plough, but its temper is too uncertain to render it a pleasant animal to manage. As is the case with all half-wild cattle, its milk is very scanty, but compensates **by the richness of the quality for the lack of quantity.**

In the picture which appears on a following page, one of these domesticated Buffaloes is represented, harnessed with a camel, to a rude form of plough used in the East.

THE BHAINSA, OR DOMESTIC BUFFALO, AND CAMEL, DRAWING THE PLOUGH.

THE WILD BULL.

The Tô, Wild Bull of the Old Testament—Passages in which it is mentioned—The Wild Bull in the net—Hunting with nets in the East—The Oryx supposed to be the Tô of Scripture—Description of the Oryx, its locality, appearance, and habits—The points in which the Oryx agrees with the Tô—The "snare" in which the foot is taken, as distinguished from the net.

IN two passages of the Old Testament an animal is mentioned, respecting which the translators and commentators have been somewhat perplexed, in one passage being translated as the "Wild Ox," and in the other as the "Wild Bull." In the Jewish Bible the same rendering is preserved, but the sign of doubt is added to the word in both cases, showing that the translation is an uncertain one.

The first of these passages occurs in Deut. xiv. 5, where it is classed together with the ox, sheep, goats, and other ruminants, as one of the beasts which were lawful for food. Now, although we cannot identify it by this passage, we can at all events ascertain two important points—the first, that it was a true ruminant, and the second, that it was not the ox, the sheep, or the goat. It was, therefore, some wild ruminant, and we now have to ask how we are to find out the species.

If we turn to Isa. li. 20, we shall find a passage which will help us considerably. Addressing Jerusalem, the prophet uses these words, "By whom shall I comfort thee? Thy sons have fainted, they lie at the head of all the streets, as a wild bull in a net; they are full of the fury of the Lord, the rebuke of thy God." We now see that the Tô or Teô must be an animal which is captured by means of nets, and therefore must inhabit spots wherein the toils can be used. Moreover, it is evidently a powerful animal, or the force of the simile would be lost. The prophet evidently refers to some large and strong beast which has been entangled in the hunter's nets, and which lies helplessly struggling in them. We are, therefore, almost perforce driven to recognise it as some large antelope.

The expression used by the prophet is so characteristic that it needs a short explanation. In this country, and at the present day, the use of the net is almost entirely restricted to fishing and bird-catching; but in the East nets are still employed in the capture of very large game.

A brief allusion to the hunting-net is made at page 31, but, as the passage in Isaiah li. requires a more detailed account of this mode of catching large animals, it will be as well to describe the sport as at present practised in the East.

When a king or some wealthy man determines to hunt game without taking much trouble himself, he gives orders to his men to prepare their nets, which vary in size or strength according to the particular animal for which they are intended. If, for example, only the wild boar and similar animals are to be hunted, the nets need not be of very great width; but for agile creatures, such as the antelope, they must be exceedingly wide, or the intended prey will leap over them. As the net is much used in India for the purpose of catching game, Captain Williamson's description of it will explain many of the passages of Scripture wherein it is mentioned.

The material of the net is hemp, twisted loosely into a kind of rope, and the mode in which it is formed is rather peculiar. The meshes are not knotted together, but only twisted round each other, much after the fashion of the South American hammocks, so as to obtain considerable elasticity, and to prevent a powerful animal from snapping the cord in its struggles. Some of these nets are thirteen feet or more in width, and even such a net as this has been overleaped by a herd of antelopes. Their length is variable, but, as they can be joined in any number when set end to end, the length is not so important as the width.

The mode of setting the nets is singularly ingenious. When a suitable spot has been selected, the first care of the hunters is to stretch a rope as tightly as possible along the ground. For this purpose stout wooden stakes or truncheons are sunk crosswise in the earth, and between these the rope is carefully strained. The favourite locality of the net is a ravine, through which the animals can be driven so as to run against the net in their efforts to escape, and across the ravine a whole row of these stakes is sunk. The net is now brought to the spot, and its lower edge fastened strongly to the ground rope.

The strength of this mode of fastening is astonishing, and, although the stakes are buried scarcely a foot below the surface, they cannot be torn up by any force which can be applied to them; and, however strong the rope may be, it would be broken before the stakes could be dragged out of the ground.

A smaller rope is now attached to the upper edge of the net, which is raised upon a series of slight poles. It is not stretched quite tightly, but droops between each pair of poles, so that a net which is some thirteen feet in width will only give nine or ten feet of clear height when the upper edge is supported on the poles. These latter are not fixed in the ground, but merely held in their places by the weight of the net resting upon them.

When the nets have been properly set, the beaters make a wide circuit through the country, gradually advancing towards the fatal spot, and driving before them all the wild animals that inhabit the neighbourhood. As soon as any large beast, such, for example, as an antelope, strikes against the net, the supporting pole falls, and the net collapses upon the unfortunate animal, whose struggles—especially if he be one of the horned animals—only entangle him more and more in the toils.

As soon as the hunters see a portion of the net fall, they run to the spot, kill the helpless creature that lies enveloped in the elastic meshes, drag away the body, and set up the net again in readiness for the next comer. Sometimes the line of nets will extend for half a mile or more, and give employment to a large staff of hunters, in killing the entangled animals, and raising afresh those portions of the net which had fallen.

Accepting the theory that the Tô is one of the large antelopes that inhabit, or used to inhabit, the Holy Land and its neighbourhood, we may safely conjecture that it may signify the beautiful animal known as the ORYX (*Oryx leucoryx*), an animal which has a tolerably wide range, and is even now found on the borders of the Holy Land. It is a large and powerful antelope, and is remarkable for its beautiful horns, which sometimes exceed a yard in length, and sweep in a most graceful curve over the back.

Sharp as they are, and evidently formidable weapons, the manner in which they are set on the head renders them apparently unserviceable for combat. When, however, the Oryx is brought to bay, or wishes to fight, it stoops its head until the nose is close to the ground, the points of the horns being thus

WILD BULL, OR ORYX.

brought to the front. As the head is swung from side to side, the curved horns sweep through a considerable space, and are so formidable that even the lion is chary of attacking their owner. Indeed, instances are known where the lion has been transfixed and killed by the horns of the Oryx. Sometimes the animal is not content with merely standing to repel the attacks of its adversaries, but suddenly charges forward with astonishing rapidity, and strikes upwards with its horns as it makes the leap.

But these horns, which can be used with such terrible effect in battle, are worse than useless when the animal is hampered in the net. In vain does the Oryx attempt its usual defence: the curved horns get more and more entangled in the elastic meshes, and become a source of weakness rather than strength. We see now how singularly appropriate is the passage, "Thy sons lie at the heads of all the streets, as a wild bull (or Oryx) in a net," and how completely the force of the metaphor is lost without a knowledge of the precise mode of fixing the nets, of driving the animals into them, and of the manner in which they render even the large and powerful animals helpless.

The height of the Oryx at the shoulder is between three and four feet, and its colour is greyish white, mottled profusely with black and brown in bold patches. It is plentiful in Northern Africa, and, like many other antelopes, lives in herds, so that it is peculiarly suited to that mode of hunting which consists in surrounding a number of animals, and driving them into a trap of some kind, whether a fenced enclosure, a pitfall, or a net.

There is, by the way, the term "snare," which is specially used with especial reference to catching the foot as distinguished from the net which enveloped the whole body. For example, in Job xviii. 8, "He is cast into a net, he walketh on a snare," where a bold distinction is drawn between the two and their mode of action. And in ver. 10, "The snare is laid for him in the ground." Though I would not state definitely that such is the case, I believe that the snare which is here mentioned is one which is still used in several parts of the world.

It is simply a hoop, to the inner edge of which are fastened a number of elastic spikes, the points being directed towards the centre. This is merely laid in the path which the animal will take, and is tied by a short cord to a log of wood. As the deer or antelope treads on the snare, the foot passes easily through the elastic spikes, but, when the foot is raised, the spikes run into the joint and hold the hoop upon the limb. Terrified by the check and the sudden pang, the animal tries to run away, but, by the united influence of sharp spikes and the heavy log, it is soon forced to halt, and so becomes an easy prey to its pursuers.

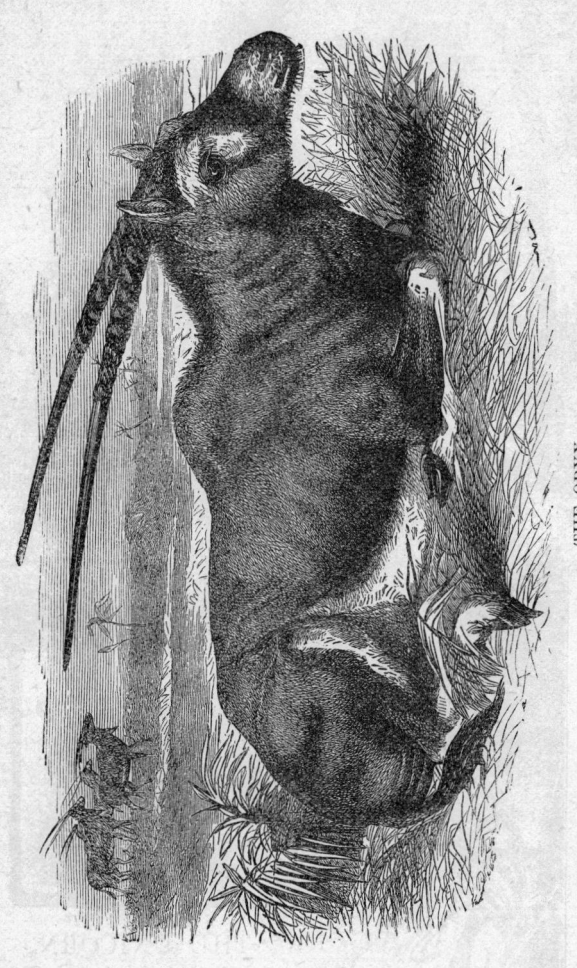

THE ORYX.

THE UNICORN.

The Unicorn apparently known to the Jews—
Its evident connection with the Ox tribe—
Its presumed identity with the now extinct Urus—Enormous size and dangerous character of the Urus.

THERE are many animals mentioned in the Scriptures which are identified with difficulty, partly because their names occur only once or twice in the sacred writings, and partly because, when they are mentioned, the context affords no clue to their identity by giving any hint as to their appearance or habits. In such cases, although the translators would have done better if they had simply given the Hebrew word without endeavouring to identify it with any known animal, they may be excused for committing errors in their nomenclature. There is one animal, however, for which no such excuse can be found, and this is the Reêm of Scripture, translated as Unicorn in the authorized version.

Even in late years the Unicorn has been erroneously supposed to be identical with the Rhinoceros of India. It is, however, now certain that the Unicorn was not the Rhinoceros, and that it can be almost certainly identified with an animal which, at the time when the passages in question were written, was plentiful in Palestine, although, like the Lion, it is now extinct.

On turning to the Jewish Bible we find that the word Reêm is translated as buffalo, and there is no doubt that this rendering is nearly the correct one. At the present day naturalists are nearly all agreed that the Unicorn of the Old Testament must have been of the Ox tribe. Probably the Urus, a species now extinct, was the animal alluded to. A smaller animal, the Bonassus or Bison, also existed in Palestine, and even to the present day continues to maintain itself in one or two spots, though it will probably be as soon completely erased from the surface of the earth as its gigantic congener.

That the Unicorn was one of the two animals is certain, and that it was the larger is nearly as certain. The reason for deciding upon the Urus is, that its horns were of great size and strength, and therefore agree with the description of the Unicorn; whereas those of the Bonassus, although powerful, are short, and not conspicuous enough to deserve the notice which is taken of them by the sacred writers.

Of the extinct variety we know but little. We do know, however, that it was a huge and most formidable beast, as is evident from the skulls and other bones which have been discovered. Their character also indicates that the creature was nothing more than a very large Ox, probably measuring twelve feet in length, and six feet in height. Such a wild animal, armed, as it was, with enormous horns, would prove a most formidable antagonist.

THE BISON.

The Bison tribe and its distinguishing marks—Its former existence in Palestine—Its general habits—Origin of its name—Its musky odour - Size and speed of the Bison—Its dangerous character when brought to bay—Its defence against the wolf—Its untameable disposition.

A FEW words are now needful respecting the second animal which has been mentioned in connexion with the Reêm; namely, the Bison, or Bonassus. The Bisons are distinguishable from ordinary cattle by the thick and heavy mane which covers the neck and shoulders, and which is more conspicuous in the male than in the female. The general coating of the body is also rather different, being thick and woolly instead of lying closely to the skin like that of the other oxen. The Bison certainly inhabited Palestine, as its bones have been found in that country. It has, however, been extinct in the Holy Land for many years, and, not being an animal that is capable of withstanding the encroachments of man, it has gradually died out from the greater part of Europe and Asia, and is now to be found only in a very limited locality, chiefly in a Lithuanian forest, where it is strictly preserved, and in some parts of the Caucasus. There it still preserves the habits which made its ancient and gigantic relative so dangerous an animal. Unlike the buffalo, which loves the low-lying and marshy lands, the Bison prefers the high wooded localities, where it lives in small troops.

Its name of Bison is a modification of the word Bisam, or musk, which was given to it on account of the strong musky

BISON KILLING WOLF.

odour of its flesh, which is especially powerful about the head and neck. This odour is not so unpleasant as might be supposed, and those who have had personal experience of the animal say that it bears some resemblance to the perfume of violets. It is developed most strongly in the adult bulls, the cows and young male calves only possessing it in a slight degree.

It is a tolerably large animal, being about six feet high at the shoulder—a stature nearly equivalent to that of the ordinary Asiatic elephant; and, in spite of its great bulk, is a fleet and active animal, as indeed is generally the case with those oxen which inhabit elevated localities. Still, though it can run with considerable speed, it is not able to keep up the pace for any great distance, and at the end of a mile or two can be brought to bay.

Like most animals, however large and powerful they may be, it fears the presence of man, and, if it sees or scents a human being, will try to slip quietly away; but when it is baffled in this attempt, and forced to fight, it becomes a fierce and dangerous antagonist, charging with wonderful quickness, and using its short and powerful horns with great effect. A wounded Bison, when fairly brought to bay, is perhaps as awkward an opponent as can be found, and to kill it without the aid of fire-arms is no easy matter.

Although the countries in which it lives are infested with wolves, it seems to have no fear of them when in health; and, even when pressed by their winter's hunger, the wolves do not venture to attack even a single Bison, much less a herd of them. Like other wild cattle, it likes to dabble in muddy pools, and is fond of harbouring in thickets near such localities; and those who have to travel through the forest keep clear of such spots, unless they desire to drive out the animal for the purpose of killing it.

Like the extinct Aurochs, the Bison has never been domesticated, and, although the calves have been captured while very young, and attempts have been made to train them to harness, their innate wildness of disposition has always baffled such efforts.

THE GAZELLE, OR ROE OF SCRIPTURE.

Its swiftness, its beauty, and the quality of its flesh—Different varieties of the Gazelle—How the Gazelle defends itself against wild beasts—Chase of the Gazelle.

WE now leave the Ox tribe, and come to the Antelopes, several species of which are mentioned in the Scriptures. Four kinds of antelope are found in or near the Holy Land, and there is little doubt that all of them are mentioned in the sacred volume.

The first that will be described is the GAZELLE, which is acknowledged to be the animal that is represented by the word *Tsebi*, or *Tsebiyah*. The Jewish Bible accepts the same rendering.

This word occurs many times, sometimes as a metaphor, and sometimes representing some animal which was lawful food, and which therefore belonged to the true ruminants. Moreover, its flesh was not only legally capable of being eaten, but was held in such estimation that it was provided for the table of Solomon himself, together with other animals which will be described in their turn.

THE GAZELLE.

It is even now considered a great dainty, although it is not at all agreeable to European taste, being hard, dry, and without flavour. Still, as has been well remarked, tastes differ as well as localities, and an article of food which is a costly luxury in one land is utterly disdained in another, and will hardly be eaten except by one who is absolutely dying of starvation.

The Gazelle is very common in Palestine in the present day, and, in the ancient times, must have been even more plentiful. There are several varieties of it, which were once thought to be distinct species, but are now acknowledged to be mere varieties, all of which are referable to the single species *Gazella Dorcas*. There is, for example, the Corinna, or Corine Antelope, which is a rather boldly-spotted female; the Kevella Antelope, in which the horns are slightly flattened; the small variety called the Ariel, or Cora; the grey Kevel, which is a rather large variety; and the Long-horned Gazelle, which owes its name to a rather large development of the horns.

Whatever variety may inhabit any given spot, they all have the same habits. They are gregarious animals, associating together in herds often of considerable size, and deriving from their numbers an element of strength which would otherwise be wanting. Against mankind, numbers are of no avail; but when the agile though feeble Gazelle has to defend itself against the predatory animals of its own land, it can only defend itself by the concerted action of the whole herd. Should, for example, the wolves prowl round a herd of Gazelles, after their treacherous wont, the Gazelles instantly assume a posture of self-defence. They form themselves into a compact phalanx, all the males coming to the front, and the strongest and boldest taking on themselves the honourable duty of facing the foe. The does and the young are kept within their ranks, and so formidable is the array of sharp, menacing horns, that beasts as voracious as the wolf, and far more powerful, have been known to retire without attempting to charge.

As a rule, however, the Gazelle does not desire to resist, and prefers its legs to its horns as a mode of insuring safety. So fleet is the animal, that it seems to fly over the ground as if propelled by volition alone, and its light, agile frame is so enduring, that a fair chase has hardly any prospect of success. Hunters, therefore, prefer a trap of some kind, if they chase the animal merely for food or for the sake of its skin, and contrive to kill considerable numbers at once. Sometimes they dig pitfalls, and drive the Gazelles into them by beating a large tract of country, and gradually narrowing the circle. Sometimes they use nets, such as have already been described, and sometimes they line the sides of a ravine with archers and spearmen, and drive the herd of Gazelles through the treacherous defile.

These modes of slaughter are, however, condemned by the true hunter, who looks upon those who use them much in the same light as an English sportsman looks on a man who shoots foxes. The greyhound and the falcon are both employed in the legitimate capture of the Gazelle, and in some cases both are trained to work together. Hunting the Gazelle with the greyhound very much resembles coursing in our own country, and chasing it with the hawk is exactly like the system of falconry that was once so popular an English sport, and which even now shows signs of revival.

It is, however, when the dog and the bird are trained to work together that the spectacle becomes really novel and interesting to an English spectator.

As soon as the Gazelles are fairly in view, the hunter unhoods his hawk, and holds it up so that it may see the animals. The bird fixes its eye on one Gazelle, and by that glance the animal's doom is settled. The falcon darts after the Gazelles, followed by the dog, who keeps his eye on the hawk, and holds himself in readiness to attack the animal that his feathered ally may select. Suddenly the falcon, which has been for some few seconds hovering over the herd of Gazelles, makes a stoop upon the selected victim, fastening its talons in its forehead, and, as it tries to shake off its strange foe, flaps its wings into the Gazelle's eyes so as to blind it. Consequently, the rapid course of the antelope is arrested, so that the dog is able to come up and secure the animal while it is struggling to escape from its feathered enemy. Sometimes, though rarely, a young and inexperienced hawk swoops down with such reckless force that it misses the forehead of the Gazelle, and impales itself upon the sharp horns, just as in England the falcon is apt to be spitted on the bill of the heron.

The most sportsmanlike mode of hunting the Gazelle is to use the falcon alone ; but for this sport a bird must possess exceptional strength, swiftness, and intelligence. A very spirited account of such a chase is given by Mr. G. W. Chasseaud, in his " Druses of the Lebanon :"—

" Whilst reposing here, our old friend with the falcon informs us that at a short distance from this spot is a khan called Nebbi Youni, from a supposition that the prophet Jonah was here landed by the whale ; but the old man is very indignant when we identify the place with a fable, and declare to him that similar sights are to be seen at Gaza and Scanderoon. But his good humour is speedily recovered by reverting to the subject of the exploits and cleverness of his falcon. This reminds him that we have not much time to waste in idle talk, as the greater heats will drive the gazelles from the plains to the mountain retreats, and lose us the opportunity of enjoying the most sportsmanlike amusement in Syria. Accordingly, bestriding our animals again, we ford the river at that point where a bridge once stood.

"We have barely proceeded twenty minutes before the keen eye of the falconer has descried a herd of gazelles quietly grazing in the distance. Immediately he reins in his horse, and enjoining silence, instead of riding at them, as we might have felt inclined to do, he skirts along the banks of the river, so as to cut off, if possible, the retreat of these fleet animals where the banks are narrowest, though very deep, but which would be cleared at a single leap by the gazelles. Having successfully accomplished this manœuvre, he again removes the hood from the hawk, and indicates to us that precaution is no longer necessary. Accordingly, first adding a few slugs to the charges in our barrels, we balance our guns in an easy posture, and, giving the horses their reins, set off at full gallop, and with a loud hurrah, right towards the already startled gazelles.

"The timid animals, at first paralysed by our appearance, stand and gaze for a second terror-stricken at our approach; but their pause is only momentary; they perceive in an instant that the retreat to their favourite haunts has been secured, and so they dash wildly forward with all the fleetness of despair, coursing over the plain with no fixed refuge in view, and nothing but their fleetness to aid in their delivery. A stern chase is a long chase, and so, doubtless, on the present occasion it would prove with ourselves, for there is many and many a mile of level country before us, and our horses, though swift of foot, stand no chance in this respect with the gazelles.

"Now, however, the old man has watched for a good opportunity to display the prowess and skill of his falcon: he has followed us only at a hand-gallop; but the hawk, long inured to such pastime, stretches forth its neck eagerly in the direction of the flying prey, and being loosened from its pinions, sweeps up into the air like a shot, and passes overhead with incredible velocity. Five minutes more, and the bird has outstripped even the speed of the light-footed gazelle; we see him through the dust and haze that our own speed throws around us, hovering but an instant over the terrified herd; he has singled out his

THE FALCON USED IN OUR HUNT.

prey, and, diving with unerring aim, fixes his iron talons into the head of the terrified animal.

"This is the signal for the others to break up their orderly retreat, and to speed over the plain in every direction. Some, despite the danger that hovers on their track, make straight for their old and familiar haunts, and passing within twenty yards of where we ride, afford us an opportunity of displaying our skill as amateur huntsmen on horseback; nor does it require but little nerve and dexterity to fix our aim whilst our horses are tearing over the ground. However, the moment presents itself, the loud report of barrel after barrel startles the unaccustomed inmates of that unfrequented waste; one gazelle leaps twice its own height into the air, and then rolls over, shot through the heart; another bounds on yet a dozen paces, but,

THE GAZELLE. 169

wounded mortally, staggering, halts, and then falls to the ground.

"This is no time for us to pull in and see what is the amount of damage done, for the falcon, heedless of all surrounding incidents, clings firmly to the head of its terrified victim, flapping its strong wings awhile before the poor brute's terrified eyes, half blinding it and rendering its head dizzy; till, after tearing round and round with incredible speed, the poor creature stops, panting for breath, and, overcome with excessive terror,

THE ARAB IS DELIGHTED AT THE SUCCESS OF THE HUNT.

drops down fainting upon the earth. Now the air resounds with the acclamations and hootings of the ruthless victors.

"The Arab is wild in his transports of delight. More certain of the prowess of his bird than ourselves, he had stopped awhile to gather together the fruits of our booty, and now galloped furiously up, waving his long gun, and shouting lustily the while the praises of his infallible hawk; then getting down, and hoodwinking the bird again, he first of all takes the precaution of fastening together the legs of the fallen gazelle, and then he humanely blows up into its nostrils. Gradually the natural brilliancy returns to the dimmed eyes of the gazelle, then it struggles valiantly, but vainly, to disentangle itself from its fetters.

"Pitying its efforts, the falconer throws a handkerchief over its head, and, securing this prize, claims it as his own, declaring that he will bear it home to his house in the mountains, where, after a few weeks' kind treatment and care, it will become as domesticated and affectionate as a spaniel. Meanwhile, Abou Shein gathers together the fallen booty, and, tying them securely with cords, fastens them behind his own saddle, declaring, with a triumphant laugh, that we shall return that evening to the city of Beyrout with such game as few sportsmen can boast of having carried thither in one day."

The gentle nature of the Gazelle is as proverbial as its grace and swiftness, and is well expressed in the large, soft, liquid eye, which has formed from time immemorial the stock comparison of Oriental poets when describing the eyes of beauty.

THE GAZELLE.

THE PYGARG, OR ADDAX.

The Dishon or Dyshon—Signification of the word Pygarg—Certainty that the Dishon is an antelope, and that it must be one of a few species—Former and present range of the Addax—Description of the Addax

THERE is a species of animal mentioned once in the Scriptures under the name of Dishon which the Jewish Bible leaves untranslated, and merely gives as Dyshon, and which is rendered in the Septuagint by Pugargos, or PYGARG, as one version gives it. Now, the meaning of the word Pygarg is white-crouped, and for that reason the Pygarg of the Scriptures is usually held to be one of the white-crouped antelopes, of which several species are known. Perhaps it may be one of them—it may possibly be neither, and it may probably refer to all of them.

But that an antelope of some kind is meant by the word Dishon is evident enough, and it is also evident that the Dishon must have been one of the antelopes which could be obtained by the Jews. Now as the species of antelope which could have furnished food for that nation are very few in number, it is clear that, even if we do not hit upon the exact species, we may be sure of selecting an animal that was closely allied to it. Moreover, as the nomenclature is exceedingly loose, it is probable that more than one species might have been included in the word Dishon.

Modern commentators have agreed that there is every probability that the Dishon of the Pentateuch was the antelope known by the name of Addax.

This handsome antelope is a native of Northern Africa. It has a very wide range, and, even at the present day, is found in the vicinity of Palestine, so that it evidently was one of the antelopes which could be killed by Jewish hunters. From its large size, and long twisted horns, it bears a strong resemblance to the Koodoo of Southern Africa. The horns, however, are not so long, nor so boldly twisted, the curve being comparatively slight, and not possessing the bold spiral shape which distinguishes those of the koodoo.

THE ADDAX.

The ordinary height of the Addax is three feet seven or eight inches, and the horns are almost exactly alike in the two sexes. Their length, from the head to the tips, is rather more than two feet. Its colour is mostly white, but a thick mane of dark black hair falls from the throat, a patch of similar hair grows on the forehead, and the back and shoulders are greyish brown. There is no mane on the back of the neck, as is the case with the koodoo.

The Addax is a sand-loving animal, as is shown by the wide and spreading hoofs, which afford it a firm footing on the yielding soil. In all probability, this is one of the animals which would be taken, like the wild bull, in a net, being surrounded and driven into the toils by a number of hunters. It is not, however, one of the gregarious species, and is not found in those vast herds in which some of the antelopes love to assemble.

THE FALLOW-DEER, OR BUBALE.

The word Jachmur evidently represents a species of antelope—Resemblance of the animal to the ox tribe—Its ox-like horns and mode of attack—Its capability of domestication—Former and present range of the Bubale—Its representation on the monuments of ancient Egypt—Delicacy of its flesh—Size and general appearance of the animal.

IT has already been mentioned that in the Old Testament there occur the names of three or four animals, which clearly belong to one or other of three or four antelopes. Only one of these names now remains to be identified. This is the Jachmur, or Yachmur, a word which has been rendered in the Septuagint as Boubalos, and has been translated in our Authorized Version as FALLOW DEER.

We shall presently see that the Fallow Deer is to be identified with another animal, and that the word Jachmur must find another interpretation. If we follow the Septuagint, and call it the BUBALE, we shall identify it with a well-known antelope called by the Arabs the "Bekk'r-el-Wash," and known to zoologists as the BUBALE (*Acronotus bubalis*).

This fine antelope would scarcely be recognised as such by an unskilled observer, as in its general appearance it much more resembles the ox tribe than the antelope. Indeed, the Arabic title, "Bekk'r-el-Wash," or Wild Cow, shows how close must be the resemblance to the oxen. The Arabs, and indeed all the Orientals in whose countries it lives, believe it not to be an antelope, but one of the oxen, and class it accordingly.

How much the appearance of the Bubale justifies them in this opinion may be judged by reference to the figure on page 143. The horns are thick, short, and heavy, and are first inclined forwards, and then rather suddenly bent backwards. This formation of the horns causes the Bubale to use his weapons after the manner of the bull, thereby increasing the resemblance between them. When it attacks, the Bubale lowers its head to the ground, and as soon as its antagonist is within reach, tosses its head violently upwards, or swings it with a sidelong upward blow. In either case, the sharp curved horns, impelled by the powerful neck of the animal, and assisted by the weight of the large head, become most formidable weapons.

It is said that in some places, where the Bubales have learned to endure the presence of man, they will mix with his herds for the sake of feeding with them, and by degrees become so accustomed to the companionship of their domesticated friends, that they live with the herd as if they had belonged to it all their lives. This fact shows that the animal possesses a gentle disposition, and it is said to be as easily tamed as the gazelle itself.

Even at the present day the Bubale has a very wide range, and formerly had in all probability a much wider. It is indigenous to Barbary, and has continued to spread itself over the greater part of Northern Africa, including the borders of the Sahara, the edges of the cultivated districts, and up the Nile for no small distance. In former days it was evidently a tolerably common animal of chase in Upper Egypt as there are representations of it on the monuments, drawn with the quaint truthfulness which distinguishes the monumental sculpture of that period.

THE BUBALE, OR FALLOW-DEER OF SCRIPTURE.

It is probable that in and about Palestine it was equally common, so that there is good reason why it should be specially named as one of the animals that were lawful food. Not only was its flesh permitted to be eaten, but it was evidently considered as a great dainty, inasmuch as the Jachmur is mentioned in 1 Kings iv. 23 as one of the animals which were brought to the royal table. "Harts and Roebucks and Fallow-Deer" are the wild animals mentioned in the passage alluded to.

THE SHEEP.

Importance of Sheep in the Bible—
The Sheep the chief wealth of the
pastoral tribes—Arab shepherds of the present day—Wanderings of the flocks in search of food—Value of the wells—How the Sheep are watered—The shepherd usually a part owner of the flocks—Structure of the sheepfolds—The rock caverns of Palestine—David's adventure with Saul—Use of the dogs—The broad-tailed Sheep, and its peculiarities.

We now come to a subject which will necessarily occupy us for some little time.

There is, perhaps, no animal which occupies a larger space in the Scriptures than the Sheep. Whether in religious, civil, or

THE SHEEP.

domestic life, we find that the Sheep is bound up with the Jewish nation in a way that would seem almost incomprehensible, did we not recall the light which the New Testament throws upon the Old, and the many allusions to the coming Messiah under the figure of the Lamb that taketh away the sins of the world.

In treating of the Sheep, it will be perhaps advisable to begin the account by taking the animal simply as one of those creatures which have been domesticated from time immemorial, dwelling slightly on those points on which the sheep-owners of the old days differed from those of our own time.

The only claim to the land seems, in the old times of the Scriptures, to have lain in cultivation, or perhaps in the land immediately surrounding a well. But any one appears to have taken a piece of ground and cultivated it, or to have dug a well wherever he chose, and thereby to have acquired a sort of right to the soil. The same custom prevails at the present day among the cattle-breeding races of Southern Africa. The banks of rivers, on account of their superior fertility, were considered as the property of the chiefs who lived along their course, but the inland soil was free to all.

Had it not been for this freedom of the land, it would have been impossible for the great men to have nourished the enormous flocks and herds of which their wealth consisted; but, on account of the lack of ownership of the soil, a flock could be moved to one district after another as fast as it exhausted the herbage, the shepherds thus unconsciously imitating the habits of the gregarious animals, which are always on the move from one spot to another.

Pasturage being thus free to all, Sheep had a higher comparative value than is the case with ourselves, who have to pay in some way for their keep. There is a proverb in the Talmud which may be curtly translated, "Land sell, sheep buy."

The value of a good pasture-ground for the flocks is so great, that its possession is well worth a battle, the shepherds being saved from a most weary and harassing life, and being moreover fewer in number than is needed when the pasturage is scanty. Sir S. Baker, in his work on Abyssinia, makes some very interesting remarks upon the Arab herdsmen, who are placed in conditions very similar to those of the Israelitish shepherds

"The Arabs are creatures of necessity; their nomadic life is compulsory, as the existence of their flocks and herds depends upon the pasturage. Thus, with the change of seasons they must change their localities according to the presence of fodder for their cattle. . . . The Arab cannot halt in one spot longer than the pasturage will support his flocks. The object of his life being fodder, he must wander in search of the ever-changing

ARABS JOURNEYING TO FRESH PASTURES.

supply. His wants must be few, as the constant change of encampment necessitates the transport of all his household goods; thus he reduces to a minimum his domestic furniture and utensils. . . .

"This striking similarity to the descriptions of the Old Testament is exceedingly interesting to a traveller when residing among these curious and original people. With the Bible in one's hand, and these unchanged tribes before the eyes, there is a thrilling illustration of the sacred record; the past becomes the present, the veil of three thousand years is raised, and the living picture is a witness to the exactness of the historical description. At the same time there is a light thrown upon many obscure passages in the Old Testament by the experience of the present customs and figures of speech of the Arabs, which are precisely those that were practised at the periods described. . . . .

"Should the present history of the country be written by an Arab scribe, the style of the description would be precisely that of the Old Testament. There is a fascination in the

VIEW OF THE PYRAMIDS.

unchangeable features of the Nile regions. There are the vast pyramids that have defied time, the river upon which Moses was cradled in infancy, the same sandy desert through which he led his people, and the watering-places where their flocks were led to drink. The wild and wandering Arabs, who thousands of years ago dug out the wells in the wilderness, are represented by their descendants, unchanged, who now draw water from the deep wells of their forefathers, with the skins that have never altered their fashion.

"The Arabs, gathering with their goats and sheep around the

wells to-day, recall the recollection of that distant time when 'Jacob went on his journey, and came into the land of the people of the east. And he looked, and behold a well in the field, and lo! there were three flocks of sheep lying by it,' &c. The picture of that scene would be an illustration of Arab daily life in the Nubian deserts, where the present is a mirror of the past."

Owing to the great number of Sheep which they have to tend, and the peculiar state of the country, the life of the shepherd in Palestine is even now very different from that of an English shepherd, and in the days of the early Scriptures the distinction was even more distinctly marked.

Sheep had to be tended much more carefully than we generally think. In the first place, a thoughtful shepherd had always one idea before his mind,—namely, the possibility of obtaining sufficient water for his flocks. Even pasturage is less important than water, and, however tempting a district might be, no shepherd would venture to take his charge there if he were not sure of obtaining water. In a climate such as ours, this ever-pressing anxiety respecting water can scarcely be appreciated, for in hot climates not only is water scarce, but it is needed far more than in a temperate and moist climate. Thirst does its work with terrible quickness, and there are instances recorded where men have sat down and died of thirst in sight of the river which they had not strength to reach.

In places therefore through which no stream runs, the wells are the great centres of pasturage, around which are to be seen vast flocks extending far in every direction. These wells are kept carefully closed by their owners, and are only opened for the use of those who are entitled to water their flocks at them.

Noontide is the general time for watering the Sheep, and towards that hour all the flocks may be seen converging towards their respective wells, the shepherd at the head of each flock, and the Sheep following him. See how forcible becomes the imagery of David, the shepherd poet, "The Lord is my Shepherd; I shall not want. He maketh me to lie down in green pastures (or, in pastures of tender grass): He leadeth me beside the still waters" (Ps. xxiii. 1, 2). Here we have two of the principal duties of the good shepherd brought prominently before us,—namely, the

THE SHEEP.

guiding of the Sheep to green pastures and leading them to fresh water. Very many references are made in the Scriptures to the pasturage of sheep, both in a technical and a metaphorical sense; but as our space is limited, and these passages are very numerous, only one or two of each will be taken.

In the story of Joseph, we find that when his father and brothers were suffering from the famine, they seem to have cared as much for their Sheep and cattle as for themselves, inasmuch as among a pastoral people the flocks and herds constitute the only wealth. So, when Joseph at last discovered himself, and his family were admitted to the favour of Pharaoh, the first request which they made was for their flocks. "Pharaoh said unto his brethren, What is your occupation? And they said unto Pharaoh, Thy servants are shepherds, both we, and also our fathers.

"They said moreover unto Pharaoh, For to sojourn in the land are we come; for thy servants have no pasture for their flocks; for the famine is sore in the land of Canaan : now therefore, we pray thee, let thy servants dwell in the land of Goshen."

This one incident, so slightly remarked in the sacred history, gives a wonderfully clear notion of the sort of life led by Jacob and his sons. Forming, according to custom, a small tribe of their own, of which the father was the chief, they led a pastoral life, taking their continually increasing herds and flocks from place to place as they could find food for them. For example, at the memorable time when the story of Joseph begins, he was sent by his father to his brothers, who were feeding the flocks, and he wandered about for some time, not knowing where to find them. It may seem strange that he should be unable to discover such very conspicuous objects as large flocks of sheep and goats, but the fact is that they had been driven from one pasture-land to another, and had travelled in search of food all the way from Shechem to Dothan.

In 1 Chron. iv. 39, 40, we read of the still pastoral Israelites that "they went to the entrance of Gedor, even unto the east side of the valley, to seek pasture for their flocks. And they found fat pasture and good, and the land was wide, and quiet, and peaceable."

How it came to be quiet and peaceable is told in the context. It was peaceable simply because the Israelites were attracted by the good pasturage, attacked the original inhabitants, and exterminated them so effectually that none were left to offer resistance to the usurpers. And we find from this passage that the value of good pasture-land where the Sheep could feed continually without being forced to wander from one spot to another was so considerable, that the owners of the flocks engaged in war, and exposed their own lives, in order to obtain so valuable a possession.

JACOB MEETS RACHEL AT THE WELL.

We will now look at one or two of the passages that mention watering the Sheep—a duty so imperative on an Oriental shepherd, and so needless to our own.

In the first place we find that most graphic narrative which occurs in Gen. xxix. to which a passing reference has already been made. When Jacob was on his way from his parents to the home of Laban in Padan-aram, he came upon the very well which belonged to his uncle, and there saw three flocks of Sheep lying around the well, waiting until the proper hour arrived. According to custom, a large stone was laid over the well, so as to perform the double office of keeping out the sand and dust, and of guarding the precious water against those who had no right to it. And when he saw his cousin Rachel arrive with

EASTERN SHEPHERD WATCHING HIS FLOCK.

the flock of which she had the management, he, according to the courtesy of the country and the time, rolled away the ponderous barrier, and poured out water into the troughs for the Sheep which Rachel tended.

About two hundred years afterwards, we find Moses performing a similar act. When he was obliged to escape into Midian on account of his fatal quarrel with a tyrannical Egyptian, he sat down by a well, waiting for the time when the stone might be rolled away, and the water be distributed. Now it happened that this well belonged to Jethro, the chief priest of the country, whose wealth consisted principally of Sheep. He entrusted his flock to the care of his seven daughters, who led their Sheep to the well and drew water as usual into the troughs. Presuming on their weakness, other shepherds came and tried to drive them away, but were opposed by Moses, who drove them away, and with his own hands watered the flock.

Now in both these examples we find that the men who performed the courteous office of drawing the water and pouring it into the sheep-troughs married afterwards the girl to whose charge the flocks had been committed. This brings us to the Oriental custom which has been preserved to the present day.

The wells at which the cattle are watered at noon-day are the meeting-places of the tribe, and it is chiefly at the well that the young men and women meet each other. As each successive flock arrives at the well, the number of the people increases, and while the sheep and goats lie patiently round the water, waiting for the time when the last flock shall arrive, and the stone be rolled off the mouth of the well, the gossip of the tribe is discussed, and the young people have ample opportunity for the pleasing business of courtship.

As to the passages in which the wells, rivers, brooks, watersprings, are spoken of in a metaphorical sense, they are too numerous to be quoted.

And here I may observe, that in reality the whole of Scripture has its symbolical as well as its outward signification ; and that, until we have learned to read the Bible strictly according to the spirit, we cannot understand one-thousandth part of the mysteries which it conceals behind its veil of language ; nor can we appreciate one-thousandth part of the treasures of wisdom which lie hidden in its pages

THE SHEEP.

Another duty of the shepherd of ancient Palestine was to guard his flock from depredators, whether man or beast. Therefore the shepherd was forced to carry arms; to act as a sentry during the night; and, in fact, to be a sort of irregular soldier. A fully-armed shepherd had with him his bow, his spear, and his sword, and not even a shepherd lad was without his sling and the great quarter-staff which is even now universally carried by the tribes along the Nile—a staff as thick as a man's wrist, and six or seven feet in length. He was skilled in the use of all these weapons, especially in that of the sling.

In these days, the sling is only considered as a mere toy, whereas, before the introduction of fire-arms, it was one of the most formidable weapons that could be wielded by light troops. Round and smooth stones weighing three or four ounces were the usual projectiles, and, by dint of constant practice from childhood, the slingers could aim with a marvellous precision.

DAVID GATHERS STONES FROM THE BROOK TO CAST AT GOLIATH.

Of this fact we have a notable instance in David, who knew that the sling and the five stones in the hand of an active youth unencumbered by armour, and wearing merely the shepherd's simple tunic, were more than a match for all the ponderous weapons of the gigantic Philistine.

It has sometimes been the fashion to attribute the successful aim of David to a special miracle, whereas those who are acquainted with ancient weapons know well that no miracle was wrought, because none was needed; a good slinger at that time being as sure of his aim as a good rifleman of our days.

The sling was in constant requisition, being used both in directing the Sheep and in repelling enemies : a stone skilfully thrown in front of a straying Sheep being a well-understood signal that the animal had better retrace its steps if it did not want to feel the next stone on its back.

AN EASTERN SHEPHERD.

Passing his whole life with his flock, the shepherd was identified with his Sheep far more than is the case in this country. He knew all his Sheep by sight, he called them all by their names, and they all knew him and recognised his voice. He did not drive them, but he led them, walking in their front, and they following him. Sometimes he would play with them, pretending to run away while they pursued him, exactly as an infant-school teacher plays with the children.

Consequently, they looked upon him as their protector as well as their feeder, and were sure to follow wherever he led them.

We must all remember how David, who had passed all his early years as a shepherd, speaks of God as the Shepherd of

SHEEP FOLLOWING THEIR SHEPHERD.

Israel, and the people as Sheep; never mentioning the Sheep as being driven, but always as being led. "Thou leddest Thy people like a flock, by the hands of Moses and Aaron" (Ps. lxxvii. 20); "The Lord is my Shepherd. . . . He leadeth me beside the still waters" (Ps. xxiii. 1, 2); "Lead me in a plain path, because of mine enemies" (Ps. xxvii. 11); together with many other passages too numerous to be quoted.

Our Lord Himself makes a familiar use of the same image: "He calleth his own sheep by name, and leadeth them out And when he putteth forth his own sheep, he goeth before them, and the sheep follow him: for they know his voice,

Although the shepherds of our own country know their Sheep by sight, and say that there is as much difference in the faces of Sheep as of men, they have not, as a rule, attained the art of teaching their Sheep to recognise their names. This custom, however, is still retained, as may be seen from a well-known passage in Hartley's "Researches in Greece and the Levant:"—

"Having had my attention directed last night to the words in John x. 3, I asked my man if it were usual in Greece to give names to the sheep. He informed me that it was, and that the sheep obeyed the shepherd when he called them by their names. This morning I had an opportunity of verifying the truth of this remark. Passing by a flock of sheep, I asked the shepherd the same question which I had put to the servant, and he gave me the same answer. I then bade him call one of his sheep. He did so, and it instantly left its pasturage and its companions, and ran up to the hands of the shepherd, with signs of pleasure, and with a prompt obedience which I had never before observed in any other animal.

"It is also true that in this country, 'a stranger will they not follow, but will flee from him.' The shepherd told me that many of his sheep were still wild, that they had not learned their names, but that by teaching them they would all learn them."

Generally, the shepherd was either the proprietor of the flock, or had at all events a share in it, of which latter arrangement we find a well-known example in the bargain which Jacob made with Laban, all the white Sheep belonging to his father-in-law, and all the dark and spotted Sheep being his wages as shepherd. Such a man was far more likely to take care of the Sheep than if he were merely a paid labourer; especially in a country where the life of a shepherd was a life of actual danger, and he might at any time be obliged to fight against armed robbers, or to oppose the wolf, the lion, or the bear. The combat of the shepherd David with the last-mentioned animals has already been noticed.

In allusion to the continual risks run by the Oriental shepherd, our Lord makes use of the following well-known words:—"The thief cometh not but for to steal, and to kill, and to destroy: I am come that they might have life, and have it more abundantly. I am the Good Shepherd: the good shepherd giveth his life for the sheep. But he that is an hireling, ... whose own the sheep are not, seeth the wolf coming, and leaveth the sheep, and fleeth: and the wolf catcheth them, and scattereth the sheep. The hireling fleeth because he is an hireling, and careth not for the sheep."

Owing to the continual moving of the Sheep, the shepherd had very hard work during the lambing time, and was obliged to carry in his arms the young lambs which were too feeble to accompany their parents, and to keep close to him those Sheep who were expected soon to become mothers. At that time of year the shepherd might constantly be seen at the head of his flock, carrying one or two lambs in his arms, accompanied by their mothers.

In allusion to this fact Isaiah writes: "His reward is with Him, and His work before Him. He shall feed His flock like a shepherd; He shall gather the lambs with His arms and carry them in His bosom, and shall gently lead them that are with young" (or, "that give suck," according to the marginal reading). Here we have presented at once before us the good shepherd who is no hireling, but owns the Sheep; and who therefore has "his reward with him, and his work before him;" who bears the tender lambs in his arms, or lays them in the folds of his mantle, and so carries them in his bosom, and leads by his side their yet feeble mothers.

Frequent mention is made of the folds in which the Sheep are penned; and as these folds differed—and still differ—materially from those of our own land, we shall miss the force of several passages of Scripture if we do not understand their form, and the materials of which they were built. Our folds consist merely of hurdles, moveable at pleasure, and so low that a man can easily jump over them, and so fragile that he can easily pull them down. Moreover, the Sheep are frequently enclosed within the fold while they are at pasture.

If any one should entertain such an idea of the Oriental fold, he would not see the force of the well-known passage in which our Lord compares the Church to a sheepfold, and Himself to the door. "He that entereth not by the door into the sheepfold, but climbeth up some other way, the same is a thief and a robber. But he that entereth in by the door is the shepherd of the sheep. To him the porter openeth, and the sheep hear his voice. . . . All that ever came before me are thieves and robbers: but the sheep did not hear them. I am the door: by me if any man enter in, he shall be saved, and shall go in and out, and find pasture."

ANCIENT SHEEP PEN.

Had the fold here mentioned been a simple enclosure of hurdles, such an image could not have been used. It is evident that the fold to which allusion was made, and which was probably in sight at the time when Jesus was disputing with the Pharisees, was a structure of some pretensions; that it had walls which a thief could only enter by climbing over them—not by "breaking through" them, as in the case of a mud-walled private house; and that it had a gate, which was guarded by a watchman.

In fact, the fold was a solid and enduring building, made of stone. Thus in Numbers xxxii. it is related that the tribes of Reuben and Gad, who had great quantities of Sheep and other cattle, asked for the eastward side of Jordan as a pasture-ground, promising to go and fight for the people, but previously to build fortified cities for their families, and folds for their cattle, the folds being evidently, like the cities, buildings of an enduring nature.

In some places the folds are simply rock caverns, partly natural and partly artificial, often enlarged by a stone wall built outside it. It was the absence of these rock caverns on the east side of Jordan that compelled the Reubenites and Gadites to build folds for themselves, whereas on the opposite side places of refuge were comparatively abundant.

See, for example, the well-known history related in 1 Sam. xxiii. xxiv. David and his miscellaneous band of warriors, some six hundred in number, were driven out of the cities by the fear of Saul, and were obliged to pass their time in the wilderness, living in the "strong holds" (xxiii. 14, 19), which we find immediately afterwards to be rock caves (ver. 25). These caves were of large extent, being able to shelter these six hundred warriors, and, on one memorable occasion, to conceal them so completely as they stood along the sides, that Saul, who had just come out of the open air, was not able to discern them in the dim light, and David even managed to approach him unseen, and cut off a portion of his outer robe.

That this particular cave was a sheepfold we learn from xxiv. 2-4: "Then Saul took three thousand chosen men out of all Israel, and went to seek David and his men upon the rocks of the wild goats. And he came to the sheepcotes by the way." Into these strongholds the Sheep are driven towards nightfall, and, as the flocks converge towards their resting-place, the bleatings of the sheep are almost deafening.

The shepherds as well as their flocks found shelter in these caves, making them their resting-places while they were living the strange, wild, pastoral life among the hills; and at the present day many of the smaller caves and "holes of the rock" exhibit the vestiges of human habitation in the shape of straw, hay, and other dried herbage, which has been used for beds, just as we now find the rude couches of the coast-guard men in the cliff caves of our shores.

The dogs which are attached to the sheepfolds were, as they are now, the faithful servants of man, although, as has already been related, they are not made the companions of man as is the case with ourselves. Lean, gaunt, hungry, and treated with but scant kindness, they are yet faithful guardians against the attack of enemies. They do not, as do our sheepdogs, assist in driving the flocks, because the Sheep are not driven, but led, but they are invaluable as nocturnal sentries. Crouching together outside the fold, in little knots of six or seven together, they detect the approach of wild animals, and at the first sign of the wolf or the jackal they bark out a defiance, and scare away the invaders. It is strange that the old superstitious idea of their uncleanness should have held its ground through so many tens of centuries; but, down to the present day, the shepherd of Palestine, though making use of the dog as a guardian of his flock, treats the animal with utter contempt, not to say cruelty, beating and kicking the faithful creature on the least provocation, and scarcely giving it sufficient food to keep it alive.

Sometimes the Sheep are brought up by hand at home. "House-lamb," as we call it, is even now common, and the practice of house-feeding peculiar in the old Scriptural times.

We have an allusion to this custom in the well-known parable of the prophet Nathan: "The poor man had nothing, save one little ewe lamb, which he had bought and nourished up: and it grew up together with him, and with his children; it did eat of his own meat, and drank of his own cup, and lay in his bosom, and was unto him as a daughter" (2 Sam. xii. 3). A further, though less distinct, allusion is made to this practice in Isaiah vii. 21: "It shall come to pass in that day, that a man shall nourish a young cow, and two sheep."

How the Sheep thus brought up by hand were fattened may be conjectured from the following passage in Mr. D. Urquhart's valuable work on the Lebanon:—

"In the month of June, they buy from the shepherds, when pasturage has become scarce and sheep are cheap, two or three sheep; these they feed by hand. After they have eaten up the old grass and the provender about the doors, they get vine leaves, and, after the silkworms have begun to spin, mulberry leaves. They purchase them on trial, and the test is appetite If a sheep does not feed well, they return it after three days To increase their appetite they wash them twice a day, morning and evening, a care they never bestow on their own bodies.

THE POOR MAN'S LAMB.

THE RICH MAN'S FEAST.

"If the sheep's appetite does not come up to their standard, they use a little gentle violence, folding for them forced leaf-balls and introducing them into their mouths. The mulberry has the property of making them fat and tender. At the end of four months the sheep they had bought at eighty piastres will sell for one hundred and forty, or will realize one hundred and fifty.

"The sheep is killed, skinned, and hung up. The fat is then removed; the flesh is cut from the bones, and hung up in the sun. Meanwhile, the fat has been put in a cauldron on the fire, and as soon as it has come to boil, the meat is laid on. The proportion of the fat to the lean is as four to ten, eight 'okes' fat and twenty lean. A little salt is added, it is simmered for an hour, and then placed in jars for the use of the family during the year.

"The large joints are separated and used first, as not fit for keeping long. The fat, with a portion of the lean, chopped fine, is what serves for cooking the 'bourgoul,' and is called *Dehen*. The sheep are of the fat-tailed variety, and the tails are the great delicacy."

This last sentence reminds us that there are two breeds of Sheep in Palestine. One much resembles the ordinary English Sheep, while the other is a very different animal. It is much taller on its legs, larger-boned, and long-nosed. Only the rams have horns, and they are not twisted spirally like those of our own Sheep, but come backwards, and then curl round so that the point comes under the ear. The great peculiarity of this Sheep is the tail, which is simply prodigious in point of size, and is an enormous mass of fat. Indeed, the long-legged and otherwise lean animal seems to concentrate all its fat in the tail, which, as has been well observed, appears to abstract both flesh and fat from the rest of the body. So great is this strange development, that the tail alone will sometimes weigh one-fifth as much as the entire animal. A similar breed of Sheep is found in Southern Africa and other parts of the world. In some places, the tail grows to such an enormous size that, in order to keep so valuable a part of the animal from injury, it is fastened to a small board, supported by a couple of wheels, so that the Sheep literally wheels its own tail in a cart.

Frequent reference to the fat of the tail is made in the Authorized Version of the Scriptures, though in terms which

FLOCKS OF SHEEP BEING TAKEN INTO JERUSALEM.

would not be understood did we not know that the Sheep which is mentioned in those passages is the long-tailed Sheep of Syria. See, for example, the history narrated in Exod. xxix. 22, where special details are given as to the ceremony by which Aaron and his sons were consecrated to the priesthood. "Thou shalt take of the ram the fat and the rump, and the fat that covereth the inwards, and the caul above the liver, and the two kidneys, and the fat that is upon them."

Though this particular breed is not very distinctly mentioned in the Bible, the Talmudical writers have many allusions to it. In the Mischna these broad-tailed Sheep are not allowed to leave their folds on the Sabbath-day, because by wheeling their little tail-waggons behind them they would break the Sabbath. The writers describe the tail very graphically, comparing its shape to that of a saddle, and saying that it is fat, without bones, heavy and long, and looks as if the whole body were continued beyond the hind-legs, and thence hung down in place of a tail.

The Rabbinical writers treat rather fully of the Sheep, and

give some very amusing advice respecting their management. If the ewes cannot be fattened in the ordinary manner, that end may be achieved by tying up the udder so that the milk cannot flow, and the elements which would have furnished milk are forced to produce fat. If the weather should be chilly at the shearing time, and there is danger of taking cold after the wool is removed, the shepherd should dip a sponge in oil and tie it on the forehead of the newly-shorn animal. Or, if he should not have a sponge by him, a woollen rag will do as well. The same potent remedy is also efficacious if the Sheep should be ill in lambing time.

That the Sheep is liable to the attack of the gadfly, which deposits its eggs in the nostrils of the unfortunate animal, was as well known in the ancient as in modern times. It is scarcely necessary to mention that the insect in question is the *Æstrus ovis*. Instinctively aware of the presence of this insidious and dreaded enemy, which, though so apparently insignificant, is as formidable a foe as any of the beasts of prey, the Sheep display the greatest terror at the sharp, menacing sound produced by the gadfly's wings as the insect sweeps through the air towards its destination. They congregate together, placing their heads almost in contact with each other, snort and paw the ground in their terror, and use all means in their power to prevent the fly from accomplishing its purpose.

When a gadfly succeeds in attaining its aim, it rapidly deposits an egg or two in the nostril, and then leaves them. The tiny eggs are soon hatched by the natural heat of the animal, and the young larvæ crawl up the nostril towards the frontal sinus. There they remain until they are full-grown, when they crawl through the nostrils, fall on the ground, burrow therein, and in the earth undergo their changes into the pupal and perfect stages.

It need hardly be said that an intelligent shepherd would devote himself to the task of killing every gadfly which he could find, and, as these insects are fond of basking on sunny rocks or tree-trunks, this is no very difficult matter.

The Rabbinical writers, however, being totally ignorant of practical entomology, do not seem to have recognised the insect until it had reached its full larval growth. They say that the rams manage to shake the grubs out of their nostrils by butting at one another in mimic warfare, and that the ewes, which are hornless, and are therefore incapable of relieving themselves by such means, ought to be supplied with plants which will make them sneeze, so that they may shake out the grubs by the convulsive jerkings of the head caused by inhaling the irritating substance.

The same writers also recommend that the rams should be furnished with strong leathern collars.

When the flock is on the march, the rams always go in the van, and, being instinctively afraid of their ancient enemy the wolf, they continually raise their heads and look about them. This line of conduct irritates the wolves, who attack the foremost rams and seize them by the throat. If, therefore, a piece of stout leather be fastened round the ram's neck, the wolf is baffled, and runs off in sullen despair.

Generally, the oldest ram is distinguished by a bell, and, when the flock moves over the hilly slopes, the Sheep walk in file after the leader, making narrow paths, which are very distinct from a distance, but are scarcely perceptible when the foot of the traveller is actually upon them. From this habit has arisen an ancient proverb, "As the sheep after the sheep, so the daughter after the mother," a saying which is another form of our own familiar proverb, "What is bred in the bone will not come out of the flesh."

WE now come to the Sheep considered with reference to its uses. First and foremost the Sheep was, and still is, one of the chief means of subsistence, being to the pastoral inhabitants of Palestine what the oxen are to the pastoral inhabitants of Southern Africa.

To ordinary persons the flesh of the Sheep was a seldom-tasted luxury; great men might eat it habitually, "faring sumptuously every day," and we find that, among the glories of Solomon's reign, the sacred chronicler has thought it worth while to mention that part of the daily provision for his household included one hundred Sheep. No particular pains seem to have been taken about the cooking of the animal, which seems generally to have been boiled. As, however, in such a climate the flesh could not be kept for the purpose of making it tender, as is the case in this part of the world, it was cooked as soon as the animal was killed, the fibres not having time to settle into the rigidity of death.

Generally, when ordinary people had the opportunity of tasting the flesh of the Sheep, it was on the occasion of some rejoicing,—such, for example, as a marriage feast, or the advent of a guest, for whom a lamb or a kid was slain and cooked on the spot, a young male lamb being almost invariably chosen as less injurious than the ewe to the future prospects of the flock. Roasting over a fire was sometimes adopted, as was baking in an oven sunk in the ground, a remarkable instance of which we shall see when we come to the Jewish sacrifices. Boiling, however, was the principal mode; so much so, indeed, that the Hebrew word which signifies boiling is used to signify any kind of cooking, even when the meat was roasted.

The process of cooking and eating the Sheep was as follows.

The animal having been killed according to the legal form, the skin was stripped off, and the body separated joint from joint, the right shoulder being first removed. This, it will be remembered, was the priest's portion; see Lev. vii. 32 : " The right shoulder shall ye give unto the priest for an heave offering of the sacrifices of your peace offerings." The whole of the flesh was then separated from the bones, and chopped small, and even the bones themselves broken up, so that the marrow might not be lost.

A reference to this custom is found in Micah iii. 2, 3, " Who pluck off their skin from off them, and their flesh from off their bones; who also eat the flesh of my people . . . . and they break their bones, and chop them in pieces, as for the pot, and as flesh within the caldron." The reader will now understand more fully the force of the prophecy, " He keepeth all His bones: not one of them is broken " (Psa. xxxiv. 20).

The mixed mass of bones and flesh was then put into the caldron, which was generally filled with water, but sometimes with milk, as is the custom with the Bedouins of the present day, whose manners are in many respects identical with those of the early Jews. It has been thought by some commentators that the injunction not to "seethe a kid in his mother's milk" (Deut. xiv. 21) referred to this custom. I believe, however, that the expression "in his mother's milk" does not signify that the flesh of the kid might not be boiled in its mother's milk, but

THE SHEEP.

that a kid might not be taken which was still in its mother's milk, *i.e.* unweaned.

Salt and spices were generally added to it; see Ezek. xxiv. 10: "Heap on wood, kindle the fire, consume the flesh, and spice it well." The surface was carefully skimmed, and, when the meat was thoroughly cooked, it and the broth were served up separately. The latter was used as a sort of sauce, into which unleavened bread was dipped. So in Judges vi. 19 we read that when Gideon was visited by the angel, according to the hospitable custom of the land, he "made ready a kid, and unleavened cakes of an ephah of flour: the flesh he put in a basket, and he put the broth in a pot, and brought it out unto him under the oak, and presented it to him."

Valuable, however, as was the Sheep for this purpose, there has always existed a great reluctance to kill the animal, the very sight of the flocks being an intense gratification to a pastoral Oriental. The principal part of the food supplied by the Sheep was, and is still, the milk; which afforded abundant food without thinning the number of the flock. As all know who have tasted it, the milk of the Sheep is peculiarly rich, and in the East is valued much more highly than that of cattle. The milk was seldom drunk in a fresh state, as is usually the case with ourselves, but was suffered to become sour, curdled, and semi-solid.

We now come to a portion of the Sheep scarcely less important than the flesh and the milk, *i.e.* the fleece, or wool.

In the ancient times nearly the whole of the clothing was made of wool, especially the most valuable part of it, namely the large mantle, or "haick," in which the whole person could be folded, and which was the usual covering during sleep. The wool, therefore, would be an article of great national value; and so we find that when the king of Moab paid his tribute in kind to the king of Israel, it was carefully specified that the Sheep should not be shorn. "And Mesha king of Moab was a sheepmaster, and rendered unto the king of Israel an hundred thousand lambs, and an hundred thousand rams, with the wool."

The wool of the Sheep of Palestine differed extremely in value; some kinds being coarse and rough, while others were fine.

The wool was dressed in those times much as it is at present, being carded and then spun with the spindle, the distaff being apparently unused, and the wool simply drawn out by the hand. The shape of the spindle was much like that of the well-known flat spinning-tops that come from Japan—namely, a disc through which passes an axle. A smart twirl given by the fingers to the axle makes the disc revolve very rapidly, and its weight causes the rotation to continue for a considerable time Spinning the wool was exclusively the task of the women, a custom which prevailed in this country up to a very recent time, and which still traditionally survives in the term "spinster," and in the metaphorical use of the word "distaff" as synonymous with a woman's proper work.

When spun into threads, the wool was woven in the simple loom which has existed up to our own day, and which is identical in its general principles throughout a very large portion of the world. It consisted of a framework of wood, at one end of which was placed the "beam" to which the warp was attached; and at the other end was the "pin" on which the cloth was rolled as it was finished.

The reader may remember that when Delilah was cajoling Samson to tell her the secret of his strength, he said, "If thou weavest the seven locks of my head with the web." So, as he slept, she interwove his long hair with the fabric which was on her loom, and, to make sure, "fastened it with the pin," *i.e.* wove it completely into the cloth which was rolled round the pin. So firmly had she done so, that when he awoke he could not disentangle his hair, but left the house with the whole of the loom, the beam and the pin, and the web hanging to his head.

Wool was often dyed of various colours; blue, purple, and scarlet being those which were generally employed. The rams' skins which formed part of the covering of the Tabernacle were ordered to be dyed scarlet, partly on account of the significance of the colour, and partly because none but the best and purest fleeces would be chosen for so rare and costly a dye. How the colour was produced we shall learn towards the end of the volume.

Sheep-shearing was always a time of great rejoicing and revelry, which seem often to have been carried beyond the bounds of sobriety. Thus when Nabal had gathered together his three thousand Sheep in Carmel, and held a shearing festival, David sent to ask for some provisions for his band, and was refused in accordance with the disposition of the man, who had inflamed his naturally churlish nature with wine. "He held a feast in his house, like the feast of a king: and Nabal's heart was merry within him, for he was very drunken" (1 Sam. xxv. 36).

The same was probably the case when Laban was shearing his Sheep (Gen. xxxi. 19). Otherwise it would scarcely have been possible for Jacob to have gone away unknown to Laban, taking with him his wives and children, his servants, his camels, and his flocks, the rapid increase of which had excited the jealousy of his uncle, and which were so numerous that, in fear of his brother Esau, he divided them into two bands, and yet was able to select from them a present to his brother, consisting in all of nearly six hundred sheep, camels, oxen, goats, and asses.

Sometimes the shepherds and others who lived in pastoral districts made themselves coats of the skins of the Sheep, with the wool still adhering to it. The custom extends to the present day, and even in many parts of Europe the sheep-skin dress of the shepherds is a familiar sight to the traveller. The skin was sometimes tanned and used as leather, but was considered as inferior to that of the goat. Mr. Tristram conjectures that the leathern "girdle" worn by St. John the Baptist was probably the untanned sheep-skin coat which has been just mentioned. So it is said of the early Christians, that "they wandered about in sheep-skins and goat-skins, being destitute, afflicted, tormented," the sheep-skins in question being evidently the rude shepherd's coats.

The horn of the ram had a national value, as from it were made the sacred trumpets which played so important a part in the history of the Jewish nation. There is no doubt that the primitive trumpets were originally formed either from the horn of an animal, such as the ox, the large-horned antelopes, the sheep, and the goat, and that in process of time they were made of metal, generally copper or silver.

References are frequently made in the Bible to these trumpets, for which there were different names, probably on account of their different forms. These names are, however, very loosely rendered in our version, the same word being sometimes translated the "cornet," and sometimes the "trumpet."

SOUNDING THE TRUMPETS IN THE YEAR OF JUBILEE.

The jubilee year was always ushered in by the blasts of the sacred trumpets. "Then shalt thou cause the trumpet of the jubilee to sound on the tenth day of the seventh month, in the day of atonement shall ye make the trumpet sound throughout all your land" (Lev. xxv. 9). Then there was the festival known as the Feast of Trumpets. "In the seventh month, on the first day of the month, ye shall have an holy convocation; ye shall do no servile work: it is a day of blowing the trumpets unto you" (Numb. xxix. 1).

One of these trumpets is now before me, and is shown in the accompanying illustration.

In length it measures eighteen inches, *i.e.* a cubit, and it is formed entirely in one piece. As far as I can judge, it is made from the left horn of the broad-tailed Sheep, which, as has already been remarked, is not spiral, but flattish, curved backwards, and forming nearly a circle, the point passing under the ear. This structure, added to the large size of the horn, adapts it well for its purpose. In order to bring it to the proper shape, the horn is softened by heat, and is then modelled into the very form which was used by the Jewish priests who blew the trumpet before the ark.

RAM'S HORN TRUMPET.

At the present day one such trumpet, at least, is found in every Jewish community, and is kept by the man who has the privilege of blowing it.

WE now come to the important subject, the use of the Sheep in sacrifice.

No animal was used so frequently for this purpose as the Sheep, and in many passages of the Mosaic law are specified the precise age as well as the sex of the Sheep which was to be sacrificed in certain circumstances. Sometimes the Sheep was sacrificed as an offering of thanksgiving, sometimes as an expiation for sin, and sometimes as a redemption for some more valuable animal. The young male lamb was the usual sacrifice;

and almost the only sacrifice for which a Sheep might not be offered was that of the two goats on the great Day of Atonement.

A LAMB UPON THE ALTAR OF BURNT OFFERING.

To mention all the passages in which the Sheep is ordered for sacrifice would occupy too much of our space, and we will therefore restrict ourselves to the one central rite of the Jewish nation, the sacrifice of the Paschal lamb, the precursor of the Lamb of God, who taketh away the sins of the world.

Without examining in full the various ceremonies of the Paschal sacrifice, we will glance over the salient points which distinguish it from any other sacrifice.

The lamb must be a male, which is selected and examined with the minutest care, that it may be free from all blemish, and must be of the first year. It must be killed on the fourteenth of the month Abib as the sun is setting, and the blood must be sprinkled with hyssop. In the first or Egyptian Passover the blood was sprinkled on the lintels and doorposts of the houses, but afterwards on the altar. It must be roasted with fire, and not boiled, after the usual custom in the East; not a bone must be broken. It must be eaten by the household in haste, as if they were just starting on a journey, and if any of it should be left, it must be consumed in the fire, and not eaten on the following day.

Such are the chief points in connexion with the Paschal rite, at once a sacrifice and a feast. The original directions not being sufficiently minute to meet all the practical difficulties which might hinder the correct performance of the rite, a vast number of directions are given by the Rabbinical writers. In order, for example, to guard against the destruction of any part of the animal by careless cooking over a fire, or the possible fracture of a bone by a sudden jet of flame, the Paschal lamb was rather baked than roasted, being placed in an earthen oven from which the ashes had been removed. In order to prevent it from being burned or blackened against the sides of the oven, (in which case it would be cooked with earthenware and not with fire), it was transfixed with a wooden stake, made from the pomegranate-tree, and a transverse spit was thrust through the shoulders. These spits were made of wood, because a metal spit would become heated in the oven, and would cause all the flesh which it touched to be roasted with metal, and not with fire; and the wood of the pomegranate was chosen, because that wood was supposed not to emit any sap when heated. If a drop of water had fallen on the flesh, the law would have been broken, as that part of the flesh would be considered as boiled, and not roasted.

As to the eating of unleavened bread and bitter herbs with the lamb, the custom does not bear on the present subject. In shape the oven seems to have resembled a straw beehive, having an opening at the side by which the fuel could be removed and the lamb inserted.

The ceremony of the Passover has been described by several persons, such as the late Consul Rogers and the Dean of Westminster, the latter of whom has given a most striking and vivid account of the rite in his "Lectures on the Jewish Church."

The place which is now employed in the celebration of this rite is a level spot about two hundred yards from the summit of the mountain, a place which is apparently selected on account of its comparative quiet and seclusion. Dean Stanley thinks that in former times, when the Samaritans were the masters of the country, they celebrated the sacrifice on the sacred plateau on the very summit of the mountain, so that the rite could be seen for a vast distance on every side. Now, however, the less conspicuous place is preferred. By the kindness of the Palestine Exploration Society, I am enabled to present the reader with a view of this sacred spot, taken from a photograph made an hour or two before the time of sacrifice. The rough, rugged character of the mountain is shown by this illustration, though not so well as in several other photographs of Gerizim, in which the entire surface seems to be loosely covered with stones like those of which the low wall is built. Near the centre of the illustration may be seen a pile of sticks and the tops of two

THE PLACE OF SACRIFICE.

caldrons, on each of which a stone is laid to keep the cover from being blown off by the wind. These sticks nearly fill a trench in which the caldrons are sunk, and their use will be presently seen on reading Dean Stanley's narrative. In the far distance are the plains of Samaria, and the long-drawn shadows of the priest and his nephew, and probable successor, show that the time of sacrifice is rapidly approaching.

On the previous day the whole of the community had pitched their tents on the mountain, and as the time of sunset approached the women retired to the tents, and all the males, except those who were unclean according to the provisions of the Mosaic law, assembled near a long deep trench that had been dug in the ground. The men are clothed in long white garments, and the six young men who are selected as the actual sacrificers are dressed in white drawers and shirts. These youths are trained to the duty, but whether they hold any sacred office could not be ascertained.

Then, according to the narrative of Dean Stanley, "the priest, ascending a large rough stone in front of the congregation, recited in a loud chant or scream, in which the others joined, prayers or praises chiefly turning on the glories of Abraham and Isaac. Their attitude was that of all Orientals in prayer; standing, occasionally diversified by the stretching out of the hands, and more rarely by kneeling or crouching, with their knees wrapped in their clothes and bent to the ground, towards the Holy Place on the summit of Gerizim. The priest recited his prayers by heart; the others had mostly books in Hebrew and Arabic.

"Presently, suddenly there appeared amongst the worshippers six sheep, driven up by the side of the youths before mentioned. The unconscious innocence with which they wandered to and fro amongst the bystanders, and the simplicity in aspect and manner of the young men who tended them, more recalled a pastoral scene in Arcadia, or one of those inimitable patriarchal *tableaux* represented in the Ammergau Mystery, than a religious ceremonial.

"The sun, meanwhile, which had hitherto burnished up the Mediterranean in the distance, now sank very nearly to the farthest western ridge overhanging the plain of Sharon. The recitation became more vehement. The priest turned about, facing his brethren, and the whole history of the Exodus from the beginning of the plagues of Egypt was rapidly, almost furiously, chanted. The sheep, still innocently playful, were driven more closely together.

"The setting sun now touched the ridge. The youths burst into a wild murmur of their own, drew forth their long bright knives, and brandished them aloft. In a moment the sheep were thrown on their backs, and the flashing knives rapidly drawn across their throats. Then a few convulsive but silent struggles—'as a sheep ... dumb ... that openeth not his mouth,' —and the six forms lay lifeless on the ground, the blood streaming from them; the one only Jewish sacrifice lingering in the world. In the blood the young men dipped their fingers, and a small spot was marked on the foreheads and noses of the children. A few years ago the red stain was placed on all. But this had now dwindled away into the present practice, preserved, we were told, as a relic or emblem of the whole. Then, as if in congratulation at the completion of the ceremony, they all kissed each other, in the Oriental fashion, on each side of the head.

"The next process was that of the fleecing and roasting of the slaughtered animals, for which the ancient temple furnished such ample provisions. Two holes on the mountain side had been dug; one at some distance, of considerable depth, the other, close to the scene of the sacrifice, comparatively shallow. In this latter cavity, after a short prayer, a fire was kindled, out of the mass of dry heath, juniper, and briers, such as furnished the materials for the conflagration in Jotham's parable, delivered not far from this spot.

"Over the fire were placed two caldrons full of water. Whilst the water boiled, the congregation again stood around, and (as if for economy of time) continued the recitation of the Book of Exodus, and bitter herbs were handed round wrapped in a strip of unleavened bread—'with unleavened bread and bitter herbs shall they eat it.' Then was chanted another short prayer; after which the six youths again appeared, poured the boiling water over the sheep, and plucked off their fleeces. The right forelegs of the sheep, with the entrails, were thrown aside and burnt. The liver was carefully put back. Long poles were brought, on which the animals were spitted; near the bottom of each pole was a transverse peg or stick, to prevent the body from slipping off."

This cross-piece does not, however, penetrate the body, which in most cases scarcely touches it, so that there is little or no resemblance to a crucifixion. The writer lays especial stress on this point, because the early Christians saw in the transverse spit an emblem of the cross. In the Jewish Passover this emblem would have been more appropriate, as in that ceremony the cross-piece was passed through the shoulders, and the forefeet tied to it.

The Sheep being now prepared, they were carried to the oven, which on this occasion was a deep, circular pit, in which a fire had been previously kindled. Into this the victims were carefully lowered, the stakes on which they were impaled guarding their bodies from touching the sides of the oven, and the cross-piece at the end preventing them from slipping off the stake to the bottom of the pit among the ashes. A hurdle was then laid on the mouth of the pit, and wet earth was heaped upon it so as to close it completely. The greater part of the community then retired to rest. In about five hours, the Paschal moon being high in the heavens, announcement was made that the feast was about to begin. Then, to resume Dean Stanley's narrative,

"Suddenly the covering of the hole was torn off, and up rose into the still moonlit sky a vast column of smoke and steam; recalling, with a shock of surprise, that, even by an accidental coincidence, Reginald Heber should have so well caught this striking feature of so remote and unknown a ritual:

Smokes on Gerizim's mount Samaria's sacrifice.'

"Out of the pit were dragged successively the six sheep, on their long spits, black from the oven. The outlines of their heads, their ears, their legs, were still visible—'his head, with his legs, and with the inward parts thereof.' They were hoisted aloft, and then thrown on large square brown mats, previously prepared for their reception, on which we were carefully prevented from treading, as also from touching even the extremities of the spit.

"The bodies thus wrapped in the mats were hurried down to the trench where the sacrifice had taken place, and laid out upon them in a line between two files of the Samaritans. Those who had before been dressed in white robes still retained them, with the addition now of shoes on their feet and staves in their hands, and ropes round their waists—'thus shall ye eat it; with your loins girded, your shoes on your feet, your staff in your hand.' The recitation of prayers or of the Pentateuch recommenced, and continued till it suddenly terminated in their all sitting down on their haunches, after the Arab fashion at meals, and beginning to eat. This, too, is a deviation from the practice of only a few years since, when they retained the Mosaic ritual of standing whilst they ate. The actual feast was conducted in rapid silence, as of men in hunger, as no doubt most of them were, and so as soon to consume every portion of the blackened masses, which they tore away piecemeal with their fingers—'ye shall eat in haste.' There was a general merriment, as of a hearty and welcome meal.

"In ten minutes all was gone but a few remnants. To the priest and to the women, who, all but two (probably his two wives), remained in the tents, separate morsels were carried round. The remnants were gathered into the mats, and put on a wooden grate, or hurdle, over the hole where the water had been originally boiled; the fire was again lit, and a huge bonfire was kindled. By its blaze, and by candles lighted for the purpose, the ground was searched in every direction, as for the consecrated particles of sacramental elements; and these fragments of flesh and bone were thrown upon the burning mass—'ye shall let nothing remain until the morning; and that which remaineth until the morning ye shall burn with fire;' 'there shall not anything of the flesh which thou sacrificest the first day at even remain all night until the morning;' 'thou shalt not carry forth aught of the flesh abroad out of the house.' The flames blazed up once more, and then gradually sank away.

"Perhaps in another century the fire on Mount Gerizim will be the only relic left of this most interesting and ancient rite."

THE CHAMOIS.

The Zemer or Chamois only once mentioned in the Bible—Signification of the word Zemer—Probability that the Zemer is the Aoudad—Its strength and activity—The Mouflon probably classed with the Aoudad under the name of Zemer.

AMONG the animals which may be used for food is mentioned one which in our version is rendered Chamois. See Deut. xiv. 5, a passage which has several times been quoted.

It is evident to any one acquainted with zoology that, whatever may be the Hebrew word, "Chamois" cannot be the correct rendering, inasmuch as this animal does not inhabit Palestine, nor are there any proofs that it ever did so. The Chamois frequents the lofty inaccessible crags of the highest mountains, finding its food in the scanty herbage which grows in such regions, appearing on the brink of awful precipices, and leaping from ledge to ledge with ease and safety. We must, therefore, look for some other animal.

The Chamois is one of the most wary of Antelopes, and possesses the power of scenting mankind at what would seem to be an impossible distance.

Its ears are as acute as its nostrils, so that there are few animals which are so difficult to approach.

Only those who have been trained to climb the giddy heights of the Alpine Mountains, to traverse the most fearful precipices with a quiet pulse and steady head, to exist for days amid the terrible solitudes of ice, rock, and snow,—only these, can hope to come within sight of the Chamois, when the animal is at large upon its native cliffs.

The Hebrew word, which has been rendered Chamois, is Zamar, or Zemer, *i.e.* the leaper, and therefore an animal which is conspicuous for its agility. Zoologists have now agreed in the opinion that the Zamer of Deuteronomy is the handsome wild sheep which we know under the name of Aoudad (*Ammotragus Tragelaphus*). This splendid sheep is known by various names. It is the Jaela of some authors, and the Bearded Sheep of others. It is also called the Fichtall, or Lerwea; and the French zoologists describe it under the name of *Mouflon à manchettes*, in allusion to the fringe of long hair that ornaments the fore limbs.

The Aoudad is a large and powerful animal, exceedingly active, and has the habits of the goat rather than of the sheep, on which account it is reckoned among the goats by the Arabs of the present day, and doubtless was similarly classed by the ancient inhabitants of Palestine. The height of the adult Aoudad is about three feet, and its general colour is pale dun, relieved by the dark masses of long hair that fall from the neck and the tufts of similar hair which decorate the knees of the male. The female is also bearded and tufted, but the hair, which in the male looks like the mane of the lion, in the female is but slightly developed.

It is so powerful and active an animal, that an adult male which lived for some time in the Zoological Gardens was much dreaded by the keepers, not even the man who fed it liking to enter the enclosure if he could help himself. The animal was given to making unexpected charges, and would do so with astonishing quickness, springing round and leaping at the object of his hate with tremendous force, and with such rapidity that

CHAMOIS DEFENDING ITS YOUNG.

even the experienced keeper, who knew all the ways of the animals under his charge, had often some difficulty in slipping behind the door, against which the horns of the Aoudad would clatter as if they would break the door to pieces. So fond was he of attacking something that he would often butt repeatedly

CHASING THE AOUDAD.

at the wooden side of the shed, hurling himself against it with eager fury.

The horns of the Aoudad are about two feet in length, and are of considerable diameter. They curve boldly and gracefully backwards, their points diverging considerably from each other, so that when the animal throws its head up, the points of the horns come on either side of the back. This divergence of the horns has another object. They cover a considerable space, so that when the animal makes its charge the object of its anger has much more difficulty in escaping the blow than if the horns were closer together.

Whether these horns were used as musical instruments is doubtful, simply because we are not absolutely sure that the Zamar and the Aoudad are identical, however great may be the probability. But inasmuch as the horn-trumpets were evidently of various sizes, it is certain that the Jewish musicians would never have neglected to take advantage of such magnificent materials as they would obtain from the horns of this animal Perhaps the Chaldaic "keren" may have been the horn of the Aoudad, or of the animal which will next be mentioned.

The Aoudad is wonderfully active, and even the young ones bound to an astonishing height. I have seen the marks of their hoofs eight feet from the ground.

In its wild state the Aoudad lives in little flocks or herds, and prefers the high and rocky ground, over which it leaps with a sure-footed agility equal to that of the Chamois itself. These flocks are chased by hunters, who try to get it upon the lowest and least broken ground, where it is at a disadvantage, and then run it down with their horses, as seen in the illustration on page 214.

The Aoudad was formerly plentiful in Egypt, and even now is found along the Atlas mountain-range. It is seen on the Egyptian monuments, and, owing to its evident profusion, we have every reason to conjecture that it was one of those animals which were specially indicated as chewing the cud and cleaving the hoof.

PERHAPS the MOUFLON (*Caprovis Musimon*) may be the animal which is meant by the Hebrew word Zamar, and it is not unlikely that both animals may have been included in one name.

This animal, which is nearly allied to the Aoudad, is also very goatlike in general aspect. It is indeed to this resemblance that the name Caprovis, or goat-sheep, has been given to it. The name Ammotragus, which, as mentioned above, belongs to the Aoudad, has a similar signification.

The horns of the Mouflon belong only to the male animal,

and are of enormous size, so that if trumpets of deep tone and great power were needed, they could be obtained from the horns of this animal. Those of the Aoudad are very large, and would be well adapted for the same purpose, but they would not furnish

THE MOUFLON.

such instruments as the horns of the Mouflon, which are so large that they seem almost unwieldy for an animal of twice the Mouflon's size, and give visible proofs of the strength and agility of an animal which can carry them so lightly and leap about under their weight so easily as does the Mouflon.

At the present time the Mouflon is only to be found in Crete, Sardinia, and Corsica, but formerly it was known to inhabit many other parts of the earth, and was almost certainly one of the many animals which then haunted the Lebanon, but which have in later days been extirpated.

THE GOAT.

Value of the Goat—Its use in furnishing food—The male kid the usual animal of slaughter—Excellence of the flesh and deception of Isaac—Milk of the Goat—An Oriental milking scene—The hair of the goat, and the uses to which it is put—The Goat's skin used for leather—The "bottle" of Scripture—Mode of making and repairing the bottles—Ruse of the Gibeonites—The "bottle in the smoke"—The sacks and the kneading troughs—The Goat as used for sacrifice—General habits of the Goat—Separation of the Goats from the sheep—Performing Goats—Different breeds of Goats in Palestine.

WHETHER considered in reference to food, to clothing, or to sacrifice, the GOAT was scarcely a less important animal than the sheep. It was especially valuable in such a country as Palestine, in which the soil and the climate vary so much according to the locality. Upon the large fertile plains the sheep are bred in vast flocks, the rich and succulent grass being exactly to their taste; while in the hilly and craggy districts the Goats abound, and delight in browsing upon the scanty herbage that grows upon the mountain-side.

For food the Goat was even more extensively used than the sheep. The adult male was, of course, not eaten, being very tough, and having an odour which would repel any but an actually starving man. Neither were the females generally eaten, as they were needed for the future increase of the flocks. The young male kid formed the principal material of a feast, and as soon as a stranger claimed the hospitality of a man in good circumstances, the first thing that was done was to take a young male kid and dress it for him.

For example, when the angel visited Gideon in the guise of a stranger, Gideon "went in and made ready a kid, and unleavened cakes of an ephah of flour," and brought them to his guest (Judges vi. 19). And when Isaac was on his death-bed and asked Esau to take his bow and arrows and hunt for "venison," which was probably the flesh of one of the antelopes which have already been mentioned, a ready substitute was found in the two kids, from whose flesh Rebekah made the dish for which he longed. The imposition might easily pass without

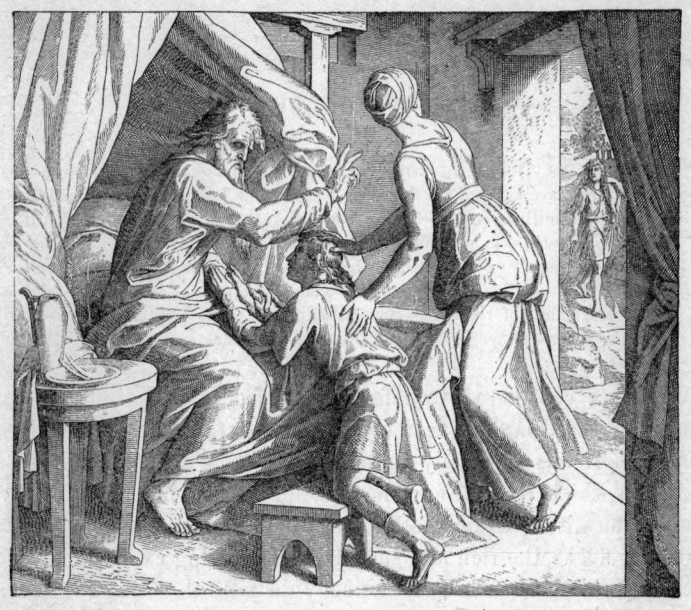

JACOB DECEIVES HIS FATHER AND TAKES ESAU'S BLESSING.

detection, because the flesh of the kid is peculiarly tender, and can scarcely be distinguished from lamb, even when simply roasted. Isaac, therefore, with his senses dulled by his great age, was the less likely to discover the imposture, when the flesh of the kids was stewed into "savoury meat such as he loved."

A curious illustration of the prevalence of kid's flesh as food is given in the parable of the prodigal son, for whom his father had killed the fatted calf. "And he answering said to his father, Lo, these many years do I serve thee, neither transgressed I at any time thy commandment: and yet thou never gavest me a kid, that I might make merry with my friends" (Luke xv. 29). The force of the reproval cannot be properly understood unless we are acquainted with the customs of the East. The kid was the least valuable animal that could have been given, less valuable than a lamb, and infinitely inferior to the fatted calf, which was kept in wealthy households for some feast of more than ordinary magnificence.

The kid was cooked exactly in the same manner as the sheep, namely, by cutting to pieces and stewing in a caldron, the meat and broth being served separately. See, for example, the case of Gideon, to whom a reference has already been made. When he brought the banquet to his guest, "the flesh he put in a basket, and he put the broth in a pot, and brought it out unto him under the oak, and presented it. And the angel of God said unto him, Take the flesh and the unleavened cakes, and lay them upon this rock, and pour out the broth."

THE ANGEL APPEARS TO GIDEON.

Gideon did so, and the angel reached forth the staff that was in his hand, and touched the flesh, and there rose up fire out of the rock and burnt up the offering.

The same custom exists at the present day. When an Arab chief receives a guest, a kid is immediately killed and given to the women to be cooked, and the guest is pressed to stay until it is ready, in the very words used by Gideon three thousand years ago. "Depart not hence, I pray thee, until I come unto thee, and bring forth my present, and set it before thee." The refusal of proffered hospitality would be, and still is considered to be, either a studied insult, or a proof of bad manners, and no one with any claims to breeding would commit such an action without urgent cause and much apology.

Like the sheep, the Goat is extremely valuable as a milk-producer, and at the present day the milk of the Goat is used as largely as that of the sheep. "At Rasheiya, under Mount Hermon," writes Mr. Tristram, "we saw some hundreds of goats gathering for the night in the wide open market-place beneath the castle. It was no easy matter to thread our way among them, as they had no idea of moving for such belated intruders on their rest. All the she-goats of the neighbouring hills are driven in every evening, and remain for their morning's milking, after which they set forth on their day's excursion.

"Each house possesses several, and all know their owners. The evening milking is a picturesque scene. Every street and open space is filled with the goats; and women, boys, and girls are everywhere milking with their small pewter pots, while the goats are anxiously awaiting their turn, or lying down to chew the cud as soon as it is over. As no kids or he-goats are admitted, the scene is very orderly, and there is none of the deafening bleating which usually characterises large flocks.

"These mountain goats are a solemn set, and by the gravity of their demeanour excite a suspicion that they have had no youth, and never were kids. They need no herdsman to bring them home in the evening, for, fully sensible of the danger of remaining unprotected, they hurry homewards of their own accord as soon as the sun begins to decline."

LIKE the wool of the sheep, the hair of the Goat is used for the manufacture of clothing; and, as is the case with wool, its quality differs according to the particular breed of the animal, which assumes almost as many varieties as the sheep or the dog. The hair of some varieties is thick and rough, and can only be made into coarse cloths, while others, of which the mohair Goat and Cashmere Goat are familiar examples, furnish a staple of surpassing delicacy and fineness. It is most likely that the covering and curtains of the Tabernacle mentioned in Exod. xxvi. 7 were of the latter kind, as otherwise they would have been out of character with the fine linen, and blue and scarlet, their golden clasps, and the profuse magnificence which distinguished every part of the sacred building. Moreover, the hair of the Goat is classed among the costly offerings which were made when the Tabernacle was built. "And they came forth, men and women, as many as were willing hearted, and brought bracelets, and earrings, and rings, and tablets, all jewels of gold: and every man that offered offered an offering of gold unto the Lord. And every man, with whom was found blue, and purple, and scarlet, and fine linen, and goats' hair, and red skins of rams, and badgers' skins, brought them" to be used in the structure of that wonderful building, in which nothing might be used except the finest and costliest that could be procured.

One of the principal uses to which the goat-skin was applied was the manufacture of leather, for which purpose it is still used, and is considered far better than that of the sheep. Perhaps the most common form in which this leather is used is the well-known water-vessel, or "bottle" of the Bible.

These so-called bottles are made from the entire skin of the animal, which is prepared in slightly different methods according to the locality in which the manufacture is carried on. In Palestine they are soaked for some little time in the tanning mixture, and are then filled with water, after the seams have been pitched. In this state they are kept for some time, and are kept exposed to the sun, covered entirely with the tanning fluid, and filled up with water to supply the loss caused by evaporation and leakage.

The hair is allowed to remain on the skins, because it acts as a preservative against the rough usage to which they are subject at the hard hands of the water-carriers. By degrees the hairy covering wears off, first in patches, and then over the entire surface, so that a new bottle can be recognised at a glance, and any one who wished to sell an old bottle at the price of a new one would be at once detected.

Vessels made in this rude manner are absolutely necessary in the countries wherein they are used. Wooden or metal vessels would be too heavy, and, besides, the slight though constant evaporation that always takes place through the pores of the leather keeps down the temperature of the water, even under a burning sun, the slight loss which is caused by the porousness of the skin being more than counterbalanced by the coolness of the water. It is true that the goat-skin communicates to the liquid a flavour far from pleasant, but in those countries the quality of the water is of little consequence, provided that it is plentiful in quantity, and tolerably cool.

In all parts of the world where the skin is used for this purpose the mode of manufacture is practically identical. An account of the art of preparing the goat-skin as practised in Abyssinia is given by Mr. C. Johnston, in his "Travels in Southern Abyssinia:"—

"To be of any value it must be taken off uncut, except around the neck, and in those situations necessary to enable the butchers to draw the legs out of the skin; also, of course, where the first incision is made to commence the process, and which is a circular cut carried around both haunches, not many inches from and having the tail for a centre. The hide is then stripped over the thighs, and two smaller incisions being made round the middle joint of the hind-legs enable them to be drawn out.

"A stick is now placed to extend these extremities, and by this, for the convenience of the operators, the whole carcase is suspended from the branch of a tree, and, by some easy pulls around the body, the skin is gradually withdrawn over the fore-legs, which are incised around the knees, to admit of their being taken out; after which, the head being removed, the whole business concludes by the skin being pulled inside out over the decollated neck. One of the parties now takes a rough stone and well rubs the inside surface, to divest it of a few fibres of the subcutaneous muscle which are inserted into the skin, and after this operation it is laid aside until the next day; the more interesting business of attending to the meat calling for immediate attention.

"These entire skins are afterwards made into sacks by the apertures around the neck and legs being secured by a double fold of the skin being sewed upon each other, by means of a slender but very tough thong. These small seams are rendered quite air-tight, and the larger orifice around the haunches being gathered together by the hands, the yet raw skin is distended with air; and the orifice being then tied up, the swollen bag is left in that state for a few days, until slight putrefaction has commenced, when the application of the rough stone soon divests its surface of the hair. After this has been effected, a deal of labour, during at least one day, is required to soften the distended skin by beating it with heavy sticks, or trampling upon it for hours together, the labourer supporting himself by clinging to the bough of a tree overhead, or holding on by the wall of the house.

" In this manner, whilst the skin is drying, it is prevented from getting stiff, and, still further to secure it from this evil condition, it is frequently rubbed with small quantities of butter. When it is supposed that there is no chance of the skin becoming hard and easily broken, the orifice is opened, the air escapes, and a very soft, flaccid leather bag is produced, but which, for several days after, affords an amusement to the owner, when otherwise unemployed, by well rubbing it all over with his hands."

The reader will see that the two processes are practically identical, the chief difference being that in one country the skins are distended with water and in the other with air.

As these bottles are rather apt to be damaged by the thorns, branches, rocks, and similar objects with which they come in contact, and are much too valuable to be thrown away as useless, their owners have discovered methods of patching and repairing them, which enable them to be used for some time longer. Patches of considerable size are sometimes inserted, if the rent should be of importance, while the wound caused by a thorn is mended by a simple and efficacious expedient. The skin is first emptied, and a round flat piece of wood, or even a stone of suitable shape, is put into it. The skin is then held with the wounded part downwards, and the stone shaken about until it comes exactly upon the hole. It is then grasped, the still wet hide gathered tightly under it, so as to pucker up the skin, and a ligature is tied firmly round it. Perhaps some of my readers may have practised the same method of mending a punctured football.

Allusion to this mode of mending the skin bottles is made in Josh. ix. 4, 13. The Gibeonites " did work wilily, and went and made as if they had been ambassadors, and took old sacks upon their asses, and wine bottles, old, and rent, and bound up . . . and said . . . these bottles of wine, which we filled, were new; and, behold, they be rent."

If these skin bottles be allowed to become dry, as is sometimes the case when they are hung up in the smoky tents, they shrivel up, and become rotten and weak, and are no longer enabled to bear the pressure caused by the fermentation of new

EASTERN WATER-CARRIERS WITH BOTTLES MADE OF GOAT-SKIN.

wine. So, in Ps. cxix. 81—83: "My soul fainteth for Thy salvation: but I hope in Thy word.

"Mine eyes fail for Thy word, saying, When wilt Thou comfort me?

"For I am become like a bottle in the smoke; yet do I not forget Thy statutes."

How forcible does not this image become, when we realize the early life of the shepherd poet, his dwelling in tents wherein are no windows nor chimneys, and in which the smoke rolls to and fro until it settles in the form of soot upon the leathern bottles and other rude articles of furniture that are hung from the poles!

In the New Testament there is a well-known allusion to the weakness of old bottles: "Neither do men put new wine into old bottles, or the bottles break and the wine runneth out, and the bottles perish; but they put new wine into new bottles, and both are preserved." It would be impossible to understand the meaning of this passage unless we knew that the "bottles" in question were not vessels of glass or earthenware, but merely the partly-tanned skins of goats.

Another allusion to the use of the goat-skin is made in that part of the Book of Joshua which has already been mentioned. If the reader will refer to Josh. ix. 4, he will see that the Gibeonites took with them not only old bottles, but old sacks. Now, these sacks bore no resemblance to the hempen bags with which we are so familiar, but were nothing more than the same goat-skins that were employed in the manufacture of bottles, but with the opening at the neck left open. They were, in fact, skin-bottles for holding solids instead of liquids. The sacks which Joseph's brethren took with them, and in the mouths of which they found their money, were simply goat-skin bags, made as described.

Yet another use for the goat-skin. It is almost certain that the "kneading-troughs" of the ancient Israelites were simply circular pieces of goat-skin, which could be laid on the ground when wanted, and rolled up and carried away when out of use. Thus, the fact that "the people took their dough before it was leavened, their kneading-troughs being bound up in their clothing upon their shoulders," need cause no surprise.

Nothing could be more in accordance with probability. The women were all hard at work, preparing the bread for the expected journey, when the terrified Pharaoh "called for Moses and Aaron by night, and said, Rise up, and get you forth from among my people, both ye and the children of Israel, and go, serve the Lord. as ye have said. . . . And the Egyptians were urgent upon the people that they might send them out of the land in haste; for they said, We be all dead men."

So the women, being disturbed at their work, and being driven out of the country before they had leavened, much less baked, their bread, had no alternative but to roll up the dough in the leathern " kneading-troughs," tie them up in a bundle with their spare clothing, and carry them on their shoulders; whereas, if we connect the kneading-troughs with the large heavy wooden implements used in this country, we shall form an entirely erroneous idea of the proceeding. As soon as they came to their first halting-place at Succoth, they took the leathern kneading-troughs out of their clothes, unrolled them, took the dough which had not even been leavened, so unexpectedly had the order for marching arrived, made it into flat cakes, and baked them as they best could. The same kind of "kneading-trough" is still in use in many parts of the world.

Stone as well as earthenware jars were also used by the inhabitants of ancient Palestine; but they were only employed for the storage of wine in houses, whereas the bottles that were used in carrying wine from one place to another were invariably made of leather. Water also was stored in stone or earthenware jars. See, for example, John ii. 6: "And there were set there six waterpots of stone, after the manner of the purifying of the Jews, containing two or three firkins apiece." Whereas, when it was carried about, it was poured into bottles made of skin. Such was probably the "bottle of water" that Abraham put on Hagar's shoulder, when she was driven away by the jealousy of Sarah, and such was the "bottle of wine" that Hannah brought as her offering when she dedicated Samuel to the service of God.

IN sacrifices, the Goat was in nearly as much requisition as the lamb, and in one—namely, that which was celebrated on the Great Day of Atonement—the Goat was specially mentioned as the only animal which could be sacrificed. The reader will, perhaps, remember that for this peculiar sacrifice two Goats were required, on which two lots were cast, one for the Lord, *i.e.* with the word "Jehovah" upon it, and the other for the scapegoat, *i.e.* inscribed with the word "Azazel." The latter term is derived from two Hebrew words, the former being "Az," which is the general name for the Goat, and the second "azel," signifying "he departed." The former, which belonged to Jehovah, was sacrificed, and its blood sprinkled upon the mercy-seat and the altar of incense; and the Goat Azazel was led away into the wilderness, bearing upon its head the sins of the people, and there let loose.

THESE being the uses of the Goat, it may naturally be imagined that the animal is one of extreme importance, and that it is watched as carefully by its owners as the sheep. Indeed, both sheep and Goats belong to the same master, and are tended by the same shepherd, who exercises the same sway over them that he does over the sheep.

They are, however, erratic animals, and, although they will follow the shepherd wherever he may lead them, they will not mix with the sheep. The latter will walk in a compact flock along the valley, the shepherd leading the way, and the sheep following him, led in their turn by the sound of the bell tied round the neck of the master-ram of the flock. The Goats, however, will not submit to walk in so quiet a manner, but prefer to climb along the sides of the rocks that skirt the valleys, skipping and jumping as they go, and seeming to take delight in getting themselves into dangerous places, where a man could not venture to set his foot.

In the evening, when the shepherds call their flocks to repose, they often make use of the caverns which exist at some height in the precipitous side of the hills, as being safe strongholds, where the jackal and the hyæna will not venture to attack them. When such is the case, the shepherds take their station by the mouth of the cave, and assist the sheep as they come sedately up the narrow path that leads to the cavern. The Goats, however, need no assistance, but come scrambling along by paths where no foot but a Goat's could tread, mostly descending from a considerable height above the cave, and, as if in exultation at their superior agility, jumping over the backs of the sheep as they slowly file into the accustomed fold.

Friendly as they are, the Goats and sheep never mingle together. There may be large flocks of them feeding in the same pasturage, but the Goats always take the highest spots on which verdure grows, while the sheep graze quietly below. Goats are specially fond of the tender shoots of trees, which they find in plenty upon the mountain side; and, according to Mr. Tristram,

GOATS ON THE MARCH.

by their continual browsing, they have extirpated many species of trees which were once common on the hills of Palestine, and which now can only be found in Lebanon on the east of the Jordan.

Even when folded together in the same enclosure, the Goats never mix with the sheep, but gather together by themselves, and they instinctively take the same order when assembled round the wells at mid-day.

THE GOAT. 229

This instinctive separation of the sheep and the goats naturally recalls to our minds the well-known saying of our Lord that "before Him shall be gathered all nations, and He shall separate them one from another, as a shepherd divideth his sheep from the goats : and He shall set the sheep on His right hand, and the goats on His left."

The image thus used was one that was familiar to all the hearers, who were accustomed daily to see the herds of sheep and Goats under one shepherd, yet totally distinct from each other. At feeding-time the Goats will be browsing in long lines on the mountain sides, while the sheep are grazing in the plain or valley; at mid-day, when the flocks are gathered round the wells to await the rolling away of the stone that guards the water, the Goats assemble on one side and the sheep on the other. And at night, when they are all gathered into one fold by one shepherd, they are still separated from each other. The same image is employed by the prophet Ezekiel : " As for you, O my flock, thus said the Lord God, Behold I judge between cattle and cattle, between rams and the he-goats.'

Generally, the leading Goat was distinguished by a bell as well as the leading sheep, and in reference to this custom there was an old proverb, " If the shepherd takes the lead, he blinds the bell-goat," while another proverb is based upon the inferior docility of the animal—"If the shepherd be lame, the Goats will run away."

Yet the Goat can be tamed very effectively, and can even be taught to perform many tricks. " We saw just below us, on the rudely-constructed 'parade,' a crowd of men and children, surrounding a fantastically-dressed man exhibiting a Goat, which had been tutored to perform some cunning trick. It stood with its four feet close together on the top of a very long pole, and allowed the man to lift it up and carry it round and round within the circle ; then the Goat was perched on four sticks, and again carried about. A little band of music—pipes, drums, and tambourines—called together the people from all parts of the town to witness this performance.

" The Goat danced and balanced himself obediently and perfectly, in very unnatural-looking positions, as if thoroughly understanding the words and commands of his master. The men who watched the actions of the Goat looked as grave and serious as if they were attending a philosophical or scientific lecture." ("Domestic Life in Palestine," by Miss Rogers.)

Another feat is a favourite with the proprietors of trained Goats. The man takes a stool and plants it carefully on the ground, so as to be perfectly level, and then orders the Goat to stand upon it. A piece of wood about six inches in length, and shaped something like a dice-box, is then placed on the stool, and the Goat manages to stand on it, all his sharp, hard hoofs being pressed closely together on the tiny surface. The man then takes another piece of wood and holds it to the Goat's feet. The animal gently removes first one foot and then another, and, by careful shifting of the feet, enables its master to place the second piece of wood on the first. Successive additions are made, until at the last the Goat is perched on the topmost of some nine or ten pieces of wood balanced on each other, the whole looking like a stout reed marked off with joints.

The stately steps and bold bearing of the old he-goat is mentioned in the Proverbs: "There be three things which go well, yea, four are comely in going:

" A lion, which is strongest among beasts, and turneth not away for any;

" A greyhound; an he goat also; and a king, against whom there is no rising up." (Prov. xxx. 29–31.) The word which is here rendered as he-goat signifies literally the "Butter," and is given to the animal on account of the mode in which it uses its formidable horns. The word is not common in the Bible, but it is used even at the present day among the Arabs.

Several herds of goats exist in Palestine, the most valuable of which is the Mohair Goat, and the most common the Syrian Goat. These, however dissimilar they may be in appearance, are only varieties of the ordinary domestic animal, the former being produced artificially by carefully selecting those specimens for breeding which have the longest and finest hair. It was from the hair of this breed that the costly fabrics used in the Tabernacle were woven, and it is probably to this breed that reference is made in Solomon's Song, iv. 1, 2: "Behold, thou art fair, my love; behold, thou art fair; thou hast doves' eyes within thy locks: thy hair is as a flock of goats, that appear from Mount Gilead.

"Thy teeth are like a flock of sheep that are even shorn, which

HERD OF GOATS ATTACKED BY A LION.

came up from the washing." In this passage the careful reader will also note another reference to the habits of the Goats and sheep, the hair being compared to the dark-haired Goats that wander on the tops of the hills, while the teeth are compared to sheep that are ranged in regular order below. The Mohair Goat is known scientifically as *Capra Angorensis*. The same image is used again in chap. vi. 5.

The second breed is that which is commonest throughout the country. It is known by the name of the Syrian Goat, and is remarkable for the enormous length of its ears, which sometimes exceed a foot from root to tip. This variety has been described as a separate species under the name of *Capra Mambrica*, or *C. Syriaca*, but, like the Mohair Goat, and twenty-three other so-called species, is simply a variety of the common Goat, *Hircus œgragus*.

Reference is made to the long ears of the Syrian Goat in Amos iii. 12: "Thus saith the Lord: As the shepherd taketh out of the mouth of the lion two legs, or a piece of an ear; so shall the children of Israel be taken out that dwell in Samaria." Such a scene, which was familiar to Amos, the shepherd as well as the prophet, is represented in the illustration. In the foreground is the goat on which the lion has sprung, and from which one of the long ears has been torn away. Its companions are gathering round it in sympathy, while its kid is trying to discover the cause of its mother's uneasiness. In the background is a group of armed shepherds, standing round the lion which they have just killed, while one of them is holding up the torn ear which he has taken out of the lion's mouth.

THE WILD GOAT.

The Azelim or Wild Goats of Scripture identical with the Beden or Arabian Ibex—Different names of the Beden—Its appearance and general habits—En-gedi, or Goats' Fountain—The Beden formerly very plentiful in Palestine, and now tolerably common—Its agility—Difficulty of catching or killing it—How the young are captured—Flesh of the Beden—Use of the horns at the present day—The Ako of Deuteronomy.

In three passages of the Old Testament occurs a word, "Azelim," which is variously translated in our Authorized Version.

It is first seen in 1 Sam. xxiv. 2, in which it is rendered as "Wild Goats." "It was told Saul, saying, Behold, David is in the wilderness of En-gedi [*i.e.* the Fountain of the Goat]. Then Saul took three thousand chosen men out of all Israel, and went to seek David and his men upon the rocks of the wild goats (*azelim*)." The same word occurs in Job xxxix. 1: "Knowest thou the time when the wild goats of the rock bring forth?" It is also found in Ps. civ. 18: "The high hills are a refuge for the wild goats." In all these passages it is rendered as "wild goats." But, in Prov. v. 19, it is translated as roe: "Rejoice with the wife of thy youth. Let her be as the loving hind and pleasant roe (*azelah*)." The Jewish Bible follows the same diverse renderings.

We now have to discover the animal which was signified by the word Azel. According to its etymology, it is the Climber, just as the adult he-goat is called the Butter.

That it was a climbing animal is evident from its name, and that it loved to clamber among precipices is equally evident from the repeated connexion of the word rock with the name of the animal. We also see, from the passage in Job, that it is a wild animal whose habits were not known. There is scarcely any doubt that the Azel of the Old Testament is the ARABIAN IBEX or BEDEN (*Capra Nubiana*). This animal is very closely allied to the well-known Ibex of the Alps, or Steinbock, but may be distinguished from it by one or two slight differences, such as the black beard and the slighter make of the horns, which moreover have three angles instead of four, as is the case with the Alpine Ibex.

The Beden is known by several names. It is sometimes called the Jaela, sometimes the Nubian Wild Goat, and is also known as the Wild Goat of Sinai. The general colour of the Beden is grey, becoming brownish in winter, and being whitish grey beneath. The feet are spotted with black and white, and the beard of the male is black, differing from that of the Alpine Ibex, which is brown. The female is beardless. The lines along the back and the sides of the tail are black, and there are three streaks on each ear.

The Beden generally lives in little herds of eight or ten, and is even now to be found in Palestine. At the strange, wild, weird-looking En-gedi (Ain Jiddy), or Fountain of the Goats, the Beden is still to be seen. Mr. Tristram suggests that David and his followers took up their residence at En-gedi for the sake of the Wild Goats that were plentiful upon the spot, and which would furnish food for himself and his hardy band of outlaws. "In the neighbourhood of En-gedi," remarks this traveller, "while encamped by the Dead Sea shore, we obtained several fine specimens, and very interesting it was to find the graceful creature by the very fountain to which it gave name.

"When clambering over the heights above En-gedi, I often, by the help of my glass, saw the Ibex from a distance, and once, when near Mar-saba, only a few miles from Jerusalem, started one at a distance of four hundred yards. At the south end of the Dead Sea they were common, and I have picked up a horn both near Jericho on the hills and also on the hills of Moab on the eastern side. At Jericho, too, I obtained a young one which I hoped to rear, but which died after I had had it for ten days, owing, I believe, to the milk with which it was fed being sour. Further north and west we did not find it, though I have reason to believe that a few linger on the mountains between Samaria and the Jordan, and perhaps also on some of the spurs of Lebanon. We found its teeth in the breccia of bone occurring in the Lebanon, proving its former abundance there."

As the Beden was found so plentifully even in these days when fire-arms have rendered many wild animals scarce and wary, so that they will not show themselves within range of a bullet, it is evident that in the time when David lived at En-gedi and drank of the Goats' Fountain they were far more numerous, and could afford nourishment to him and his soldiers. Travellers, moreover, who do not happen to be experienced hunters, will often fail in seeing the Beden, even in places where it is tolerably plentiful. The colour of its coat resembles so nearly that of the rocks, that an inexperienced eye would see nothing but bare stones and sticks where a practised hunter would see numbers of Beden, conspicuous by their beautifully curved horns.

The agility of the Beden is extraordinary. Loving the highest and most craggy parts of the mountain ridge, it flings itself from spot to spot with a recklessness that startles one who has not been accustomed to the animal, and the wonderful certainty of its foot. It will, for example, dash at the face of a perpendicular precipice that looks as smooth as a brick wall, for the purpose of reaching a tiny ledge which is hardly perceptible, and which is some fifteen feet or so above the spot whence the animal sprang. Its eye, however, has marked certain little cracks and projections on the face of the rock, and as the animal makes its leap, it takes these little points of vantage in rapid succession, just touching them as it passes upwards, and by the slight stroke of its foot keeping up the original impulse of its leap. Similarly, the Ibex comes sliding and leaping down precipitous sides of the mountains, sometimes halting with all the four feet drawn together, on a little projection scarcely larger than a penny, and sometimes springing boldly over a wide crevasse, and alighting with exact precision upon a projecting piece of rock that seems scarcely large enough to sustain a rat comfortably.

The young of the Ibex are sometimes captured and tamed. They are, however, difficult to rear, and give much more trouble than the young gazelles when taken in a similar manner. The natives can generally procure the kids at the proper time of year, and sell them at a very cheap rate. They seldom, however, can be reared, and even those who live in the country experience the greatest difficulty in keeping the young Beden alive until it attains maturity.

Were it not for the curious habits of the Beden, the young could scarcely ever be obtained alive, as they are so agile that they could easily leap away from their slow two-legged pursuers. But the mother Ibex has a habit of leading a very independent life, wandering to considerable distances, and leaving her kid snugly hidden in some rock-cleft. The hunters watch the mother as she starts off in the morning, clamber up to the spot where the kid is concealed, and secure it without difficulty The Arabs say that there are always two kids at a birth, but

ARABIAN IBEX, OR BEDEN; THE WILD GOAT OF SCRIPTURE.

there is considerable discrepancy of evidence on this point, which, after all, is of very little importance.

The flesh of the Beden is really excellent. It is far superior to that of the gazelle, which is comparatively dry and hard, and it has been happily suggested that the Beden was the animal in search of which Esau was sent to hunt with his quiver and his bow, and which furnished the "savoury meat" which Isaac loved. None but a true hunter can hope to secure the Beden, and even all the knowledge, patience, and energy of the best hunters are tried before they can kill their prey. It was therefore no matter of wonder that Isaac should be surprised when he thought that he heard Esau return so soon from the hunting-grounds. " How is it that thou hast found it so quickly, my son ? "

There are few animals more wary than the Beden, and even the chamois ot the Alps does not exercise the finest qualities of a hunter more than does the Beden of Palestine. It is gifted with very keen eyes, which can discern the approach of an enemy long before its grey coat and curved horns can be distinguished from the stones and gnarled boughs of the mountain side. And, even if the enemy be not within range of the animal's sight, its nostrils are so keen that it can detect a man by scent alone at a considerable distance. Like all gregarious animals, the Beden insures the safety of the flock by stationing sentries, which are posted on places that command the whole surrounding country, and to deceive the watchful senses of these wary guardians tests all the qualities of the hunter.

The dawn of day is the time that is generally chosen for approaching a herd, because the animals are then feeding, and if the hunter can manage to approach them against the wind, he may chance to come within range. Should however the wind change its direction, he may quietly walk home again, for at the first breath of the tainted gale the sentinels utter their shrill whistle of alarm, and the whole party dash off with a speed that renders pursuit useless.

The horns of the Beden are of very great size, and from their bold curves, with the large rings and ridges which cover their front, are remarkably handsome objects. In their own country they are in great request as handles to knives, and even in England they may be occasionally seen serving as handles to carving-knives and forks.

As to the word Ako, which occurs in Deut. xiv. 5, together with other animals, and is rendered as "Wild Goat," there is so much doubt about the correct translation that I can do no more than mention that the Jewish Bible follows our authorized edition in translating Ako as Wild Goat, but adds the doubtful mark to the word.

THE DEER.

The Hart and Hind of Scripture—Species of Deer existing in Palestine—Earliest mention of the Hind—The Hart classed among the clean animals—Passages alluding to its speed—Care of the mother for her young, and her custom of secreting it—Tameable character of the Deer—

WE now come to the DEER which are mentioned in Scripture. There are not many passages in which they are mentioned, and one of them is rather doubtful, as we shall see when we come to it.

There is no doubt that the two words HART and HIND (in the Hebrew *Ayzal* and *Ayzalah*) represent Deer of some kind, and the question is to find out what kind of Deer is signified by these words. I think that we may safely determine that no particular species is meant, but that under the word Ayzal are

RED DEER.

comprehended any kinds of Deer that inhabit Palestine, and were likely to be known to those to whom the earlier Scriptures were addressed. That some kind of Deer was plentiful is evident from the references which are made to it, and specially by the familiar word Ajala or Ayala, as it is pronounced, which signifies the Deer-ground or pasture. But the attempt to discriminate between one species and another is simply impossible, and the more careful the search the more impracticable the task appears.

As far as can be ascertained, at least two kinds of Deer inhabited Palestine in the earlier days of the Jewish history, one belonging to the division which is known by its branched horns, and the other to that in which the horns are flat or palmated over the tips. Examples of both kinds are familiar to us under the titles of the RED DEER and the FALLOW DEER, and it is tolerably certain that both these animals were formerly found in Palestine, or that at all events the Deer which did exist there were so closely allied to them as to be mere varieties occasioned by the different conditions in which they were placed.

We will now proceed to the various passages in which the Hart and Hind are mentioned in the Bible.

FALLOW-DEER, OR HIND OF SCRIPTURE.

As might be expected, we come upon it among the number of the beasts which divided the hoof and chewed the cud, and were specially indicated as fit for food; see Deut. xii. 15: "Notwithstanding thou mayest kill and eat flesh in all thy gates, ... the unclean and the clean may eat thereof, as of the roebuck, and as of the hart."

There is, however, an earlier mention of the word in Gen. xlix. 21. It occurs in that splendid series of imagery in which

A QUIET SPOT.

Jacob blesses his sons, and prophesies their future, each image serving ever afterwards as the emblem of the tribe: "Naphtali is a hind let loose: he giveth goodly words;"—or, according to the Jewish Bible, "Naphtali is a hind sent forth: he giveth sayings of pleasantness." Now, such an image as this would never have been used, had not the spectacle of the "hind let loose" been perfectly familiar to the eyes both of the dying patriarch and his hearers, and equally so with the lion, the ass, the vine, the serpent, and other objects used emblematically in the same prophetic poem.

The excellence of the Hart's flesh is shown by its occurrence among the animals used for King Solomon's table; see 1 Kings iv. 23, a passage which has been quoted several times, and therefore need only be mentioned.

Allusion is made to the speed and agility of the Deer in several passages. See, for example, Isa. xxxv. 6: "Then shall the lame man leap as an hart, and the tongue of the dumb sing." Again, in 2 Sam. xxii. 33, 34: "God is my strength and power: and He maketh my way perfect.

"He maketh my feet like hinds' feet: and setteth me upon my high places."

Nearly four hundred years afterwards we find Habakkuk using precisely the same image, evidently quoting David's Psalm of Thanksgiving:—"Yet I will rejoice in the Lord, I will joy in the God of my salvation.

"The Lord God is my strength, and He will make my feet like hinds' feet, and He will make me to walk upon mine high places." (iii. 18, 19.)

A passage of a similar character may be found in Solomon's Song, ii. 8, 9: "The voice of my beloved! behold, he cometh leaping upon the mountains, skipping upon the hills.

"My beloved is like a roe or a young hart."

There is one passage in the Psalms which is familiar to us in many ways, and not the least in that it has been chosen as the text for so many well-known anthems. "As the hart panteth after the water-brooks, so panteth my soul after Thee, O God.

"My soul thirsteth for God, for the living God: when shall I come and appear before God?" (Ps. xlii. 1, 2.)

Beautiful as this passage is, it cannot be fully understood without the context.

RED DEER AND FAWN.

David wrote this psalm before he had risen to royal power, and while he was fleeing from his enemies from place to place, and seeking an uncertain shelter in the rock-caves. In verse 6 he enumerates some of the spots in which he has been forced to reside, far away from the altar, the priests, and the sacrifice. He has been hunted about from place to place by his enemies as a stag is hunted by the hounds, and his very soul thirsted for the distant Tabernacle, in which the Shekinah, the visible presence of God, rested on the mercy-seat between the golden cherubim.

Wild and unsettled as was the early life of David, this was ever the reigning thought in his mind, and there is scarcely a psalm that he wrote in which we do not find some allusion to the visible presence of God among men. No matter what might be the troubles through which he had to pass, even though he trod the valley of the shadow of death, the thought of his God was soothing as water to the hunted stag, and in that thought he ever found repose. Through all his many trials and adversities, through his deep remorse for his sins, through his wounded paternal affections, through his success and prosperity, that one thought is the ruling power. He begins his career with it when he opposed Goliath: "Thou comest to me with a sword, and with a spear, and with a shield: but I come to thee in the name of the Lord of hosts, the God of the armies of Israel." He closes his career with the same thought, and, in the "last words" that are recorded, he charged his son to keep the commandments of the Lord, that he might do wisely all that he did.

We now come to another point in the Deer's character; namely, the watchful care of the mother over her young. She always retires to some secret place when she instinctively knows that the birth is at hand, and she hides it from all eyes until it is able to take care of itself. By some strange instinct, the little one, almost as soon as it is born, is able to comprehend the signals of its mother, and there is an instance, well known to naturalists, where a newly-born Deer, hardly an hour old, crouched low to the earth in obedience to a light tap on its shoulder from its mother's hoof. She, with the intense watchfulness of her kind, had seen a possible danger, and so warned her young one to hide itself.

There is scarcely any animal so watchful as the female Deer, as all hunters know by practical experience. It is comparatively

THE LEADER OF THE HERD.

easy to deceive the stag who leads the herd, but to evade the eyes and ears of the hinds is a very different business, and taxes all the resources of a practised hunter. If they take such care of the herd in general, it may be imagined that their watchfulness would be multiplied tenfold when the object of their anxiety is their own young.

It is in allusion to this well-known characteristic that a passage in the Book of Job refers: "Knowest thou the time when the wild goats of the rock bring forth? or canst thou mark when the hinds do calve?" (xxxix. 1.) A similar image is used in Psa. xxix. 9. After enumerating the wonders that are done by the voice of the Lord, the thunders and rain torrents, the devastating tempests, the forked lightning, and the earthquake "that shaketh the wilderness of Kadesh," the Psalmist proceeds: "The voice of the Lord maketh the hinds to calve, and discovereth the forests,"—this being as mysterious to the writer as the more conspicuous wonders which he had previously mentioned.

So familiar to the Hebrews was the watchful care which the female Deer exercised over her young, that it forms the subject of a powerful image in one of Jeremiah's mournful prophecies: "Yea, the hind also calved in the field, and forsook it, because there was no grass." (xiv. 5.) To those who understand the habits of the animal, this is a most telling and picturesque image. In the first place, the Hind, a wild animal that could find food where less active creatures would starve, was reduced to such straits that she was obliged to remain in the fields at the time when her young was born, instead of retiring to some sheltered spot, according to her custom. And when it was born, instead of nurturing it carefully, according to the natural maternal instinct, she was forced from sheer hunger to abandon it in order to find a sufficiency of food for herself.

That the Deer could be tamed, and its naturally affectionate disposition cultivated, is evident from a passage in the Proverbs (v. 18, 19): "Let thy fountain be blessed: and rejoice with the wife of thy youth. Let her be as the loving hind and pleasant roe."

We might naturally expect that the Rabbinical writers would have much to say on the subject of the Hart and Hind. Among much that is irrelevant to the object of the present work there are a few passages that deserve mention. Alluding to the annual shedding of the Deer's horns, there is a proverb respecting one who ventures his money too freely in trade, that "he has hung it on the stag's horns," meaning thereby that he will never

THE WATCHFUL DOE.

see it again. It is remarkable that in Western Africa there is a proverb of a similar character, the imprudent merchant being told to look for his money in the place where Deer shed their horns.

A KNEELING CAMEL.

THE CAMEL.

CHAPTER I.

The two species of Camel, and the mode of distinguishing them—Value of the Camel in the East—Thirst-enduring capability—The hump, and its use to the animal—The Camel as a beast of draught and burden—How the Camel is laden—Camels for riding—Difficulty of sitting a Camel—A rough-paced steed—Method of guiding the Camel—The swift dromedary—Young Camels and their appearance—The deserted Camel.

BEFORE treating of the Scriptural references to the Camel, it will be as well to clear the ground by noticing that two distinct species of Camel are known to zoologists; namely, the common Camel (*Camelus dromedarius*), which has one hump, and the Bactrian Camel (*Camelus Bactrianus*), which has two of these curious projections. There is a popular but erroneous idea that the dromedary and the Camel are two distinct animals, the latter being distinguished by its huge hump, whereas the fact is, that the dromedary is simply a lighter and more valuable breed of the one-humped Camel of Arabia, the two-humped Bactrian Camel being altogether a different animal, inhabiting Central Asia, Thibet, and China.

THE Camel is still one of the most valued animals that inhabit Palestine, and in former times it played a part in Jewish history scarcely inferior to that of the ox or sheep. We shall, therefore, devote some space to it.

In some parts of the land it even exceeded in value the sheep, and was infinitely more useful than the goat. At the very beginning of Jewish history we read of this animal, and it is mentioned in the New Testament nearly two thousand years

JACOB LEAVES LABAN AND RETURNS TO CANAAN WITH HIS CAMELS, SHEEP, AND CATTLE

after we meet with it in the Book of Genesis. The earliest mention of the Camel occurs in Gen. xii. 16, where is related the journey of Abram: "He had sheep, and oxen, and he-asses, and men-servants, and maid-servants, and she-asses, and camels."

Belonging, as he did, to the nomad race which lives almost wholly on the produce of their herds, Abram needed Camels, not only for their milk, and, for all we know, for their flesh, but for their extreme use as beasts of burden, without which he could never have travelled over that wild and pathless land. The whole of Abram's outer life was exactly that of a Bedouin sheikh of the present day, in whom we find reproduced the habits, the tone of thought, and the very verbiage of the ancient Scriptures.

Many years afterwards, when the son of his old age was desirous of marrying a wife of his own kindred, we find that he sent his trusted servants with ten of his Camels to Mesopotamia, and it was by the offering of water to these Camels, that Rebekah was selected as Isaac's wife (see Gen. xxiv. 10, 19). In after days, when Jacob was about to leave Laban, these animals are mentioned as an important part of his wealth: "And the man increased exceedingly, and had much cattle, and maid-servants, and men-servants, and camels, and asses" (Gen. xxx. 43).

It is thought worthy of mention in the sacred narrative that Job had three thousand, and afterwards six thousand Camels (Job i. 3, and xlii. 12); that the Midianites and Amalekites possessed camels without number, as the sand by the seaside.

A CAMP IN THE DESERT.

They were valuable enough to be sent as presents from one potentate to another. For example, when Jacob went to meet Esau, he gave as his present two hundred and twenty sheep, the same number of goats, fifty oxen, thirty asses, and sixty camels, *i.e.* thirty mothers, each with her calf. They were important enough to be guarded by men of position. In 1 Chron. xxvii. 30, we find that the charge of David's Camels was confided to one of his officers, Obil the Ishmaelite, who, from his origin, might be supposed to be skilful in the management of these animals. Bochart, however, conjectures that the word Obil ought to be read as Abal, *i.e.* the camel-keeper, and that the passage would therefore read as follows: "Over the camels was an Ishmaelitish camel-keeper."

We will now proceed to the uses of the Camel, and first take it in the light of food.

By the Mosaic law, the Camel was a forbidden animal, because it did not divide the hoof, although it chewed the cud. Yet, although the Jews might not eat its flesh, they probably used the milk for food, as they do at the present day. No distinct Scriptural reference is made to the milk of the Camel; but, as the Jews of the present day are quite as fastidious as their ancestors in keeping the Mosaic law, we are justified in concluding that, although they would not eat the flesh of the animal, they drank its milk. At the present time, the milk is used, like that of the sheep, goat, and cow, both in a fresh and curdled state, the latter being generally preferred to the former. A kind of cheese is made from it, but is not much to the taste of the European traveller, on account of the quantity of salt which is put in it. Butter is churned in a very simple manner, the fresh milk being poured into a skin bag, and the bag beaten with a stick until the butter makes its appearance.

That it was really used in the patriarchal times is evident by the passage which has already been mentioned, where Jacob is related to have brought as a present to his brother Esau thirty milch Camels, together with their young. So decided a stress would certainly not have been laid upon the fact that the animals were milch Camels unless the milk were intended for use.

Perhaps the use of the Camel's milk might be justified by saying that the prohibition extended only to eating and not to drinking, and that therefore the milk might be used though the flesh was prohibited.

There was another mode in which the Camel might be used by travellers to sustain life.

The reader is probably aware that, even in the burning climate in which it dwells, the Camel is able to go for a long time without drinking,—not that it requires less liquid nourishment than other animals, but that it is able, by means of its internal construction, to imbibe at one draught a quantity of water which will last for a considerable time. It is furnished with a series of cells, into which the water runs as fast as it is drunk, and in which it can be kept for some time without losing its life-preserving qualities. As much as twenty gallons have been imbibed by a Camel at one draught, and this amount will serve it for several days, as it has the power of consuming by degrees the water which it has drunk in a few minutes.

This curious power of the Camel has often proved to be the salvation of its owner. It has often happened that, when travellers have been passing over the desert, their supply of water has been exhausted, partly by the travellers and partly by the burning heat which causes it to evaporate through the pores of the goat-skin bottle in which it was carried. Then the next well, where they had intended to refill their skins and refresh themselves, has proved dry, and the whole party seemed doomed to die of thirst.

Under these circumstances, only one chance of escape is left them. They kill a Camel, and from its stomach they procure water enough to sustain life for a little longer, and perhaps to enable them to reach a well or fountain in which water still remains. The water which is thus obtained is unaltered, except by a greenish hue, the result of mixing with the remains of herbage in the cells. It is, of course, very disagreeable, but those who are dying from thirst cannot afford to be fastidious, and to them the water is a most delicious draught.

It is rather curious that, if any of the water which is taken out of a dead Camel can be kept for a few days, both the green hue and the unpleasant flavour disappear, and the water becomes fresh, clear, and limpid. So wonderfully well do the internal cells preserve the water, that after a Camel has been dead for ten days—and in that hot climate ten days after death are equal to a month here—the water within it has been quite pure and drinkable.

Many persons believe in the popular though erroneous idea that the Camel does not require as much water as ordinary animals. He will see, however, from the foregoing account that it needs quite as much water as the horse or the ox, but that it possesses the capability of taking in at one time as much as

A GRATEFUL SHADE.

either of these animals would drink in several days. So far from being independent of water, there is no animal that requires it more, or displays a stronger desire for it. A thirsty Camel possesses the power of scenting water at a very great distance, and, when it does so, its instincts conquer its education, and it goes off at full speed towards the spot, wholly ignoring its rider or driver. Many a desert spring has been discovered, and many a life saved, by this wonderful instinct, the animal having scented the distant water when its rider had lost all hope, and was resigning himself to that terrible end, the death by thirst. The sacred Zemzem fountain at Mecca was discovered by two thirsty Camels.

Except by the Jews, the flesh of the Camel is eaten throughout Palestine and the neighbouring countries, and is looked upon as a great luxury. The Arab, for example, can scarcely have a greater treat than a Camel-feast, and looks forward to it in a state of wonderful excitement. He is so impatient, that scarcely is the animal dead before it is skinned, cut up, and the various parts prepared for cooking.

To European palates the flesh of the Camel is rather unpleasant, being tough, stringy, and without much flavour. The fatty hump is universally considered as the best part of the animal, and is always offered to the chief among the guests, just as the North American Indian offers the hump of the bison to the most important man in the assembly. The heart and the tongue, however, are always eatable, and, however old a Camel may be, these parts can be cooked and eaten without fear.

The hump, or "bunch" as it is called in the Bible, has no connexion with the spine, and is a supplementary growth, which varies in size, not only in the species, but in the individual. It is analogous to the hump upon the shoulders of the American bison and the Indian zebra, and in the best-bred Camels it is the smallest though the finest and most elastic.

This hump, by the way, affords one of the points by which the value of the Camel is decided. When it is well fed and properly cared for, the hump projects boldly, and is firm and elastic to the touch. But if the Camel be ill, or if it be badly fed or overworked, the hump becomes soft and flaccid, and in bad cases hangs down on one side like a thick flap of skin. Consequently, the dealers in Camels always try to produce their animals in the market with their humps well developed; and, if they find that this important part does not look satisfactory, they use various means to give it the required fulness, inflating it with air being the most common. In fact, there is as much deception among Camel-dealers in Palestine as with dog or pigeon fanciers in England.

Here perhaps I may remark that the hump has given rise to some strange but prevalent views respecting the Camel. Many persons think that the dromedary has one hump and the Camel two—in fact, that they are two totally distinct animals. Now the fact is that the Camel of Palestine is of one species only, the dromedary being a lighter and swifter breed, and differing from the ordinary Camel just as a hunter or racer differs from a cart-horse. The two-humped Camel is a different species altogether, which will be briefly described at the end of the present article.

The Camel is also used as a beast of draught, and, as we find, not only from the Scriptures, but from ancient monuments, was employed to draw chariots and drag the plough. Thus in Isa. xxi. 7: "And he saw a chariot with a couple of horsemen, a chariot of asses, and a chariot of camels." It is evident that in this passage some chariots were drawn by Camels and some by asses. It is, however, remarkable that in Kennard's "Eastern Experiences," these two very useful animals are mentioned as being yoked together: "We passed through a fertile country, watching the fellaheen at their agricultural labours, and not a little amused at sometimes remarking a very tall camel and a very small donkey yoked together in double harness, dragging a plough through the rich brown soil." Camels drawing chariots are still to be seen in the Assyrian sculptures. In Palestine—at all events at the present time—the Camel is seldom if ever used as a beast of draught, being exclusively employed for bearing burdens and carrying riders.

Taking it first as a beast of burden, we find several references in different parts of the Scriptures. For example, see 2 Kings viii. 9: "So Hazael went to meet him, and took a present with him, even of every good thing of Damascus, forty camels' burden." Again, in 1 Chron. xii. 40: "Moreover they that were nigh them, even unto Issachar and Zebulun and Naphtali, brought bread on asses, and on camels, and on mules, and on oxen." Another allusion to the same custom is made in Isaiah: "They will carry their riches upon the shoulders of young asses, and their treasures upon the bunches (or humps) of camels."

The Camel can carry a considerable load, though not so much as is generally fancied. A sort of a pack-saddle of a very simple description is used, in order to keep the burden upon so strangely-shaped an animal. A narrow bag about eight feet long is made, and rather loosely stuffed with straw or similar material. It is then doubled, and the ends firmly sewn together, so as to form a great ring, which is placed over the hump, and forms a tolerably flat surface. A wooden framework is tied on the pack-saddle, and is kept in its place by a girth and a crupper. The packages which the Camel is to carry are fastened together by cords, and slung over the saddle. They are only connected by those semi-knots called "hitches," so that, when the Camel is to be unloaded, all that is needed is to pull the lower end of the rope, and the packages fall on either side of the animal. So quickly is the operation of loading performed, that a couple of experienced men can load a Camel in very little more than a minute.

As is the case with the horse in England, the Camels that are used as beasts of burden are of a heavier, slower, and altogether inferior breed to those which are employed to carry riders, and all their accoutrements are of a ruder and meaner order, devoid of the fantastic ornaments with which Oriental riders are fond of decorating their favourite animals.

In the large illustration are represented four of the ordinary Camels of burden, as they appear when laden with boughs for the Feast of Tabernacles. The branches are those of the Hebrew pine, and, as may be seen, the animals are so heavily laden with them that their forms are quite hidden under their leafy burdens. The weight which a Camel will carry varies much, according to the strength of the individual, which has given rise to the Oriental proverb, "As the camel, so the load." But an animal of ordinary strength is supposed to be able to carry from five to six hundred pounds for a short journey, and half as much for a long one,—a quantity which, as the reader will see, is not so very great when the bulk of the animal is taken into consideration. It is remarkable that the Camel knows its own

CAMELS LADEN WITH BOUGHS.

powers, and instinctively refuses to move if its correct load be exceeded. But, when it is properly loaded, it will carry its

MORNING IN THE DESERT: STARTING OF THE CARAVAN.

burden for hours together at exactly the same pace, and without seeming more fatigued than it was when it started.

The riding Camels are always of a better breed than those which are used for burden, and may be divided into two classes; namely, those which are meant for ordinary purposes, and those which are specially bred for speed and endurance. There is as much difference between the ordinary riding Camel and the swift Camel as there is between the road hack and the race-horse. We will first begin with the description of the common riding Camel and its accoutrements.

The saddle which is intended for a rider is very different from the pack-saddle on which burdens are carried, and has a long upright projection in front, to which the rider can hold if he wishes it.

The art of riding the Camel is far more difficult of accomplishment than that of riding the horse, and the preliminary operation of mounting is not the least difficult portion of it. Of

THE CAMEL.

course, to mount a Camel while the animal is standing is impossible, and accordingly it is taught to kneel until the rider is seated. Kneeling is a natural position with the Camel, which is furnished with large callosities or warts on the legs and breast, which act as cushions on which it may rest its great weight without abrading the skin. These callosities are not formed, as some have imagined, by the constant kneeling to which the Camel is subjected, but are born with it, though of course less developed than they are after they have been hardened by frequent pressure against the hot sand.

When the Camel kneels, it first drops on its knees, and then on the joints of the hind legs. Next it drops on its breast, and then again on the bent hind legs. In rising it reverses the process, so that a novice is first pitched forward, then backward, then forward, and then backward again, to the very great disarrangement of his garments, and the probable loss of his seat altogether. Then when the animal kneels he is in danger of being thrown over its head by the first movement, and jerked over its tail by the second; but after a time he learns to keep his seat mechanically.

As to the movement of the animal, it is at first almost as unpleasant as can be conceived, and has been described by several travellers, some of whose accounts will be here given. One well-known traveller declares that any person desiring to practise Camel-riding can readily do so by taking a music-stool, screwing it up as high as possible, putting it into a cart without springs, sitting on the top of it cross-legged, and having the cart driven at full speed transversely over a newly-ploughed field.

There is, however, as great a difference in the gait of Camels as of horses, some animals having a quiet, regular, easy movement, while others are rough and high-stepping, harassing their riders grievously in the saddle. Even the smooth-going Camel is, however, very trying at first, on account of its long swinging strides, which are taken with the legs of each side alternately, causing the body of the rider to swing backwards and forwards as if he were rowing in a boat.

Those who suffer from sea-sickness are generally attacked with the same malady when they make their first attempts at Camel-riding, while even those who are proof against this particular form of discomfort soon begin to find that their backs are aching, and that the pain becomes steadily worse. Change of attitude is but little use, and the wretched traveller derives but scant comfort from the advice of his guide, who tells him to allow his body to swing freely, and that in a short time he will become used to it. Some days, however, are generally consumed before he succeeds in training his spine to the continual unaccustomed movement, and he finds that, when he wakes on the morning that succeeds his first essay, his back is so stiff that he can scarcely move without screaming with pain, and that the prospect of mounting the Camel afresh is anything but a pleasant one.

"I tried to sit erect without moving," writes Mr. Kennard, when describing his experience of Camel-riding. "This proved a relief for a few minutes, but, finding the effort too great to continue long in this position, I attempted to recline with my head resting upon my hand. This last manœuvre I found would not do, for the motion of the camel's hind legs was so utterly at variance with the motion of his fore-legs that I was jerked upwards, and forwards, and sideways, and finally ended in nearly rolling off altogether.

"Without going into the details of all that I suffered for the next two or three days—how that on several occasions I slid from the camel's back to the ground, in despair of ever accustoming my half-dislocated joints to the ceaseless jerking and swaying to and fro, and how that I often determined to trudge on foot over the hot desert sand all the way to Jerusalem rather than endure it longer—I shall merely say that the day did at last arrive when I descended from my camel, after many hours' riding, in as happy and comfortable a state of mind as if I had been lolling in the easiest of arm-chairs."

A very similar description of the transition from acute and constant suffering to perfect ease is given by Albert Smith, who states that more than once he has dozed on the back of his Camel, in spite of the swaying backwards and forwards to which his body was subjected.

If such be the discomfort of riding a smooth-going and good-tempered Camel, it may be imagined that to ride a hard-going and cross-grained animal must be a very severe trial to an inexperienced rider. A very amusing account of a ride on such a

THE CAMEL POST.

Camel, and of a fall from its back, is given by Mr. Hamilton in his "Sinai, the Hedjaz, and Soudan:"—

"A dromedary I had obtained at Suk Abu Sin for my own riding did not answer my expectations, or rather the saddle was badly put on—not an easy thing to do well, by the way—and one of my servants, who saw how out of patience I was at the many times I had had to dismount to have it arranged, persuaded me to try the one he was riding, the Sheik's present. I had my large saddle transferred to his beast, and, nothing doubting, mounted it.

"He had not only no nose-string, but was besides a vicious brute, rising with a violent jerk before I was well in the saddle, and anxious to gain the caravan, which was a little way ahead, he set off at his roughest gallop. Carpets, kufieh, tarbush, all went off in the jolting; at every step I was thrown a foot into the air, glad to come down again, bump, bump, on the saddle, by dint of holding on to the front pommel with the left hand, while the right was engaged with the bridle, which in the violence of the exercise it was impossible to change to its proper hand. I had almost reached the caravan, and had no doubt my humpbacked Pegasus would relax his exertions, when a camel-driver, one of the sons of iniquity, seeing me come up at full speed, and evidently quite run away with, took it into his head to come to my assistance.

"I saw what he was at, and called out to him to get out of the way, but instead of this he stuck himself straight before me, stretching himself out like a St. Andrew's cross, with one hand armed with a huge club, and making most diabolical grimaces. Of course the camel was frightened, it was enough to frighten a much more reasonable being; so, wheeling quickly round, it upset my unstable equilibrium. Down I came head foremost to the ground, and when I looked up, my forehead streaming with blood, the first thing I saw was my Arab with the camel, which he seemed mightily pleased with himself for having so cleverly captured, while the servant who had suggested the unlucky experiment came ambling along on my easy-paced dromedary, and consoled me by saying that he knew it was a runaway beast, which there was no riding without a nose-string.

"I now began to study the way of keeping one's seat in such an emergency. An Arab, when he gallops his dromedary with one of these saddles, holds hard on with the right hand to the back part of the seat, not to the pommel, and grasps the bridle tightly in the other. The movement of the camel in galloping

A RUNAWAY.

throws one violently forward, and without holding on, excepting on the naked back, when the rider sits behind the hump, it is impossible to retain one's seat. I afterwards thought myself lucky in not having studied this point sooner, as, from the greater resistance I should have offered, my tumble, since it was *fated* I should have one, would probably have been much more severe. It is true I might also have escaped it, but in the chapter of probabilities I always think a mishap the most probable."

264　　　　　*STORY OF THE BIBLE ANIMALS.*

AN ARAB SHEIK MOUNTED UPON HIS CAMEL.

It may be imagined that a fall from a Camel's back is not a trifle, and, even if the unskilful rider be fortunate enough to fall on soft sand instead of hard rock, he receives a tolerably severe shock, and runs no little risk of breaking a limb. For the average height of a Camel's back is rather more than six feet, while some animals measure seven feet from the ground to the top of the hump.

This height, however, is of material advantage to the traveller. In the first place it lifts him above the waves of heated air that are continually rolling over the sand on which the burning rays of the sun are poured throughout the day; and in the second place it brings him within reach of the slightest breeze that passes above the stratum of hot air, and which comes to the traveller like the breath of life. Moreover, his elevated position enables him to see for a very great distance, which is an invaluable advantage in a land where every stranger may be a robber, and is probably a murderer besides.

The best mode of avoiding a fall is to follow the Arab mode of riding,—namely, to pass one leg over the upright pommel, which, as has been mentioned, is a mere wooden peg or stake, and hitching the other leg over the dangling foot. Perhaps the safest, though not the most comfortable, mode of sitting is by crossing the legs in front, and merely grasping the pommel with the hands.

Yet, fatiguing as is the seat on the Camel's back to the beginner, it is less so than that on the horse's saddle, inasmuch as in the latter case one position is preserved, while in the former an infinite variety of seat is attainable when the rider has fairly mastered the art of riding.

The Camel is not held by the bit and bridle like the horse, but by a rope tied like a halter round the muzzle, and having a knot on the left or "near" side. This is held in the left hand, and is used chiefly for the purpose of stopping the animal. The Camel is guided partly by the voice of its rider, and partly by a driving-stick, with which the neck is lightly touched on the opposite side to that which its rider wishes it to take. A pressure of the heel on the shoulder-bone tells it to quicken its pace, and a little tap on the head followed by a touch on the short ears are the signals for full speed.

There are three different kinds of stick with which the Camel is driven; one of them, a mere almond branch with the bark, and an oblique head, is the sceptre or emblem of sovereignty of the Prince of Mecca. Mr. Hamilton suggests that this stick, called the "*mesh'ab*," is the original of the jackal-headed stick with which so many of the Egyptian deities are represented; and that Aaron's rod that "brought forth buds, and bloomed blossoms, and yielded almonds," was the *mesh'ab*, the almond-branch sceptre, the emblem of his almost regal rank and authority.

AARON'S ROD BEARS ALMONDS.

The women mostly ride in a different manner from the men. Sometimes they are hardy enough to sit the animal in the same way as their husbands, but as a rule they are carried by the animal rather than ride it, sitting in great basket-like appendages which are slung on either side of the Camel. These constitute the "furniture" which is mentioned in Gen. xxxi. 34. When Jacob left the house of Laban, to lead an independent life, Rachel stole her father's images, or "teraphim," and carried them away with her, true to her affectionate though deceptive nature, which impelled her to incur the guilt of robbery for the sake of enriching her husband with the cherished teraphim of her father. From the most careful researches we learn that these teraphim were used for divining the future, and that they were made in the human form. That they were of considerable size is evident from the fact that, when Saul was hunting after David, his wife Michal contrived to convey him out of the house, and for a time to conceal her fraud by putting an image (or teraph) into the bed as a representative of her husband. Had not, therefore, the camel-furniture been of considerable dimensions, images of such a size could not be hidden, but they could well be stowed away in the great panniers, as long as their

CAMEL-RIDING.

mistress sat upon them, after the custom of Oriental travellers and declined to rise on the ready plea of indisposition.

This sort of carriage is still used for the women and children. "The wife and child came by in the string of camels, the former reclining in an immense circular box, stuffed and padded, covered with red cotton, and dressed with yellow worsted ornaments. This family nest was mounted on a large camel. It seemed a most commodious and well-arranged travelling carriage, and very superior as a mode of camel-riding to that which our Sitteen rejoiced in (*i.e.* riding upon a saddle). The Arab wife could change her position at pleasure, and the child had room to walk about and could not fall out, the sides of the box just reaching to its shoulders. Various jugs and skins and articles of domestic use hung suspended about it, and trappings of fringe and finery ornamented it."

This last sentence brings us to another point which is several times mentioned in the Bible; namely, the ornaments with which the proprietors of Camels are fond of bedizening their favourite animals.

Their leathern collars are covered with cowrie shells sewn on them in various fantastic patterns. Crescent-shaped ornaments are made of shells sewn on red cloth, and hung so abundantly upon the harness of the animal that they jingle at every step which it takes. Sheiks and other men of rank often have these ornaments made of silver, so that the cost of the entire trappings is very great.

THE DELOUL, OR SWIFT CAMEL.

WE now come to the Swift Camel, or Deloul.

The limbs of the Deloul are long and wiry, having not an ounce of superfluous fat upon them, the shoulders are very broad, and the hump, though firm and hard, is very small.

A thoroughbred Deloul, in good travelling condition, is not

at all a pleasing animal to an ordinary eye, being a lank, gaunt, and ungainly-looking creature, the very conformation which insures its swiftness and endurance being that which detracts from its beauty. An Arab of the desert, however, thinks a good Deloul one of the finest sights in the world. As the talk of the pastoral tribes is of sheep and oxen, so is the talk of the nomads about Camels. It is a subject which is for ever on their lips, and a true Bedouin may be seen to contemplate the beauties of one of these favourite animals for hours at a time,—if his own, with the rapture of a possessor, or, if another's, with the determination of stealing it when he can find an opportunity.

Instead of plodding along at the rate of three miles an hour, which is the average speed of the common Camel, the Deloul can cover, if lightly loaded, nine or ten miles an hour, and go on at the same pace for a wonderful time, its long legs swinging, and its body swaying, as if it were but an animated machine. Delouls have been reported to have journeyed for nearly fifty hours without a single stop for rest, during which time the animals must have traversed nearly five hundred miles. Such examples must, however, be exceptional, implying, as they do, an amount of endurance on the part of the rider equal to that of the animal; and even a journey of half that distance is scarcely possible to ordinary men on Delouls.

For the movements of the Deloul are very rough, and the rider is obliged to prepare himself for a long journey by belting himself tightly with two leathern bands, one just under the arms, and the other round the pit of the stomach. Without these precautions, the rider would be likely to suffer serious injuries, and, even with them, the exercise is so severe, that an Arab makes it a matter of special boast that he can ride a Deloul for a whole day.

A courier belonging to the Sherif of Mecca told Mr. Hamilton that he often went on the same dromedary from Mecca to Medina in forty-eight hours, the distance being two hundred and forty miles. And a thoroughbred Deloul will travel for seven or eight weeks with only four or five days of rest.

Even at the present time, these Camels are used for the conveyance of special messages, and in the remarkable Bornu kingdom a regular service of these animals is established, two couriers always travelling in company, so that if one rider or Camel should fail or be captured by the Arabs, who are always on the alert for so valuable a prey, the other may post on and carry the message to its destination.

The swift dromedary, or Deloul, is mentioned several times in the Old Testament. One of them occurs in Isa. lx. 6: "The multitude of camels shall cover thee, the dromedaries of Midian

ANOTHER MODE OF RIDING THE CAMEL.

and Ephah." In this passage a distinction is drawn between the ordinary Camel and the swift dromedary, the former being the word "gamel," and the latter the word "beker," which is again used in Jer. ii. 23: "See thy way in the valley, know what thou hast done: thou art a swift dromedary."

There is a passage in the Book of Esther which looks as if it referred to the ordinary Camel and the swift dromedary, but there is considerable uncertainty about the proper rendering. It runs as follows: "And he wrote in king Ahasuerus' name, and sealed it with the king's ring, and sent letters and posts on horseback, and riders on mules, camels, and young dromedaries."

The Jewish Bible, however, translates this passage as follows: 'And sent letters by the runners on the horses, and riders on the racers, mules, and young mares." Now, the word *rekesh*, which is translated as "racer," is rendered by Buxtorf as "a swift horse or mule," and the word *beni-rammachim*, which is translated as "young mares," literally signifies "those born of mares."

The Camel-drivers behave towards their animals with the curious inconsistency which forms so large a part of the Oriental character.

Prizing them above nearly all earthly things, proud of them, and loving them after their own fashion, the drivers will talk to them, cheer them, and sing interminable songs for their benefit. Towards the afternoon the singing generally begins, and it goes on without cessation in a sort of monotonous hum, as Dr. Bonar calls it. The same traveller calls attention to a passage in Caussinus' "Polyhistor Symbolicus," in which the learned and didactic author symbolizes the maxim that more can be done by kindness than by blows. "The Camel is greatly taken with music and melody. So much so, indeed, that if it halts through weariness, the driver does not urge it with stripes and blows, but soothes it by his songs."

Several travellers have mentioned these songs. See, for example, Miss Rogers' account of some Bedouins: "Their songs were already subdued to harmonize with their monotonous swinging pace, and chimed softly and plaintively with the tinkling of camel-bells, thus—

> "'Dear unto me as the sight of mine eyes,
> Art thou, O my Camel!
> Precious to me as the health of my life,
> Art thou, O my Camel!
> Sweet to my ears is the sound
> Of thy tinkling bells, O my Camel!
> And sweet to thy listening ears
> Is the sound of my evening song.'

And so on, *ad libitum*."

Sometimes a female Camel gives birth to a colt on the journey. In such a case, a brief pause is made, and then the train proceeds on its journey, the owner of the Camel carrying the young one in his arms until the evening halt. He then gives it to its mother, and on the following day it is able to follow her without further assistance. The young Camels are almost pretty, their hair being paler than that of the adult animal, and their limbs more slender.

Although the young Camel is better-looking than its parents, it is not one whit more playful. Unlike almost all other animals, the Camel seems to have no idea of play, and even the young Camel of a month or two old follows its mother with the same steady, regular pace which she herself maintains.

In spite of all the kindness with which a driver treats his Camels, he can at times be exceedingly cruel to them, persisting in over-loading and over-driving them, and then, if a Camel fall exhausted, removing its load, and distributing it among the other Camels. As soon as this is done, he gives the signal to proceed, and goes on his way, abandoning the wretched animal to its fate—*i.e.* to thirst and the vultures. He will not even have the humanity to kill it, but simply leaves it on the ground, muttering that it is "his fate!"

THE CAMEL.

CHAPTER II.

The Camel and its master—Occasional fury of the animal—A boy killed by a Camel—Another instance of an infuriated Camel—Theory respecting the Arab and his Camel—Apparent stupidity of the Camel—Its hatred of a load, and mode of expressing its disapprobation—Riding a Camel through the streets—A narrow escape—Ceremony of weaning a young Camel—The Camel's favourite food—Structure of the foot and adaptation to locality—Difficulty in provisioning—Camel's hair and skin—Sal-ammoniac and Desert fuel—The Camel and the needle's eye—Straining at a gnat and swallowing a Camel.

WE now come to the general characteristics of the Camel.

The Camels know their master well, some of them being much more affectionate than others. But they are liable to fits

THE CAMEL.

of strange fury, in which case even their own masters are not safe from them. They are also of a revengeful nature, and have an unpleasant faculty of treasuring up an injury until they can find a time of repaying it. Signor Pierotti gives a curious example of this trait of character. As he was going to the Jordan, he found a dead Camel lying on the roadside, the head nearly separated from the body. On inquiry he found that the animal had a master who ill-treated it, and had several times tried to bite him. One evening, after the Camels had been unloaded, the drivers lay down to sleep as usual.

The Camel made its way to its master, and stamped on him as he slept. The man uttered one startled cry, but had no time for another. The infuriated Camel followed up its attack by grasping his throat in its powerful jaws, and shaking him to death. The whole scene passed so rapidly, that before the other drivers could come to the man's assistance he was hanging dead from the jaws of the Camel, who was shaking him as a dog shakes a rat, and would not release its victim until its head had been nearly severed from its body by sword-cuts.

A similar anecdote is told by Mr. Palgrave, in his "Central and Eastern Arabia:"—

"One passion alone he possesses, namely, revenge, of which he gives many a hideous example; while, in carrying it out, he shows an unexpected degree of forethoughted malice, united meanwhile with all the cold stupidity of his usual character. One instance of this I well remember—it occurred hard by a small town in the plain of Baalbec, where I was at the time residing.

"A lad of about fourteen had conducted a large camel, laden with wood, from that very village to another at half an hour's distance or so. As the animal loitered or turned out of the way, its conductor struck it repeatedly, and harder than it seems to have thought he had a right to do. But, not finding the occasion favourable for taking immediate quits, it 'bided its time,' nor was that time long in coming.

"A few days later, the same lad had to re-conduct the beast, but unladen, to his own village. When they were about half way on the road, and at some distance from any habitation, the camel suddenly stopped, looked deliberately round in every direction to assure itself that no one was in sight, and, finding the road clear of passers-by, made a step forward, seized the unlucky boy's head in its monstrous mouth, and, lifting him up in the air, flung him down again on the earth, with the upper part of his head completely torn off, and his brains scattered on the ground. Having thus satisfied its revenge, the brute quietly resumed its pace towards the village, as though nothing were the matter, till some men, who had observed the whole, though unfortunately at too great a distance to be able to afford timely help, came up and killed it.

"Indeed, so marked is this unamiable propensity, that some philosophers have ascribed the revengeful character of the Arabs to the great share which the flesh and milk of the camel have in their sustenance, and which are supposed to communicate, to those who partake of them over-largely, the moral or immoral qualities of the animal to which they belonged. I do not feel myself capable of pronouncing an opinion on so intricate a question, but thus much I can say, that the camel and its Bedouin master do afford so many and such divers points of resemblance, that I do not think our Arab of Shomer far in the wrong, when I once on a time heard him say, 'God created the Bedouin for the camel, and the camel for the Bedouin.'"

The reader will observe that Mr. Palgrave in this anecdote makes reference to the stupidity of the Camel. There is no doubt that the Camel is by no means an intellectual animal; but it is very possible that its stupidity may in a great measure be owing to the fact that no one has tried to cultivate its intellectual powers. The preceding anecdotes show clearly that the Camel must possess a strong memory, and be capable of exercising considerable ingenuity.

Still it is not a clever animal. If its master should fall off its back, it never dreams of stopping, as a well-trained horse would do, but proceeds at the same plodding pace, leaving his master to catch it if he can. Should it turn out of the way to crop some green thorn-bush, it will go on in the same direction, never thinking of turning back into the right road unless directed by its rider. Should the Camel stray, "it is a thousand to one that he will never find his way back to his accustomed home or pasture, and the first man who picks him up will have no particular shyness to get over; . . . and the losing of his old master and of his former cameline companions gives him no regret, and occasions no endeavour to find them again."

He has the strongest objection to being laden at all, no matter how light may be the burden, and expresses his disapprobation by growling and groaning, and attempting to bite. So habitual is this conduct that if a kneeling Camel be only approached, and a stone as large as a walnut laid on its back, it begins to remonstrate in its usual manner, groaning as if it were crushed to the earth with its load.

The Camel never makes way for any one, its instinct leading it to plod onward in its direct course. What may have been its habits in a state of nature no one can tell, for such a phenomenon as a wild Camel has never been known in the memory of man. There are wild oxen, wild goats, wild sheep, wild horses, and wild asses, but there is no spot on the face of the earth where the Camel is found except as the servant of man. Through innate stupidity, according to Mr. Palgrave, it goes straight forwards in the direction to which its head happens to be pointed, and is too foolish even to think of stopping unless it hears the signal for halt.

As it passes through the narrow streets of an Oriental city, laden with goods that project on either side, and nearly fill up the thoroughfare, it causes singular inconvenience, forcing every one who is in front of it to press himself closely to the wall, and to make way for the enormous beast as it plods along. The driver or rider generally gives notice by continually calling to the pedestrians to get out of the way, but a laden Camel rarely passes through a long street without having knocked down a man or two, or driven before it a few riders on asses who cannot pass between the Camel and the wall.

One source of danger to its rider is to be found in the low archways which span so many of the streets. They are just high enough to permit a laden Camel to pass under them, but are so low that they leave no room for a rider. The natives, who are accustomed to this style of architecture, are always ready for an archway, and, when the rider sees an archway which will not allow him to retain his seat, he slips to the ground, and remounts on the other side of the obstacle.

Mr. Kennard had a very narrow escape with one of these archways. "I had passed beneath one or two in perfect safety, without being obliged to do more than just bend my head forward, and was in the act of conversing with one of my companions behind, and was therefore in a happy state of ignorance as to what was immediately before me, when the shouting and running together of the people in the street on either side made me turn my head quickly, but only just in time to feel my breath thrown back on my face against the keystone of a gateway, beneath which my camel, with too much way on him to be stopped immediately, had already commenced to pass.

"With a sort of feeling that it was all over with me, I threw myself back as far as I could, and was carried through in an almost breathless state, my shirt-studs actually scraping along against the stonework. On emerging again into the open street, I could hardly realize my escape, for if there had been a single projecting stone to stop my progress, the camel would have struggled to get free, and my chest must have been crushed in."

It will be seen from these instances that the charge of stupidity is not an undeserved one. Still the animal has enough intellect to receive all the education which it needs for the service of man, and which it receives at a very early age. The ordinary Camel of burden is merely taught to follow its conductor, to obey the various words and gestures of command, and to endure a load. The Deloul, however, is more carefully trained. It is allowed to follow its mother for a whole year in perfect liberty. Towards the expiration of that time the young animal is gradually stinted in its supply of milk, and forced to browse for its nourishment. On the anniversary of its birth, the young Deloul is turned with its head towards Canopus, and its ears solemnly boxed, its master saying at the same time, "Henceforth drinkest thou no drop of milk." For this reason the newly-weaned Camel is called Lathim, or the "ear-boxed." It is then prevented from sucking by a simple though cruel experiment. A wooden peg is sharpened at both ends, and one end thrust into the young animal's nose. When it tries to suck, it pricks its mother with the projecting end, and at the same time forces the other end more deeply into the wound, so that the mother drives away her offspring, and the young soon ceases to make the attempt.

The food of the Camel is very simple, being, in fact, anything that it can get. As it proceeds on its journey, it manages to browse as it goes along, bending its long neck to the ground, and

PASSING A CAMEL IN A NARROW STREET OF AN EASTERN CITY.

cropping the scanty herbage without a pause. Camels have been known to travel for twenty successive days, passing over some eight hundred miles of ground, without receiving any food except that which they gathered for themselves by the way. The favourite food of the Camel is a shrub called the ghada, growing to six feet or so in height, and forming a feathery tuft of innumerable little green twigs, very slender and flexible. It is so fond of this shrub that a Camel can scarcely ever pass a bush without turning aside to crop it; and even though it be beaten severely for its misconduct, it will repeat the process at the next shrub that comes in sight.

It also feeds abundantly on the thorn-bushes which grow so plentifully in that part of the world; and though the thorns are an inch or two in length, very strong, and as sharp as needles, the hard, horny palate of the animal enables it to devour them with perfect ease.

There are several species of these thorn-shrubs, which are scattered profusely over the ground, and are, in fact, the commonest growth of the place. After they die, being under the fierce sun of that climate, they dry up so completely, that if a light be set to them they blaze up in a moment, with a sharp cracking sound and a roar of flame, and in a moment or two are nothing but a heap of light ashes. No wonder was it that when

MOSES AT THE BURNING BUSH.

Moses saw the thorn-bush burning without being consumed he was struck with awe at the miracle. These withered bushes are the common fuel of the desert, giving out a fierce but brief heat, and then suddenly sinking into ashes. "For as the crackling of thorns under a pot, so is the laughter of the fool" (Eccl. vii. 6).

The dried and withered twigs of these bushes are also eaten by the Camel, which seems to have a power of extracting nutriment from every sort of vegetable substance. It has been fed

AN ARAB ENCAMPMENT.

on charcoal, and, as has been happily remarked, could thrive on the shavings of a carpenter's workshop.

Still, when food is plentiful, it is fed as regularly as can be managed, and generally after a rather peculiar manner. "Our guide," writes Mr. Hamilton, in the work which has already been mentioned, "is an elderly man, the least uncouth of our cameldrivers. He has three camels in the caravan, and it was amusing to see his preparations for their evening's entertainment. The table-cloth, a circular piece of leather, was duly spread on the ground; on this he poured the quantity of dourrah destined for their meal, and calling his camels, they came and took each its place at the feast. It is quaint to see how each in his turn eats, so gravely and so quietly, stretching his long neck into the middle of the heap, then raising his head to masticate each mouthful; all so slowly and with such gusto, that we could swear it was a party of epicures sitting in judgment on one of Vachette's *chefs d'œuvre*."

The foregoing passages will show the reader how wonderfully adapted is the constitution of the Camel for the country in which it lives, and how indispensable it is to the inhabitants. It has been called "the ship of the desert," for without the Camel the desert would be as impassable as the sea without ships. No water being found for several days' journey together, the animal is able to carry within itself a supply of water which will last it for several days, and, as no green thing grows far from the presence of water, the Camel is able to feed upon the brief-lived thorn-shrubs which have sprung up and died, and which, from their hard and sharp prickles, are safe from every animal except the hard-mouthed Camel.

But these advantages would be useless without another—*i.e.* the foot. The mixed stones and sand of the desert would ruin the feet of almost any animal, and it is necessary that the Camel should be furnished with a foot that cannot be split by heat like the hoof of a horse, that is broad enough to prevent the creature from sinking into the sand, and is tough enough to withstand the action of the rough and burning soil.

Such a foot does the Camel possess. It consists of two long toes resting upon a hard elastic cushion with a tough and horny sole. This cushion is so soft that the tread of the huge animal is as noiseless as that of a cat, and, owing to the division of the toes, it spreads as the weight comes upon it, and thus gives a firm footing on loose ground. The foot of the moose-deer has a similar property, in order to enable the animal to walk upon the snow.

In consequence of this structure, the Camel sinks less deeply into the ground than any other animal; but yet it does sink in it, and dislikes a deep and loose sand, groaning at every step, and being wearied by the exertion of dragging its hard foot out of the holes into which they sink. It is popularly thought that hills are impracticable to the Camel; but it is able to climb even rocky ground from which a horse would recoil. Mr. Marsh, an American traveller, was much surprised by seeing a caravan of

ON THE MARCH.

fifty camels pass over a long ascent in Arabia Petræa. The rock was as smooth as polished marble, and the angle was on an average fifteen degrees; but the whole caravan passed over it without an accident.

The soil that a Camel most hates is a wet and muddy ground, on which it is nearly sure to slip. If the reader will look at a Camel from behind, he will see that the hinder legs are close together until the ankle-joint, when they separate so widely that the feet are set on the ground at a considerable distance from each other. On dry ground this structure increases the stability of the animal by increasing its base; but on wet ground the effect is singularly unpleasant. The soft, padded feet have no hold, and slip sideways at every step, often with such violence as to dislocate a joint and cause the death of the animal. When such ground has to be traversed, the driver generally passes a bandage round the hind legs just below the ankle-joint, so as to prevent them from diverging too far.

It must be remarked, however, that the country in which the animal lives is essentially a dry one, and that moist and muddy ground is so exceptional that the generality of Camels never see it in their lives. Camels do not object to mud an inch or two deep, provided that there is firm ground below; and they have been seen to walk with confident safety over pavements covered with mud and half-frozen snow.

The animals can ford rivers well enough, provided that the bed be stony or gravelly; but they are bad swimmers, their round bodies and long necks being scarcely balanced by their legs, so that they are apt to roll over on their sides, and in such a case they are sure to be drowned. When swimming is a necessity, the head is generally tied to the stern of a boat, or guided by the driver swimming in front, while another often clings to the tail, so as to depress the rump and elevate the head. It is rather curious that the Camels of the Sahara cannot be safely entrusted to the water. They will swim the river readily enough; but they are apt to be seized with illness afterwards, and to die in a few hours.

WE now come to some other uses of the Camel.

Its hair is of the greatest importance, as it is used for many purposes. In this country, all that we know practically of the Camel's hair is that it is employed in making brushes for painters; but in its own land the hair plays a really important part. At the proper season it is removed from the animal, usually by being pulled away in tufts, but sometimes by being shorn, and it is then spun by the women into strong thread.

From this thread are made sundry fabrics where strength is required and coarseness is not an objection. The "black tents" of the Bedouin Arabs, similar to those in which Abraham lived, are made of Camel's hair, and so are the rugs, carpets, and cordage used by the nomad tribes. Even mantles for rainy or cold weather are made of Camel's hair, and it was in a dress of this coarse and rough material that St. John the Baptist was clad.

HAIR OF THE CAMEL.

The best part of the Camel's hair is that which grows in tufts on the back and about the hump, the fibre being much longer than that which covers the body. There is also a little very fine under-wool which is carefully gathered, and, when a sufficient quantity is procured, it is spun and woven into garments. Shawls of this material are even now as valuable as those which are made from the Cachmire goat.

The skin of the Camel is made into a sort of leather. It is simply tanned by being pegged out in the sun and rubbed with salt.

Sandals and leggings are made of this leather, and in some places water-bottles are manufactured from it, the leather being thicker and less porous than that of the goat, and therefore wasting less of the water by evaporation. The bones are utilized, being made into various articles of commerce.

So universally valuable is the Camel that even its dung is important to its owners. Owing to the substances on which the animal feeds, it consists of little but macerated fragments of aromatic shrubs. It is much used as poultices in case of bruises or rheumatic pains, and is even applied with some success to simple fractures. It is largely employed for fuel, and the desert couriers use nothing else, their Camels being furnished with a net, so that none of this useful substance shall be lost. For this purpose it is carefully collected, mixed with bits of straw, and made into little rolls, which are dried in the sun, and can then be laid by for any time until they are needed.

Mixed with clay and straw, it is most valuable as a kind of mortar or cement with which the walls of huts are rendered weather-proof, and the same material is used in the better-class houses to make a sort of terrace on the flat roof. This must be waterproof in order to withstand the wet of the rainy season, and no material answers the purpose so well as that which has been mentioned. So strangely hard and firm is this composition, that stoves are made of it. These stoves are made like jars, and have the faculty of resisting the power of the inclosed fire. Even after it is burned it has its uses, the ashes being employed in the manufacture of sal-ammoniac.

THERE are two passages in the New Testament which mention the Camel in an allegorical sense. The first of these is the proverbial saying of our Lord, "A rich man shall hardly enter into the kingdom of heaven. Again I say unto you, It is easier for a camel to go through the eye of a needle, than for a rich man to enter into the kingdom of God" (Matt. xix. 23, 24).

Now, this well-known but scarcely understood passage requires some little dissection. If the reader will refer to the context, he will see that this saying was spoken in allusion to the young and wealthy man who desired to be one of the disciples, but clung too tightly to his wealth to accept the only conditions on which he could be received. His possessions were a snare to him, as was proved by his refusal to part with them at Christ's command. On his retiring, the expression was used, "that a rich man shall hardly (or, with difficulty) enter the kingdom of heaven," followed by the simile of the Camel and the needle's eye.

Now, if we are to take this passage literally, we can but draw one conclusion from it, that a rich man can no more enter heaven than a camel pass through the eye of a needle, *i.e.* that it is impossible for him to do so. Whereas, in the previous sentence, Christ says not that it is impossible, but difficult ($\delta\upsilon\sigma\kappa\delta\lambda\omega\varsigma$) for him to do so. It is difficult for a man to use his money for the service of God, the only purpose for which it was given him, and the difficulty increases in proportion to its amount. But wealth in itself is no more a bar to heaven than intellect, health, strength, or any other gift, and, if it be rightly used, is one of the most powerful tools that can be used in the service of God. Our Lord did not condemn all wealthy men alike. He knew many; but there was only one whom He advised to sell his possessions and give them to the poor as the condition of being admitted among the disciples.

CAMEL GOING THROUGH A "NEEDLE'S EYE."

We will now turn to the metaphor of the Camel and the needle's eye. Of course it can be taken merely as a very bold metaphor, but it may also be understood in a simpler sense, the sense in which it was probably understood by those who heard it. In Oriental cities, there are in the large gates small and very low apertures called metaphorically "needle's-eyes," just as we talk of certain windows as "bull's-eyes." These entrances are too narrow for a Camel to pass through them in the ordinary manner, especially if loaded. When a laden Camel has to pass through one of these entrances, it kneels down, its load is removed, and then it shuffles through on its knees. "Yesterday," writes Lady Duff-Gordon from Cairo, "I saw a camel go through the eye of a needle, *i.e.* the low-arched door of an enclosure. He must kneel, and bow his head to creep through; and thus the rich man must humble himself."

There is another passage in which the Camel is used by our Lord in a metaphorical sense. This is the well-known sentence: "Ye blind guides, which strain at a gnat, and swallow a camel" (Matt. xxiii. 24). It is remarkable that an accidental misprint has robbed this passage of its true force. The real translation is: "which strain *out* the gnat, and swallow the camel." The Greek word is διυλίζω, which signifies to filter thoroughly; and the allusion is made to the pharisaical custom of filtering liquids before drinking them, lest by chance a gnat or some such insect which was forbidden as food might be accidentally swallowed.

THE BACTRIAN CAMEL.

General description of the animal—Its use in mountain roads—Peculiar formation of the foot—Uses of a mixed breed—Its power of enduring cold—Used chiefly as a beast of draught—Unfitness for the plough—The cart and mode of harnessing—The load which it can draw—Camel-skin ropes—A Rabbinical legend.

THE second kind of Camel—namely, the Bactrian species—was probably unknown to the Jews until a comparatively late portion of their history. This species was employed by the Assyrians, as we find by the sculptures upon the ruins, and if in no other way the Jews would become acquainted with them through the nation by whom they were conquered, and in whose **land** they abode for so long.

The Bactrian Camel is at once to be distinguished from that which has already been described by the two humps and the clumsier and sturdier form. Still the skeletons of the Bactrian and Arabian species are so similar that none but a very skilful **anatomist** can distinguish between them, and several learned

A REST IN THE DESERT.

zoologists have expressed an opinion, in which I entirely coincide, that the Bactrian and Arabian Camels are but simple varieties of one and the same species, not nearly so dissimilar as the greyhound and the bulldog.

Unlike the one-humped Camel, the Bactrian species is quite at home in a cold climate, and walks over ice as easily as its congener does over smooth stone. It is an admirable rock-climber, and is said even to surpass the mule in the sureness of its tread. This quality is probably occasioned by the peculiar structure of the foot, which has an elongated toe projecting beyond the soft pad, and forming a sort of claw. In the winter time the riders much prefer them to horses, because their long legs enable them to walk easily through snow, in which a horse could only plunge helplessly, and would in all probability sink and perish.

A mixed breed of the one-humped and the Bactrian animals is thought to be the best for hill work in winter time, and General Harlan actually took two thousand of these animals in winter time for a distance of three hundred and sixty miles over the snowy tops of the Indian Caucasus; and though the campaign lasted for seven months, he only lost one Camel, and that was accidentally killed. Owing to its use among the hills, the Bactrian species is sometimes called the Mountain Camel.

It very much dislikes the commencement of spring, because the warm mid-day sun slightly melts the surface of the snow, and the frost of night converts it into a thin plate of ice. When the Camel walks upon this semi-frozen snow, its feet plunge into the soft substratum through the icy crust, against which its legs are severely cut. The beginning of the winter is liable to the same objection.

The mixed breed which has just been mentioned must be procured from a male Bactrian and a female Arabian Camel. If the parentage be reversed, the offspring is useless, being weak, ill-tempered, and disobedient.

The Bactrian Camel is, as has been mentioned, tolerant of cold, and is indeed so hardy an animal that it bears the severest winters without seeming to suffer distress, and has been seen quietly feeding when the thermometer has reached a temperature several degrees below zero. Sometimes, when the cold is more than usually sharp, the owners sew a thick cloth round its body, but even in such extreme cases the animal is left to find

THE BACTRIAN CAMEL.

its own food as it best can. And, however severe the weather may be, the Bactrian Camel never sleeps under a roof.

This Camel is sometimes employed as a beast of burden, but its general use is for draught. It is not often used alone for the plough, because it has an uncertain and jerking mode of pulling, and does not possess the steady dragging movement which is obtained by the use of the horse or ox.

BACTRIAN CAMELS DRAWING CART.

It is almost invariably harnessed to carts, and always in pairs. The mode of yoking the animals is as simple as can well be conceived. A pole runs between them from the front of the vehicle, and the Camels are attached to it by means of a pole which passes over their necks. Oxen were harnessed in a similar manner. It was probably one of these cars or chariots that was mentioned by Isaiah in his prophecy respecting Assyria:—"And he saw a chariot with a couple of horsemen, a chariot of asses, and a chariot of camels" (Isa. xxi. 7). The cars themselves are as simple as the mode of harnessing them, being almost exactly like the ox carts which have already been described.

The weight which can be drawn by a pair of these Camels is really considerable. On a tolerably made road a good pair of Camels are expected to draw from twenty-six to twenty-eight hundred weight, and to continue their labours for twenty or thirty successive days, traversing each day an average of thirty miles. It is much slower than the Arabian Camel, seldom going at more than two and a half miles per hour. If, however, the vehicle to which a pair of Bactrians are harnessed were well made, the wheels truly circular, and the axles kept greased so as to diminish the friction, there is no doubt that the animals could draw a still greater load to longer distances, and with less trouble to themselves. As it is, the wheels are wretchedly fitted, and their ungreased axles keep up a continual creaking that is most painful to an unaccustomed ear, and totally unheeded by the drivers.

The hair of the Bactrian Camel is long, coarse, and strong; and, like that of the Arabian animal, is made into rough cloth. It is plucked off by hand in the summer time, when it naturally becomes loose in readiness for its annual renewal, and the weight of the entire crop of hair ought to be about ten pounds. The skin is not much valued, and is seldom used for any purpose except for making ropes, straps, and thongs, and is not thought worth the trouble of tanning. The milk, like that of the Arabian animal, is much used for food, but the quantity is very trifling, barely two quarts per diem being procured from each Camel.

There is but little that is generally interesting in the Rabbinical writers on the Camel. They have one proverbial saying upon the shortness of its ears. When any one makes a request that is likely to be refused, they quote the instance of the Camel, who, it seems, was dissatisfied with its appearance, and asked for horns to match its long ears. The result of the request was, that it was deprived of its ears, and got no horns.

THE HORSE.

The Hebrew words which signify the Horse—The Horse introduced into Palestine from Egypt—Similarity of the war-horse of Scripture and the Arab horse of the present day—Characteristics of the Horse—Courage and endurance of the Horse—Hardness of its unshod hoofs—Love of the Arab for his Horse—Difficulty of purchasing the animal—The Horse prohibited to the Israelites—Solomon's disregard of the edict—The war-chariot, its form and use—Probable construction of the iron chariot—The cavalry Horse—Lack of personal interest in the animal.

SEVERAL Hebrew words are used by the various Scriptural writers to signify the Horse, and, like our own terms of horse, mare, pony, charger, &c., are used to express the different qualities of the animal. The chief distinction of the Horse seemed to lie in its use for riding or driving, the larger and heavier animals being naturally required for drawing the weighty springless chariots. The chariot horse was represented by the word *Sus*, and the cavalry horse by the word *Parash*, and in several passages both these words occur in bold contrast to each other. See, for example, 1 Kings iv. 26, &c.

AMONG the many passages of Scripture in which the Horse is mentioned, there are few which do not treat of it as an adjunct of war, and therefore it is chiefly in that light that we must regard it.

The Horse of the Scriptures was evidently a similar animal to the Arab Horse of the present day, as we find not only from internal evidence, but from the sculptures and paintings which still remain to tell us of the vanished glories of Egypt and Assyria. It is remarkable, by the way, that the first mention of the Horse in the Scriptures alludes to it as an Egyptian animal. During the terrible famine which Joseph had foretold, the Egyptians and the inhabitants of neighbouring countries were unable to find food for themselves or fodder for their cattle, and, accordingly, they sold all their beasts for bread. "And they brought their cattle unto Joseph, and Joseph gave them bread in exchange for horses and the flocks, and for the cattle of herds, and for the asses, and he fed them with bread for all their cattle for that year."

This particular breed of Horses is peculiarly fitted for the purposes of war, and is much less apt for peaceful duties than the heavier and more powerful breeds, which are found in different parts of the world. It is remarkable for the flexible agility of its movements, which enable it to adapt itself to every movement of the rider, whose intentions it seems to divine

TRIAL OF ARAB HORSES.

by a sort of instinct, and who guides it not so much by the bridle as by the pressure of the knees and the voice. Examples of a similar mode of guidance may be seen on the well-known frieze of the Parthenon, where, in the Procession of Horsemen, the riders may be seen directing their steeds by touching the side of the neck with one finger, thus showing their own skill and the well-trained quality of the animals which they ride.

Its endurance is really wonderful, and a horse of the Kochlani breed will go through an amount of work which is almost incredible. Even the trial by which a Horse is tested is so

AN ARAB HORSE OF THE KOCHLANI BREED.

severe, that any other animal would be either killed on the spot or ruined for life. When a young mare is tried for the first time, her owner rides her for some fifty or sixty miles at full speed, always finishing by swimming her through a river. After this trial she is expected to feed freely; and should she refuse her food, she is rejected as an animal unworthy of the name of Kochlani.

Partly from native qualities, and partly from constant association with mankind, the Arab Horse is a singularly intelligent animal. In Europe we scarcely give the Horse credit for the sensitive intelligence with which it is endowed, and look upon it rather as a machine for draught and carriage than a companion to man. The Arab, however, lives with his horse, and finds in it the docility and intelligence which we are accustomed to associate with the dog rather than the Horse. It will follow him about and come at his call. It will stand for any length of time and await its rider without moving. Should he fall from its back, it will stop and stand patiently by him until he can remount; and there is a well-authenticated instance of an Arab Horse whose master had been wounded in battle, taking him up by his clothes and carrying him away to a place of safety.

Even in the very heat and turmoil of the combat, the true Arab Horse seems to be in his true element, and fully deserves the splendid eulogium in the Book of Job (xxxix. 19—25): " Hast thou given the horse strength? hast thou clothed his neck with thunder?

" Canst thou make him afraid as a grasshopper? the glory of his nostrils is terror.

" He paweth in the valley, and rejoiceth in his strength: he goeth on to meet the armed men.

" He mocketh at fear, and is not affrighted; neither turneth he back from the sword.

" The quiver rattleth against him, the glittering spear and the shield.

" He walketh the ground with fierceness and rage: neither believeth he that it is the sound of the trumpet.

" He saith among the trumpets, Ha, ha; and he smelleth the battle afar off, the thunder of the captains, and the shouting."

In another passage an allusion is made to the courage of the

Horse, and its love for the battle. "I hearkened and heard, but they spake not aright: no man repented him of his wickedness, saying, What have I done? Every one turned to his course, as

THE WAR HORSE.

the horse rusheth into the battle." (Jer. viii. 6.) Even in the mimic battle of the djereed the Horse seems to exult in the conflict as much as his rider, and wheels or halts almost without the slightest intimation.

The hoofs of the Arab Horses are never shod, their owners thinking that that act is not likely to improve nature, and even among the burning sands and hard rocks the Horse treads with unbroken hoof. In such a climate, indeed, an iron shoe would be worse than useless, as it would only scorch the hoof by day, and in consequence of the rapid change of temperature by day or night, the continual expansion and contraction of the metal would soon work the nails loose, and cause the shoe to fall off.

A tender-footed Horse would be of little value, and so we often find in the Scriptures that the hardness of the hoof is reckoned among one of the best qualities of a Horse. See, for example, Isa. v. 28: "Whose arrows are sharp, and all their bows bent, their horses' hoofs shall be counted like flint, and their wheels like a whirlwind." Again, in Micah iv. 13: "Arise and thresh, O daughter of Zion: for I will make thine horn iron, and I will make thy hoofs brass: and thou shalt beat in pieces many people." Allusion is here made to one mode of threshing, in which a number of Horses were turned into the threshing-floor, and driven about at random among the wheat, instead of walking steadily like the oxen.

In Judges v. 22 there is a curious allusion to the hoofs of the Horse. It occurs in the Psalm of Thanksgiving sung by Deborah and Barak after the death of Sisera: "Then were the horse-hoofs broken by the means of the prancings, the prancings of their mighty ones."

Horses possessed of the qualities of courage, endurance, and sureness of foot are naturally invaluable; and even at the present day the Arab warrior esteems above all things a Horse of the purest breed, and, whether he buys or sells one, takes care to have its genealogy made out and hung on the animal's neck.

As to the mare, scarcely any inducement is strong enough to make an Arab part with it, even to a countryman, and the sale of the animal is hindered by a number of impediments which in point of fact are almost prohibitory. Signor Pierotti, whose long residence in Palestine has given him a deep insight into the character of the people, speaks in the most glowing terms of the pure Arab Horse, and of its inestimable value to its owner. Of the difficulties with which the sale of the animal is surrounded, he gives a very amusing account:—

"After this enumeration of the merits of the horse, I will describe the manner in which a sale is conducted, choosing the case of the mare, as that is the more valuable animal. The price varies with the purity of blood of the steed, and the fortunes of its owner. When he is requested to fix a value, his first reply is, 'It is yours, and belongs to you, I am your servant;' because, perhaps, he does not think that the question is asked with any real design of purchasing; when the demand is repeated, he either makes no answer or puts the question by; at the third demand he generally responds rudely with a sardonic smile, which is not a pleasant thing to see, as it is a sign of anger; and

ARAB HORSES.

then says that he would sooner sell his family than his mare. This remark is not meant as a mere jest; for it is no uncommon thing for a Bedawy to give his parents as hostages rather than separate himself from his friend.

"If, however, owing to some misfortune, he determines on selling his mare, it is very doubtful whether he or his parents will allow her to leave their country without taking the precaution to render her unfit for breeding.

"There are many methods of arranging the sale, all of which I should like to describe particularly; however, I will confine myself to a general statement. Before the purchaser enters upon the question of the price to be paid, he must ascertain that the parents, friends, and allies of the owners give their consent to the sale, without which some difficulty or other may arise, or perhaps the mare may be stolen from her new master. He must also obtain an unquestionable warranty that she is fit for breeding purposes, and that no other has a prior claim to any part of her body. This last precaution may seem rather strange, but it arises from the following custom. It sometimes happens that, when a Bedawy is greatly in want of money, he raises it most easily by selling a member of his horse; so that very frequently a horse belongs to a number of owners, one of whom has purchased the right fore-leg, another the left, another the hind-leg, or the tail, or an ear, or the like; and the proprietors have each a proportionate interest in the profits of its labour or sale.

"So also the offspring are sold in a similar manner; sometimes only the first-born, sometimes the first three; and then it occasionally happens that two or three members of the foal are, as it were, mortgaged. Consequently, any one who is ignorant of this custom may find that, after he has paid the price of the mare to her supposed owner, a third person arises who demands to be paid the value of his part; and, if the purchaser refuse to comply, he may find himself in a very unpleasant situation, without any possibility of obtaining help from the local government. Whoever sells his mare entirely, without reserving to himself one or two parts, must be on good terms with the confederate chiefs in the neighbourhood, and must have obtained their formal sanction, otherwise they would universally despise him, and perhaps lie in wait to kill him, so that his only hope of escape would be a disgraceful flight, just as if he had committed

BUYING AN ARAB HORSE.

some great crime. It is an easier matter to purchase a stallion; but even in this case the above formalities must be observed.

"These remarks only apply to buying horses of the purest blood; those of inferior race are obtained without difficulty, and at fair prices."

For some reason, perhaps the total severance of the Israelites from the people among whom they had lived so long in captivity, the use of the Horse, or, at all events, the breeding of it, was forbidden to the Israelites; see Deut. xvi. 16. After prophesying that the Israelites, when they had settled themselves in the Promised Land, would want a king, the inspired writer next ordains that the new king must be chosen by Divine command, and must belong to one of the twelve tribes. He then proceeds as follows:—"But he shall not multiply horses to himself, nor cause the people to return to Egypt, to the end that he should multiply horses: forasmuch as the Lord hath said unto you, Ye shall henceforth return no more that way."

The foresight of this prophetical writer was afterwards shown by the fact that many kings of Israel did send to Egypt for Horses, Egypt being the chief source from which these animals were obtained. And, judging from the monuments to which reference has been made, the Horse of Egypt was precisely the same animal as the Arab Horse of the present day, and was probably obtained from nomad breeders.

In spite of the prohibitory edict, both David and Solomon used Horses in battle, and the latter supplied himself largely from Egypt, disregarding as utterly the interdict against plurality of Horses as that against plurality of wives, which immediately follows.

David seems to have been the first king who established a force of chariots, and this he evidently did for the purpose of action on the flat grounds of Palestine, where infantry were at a great disadvantage when attacked by the dreaded chariots; yet he did not controvert the law by multiplying to himself Horses, or even by importing them from Egypt; and when he had an opportunity of adding to his army an enormous force of chariots, he only employed as many as he thought were sufficient for his purpose. After he defeated Hadadezer, and had taken from him a thousand chariots with their Horses, together with seven

THE ARAB'S FAVOURITE STEEDS.

hundred cavalry, he houghed all the Horses except those which were needed for one hundred chariots.

Solomon, however, was more lax, and systematically broke the ancient law by multiplying Horses exceedingly, and sending to Egypt for them. We learn from 1 Kings iv. 26 of the enormous establishment which he kept up both for chariots and cavalry. Besides those which were given to him as tribute, he purchased both chariots and their Horses from Egypt and Syria.

Chariots were far more valued in battle than horsemen, probably because their weight made their onset irresistible against infantry, who had no better weapons than bows and spears. The slingers themselves could make little impression on the chariots; and even if the driver, or the warrior who fought in the chariot, or his attendant, happened to be killed, the weighty machine, with its two Horses, still went on its destructive way.

Of their use in battle we find very early mention. For example, in Exod. xiv. 6 it is mentioned that Pharaoh made ready

PHARAOH PURSUES THE ISRAELITES WITH CHARIOTS AND HORSES, AND THE SEA COVERS THEM.

his chariot to pursue the Israelites; and in a subsequent part of the same chapter we find that six hundred of the Egyptian chariot force accompanied their master in the pursuit, and that the whole army was delayed because the loss of the chariot wheels made them drive heavily.

Then in the familiar story of Sisera and Jael the vanquished general is mentioned as alighting from his chariot, in which he would be conspicuous, and taking flight on foot; and, after his death, his mother is represented as awaiting his arrival, and saying to the women of the household, "Why is his chariot so long in coming? Why tarry the wheels of his chariot?"

During the war of conquest which Joshua led, the chariot plays a somewhat important part. As long as the war was carried on in the rugged mountainous parts of the land, no mention of the chariot is made; but when the battles had to be fought on level ground, the enemy brought the dreaded chariots to bear upon the Israelites. In spite of these adjuncts, Joshua won the battles, and, unlike David, destroyed the whole of the Horses and burned the chariots.

Many years afterwards, a still more dreadful weapon, the iron chariot, was used against the Israelites by Jabin. This new instrument of war seems to have cowed the people completely; for we find that by means of his nine hundred chariots of iron Jabin "mightily oppressed the children of Israel" for twenty years. It has been well suggested that the possession of the war chariot gave rise to the saying of Benhadad's councillors, that the gods of Israel were gods of the hills, and so their army had been defeated; but that if the battle were fought in the plain, where the chariots and Horses could act, they would be victorious.

So dreaded were these weapons, even by those who were familiar with them and were accustomed to use them, that when the Syrians had besieged Samaria, and had nearly reduced it by starvation, the fancied sound of a host of chariots and Horses that they heard in the night caused them all to flee and evacuate the camp, leaving their booty and all their property in the hands of the Israelites.

Whether the Jews ever employed the terrible scythe chariots is not quite certain, though it is probable that they may have done so; and this conjecture is strengthened by the fact that they were employed against the Jews by Antiochus, who had "footmen an hundred and ten thousand, and horsemen five thousand and three hundred, and elephants two and twenty, and three hundred chariots armed with hooks" (2 Macc. xiii. 2). Some commentators think that by the iron chariots mentioned above were signified ordinary chariots armed with iron scythes projecting from the sides.

By degrees the chariot came to be one of the recognised forces in war, and we find it mentioned throughout the books of the Scriptures, not only in its literal sense, but as a metaphor which every one could understand. In the Psalms, for example, are

ELIJAH IS CARRIED UP.

several allusions to the war-chariot. "He maketh wars to cease unto the end of the earth; He breaketh the bow, and cutteth the spear in sunder; He burneth the chariot in the fire" (Ps. xlvi. 9). Again: "At Thy rebuke, O God of Jacob, both the chariot and horse are cast into a dead sleep" (Ps. lxxvi. 6). And: "Some trust in chariots, and some in horses: but we will remember the name of the Lord our God" (Ps. xx. 7). Now, the force of these passages cannot be properly appreciated unless we realize to ourselves the dread in which the war-chariot was held by the foot-soldiers. Even cavalry were much feared; but the chariots were objects of almost superstitious fear, and the rushing sound of their wheels, the noise of the Horses' hoofs, and the shaking of the ground as the "prancing horses and jumping chariots" (Nah. iii. 2) thundered along, are repeatedly mentioned.

See, for example, Ezek. xxvi. 10 : " By reason of the abundance of his horses their dust shall cover thee : thy walls shall shake at the noise of the horsemen, and of the wheels, and of the chariots." Also, Jer. xlvii. 3 : " At the noise of the stamping of the hoofs of his strong horses, at the rushing of his chariots, and at the rumbling of his wheels, the fathers shall not look back to their children for feebleness of hands." See also Joel ii. 4, 5 : " The appearance of them is as the appearance of horses; and as horsemen, so shall they run.

" Like the noise of chariots on the tops of mountains shall they leap, like the noise of a flame of fire that devoureth the stubble, as a strong people set in battle array."

In several passages the chariot and Horse are used in bold imagery as expressions of Divine power: " The chariots of God are twenty thousand, even thousands of angels: the Lord is among them, as in Sinai, in the holy place" (Ps. lxviii. 17). A similar image is employed in Ps. civ. 3: " Who maketh the clouds His chariot : who walketh upon the wings of the wind." In connexion with these passages, we cannot but call to mind that wonderful day when the unseen power of the Almighty was made manifest to the servant of Elisha, whose eyes were suddenly opened, and he saw that the mountain was full of Horses and chariots of fire round about Elisha.

The chariot and horses of fire by which Elijah was taken from earth are also familiar to us, and in connexion with the passage which describes that wonderful event, we may mention one which occurs in the splendid prayer of Habakkuk (iii. 8) : " Was the Lord displeased against the rivers? was Thine anger against the rivers? was Thy wrath against the sea, that Thou didst ride upon Thine horses and Thy chariots of salvation?"

By degrees the chariot came to be used for peaceful purposes, and was employed as our carriages of the present day, in carrying persons of wealth. That this was the case in Egypt from very early times is evident from Gen. xli. 43, in which we are told that after Pharaoh had taken Joseph out of prison and raised him to be next in rank to himself, the king caused him to ride in the second chariot which he had, and so to be proclaimed ruler over Egypt. Many years afterwards we find him travelling in his chariot to the land of Goshen, whither he went to meet Jacob and to conduct him to the presence of Pharaoh.

At first the chariot seems to have been too valuable to the Israelites to have been used for any purpose except war, and it is not until a comparatively late time that we find it employed as a carriage, and even then it is only used by the noble and wealthy. Absalom had such chariots, but it is evident that he used them for purposes of state, and as appendages of his regal rank. Chariots or carriages were, however, afterwards employed by the Israelites as freely as by the Egyptians, from whom they were originally procured; and accordingly we find Rehoboam mounting his chariot and fleeing to Jerusalem, Ahab riding in his chariot from Samaria to Jezreel, with Elijah running before him; and in the New Testament we read of the chariot in which sat the chief eunuch of Ethiopia whom Philip baptized (Acts viii. 28).

As to the precise form and character of these chariots, they are made familiar to us by the sculptures and paintings of Egypt and Assyria, from both of which countries the Jews procured the vehicles. Differing very slightly in shape, the principle of the chariot was the same; and it strikes us with some surprise that the Assyrians, the Egyptians, and the Jews, the three wealthiest and most powerful nations of the world, should not have invented a better carriage. They lavished the costliest materials and the most artistic skill in decorating the chariots, but had no idea of making them comfortable for the occupants.

They were nothing but semicircular boxes on wheels, and of very small size. They were hung very low, so that the occupants could step in and out without trouble, though they do not seem to have had the sloping floor of the Greek or Roman chariot. They had no springs, but, in order to render the jolting of the carriage less disagreeable, the floor was made of a sort of network of leathern ropes, very tightly stretched so as to be elastic. The wheels were always two in number, and generally had six spokes.

To the side of the chariot was attached the case which contained the bow and quiver of arrows, and in the case of a rich man these bow-cases were covered with gold and silver, and adorned with figures of lions and other animals. Should the chariot be intended for two persons, two bow-cases were fastened to it, the one crossing the other. The spear had also its tubular case, in which it was kept upright, like the whip of a modern carriage.

Two Horses were generally used with each chariot, though three were sometimes employed. They were harnessed very simply, having no traces, and being attached to the central pole by a breast-band, a very slight saddle, and a loose girth. On their heads were generally fixed ornaments, such as tufts of feathers, and similar decorations, and tassels hung to the harness served to drive away the flies. Round the neck of each Horse passed a strap, to the end of which was attached a bell. This ornament is mentioned in Zech. xiv. 20: "In that day shall there be upon the bells of the horses, Holiness unto the Lord" —*i.e.* the greeting of peace shall be on the bells of the animals once used in war.

Sometimes the owner drove his own chariot, even when going into battle, but the usual plan was to have a driver, who managed the Horses while the owner or occupant could fight with both his hands at liberty. In case he drove his own Horse, the reins passed round his waist, and the whip was fastened to the wrist by a thong, so that when the charioteer used the bow, his principal weapon, he could do so without danger of losing his whip.

Thus much for the use of the chariot in war; we have now the Horse as the animal ridden by the cavalry.

As was the case with the chariot, the war-horse was not employed by the Jews until a comparatively late period of their history. They had been familiarized with cavalry during their long sojourn in Egypt, and in the course of their war of conquest had often suffered defeat from the horsemen of the enemy. But we do not find any mention of a mounted force as forming part of the Jewish army until the days of David, although after that time the successive kings possessed large forces of cavalry.

Many references to mounted soldiers are made by the prophets, sometimes allegorically, sometimes metaphorically. See, for example, Jer. vi. 23: "They shall lay hold on bow and spear; they are cruel, and have no mercy; their voice roareth like the sea; and they ride upon horses, set in array as men for war against thee, O daughter of Zion." The same prophet has a similar passage in chap. l. 42, couched in almost precisely the same words. And in chap. xlvi. 4, there is a further reference to the cavalry, which is specially valuable as mentioning the weapons used by them. The first call of the prophet is to the infantry: "Order ye the buckler and shield, and draw near to battle" (verse 3); and then follows the command to the cavalry,

THE ISRAELITES, LED BY JOSHUA, TAKE JERICHO.

"Harness the horses; and get up, ye horsemen, and stand forth with your helmets; furbish the spears, and put on the brigandines." The chief arms of the Jewish soldier were therefore the cuirass, the helmet, and the lance, the weapons which in all ages, and in all countries, have been found to be peculiarly suitable to the horse-soldier.

BEING desirous of affording the reader a pictorial representation of the war and state chariots, I have selected Egypt as the typical country of the former, and Assyria of the latter. Both drawings have been executed with the greatest care in details, every one of which, even to the harness of the Horses, the mode of holding the reins, the form of the whip, and the offensive and defensive armour, has been copied from the ancient records of Egypt and Nineveh.

We will first take the war-chariot of Egypt.

ANCIENT BATTLE-FIELD.

This form has been selected as the type of the war-chariot because the earliest account of such a force mentions the war-chariots of Egypt, and because, after the Israelites had adopted chariots as an acknowledged part of their army, the vehicles, as well as the trained Horses, and probably their occupants, were procured from Egypt.

The scene represents a battle between the imperial forces and a revolted province, so that the reader may have the opportunity of seeing the various kinds of weapons and armour which were in use in Egypt at the time of Joseph. In the foreground is the chariot of the general, driven at headlong speed, the Horses at full gallop, and the springless chariot leaping off the ground as the Horses bound along. The royal rank of the general in question is shown by the feather fan which denotes his high birth, and which is fixed in a socket at the back of his chariot, much as a coachman fixes his whip. The rank of the rider is further shown by the feather plumes on the heads of his Horses.

By the side of the chariot are seen the quiver and bow-case, the former being covered with decorations, and having the figure of a recumbent lion along its sides. The simple but effective harness of the Horses is especially worthy of notice, as showing how the ancients knew, better than the moderns, that to cover a Horse with a complicated apparatus of straps and metal only deteriorates from the powers of the animal, and that a Horse is more likely to behave well if he can see freely on all sides, than if all lateral vision be cut off by the use of blinkers.

Just behind the general is the chariot of another officer, one of whose Horses has been struck, and is lying struggling on the ground. The general is hastily giving his orders as he dashes past the fallen animal. On the ground are lying the bodies of some slain enemies, and the Horses are snorting and shaking their heads, significative of their unwillingness to trample on a human being. By the side of the dead man are his shield, bow, and quiver, and it is worthy of notice that the form of these weapons, as depicted upon the ancient Egyptian monuments, is identical with that which is still found among several half-savage tribes of Africa.

In the background is seen the fight raging round the standards. One chief has been killed, and while the infantry are pressing round the body of the rebel leader and his banner on one side, on the other the imperial chariots are thundering along to support the attack, and are driving their enemies before them. In the distance are seen the clouds of dust whirled into the air by the hoofs and wheels, and circling in clouds by the eddies caused by the fierce rush of the vehicles, thus illustrating the passage in Jer. iv. 13: "Behold, he shall come up as clouds, and his chariots shall be as a whirlwind: his horses are swifter than eagles. Woe unto us! for we are spoiled." The reader will see, by reference to the illustration, how wonderfully true and forcible is this statement, the writer evidently having been an eye-witness of the scene which he so powerfully depicts.

CHARIOT OF STATE.

THE second scene is intentionally chosen as affording a strong contrast to the former. Here, instead of the furious rush, the galloping Horses, the chariots leaping off the ground, the archers bending their bows, and all imbued with the fierce ardour of battle, we have a scene of quiet grandeur, the Assyrian king making a solemn progress in his chariot after a victory, accompanied by his attendants, and surrounded by his troops, in all the placid splendour of Eastern state.

Chief object in the illustration stands the great king in his chariot, wearing the regal crown, or mitre, and sheltered from the sun by the umbrella, which in ancient Nineveh, as in more modern times, was the emblem of royalty. By his side is his charioteer, evidently a man of high rank, holding the reins in a business-like manner; and in front marches the shield-bearer. In one of the sculptures from which this illustration was composed, the shield-bearer was clearly a man of rank, fat, fussy, full of importance, and evidently a portrait of some well-known individual.

The Horses are harnessed with remarkable lightness, but they bear the gorgeous trappings which befit the rank of the rider, their heads being decorated with the curious successive plumes with which the Assyrian princes distinguished their chariot Horses, and the breast-straps being adorned with tassels, repeated in successive rows like the plumes of the head

The reader will probably notice the peculiar high action of the Horses. This accomplishment seems to have been even more valued among the ancients than by ourselves, and some of the sculptures show the Horses with their knees almost touching their noses. Of course the artist exaggerrated the effect that he wanted to produce; but the very fact of the exaggeration shows the value that was set on a high and showy action in a Horse that was attached to a chariot of state. The old Assyrian sculptors knew the Horse well, and delineated it in a most spirited and graphic style, though they treated it rather conventionally. The variety of attitude is really wonderful, considering that all the figures are profile views, as indeed seemed to have been a law of the historical sculptures.

BEFORE closing this account of the Horse, it may be as well to remark the singular absence of detail in the Scriptural accounts. Of the other domesticated animals many such details are given, but of the Horse we hear but little, except in connexion with war. There are few exceptions to this rule, and even the oft-quoted passage in Job, which goes deeper into the character of the Horse than any other portion of the Scriptures, only considers the Horse as an auxiliary in battle. We miss the personal interest in the animal which distinguishes the many references to the ox, the sheep, and the goat; and it is remarkable that even in the Book of Proverbs, which is so rich in references to various animals, very little is said of the Horse.

THE HORSE. 313

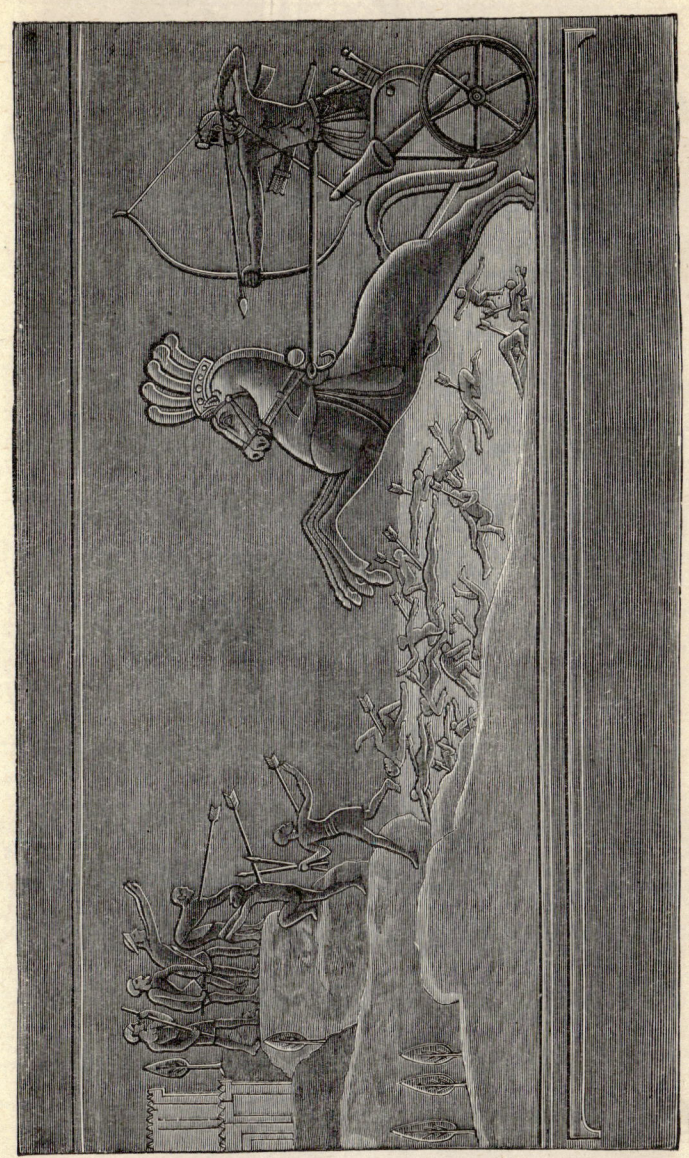

ANCIENT EGYPTIAN SCULPTURE REPRESENTING A VICTORIOUS KING IN HIS CHARIOT SLAYING HIS ENEMIES.

MUMMY OF AN EGYPTIAN KING (OVER THREE THOUSAND YEARS OLD).

THE ASS.

Importance of the Ass in the East—Its general use for the saddle—Riding the Ass not a mark of humility—The triumphal entry—White Asses—Character of the Scriptural Ass—Saddling the Ass—Samson and Balaam.

In the Scriptures we read of two breeds of Ass, namely, the Domesticated and the Wild Ass. As the former is the more important of the two, we will give it precedence.

In the East, the Ass has always played a much more important part than among us Westerns, and on that account we find it so frequently mentioned in the Bible. In the first place, it is the universal saddle-animal of the East. Among us the Ass has ceased to be regularly used for the purposes of the saddle, and is only casually employed by holiday-makers and the like. Some persons certainly ride it habitually, but they almost invariably belong to the lower orders, and are content to ride without a saddle, balancing themselves in some extraordinary manner just over the animal's tail. In the East, however, it is ridden by persons of the highest rank, and is decorated with saddle and harness as rich as those of the horse.

So far from the use of the Ass as a saddle-animal being a mark of humility, it ought to be viewed in precisely the opposite light. In consequence of the very natural habit of reading, according to Western ideas, the Scriptures, which are books essentially Oriental in all their allusions and tone of thought, many persons have entirely perverted the sense of one very familiar passage, the prophecy of Zechariah concerning the future Messiah. "Rejoice greatly, O daughter of Zion; shout, O daughter of Jerusalem: behold, thy King cometh unto thee: He is just, and having salvation; lowly, and riding upon an ass, and upon a colt the foal of an ass" (Zech. ix. 9).

Now this passage, as well as the one which describes its fulfilment so many years afterwards, has often been seized upon as a proof of the meekness and lowliness of our Saviour, in riding upon so humble an animal when He made His entry into Jerusalem. The fact is, that there was no humility in the case, neither was the act so understood by the people. He rode upon an Ass as any prince or ruler would have done who was engaged on a peaceful journey, the horse being reserved for war purposes. He rode on the Ass, and not on the horse, because He was the Prince of Peace and not of war, as indeed is shown very clearly in the context. For, after writing the words which have just been quoted, Zechariah proceeds as follows (ver. 10): "And I will cut off the chariot from Ephraim, and the horse from Jerusalem, and the battle bow shall be cut off: and He shall speak peace unto the heathen: and His dominion shall be from sea even to sea, and from the river even to the ends of the earth."

Meek and lowly was He, as became the new character, hitherto unknown to the warlike and restless Jews, a Prince, not of war, as had been all other celebrated kings, but of peace. Had He come as the Jews expected—despite so many prophecies—their Messiah to come, as a great king and conqueror, He might have ridden the war-horse, and been surrounded with countless legions of armed men. But He came as the herald of peace, and not of war; and, though meek and lowly, yet a Prince, riding as became a prince, on an Ass colt which had borne no inferior burden.

That the act was not considered as one of lowliness is evident from the manner in which it was received by the people, accepting Him as the Son of David, coming in the name of the

Highest, and greeting Him with the cry of "Hosanna!" ("Save us now,") quoted from verses 25, 26 of Ps. cxviii.: "Save now, I beseech Thee, O Lord: O Lord, I beseech Thee, send now prosperity."

"Blessed be He that cometh in the name of the Lord."

ENTERING JERUSALEM.

The palm-branches which they strewed upon the road were not chosen by the attendant crowd merely as a means of doing honour to Him whom they acknowledged as the Son of David. They were necessarily connected with the cry of "Hosanna!" At the Feast of Tabernacles, it was customary for the people to assemble with branches of palms and willows in their hands, and for one of the priests to recite the Great Hallel, *i.e.* Ps. cxiii. and cxviii. At certain intervals, the people responded with the cry of "Hosanna!" waving at the same time their palm-branches. For the whole of the seven days through which the feast lasted they repeated their Hosannas, always accompanying the shout with the waving of palm-branches, and setting them towards the altar as they went in procession round it.

Every child who could hold a palm-branch was expected to take part in the solemnity, just as did the children on the occasion of the triumphal entry. By degrees, the name of Hosanna was transferred to the palm-branches themselves, as well as to the feast, the last day being called the Great Hosanna.

The reader will now see the importance of this carrying of palm-branches, accompanied with Hosannas, and that those who used them in honour of Him whom they followed into Jerusalem had no idea that He was acting any lowly part.

Again, the woman of Shunem, who rode on an Ass to meet Elisha, a mission in which the life of her only child was involved, was a woman of great wealth (2 Kings iv. 8), who was able not only to receive the prophet, but to build a chamber, and furnish it for him.

Not to multiply examples, we see from these passages that the Ass of the East was held in comparatively high estimation, being used for the purposes of the saddle, just as would a high-bred horse among ourselves.

Consequently, the Ass is really a different animal. In this country he is repressed, and seldom has an opportunity for displaying the intellectual powers which he possesses, and which are of a much higher order than is generally imagined. It is rather remarkable, that when we wish to speak slightingly of intellect we liken the individual to an Ass or a goose, not knowing that we have selected just the quadruped and the bird which are least worthy of such a distinction.

Putting aside the bird, as being at present out of place, we shall find that the Ass is one of the cleverest of our domesticated animals. We are apt to speak of the horse with a sort of reverence, and of the Ass with contemptuous pity, not knowing that, of the two animals, the Ass is by far the superior in point of intellect. It has been well remarked by a keen observer of nature, that if four or five horses are in a field, together with one Ass, and there be an assailable point in the fence, the Ass is sure to be the animal that discovers it, and leads the way through it.

Take even one of our own toil-worn animals, turned out in a common to graze, and see the ingenuity which it displays when persecuted by the idle boys who generally frequent such places, and who try to ride every beast that is within their reach. It seems to divine at once the object of the boy as he steals up to it, and he takes a pleasure in baffling him just as he fancies that he has succeeded in his attempt.

SYRIAN ASSES.

Should the Ass be kindly treated, there is not an animal that proves more docile, or even affectionate. Stripes and kicks it resents, and sets itself distinctly against them; and, being nothing but a slave, it follows the slavish principle of doing no work that it can possibly avoid.

Now, in the East the Ass takes so much higher rank than our own animal, that its whole demeanour and gait are different from those displayed by the generality of its brethren. "Why, the very slave of slaves," writes Mr. Lowth, in his "Wanderer in Arabia," "the crushed and grief-stricken, is so no more in Egypt: the battered drudge has become the willing servant. Is that active little fellow, who, with race-horse coat and full flanks, moves under his rider with the light step and the action of a pony—is he the same animal as that starved and head-bowed object of the North, subject for all pity and cruelty, and clothed with rags and insult?

"Look at him now. On he goes, rapid and free, with his small head well up, and as gay as a crimson saddle and a bridle of light chains and red leather can make him. It was a gladdening sight to see the unfortunate as a new animal in Egypt."

Hardy animal as is the Ass, it is not well adapted for tolerance of cold, and seems to degenerate in size, strength, speed, and spirit in proportion as the climate becomes colder. Whether it might equal the horse in its endurance of cold provided that it were as carefully treated, is perhaps a doubtful point; but it is a well-known fact that the horse does not necessarily degenerate by moving towards a colder climate, though the Ass has always been found to do so.

There is, of course, a variety in the treatment which the Ass receives even in the East. Signor Pierotti, whose work on the customs and traditions of Palestine has already been mentioned, writes in very glowing terms of the animal. He states that he formed a very high opinion of the Ass while he was in Egypt, not only from its spirited aspect and its speed, but because it was employed even by the Viceroy and the great Court officers, who may be said to use Asses of more or less intelligence for every occasion. He even goes so far as to say that, if all the Asses were taken away from Egypt, travel would be impossible.

The same traveller gives an admirable summary of the character of the Ass, as it exists in Egypt and Palestine. "What, then, are the characteristics of the ass? Much the same as those which adorn it in other parts of the East—namely, it is useful for riding and for carrying burdens; it is sensible of kindness, and shows gratitude; it is very steady, and is larger, stronger, and more tractable than its European congener; its pace is easy and pleasant; and it will shrink from no labour, if only its poor daily feed of straw and barley is fairly given.

"If well and liberally supplied, it is capable of any enterprise, and wears an altered and dignified mien, apparently forgetful of its extraction, except when undeservedly beaten by its masters, who, however, are not so much to be blamed, because, having learned to live among sticks, thongs, and rods, they follow the same system of education with their miserable dependants.

"The wealthy feed him well, deck him with fine harness and silver trappings, and cover him, when his work is done, with rich Persian carpets. The poor do the best they can for him, steal for his benefit, give him a corner at their fireside, and in cold weather sleep with him for more warmth. In Palestine, all the rich men, whether monarchs or chiefs of villages, possess a number of asses, keeping them with their flocks, like the patriarchs of old. No one can travel in that country, and observe how the ass is employed for all purposes, without being struck with the exactness with which the Arabs retain the Hebrew customs."

The result of this treatment is, that the Eastern Ass is an enduring and tolerably swift animal, vying with the camel itself in its powers of long-continued travel, its usual pace being a sort of easy canter. On rough ground, or up an ascent, it is said even to gain on the horse, probably because its little sharp hoofs give it a firm footing where the larger hoof of the horse is liable to slip.

The familiar term "saddling the Ass" requires some little explanation.

The saddle is not in the least like the article which we know by that name, but is very large and complicated in structure. Over the animal's back is first spread a cloth, made of thick woollen stuff, and folded several times. The saddle itself is a very thick pad of straw, covered with carpet, and flat at the top, instead of being rounded as is the case with our saddles. The pommel is very high, and when the rider is seated on it, he is perched high above the back of the animal. Over the saddle is thrown a cloth or carpet, always of bright colours, and varying in costliness of material and ornament according to the wealth of the possessor. It is mostly edged with a fringe and tassels.

The bridle is decorated, like that of the horse, with bells, embroidery, tassels, shells, and other ornaments.

As we may see from 2 Kings iv. 24, the Ass was generally

guided by a driver who ran behind it, just as is done with donkeys hired to children here. Owing to the unchanging character of the East, there is no doubt that the "riders on asses" of the Scriptures

A STREET IN CAIRO, EGYPT.

rode exactly after the mode which is adopted at the present day. What that mode is, we may learn from Mr. Bayard Taylor's amusing and vivid description of a ride through the streets of Cairo:—

"To see Cairo thoroughly, one must first accustom himself to the ways of these long-eared cabs, without the use of which I would advise no one to trust himself in the bazaars. Donkey-riding is universal, and no one thinks of going beyond the Frank quarters on foot. If he does, he must submit to be followed by not less than six donkeys with their drivers. A friend of mine who was attended by such a cavalcade for two hours, was obliged to yield at last, and made no second attempt. When we first appeared in the gateway of an hotel, equipped for an excursion, the rush of men and animals was so great that we were forced to retreat until our servant and the porter whipped us a path through the yelling and braying mob. After one or two trials I found an intelligent Arab boy named Kish, who for five piastres a day furnished strong and ambitious donkeys, which he kept ready at the door from morning till night. The other drivers respected Kish's privilege, and henceforth I had no trouble.

"The donkeys are so small that my feet nearly touched the ground, but there is no end to their strength and endurance. Their gait, whether in pace or in gallop, is so easy and light that fatigue is impossible. The drivers take great pride in having high-cushioned red saddles, and in hanging bits of jingling brass to the bridles. They keep their donkeys close shorn, and frequently beautify them by painting them various colours. The first animal I rode had legs barred like a zebra's, and my friend's rejoiced in purple flanks and a yellow belly. The drivers ran behind them with a short stick, punching them from time to time, or giving them a sharp pinch on the rump. Very few of them own their donkeys, and I understood their pertinacity when I learned that they frequently received a beating on returning home empty-handed.

"The passage of the bazaars seems at first quite as hazardous on donkey-back as on foot; but it is the difference between knocking somebody down and being knocked down yourself, and one certainly prefers the former alternative. There is no use in attempting to guide the donkey, for he won't be guided. The driver shouts behind, and you are dashed at full speed into a confusion of other donkeys, camels, horses, carts, water-carriers, and footmen. In vain you cry out '*Bess*' (enough), '*Piacco*,' and other desperate adjurations; the driver's only reply is: 'Let the bridle hang loose!' You dodge your head under a camel-load of planks; your leg brushes the wheel of a dust-cart; you strike a fat Turk plump in the back; you miraculously escape up-

BEGGAR IN THE STREETS OF CAIRO.

setting a fruit-stand; you scatter a company of spectral, white-masked women; and at last reach some more quiet street, with the sensations of a man who has stormed a battery.

"At first this sort of riding made me very nervous, but presently I let the donkey go his own way, and took a curious interest in seeing how near a chance I ran of striking or being struck. Sometimes there seemed no hope of avoiding a violent collision; but, by a series of the most remarkable dodges, he

NIGHT-WATCH IN CAIRO.

generally carried you through in safety. The cries of the driver running behind gave me no little amusement. 'The hawadji comes! Take care on the right hand! Take care on the left hand! O man, take care! O maiden, take care! O boy, get out of the way! The hawadji comes!' Kish had strong lungs, and his donkey would let nothing pass him; and so wherever we went we contributed our full share to the universal noise and confusion."

This description explains several allusions which are made in the Scriptures to treading down the enemies in the streets, and to the chariots raging and jostling against each other in the ways.

The Ass was used in the olden time for carrying burdens, as it is at present, and, in all probability, carried them in the same way. Sacks and bundles are tied firmly to the pack-saddle; but poles, planks, and objects of similar shape are tied in a sloping direction on the side of the saddle, the longer ends trailing on the ground, and the shorter projecting at either side of the animal's head. The North American Indians carry the poles of their huts, or wigwams, in precisely the same way, tying them on either side of their horses, and making them into rude sledges, upon which are fastened the skins that form the walls of their huts. The same system of carriage is also found among the Esquimaux, and the hunters of the extreme North, who harness their dogs in precisely the same manner. The Ass, thus laden, becomes a very unpleasant passenger through the narrow and crowded streets of an Oriental city; and many an unwary traveller has found reason to remember the description of Issachar as the strong Ass between two burdens.

The Ass was also used for agriculture, and was employed in the plough, as we find from many passages. See for example, " Blessed are ye that sow beside all waters, that send forth thither the feet of the ox and the ass" (Isa. xxxii. 20). Sowing beside the waters is a custom that still prevails in all hot countries, the margins of rivers being tilled, while outside this cultivated belt there is nothing but desert ground.

The ox and the Ass were used in the first place for irrigation, turning the machines by which water was lifted from the river, and poured into the trenches which conveyed it to all parts of the tilled land. If, as is nearly certain, the rude machinery of the East is at the present day identical with those which were used in the old Scriptural times, they were yoked to the machine in rather an ingenious manner. The machine consists of an upright pivot, and to it is attached the horizontal pole to which the ox or Ass is harnessed. A machine exactly similar in principle may be seen in almost any brick-field in England; but the ingenious part of the Eastern water-machine is the mode in which the animal is made to believe that it is being driven by its keeper, whereas the man in question might be at a distance, or fast asleep.

The animal is first blindfolded, and then yoked to the end of the horizontal bar. Fixed to the pivot, and rather in front of the bar, is one end of a slight and elastic strip of wood. The projecting end, being drawn forward and tied to the bridle of the animal, keeps up a continual pull, and makes the blinded animal believe that it is being drawn forward by the hand of a driver. Some ingenious but lazy attendants have even invented a sort of self-acting whip, *i.e.* a stick which is lifted and allowed to fall on the animal's back by the action of the wheel once every round.

The field being properly supplied with water, the Ass is used for ploughing it. It is worthy of mention that at the present day the prohibition against yoking an ox and an Ass together is often disregarded. The practice, however, is not a judicious one, as the slow and heavy ox does not act well with the lighter and more active animal, and, moreover, is apt to butt at its companion with its horns in order to stimulate it to do more than its fair proportion of the work.

There is a custom now in Palestine which probably existed in the days of the Scriptures, though I have not been able to find any reference to it. Whenever an Ass is disobedient and strays from its master, the man who captures the trespasser on his grounds clips a piece out of its ear before he returns it to its owner. Each time that the animal is caught on forbidden grounds it receives a fresh clip of the ear. By looking at the ears of an Ass, therefore, any one can tell whether it has ever been a straggler ; and if so, he knows the number of times that it has strayed, by merely counting the clip-marks, which always begin at the tip of the ear, and extend along the edges. Any Ass, no matter how handsome it may be, that has many of those clips, is always rejected by experienced travellers, as it is sure to be a dull as well as a disobedient beast.

There are recorded in the Scriptures two remarkable circumstances connected with the Ass, which, however, need but a few words. The first is the journey of Balaam from Pethor to Moab, in the course of which there occurred that singular incident of the Ass speaking in human language (see Numb. xxii. 21, 35). The second is the well-known episode in the story of Samson, where he is recorded as breaking the cords with which his enemies had bound him, and killing a thousand Philistines with the fresh jaw-bone of an Ass.

THE WILD ASS.

Various allusions to the Wild Ass—Its swiftness and wildness—The Wild Ass of Asia and Africa—How the Wild Ass is hunted—Excellence of its flesh—Meeting a Wild Ass—Origin of the domestic Ass—The Wild Asses of Quito.

THERE are several passages of Scripture in which the Wild Ass is distinguished from the domesticated animal, and in all of them there is some reference made to its swiftness, its intractable nature, and love of freedom. It is an astonishingly swift animal, so that on the level ground even the best horse has scarcely a chance of overtaking it. It is exceedingly wary, its sight, hearing, and sense of scent being equally keen, so that to approach it by craft is a most difficult task.

Like many other wild animals, it has a custom of ascending hills or rising grounds, and thence surveying the country, and even in the plains it will generally contrive to discover some earth-mound or heap of sand from which it may act as sentinel and give the alarm in case of danger. It is a gregarious animal, always assembling in herds, varying from two or three to several hundred in number, and has a habit of partial migration in search of green food, traversing large tracts of country in its passage.

It has a curiously intractable disposition, and, even when captured very young, can scarcely ever be brought to bear a burden or draw a vehicle.

Attempts have been often made to domesticate the young that have been born in captivity, but with very slight success, the wild nature of the animal constantly breaking out, even when it appears to have become moderately tractable.

Although the Wild Ass does not seem to have lived within the limits of the Holy Land, it was common enough in the surrounding country, and, from the frequent references made to it in Scriptures, was well known to the ancient Jews.

We will now look at the various passages in which the Wild Ass is mentioned, and begin with the splendid description in Job xxxix. 5–8:

" Who hath sent out the wild ass free? or who hath loosed the bands of the wild ass?

" Whose house I have made the wilderness, and the barren lands (or salt places) his dwellings.

" He scorneth the multitude of the city, neither regardeth he the crying of the driver.

" The range of the mountains is his pasture, and he searcheth after every green thing."

Here we have the animal described with the minuteness and truth of detail that can only be found in personal knowledge; its love of freedom, its avoidance of mankind, and its migration in search of pasture.

Another allusion to the pasture-seeking habits of the animal is to be found in chapter vi. of the same book, verse 5: " Doth the wild ass bray when he hath grass?" or, according to the version of the Jewish Bible, " over tender grass?"

A very vívid account of the appearance of the animal in its wild state is given by Sir R. Kerr Porter, who was allowed by a Wild Ass to approach within a moderate distance, the animal evidently seeing that he was not one of the people to whom it was accustomed, and being curious enough to allow the stranger to approach him.

"The sun was just rising over the summit of the eastern mountains, when my greyhound started off in pursuit of an animal which, my Persians said, from the glimpse they had of it, was an antelope. I instantly put spurs to my horse, and with my attendants gave chase. After an unrelaxed gallop of three miles, we came up with the dog, who was then within a short stretch of the creature he pursued; and to my surprise, and at first vexation, I saw it to be an ass.

"Upon reflection, however, judging from its fleetness that it must be a wild one, a creature little known in Europe, but which the Persians prize above all other animals as an object of chase, I determined to approach as near to it as the very swift Arab I was on could carry me. But the single instant of checking my horse to consider had given our game such a head of us that, notwithstanding our speed, we could not recover our ground on him.

"I, however, happened to be considerably before my companions, when, at a certain distance, the animal in its turn made a pause, and allowed me to approach within pistol-shot of him. He then darted off again with the quickness of thought, capering, kicking, and sporting in his flight, as if he were not blown in the least, and the chase was his pastime. When my followers of the country came up, they regretted that I had not shot the creature when he was within my aim, telling me that his flesh is one of the greatest delicacies in Persia.

"The prodigious swiftness and the peculiar manner in which he fled across the plain coincided exactly with the description that Xenophon gives of the same animal in Arabia. But above all, it reminded me of the striking portrait drawn by the author of the Book of Job. I was informed by the Mehnander, who had been in the desert when making a pilgrimage to the shrine of Ali, that the wild ass of Irak Arabi differs in nothing from the one I had just seen. He had observed them often for a short time in the possession of the Arabs, who told him the creature was perfectly untameable.

"A few days after this discussion, we saw another of these animals, and, pursuing it determinately, had the good fortune to kill it."

It has been suggested by many zoologists that the Wild Ass is the progenitor of the domesticated species. The origin of the domesticated animal, however, is so very ancient, that we have

HUNTING WILD ASSES.

no data whereon even a theory can be built. It is true that the Wild and the Domesticated Ass are exactly similar in appearance, and that an *Asinus hemippus*, or Wild Ass, looks so like an Asiatic *Asinus vulgaris*, or Domesticated Ass, that by the eye alone the two are hardly distinguishable from each other. But with their appearance the resemblance ends, the domestic animal being quiet, docile, and fond of man, while the wild animal is savage, intractable, and has an invincible repugnance to human beings.

This diversity of spirit in similar forms is very curious, and is strongly exemplified by the semi-wild Asses of Quito. They are the descendants of the animals that were imported by the Spaniards, and live in herds, just as do the horses. They combine the habits of the Wild Ass with the disposition of the tame animal. They are as swift of foot as the Wild Ass of Syria or Africa, and have the same habit of frequenting lofty situations, leaping about among rocks and ravines, which seem only fitted for the wild goat, and into which no horse can follow them.

Nominally, they are private property, but practically they may be taken by any one who chooses to capture them. The lasso is employed for the purpose, and when the animals are caught they bite, and kick, and plunge, and behave exactly like their wild relations of the Old World, giving their captors infinite trouble in avoiding the teeth and hoofs which they wield so skilfully. But, as soon as a load has once been bound on the back of one of these furious creatures, the wild spirit dies out of it, the head droops, the gait becomes steady, and the animal behaves as if it had led a domesticated life all its days.

THE MULE.

Ancient use of the Mule—Various breeds of Mule—Supposed date of its introduction into Palestine—Mule-breeding forbidden to the Jews—The Mule as a saddle-animal—Its use on occasions of state—The king's Mule—Obstinacy of the Mule.

THERE are several references to the MULE in the Holy Scriptures, but it is remarkable that the animal is not mentioned at all until the time of David, and that in the New Testament the name does not occur at all.

The origin of the Mule is unknown, but that the mixed breed between the horse and the ass has been employed in many countries from very ancient times is a familiar fact. It is a very strange circumstance that the offspring of these two animals should be, for some purposes, far superior to either of the parents, a well-bred Mule having the lightness, surefootedness, and hardy endurance of the ass, together with the increased size and muscular development of the horse. Thus it is peculiarly adapted either for the saddle or for the conveyance of burdens over a rough or desert country.

The Mules that are most generally serviceable are bred from the male ass and the mare, those which have the horse as the father and the ass as the mother being small, and comparatively valueless. At the present day, Mules are largely employed in Spain and the Spanish dependencies, and there are some breeds which are of very great size and singular beauty, those of Andalusia being especially celebrated. In the Andes, the Mule has actually superseded the llama as a beast of burden.

Its appearance in the sacred narrative is quite sudden. In Gen. xxxvi. 24, there is a passage which seems as if it referred to the Mule: "This was that Anah that found the mules in the wilderness." Now the word which is here rendered as Mules is

"Yemim," a word which is not found elsewhere in the Hebrew Scriptures. The best Hebraists are agreed that, whatever interpretation may be put upon the word, it cannot possibly have the signification that is here assigned to it. Some translate the word as "hot springs," while the editors of the Jewish Bible

MULES OF THE EAST.

prefer to leave it untranslated, thus signifying that they are not satisfied with any rendering.

The word which is properly translated as Mule is "Pered;" and the first place where it occurs is 2 Sam. xiii. 29. Absalom had taken advantage of a sheep-shearing feast to kill his brother Amnon in revenge for the insult offered to Tamar: "And the servants of Absalom did unto Amnon as Absalom had commanded. Then all the king's sons arose, and every man gat him up upon his mule, and fled." It is evident from this passage that the Mule must have been in use for a considerable time, as the sacred writer mentions, as a matter of course, that the king's sons had each his own riding mule.

ABSALOM IS CAUGHT IN THE BOUGHS OF AN OAK TREE.

Farther on, chap. xviii. 9 records the event which led to the death of Absalom by the hand of Joab. "And Absalom met the servants of David. And Absalom rode upon a mule, and the mule went under the thick boughs of a great oak, and his head caught hold of the oak, and he was taken up between the heaven and the earth; and the mule that was under him went away."

We see by these passages that the Mule was held in such high estimation that it was used by the royal princes for the saddle, and had indeed superseded the ass. In another passage we shall find that the Mule was ridden by the king himself when he travelled in state, and that to ride upon the king's Mule was considered as equivalent to sitting upon the king's throne. See, for example, 1 Kings i. in which there are several passages illustrative of this curious fact. See first, ver. 33, in which David gives to Zadok the priest, Nathan the prophet, and Benaiah the captain of the hosts, instructions for bringing his son Solomon to Gihon, and anointing him king in the stead of his father: "Take with you the servants of your lord, and cause Solomon my son to ride upon mine own mule, and bring him down to Gihon."

That the Mule was as obstinate and contentious an animal in Palestine as it is in Europe is evident from the fact that the Eastern mules of the present day are quite as troublesome as their European brethren. They are very apt to shy at anything, or nothing at all; they bite fiercely, and every now and then they indulge in a violent kicking fit, flinging out their heels with wonderful force and rapidity, and turning round and round on their fore-feet so quickly that it is hardly possible to approach them. There is scarcely a traveller in the Holy Land who has not some story to tell about the Mule and its perverse disposition; but, as these anecdotes have but very slight bearing on the subject of the Mule as mentioned in the Scriptures, they will not be given in these pages.

DANIEL REFUSES TO EAT THE KING'S MEAT.

SWINE.

The Mosaic prohibition of the pig—Hatred of Swine by Jews and Mahometans—The prodigal son—Supposed connexion between Swine and diseases of the skin—Destruction of the herd of Swine—The wild boar of the woods—The damage which it does to the vines.

MANY are the animals which are specially mentioned in the Mosaic law as unfit for food, beside those that come under the general head of being unclean because they do not divide the hoof and chew the cud. There is none, however, that excited such abhorrence as the hog, or that was more utterly detested.

It is utterly impossible for a European, especially one of the present day, to form even an idea of the utter horror and loathing with which the hog was regarded by the ancient Jews.

Even at the present day, a zealous Jew or Mahometan looks upon the hog, or anything that belongs to the hog, with an abhorrence too deep for words. The older and stricter Jews felt so deeply on this subject, that they would never even mention the name of the hog, but always substituted for the objectionable word the term "the abomination."

Several references are made in the Scriptures to the exceeding disgust felt by the Jews towards the Swine. The portion of the Mosaic law on which a Jew would ground his antipathy to the flesh of Swine is that passage which occurs in Lev. xi. 7: "And the swine, though he divide the hoof, and be clovenfooted, yet he cheweth not the cud ; he is unclean to you." But the very same paragraph, of which this passage forms the termination, treats of other unclean beasts, such as the coney (or hyrax) and the hare, neither of which animals are held in such abhorrence as the Swine

This enactment could not therefore have produced the singular feeling with which the Swine were regarded by the Jews, and in all probability the antipathy was of far greater antiquity than the time of Moses.

How hateful to the Jewish mind was the hog we may infer from many passages, several of which occur in the Book of Isaiah. See, for example, lxv. 3, 4: "A people that provoketh me to anger continually to my face; that sacrificeth in gardens, and burneth incense upon altars of brick;

"Which remain among the graves, and lodge in the monuments, which eat swine's flesh, and broth of abominable things is in their vessels." Here we have the people heaping one abomination upon another—the sacrifice to idols in the gardens, the burning of incense upon a forbidden altar and with strange fire, the living among the tombs, where none but madmen and evil spirits were supposed to reside, and, as the culminating point of iniquity, eating Swine's flesh, and drinking the broth in which it was boiled.

In the next chapter, verse 3, we have another reference to the Swine. Speaking of the wickedness of the people, and the uselessness of their sacrifices, the prophet proceeds to say : "He that killeth an ox is as if he slew a man ; he that sacrificeth a lamb, as if he had cut off a dog's neck ; he that offereth an oblation, as if he offered swine's blood." We see here how the prophet proceeds from one image to another: the murder of a man, the offering of a dog instead of a lamb, and the pouring out of Swine's blood upon the altar instead of wine—the last-mentioned crime being evidently held as the worst of the three. Another reference to the Swine occurs in the same chapter, verse 17: " They that sanctify themselves, and purify themselves in the gardens behind one tree in the midst, eating swine's flesh, and the abomination, and the mouse, shall be consumed together, saith the Lord."

Not only did the Jews refuse to eat the flesh of the hog, but they held in utter abomination everything that belonged to it, and would have thought themselves polluted had they been even touched with a hog's bristle. Even at the present day this feeling has not diminished, and both by Jews and Mahometans the hog is held in utter abhorrence.

Some recent travellers have made great use of this feeling. Signor Pierotti, for example, during his long sojourn in Palestine, found the flesh of the hog extremely beneficial to him. " How often has the flesh of this animal supported me, especially during the earlier part of my stay in Palestine, before I had learned to like the mutton and the goats' flesh! I give the preference to this meat because it has often saved me time by rendering a fire unnecessary, and freed me from importunate, dirty, and unsavoury guests, who used their hands for spoons, knives, and forks.

"A little piece of bacon laid conspicuously upon the cloth that served me for a table was always my best friend. Without this talisman I should never have freed myself from unwelcome company, at least without breaking all the laws of hospitality by not inviting the chiefs of my escort or the guides to share my meal; a thing neither prudent nor safe in the open country. Therefore, on the contrary, when thus provided I pressed them with the utmost earnestness to eat with me, but of course never succeeded in persuading them; and so dined in peace, keeping on good terms with them, although they did call me behind my back a ' dog of a Frank ' for eating pork.

" Besides, I had then no fear of my stores failing, as I always took care to carry a stock large enough to supply the real wants of my party. So a piece of bacon was more service to me than a revolver, a rifle, or a sword; and I recommend all travellers in Palestine to carry bacon rather than arms.

Such being the feelings of the Jews, we may conceive the abject degradation to which the Prodigal Son of the parable

THE PRODIGAL SON.

must have descended, when he was compelled to become a swine-herd for a living, and would have been glad even to have eaten the very husks on which the Swine fed. These husks, by the way, were evidently the pods of the locust-tree, or carob, of which we shall have more to say in a future page. We have in our language no words to express the depths of ignominy into which this young man must have fallen, nor can we conceive any office which in our estimation would be so degrading as would be that of swine-herd to a Jew.

How deeply rooted was the abhorrence of the Swine's flesh we can see from a passage in 2 Maccabees, in which is related a series of insults offered to the religion of the Jews. The temple in Jerusalem was to be called the Temple of Jupiter Olympus, and that on Gerizim was to be dedicated to Jupiter, the defender of strangers. The altars were defiled by forbidden things, and the celebration of the Sabbath, or of any Jewish ceremony, was punishable with death.

Severe as were all these afflictions, there was one which the Jews seem, from the stress laid upon it, to have felt more keenly than any other. This was the compulsory eating of Swine's flesh, an act which was so abhorrent to the Jews that in attempting to enforce it, Antiochus found that he was foiled by the passive resistance offered to him. The Jews had allowed their temples to be dedicated to the worship of heathen deities, they had submitted to the deprivation of their sacred rites, they had even consented to walk in procession on the Feast of Bacchus, carrying ivy like the rest of the worshippers in that most licentious festival. It might be thought that any people who submit to such degradation would suffer any similar in-

SWINE. 341

dignity. But even their forbearance had reached its limits, and nothing could induce them to eat the flesh of Swine.

Several examples of the resistance offered by them are recorded in the book just mentioned. Eleazer, for example, a man ninety years old, sternly refused to partake of the abominable

ELEAZAR REFUSES TO EAT SWINE'S FLESH.

food. Some of the officials, in compassion for his great age, advised him to take lawful meat with him and to exchange it for the Swine's flesh. This he refused to do, saying that his age was only a reason for particular care on his part, lest the young should be led away by his example. His persecutors then forced the meat into his mouth, but he rejected it, and died under the lash.

Another example of similar, but far greater heroism, is given by the same chronicler. A mother and her seven sons were urged with blows to eat the forbidden food, and refused to do so. Thinking that the mother would not be able to endure the

A MOTHER AND HER SEVEN SONS TORTURED FOR REFUSING TO EAT SWINE'S FLESH.

sight of her sons' sufferings, the officers took them in succession, and inflicted a series of horrible tortures upon them, beginning by cutting off their tongues, hands, and feet, and ending by roasting them while still alive. Their mother, far from counselling her sons to yield, even though they were bribed by promises of wealth and rank, only encouraged them to persevere, and, when the last of her sons was dead, passed herself through the same fiery trial.

It has been conjectured, and with plausibility, that the pig was prohibited by Moses on account of the unwholesomeness of its flesh in a hot country, and that its almost universal repudiation in such lands is a proof of its unfitness for food. In countries where diseases of the skin are so common, and where the dreaded leprosy still maintains its hold, the flesh of the pig is

SWINE. 343

thought, whether rightly or wrongly, to increase the tendency to such diseases, and on that account alone would be avoided.

It has, however, been shown that the flesh of Swine can be habitually consumed in hot countries without producing any

THE EVIL SPIRITS ENTER A HERD OF SWINE.

evil results; and, moreover, that the prohibition of Moses was not confined to the Swine, but included many other animals whose flesh is used without scruple by those very persons who reject that of the pig.

Knowing the deep hatred of the Jews towards this animal, we may naturally wonder how we come to hear of herds of Swine kept in Jewish lands.

Of this custom there is a familiar example in the herd of Swine that was drowned in the sea (Matt. viii. 28—34). It is an open question whether those who possessed the Swine were Jews of lax principles, who disregarded the Law for the sake of gain, or whether they were Gentiles, who, of course, were not bound by the Law. The former seems the likelier interpretation, the destruction of the Swine being a fitting punishment for their owners. It must be here remarked, that our Lord did not, as is often said, destroy the Swine, neither did He send the devils into them, so that the death of these animals cannot be reckoned as one of the divine miracles. Ejecting the evil spirits from the maniacs was an exercise of His divine authority; the destruction of the Swine was a manifestation of diabolical anger, permitted, but not dictated.

Swine are at the present day much neglected in Palestine, because the Mahometans and Jews may not eat the flesh, and the Christians, as a rule, abstain from it, so that they may not hurt the feelings of their neighbours. Pigs are, however, reared in the various monasteries, and by the Arabs attached to them.

WILD BOARS DEVOURING THE CARCASE OF A DEER.

WE now come to the wild animal. There is only one passage in the Scriptures in which the WILD BOAR is definitely mentioned, and another in which a reference is made to it in a paraphrase.

WILD BOARS.

The former of these is the well-known verse of the Psalms: "Why hast thou broken down her hedges, so that all they which pass by the way do pluck her?

"The boar out of the wood doth waste it, and the wild beast of the field doth devour it" (Ps. lxxx. 12, 13). The second passage is to be found in Ps. lxviii. 30. In the Authorized Version it is thus rendered: "Rebuke the company of spearmen, the multitude of bulls, with the calves of the people." If the reader will refer to the marginal translation (which, it must be remarked, is of equal authority with the text), the passage runs thus: "Rebuke the beasts of the reeds," &c. Now, this is undoubtedly the correct rendering, and is accepted in the Jewish Bible.

Having quoted these two passages, we will proceed to the description and character of the animal.

In the former times, the Wild Boar was necessarily much more plentiful than is the case in these days, owing to the greater abundance of woods, many of which have disappeared by degrees, and others been greatly thinned by the encroachments of mankind. Woods and reed-beds are always the habitations of the Wild Boar, which resides in these fastnesses, and seems always to prefer the reed-bed to the wood, probably because it can find plenty of mud, in which it wallows after the fashion of its kind. There is no doubt whatever that the "beast of the reeds" is simply a poetical phrase for the Wild Boar.

If there should be any cultivated ground in the neighbourhood, the Boar is sure to sally out and do enormous damage to the crops. It is perhaps more dreaded in the vineyards than in any other ground, as it not only devours the grapes, but tears down and destroys the vines, trampling them under foot, and destroying a hundredfold as much as it eats.

If the reader will refer again to Ps. lxxx. he will see that the Jewish nation is described under the image of a vine: "Thou hast brought a vine out of Egypt: Thou hast cast out the heathen and planted it," &c. No image of a destructive enemy could therefore be more appropriate than that which is used. We have read of the little foxes that spoil the vines, but the Wild Boar is a much more destructive enemy, breaking its way through the fences, rooting up the ground, tearing down the vines themselves, and treading them under its feet. A single party

WILD BOARS DESTROYING A VINEYARD.

of these animals will sometimes destroy an entire vineyard in a single night.

We can well imagine the damage that would be done to a vineyard even by the domesticated Swine, but the Wild Boar is infinitely more destructive. It is of very great size, often resembling a donkey rather than a boar, and is swift and active beyond conception. The Wild Boar is scarcely recognisable as the very near relation of the domestic species. It runs with such speed, that a high-bred horse finds some difficulty in overtaking it, while an indifferent steed would be left hopelessly behind. Even on level ground the hunter has hard work to overtake it; and if it can get upon broken or hilly ground, no horse can catch it. The Wild Boar can leap to a considerable distance, and can wheel and turn when at full speed, with an agility that makes it a singularly dangerous foe. Indeed, the inhabitants of countries where the Wild Boar flourishes would as soon face a lion as one of these animals, the stroke of whose razor-like tusks is made with lightning swiftness, and which is sufficient to rip up a horse, and cut a dog nearly asunder.

Although the Wild Boar is not as plentiful in Palestine as used to be the case, it is still found in considerable numbers. Whenever the inhabitants can contrive to cut off the retreat of marauding parties among the crops, they turn out for a general hunt, and kill as many as they can manage to slay. After one of these hunts, the bodies are mostly exposed for sale, but, as the demand for them is very small, they can be purchased at a very cheap rate. Signor Pierotti bought one in the plains of Jericho for five shillings. For the few who may eat the hog, this is a fortunate circumstance, the flesh being very excellent, and as superior to ordinary pork as is a pheasant to a barn-door fowl, or venison to mutton.

INDIAN ELEPHANT.

THE ELEPHANT.

The Elephant indirectly mentioned in the Authorized Version—The Elephant as an engine of war—Antiochus and his Elephants—Oriental exaggeration—Self-devotion of Eleazar—Attacking the Elephants, and their gradual abandonment in war.

EXCEPT indirectly, the Elephant is never mentioned in the Authorized Version of the Canonical Scriptures, although frequent references are made to ivory, the product of that animal.

The earliest mention of ivory in the Scriptures is to be found in 1 Kings x. 18: "Moreover the king (*i.e.* Solomon) made a great throne of ivory, and overlaid it with the best gold." This passage forms a portion of the description given by the sacred historian of the glories of Solomon's palace, of which this celebrated throne, with the six steps and the twelve lions on the steps, was the central and most magnificent object. It is named together with the three hundred golden shields, the golden vessel of the royal palace, and the wonderful arched viaduct crossing the valley of the Tyropœon, "the ascent by which he went up unto the house of the Lord," all of which glories so overcame the Queen of Sheba that "there was no more spirit in her."

KING SOLOMON, SEATED UPON HIS THRONE, RECEIVES THE QUEEN OF SHEBA.

We see, therefore, that in the time of Solomon ivory was so precious an article that it was named among the chief of the wonders to be seen in the palace of Solomon, the wealthiest and most magnificent monarch of sacred or profane history.

That it should not have been previously mentioned is very singular. Five hundred years had elapsed since the Israelites escaped from the power of Egypt, and during the whole of that time, though gold and silver and precious stones and costly raiment are repeatedly mentioned, we do not find a single passage in which any allusion is made to ivory. Had we not known that ivory was largely used among the Egyptians, such an omission would cause no surprise. But the researches of modern travellers have brought to light many articles of ivory that were in actual use in Egypt, and we therefore cannot but wonder that a material so valued and so beautiful does not seem to have been reckoned among the treasures which were brought by the Israelites from the land of their captivity, and which

INDIAN ELEPHANTS.

were so abundant that the Tabernacle was entirely formed of them.

In the various collections of Europe are many specimens of ivory used by the ancient Egyptians, among the chief of which may be mentioned an ivory box in the Louvre, having on its lid the name of the dynasty in which it was carved, and the ivory-tipped lynch-pins of the splendid war-chariot in Florence, from which the illustration on page 309 has been drawn.

The ivory used by the Egyptians was, of course, that of the African Elephant; and was obtained chiefly from Ethiopia, as we find in Herodotus ("Thalia," 114):—" Where the meridian declines towards the setting sun, the Ethiopian territory reaches, being the extreme part of the habitable world. It produces much gold, huge elephants, wild trees of all kinds, ebony, and men of large stature, very handsome and long-lived."

The passages in the Bible in which the Elephant itself is named are only to be found in the Apocrypha, and in all of them the Elephant is described as an engine of war. If the reader will refer to the First Book of the Maccabees, he will find that the Elephant is mentioned at the very commencement of the book. "Now when the kingdom was established before Antiochus, he thought to reign over Egypt, that he might have the dominion of two realms.

"Wherefore he entered into Egypt with a great multitude, with chariots, and elephants, and horsemen, and a great navy." (i. 16, 17.)

Here we see that the Elephant was considered as a most potent engine of war, and, as we may perceive by the context, the King of Egypt was so alarmed by the invading force, that he ran away, and allowed Antiochus to take possession of the country.

After this, Antiochus Eupator marched against Jerusalem with a vast army, which is thus described in detail:—"The number of his army was one hundred thousand footmen, and twenty thousand horsemen, and two and thirty elephants exercised in battle.

"And to the end that they might provoke the elephants to fight, they showed them the blood of grapes and mulberries.

"Moreover, they divided the beasts among the armies, and for every elephant they appointed a thousand men, armed with coats of mail, and with helmets of brass on their heads; and, besides this, for every beast were ordained five hundred horsemen of the best.

"These were ready at every occasion wheresoever the beast was; and whithersoever the beast went they went also, neither departed they from him.

"And upon the beasts were there strong towers of wood, which covered every one of them, and were girt fast unto them with devices; there were also upon every one two and thirty strong men that fought upon them, beside the Indian that ruled him.

"As for the remnant of the horsemen, they set them on this side and that side at the two fronts of the host, giving them signs what to do, and being harnessed all over amidst the ranks." (1 Macc. vi. 30, &c.)

It is evident from this description that, in the opinion of the writer, the Elephants formed the principal arms of the opposing force, these animals being prominently mentioned, and the rest of the army being reckoned as merely subsidiaries of the terrible beasts. The thirty-two Elephants appear to have taken such a hold of the narrator's mind, that he evidently looked upon them in the same light that the ancient Jews regarded chariots of war, or as at the present day savages regard artillery. According to his ideas, the thirty-two Elephants constituted the real army, the hundred thousand infantry and twenty thousand cavalry being only in attendance upon these animals.

Taken as a whole, the description of the war Elephant is a good one, though slightly exaggerated, and is evidently written by an eye-witness. The mention of the native mahout, or "Indian that guided him," is characteristic enough, as is the account of the howdah, or wooden carriage on the back of the animal.

The number of warriors, however, is evidently exaggerated, though not to such an extent as the account of Julius Cæsar's Elephants, which are said to have carried on their backs sixty soldiers, beside the wooden tower in which they fought. It is evident that, in the first place, no Elephant could carry a tower large enough to hold so many fighting men, much less one which would afford space for them to use their weapons.

A good account of the fighting Elephant is given by Topsel (p. 157):—"There were certain officers and guides of the Elephants, who were called *Elephantarchœ,* who were the governors of sixteen Elephants, and they which did institute and teach them martial discipline were called *Elephantagogi.*

"The Military Elephant did carry four persons on his bare back, one fighting on the right hand, another fighting on the left hand, a third, which stood fighting backwards from the Elephant's head, and a fourth in the middle of these, holding the rains, and guiding the Beast to the discretion of the Souldiers, even as the Pilot in a ship guideth the stem, wherein was required an equall knowledge and dexterity; for when the Indian which ruled them said, Strike here on the right hand, or else on the left, or refrain and stand still, no reasonable man could yield readier obedience."

This description is really a very accurate as well as spirited one, and conveys a good idea of the fighting Elephant as it appeared when brought into action.

Strangely enough, after giving this temperate and really excellent account of the war Elephant, the writer seems to have been unable to resist the fascination of his theme, and proceeds to describe, with great truth and spirit, the mode of fighting adopted by the animal, intermixed with a considerable amount of the exaggeration from which the former part of his account is free.

"They did fasten iron chains, first of all, upon the Elephant that was to bear ten, fifteen, twenty, or thirty men, on either side two panniers of iron bound underneath their belly, and upon them the like panniers of wood, hollow, wherein they placed their men at armes, and covered them over with small boards (for the trunck of the Elephant was covered with a mail for defence, and upon that a broadsword two cubits long); this (as also the wooden Castle, or pannier aforesaid) were fastened first to the neck and then to the rump of the Elephant.

"Being thus armed, they entered the battel, and they shewed unto the Beasts, to make them more fierce, wine, liquor made of Rice, and white cloth, for at the sight of any of these his courage and rage increaseth above all measure. Then at the sound of the Trumpet, he beginneth with teeth to strike, tear, beat, spoil, take up into the air, cast down again, stamp upon men under feet, overthrow with his trunck, and make way for his riders to pierce with Spear, Shield, and Sword; so that his horrible voice.

THE WAR ELEPHANT.

his wonderful body, his terrible force, his admirable skill, his ready and inestimable obedience, and his strange and seldom-seen shape, produced in a main battel no mean accidents and overturns."

In this account there is a curious mixture of truth and exaggeration. As we have already seen, the number of soldiers which the animal was supposed to carry is greatly exaggerated, and it is rather amusing to note how the "towers" in which they fought are modified into "panniers." Then the method by which the animal is incited to the combat is partly true, and partly false. Of course an Elephant is not angered by seeing a piece of white cloth, or by looking at wine, or a liquor made of rice.

But that the wine, or the "liquor made of rice," *i.e.* arrack, was administered to the Elephant before it was brought into the battle-field, is likely enough. Elephants are wonderfully fond of strong drink. They can be incited to perform any task within their powers by a provision of arrack, and when stimulated by a plentiful supply of their favourite drink they would be in good fighting condition.

Next we find the writer describing the Elephant as being furnished with a coating of mail armour on its proboscis, the end of which was armed with a sword a yard in length. Now any one who is acquainted with the Elephant will see at once that such offensive and defensive armour would deprive the animal of the full use of the proboscis, and would, therefore, only weaken, and not strengthen, its use in battle. Accordingly we find that the writer, when describing with perfect accuracy the mode in which the Elephant fights, utterly omits all mention of the sword and the mailed proboscis, and describes the animal, not as striking or thrusting with the sword, but as overthrowing with the trunk, taking up into the air, and casting down again—acts which could only be performed when the proboscis was unencumbered by armour. The use of weapons was left to the soldiers that fought upon its back, the principal object of the huge animal being to trample its way through the opposing ranks, and to make a way for the soldiers that followed.

It may be easily imagined that, before soldiers become familiarized with the appearance of the Elephant, they might be pardoned for being panic-struck at the sight of so strange an animal. Not only was it formidable for its vast size, and for the armed men which it carried, but for the obedience which it rendered to its keeper, and the skill with which it wielded the strange but powerful weapon with which Nature had armed it.

At first, the very approach of so terrible a foe struck consternation into the soldiers, who knew of no mode by which they could oppose the gigantic beast, which came on in its swift, swinging pace, crushing its way by sheer weight through the ranks, and striking right and left with its proboscis. No other method of checking the Elephant, except by self-sacrifice, could be found; and in 1 Macc. vi. 43—46, we read how Eleazar, the son of Mattathias, nobly devoted himself for his country.

"Eleazar also, surnamed Savaran, perceiving that one of the beasts, armed with royal harness, was higher than all the rest, and supposing that the king was upon him,

"Put himself in jeopardy, to the end he might deliver his people, and get him a perpetual name.

"Whereupon he ran upon him courageously, through the midst of the battle, slaying on the right hand and on the left, so that they were divided from him on both sides.

"Which done, he crept under the elephant, and thrust him under, and slew him; whereupon the elephant fell down upon him, and he died."

I may here mention that the surname of Savaran, or Avaran, as it ought to be called, signifies one who pierces an animal from behind, and was given to him after his death, in honour of his exploit.

At first, then, Elephants were the most formidable engines of war that could be brought into the battle-field, and the very sight of these huge beasts, towering above even the helmets of the cavalry, disheartened the enemy so much that victory became easy.

After a while, however, when time for reflection had been allowed, the more intellectual among the soldiers began to think that, after all, the Elephant was not a mere engine, but a living animal, and, as such, subject to the infirmities of the lower animals. So they invented scheme after scheme, by which they baffled the attacks of these once dreaded foes, and sometimes even succeeded in driving them back among the ranks of their own soldiery, so maddened with pain and anger, that they dealt destruction among the soldiers for whom they were fighting, and so broke up their order of battle that the foe easily overcame them.

The vulnerable nature of the proboscis was soon discovered, and soldiers were armed with very sharp swords, set on long handles, with which they continually attacked the Elephants' trunks. Others were mounted on swift horses, dashed past the Elephant, and hurled their darts before the animal could strike them. Others, again, were placed in chariots, and armed with very long and sharply-pointed spears. Several of these chariots would be driven simultaneously against an Elephant, and sometimes succeeded in killing the animal. Slingers also were told off for the express purpose of clearing the "castles," or howdahs, of the soldiers who fought on the Elephants' backs, and their especial object was the native mahout, who sat on the animal's neck.

Sometimes they made way for the Elephant as it pressed forward, and then closed round it, so as to make it the central mark, on which converged a hail of javelins, arrows, and stones on every side, until the huge animal sank beneath its many wounds. By degrees, therefore, the Elephant was found to be so uncertain an engine of war, that its use was gradually discontinued, and finally abandoned altogether.

The Elephant which was employed in these wars was the Indian species, *Elephas Indicus*, which is thought to be more susceptible of education than the African Elephant. The latter, however, has been tamed, and, in the days of Rome's greatest splendour, was taught to perform a series of tricks that seem almost incredible. As, however, the Indian species is that with which we have here to do, I have selected it for the principal illustrations.

It may be at once distinguished from its African relative by the comparatively small ears, those of the African Elephant reaching above the back of the head, and drooping well below the neck. The shape of the head, too, is different. In the Indian species, only the males bear tusks, and even many of them are unarmed. In the African species, however, both sexes bear tusks, those of the male furnishing the best ivory, with its

THE ELEPHANT. 359

peculiar creamy colour and beautiful graining, and those of the female being smaller in size, and producing ivory of a much inferior quality.

AFRICAN ELEPHANTS.

The Elephant, whether of Asia or Africa, always lives in herds varying greatly in numbers, and invariably found in the deepest forests, or in their near vicinity. Both species are fond of water, and never wander far from some stream or fountain, although they can, and do, make tolerably long journeys for the purpose of obtaining the needful supply of liquid.

They have a curious capability of laying up a store of water in their interior, somewhat after the fashion of the camel, but also possess the strange accomplishment of drawing the liquid supply from their stomachs by means of their trunks, and scattering it in a shower over their backs to cool their heated bodies.

When drinking, the Elephant inserts the tip of his trunk into the stream, fills it with water, and then, turning it into his throat, discharges the contents.

The strangest portion of the Elephant is the trunk, or proboscis. This wonderful appendage is furnished at its extremity with a finger-like projection, with which the animal can pluck a single blade of grass or pick up a small object from the ground.

The value of the proboscis to the Elephant can be estimated when it is considered that without its aid the animal must soon starve to death. The short, thick neck and projecting tusks would entirely prevent it from reaching any of the vegetation upon which it feeds.

With the trunk, however, the Elephant readily carries its food to its mouth, and employs the useful member just as if it were a long and flexible arm.

The Elephant bears a worldwide fame for its capabilities as a servant and companion of man, and for the extraordinary development of its intellectual faculties. The Indian or Asiatic Elephant is the variety that is considered most docile and easy to train; these are almost invariably taken in a wild state from their native forests. The Indian hunters usually proceed into the woods with trained female Elephants. These advance quietly, and by their blandishments so occupy the attention of any unfortunate male that they meet that the hunters are enabled to tie his legs together and fasten him to a tree. His treacherous companions now leave him to struggle in impotent rage until he is so subdued by hunger and fatigue that the hunters can drive him home between two tame elephants. When once captured, he is easily trained.

The following curious instance of intelligence in an Elephant is given by a traveller in Ceylon:

"One evening, while riding in the vicinity of Kandy, my horse showed some excitement at a noise which was heard in the thick jungle, sounding something like '*Urmph! Urmph!*' uttered in a hoarse and dissatisfied tone. A turn in the forest explained the mystery, by bringing me face to face with a tame working Elephant unaccompanied by any driver or attendant. He was laboring painfully with a heavy beam of timber, which he had balanced across his tusks and was carrying to the village from which I had come.

"The pathway being narrow, he was compelled to bend his head

ELEPHANTS' WATERING-PLACE.

to one side to permit the passage of the long piece of wood, and the exertion and inconvenience combined, led him to utter the dissatisfied sounds which had frightened my horse.

"On seeing us halt, the Elephant raised his head, looked at us for a moment, then dropped the timber, and forced himself backward among the bushes at the side of the road, so as to leave us plenty of room to pass.

"My horse still hesitated; the Elephant observed this, and impatiently crowded himself still deeper in the jungle, repeating his cry of, 'Urmph! Urmph!' but in a voice evidently meant to encourage us to come on. Still the horse trembled; and, anxious to observe the conduct of the two sagacious creatures, I forbore any interference. Again the Elephant wedged himself farther in among the trees and waited for us to pass him. At last the horse timidly did so, after which I saw the wise Elephant come out of the wood, take up the heavy timber upon his tusks, and resume his route, hoarsely snorting, as before, his discontented remonstrance."

Although so valuable an animal for certain kinds of work, the Elephant is hardly so effective an assistant as might be supposed. The working Elephant is always a delicate animal, and requires watchfulness and care; as a beast of burden he is unsatisfactory, for, although in the matter of mere strength there is hardly any weight that could be conveniently placed on him which he could not carry, it is difficult to pack it without causing abrasions of the Elephant's skin, which afterwards ulcerate.

His skin is easily chafed by harness, especially in wet weather. Either during long droughts, or too much moisture, his feet are also liable to sores which render him useless for months.

In India the Elephant is used more for purposes of state display or for hunting than for hard labor. It is especially trained for tiger-hunting, and, as there is a natural dread of the terrible tiger deeply implanted in almost all Elephants, it is no easy matter to teach the animal to approach his powerful foe.

A stuffed tiger-skin is employed for this purpose, and is continually shown to the Elephant until he learns to lose all distrust of the inanimate object, and to strike it, to crush it with his feet, or to pierce it with his tusks.

After a while a boy is put inside the tiger-skin, in order to accustom the Elephant to the sight of the tiger in motion.

TIGER.

The last stage in the proceedings is to procure a dead tiger, and to substitute it for the stuffed skin. Even with all this training, it most frequently happens that when the Elephant is brought to face a veritable living tiger the furious bounds, the savage yells, and gleaming eyes of the beast are so terrifying that he turns tail and makes a hasty retreat. Hardly one Elephant out of ten will face an angry tiger. The Elephant, when used in tiger-hunting, is always guided by a native driver, called a mahout, who sits astride of the animal's neck and guides its movements by means of the voice and the use of an iron hook at the end of a short stick.

The hunters who ride upon the Elephant sit in a kind of box called a howdah, which is strapped firmly upon the animal's back, or else merely rests upon a large flat pad furnished with cross-ropes for maintaining a firm hold. The Elephant generally kneels to

THE TIGER IN THE REEDS.

enable the riders to mount, and then rises from the ground with a peculiar swinging motion that is most discomposing to beginners in the art.

The chase of the tiger is among the most exciting and favourite sports in India. When starting on a hunt, a number of hunters usually assemble, mounted on Elephants trained for the purpose, and carrying with them a supply of loaded rifles in their howdahs, or carriages mounted on the Elephants' backs. Thus armed, they proceed to the spot where a tiger has been seen. The animal is usually found hidden in the long grass or jungle, which is frequently eight or more feet in height; and when roused, it endeavours to creep away under the grass. The movement of the leaves betrays him, and he is checked by a rifle-ball aimed at him through the jungle. Finding that he cannot escape without being seen, he turns round and springs at the nearest Elephant, endeavouring to clamber up it and attack the party in the howdah. This is the most dangerous part of the proceedings, as many Elephants will turn round and run away, regardless of the efforts of their drivers to make them face the tiger. Should, however, the Elephant stand firm, a well-directed ball checks the tiger in his spring; and he then endeavours to again escape, but a volley of rifle-balls from the backs of the other Elephants, who by this time have come up, lays the savage animal prostrate, and in a very short time his skin decorates the successful marksman's howdah.

THE CONEY, OR HYRAX.

The Shaphan of Scripture, and the correct meaning of the word—Identification of the Shaphan with the Syrian Hyrax—Description of the animal—Its feet, teeth, and apparent rumination—Passages in which the Coney is mentioned—Habits of the animal—Its activity and wariness—The South African Hyrax, and its mode of life—Difficulty of procuring it—Similarity in appearance and habits of the Syrian species—Three species of Hyrax known to naturalists

AMONG the many animals mentioned in the Bible, there is one which is evidently of some importance in the Jewish code, inasmuch as it is twice named in the Mosaic law.

That it was also familiar to the Jews is evident from other references which are made to its habits. This animal is the Shaphan of the Hebrew language, a word which has very wrongly been translated in the Authorized Version as Coney, *i.e.* Rabbit, the creature in question not being a rabbit, nor even a rodent. No rabbit has ever been discovered in Palestine, and naturalists have agreed that the true Coney or Rabbit has never inhabited the Holy Land. There is no doubt that the Shaphan of the Hebrew Scripture, and the Coney of the Vulgate, was the SYRIAN HYRAX (*Hyrax Syriacus*). This little animal is rather larger than an ordinary rabbit, is not unlike it in appearance, and has many of its habits. It is clothed with brown fur, it is very active, it inhabits holes and clefts in rocks, and it has in the front of its mouth long chisel-shaped teeth, very much like those of the rabbit. Consequently, it was classed by naturalists

THE HYRAX.

among the rodents for many years, under the name of Rock Rabbit. Yet, as I have already mentioned, it is not even a rodent, but belongs to the pachydermatous group of animals, and occupies an intermediate place between the rhinoceros and the hippopotamus.

If it be examined carefully, the rodent-like teeth will be seen to resemble exactly the long curved tusks of the hippopotamus, with their sharp and chisel-edged tips; the little feet, on a close inspection, are seen to be furnished with a set of tiny hoofs just like those of the rhinoceros; and there are many other points in its structure which, to the eye of a naturalist, point out its true place in nature.

In common with the rodents, and other animals which have similarly-shaped teeth, the Hyrax, when at rest, is continually working its jaws from side to side, a movement which it instinctively performs, in order that the chiselled edges of the upper and lower teeth may be preserved sharp by continually rubbing against each other, and that they may not be suffered to grow too long, and so to deprive the animal of the means whereby it gains its food. But for this peculiar movement, which looks very like the action of ruminating, the teeth would grow far beyond the mouth, as they rapidly deposit dental material in their bases in order to supply the waste caused at their tips by the continual friction of the edges against each other.

It may seem strange that an animal which is classed with the elephant, the rhinoceros, and the hippopotamus, all bare-skinned animals, should be clothed with a furry coat. The reader may perhaps remember that the Hyrax does not afford a solitary instance of this structure, and that, although the elephants of our day have only a few bristly hairs thinly scattered over the body, those of former days were clad in a thick and treble coat of fur and hair.

THERE are four passages of Scripture in which the CONEY is mentioned—two in which it is prohibited as food, and two in which allusion is made to its manner of life. In order to understand the subject better, we will take them in their order.

The first mention of the Coney occurs in Leviticus xi. 5, among the list of clean and unclean animals: "The coney, because he cheweth the cud, but divideth not the hoof; he is unclean unto you." The second is of a like nature, and is to be found in Deut. xiv. 7: "These ye shall not eat of them that chew the cud, or of them that divide the cloven hoof; as the camel, and the hare, and the coney: for they chew the cud, but divide not the hoof; therefore they are unclean unto you."

The remaining passages, which describe the habits of the Coney, are as follow. The first alludes to the rock-loving habits of the animal: "The high hills are a refuge for the wild goats, and the rocks for the conies." (Ps. civ. 18.) The second makes a similar mention of the localities which the animal frequents, and in addition speaks of its wariness, including it among the "four things which are little upon the earth, but they are exceedingly wise." The four are the ants, the locusts, the spiders, and the Conies, which "are but a feeble folk, yet make they their houses in the rocks."

We will take these passages in their order.

It has already been mentioned that the Hyrax, a true pachyderm, does not merely chew the cud, but that the peculiar and constant movement of its jaws strongly resembles the act of rumination. The Jews, ignorant as they were of scientific zoology, would naturally set down the Hyrax as a ruminant, and would have been likely to eat it, as its flesh is very good. It must be remembered that two conditions were needful to render an animal fit to be eaten by a Jew, the one that it must be a ruminant, and the second that it should have a divided hoof. Granting, therefore, the presence of the former qualification, Moses points out the absence of the latter, thereby prohibiting the animal as effectually as if he had entered into a question of comparative anatomy, and proved that the Hyrax was incapable of rumination.

We now come to the habits of the animal.

As we may gather from the passages of Scripture which have already been mentioned, the Hyrax inhabits rocky places, and lives in the clefts that are always found in such localities. It is an exceedingly active creature, leaping from rock to rock with wonderful rapidity, its little sharp hoofs giving it a firm hold of the hard and irregular surface of the stony ground. Even in captivity it retains much of its activity, and flies about its cage with a rapidity that seems more suitable to a squirrel than to an animal allied to the rhinoceros and hippopotamus.

There are several species—perhaps only varieties—of the Hyrax, all of them identical in habits, and almost precisely similar in appearance. The best known of these animals is that which inhabits Southern Africa (*Hyrax Capensis*), and which is familiar to the colonists by its name of Klip-das, or Rock-rabbit. In situations which suit it, the Hyrax is very plentiful, and is much hunted by the natives, who esteem its flesh very highly.

Small and insignificant as it appears to be, even Europeans think that to kill the Hyrax is a tolerable test of sportsmanship, the wariness of the animal being so great that much hunter's craft is required to approach it.

The following account of the Hyrax has been furnished to me by Major A. W. Drayson, R.A.:—" In the Cape Colony, and over a great portion of Southern Africa, this little creature is found. It is never, as far as my experience goes, seen in great numbers, as we find rabbits in England, though the caution of the animal is such as to enable it to remain safe in districts from which other animals are soon exterminated.

" As its name implies, it is found among rocks, in the crevices and holes of which it finds a retreat. When a natural cavity is not found, the klip-das scratches a hole in the ground under the rocks, and burrows like a common rabbit. In size it is about equal to a hare, though it is much shorter in the legs, and has ears more like those of a rat than a rabbit. Its skin is covered with fur, thick and woolly, as though intended for a colder climate than that in which it is usually found; and, when seen from a distance, it looks nearly black.

" The rock-rabbit is a very watchful creature, and usually feeds on the summit of any piece of rock near its home, always choosing one from which it can obtain a good view of the surrounding country. When it sees an enemy approaching, it sits rigidly on the rock and watches him without moving, so that at a little distance it is almost impossible to distinguish it from the rock on which it sits. When it does move, it darts quickly out of sight, and disappears into its burrow with a sudden leap.

" In consequence of its activity and cunning, the rock-rabbit is seldom killed by white men; and when a hunter does secure one, it is generally by means of a long shot. The natives usually watch near its burrow, or noiselessly stalk it.

" I once killed one of these animals by a very long shot from a rifle, as it was sitting watching us from the top of a large boulder, at a distance of a hundred and fifty yards or thereabouts. The Dutch Boers who were with me were delighted at the sight of it, as they said it was good eating; and so it proved to be, the flesh being somewhat like that of a hare, though in our rough field-cookery we could not do justice to it."

This short narrative excellently illustrates the character of the animal, which is classed among the "four things which be exceeding wise." It is so crafty that no trap or snare ever set has induced a Hyrax to enter it, and so wary that it is with difficulty to be killed even with the aid of fire-arms. "No animal," writes Mr. Tristram, "ever gave us so much trouble to secure. . . . The only chance of securing one is to be concealed, particularly about sunset or before sunrise, on some overhanging cliff, taking care not to let the shadow be cast below, and then to wait until the little creatures cautiously peep forth from their holes. They are said to be common by those who have not looked for them, but are certainly not abundant in Palestine, and few writers have ever had more than a single glimpse of one. I had the good fortune to see one feeding in the gorge of the Kedron, and then to watch it as it sat at the mouth of its hole, ruminating, metaphorically if not literally, while waiting for sunset."

Should the Hyrax manage to catch a glimpse of the enemy, it utters a shrill cry or squeal, and darts at once to its hole—an action which is followed by all its companions as soon as they hear the warning cry. It is a tolerably prolific animal, rearing four or five young at a birth, and keeping them in a soft bed of hay and fur, in which they are almost hidden. If surprised in its hole and seized, the Hyrax will bite very sharply, its long chisel-edged teeth inflicting severe wounds on the hand that attempts to grasp it. But it is of a tolerably docile disposition, and in a short time learns to know its owner, and to delight in receiving his caresses.

Three species of Hyrax are known to naturalists. One is the Klip-das, or Rock-rabbit, of Southern Africa; the second is the Ashkoko of Abyssinia; and the third is the Syrian Hyrax, or the Coney of the Bible. The two last species have often been confounded together, but the Syrian animal may be known by the oblong pale spot on the middle of its back.

HIPPOPOTAMUS.

BEHEMOTH.

Literal translation of the word Behemoth—Various theories respecting the identity of the animal—The Hippopotamus known to the ancient Hebrews—Geographical range of the animal—"He eateth grass like the ox"—Ravages of the Hippopotamus among the crops—Structure of the mouth and teeth—The "sword or scythe" of the Hippopotamus—Some strange theories—Haunts of the Hippopotamus—The Egyptian hunter—A valuable painting—Strength of the Hippopotamus—Rising of the Nile—Modern hunters—Wariness of the Hippopotamus—The pitfall and the drop-trap.

IN the concluding part of that wonderful poem which is so familiar to us as the Book of Job, the Lord is represented as reproving the murmurs of Job, by showing that he could not even understand the mysteries of the universe, much less the purposes of the Creator. By presuming to bring a charge of injustice against his Maker, he in fact inferred that the accuser was more competent to govern the world than was the Creator, and thus laid himself open to the unanswerable irony of the splendid passages contained in chapters xl. xli., which show that man cannot even rule the animals, his fellow-creatures, much less control the destinies of the human race.

The passages with which we are at present concerned are to be found at the end of the fortieth chapter, and contain a most powerful description of some animal which is called by the name of Behemoth. Now this word only occurs once in the whole of the Scriptures, *i.e.* in Job xl. 15 : " Behold now behemoth, which I made with thee," &c. Some commentators, in consequence of the plural termination of the word, which may be literally translated as " beasts," have thought that it was a collective term for all the largest beasts of the world, such as the elephant, the hippopotamus, the wild cattle, and their like. Others have thought that the elephant was signified by the word Behemoth ; and some later writers, acquainted with palæontology, have put forward a conjecture that the Behemoth must have been some extinct pachydermatous animal, like the dinotherium, in which might be combined many of the qualities of the elephant and hippopotamus.

It is now, however, agreed by all Biblical scholars and naturalists, that the hippopotamus, and no other animal, is the creature which was signified by the word Behemoth, and this interpretation is followed in the Jewish Bible.

We will now take the whole of the passage, and afterwards examine it by degrees, comparing the Authorized Version with the Jewish Bible, and noting at the same time one or two variations in the rendering of certain phrases. The passage is given as follows in the Jewish Bible, and may be compared with our Authorized Version :—

" Behold now the river-horse, which I have made with thee : he eateth grass like an ox.

" Lo now, his strength is in his loins, and his vigour is in the muscles of his body.

" He moveth his tail like a cedar : the sinews of his thighs are wrapped together.

" His bones are pipes of copper ; his bones are like bars of iron.

" He is the chief of the ways of God : he that made him can alone reach his sword.

" That the mountains should bring forth food for him, and all the beasts of the field play there.

" He lieth under wild lotuses, in the covert of the reed, and fens.

" Wild lotuses cover him with their shadow ; willows of the brook compass him about.

"Behold, should a river overflow, he hasteth not: he feels secure should Jordan burst forth up to his mouth.

"He taketh it in with his eyes: his nose pierceth through snares."

We will now take this description in detail, and see how far it applies to the now familiar habits of the hippopotamus. A little allowance must of course be made for poetical imagery, but we shall find that in all important details the account of the Behemoth agrees perfectly with the appearance and habits of the hippopotamus.

In the first place, it is evident that we may dismiss from our minds the idea that the Behemoth was an extinct pachyderm The whole tenor of the passage shows that it must have been an animal then existing, and whose habits were familiar to Job and his friends. Now the date of the Book of Job could not have been earlier than about 1500 B.C., and in, consequence, the ideas of a palæozoic animal must be discarded.

We may also dismiss the elephant, inasmuch as it was most unlikely that Job should have known anything about the animal, and it is certain that he could not have attained the familiarity with its appearance and habits which is inferred by the context. Moreover, it cannot be said of the elephant that "he eateth grass as an ox." The elephant feeds chiefly on the leaves of trees, and when he does eat grass, he cannot do so "like an ox," but plucks it with his proboscis, and then puts the green tufts into his mouth. So characteristic a gesture as this would never have passed unnoticed in a description so full of detail.

That the hippopotamus was known to the ancient Hebrews is certain. After their sojourn in Egypt they had necessarily become familiarized with it; and if, as most commentators believe, the date of the Book of Job be subsequent to the liberation of the Israelites, there is no difficulty in assuming that Job and his companions were well acquainted with the animal. Even if the book be of an earlier date, it is still possible that the hippopotamus may, in those days, have lived in rivers where it is now as much extinct as it is in England. Mr. Tristram remarks on this point: "No hippopotamus is found in Asia, but there is no reason for asserting that it may not have had an eastern range as far as Palestine, and wallowed in the Jordan; for its bones are

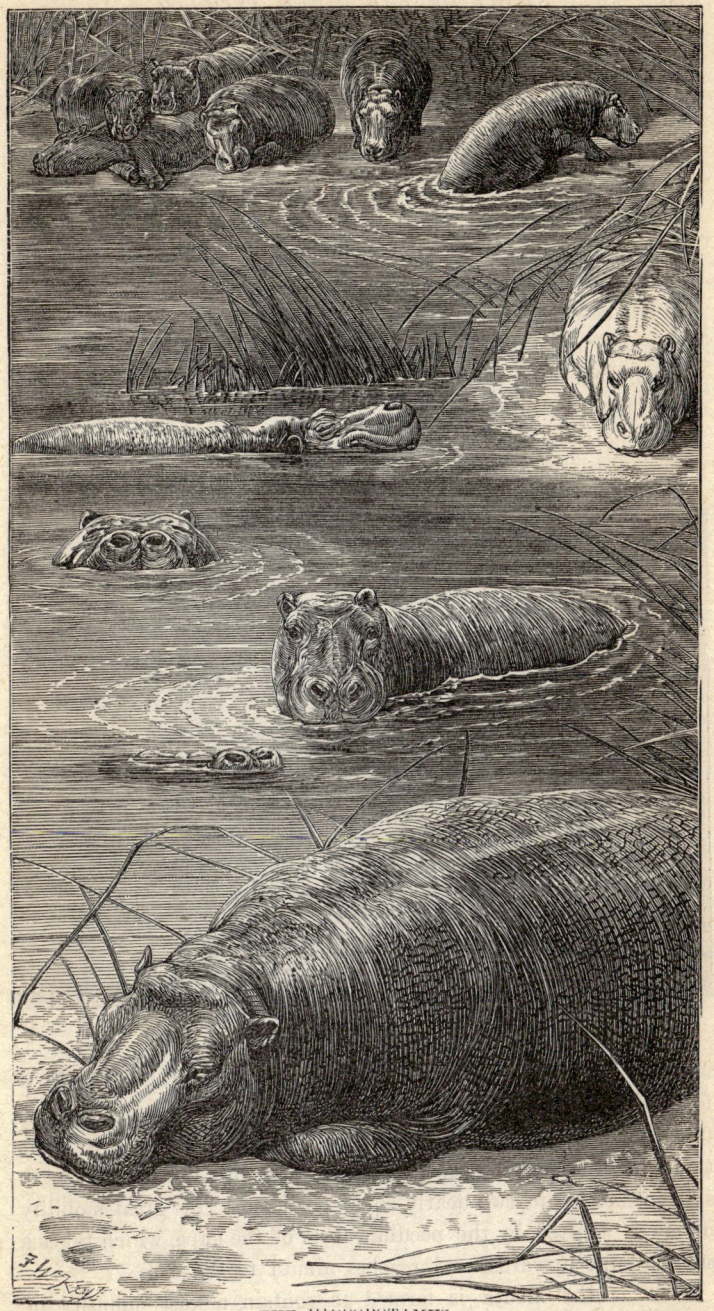

THE HIPPOPOTAMUS.

found in the *débris* of the rivers of Algeria, flowing into the Mediterranean, when tradition is quite silent as to its former existence.

There is no doubt that the hippopotamus and the urus were the two largest animals known to the Jews, and it is probably on that account that the former received the name of Behemoth.

Assuming, therefore, that the Behemoth is identical with the hippopotamus, we will proceed with the description.

"He eateth grass like the ox." The word which is here rendered "grass" is translated in Numb. xi. 5 as "leeks." It means, something that is green, and is probably used to signify green herbage of any description. Now it is perfectly true of the hippopotamus that it eats grass like an ox, or like cattle, as the passage may be translated. In order to supply its huge

THE GREAT JAWS OF THE HIPPOPOTAMUS.

massive body with nourishment, it consumes vast quantities of food. The mouth is enormously broad and shovel-shaped, so as to take in a large quantity of food at once; and the gape is so wide, that when the animal opens its jaws to their full extent it seems to split its head into two nearly equal portions. This great mobility of jaw is assisted by the peculiar form of the gape, which takes a sudden turn upwards, and reaches almost to the eyes.

Just as the mouth is formed to contain a vast quantity of

THE HIPPOPOTAMUS.

food, so the jaws and teeth are made to procure it. From the front of the lower jaw the incisor teeth project horizontally, no longer performing the ordinary duties of teeth, but being modified into tusks, which are in all probability used as levers for prising up the vegetables on which the animal lives. But the most singular portion of the jaw is the mode in which the canine teeth are modified so as to resemble the incisor teeth of rodents, and to perform a similar office.

These teeth are very long, curved, and chisel-edged at their tips, their shape being preserved by continual attrition, just as has been mentioned of the hyrax. The material of the teeth is peculiarly hard, so much so, indeed, that it is in great request for artificial teeth, the "verniers" of philosophical instruments, and similar purposes. Consequently, with these teeth the hippopotamus can cut through the stems of thick and strong herbage as with shears, and the strength of its jaws is so great that an angered hippopotamus has been known to bite a man completely in two, and to crush a canoe to fragments with a single movement of its enormous jaws.

Keeping this description in our minds, we shall see how true is the statement in verse 19. This passage is not adequately rendered in the Authorized Version: the word which is translated as "sword" also signifies a scythe, and evidently having that meaning in the text. The passage is best translated thus: "His Maker hath furnished him with his scythe."

The havoc which such an animal can make among growing crops may be easily imagined. It is fond of leaving the river, and forcing its way into cultivated grounds, where it eats vast quantities of green food, and destroys as much as it eats, by the trampling of its heavy feet. Owing to the width of the animal, the feet are placed very far apart, and the consequence is that the hippopotamus makes a double path, the feet of each side trampling down the herbage, and causing the track to look like a double rut, with an elevated ridge between them.

Some little difficulty has been made respecting the passage in verse 20, "Surely the mountains bring him forth food." Commentators ignorant of the habits of the hippopotamus, and not acquainted with the character of the country where it lives, have thought that the animal only lived in the rivers, and merely found its food along its banks, or at most upon the marshes at the river-side. The hippopotamus, say they, is not a dweller on the mountains, but an inhabitant of the river, and therefore this passage cannot rightly be applied to the animal.

Now, in the first place, the word *harim*, which is translated as "mountains" in the Authorized Version, is rendered as "hills" by many Hebraists. Moreover, as we know from many passages of Scripture, the word "mountain" is applied to any elevated spot, without reference to its height. Such places are very common along the banks of the Nile, and are employed for the culture of vegetables, which would not grow properly upon the flat and marshy lands around them. These spots are very attractive to the hippopotamus, who likes a change of diet, and thus finds food upon the mountains. In many parts of Egypt the river runs through a mountainous country, so that the hills are within a very short distance of the water, and are easily reached by the hippopotamus.

THE HIPPOPOTAMUS EATING GRASS.

We will now proceed to the next verse. After mentioning that the Behemoth can eat grass like an ox, and finds its food upon the hills, the sacred writer proceeds to show that in its moments of repose it is an inhabitant of the rivers and marshy ground: "He lieth under the shady trees, in the covert of the reed, and fens.

"The shady trees cover him with their shadow; the willows of the brook compass him about."

Here I may remind the reader that the compound Hebrew word which is rendered in the Authorized Version as "shady trees" is translated by some persons as "wild lotuses"—a rendering which is followed by the editor of the Jewish Bible. Apparently, however, the Authorized Version gives a more correct meaning of the term. Judging from a well-known Egyptian painting, which represents a hunter in the act of harpooning the hippopotamus, the tall papyrus reeds are the plants that are signified by this word, which occurs in no other place in the Scriptures.

Nothing can be more accurate than this description of the habits of the animal. I have now before me a number of sketches by Mr. T. Baines, representing various incidents in the life of the hippopotamus; and in one or two of them, the little islands that stud the river, as well as the banks themselves, are thickly clothed with reeds mixed with papyrus, the whole being exactly similar to those which are represented in the conventional style of Egyptian art. These spots are the favourite haunts of the hippopotamus, which loves to lie under their shadow, its whole body remaining concealed in the water, and only the eyes, ears, and nostrils appearing above the surface.

As reference will be made to this painting when we come to the Leviathan, it will be as well to describe it in detail. In order that the reader should fully understand it, I have had it translated, so to speak, from the conventional outline of Egyptian art into perspective, exactly as has been done with the Assyrian and Egyptian chariots.

In the foreground is seen the hunter, standing on a boat that closely resembles the raft-boat which is still in use in several parts of Africa. It is made of the very light wood called ambatch, by cutting down the requisite number of trees, laying them side by side so that their bases form the stern and their points the bow of the extemporized boat. They are then firmly lashed together, the pointed ends turned upwards, and the simple vessel is complete. It is, in fact, nothing more than a raft of triangular shape, but the wood is so buoyant that it answers every purpose.

In his hand the hunter grasps the harpoon which he is about to launch at the hippopotamus. This is evidently the same weapon which is still employed for that purpose. It consists of a long shaft, into the end of which a barbed iron point is loosely inserted. To the iron point is attached one end of a rope, and to the other end, which is held in the left hand of the harpooner, a float of ambatch wood is fastened.

When the weapon is thrown, the furious struggles of the wounded animal disengage the shaft of the harpoon, which is regained by the hunter; and as it dashes through the water, throwing up spray as it goes, the ambatch float keeps the end of the rope at the surface, so that it can be seen as soon as the animal becomes quieter. Sometimes it dives to the bottom, and remains there as long as its breath can hold out; and when it

A HIPPOPOTAMUS HUNT IN EGYPT.

(This picture is taken from an ancient Egyptian painting.)

comes up to breathe, it only pushes the nostrils out of the water under the shadow of the reeds, so that but for the float it might manage to escape.

In the meantime, guided by the float, the hunter follows the course of the animal, and, as soon as it comes within reach of his weapon, drives another spear into it, and so proceeds until the animal dies from loss of blood. The modern hunters never throw a second harpoon unless the one already fixed gives way, mainly employing a spear to inflict the last wounds. But if we may judge from this painting, the Egyptian hunter attached a new rope with every cast of his weapon, and, when the hippopotamus became weak from its wounds, gathered up the ropes and came to close quarters.

In the bow of the boat is the hunter's assistant, armed with a rope made lasso-wise into a noose, which he is throwing over the head of the hippopotamus, whose attitude and expression show evidently, in spite of the rudeness of the drawing, the impotent anger of the weakened animal.

Behind the hippopotamus are the tall and dense reeds and papyrus under the shelter of which the animal loves to lie, and on the surface of the water float the beautiful white flowers of the lotus.

In the Egyptian painting, the artist, in spite of the conventionalities to which he was bound, has depicted the whole scene with skill and spirit. The head and open mouth of the hippopotamus are remarkably fine, and show that the artist who drew the animal must have seen it when half mad with pain, and half dead from loss of blood.

The enormous strength of the hippopotamus is shown in verses 16, 18, the last of which passages requires a little explanation. Two different words are used here to express the bones of the animal. The first is derived from a word signifying strength, and means the "strong bones," *i.e.* those of the legs. These are hollow, and are therefore aptly compared to tubes or pipes of copper. The second term is thought by some Hebraists to refer to the rib-bones, which are solid, and therefore are not likened to tubes, but to bars of iron.

The 23d verse has been translated rather variously. The Authorized Version can be seen by reference to a Bible, and another translation, that of the Jewish Bible, is given on page 374. A third, and perhaps the best rendering of this passage is given by the Rev. W. Drake, in Smith's "Dictionary of the Bible:" "Lo, the river swelleth proudly against him, yet he is not alarmed; he is securely confident though a Jordan burst forth against his mouth."

In all probability reference is here made to the annual rising of the Nile, and the inundations which it causes. In some years, when it rises much above its usual height, the floods become most disastrous. Whole villages are swept away, and scarcely a vestige of the mud-built houses is left; the dead bodies of human beings are seen intermixed with those of cattle, and the whole country is one scene of desolation. Yet the almost amphibious hippopotamus cares nothing for the floods, as long as it can find food, and so, " though the river swelleth proudly against him," he is not alarmed.

From the use of the word "Jordan" in the same verse, it might be thought that the river of Palestine was intended. This, however, is not the case. The word "Jordan" is simply used as a poetical term for any river, and is derived from a Hebrew word which signifies " descending quickly."

We now come to the last verse of this noble description: "He taketh it in with his eyes." These words have also been variously rendered, some translating them as " He receiveth it (*i.e.* the river) up to his eyes." But the translation which seems to suit the context best is, " Who will take him when in his sight ? His nose pierceth through (*i.e.* detects) snares." Now, this faculty of detecting snares is one of the chief characteristics of the hippopotamus, when it lives near places inhabited by mankind, who are always doing their best to destroy it. In the first place, its body gives them an almost unlimited supply of flesh, the fat is very highly valued for many purposes, the teeth are sold to the ivory-dealers, and the hide is cut up into whips, or khoorbashes.

There is now before me a khoorbash, purchased from a native Egyptian who was beating a servant with it. The whip is identical with that which was used by the ancient Egyptians in urging the Israelites to their tasks, and the scene reminded the traveller so forcibly of the old Scriptural times that he rescued the unfortunate servant, and purchased the khoorbash, which is now in my collection.

Not content with hunting the hippopotamus, the natives contrive various traps, either pitfalls or drop-traps. The former are simply pits dug in the path of the animal, covered with sticks and reeds, and having at the bottom a sharp stake on which the victim is impaled, and so effectually prevented from escaping or damaging the pit by its struggles.

The drop-trap is a log of wood, weighted with stones, and

having at one end an iron spike, which is sometimes poisoned. The path which the animal takes is watched, a conveniently overhanging branch is selected, and from that branch the cruel spear is suspended, by a catch or trigger, exactly over the centre of the path. There is no difficulty in finding the precise centre

HIPPOPOTAMUS AND TRAP.

of the path, owing to the peculiar gait of the animal, which has already been described. One end of the trigger supports the spear, and to the other is attached a rope, which is brought across the path in such a way that when touched it relieves the spear, which is driven deeply into the animal's back. If well hung, the spear-blade divides the spine, and the wounded animal falls on the spot, but, even if it should miss a vital part, the poison soon does its fatal work.

In consequence of the continual persecution to which it is subjected, the hippopotamus becomes exceedingly wary, and, huge, clumsy, and blundering as it looks, is clever enough to detect either pitfall or drop-trap that have not been contrived with especial care. An old and experienced hippopotamus becomes so wary that he will be suspicious even of a bent twig, and, rather than venture across it, he will leave the path, force for himself a roundabout passage, and return to the path beyond the object that alarmed him.

Mr. T. Baines, to whose sketches I am indebted for the illustration, told me that the hippopotamus is possessed of much more intellect than might be expected from a creature of so dull, clumsy, and unpromising aspect. Apathetic it generally is, and, as long as it is left unmolested, does not care to molest even the human beings that intrude upon its repose.

It likes to lie in the shade of the reeds and rushes, and may be seen floating in the water, with only the nostrils, the eyes, and the ears above the surface, these organs being set in a line along the head, evidently for the purpose of allowing the whole body to be hidden under water while the three most important senses are capable of acting.

A canoe-man who knows the habits of the hippopotamus will fearlessly take his fragile vessel through a herd of the animals, knowing that, if he only avoids contact with them, they will not interfere with him. The only danger is, that a hippopotamus may rise under the canoe, and strike itself against the boat, in which case the animal is rather apt to consider the intruding object as an enemy, and to attack it, sometimes crushing the canoe between its teeth, and mostly upsetting it, and throwing the crew into the water. In such a case, the men always dive at once to the bottom of the river, and hold on to some weed or rock as long as they can exist without breathing. The reason for this proceeding is, that the hippopotamus always looks for its enemy upon the surface of the water, and, if the men were to swim to shore, they would be caught and killed before they had swum many strokes. But, as it sees nothing but the damaged canoe, its short-lived anger vanishes, and it sinks again into the river, leaving the men at liberty to regain and repair their vessel.

There is one passage in the description of the Behemoth which requires a few words of explanation: "He moveth his tail like a cedar" (v. 17).

Several commentators have imagined that this expression shows that the Behemoth must have been an animal which had a very long and powerful tail, and have adduced the passage as a proof that the crocodile was the animal that was signified by the Behemoth. Others, again, have shifted the position of the tail, and, by rendering it as the "proboscis," have identified the Behemoth with the elephant. There is, however, no necessity for straining the interpretation, the passage evidently signifying that the member in question is stiff and inflexible as the cedar-stem.

BABOON.

THE APE.

The Monkey tribe rarely mentioned in Scripture—Why the Ape was introduced into Palestine—Solomon's ships, and their cargo of Apes, peacocks, ivory, and gold—Various species of Monkey that might have been imported—Habits of the Monkey, and reverence in which it is held by the natives—The Egyptians and their Baboon worship—Idols and memorials—The Wanderoo—its singular aspect—Reasons why it should be introduced into Palestine—General habits of the Wanderoo—Various species of Monkey that may be included in the term "Kophim."

ANIMALS belonging to the monkey tribe are but sparingly mentioned in Holy Writ. If, as is possible, the Satyr of Scripture signifies some species of baboon, there are but three passages either in the Old or New Testament where these animals are mentioned. In 1 Kings x. 22, and the parallel passage 2 Chron. ix. 21, the sacred historian makes a passing allusion to apes as forming part of the valuable cargoes which were brought by Solomon's fleet to Tharshish, the remaining articles being gold, ivory, and peacocks. The remaining passage occurs in Is. xiii. 21, where the prophet foretells that on the site of Babylon satyrs shall dance.

The reason for this reticence is simple enough. No monkey was indigenous to Palestine when the various writers of the Bible lived, and all their knowledge of such animals must have been derived either from the description of sailors, or from the sight of the few specimens that were brought as curiosities from foreign lands. Such specimens must have been extremely rare, or they would not have been mentioned as adjuncts to the wealth of Solomon, the wealthiest, as well as the wisest monarch of his time. To the mass of the people they must have been practically unknown, and therefore hold but a very inferior place in the Scriptures, which were addressed to all mankind.

There is scarcely any familiar animal, bird, reptile or insect, which is not used in some metaphorical sense in the imagery which pervades the whole of the Scriptures. For example, the various carnivorous animals, such as the lion, wolf, and bear, are used as emblems of destruction in various ways; while the carnivorous birds, such as the eagle and hawk, and the destructive insects, such as the locust and the caterpillar, are all similarly employed in strengthening and illustrating the words of Holy Writ.

But we never find any animal of the monkey tribe mentioned metaphorically, possibly because any monkeys that were imported into Palestine must only have been intended as objects of curiosity, just as the peacocks which accompanied them were objects of beauty, and the gold and ivory objects of value—all being employed in the decoration of the king's palace.

The question that now comes before us is the species of monkey that is signified by the Hebrew word Kophim. In modern days, we distinguish this tribe of animals into three great sections, namely, the apes, the baboons, and the monkey; and according to this arrangement the ape, being without tails, must have been either the chimpanzee of Africa, the orang-outan of Sumatra, or one of the Gibbons. But there is no reason to imagine that the word Kophim was intended to represent any one of these animals, and it seems evident that the word was applied to any species of monkey, whether it had a tail or not.

Perhaps the best method of ascertaining approximately the

particular species of monkey, is to notice the land from which the animals came. Accordingly, we find that the ships of Solomon brought gold, ivory, apes, and peacocks, and that they evidently brought their cargoes from the same country. Consequently, the country in question must produce gold, and must be inhabited by the monkey tribe, by the elephant, and by the peacock. If the peacock had not been thus casually mentioned, we should have been at a loss to identify the particular country to which reference is made; but the mention of that bird shows that some part of Asia must be signified. It is most probable

THE RHESUS MONKEY.

that the vessels in question visited both India and Ceylon, although, owing to the very imperfect geographical knowledge of the period, it is not possible to assert absolutely that this is the case. In India, however, and the large island of Ceylon, gold, elephants, peacocks, and monkeys exist; and therefore we will endeavour to identify the animals which are mentioned under the general term Apes, or Kophim.

We are quite safe in suggesting that some of the apes in question must have belonged to the Macaques, and it is most likely that one of them was the RHESUS MONKEY.

390   STORY OF THE BIBLE ANIMALS.

This animal is very plentiful in India, and is one of the many creatures which are held sacred by the natives. Consequently, it takes up its quarters near human habitations, feeling sure that it will not be injured, and knowing that plenty of food is at hand. It is said that in some parts of India the natives always leave one-tenth of their grain-crops for the monkeys, and thus

FEEDING THE MONKEYS IN INDIA.

the animals content themselves with this offering, and refrain from devastating the fields, as they would otherwise do. This story may be true or not. It is certainly possible that in a long series of years the monkeys of that neighbourhood have come to look upon their tithe as a matter belonging to the ordinary course of things; but whether it be true or not, it illustrates the reverence entertained by the Hindoos for their monkeys.

In many places where grain and fruit crops are cultivated, the monkeys get rather more than their share, plundering without scruple, and finding no hindrance from the rightful owners, who dare not drive them away, lest they should injure any of these sacred beings. However, being of the opinion that no evil will follow a foreigner's action, they are only too glad to avail themselves of the assistance of Europeans, who have no scruples on the subject. Still, although they are pleased to see the

TROUBLESOME NEIGHBORS.

monkeys driven off, and their crops saved, they would rather lose all their harvest than allow a single monkey to be killed, and in the earlier years of the Indian colony, several riots took place between the natives and the English, because the latter had killed a monkey through ignorance of the reverence in which it was held.

Another monkey which may probably have been brought to Palestine from India is the HOONUMAN, ENTELLUS, or MAKUR, which is more reverenced by the Hindoos than any other species. Its scientific title is *Presbytes entellus*. In some parts of India it is worshipped as a form of divinity, and in all it is reverenced and protected to such an extent that it becomes a

MONKEYS ENTERING A PLANTATION.

positive nuisance to Europeans who are not influenced by the same superstitious ideas as those which are so prevalent in India. Being a very common species, it could easily be captured, especially if, as is likely to be the case, it was fearless of man through long immunity from harm. The sailors who manned Solomon's navy would not trouble themselves about the sacred character of the monkeys, but would take them without the least scruple wherever they could be found.

The Hoonuman would also be valued by them on account of its docility when taken young, and the amusing tricks which it is fond of displaying in captivity as well as in a state of freedom. Moreover, it is rather a pretty creature, the general colour being yellowish, and the face black.

THE APE. 393

Perfectly aware of the impunity with which they are permitted to act, these monkeys prefer human habitations to the forests which form the natural home of their race, and crowd into the villages and temples, the latter being always swarming with the long-tailed host. As is the case with the Rhesus, the Hoonuman monkeys are much too fond of helping themselves

SLOTHFUL MONKEYS.

from the shops and stalls, and if they can find a convenient roof, will sit there and watch for the arrival of the most dainty fruits.

However, the natives, superstitious as they are, and unwilling to inflict personal injury on a monkey, have no scruple in making arrangements by which a monkey that trespasses on forbidden spots will inflict injury on itself. They may not shoot or wound in any way the monkeys which cluster on their roofs, and the animals are so perfectly aware of the fact, that they refuse to be driven away by shouts and menacing gestures. But, they contrive to make the roofs so uncomfortable by covering them with thorns, that the monkeys are obliged to quit their points of vantage, and to choose some spot where they can sit down without fear of hurting themselves.

A PRIVILEGED RACE.

That the Hindoos should pay homage almost divine to a monkey, does seem equally absurd and contemptible. But, strange as this superstition may be, and the more strange because the intellectual powers of the educated Hindoos are peculiarly subtle and penetrating, it was shared by a greater, a mightier, and a still more intellectual race, now extinct as a nation. The ancient Egyptians worshipped the baboon, and ranked it among the most potent of their deities; and it can but strike us with wonder when we reflect that a people who could erect buildings perfectly unique in the history of the world, who held the foremost place in civilization, who perfected arts which we, at a distance of three thousand years, have only just learned, should pay divine honours to monkeys, bulls, and snakes. Such, however, was the case; and we find that the modern Hindoo shows as great reverence for the identical animals as did the Egyptian when Pharaoh was king, and Joseph his prime minister.

It is said by some, that neither the Egyptian of the ancient times, nor the Hindoo of the present day, actually worshipped these creatures, but that they reverenced them as external signs of some attribute of God. Precisely the same remarks have been made as to the worship of idols, and it is likely enough that the highly educated among the worshippers did look upon a serpent merely as an emblem of divine wisdom, a bull as an image of divine strength, and a monkey as an external memorial of the promised incarnation of divinity So with idols, which to the man of educated and enlarged mind were nothing but visible symbols employed for the purpose of directing the mind in worship. But, though this was the case with the educated and intellectual, the ignorant and uncultivated, who compose the great mass of a nation, did undoubtedly believe that both the living animal and the lifeless idol were themselves divine, and did worship them accordingly.

There is one species of monkey, which is extremely likely to have been brought to Palestine, and used for the adornment of a luxurious monarch's palace. This is the WANDEROO. or NIL-BHUNDER (*Silenus veter*). The Wanderoo, or Ouanderoo, as the name is sometimes spelled, is a very conspicuous animal, on account of the curious mane that covers its neck and head, and the peculiarly formed tail, which is rather long and tufted, like that of a baboon, and has caused it to be ranked among those animals by several writers, under the name of the Liontailed Baboon. That part of the hairy mass which rolls over the head is nearly black, but as it descends over the shoulders, it assumes a greyer tinge, and in some specimens is nearly white. As is the case with many animals, the mane is not noticeable in the young specimens, but increases in size with age, only reaching its full dimensions when the animal has attained adult age. Only in the oldest specimens is the full, white, venerable, wig-like mane to be seen in perfection.

In captivity, the general demeanour of this monkey corresponds with its grave and dignified aspect. It seems to be more sedate than the ordinary monkeys, to judge from the specimens which have lived in the Zoological Gardens, and sits peering with its shiny brown eyes out of the enormous mane, with as much gravity as if it were really a judge deciding an important case in law. Not that it will not condescend to the little tricks and playful sallies for which the monkeys are so celebrated; but it soon loses the vivacity of youth, and when full-

THE WANDEROO.

grown, presents as great a contrast to its former vivacity, as does a staid full-grown cat sitting by the fire, to the restless, lively, playful kitten of three months old. During its growth, it can be taught to go through several amusing performances, but it has little of the quick, mercurial manner, which is generally found among the monkey tribe.

The docility of the Wanderoo often vanishes together with its youth. The same animal may be gentle, tractable, and teachable when young, and yet, when a few years have passed over its head and whitened its mane, may be totally obstinate and dull.

THE ENEMY DISCOVERED.

The natives of the country in which the Wanderoo lives, attribute to it the wisdom which its venerable aspect seems to imply, much as the ancient Athenians venerated the owl as the bird of wisdom, and the chosen companion of the learned Minerva. In many places, the Wanderoo is thought to be a sort of king among monkeys, and to enjoy the same supremacy over its maneless kinsfolk, that the king-vulture maintains over the other vultures which are destitute of the brilliant crest that marks its rank.

I am induced to believe that the Wanderoo must have been one of the monkeys which were brought to Solomon, for two reasons.

In the first place, it is a native both of India and Ceylon, and therefore might have formed an article of merchandise, together with the peacock, gold, and ivory. And if, as is extremely probable, the Tharshish of the Scripture is identical with Ceylon, it is almost certain that the Wanderoo would have been brought to Solomon, in order to increase the glories of his palace. Sir Emerson Tennant points out very forcibly, that in the Tamil language, the words for apes, ivory, and peacocks, are identical with the Hebrew names for the same objects, and thus gives a very strong reason for supposing that Ceylon was the country from which Solomon's fleet drew its supplies.

Another reason for conjecturing that the Wanderoo would have been one of the animals sent to grace the palace of Solomon is this. In the days when that mighty sovereign lived, as indeed has been the case in all partially civilized countries, the kings and rulers have felt a pride in collecting together the rarest objects which they could purchase, giving the preference to those which were in any way conspicuous, whether for intrinsic value, for size, for beauty, or for ugliness. Thus, giants, dwarfs, and deformed persons of either sex, and even idiots, were seen as regular attendants at royal courts, a custom which extended even into the modern history of England, the "Fool" being an indispensable appendage to the train of every person of rank. Animals from foreign lands were also prized, and value was set upon them, not only for their variety, but for any external characteristic which would make them especially conspicuous.

Ordinary sovereigns would make collections of such objects, simply because they were rare, and in accordance with the

BONNET MONKEYS.

general custom; and in importing the "apes" and peacocks together with the gold and ivory, Solomon but followed the usual custom. He, however, on whom the gift of wisdom had been especially bestowed, would have another motive besides ostentation or curiosity. He was learned in the study of that science which we now call Natural History. It is, therefore, extremely probable, that he would not neglect any opportunities of procuring animals from distant lands, in order that he might study the products of countries which he had not personally visited, and it is not likely that so conspicuous an animal as the Wanderoo would have escaped the notice of those who provided the cargo for which so wealthy a king could pay, and for which they would demand a price proportionate to its variety.

There is perhaps no monkey which is so conspicuous among its kin as the Wanderoo, and certainly no monkey or ape inhabiting those parts of the world to which the fleet of Solomon would have access. Its staid, sedate manners, its black body, lion-like tail, and huge white-edged mane, would distinguish it so boldly from its kinsfolk, that the sailors would use all their efforts to capture an animal for which they would be likely to obtain a high price.

The peculiar and unique character of Solomon affords good reason for conjecture that, not only were several species of the monkey tribe included under the general word Kophim, but that the number of species must have been very great. He wrote largely of the various productions of the earth, and, to judge him by ourselves, it is certain that with such magnificent means at his command, he would have ransacked every country that his ships could visit, for the purpose of collecting materials for his works. It is therefore almost certain that under the word Kophim may be included all the most plentiful species of monkey which inhabit the countries to which his fleet had access, and that in his palace were collected together specimens of each monkey which has here been mentioned, besides many others of which no special notice need be taken, such as the Bonnet Monkeys, and other Macaques.

THE BAT.

THE BAT.

The Bat mentioned always with abhorrence—Meaning of the Hebrew name—The prohibition against eating Bats—The edible species, their food and mode of life—The noisome character of the Bat, and the nature of its dwelling-place—Its hatred of light—Mr. Tristram's discoveries—Bats found in the quarries from which the stone of the Temple was hewn—Edible Bats in a cave near the centre of Palestine—Another species of long-tailed Bat captured in the rock caves where hermits had been buried—Other species which probably inhabit Palestine.

AMONG the animals that are forbidden to be eaten by the Israelites we find the BAT prominently mentioned, and in one or two parts of Scripture the same creature is alluded to with evident abhorrence. In Isaiah ii. 20, for example, it is prophesied that when the day of the Lord comes, the worshippers of idols will try to hide themselves from the presence of the Lord, and will cast their false gods to the bats and the moles, both animals being evidently used as emblems of darkness and ignorance, and associated together for a reason which will be given when treating of the mole. The Hebrew name of the Bat is expressive of its nocturnal habits, and literally signifies some being that flies by night, and it is a notable fact that the

Greek and Latin names for the bat have also a similar derivation.

In Lev. xi. 20, the words, "All fowls that creep, going upon all four, shall be an abomination unto you," are evidently intended to apply to the bat, which, as is now well known, is not a bird with wings, but a mammal with very long toes, and a well developed membrane between them. Like other mammals, the Bat crawls, or walks, on all four legs, though the movement is but a clumsy one, and greatly different from the graceful ease with which the creature urges its course through the evening air in search of food.

Perhaps the prohibition to eat so unsightly an animal may seem almost needless; but it must be remembered that in several parts of the earth, certain species of Bat are used as food. These are chiefly the large species, that are called Kalongs, and which feed almost entirely on fruit, thus being to their insectivorous relatives what the fruit-loving bear is among the larger carnivora. These edible Bats have other habits not shared by the generality of their kin. Some of the species do not retire to caves and hollow trees for shelter during their hours of sleep, but suspend themselves by their hind legs from the topmost branches of the trees whose fruit affords them nourishment. In this position they have a most singular aspect, looking much as if they themselves were large bunches of fruit hanging from the boughs. Thus, they are cleanly animals, and are as little repulsive as bats can be expected to be.

But the ordinary bats, such as are signified by the "night-fliers" of the Scriptures, are, when in a state of nature, exceedingly unpleasant creatures. Almost all animals are infested with parasitic insects, but the Bat absolutely swarms with them, so that it is impossible to handle a Bat recently dead without finding some of them on the hands. Also, the bats are in the habit of resorting to caverns, clefts in the rocks, deserted ruins, and similar dark places, wherein they pass the hours of daylight, and will frequent the same spots for a long series of years. In consequence of this habit, the spots which they select for their resting place become inconceivably noisome, and can scarcely be entered by human beings, so powerful is the odour with which they are imbued.

Sometimes, when travellers have been exploring the chambers

of ruined buildings, or have endeavoured to penetrate into the recesses of rocky caves, they have been repelled by the bats which had taken up their habitation therein. No sooner does the light of the torch or lamp shine upon the walls, than the

BATS' RESTING-PLACE.

clusters of bats detach themselves from the spots to which they had been clinging, and fly to the light like moths to a candle. No torch can withstand the multitude of wings that come flapping about it, sounding like the rushing of a strong wind, while the bats that do not crowd around the light, dash against the explorers, beating their leathery wings against their faces, and clinging in numbers to their dress. They would even settle on the face unless kept off by the hands, and sometimes they force the in truders to beat a retreat. They do not intend to attack, for they are quite incapable of doing any real damage; and, in point of fact, they are much more alarmed than those whom they annoy. Nocturnal in their habits, they cannot endure the light, which completely dazzles them, so that they dash about at random, and fly blindly towards the torches in their endeavours to escape.

If, then, we keep in mind the habits of the bats, we shall comprehend that their habitations must be inexpressibly revolting to human beings, and shall the better understand the force of the prophecy that the idols shall be cast to the bats and the moles.

No particular species of Bat seems to be indicated by the Hebrew word Hatalleph, which is evidently used in a comprehensive sense, and signifies all and any species of Bat. Until very lately, the exact species of Bats which inhabit Palestine were not definitely ascertained, and could only be conjectured. But, Mr. Tristram, who travelled in the Holy Land for the express purpose of investigating its physical history, has set this point at rest, in his invaluable work, " The Land of Israel," to which frequent reference will be made in the course of the following pages.

Almost every cavern which he entered was tenanted by bats, and he procured several species of these repulsive but interesting animals. While exploring the vast quarries in which the stone for the Temple was worked beneath the earth, so that no sound of tool was heard during the building, numbers of bats were disturbed by the lights, and fluttered over the heads of the exploring party.

On another occasion, he was exploring a cave near the centre of Palestine, when he succeeded in procuring some specimens, and therefore in identifying at least one species. " In climbing the rocks soon afterwards, to examine a cave, I heard a singular whining chatter within, and on creeping into its recesses, a stone thrown up roused from their roosting-places a colony of large bats, the soft waving flap of whose wings I could hear in the darkness. How to obtain one I knew not; but on vigorously plying my signal whistle, all the party soon gathered to my help. B. suggested smoking them, so a fire of brushwood was kindled, and soon two or three rushed out. Two fell to our shot, and I was delighted to find myself the possessor of a couple of large fox-headed bats of the genus Pteropus (*Xantharpya œgyptiaca*), and

GREAT FOX-HEADED BAT, OR FLYING FOX.

extending twenty and a half inches from wing to wing. As none of the bats of Palestine are yet known, this was a great prize, and another instance of the extension westward of the Indian fauna." These Bats belong to the fruit-eating tribe, and are closely allied to the Flying Foxes of Java, Australia, and Southern Africa. Therefore, this would be one of the species commonly used for food, and hence the necessity for the prohibition. The present species extends over the greater part of Northern Africa and into parts of Asia.

The same traveller subsequently discovered several more species of bats. On one occasion, he was exploring some caves, near the site of the ancient Jericho. On the eastern face of the cliffs are a number of caves, arranged in regular tiers, and originally approached by steps cut out of the face of the rock. These staircases are, however, washed away by time and the rains, and in consequence the upper tiers were almost inacces-

CAVE NEAR THE SITE OF ANCIENT JERICHO.

sible. In some of these caves the walls were covered with brilliant, but mutilated frescoes; and in others, hermits had lived and died and been buried. Mr. Tristram and his companions had penetrated to the second tier, and there made a curious discovery.

"In the roof of this was a small hole, athwart which lay a stick. After many efforts, we got a string across it, and so hauled up a rope, by which, finding the stick strong enough, we climbed, and with a short exercise of the chimney-sweeper's art, we found ourselves in a third tier of cells, similar to the lower ones, and covered with the undisturbed dust of ages. Behind the chapel was a dark cave, with an entrance eighteen inches high. Having lighted our lantern, we crept in on our faces, and found the place full of human bones and skulls; with dust several inches deep. We were in an ancient burying-place of the Anchorites, or hermits of the country, whose custom it was to retire to such desert and solitary places.

"Their bones lay in undisturbed order, probably as the corpses had been stretched after death.

"After capturing two or three long-tailed bats, of a species new to us, which were the only living occupants of the cave, we crept out, with a feeling of religious awe, from this strange, sepulchral cavern."

Besides the species of bats that have been described, it is probable that representatives of several more families of bats inhabit Palestine.

LEOPARDS.

BIRDS.

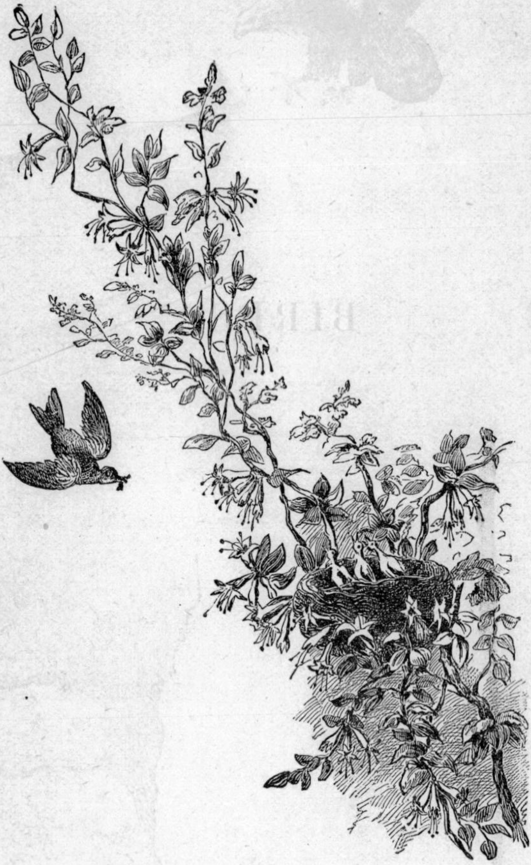

THE

LÄMMERGEIER, OR OSSIFRAGE OF SCRIPTURE.

Difficulty of identifying the various birds mentioned in Scripture—The vultures of Palestine—The Lämmergeier, or Ossifrage of Scripture—Appearance of the Lämmergeier—Its flight and mode of feeding—Nest of the Lämmergeier.

It has already been mentioned that even the best Biblical scholars have found very great difficulties in identifying several of the animals which are named in Scripture. This difficulty is greatly increased when we come to the BIRDS, and in many instances it is absolutely impossible to identify the Hebrew word with any precise species. In all probability, however, the nomenclature of the birds is a very loose one, several species being classed under the same title.

THE LAMMERGEIER.

Keeping this difficulty in mind, I shall mention all the species which are likely to have been classed under a single title, giving a general description of the whole, and a detailed account of the particular species which seems to answer most closely to the Hebrew word.

FOLLOWING the arrangement which has been employed in this work, I shall begin with the bird which has been placed by zoologists at the head of its class, namely, the LAMMERGEIER, the bird which may be safely identified with the Ossifrage of Scripture. The Hebrew word is "Peres," a term which only occurs twice when signifying a species of bird ; namely, in Lev. xi. 13, and the parallel passage in Deut. xiv. 12. The first of these passages runs as follows : " These ye shall have in abomination among the fowls ; they shall not be eaten, they are an abomination : the eagle, and the ossifrage, and the ospray." The corresponding passage in Deuteronomy has precisely the same signification, though rather differently worded : " These are they of which ye shall not eat : the eagle, and the ossifrage, and the ospray."

The word *peres* signifies a breaker ; and the Latin term Ossifraga, or Bone-breaker, is a very good translation of the word. How it applies to the Lämmergeier we shall presently see.

The Lämmergeier belongs to the vultures, but has much more the appearance of an eagle than a vulture, the neck being clothed with feathers, instead of being naked or only covered with down. It may at once be known by the tuft of long, hair-like feathers which depends from the beak, and which has gained for the bird the title of Bearded Vulture. The colour of the plumage is a mixture of different browns and greys, tawny below and beautifully pencilled above, a line of pure white running along the middle of each feather. When young it is nearly black, and indeed has been treated as a separate species under the name of Black Vulture.

It is one of the largest of the flying birds, its length often exceeding four feet, and the expanse of its wings being rather more than ten feet. In consequence of this great spread of wing, it looks when flying like a much larger bird than it really is, and its size has often been variously misstated. Its flight, as may be imagined from the possession of such wings, is equally grand and graceful, and it sweeps through the air with great force, apparently unaccompanied by effort.

The Lämmergeier extends through a very large range of country, and is found throughout many parts of Europe and Asia. It is spread over the Holy Land, never congregating in numbers, like ordinary vultures, but living in pairs, and scarcely any ravine being uninhabited by at least one pair of Lämmergeiers.

The food of the Lämmergeier is, like that of other vultures, the flesh of dead animals, though it does not feed quite in the same manner that they do. When the ordinary vultures have found a carcase they tear it to pieces, and soon remove all the flesh. This having been done, the Lämmergeier comes to the half-picked bones, eats the remaining flesh from them, and finishes by breaking them and eating the marrow. That a bird should be able to break a bone as thick and hard as the thighbone of a horse or ox seems rather problematical, but the bird achieves the feat in a simple and effectual manner.

Seizing the bone in its claws, it rises to an immense height in the air, and then, balancing itself over some piece of rock, it lets the bone fall, and sweeps after it with scarce less rapidity than the bone falls. Should the bone be broken by the fall, the bird picks the marrow out of the fragments; and should it have escaped fracture by reason of falling on a soft piece of ground instead of a hard rock, the bird picks it up, and renews the process until it has attained its object. It will be seen, therefore, that the name of Ossifrage, or Bone-breaker, may very properly be given to this bird.

Not only does it extract the marrow from bones in this peculiar manner, but it procures other articles of food by employing precisely the same system. If it sees a tortoise, many of which reptiles are found in the countries which it inhabits, it does not waste time and trouble by trying to peck the shell open, but carries its prey high in the air, drops it on the ground, and so breaks its shell to pieces. Tortoises are often very hard-shelled creatures, and the Lämmergeier has been observed to raise one of them and drop it six or seven times before the stubborn armour would yield. Snakes, too, are killed in a similar manner, being seized by the neck, and then dropped from a height upon rocks or hard ground. The reader may perhaps be aware that the Hooded Crow of England breaks bones and the shells of bivalve molluscs in a similar manner.

Mr. Tristram suggests, with much probability, that the "eagle" which mistook the bald head of the poet Æschylus for a white stone, and killed him by dropping a tortoise upon it, was in all likelihood a Lämmergeier, the bird being a denizen of the same country, and the act of tortoise-dropping being its usual mode of killing those reptiles.

A SUCCESSFUL DEFENCE.

We now see why the Lämmergeier is furnished with such enormous wings, and so great a power of flight, these attributes being needful in order to enable it to lift its prey to a sufficient height. The air, as we all know, becomes more and more attenuated in exact proportion to the height above the earth; and did not the bird possess such great powers of flight, it would not be able to carry a heavy tortoise into the thinner strata of air which are found at the height to which it soars.

The instinct of killing its prey by a fall is employed against other animals besides snakes and tortoises, though exerted in a somewhat different manner. The bird, as has already been mentioned, lives among mountain ranges, and it may be seen floating about them for hours together, watching each inch of ground in search of prey. Should it see a goat or other inhabitant of the rocks standing near a precipice, the Lämmergeier sweeps rapidly upon it, and with a blow of its wing knocks the animal off the rock into the valley beneath, where it lies helplessly maimed, even if not killed by the fall.

Even hares and lambs are killed in this manner, and it is from the havoc which the Lämmergeier makes among the sheep that it has obtained the name of Lämmergeier, or Lamb-Vulture. So swift and noiseless is the rush of the bird, that an animal which has once been marked by its blood-red eye seldom escapes from the swoop; and even the Alpine hunters, who spend their lives in pursuit of the chamois, have occasionally been put in great jeopardy by the sudden attack of a Lämmergeier, the bird having mistaken their crouching forms for the chamois, and only turned aside at the last moment.

The reason for employing so remarkable a mode of attack is to be found in the structure of the feet, which, although belonging to so large and powerful a bird, are comparatively feeble, and are unable, like those of the eagle, to grasp the living animal in a deadly hold, and to drive the sharp talons into its vitals. They are not well adapted for holding prey, the talons not possessing the hook-like form or the sharp points which characterise those of the eagle. The feet, by the way, are feathered down to the toes. The beak, too, is weak when compared with the rest of the body, and could not perform its work were not the object which it tears previously shattered by the fall from a height.

STRUCK FROM A DIZZY HEIGHT.

The nest of the Lämmergeier is made of sticks and sods, and is of enormous dimensions. It is almost always placed upon a lofty cliff, and contains about a wagon-load or so of sticks rudely interwoven, and supporting a nearly equal amount of sods and moss.

An allied species lives in Northern Africa, where it is called by a name which signifies Father Longbeard, in allusion to the beard-like tufts of the bill.

THE EGYPTIAN VULTURE, OR GIER-EAGLE.

The Râchâm or Gier-Eagle identified with the Egyptian Vulture—Its appearance on the Egyptian monuments—The shape, size, and colour of the bird—Its value as a scavenger, and its general habits—The Egyptian Vultures and the griffons—Its fondness for the society of man—Nest of the Egyptian Vulture.

In the same list of unclean birds which has already been given, we find the name of a bird which we can identify without much difficulty, although there has been some little controversy about it. This is the so-called Gier-Eagle, which is named with the cormorant and the pelican as one of the birds which the Jews are forbidden to eat. The word which is translated as Gier-Eagle is Râchâm, a name which is almost identical with the Arabic name of the EGYPTIAN VULTURE, sometimes called Pharaoh's Chicken, because it is so often sculptured on the ancient monuments of Egypt. It is called by the Turks by a name which signifies White Father, in allusion to the colour of its plumage.

This bird is not a very large one, being about equal to a raven in size, though its enormously long wings give it an appearance of much greater size. Its colour is white, with the exception of the quill feathers of the wings, which are dark-brown. The bill and the naked face and legs are bright ochreous yellow. It does not attain this white plumage until its third year, its colour before reaching adult age being brown, with a grey neck and dull yellow legs and face.

The Egyptian Vulture, although not large, is a really handsome bird, the bold contrast of pure white and dark brown being very conspicuous when it is on the wing. In this plumage it has never been seen in England, but one or two examples are known of the Egyptian Vulture being killed in England while still in its dark-brown clothing.

It inhabits a very wide range of country, being found throughout all the warmer parts of the Old World. Although it is tolerably plentiful, it is never seen in great numbers, as is the case with several of the vultures, but is always to be found in pairs, the male and female never separating, and invariably being seen close together. In fact, in places where it is common it is hardly possible to travel more than a mile or two without seeing a pair of Egyptian Vultures. Should more than two of these birds be seen together, the spectator may be sure that they

EGYPTIAN VULTURE, OR GIER-EAGLE.

have congregated over some food. It has been well suggested that its Hebrew name of Râchâm, or Love, has been given to it in consequence of this constant association of the male and female.

The Egyptian Vulture is one of the best of scavengers, not only devouring the carcases of dead animals, but feeding on every kind of offal or garbage. Indeed, its teeth and claws are much too feeble to enable it to cope with the true vultures in tearing up a large carcase, and in consequence it never really associates with them, although it may be seen hovering near them, and it never ventures to feed in their company, keeping at a respectful distance while they feed, and, when they retire, humbly making a meal on the scraps which they have left.

Mr. Tristram narrates an amusing instance of this trait of character. "On a subsequent occasion, on the north side of Hermon, we observed the griffons teaching a lesson of patience to the inferior scavengers. A long row of Egyptian vultures were sitting on some rocks, so intently watching a spot in a corn-field that they took no notice of our approach. Creeping cautiously near, we watched a score of griffons busily engaged in turning over a dead horse, one side of which they had already reduced to a skeleton.

"Their united efforts had just effected this, when we showed ourselves, and they quickly retired. The inferior birds, who dreaded us much less than them, at once darted to the repast, and, utterly regardless of our presence within ten yards of them, began to gorge. We had hardly retired two hundred yards, when the griffons came down with a swoop, and the Egyptian vultures and a pair or two of eagles hurriedly resumed their post of observation; while some black kites remained, and contrived by their superior agility to filch a few morsels from their lordly superiors."

So useful is this bird as a scavenger, that it is protected in all parts of the East by the most stringent laws, so that a naturalist who wishes for specimens has some difficulty in procuring the bird, or even its egg. It wanders about the streets of the villages, and may generally be found investigating the heaps of refuse which are left to be cleared away by the animals and birds which constitute the scavengers of the East.

It not only eats dead animal substances, but kills and devours great quantities of rats, mice, lizards, and other pests that swarm in hot countries. So tame is it, that it may even be observed, like the gull and the rook of our own country, following the ploughman as he turns up the ground, and examining the furrow for the purpose of picking up the worms, grubs, and similar creatures that are disturbed by the share.

Being thus protected and encouraged by man, there is good

reason why it should have learned in course of time to fear him far less than its own kind. Indeed, it is so utterly fearless with regard to human beings, that it habitually follows the caravans as they pass from one town to another, for the sake of feeding on the refuse food and other offal which is thrown aside on the road.

Two articles of diet which certainly do not seem to fall within the ordinary range of vulture's food are said to be consumed by this bird. The first is the egg of the ostrich, the shell of which is too hard to be broken by the feeble beak of the Egyptian Vulture. The bird cannot, like the lämmergeier, carry the egg into the air and drop it on the ground, because its feet are not large enough to grasp it, and only slip off its round and polished surface. Therefore, instead of raising the egg into the air and dropping it upon a stone, it carries a stone into the air and drops it upon the egg. So at least say the natives of the country which it inhabits, and there is no reason why we should doubt the truth of the statement.

The other article of food is a sort of melon, very full of juice. This melon is called "nara," and is devoured by various creatures, such as lions, leopards, mice, ostriches, &c. and seems to serve them instead of drink.

The nest of the Egyptian Vulture is made in some rocky ledge, and the bird does not trouble itself about selecting a spot inaccessible to man, knowing well that it will not be disturbed. The nest is, like that of other vultures, a large and rude mass of sticks, sods, bones, and similar materials, to which are added any bits of rag, rope, skin, and other village refuse which it can pick up as it traverses the streets. There are two, and occasionally three, eggs, rather variously mottled with red. In its breeding, as in its general life, it is not a gregarious bird, never breeding in colonies, and, indeed, very seldom choosing a spot for its nest near one which has already been selected by another pair.

The illustration on page 420 represents part of the nest of the Egyptian Vulture, in which the curious mixture of bones and sticks is well shown. The parent birds are drawn in two characteristic attitudes taken from life, and well exhibit the feeble beak, the peculiar and intelligent, almost cunning expression of the head, and the ruff of feathers which surrounds the upper part of the neck. In the distance another bird is drawn as it appears on the wing, in order to show the contrast between the white plumage and the dark quill feathers of the wings, the bird presenting a general appearance very similar to that of the common sea-gull.

THE

GRIFFON VULTURE, OR EAGLE OF SCRIPTURE.

The Griffon Vulture identified with the Eagle of Scripture—Geographical range of the Griffon—Its mode of flight and sociable habits—The featherless head and neck of the bird—The Vulture used as an image of strength, swiftness, and rapacity—Its powers of sight—How Vultures assemble round a carcase—Nesting-places of the Griffon—Mr. Tristram's description of the Griffon—Rock-caves of the Wady Hamâm—Care of the young, and teaching them to fly—Strength of the Griffon.

THE Griffon Vulture is found throughout a large portion of the Old World, inhabiting nearly all the warmer portions of this hemisphere. The colour of the adult bird is a sort of yellowish brown, diversified by the black quill feathers and the ruff of white down that surrounds the neck. The head and neck are without feathers, but are sparingly covered with very short down of a similar character to that of the ruff.

It is really a large bird, being little short of five feet in total length, and the expanse of wing measuring about eight feet.

The Griffon Vulture is very plentiful in Palestine, and, unlike the lesser though equally useful Egyptian Vulture, congregates together in great numbers, feeding, flying, and herding in company. Large flocks of them may be seen daily, soaring high in the air, and sweeping their graceful way in the grand curves which distinguish the flight of the large birds of prey. They are best to be seen in the early morning, being in the habit of quitting their rocky homes at daybreak, and indulging in a flight for two or three hours, after which they mostly return to the rocks, and wait until evening, when they take another short flight before retiring to rest.

Allusion is made in the Scriptures to the gregarious habits of the Vultures: "Wheresoever the carcase is, there will the eagles be gathered together" (Matt. xxiv. 28). That the Vulture, and not the eagle, is here signified, is evident from the fact that the eagles do not congregate like the Vultures, never being seen in greater numbers than two or three together, while the Vultures assemble in hundreds.

There is also a curious passage in the Book of Proverbs, chap. xxx. ver. 17, which alludes to the carnivorous nature of the bird: "The eye that mocketh at his father, and despiseth to obey his mother, the ravens of the valley shall pick it out, and the young eagles shall eat it."

Allusion is made in several passages to the swiftness of the Vulture, as well as its voracity. See, for example, a portion of David's lamentation over the bodies of Saul and Jonathan, who, according to the poet's metaphor, "were lovely and pleasant in their lives, and in their death they were not divided; they were swifter than eagles, they were stronger than lions."

The "bitter" people—namely, the Chaldeans—are again mentioned in a very similar manner by the prophet Jeremiah: "Our persecutors are swifter than the eagles of the heavens; they pursued us upon the mountains, they laid wait for us in the wilderness" (Lam. iv. 19).

There is something peculiarly appropriate in employing the Vulture as an image of strength and swiftness when applied to warriors, the bird being an invariable attendant on the battle, and flying to the field of death with marvellous swiftness. All who had ever witnessed a battle were familiar with the presence of the Vulture—the scene of carnage, and the image which is employed, would be one which commended itself at once to those for whom it was intended. And, as the earlier history of the Jewish nation is essentially of a warlike character, we cannot wonder that so powerful and familiar an image should have been repeatedly introduced into the sacred writings.

Wonderful powers of sight are possessed by this bird. Its eyes

VULTURES.

are able to assume either a telescopic or a microscopic character, by means of a complex and marvellous structure, which can alter the whole shape of the organ at the will of the bird.

Not only can the eye be thus altered, but it changes instantaneously, so as to accommodate itself to the task which it is to perform. A Vulture, for example, sees from a vast height the body of a dead animal, and instantly swoops down upon it like an arrow from a bow. In order to enable the bird to see so distant an object, the eye has been exercising its telescopic powers, and yet, in a second or two, when the Vulture is close to its prey, the whole form of the eye must be changed, or the bird would mistake its distance, and dash itself to pieces on the ground.

By means of its powerful eyes, the Vulture can see to an enormous distance, and with great clearness, but neither so far nor so clearly as is popularly supposed. It is true that, as soon as a carcase is discovered, it will be covered with Vultures, who arrive from every side, looking at first like tiny specks in the air, scarcely perceptible even to practised eyes, and all directing their flight to the same point. "Where the carcase is, there will the vultures be gathered together." But, although they all fly towards the same spot, it does not follow that they have all seen the same object. The fact is, they see and understand each other's movements.

A single Vulture, for example, sees a dead or dying sheep, and swoops down upon it. The other Vultures which are flying about in search of food, and from which the animal in question may be concealed, know perfectly well that a Vulture soars high in the air when searching for food, and only darts to the earth when it has found a suitable prey. They immediately follow its example, and in their turn are followed by other Vultures, which can see their fellows from a distance, and know perfectly well why they are all converging to one spot.

In this way all the Vultures of a neighbourhood will understand, by a very intelligible telegraph, that a dead body of some animal has been found, and, aided by their wonderful powers of flight, will assemble over its body in an almost incredibly short space of time.

The resting-place of the Griffon Vulture is always on some lofty spot. The Arabian Vulture will build within easy reach, the eagle prefers lofty situations, but nothing but the highest and most inaccessible spots will satisfy the Vulture. To reach the nest of this bird is therefore a very difficult task, only to be attempted by experienced and intrepid cragsmen; and, in consequence, both the eggs and young of the Griffon Vulture cannot be obtained except for a very high price. The birds are fond of building in the rock-caves which are found in so many parts of Palestine, and in some places they fill these places as thickly as rooks fill a rookery.

In Mr. Tristram's "Land of Israel," there is a very graphic description of the Griffon's nests, and of the difficulty experienced in reaching them. "A narrow gorge, with limestone cliffs from five hundred to six hundred feet high, into which the sun never penetrates, walls the rapid brook on each side so closely that we often had to ride in the bed of the stream. The cliffs are perforated with caves at all heights, wholly inaccessible to man, the secure resting-place of hundreds of noble griffons, some lämmergeiers, lanner falcons, and several species of eagle. . . . One day in the ravine well repaid us, though so terrific were the precipices, that it was quite impossible to reach any of the nests with which it swarmed.

"We were more successful in the Wady Hamâm, the south-west end of the plain, the entrance from Hattin and the Buttauf, where we spent three days in exploration. The cliffs, though reaching the height of fifteen hundred feet, rise like terraces, with enormous masses of *débris*, and the wood is half a mile wide. By the aid of Giacomo, who proved himself an expert rope-climber, we reaped a good harvest of griffons' eggs, some of the party being let down by ropes, while those above were guided in working them by signals from others below in the valley. It required the aid of a party of a dozen to capture these nests. The idea of scaling the cliff with ropes was quite new to some Arabs who were herding cattle above, and who could not, excepting one little girl, be induced to render any assistance. She proved herself most sensible and efficient in telegraphing.

"While capturing the griffons' nests, we were re-enacting a celebrated siege in Jewish history. Close to us, at the head of the cliffs which form the limits of the celebrated Plain of Hattin, were the ruins of Irbid, the ancient Arbela, marked principally by the remains of a synagogue, of which some marble shafts and fragments of entablature, like those of Tell Hûm, are still to be seen, and were afterwards visited by us.

"Hosea mentions the place apparently as a strong fortress: 'All thy fortresses shall be spoiled, as Shalman spoiled Betharbel in the day of battle' (Hos. x. 14). Perhaps the prophet here refers to the refuges in the rocks below.

"The long series of chambers and galleries in the face of the precipice are called by the Arabs, Kulat Ibn Maân, and are very fully described by Josephus. These cliffs were the homes of a set of bandits, who resided here with their families, and for years set the power of Herod the Great at defiance. At length, when all other attempts at scaling the fortress had failed, he let down soldiers at this very spot in boxes, by chains, who attacked the robbers with long hooks, and succeeded in rooting them all out.

"The rock galleries, though now only tenanted by griffons, are very complete and perfect, and beautifully built. Long galleries wind backwards and forwards in the cliff side, their walls being built with dressed stone, flush with the precipice, and often opening into spacious chambers. Tier after tier rise one after another with projecting windows, connected by narrow staircases, carried sometimes upon arches, and in the upper portions rarely broken away. In many of the upper chambers to which we were let down, the dust of ages had accumulated, undisturbed by any foot save that of the birds of the air; and here we rested during the heat of the day, with the plains and lake set as in a frame before us. We obtained a full zoological harvest, as in three days we captured fourteeen nests of griffons."

Although these caverns and rocky passages are much more accessible than most of the places whereon the Griffons build, the natives never venture to enter them, being deterred not so much by their height, as by their superstitious fears. The Griffons instinctively found out that man never entered these caverns, and so took possession of them.

As the young Griffons are brought up in these lofty and precipitous places, it is evident that their first flight must be a dangerous experiment, requiring the aid of the parent birds. At first the young are rather nervous at the task which lies before them, and shrink from trusting themselves to the air. The parents, however, encourage them to use their wings, take short flights in order to set them an example, and, when they at last venture from the nest, accompany and encourage them in their first journey.

In flight it is one of the most magnificent birds that can be seen, and even when perched it often retains a certain look of majesty and grandeur. Sometimes, however, especially when basking in the sun, it assumes a series of attitudes which are absolutely grotesque, and convert the noble-looking bird into a positively ludicrous object. At one moment it will sit all hunched up, its head sunk between its shoulders, and one wing trailing behind it as if broken. At another it will bend its legs and sit down on the ankle-joint, pushing its feet out in front, and supporting itself by the stiff feathers of its tail. Often it will Touch nearly flat on the ground, partly spread its wings, and allow their tips to rest on the earth, and sometimes it will support nearly all the weight of its body on the wings, which rest, in a half doubled state, on the ground. I have before me a great number of sketches, taken in a single day, of the attitudes assumed by one of these birds, every one of which is strikingly different from the others, and transforms the whole shape of the bird so much that it is scarcely recognisable as the same individual.

THE EAGLE.

Signification of the word *Asniyeh*—The Golden Eagle and its habits—The Imperial Eagle—Its solitary mode of life—The Short-toed Eagle—Its domestic habits and fondness for the society of man—The Osprey, or Fishing Eagle—Its mode of catching fish—Its distribution in Palestine.

As to the EAGLE, rightly so called, there is little doubt that it is one of the many birds of prey that seem to have been classed under the general title of Asniyeh—the word which in the Authorized Version of the Bible is rendered as Osprey. A similar confusion is observable in the modern Arabic, one word, *ogab*, being applied indiscriminately to all the Eagles and the large *falconidæ*.

The chief of the true Eagles, namely, the Golden Eagle (*Aquila chrysaëtos*), is one of the inhabitants of Palestine, and is seen frequently, though never in great numbers. Indeed, its predacious habits unfit it for associating with its kind. Any animal which lives chiefly, if not wholly, by the chase, requires a large district in order to enable it to live, and thus twenty or thirty eagles will be scattered over a district of twice the number of miles. Like the lion among the mammalia, the Eagle leads an almost solitary life, scarcely ever associating with any of its kind except its mate and its young.

The whole of the Falconidæ, as the family to which the Eagles belong is called, are very destructive birds, gaining their subsistence chiefly by the chase, seldom feeding on carrion except when pressed by hunger, or when the dead animal has only recently been killed.

Herein they form a complete contrast to the vultures, whose usual food is putrefying carrion, and fresh meat the exception.

Destructive though the Eagles may be, they cannot be called cruel birds, for, although they deprive many birds and beasts of life, they effect their purpose with a single blow, sweeping down upon the doomed creature with such lightning velocity, and striking it so fiercely with their death-dealing talons, that almost instantaneous death usually results.

When the Eagle pounces on a bird, the mere shock caused by the stroke of the Eagle's body is almost invariably sufficient to cause death, and the bird, even if a large one—such as the swan, for example—falls dead upon the earth with scarcely a wound.

Smaller birds are carried off in the talons of their pursuers, and are killed by the grip of their tremendous claws, the Eagle in no case making use of its beak for killing its prey. If the great bird carries off a lamb or a hare, it grasps the body firmly with its claws, and then by a sudden exertion of its wonderful strength drives the sharp talons deep into the vitals of its prey, and does not loosen its grasp until the breath of life has fled from its victim.

The structure by means of which the Eagle is enabled to use its talons with such terrible effect is equally beautiful and simple, deserving special mention.

Now, many observant persons have been struck with the curious power possessed by birds which enables them to hold their position upon a branch or perch even while sleeping. In many instances the slumbering bird retains its hold of the perch by a single foot, the other being drawn up and buried in the feathers.

As this grasp is clearly an involuntary one, it is evidently independent of the mere will of the bird, and is due to some peculiar formation.

On removing the skin from the leg of any bird, and separating the muscles from each other, the structure in question is easily seen. The muscles which move the leg and foot, and the tendons or leaders which form the attachment of the muscles to the bones, are so arranged that whenever the bird bends its leg the foot is forcibly closed, and is opened again when the leg is straightened.

A common chicken, as it walks along, closing its toes as it lifts its foot from the ground and spreading them as the leg is unbent, cannot do otherwise, as the tendons are shortened and lengthened as each step is taken.

EAGLES.

It will be seen, therefore, that when a bird falls asleep upon a branch the legs are not only bent, but are pressed downwards by the weight of the body; so that the claws hold the perch with a firm and involuntary grasp which knows no fatigue, and which remains secure as long as the pressure from above keeps the limbs bent.

To return to the Eagle. When, therefore, the bird desires to drive his talons into the body of his prey, he needs only to sink downwards with his whole weight, and the forcible bending of his legs will contract the talons with irresistible force, without the necessity of any muscular exertion.

Exertion, indeed, is never needlessly used by the Eagle, for it is very chary of putting forth its great muscular powers, and unless roused by the sight of prey, or pressed to fly abroad in search of food, will sit upon a tree or point of rock for hours as motionless as a stuffed figure.

The Golden Eagle is a truly magnificent bird in size and appearance. A full-grown female measures about three feet six inches in length, and the expanse of her wings is nine feet. The male bird is smaller by nearly six inches. The colour of the bird is a rich blackish brown on the greater part of the body, the head and neck being covered with feathers of a golden red, which have earned for the bird its customary name.

The Golden Eagle is observed to frequent certain favourite places, and to breed regularly in the same spot, for a long series of years. The nest is always made upon some high place, generally upon a ledge of rock, and is most roughly constructed of sticks.

In hunting for their prey the Eagle and his mate assist each other. It may be also mentioned here that Eagles keep themselves to a single mate, and live together throughout their lives. Should, however, one of them die or be killed, the survivor does not long remain in a state of loneliness, but vanishes from the spot for a longer or shorter time, and then returns with a new mate.

As rabbits and hares, which form a frequent meal for the Eagle, are usually hidden under bushes and trees during the day, the birds are frequently forced to drive them from their place of concealment; this they have been observed to do in a very clever manner. One of the Eagles conceals itself near the cover, and its companion dashes among the bushes, screaming and making such a disturbance that the terrified inmates rush out in hopes of escape, and are immediately pounced upon by the watchful confederate.

The prey is immediately taken to the nest, and distributed to the young after being torn to pieces by the parent birds.

Four or five species of Eagle are known to inhabit Palestine. There is, for example, the Imperial Eagle (*Aquila mogilnik*), which may be distinguished from the Golden Eagle by a white patch on the shoulders, and the long, lancet-shaped feathers of the head and neck. These feathers are of a fawn colour, and contrast beautifully with the deep black-brown of the back and wings. It is not very often seen, being a bird that loves the forest, and that does not care to leave the shelter of the trees. It is tolerably common in Palestine.

Then there are several of the allied species, of which the best example is perhaps the Short-toed Eagle (*Circaëtus cinereus*), a bird which is extremely plentiful in the Holy Land—so plentiful indeed that, as Mr. Tristram remarks, there are probably twice as many of the Short-toed Eagles in Palestine as of all the other species put together. The genus to which this bird belongs does not take rank with the true Eagles, but is supposed by systematic naturalists to hold an intermediate place between the true Eagles and the ospreys.

The Short-toed Eagle is seldom a carrion-eater, preferring to kill its prey for itself. It feeds mostly on serpents and other reptiles, and is especially fond of frogs. It is a large and somewhat heavily built bird, lightness and swiftness being far less necessary than strength in taking the animals on which it feeds. It is rather more than two feet in length, and is a decidedly handsome bird, the back being dark brown, and the under parts white, covered with crescent-shaped black spots.

EAGLE RETURNING TO THE NEST WITH HER PREY.

THE OSPREY.

The Osprey, or Fishing Eagle—Its geographical range—Mode of securing prey—Structure of its feet—Its power of balancing itself in the air.

WE now come to the Osprey itself (*Pandion haliaëtus*), which was undoubtedly one of the birds grouped together under the collective term Asniyeh. This word occurs only in the two passages in Deut. xiv. and Lev. xi. which have been several times quoted already, and need not be mentioned again.

This fine bird is spread over a very large range of country, and is found in the New World as well as the Old. In consequence of its peculiar habits, it is often called the Fishing Eagle.

The Osprey is essentially a fish-eater. It seems very strange that a predacious bird allied to the eagles, none of which birds can swim, much less dive, should obtain its living from the water. That the cormorant and other diving birds should do so is no matter of surprise, inasmuch as they are able to pursue the fish in their own element, and catch them by superior speed. But any bird which cannot dive, and which yet lives on fish, is forced to content itself with those fish that come to the surface of the water, a mode of obtaining a livelihood which does not appear to have much chance of success. Yet the Osprey does on a large scale what the kingfisher does on a small one, and contrives to find abundant food in the water.

Its method of taking prey is almost exactly like that which is employed by the kingfisher. When it goes out in search of food, it soars into the air, and floats in circles over the water, watching every inch of it as narrowly as a kestrel watches a stubble-field. No sooner does a fish rise toward the surface to take a fly, or to leap into the air for sport, than the Osprey darts downwards, grasps the fish in its talons, drags the struggling prey from the water, and with a scream of joy and triumph bears it away to shore, where it can be devoured at leisure.

The bird never dives, neither does it seize the fish with its beak like the kingfisher. It plunges but slightly into the water, as

THE OSPREY SEARCHING FOR FISH.

otherwise it would not be able to use its strong wings and carry off its prey. In order to enable the bird to seize the hard and slippery body of the fish, it is furnished with long, very sharp, and boldly-hooked talons, which force themselves into the sides of the fish, and hold it as with grappling irons.

The flight of the Osprey is peculiarly easy and elegant, as might be expected from a bird the length of whose body is only twenty-two inches, and the expanse of wing nearly five feet and a half.

It is therefore able to hover over the water for long periods of time, and can balance itself in one spot without seeming to move a wing, having the singular facility of doing so even when a tolerably strong breeze is blowing. It has even been observed to maintain its place unmoved when a sharp squall swept over the spot.

Harmless though the Osprey be—except to the fish—it is a most persecuted bird, being everywhere annoyed by rooks and crows, and, in America, robbed by the more powerful white-headed eagle.

Such a scene is thus described by Wilson:

"Elevated on the high, dead limb of a gigantic tree that commanded a wide view of the neighbouring shore and ocean, the great white-headed eagle calmly surveys the motions of various smaller birds that pursue their busy avocations below.

"The snow-white gulls slowly winnowing the air; the trains of ducks streaming over the surface; silent and watchful cranes, intent and wading, and all the winged multitude that subsist by the bounty of this vast liquid magazine of nature.

"High over all these, hovers one whose action instantly arrests the eagle's attention. By his wide curvature of wing and sudden suspension in the air he knows him to be the Osprey, settling over some devoted victim of the deep. The eyes of the eagle kindle at the sight, and balancing himself with half-opened wings on the branch, he watches the result.

"Down, rapid as an arrow, from heaven descends the Osprey, the roar of its wings reaching the ear as it disappears in the water, making the surges foam around! At this moment the eager looks of the eagle are all ardour, and, levelling his neck for flight, he sees the Osprey once more emerge, struggling with his prey, and mounting in the air with screams of exultation.

"These are the signals for the eagle, who, launching into the

SNATCHED FROM THE DEEP; THE OSPREY RISES WITH HIS PREY.

air, instantly gives chase, and soon gains on the Osprey; each exerts his utmost to mount above the other, displaying in this encounter the most elegant and sublime aërial evolutions.

"The unencumbered eagle rapidly advances, and is just on the point of reaching his opponent, when, with a sudden scream, probably of despair and honest execration, the Osprey drops his fish.

"The eagle, poising himself for a moment, as if to take a more certain aim, descends like a whirlwind, snatches it in his grasp ere it reaches the water, and bears his ill-gotten booty silently away to the woods."

Although not very plentiful in Palestine, nor indeed in any other country, the Osprey is seen throughout the whole of that country where it can find a sufficiency of water. It prefers the sea-shore and the rivers of the coast, and is said to avoid the Sea of Galilee.

THE KITE, OR VULTURE OF SCRIPTURE.

The word *Dayah* and its signification—Dayah a collective term for different species of Kites—The Common or Red Kite plentiful in Palestine—Its piercing sight and habit of soaring—The Black Kite of Palestine and its habits—The Egyptian Kite—The Raah or Glede of Scripture—The Buzzards and their habits—The Peregrine Falcon an inhabitant of Central Palestine, and the Lanner of the eastern parts of the country.

IN Lev. xi. 14 and Deut. xiv. 13, we find the Vulture among the list of birds which the Jews were not permitted to eat. The word which is translated as Vulture is *dayah*, and we find it occurring again in Isaiah xxxiv. 15, "There shall the vultures also be gathered, every one with her mate." There is no doubt, however, that this translation of the word is an incorrect one, and that it ought to be rendered as KITE. In Job xxviii. 7, there is a similar word, *ayah*, which is also translated as Vulture, and which is acknowledged to be not a Vulture, but one of the Kites: "There is a path which no fowl knoweth, and which the vulture's eye hath not seen." Both these words are nearly identical with modern Arabic terms which are employed rather loosely to signify several species of Kite. Buxtorf, in his Hebrew Lexicon, gives the correct rendering, translating *dayah* as *Milvus*, and the Vulgate in one or two places gives the same translation, though in others it renders the word as Vulture.

Mr. Tristram, who has given much attention to this subject, is inclined to refer the word *ayah* to the Common Kite (*Milvus*

THE KITE, OR VULTURE OF SCRIPTURE.

regalis), which was once so plentiful in this country, and is now nearly extinct; and *dayah* to the Black Kite (*Milvus atra*). He founds this distinction on the different habits of the two species, the Common or Red Kite being thinly scattered, and being in the habit of soaring into the air at very great heights, and the latter being very plentiful and gregarious.

We will first take the Red Kite.

This bird is scattered all over Palestine, feeding chiefly on the smaller birds, mice, reptiles, and fish. In the capture of fish the Kite is almost as expert as the osprey, darting from a great height into the water, and bearing off the fish in its claws. The wings of this bird are very long and powerful, and bear it through the air in a peculiarly graceful flight. It is indeed in consequence of this flight that it has been called the Glede, the word being derived from its gliding movements.

The sight of this bird is remarkably keen and piercing, and, from the vast elevation to which it soars when in search of food, it is able to survey the face of the country beneath, and to detect the partridge, quail, chicken, or other creature that will serve it for food. This piercing sight and habit of soaring render the passage in Job peculiarly appropriate to this species of Kite, though it does not express the habits of the other. Should the Kite suspect danger when forced to leave its nest, it escapes by darting rapidly into the air, and soaring at a vast height above the trees among which its home is made. From that elevation it can act as a sentinel, and will not come down again until it is assured of safety.

Of the habits of the BLACK KITE (*Milvus atra*), Mr. Tristram gives an admirable description. "The habits of the bird bear out the allusion in Isa. xxxiv. 15, for it is, excepting during the winter three months, so numerous everywhere in Palestine as to be almost gregarious. It returns about the beginning of March, and scatters itself over the whole country, preferring especially the neighbourhood of valleys, where it is a welcome and unmolested guest. It does not appear to attack the poultry, among whom it may often be seen feeding on garbage. It is very sociable, and the slaughter of a sheep at one of the tents will soon attract a large party of black kites, which swoop down regardless of man and guns, and enjoy a noisy scramble for the refuse, chasing each other in a laughable fashion, and sometimes enabling the wily raven to steal off with the coveted morsel during their contentions. It is the butt of all the smaller scavengers, and is evidently most unpopular with the crows and daws, and even rollers, who enjoy the amusement of teasing it in their tumbling flight, which is a manœuvre most perplexing to the kite."

The same writer proceeds to mention that the Black Kite unlike the red species, is very careless about the position of its nest, and never even attempts to conceal it, sometimes building it in a tree, sometimes on a rock-ledge, and sometimes in a bush growing on the rocks. It seems indeed desirous of making the nest as conspicuous as possible, and hangs it all over with bits of cloth, strips of bark, wings of birds, and even the cast skins of serpents.

Another species (*Milvus Ægyptiacus*) is sometimes called the Black Kite from the dark hue of its plumage, but ought rather to retain the title of Egyptian Kite. Unlike the black kite, this bird is a great thief, and makes as much havoc among poultry as the red kite. It is also a robber of other birds, and if it should happen to see a weaker bird with food, it is sure to attack and rob it. Like the black kite, it is fond of the society of man, and haunts the villages in great numbers, for the purpose of eating the offal, which in Oriental towns is simply flung into the streets to be devoured by the dogs, vultures, kites, and other scavengers, without whom no village would be habitable for a month.

WHETHER the word *raah*, which is translated as Glede in Deut. xiv. 13, among the list of birds which may not be eaten, is one of these species of Kite, or a bird of a different group, is a very doubtful point. This is the only passage in which the word occurs, and we have but small grounds for definitely identifying it with any one species. The Hebrew Bible retains the word Glede, but affixes a mark of doubt to it, and several commentators are of opinion that the word is a wrong reading of *dayah*, which occurs in the parallel passage in Lev. xi. 14. The reading of the Septuagint follows this interpretation, and renders it as Vulture in both cases. Buxtorf translates the word *raah* as Rook, but suggests that *dayah* is the correct reading.

Accepting, however, the word *raah*, we shall find that it is derived from a root which signifies sight or vision, especially of some particular object, so that a piercing sight would therefore be the chief characteristic of the bird, which, as we know, is one of the attributes of the Kites, together with other birds of prey, so that it evidently must be classed among the group with which we are now concerned. It has been suggested that, granting the *raah* to be a species distinct from the *dayah*, it is a collective term for the larger falcons and buzzards, several species of which inhabit Palestine, and are not distinctly mentioned in the Bible.

444 STORY OF THE BIBLE ANIMALS.

Several species of buzzard inhabit the Holy Land, and there is no particular reason why they should be mentioned except by a collective name. Some of the buzzards are very large birds, and though their wings are short when compared with those of the vultures and eagles, the flight of the bird is both powerful and graceful. It is not, however, remarkable for swiftness, and

THE PEREGRINE FALCON, OR GLEDE OF SCRIPTURE.

never was employed, like the falcon, in catching other birds, being reckoned as one of the useless and cowardly birds of prey. In consonance with this opinion, to compare a man to a buzzard was thought a most cutting insult.

As a general rule, it does not chase its prey like the eagles or the large-winged falcons, but perches on a rock or tree, watches for some animal on which it can feed, pounces on it, and returns to its post, the whole movements being very like those of the flycatcher. This sluggishness of disposition, and the soft and almost owl-like plumage, have been the means of bringing the bird into contempt among falconers.

As to the large falcons, which seem to be included in the term *raah*, the chief of them is the Peregrine Falcon (*Falco peregrinus*), which is tolerably common in the Holy Land. In his "Land of Israel," Mr. Tristram gives several notices of this bird, from which we may take the following picture from a description of a scene at Endor. "Dreary and desolate looked the plain, though of exuberant fertility. Here and there might be seen a small flock of sheep or herd of cattle, tended by three or four mounted villagers, armed with their long firelocks, and pistols and swords, on the watch against any small party of marauding cattle-lifters.

"Griffon vultures were wheeling in circles far over the rounded top of Tabor; and here and there an eagle was soaring beneath them in search of food, but at a most inconvenient distance from our guns. Hariers were sweeping more rapidly and closely over the ground, where lambs appeared to be their only prey; and a noble peregrine falcon, which in Central Palestine does not give place to the more eastern lanner, was perched on an isolated rock, calmly surveying the scene, and permitting us to approach and scrutinize him at our leisure."

The habit of perching on the rock, as mentioned above, is very characteristic of the Peregrine Falcon, who loves the loftiest and most craggy cliffs, and makes its nest in spots which can only be reached by a bold and experienced climber. The nests of this bird are never built in close proximity, the Peregrine preferring to have its home at least a mile from the nest of any other of its kinsfolk. Sometimes it makes a nest in lofty trees, taking possession of the deserted home of some other bird; but it loves the cliff better than the tree, and seldom builds in the latter when the former is attainable.

In the passage from the "Land of Israel" is mentioned the LANNER FALCON (*Falco lanarius*), another of the larger falcons to which the term *raah* may have been applied.

This bird is much larger than the Peregrine Falcon, and, indeed, is very little less than the great gerfalcon itself. It is one of the birds that were reckoned among the noble falcons; and the female, which is much larger and stronger than the male, was employed for the purpose of chasing the kite, whose long and powerful wings could not always save it from such a foe.

Although the Lanner has been frequently mentioned among the British birds, and the name is therefore familiar to us, it is

THE LANNER FALCON.

not even a visitor of our island. The mistake has occurred by an error in nomenclature, the young female Peregrine Falcon which is much larger and darker than the male bird, having been erroneously called by the name of Lanner.

In the illustration, a pair of Lanner Falcons are depicted as pursuing some of the rock-pigeons which abound in Palestine, the attitudes of both birds being taken from life.

THE HAWK.

The Netz or Hawk – Number of species probably grouped under that name—**Rare** occurrence of the word—The Sparrow-Hawk and its general habits—Its place of nesting—The Kestrel, or Wind-hover—Various names by which it is known in England—Its mode of feeding and curious flight—The Hariers—Probable derivation of the name—Species of Harier known to inhabit Palestine—Falconry apparently unknown to the ancient Jews.

THERE is no doubt that a considerable number of species are grouped together under the single title Netz, or Hawk, a word which is rightly enough translated. That a great number of birds should have been thus confounded together is not surprising, seeing that even in this country and at the present time, the single word Hawk may signify any one of at least twelve different species. The various falcons, the hariers, the kestrel, the sparrow-hawk, and the hobbies, are one and all called popularly by the name of Hawk, and it is therefore likely that the Hebrew word Netz would signify as many species as

447

the English word Hawk. From them we will select one or two of the principal species.

In the first place, the word is of very rare occurrence. We only find it three times. It first occurs in Lev. xi. 16, in which it is named, together with the eagle, the ossifrage, and many other birds, as among the unclean creatures, to eat which was an abomination. It is next found in the parallel passage in Deut. xiv. 15, neither of which portions of Scripture need be quoted at length.

That the word *netz* was used in its collective sense is very evident from the addition which is made to it in both cases. The Hawk, "after its kind," is forbidden, showing therefore that several kinds or species of Hawk were meant. Indeed, any specific detail would be quite needless, as the collective term was quite a sufficient indication, and, having named the vultures, eagles, and larger birds of prey, the simple word *netz* was considered by the sacred writer as expressing the rest of the birds of prey.

We find the word once more in that part of the Bible to which we usually look for any reference to natural history. In Job xxxix. 26, we have the words, "Doth the hawk fly by thy wisdom, and turn [or stretch] her wings toward the south?" The precise signification of this passage is rather doubtful, but it is generally considered to refer to the migration of several of the Hawk tribe. That the bird in question was distinguished for its power of flight is evident from the fact that the sacred poet has selected that one attribute as the most characteristic of the Netz.

Taking first the typical example of the Hawks, we find that the SPARROW-HAWK (*Accipiter nisus*) is plentiful in Palestine, finding abundant food in the smaller birds of the country. It selects for its nest just the spots which are so plentiful in the Holy Land, *i.e.* the crannies of rocks, and the tops of tall trees. Sometimes it builds in deserted ruins, but its favourite spot seems to be the lofty tree-top, and, in default of that, the rock-crevice. It seldom builds a nest of its own, but takes possession of that which has been made by some other bird. Some ornithologists think that it looks out for a convenient nest, say of the crow or magpie, and then ejects the rightful owner. I am inclined to think, however, that it mostly takes possession of a nest that is already deserted, without running the risk of fighting such enemies as a pair of angry magpies. This opinion is strengthened by the fact that the bird resorts to the same nest year after year.

It is a bold and dashing bird, though of no great size, and when wild and free displays a courage which it seems to lose in captivity. As is the case with so many of the birds, the female is much larger than her mate, the former weighing about six ounces, and measuring about a foot in length, and the latter weighing above nine ounces, and measuring about fifteen inches in length.

KESTREL HOVERING OVER A FIELD IN SEARCH OF PREY.

THE most plentiful of the smaller Hawks of Palestine is the COMMON KESTREL. This is the same species which is known under the names of Kestrel, Wind-hover, and Stannel Hawk.

It derives its name of Wind-hover from its remarkable habit of hovering, head to windward, over some spot for many minutes together. This action is always performed at a moderate distance from the ground; some naturalists saying that the Hawk in question never hovers at an elevation exceeding forty feet, while

450   STORY OF THE BIBLE ANIMALS.

others, myself included, have seen the bird hovering at a height of twice as many yards. Generally, however, it prefers a lower distance, and is able by employing this manœuvre to survey a

THE WIND-HOVER, OR KESTREL.

tolerably large space beneath. As its food consists in a very great measure of field-mice, the Kestrel is thus able by means of its telescopic eyesight to see if a mouse rises from its hole;

and if it should do so, the bird drops on it and secures it in its claws.

Unlike the sparrow-hawk, the Kestrel is undoubtedly gregarious, and will build its nest in close proximity to the habitations of other birds, a number of nests being often found within a few yards of each other. Mr. Tristram remarks that he has found its nest in the recesses of the caverns occupied by the griffon vultures, and that the Kestrel also builds close to the eagles, and is the only bird which is permitted to do so. It also builds in company with the jackdaw.

Several species of Kestrel are known, and of them at least two inhabit the Holy Land, the second being a much smaller bird than the Common Kestrel, and feeding almost entirely on insects, which it catches with its claws, the common chafers forming its usual prey. Great numbers of these birds live together, and as they rather affect the society of mankind, they are fond of building their nests in convenient crannies in the mosques or churches. Independently of its smaller size, it may be distinguished from the Common Kestrel by the whiteness of its claws.

The illustration is drawn from a sketch taken from life. The bird hovered so near a house, and remained so long in one place, that the artist fixed a telescope and secured an exact sketch of the bird in the peculiar attitude which it is so fond of assuming. After a while, the Kestrel ascended to a higher elevation, and then resumed its hovering, in the attitude which is shown in the upper figure. In consequence of the great abundance of this species in Palestine, and the peculiarly conspicuous mode of balancing itself in the air while in search of prey, we may feel sure that the sacred writers had it specially in their minds when they used the collective term Netz.

It is easily trained, and, although in the old hawking days it was considered a bird which a noble could not carry, it can be trained to chase the smaller birds as successfully as the falcons can be taught to pursue the heron. The name Tinnunculus is supposed by some to have been given to the bird in allusion to its peculiar cry, which is clear, shrill, and consists of a single note several times repeated.

On page 444 the reader may see a representation of a pair of HARIER HAWKS flying below the rock on which the peregrine falcon has perched, and engaged in pursuing one of the smaller birds.

They have been introduced because several species of Harier are to be found in Palestine, where they take, among the plains and lowlands, the place which is occupied by the other hawks and falcons among the rocks.

The name of Harier appears to be given to these birds on account of their habit of regularly quartering the ground over which they fly when in search of prey, just like hounds when searching for hares. This bird is essentially a haunter of flat and marshy lands, where it finds frogs, mice, lizards, on which it usually feeds. It does not, however, confine itself to such food, but will chase and kill most of the smaller birds, and occasionally will catch even the leveret, the rabbit, the partridge, and the curlew.

When it chases winged prey, it seldom seizes the bird in the air, but almost invariably keeps above it, and gradually drives it to the ground. It will be seen, therefore, that its flight is mostly low, as suits the localities in which it lives, and it seldom soars to any great height, except when it amuses itself by rising and wheeling in circles together with its mate. This proceeding generally takes place before nest-building. The usual flight is a mixture of that of the kestrel and the falcon, the Harier sometimes poising itself over some particular spot, and at others shooting forwards through the air with motionless wings.

Unlike the falcons and most of the hawks, the Harier does not as a rule perch on rocks, but prefers to sit very upright on the ground, perching generally on a mole-hill, stone, or some similar elevation. Even its nest is made on the ground, and is composed of reeds, sedges, sticks, and similar matter, materials that can be procured from marshy land. The nest is always elevated a foot or so from the ground, and has occasionally been found on the top of a mound more than a yard in height. It is, however, conjectured that in such cases the mound is made by one nest being built upon the remains of another. The object of the elevated nest is probably to preserve the eggs in case of a flood.

At least five species of Hariers are known to exist in the Holy Land, two of which are among the British birds, namely, the Marsh Harier (*Circus æruginosus*), sometimes called the Duck

Hawk and the Moor Buzzard, and the Hen Harier (*Circus cyaneus*), sometimes called the White Hawk, Dove Hawk, or Blue Hawk, on account of the plumage of the male, which differs greatly according to age; and the Ring-tailed Hawk, on account of the dark bars which appear on the tail of the female. All the Hariers are remarkable for the circlet of feathers that surrounds the eyes, and which resembles in a lesser degree the bold feather-circle around the eye of the owl tribe.

BEFORE taking leave of the Hawks, it is as well to notice the entire absence in the Scriptures of any reference to falconry. Now, seeing that the art of catching birds and animals by means of Hawks is a favourite amusement among Orientals, as has already been mentioned when treating of the gazelle (page 168), and knowing the unchanging character of the East, we cannot but think it remarkable that no reference should be made to this sport in the Scriptures.

It is true that in Palestine itself there would be but little scope for falconry, the rough hilly ground and abundance of cultivated soil rendering such an amusement almost impossible. Besides, the use of the falcon implies that of the horse, and, as we have already seen, the horse was scarcely ever used except for military purposes.

Had, therefore, the experience of the Israelites been confined to Palestine, there would have been good reason for the silence of the sacred writers on this subject. But when we remember that the surrounding country is well adapted for falconry, that the amusement is practised there at the present day, and that the Israelites passed so many years as captives in other countries, we can but wonder that the Hawks should never be mentioned as aids to bird-catching. We find that other bird-catching implements are freely mentioned and employed as familiar symbols, such as the gin, the net, the snare, the trap, and so forth; but that there is not a single passage in which the Hawks are mentioned as employed in falconry.

BARN OWL.

THE OWL.

The words which have been translated as Owl—Use made of the Little Owl in bird-catching—Habits of the bird—The Barn, Screech, or White Owl a native of Palestine—The Yanshûph, or Egyptian Eagle Owl—Its food and nest.

IN various parts of the Old Testament there occur several words which are translated as OWL in the Authorized Version, and in most cases the rendering is acknowledged to be the correct one, while in one or two instances there is a difference of opinion on the subject.

In Lev. xi. 16, 17, we find the following birds reckoned among those which are an abomination, and which might not be eaten by the Israelites: "The owl, and the night-hawk, and the cuckoo, and the hawk after his kind;

"And the little owl, and the cormorant, and the great owl."

It is very likely that the Little Owl here mentioned is identical with the Boomah of the Arabs. It is a bird that is common in Europe, where it is much valued by bird-catchers, who employ it as a means of attracting small birds to their traps. They place it on the top of a long pole, and carry it into the fields, where they plant the pole in the ground. This Owl has a curious habit of swaying its body backwards and forwards, and is sure to attract the notice of all the small birds in the neighbourhood. It is well known that the smaller birds have a peculiar hatred to the Owl, and never can pass it without mobbing it, assembling in great numbers, and so intent on their occupation that they seem to be incapable of perceiving anything but the object of their hatred. Even rooks, magpies, and hawks are taken by this simple device.

Whether or not the Little Owl was used for this object by the ancient inhabitants of Palestine is rather doubtful; but as they certainly did so employ decoy birds for the purpose of attracting game, it is not unlikely that the Little Owl was found to serve as a decoy. We shall learn more about the system of decoy-birds when we come to the partridge.

The Little Owl is to be found in almost every locality, caring little whether it takes up its residence in cultivated grounds, in villages, among deserted ruins, or in places where man has never lived. As, however, it is protected by the natives, it prefers the neighbourhood of villages, and may be seen quietly perched in some favourite spot, not taking the trouble to move unless it be approached closely. And to detect a perched Owl is not at all an easy matter, as the bird has a way of selecting some spot where the colours of its plumage harmonize so well with the surrounding objects that the large eyes are often the first indication of its presence. Many a time I have gone to search after Owls, and only been made aware of them by the sharp angry snap that they make when startled.

The common and well-known Barn Owl, also inhabits Palestine. Like the Little Owl, it affects the neighbourhood of man, though it may be found in ruins and similar localities. An old ruined building is sure to be tenanted by the Barn Owl, whose nightly shrieks very often terrify the belated wanderer, and make him fancy that the place is haunted by disturbed spirits. Such being the habits of the bird, it is likely that in the East, where popular superstition has peopled every well with its jinn and every ruin with its spirit, the nocturnal cry of this bird, which is often called the Screech Owl from its note, should be exceedingly terrifying, and would impress itself on the minds of sacred writers as a fit image of solitude, terror, and desolation.

The Screech Owl is scarcely less plentiful in Palestine than the Little Owl, and, whether or not it be mentioned under a

THE LITTLE OWL.

separate name, is sure to be one of the birds to which allusion is made in the Scriptures.

ANOTHER name now rises before us: this is the Yanshûph, translated as the Great Owl, a word which occurs not only in the prohibitory passages of Leviticus and Deuteronomy, but in the Book of Isaiah. In that book, ch. xxxiv. ver. 10, 11, we find the following passage: "From generation to generation it shall lie waste; none shall pass through it for ever and ever.

CAUGHT NAPPING.

"But the cormorant and the bittern shall possess it; the owl (*yanshûph*) also and the raven shall dwell in it: and He shall stretch out upon it the line of confusion, and the stones of emptiness." The Jewish Bible follows the same reading.

It is most probable that the Great Owl or Yanshûph is the EGYPTIAN EAGLE OWL (*Bubo ascalaphus*), a bird which is closely allied to the great Eagle Owl of Europe (*Bubo maximus*), and the Virginian Eared Owl (*Bubo Virginianus*) of America. This fine bird measures some two feet in length, and looks much larger than its real size, owing to the thick coating of feathers which it wears in common with all true Owls, and the ear-like feather tufts on the top of its head, which it can raise or depress at pleasure. Its plumage is light tawny.

This bird has a special predilection for deserted places and ruins, and may at the present time be seen on the very spots of which the prophet spoke in his prediction. It is very plentiful in Egypt, where the vast ruins are the only relics of a creed long passed away or modified into other forms of religion, and its presence only intensifies rather than diminishes the feeling of loneliness that oppresses the traveller as he passes among the ruins.

The European Eagle Owl has all the habits of its Asiatic congener. It dwells in places far from the neighbourhood of man, and during the day is hidden in some deep and dark recess, its enormous eyes not being able to endure the light of day. In the evening it issues from its retreat, and begins its search after prey, which consists of various birds, quadrupeds, reptiles, fish, and even insects when it can find nothing better.

On account of its comparatively large dimensions, it is able to overcome even the full-grown hare and rabbit, while the lamb and the young fawn occasionally fall victims to its voracity. It seems never to chase any creature on the wing, but floats silently through the air, its soft and downy plumage deadening the sound of its progress, and suddenly drops on the unsuspecting prey while it is on the ground.

The nest of this Owl is made in the crevices of rocks, or in ruins, and is a very large one, composed of sticks and twigs, lined with a tolerably large heap of dried herbage, the parent Owls returning to the same spot year after year. Should it not be able to find either a rock or a ruin, it contents itself with a

RAVEN. BARN OWL. EAGLE OWL.

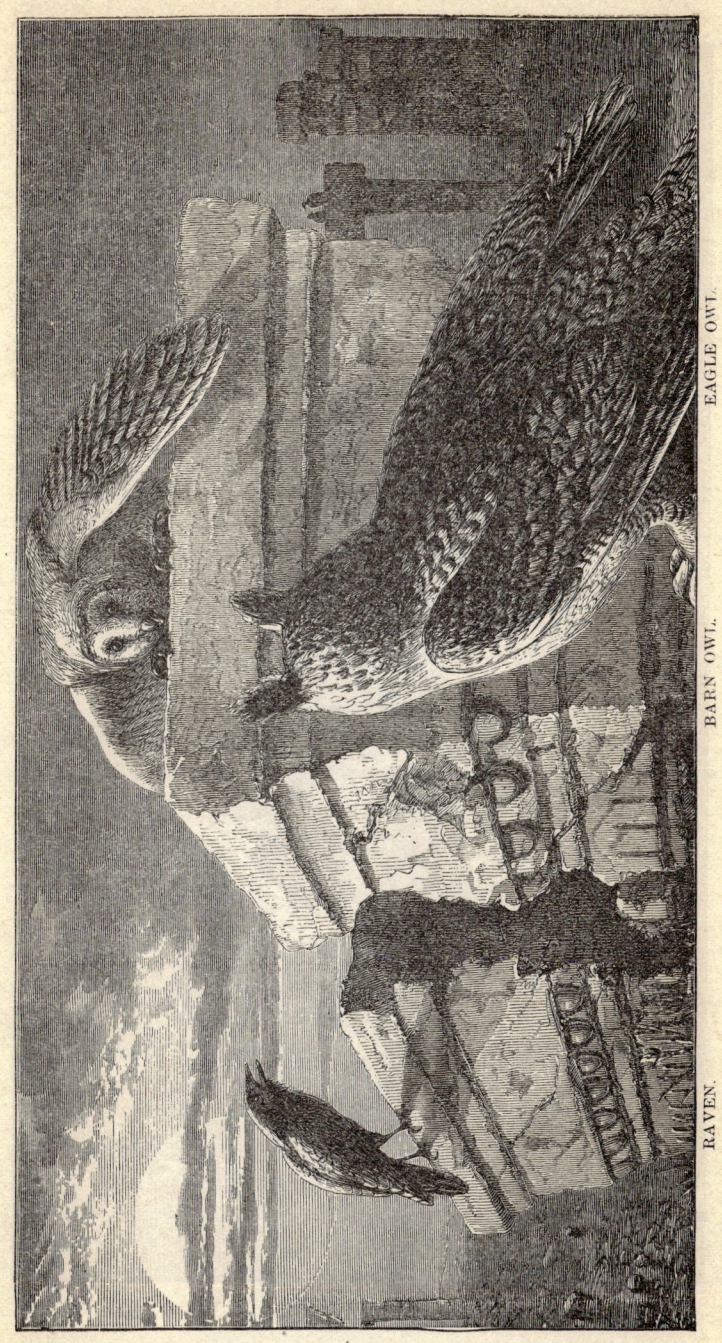

A FAMILY COUNCIL.

THE OWL.

hollow in the ground, and there lays its eggs, which are generally two in number, though occasionally a third egg is found. The Egyptian Eagle Owl does much the same thing, burrowing in sand-banks, and retreating, if it fears danger, into the hollow where its nest has been made.

In the large illustration the two last-mentioned species are given. The Egyptian Eagle Owl is seen with its back towards the spectator, grasping in its talons a dead hare, and with ear-tufts erect is looking towards the Barn Owl, which is contemplating in mingled anger and fear the proceedings of the larger bird. Near them is perched a raven, in order to carry out more fully the prophetic words, "the owl also and the raven shall dwell in it."

THE NIGHT-HAWK.

Different interpretations of the word Tachmâs—Probability that it signifies the Nightjar—Various names of the bird—Its remarkable jarring cry, and wheeling flight—Mode of feeding—Boldness of the bird—Deceptive appearance of its size.

WE next come to the vexed question of the word Tachmâs which is rendered in the Authorized Version as NIGHT-HAWK.

This word only occurs among the list of prohibited birds (see Lev. xi. 16, and Deut. xiv. 15), and has caused great controversies among commentators. The balance of probability seems to lie between two interpretations,—namely, that which considers the word *tachmâs* to signify the Night-hawk, and that which translates it as Owl. For both of these interpretations much is to be said, and it cannot be denied that of the two the latter is perhaps the preferable. If so, the White or Barn Owl is probably the particular species to which reference is made.

Still, many commentators think that the Night-hawk or Nightjar is the bird which is signified by the word *tachmâs*;

and, as we have already treated of the owls, we will accept the rendering of the Authorized Version. Moreover, the Jewish Bible follows the same translation, and renders *tachmâs* as Night-hawk, but affixes the mark of doubt.

It is not unlikely that the Jews may have reckoned this bird among the owls, just as is the case with the uneducated among ourselves, who popularly speak of the Nightjar as the Fern Owl, Churn Owl, or Jar Owl, the two last names being given to

THE NIGHT-HAWK.

it on account of its peculiar cry. There are few birds, indeed, which have received a greater variety of popular names, for, besides the Goatsucker and the five which have already been mentioned, there are the Wheel-bird and Dor-hawk, the former of these names having been given to the bird on account of its wheeling round the trees while seeking for prey, and the latter on account of the dor-beetles on which it largely feeds.

This curious variety of names is probably due to the very conspicuous character of the Nightjar, its strange, jarring, weird-like cry forcing itself on the ear of the least attentive, as it breaks the silence of night. It hardly seems like the cry of a bird, but rather resembles the sound of a pallet falling on the cogs of a rapidly-working wheel. It begins in the dusk of evening, the long, jarring note being rolled out almost interminably, until the hearer wonders how the bird can have breath enough for such a prolonged sound. The hearer may hold his breath as long as he can, take a full inspiration, hold his breath afresh, and repeat this process over and over again, and yet the Nightjar continues to trill out its rapid notes without a moment's cessation for breath, the sound now rising shrill and clear, and now sinking as if the bird were far off, but never ceasing for an instant.

This remarkable cry has caused the uneducated rustics to look upon the bird with superstitious dread, every one knowing its cry full well, though to many the bird is unknown except by its voice. It is probable that, in the days when Moses wrote the Law, so conspicuous a bird was well known to the Jews, and we may therefore conjecture that it was one of those birds which he would specially mention by name.

The general habits of the Nightjar are quite as remarkable as its note. It feeds on the wing, chasing and capturing the various moths, beetles, and other insects that fly abroad by night. It may be seen wheeling round the branches of some tree, the oak being a special favourite, sometimes circling round it, and sometimes rising high in the air, and the next moment skimming along the ground. Suddenly it will disappear, and next moment its long trilling cry is heard from among the branches of the tree round which it has been flying. To see it while singing is almost impossible, for it has a habit of sitting longitudinally on the branch, and not across it, like most birds, so that the outline of its body cannot be distinguished from that of the bough on which it is seated. As suddenly as it began, the sound ceases, and simultaneously the bird may be seen wheeling again through the air with its noiseless flight.

Being a very bold bird, and not much afraid of man, it allows a careful observer to watch its movements clearly. I have often stood close to the tree round which several Nightjars were circling, and seen them chase their prey to the ground within a yard or two of the spot on which I was standing. The flight of the Nightjar is singularly graceful. Swift as the swallow itself, it presents a command of wing that is really wonderful, gliding through the air with consummate ease, wheeling and doubling in pursuit of some active moth, whose white wings glitter against the dark background, while the sober plumage of its pursuer is scarcely visible, passing often within a few feet of the spectator, and yet not a sound or a rustle will reach his ears. Sometimes the bird is said to strike its wings together over its back, so as to produce a sharp snapping sound, intended to express anger at the presence of the intruder. I never, however, heard this sound, though I have watched the bird so often.

Owing to the soft plumage with which it is clad, this bird, like the owls, looks larger than really is the case. It is between ten and eleven inches in length, with an expanse of wing of twenty inches, and yet weighs rather less than three ounces. Its large mouth, like that of the swallow tribe, opens as far as the eyes, and is furnished with a set of *vibrissæ* or bristles, which remind the observer of the "whale-bone" which is set on the jaw of the Greenland whale.

THE SWALLOW.

Identification of the smaller birds—Oriental indifference to natural history—Use of collective terms—The Swallow—The Bird of Liberty—Swallows and Swifts—Variety of small birds found in Palestine—The Swallows of Palestine.

DIFFICULT as is the identification of the mammalia mentioned in the Bible, that of the birds is much more intricate.

Some of the larger birds can be identified with tolerable certainty, but when we come to the smaller and less conspicuous species, we are at once lost in uncertainty, and at the best can only offer conjectures. The fact is, the Jews of old had no idea of discriminating between the smaller birds, unless they happened to be tolerably conspicuous by plumage or by voice. We need not be much surprised at this. The Orientals of the present day do precisely the same thing, and not only fail to discriminate between the smaller birds, but absolutely have no names for them.

By them, the shrikes, the swallows, the starlings, the thrushes, the larks, the warblers, and all the smaller birds, are called by a common title, derived from the twittering sound of their voices, only one or two of them having any distinctive titles. They look upon the birds much as persons ignorant of entomology look at a collection of moths. There is not much difficulty in discriminating between the great hawk-moths, and perhaps in giving a name to one or two of them which are specially noticeable for any peculiarity of form or colour; but when they come to the "Rustics," the "Carpets," the "Wainscots," and similar groups, they are utterly lost; and, though they may be able to see the characteristic marks when the moths are placed side by side, they are incapable of distinguishing them separately, and, to their uneducated eyes, twenty or thirty species appear absolutely alike.

I believe that there is no country where a knowledge of practical natural history is so widely extended as in England, and yet how few educated persons are there who, if taken along a country lane, can name the commonest weed or insect, or distinguish between a sparrow, a linnet, a hedge-sparrow, and a chaffinch. Nay, how many are there who, if challenged even to repeat the names of twelve little birds, would be unable to do so without some consideration, much less to know them if the birds were placed before them.

Such being the case in a country where the capability of observation is more or less cultivated in every educated person, we may well expect that a profound ignorance on the subject should exist in countries where that faculty is absolutely neglected as a matter of education. Moreover, in England, there is a comparatively limited list of birds, whereas in Palestine are found nearly all those which are reckoned among British birds, and many other species besides. Those which reside in England reside also for the most part in Palestine, while the greater part of the migratory birds pass, as we might expect, into the Holy Land and the neighbouring countries.

If then we put together the two facts of an unobservant people and a vastly extended fauna, we shall not wonder that so many collective terms are used in the Scriptures, one word often doing duty for twenty or thirty species. The only plan, therefore, which can be adopted, is to mention generally the birds which were probably grouped under one name, and to describe briefly one or two of the most prominent.

It is, however, rather remarkable that the song of birds does not appear to be noticed by the sacred writers. We might expect that several of the prophets, especially Isaiah, the great sacred poet, who drew so many of his images from natural objects, would have found in the song of birds some metaphor expressive of sweetness or joy. We might expect that in the Book of Job, in which so many creatures are mentioned, the singing of birds would be brought as prominently forward as the neck clothed with thunder of the horse, the tameless freedom of the wild ass, the voracity of the vulture, and the swiftness of the ostrich. We might expect the song of birds to be mentioned by Amos, the herdman of Tekoa, who introduces into his rugged poem the roar of the old lion and the wail of the cub, the venom of the serpent hidden in the wattled wall of the herdman's hut, and the ravages of the palmer-worm among the olives. Above all, we might expect that in the Psalms there would be many allusions to the notes of the various birds which have formed such fruitful themes for the poets of later times. There are, however, in the whole of the Scriptures but two passages in which the song of birds is mentioned, and even in these only a passing allusion is made.

One of them occurs in Psalm civ. 12: "By them (*i.e.* the springs of water) shall the fowls of the heaven have their habitation, which sing among the branches." This passage is perhaps rendered more closely in the Jewish Bible: "Over them dwell the fowls of the heaven; they let their voices resound (or give their voice) from between the foliage."

The other occurs in Eccles. xii. 4: "And the doors shall be shut in the streets, when the sound of the grinding is low, and he shall rise up at the voice of the bird, and all the daughters of music shall be brought low." The word which is here translated as "bird," is that which is rendered in some places as "sparrow," in others as "fowl," and in others as "bird." Even in these passages, as the reader will have noticed, no marks of appreciation are employed, and we hear nothing of the sweetness, joyousness, or mournfulness of the bird's song.

WE will now proceed to the words which have been translated as Swallow in the Authorized Version.

These are two in number, namely, *derôr* and *agar*. Hebraists are, however, agreed that the latter word has been wrongly applied, the translators having interchanged the signification of two contiguous words.

We will therefore first take the word *deror*. This word signifies liberty, and is well applied to the Swallow, the bird of freedom. It is remarkable, by the way, how some of the old commentators have contrived to perplex themselves about a very simple matter. One of them comments upon the bird as being "so called, because it has the liberty of building in the houses of mankind." Another takes a somewhat similar view of the

LOST FROM THE FLOCK.

case, but puts it in a catechetical form: "Why is the swallow called the bird of liberty? Because it lives both in the house and in the field." It is scarcely necessary to point out to the reader that the "liberty" to which allusion is made is the liberty of flight, the bird coming and going at its appointed times, and not being capable of domestication.

Several kinds of Swallow are known in Palestine, including the true Swallows, the martins, and the swifts, and, as we shall presently see, it is likely that one of these groups was distinguished by a separate name. Whether or not the word *deror* included other birds beside the Swallows is rather doubtful, though not at all unlikely; and if so, it is probable that any swift-winged insectivorous bird would be called by the name of Deror, irrespective of its size or colour.

The bee-eaters, for example, are probably among the number of the birds grouped together under the word *deror*, and we may conjecture that the same is the case with the sunbirds, those bright-plumed little beings that take in the Old World the place occupied by the humming-birds in the New, and often mistaken for them by travellers who are not acquainted with ornithology. One of these birds, the *Nectarinia Oseæ*, is described by Mr. Tristram as "a tiny little creature of gorgeous plumage, rivalling the humming-birds of America in the metallic lustre of its feathers—green and purple, with brilliant red and orange plumes under its shoulders."

In order to account for the singular variety of animal life which is to be found in Palestine, and especially the exceeding diversity of species among the birds, we must remember that Palestine is a sort of microcosm in itself, comprising within its narrow boundaries the most opposite conditions of temperature, climate, and soil. Some parts are rocky, barren, and mountainous, chilly and cold at the top, and acting as channels through which the winds blow almost continuously. The cliffs are full of holes, rifts, and caverns, some natural, some artificial, and some of a mixed kind, the original caverns having been enlarged and improved by the hand of man.

As a contrast to this rough and ragged region, there lie close at hand large fertile plains, affording pasturage for unnumbered cattle, and of a tolerably equable temperature, so that the animals which are pastured in it can find food throughout the year. Through the centre of Palestine runs the Jordan, fertilizing its banks with perpetual verdure, and ending its course in the sulphurous and bituminous waters of the Dead Sea, under whose waves the ruins of the wicked cities are supposed to lie. Westward we have the shore of the Mediterranean with

THE SWALLOW AND SWIFT.

its tideless waves of the salt sea, and on the eastward of the mountain range that runs nearly parallel to the sea is the great Lake of Tiberias, so large as to have earned the name of the Sea of Galilee.

Under these favourable conditions, therefore, the number of species which are found in Palestine is perhaps greater than can be seen in any other part of the earth of the same dimensions, and it seems probable that for this reason, among many others Palestine was selected to be the Holy Land. If, for example, the Christian Church had been originated under the tropics, those who lived in a cold climate could scarcely have understood the language in which the Scriptures must necessarily have been couched. Had it, on the contrary, taken its rise in the Arctic regions, the inhabitants of the tropics and temperate regions

VIEW OF THE SEA OF GALILEE.

could not have comprehended the imagery in which the teachings of Scripture must have been conveyed. But the small and geographically insignificant Land of Palestine combines in itself many of the characteristics which belong respectively to the cold, the temperate, and the hot regions of the world, so that the terms in which the sacred writings are couched are intelligible to a very great proportion of the world's inhabitants.

This being the case, we naturally expect to find that several species of the Swallow are inhabitants of Palestine, if so migratory a bird can be said to be an inhabitant of any one country.

THE SWALLOW'S FAVOURITE HAUNT.

The chief characteristic of the Swallow, the "bird of freedom," is that it cannot endure captivity, but is forced by instinct to pass from one country to another for the purpose of preserving itself in a tolerably equable temperature, moving northwards as the spring ripens into summer, and southwards as autumn begins to sink into winter. By some marvellous instinct it traces its way over vast distances, passing over hundreds of miles where nothing but the sea is beneath it, and yet at the appointed season returning with unerring certainty to the spot where it was hatched. How it is guided no one knows, but the fact is certain, that Swallows, remarkable for some peculiarity by which they could be at once identified, have been observed to leave the country on their migration, and to return in the following year to the identical nest whence they started.

Its habit of making its nest among the habitations of mankind is mentioned in a well-known passage of the Psalms: "The sparrow hath found an house, and the swallow a nest for herself, where she may lay her young, even Thine altars, O Lord of Hosts, my King and my God" (Ps. lxxxiv. 3). The Swallow seems in all countries to have enjoyed the protection of man, and to have been suffered to build in peace under his roof. We find the same idea prevalent in the New World as well as the Old, and it is rather curious that the presence of the bird should so generally be thought to bring luck to a house.

In some parts of our country, a farmer would not dare to kill a Swallow or break down its nest, simply because he thinks that if he did so his cows would fail to give their due supply of milk. The connexion between the milking of a cow in the field and the destruction of a Swallow's nest in the house is not very easy to see, but nevertheless such is the belief. This idea ranks with that which asserts the robin and the wren to be the male and female of the same species, and to be under some special divine protection.

Whatever may be the origin of this superstition, whether it be derived from some forgotten source, or whether it be the natural result of the confiding nature of the bird, the Swallow enjoys at the present day the protection of man, and builds freely in his houses, and even his places of worship. The heathen temples, the Mahometan mosques, and the Christian churches are alike inhabited by the Swallow, who seems to know her security, and often places her nest where a child might reach it.

The bird does not, however, restrict itself to the habitations of man, though it prefers them; and in those places where no houses are to be found, and yet where insects are plentiful, it takes possession of the clefts of rocks, and therein makes its nest. Many instances are known where the Swallow has chosen the most extraordinary places for its nest. It has been known to build year after year on the frame of a picture, between the handles of a pair of shears hung on the wall, on a lamp-bracket, in a table-drawer, on a door-knocker, and similar strange localities.

The swiftness of flight for which this bird is remarkable is noticed by the sacred writers. "As the bird by wandering, as the swallow by flying, so the curse causeless shall not come" (Prov. xxvi. 2). This passage is given rather differently in the Jewish Bible, though the general sense remains the same: "As the bird is ready to flee, as the swallow to fly away; so a causeless execration, it shall not come." It is possible, however, that this passage may allude rather to the migration than the swiftness of the bird.

SWALLOWS AT HOME.

THE HOOPOE, OR LAPWING OF SCRIPTURE

The "Dukiphath" of Scripture—Various interpretations of the word—The Hoopoe—Its beauty and ill reputation—The unpleasant odour of its nest—Food of the Hoopoe—Its beautiful nest, and remarkable gestures—A curious legend of Solomon and the Hoopoe.

In the two parallel chapters, Lev. xi. and Deut. xiv., there occurs the name of a bird which is translated in the Authorized Version, Lapwing: " And the stork, the heron after her kind, the lapwing, and the bat."

The Hebrew word is *dukiphath*, and various interpretations have been proposed for it, some taking it to be the common domestic fowl, others the cock-of-the-woods, or capercailzie, while others have preferred to translate it as Hoopoe. The Jewish Bible retains the word lapwing, but adds the mark of doubt. Commentators are, however, agreed that of all these interpretations, that which renders the word as HOOPOE (*Upupa epops*) is the best.

There would be no particular object in the prohibition of such a bird as the lapwing, or any of its kin, while there would be very good reasons for the same injunction with regard to the Hoopoe.

In spite of the beauty of the bird, it has always had rather an ill reputation, and, whether in Europe or Asia, its presence seems to be regarded by the ignorant with a kind of superstitious aversion. This universal distaste for the Hoopoe is probably occasioned by an exceedingly pungent and disagreeable odour which fills the nest of the bird, and which infects for a considerable time the hand which is employed to take the eggs.

The nest is, moreover, well calculated for retaining any unpleasant smell, being generally made in the hollow of a tree, and having therefore but little of that thorough ventilation which is found in nearly all nests which are built on boughs and sprays.

The food of the Hoopoe consists almost entirely of insects They have been said to feed on earth-worms; but this notion seems to be a mistaken one, as in captivity they will not touch an earth-worm so long as they can procure an insect. Beetles of various kinds seem to be their favourite food, and when the beetles are tolerably large—say, for example, as large as the common cockchafer and dor-beetle—the bird beats them into a soft mass before it attempts to eat them. Smaller beetles are swallowed without any ceremony. The various boring insects which make their home in decaying wood are favourite articles of diet with the Hoopoe, which digs them out of the soft wood with its long curved beak.

It has already been mentioned that the nest is usually made in the hollow of a tree. In many parts of the country however, hollow trees cannot be found, and in that case the Hoopoe resorts to clefts in the rock, or even to holes in old ruins.

The bird is a peculiarly conspicuous one, not only on account of its boldly-barred plumage and its beautiful crest, but by its cry and its gestures. It has a way of elevating and depressing its crest, and bobbing its head up and down, in a manner which could not fail to attract the attention even of the most incurious, the whole aspect and expression of the bird varying with the raising and depressing of the crest.

Respecting this crest there is a curious old legend. As is the case with most of the Oriental legends, it introduces the name of King Solomon, who, according to Oriental notions, was a mighty wizard rather than a wise king, and by means of his seal, on which was engraven the mystic symbol of Divinity, held sway over the birds, the beasts, the elements, and even over the Jinns and Afreets, *i.e.* the good and evil spirits, which are too ethereal for the material world and too gross for the spiritual, and therefore hold the middle place between them.

On one of his journeys across the desert, Solomon was perishing from the heat of the sun, when the Hoopoes came to his aid, and flew in a dense mass over his head, thus forming a shelter from the fiery sunbeams. Grateful for this assistance, the monarch told the Hoopoes to ask for a boon, and it should be granted to them. The birds, after consulting together, agreed to ask that from that time every Hoopoe should wear a crown of gold like Solomon himself. The request was immediately granted, and each Hoopoe found itself adorned with a royal crown. At first, while their honours were new, great was the joy of the birds, who paused at every little puddle of water to contemplate themselves, bowing their heads over the watery mirror so as to display the crown to the best advantage.

Soon, however, they found cause to repent of their ambition. The golden crown became heavy and wearisome to them, and, besides, the wealth bestowed on the birds rendered them the prey of every fowler. The unfortunate Hoopoes were persecuted in all directions for the sake of their golden crowns which they could neither take off nor conceal.

At last, the few survivors presented themselves before Solomon, and begged him to rescind his fatal gift, which he did by substituting a crest of feathers for the crown of gold. The Hoopoe, however, never forgets its former grandeur, and is always bowing and bending itself as it used to do when contemplating its golden crown in the water.

EASTERN HOUSE-TOP.

THE SPARROW.

The Sparrow upon the house-top—Architecture of the East—Little birds exposed for sale in the market—The two Sparrows sold for a farthing—Bird-catching—The net, the snare, and the trap.

WE have already discussed the signification of the compound word *tzippor-deror*, and will now take the word *tzippor* alone.

Like many other Hebrew terms, the word is evidently used in a collective sense, signifying any small bird that is not specially designated. In several portions of Scripture it is translated as Sparrow, and to that word we will at present restrict ourselves.

On turning to Ps. cii. 5–7, we find that the word is used as an emblem of solitude and misery: "By reason of the voice of my groaning, my bones cleave to my skin.

"I am like a pelican of the wilderness: I am like an owl of the desert.

"I watch, and am as a sparrow alone upon the house-top."

The word which is here translated as "Sparrow" is *tzippor*, the same which is rendered as "bird" in Lev. xiv. 4. The Hebrew Bible more consistently uses the collective term "bird" in both instances, and renders the passage as, "I watch, and am as a lonely bird upon a roof."

Now, any one who knows the habits of the Sparrow is perfectly aware that it is a peculiarly sociable bird. It is quarrelsome enough with its fellows, and always ready to fight for a stray grain or morsel of food; but it is exceedingly gregarious, assembling together in little parties, enlivening the air with its merry though unmusical twitterings.

This cosmopolitan bird is plentiful in the coast towns of Palestine, where it haunts the habitations of men with the same dauntless confidence which it displays in this country. It is often seen upon roofs or house-tops, but is no more apt to sit alone in Palestine than it is here. On the contrary, the Sparrows collect in great numbers on the house-tops, attracted by the abundant supply of food which it finds there. This requires some little explanation.

The house-tops of the East, instead of being gabled and tiled as among ourselves, to allow the rain to run off, are quite flat, and serve as terraces or promenades in the evening, or even for sleeping-places; and from the house-tops proclamations were made. See, for example, 1 Sam. ix. 25: "And when they were come down from the high place into the city, Samuel communed with Saul upon the top of the house"—this being the ordinary place which would be chosen for a conversation. In order to keep out the heat of the mid-day sun, tents were sometimes pitched upon these flat house-tops. (See 2 Sam. xvi. 22.) Reference to the use of the house-tops as places for conversation are made in the New Testament. See, for example, Matt. x. 27: "What I tell you in darkness, that speak ye in light; and what ye hear in the ear, that preach ye upon the house-tops." Another passage of a similar nature occurs in Luke xii. 3: "Therefore whatsoever ye have spoken in darkness shall be heard in the light, and that which ye have spoken in the ear in closets shall be proclaimed on the house-tops."

These roofs, instead of being built with sloping rafters like those to which we are accustomed in this country, are made with great beams of wood laid horizontally, and crossed by planks, poles, and brushwood packed tightly together. As this roof would not keep out the rain, it is covered with a thick layer of clay mixed with straw, and beaten down as hard as possible. This covering has constantly to be renewed, as, even in the best made roofs, the heavy rains are sure to wash away some portion of the clay covering, which has to be patched up with a fresh supply of earth. A stone roller is generally kept on the roof of each house for the purpose of making a flat and even surface.

The earth which is used for this purpose is brought from the uncultivated ground, and is full of various seeds. As soon as the rains fall, these seeds spring up, and afford food to the Sparrows and other little birds, who assemble in thousands on the house-tops, and then peck away just as they do in our own streets and farm-yards.

It is now evident that the "sparrow alone and melancholy upon the house-tops" cannot be the lively, gregarious Sparrow which assembles in such numbers on these favourite feeding-places. We must therefore look for some other bird, and naturalists are now agreed that we may accept the BLUE THRUSH (*Petrocossyphus cyaneus*) as the particular Tzippor, or small bird, which sits alone on the house-tops.

The colour of this bird is a dark blue, whence it derives its popular name. Its habits exactly correspond with the idea of solitude and melancholy. The Blue Thrushes never assemble in flocks, and it is very rare to see more than a pair together. It is fond of sitting on the tops of houses, uttering its note, which, however agreeable to itself, is monotonous and melancholy to a human ear.

In connexion with the passage already quoted, "What ye hear in the ear, that preach ye upon the house-tops," I will take the opportunity of explaining the passage itself, which scarcely seems relevant to the occasion unless we understand its bearings. The context shows that our Lord was speaking of the new doctrines which He had come to teach, and the duty of spreading them, and alludes to a mode of religious teaching which was then in vogue.

The long captivity of the Jews in Babylon had caused the Hebrew language to be disused among the common people, who had learned the Chaldaic language from their captors. After their return to Palestine, the custom of publicly reading the

READING THE LAW TO THE PEOPLE AFTER THE RETURN FROM CAPTIVITY.

Scriptures was found to be positively useless, the generality of the people being ignorant of the Hebrew language.

Accordingly, the following modification was adopted. The roll of the Scriptures was brought out as usual, and the sacred words read, or rather chanted. After each passage was read, a doctor of the law whispered its meaning into the ear of a Targumista or interpreter, who repeated to the people in the Chaldaic language the explanation which the doctor had whispered in Hebrew. The reader will now see how appropriate is the metaphor, the whispering in the ear and subsequent proclamation being the customary mode of imparting religious instruction.

If the reader will now turn to Matt. x. 29, he will find that the word "sparrow" is used in a passage which has become very familiar to us. "Are not two sparrows sold for a farthing? and one of them shall not fall on the ground without your Father.

"But the very hairs of your head are all numbered.

"Fear ye not therefore, ye are of more value than many sparrows." The same sentences are given by St. Luke (xii. 6), in almost the same words.

Now the word which is translated as "Sparrow" is *strouthion*,

THE BLUE THRUSH, OR SPARROW OF SCRIPTURE.

a collective word, signifying a bird of any kind. Without the addition of some epithet, it was generally used to signify any kind of small bird, though it is occasionally employed to signify even so large a creature as an eagle, provided that the bird had been mentioned beforehand. Conjoined with the word "great," it signifies the ostrich; and when used in connexion with a word significative of running, it is employed as a general term for all cursorial birds.

In the passages above quoted it is used alone, and evidently signifies any kind of little bird, whether it be a sparrow or not. Allusion is made by our Lord to a custom, which has survived to the present day, of exposing for sale in the markets the bodies of little birds. They are stripped of their feathers, and spitted together in rows, and always have a large sale.

Various birds are sold in this manner, little if any distinction being made between them, save perhaps in respect of size, the larger species commanding a higher price than the small birds. In fact, they are arranged exactly after the manner in which the Orientals sell their "kabobs," *i.e.* little pieces of meat pierced by wooden skewers.

It is evident that to supply such a market it is necessary that the birds should be of a tolerably gregarious nature, so that a considerable number can be caught at a time. Nets were employed for this purpose, and we may safely infer that the forms of the nets and the methods of using them were identical with those which are employed in the same country at the present day.

The fowlers supply themselves with a large net supported on two sticks, and, taking a lantern with them fastened to the top of a pole, they sally out at night to the places where the small birds sleep.

Raising the net on its sticks, they lift it to the requisite height, and hold the lantern exactly opposite to it, so as to place the net between the birds and the lantern. The roosting-places are then beaten with sticks or pelted with stones, so as to awaken the sleeping birds. Startled by the sudden noise, they dash from their roosts, instinctively make towards the light, and so fall into the net. Bird-catching with nets is several times mentioned in the Old Testament, but in the New the net is only alluded to as used for taking fish.

Beside the net, several other modes of bird-catching were used by the ancient Jews, just as is the case at the present day. Boys, for example, who catch birds for their own consumption, and not for the market, can do so by means of various traps, most of which are made on the principle of the noose, or snare. Sometimes a great number of hair-nooses are set in places to which the birds are decoyed, so that in hopping about many of them are sure to become entangled in the snares. Sometimes the noose is ingeniously suspended in a narrow passage which the birds are likely to traverse, and sometimes a simple fall-trap is employed.

WE now pass to another division of the subject. In Ps. lxxxiv. 1–3, we come upon a passage in which the Sparrow is again mentioned : "How amiable are Thy tabernacles, O Lord of hosts!

"My soul longeth, yea, even fainteth for the courts of the Lord; my heart and my flesh crieth out for the living God.

"Yea, the sparrow hath found an house, and the swallow a nest for herself, where she may lay her young, even Thine altars, O Lord of hosts, my King, and my God."

It is evident that we have in this passage a different bird from the Sparrow that sitteth alone upon the house-tops; and though the same word, *tzippor*, is used in both cases, it is clear

THE TREE-SPARROW, OR SPARROW OF SCRIPTURE.

that whereas the former bird was mentioned as an emblem of sorrow, solitude, and sadness, the latter is brought forward as an image of joy and happiness. "Blessed are they," proceeds the Psalmist, "that dwell in Thy house: they will be still praising Thee. . . . For a day in Thy courts is better than a thousand. I had rather be a doorkeeper in the house of my God, than to dwell in the tents of wickedness."

According to Mr. Tristram, this is probably one of the species to which allusion is made by the Psalmist. While inspecting the ruins in the neighbourhood of the Temple, he came upon an old wall. "Near this gate I climbed on to the top of the wall, and walked along for some time, enjoying the fine view at the gorge of the Kedron, with its harvest crop of little white tombs. In a chink I discovered a sparrow's nest (*Passer cisalpinus*, var.) of a species so closely allied to our own that it is difficult to distinguish it, one of the very kind of which the Psalmist sung. . . . The swallows had departed for the winter, but the sparrow has remained pertinaciously through all the sieges and changes of Jerusalem."

The same traveller thinks that the TREE SPARROW (*Passer montanus*) may be the species to which the sacred writer refers, as it is even now very plentiful about the neighbourhood of the Temple. In all probability we may accept both these birds as representatives of the Sparrow which found a home in the Temple. The swallow is separately mentioned, possibly because its migratory habits rendered it a peculiarly conspicuous bird; but it is probable that many species of birds might make their nests in a place where they felt themselves secure from disturbance, and that all these birds would be mentioned under the collective and convenient term of Tzipporim.

THE CUCKOO.

The Cuckoo only twice mentioned in Scripture—The common species, and the Great Spotted Cuckoo—Depositing the egg.

ONLY in two instances is the word CUCKOO found in the Authorized Version of the Bible, and as they occur in parallel passages they are practically reduced to one. In Lev. xi. 16 we find it mentioned among the birds that might not be eaten, and the same prohibition is repeated in Deut. xiv. 15, the Jews being ordered to hold the bird in abomination.

It is rather remarkable that the Arabic name for the bird is exactly the same as ours, the peculiar cry having supplied the name. Its habit of laying its eggs in the nests of other birds is well known, together with the curious fact, that although so large a bird, measuring more than a foot in length, its egg is not larger than that of the little birds, such as the **hedge-sparrow**, **robin**, or **redstart**.

Besides this species, another Cuckoo inhabits Palestine, and

THE GREAT SPOTTED CUCKOO.

is much more common. This is the GREAT SPOTTED CUCKOO (*Oxylophus glandarius*). The birds belonging to this genus have been separated from the other Cuckoos because the feathers on the head are formed into a bold crest, in some species, such as Le Vaillant's Cuckoo, reminding the observer of the crest of the cockatoo. This fine bird measures nearly sixteen inches in length, and can be distinguished, not only by the crested head, but by the reddish grey of the throat and chest, and the white tips of the wing and tail feathers.

This species lays its eggs in the nests of comparatively large birds, such as the rooks, crows, and magpies;

NOAH RECEIVES THE DOVE.

THE DOVE.

Parallel between the lamb and the Dove—The Dove and the olive branch—Abram's sacrifice, and its acceptance—The Dove-sellers of the Temple—The Rock Dove and its multitudes.

In giving the Scriptural history of the Doves and Pigeons, we shall find ourselves rather perplexed in compressing the needful information into a reasonable space. There is no bird which plays a more important part, both in the Old and the New Testaments, or which is employed so largely in metaphor and symbol.

The Doves and Pigeons were to the birds what were the sheep and lambs to the animals, and, like them, derived their chief interest from their use in sacrifice. Both the lamb and the young pigeon being emblems of innocence, both were used on similar occasions, the latter being in many instances permitted when the former were too expensive for the means of the offerer. As to the rendering of the Hebrew words which have been translated as Pigeon, Dove, and Turtle Dove, there has never been any discussion. The Hebrew word *yonâh* has always been acknowledged to signify the Dove or Pigeon, and the word *tôr* to signify the Turtle Dove. Generally, the two words are used in combination, so that *tor-yonâh* signifies the Turtle Dove.

Though the interpretation of the word *yonâh* is universally accepted, there is a little difficulty about its derivation, and its signification apart from the bird. Some have thought that it is derived from a root signifying warmth, in allusion to the warmth of its affection, the Dove having from time immemorial been selected as the type of conjugal love. Others, among whom is Buxtorf, derive it from a word which signifies oppression, because the gentle nature of the Dove, together with its inability to defend itself, cause it to be oppressed, not only by man, but by many rapacious birds.

THE first passage in which we hear of the Dove occurs in the earlier part of Genesis. Indeed, the Dove and the raven are the first two creatures that are mentioned by any definite names, the word *nachosh*, which is translated as "serpent" in Gen. iii. 1, being a collective word signifying any kind of serpent, whether venomous or otherwise, and not used for the purpose of designating any particular species.

Turning to Gen. viii. 8, we come to the first mention of the Dove. The whole passage is too familiar to need quoting, and it is only needful to say that the Dove was sent out of the ark in order that Noah might learn whether the floods had subsided, and that, after she had returned once, he sent her out again seven days afterwards, and that she returned, bearing an olive-branch (or leaf, in the Jewish Bible). Seven days afterwards he sent the Dove for the third time, but she had found rest on the earth, and returned no more.

It is not within the province of this work to treat, except in the most superficial manner, of the metaphorical signification of the Scriptures. I shall, therefore, allude but very slightly to the metaphorical sense of the passages which record the exit from the ark and the sacrifice of Noah. Suffice it to say that, putting entirely aside all metaphor, the characters of the raven and the Dove are well contrasted. The one went out, and, though the trees were at that time submerged, it trusted in its strong wings, and hovered above the watery expanse until the flood had subsided. The Dove, on the contrary, fond of the society of man, and having none of the wild, predatorial habits which distinguish the raven, twice returned to its place of refuge, before it was finally able to find a resting-place for its foot.

After this, we hear nothing of the Dove until the time of Abraham, some four hundred years afterwards, when the covenant was made between the Lord and Abram, when "he believed in the Lord, and it was counted to him for righteousness." In order to ratify this covenant he was ordered to offer a sacrifice, which consisted of a young heifer, a she-goat, a ram, a turtle-dove, and a young dove or pigeon. The larger animals were severed in two, but the birds were not divided, and between the portions of the sacrifice there passed a lamp of fire as a symbol of the Divine presence.

In after days, when the promise that the seed of Abram should be as the stars of heaven for multitude had been amply fulfilled, together with the prophecy that they should be "strangers in a land that was not theirs," and should be in slavery and under oppression for many years, the Dove was specially mentioned in the new law as one of the creatures that were to be sacrificed on certain defined occasions.

Even the particular mode of offering the Dove was strictly defined. See Lev. i. 14—17: "If the burnt sacrifice for his offering to the Lord be of fowls, then he shall bring his offering of turtle-doves, or of young pigeons.

"And the priest shall bring it unto the altar, and wring off his head, and burn it on the altar; and the blood thereof shall be wrung out at the side of the altar.

"And he shall pluck away his crop with his feathers, and cast it beside the altar, on the east part, by the place of the ashes.

"And he shall cleave it with the wings thereof, but shall not divide it asunder: and the priest shall burn it upon the altar, upon the wood that is upon the fire."

Here we have a repetition not only of the sacrifice of Abram, but of the mode in which it was offered, care being taken that the body of the bird should not be divided. There is a slight, though not very important variation in one or two portions of this passage. For example, the wringing off the head of the bird is, literally, pinching off, and had to be done with the thumb nail; and the passage which is by some translators rendered as the crop and the feathers, is by others translated as the crop and its contents—a reading which seems to be more consonant with the usual ceremonial of sacrifice than the other.

As a general rule, the pigeon was only sanctioned as a sacrificial animal in case one of more value could not be afforded; and so much care was taken in this respect, that with the exception of the two "sparrows" (*tzipporim*) that were enjoined as part of the sacrifice by which the cleansed leper was received back among the people (Lev. xiv. 4), no bird might be offered in sacrifice unless it belonged to the tribe of pigeons.

It was in consequence of the poverty of the family that the Virgin Mary brought two young pigeons when she came to present her new-born Son in the Temple. For those who were able to afford it, the required sacrifice was a lamb of the first year for a burnt-offering, and a young pigeon or Turtle Dove for a sin-offering. But "if she be not able to bring a lamb, then she shall bring two turtles, or two young pigeons, the one for the burnt-offering and the other for a sin-offering." The extraordinary value which all Israelites set upon the first-born son is well known, both parents even changing their own names, and being called respectively the father and mother of Elias, or Joseph, as the case may be. If the parents who had thus attained the summit of their wishes possessed a lamb, or could have obtained one, they would most certainly have offered it in the fulness of their joy, particularly when, as in the case of Mary, there was such cause for rejoicing; and the fact that they were forced to substitute a second pigeon for the lamb is a proof of their extreme poverty.

While the Israelites were comparatively a small and compact nation, dwelling around their tabernacle, the worshippers could easily offer their sacrifices, bringing them from their homes to the altar. But in process of time, when the nation had become a large and scattered one, its members residing at great distances, and only coming to the Temple once or twice in the year to offer their sacrifices, they would have found that for even the poor to carry their pigeons with them would have greatly increased the trouble, and in many cases have been almost impossible.

For the sake of convenience, therefore, a number of dealers established themselves in the outer courts of the Temple, for the purpose of selling Doves to those who came to sacrifice. Sheep and oxen were also sold for the same purpose, and, as offerings of money could only be made in the Jewish coinage, money-changers established themselves for the purpose of exchanging foreign money brought from a distance for the legal Jewish shekel. That these people exceeded their object, and endeavoured to overreach the foreign Jews who were ignorant of the comparative value of money and goods, is evident from the

JESUS DRIVES OUT OF THE TEMPLE THE MONEY-CHANGERS AND THOSE WHO SOLD DOVES.

fact of their expulsion by our Lord, and the epithets which were applied to them.

According to some old writers, the Dove was considered as having a superiority over other birds in the instinctive certainty with which it finds its way from one place to another. At the present time, our familiarity with the variety of pigeon known as the Carrier has taught us that the eye is the real means employed by the pigeon for the direction of its flight. Those who fly pigeons for long distances always take them several times over the same ground, carrying them to an increasing distance at every journey, so that the birds shall be able to note certain objects which serve them as landmarks.

Bees and wasps have recourse to a similar plan. When a young wasp leaves its nest for the first time, it does not fly away at once, but hovers in front of the entrance for some time, getting farther and farther away from the nest until it has learned the aspect of surrounding objects. The pigeon acts in precisely the same manner, and so completely does it depend upon eyesight

THE ROCK DOVE.

that, if a heavy fog should come on, the best-trained pigeon will lose its way.

The old writers, however, made up their minds that the pigeon found its way by scent, which sense alone, according to their ideas, could guide it across the sea. They were not aware of the power possessed by birds of making their eyes telescopic at will, or of the enormous increase of range which the sight obtains by elevation. A pigeon at the elevation of several hundred yards can see to an astonishing distance, and there is no need of imagining one sense to receive a peculiar development when the ordinary powers of another are sufficient to obtain the object.

That dove-cotes were in use among the earlier Jews is well known. An allusion to the custom of keeping pigeons in cotes

BLUE ROCK PIGEONS.

is seen in Isa. lx. 8: "Who are these that fly as a cloud, and as the doves to their windows?" or, as the Jewish Bible translates the passage, "as the doves to their apertures?" In this passage the sacred writer utters a prophecy concerning the coming of the world to the Messiah, the Gentiles flocking to Him as the clouds of pigeons fly homeward to their cotes.

The practice of pigeon-keeping has survived to the present day, the houses of wealthy men being furnished with separate pigeon-houses for the protection and shelter of these popular birds.

In the Holy Land are found all the species of Pigeons with which we are familiar, together with one or two others. First, there is the Rock Pigeon, or Blue Rock Dove, which is acknowledged to be the origin of our domestic breeds of Pigeons, with all their infinite variety of colour and plumage. This species, though plentiful in Palestine, is not spread over the whole of the land, but lives chiefly on the coast and in the higher parts of the country. In these places it multiplies in amazing numbers, its increase being almost wholly unchecked by man, on account of the inaccessible cliffs in which it lays its eggs and nurtures its young, its only enemies being a few of the birds and beasts of prey, which can exercise but a trifling influence on these prolific birds.

Mr. Tristram, while visiting the Wady (or Valley) Seimûn, which lies near the Lake of Gennesaret, witnessed an amusing example of the vast number of these Pigeons.

"No description can give an adequate idea of the myriads of rock pigeons. In absolute clouds they dashed to and fro in the ravine, whirling round with a rush and a whirr that could be felt like a gust of wind. It was amusing to watch them upset the dignity and the equilibrium of the majestic griffon as they swept past him. This enormous bird, quietly sailing along, was quite turned on his back by the sudden rush of wings and wind."

In Palestine these birds are taken in nets, into which they are decoyed by a very effective though cruel device.

When one of these birds is trapped or snared, it is seized by its capturers, who spare its life for the sake of using it as a decoy. They blind it by sewing its eyelids together, and then fasten it to a perch among trees. The miserable bird utters plaintive cries, and continually flaps its wings, thus attracting others of its kind, who settle on the surrounding branches and are easily taken, their whole attention being occupied by the cries of their distressed companion.

We now come to the Turtle Doves, several of which inhabit the Holy Land; but, as they are similar in habits, we will confine ourselves to the common species, with which we are so familiar in this country. Its migratory habits are noticed in the sacred writings. See the following passage in the Song of Solomon:

"Lo, the winter is past, the rain is over and gone; the flowers appear on the earth; the time of the singing of birds is come, and the voice of the turtle is heard in our land" (Cant. ii. 11, 12). The prophet Jeremiah also refers to the migration of this bird: "Yea, the stork in the heaven knoweth her appointed times; and the turtle, and the crane, and the swallow observe the time of their coming; but my people know not the judgment of the Lord" (viii. 7).

Beside this species, there is the Collared Turtle Dove, one variety of which is known as the Barbary Dove. It is a large species,

THE TURTLE DOVE.

measuring more than a foot in length. Another species is the Palm Turtle, so called from its habit of nesting on palm-trees, when it is obliged to build at a distance from the habitations of man. It is a gregarious bird, several nests being generally found on one tree, and even, when it cannot find a palm, it will build among the thorns in multitudes. Like the common Dove, it is fond of the society of man, and is sure to make its nest among human habitations, secure in its knowledge that it will not be disturbed.

It is rather a small bird, being barely ten inches in length, and having no "collar" on the neck, like the two preceding species.

POULTRY.

Poultry plentiful in Palestine at the present day—The Domestic Fowl unknown in the early times of Israel—The eating and gathering of eggs—References to Poultry in the New Testament—The egg and the scorpion—The fatted fowl of Solomon—The hen brooding over her eggs—Poultry prohibited within Jerusalem—The cock-crowing.

AT the present day, poultry are plentiful both in Palestine and Syria, and that they were bred in the time of the Apostles is evident from one or two references which are made by our Lord. How long the Domestic Fowl had been known to the Jews is extremely uncertain, and we have very little to guide us in our search.

That it was unknown to the Jews during the earlier period of their history is evident from the utter silence of the Old Testament on the subject. A bird so conspicuous and so plentiful would certainly have been mentioned in the Law of Moses had it been known to the Israelites; but, in all its minute and detailed provisions, the Law is silent on the subject.

Neither the bird itself nor its eggs are mentioned, although there are a few references to eggs, without signifying the bird which laid them. The humane provision in Deut. xxii. 6, 7, refers not to a domesticated, but to a wild bird: "If a bird's nest chance to be before thee in any tree, or on the ground, whether they be young ones, or eggs, and the dams sitting upon the young, or upon the eggs, thou shalt not take the dam with the young: but thou shalt in any wise let the dam go, and take the young to thee; that it may be well with thee, that thou mayest prolong thy days."

THE DOMESTIC FOWL.

There is but one passage in the Old Testament which has ever been conjectured to refer to the Domestic Fowl. It occurs in 1 Kings iv. 22, 23: "And Solomon's provision for one day was thirty measures of fine flour, and threescore measures of meal,

"Ten fat oxen, and twenty oxen out of the pastures, and an hundred sheep, besides harts, and roebucks, and fallow-deer, and fatted fowl."

Many persons think that the fatted fowl mentioned in the above-quoted passage were really Domestic Fowl, which Solomon had introduced into Palestine, together with various other birds and animals, by means of his fleet. There may be truth in this conjecture, but, as there can be no certainty, we will pass from the Old Testament to the New.

We are all familiar with the passages in which the Domestic Fowl is mentioned in the New Testament. There is, for example, that touching image employed by our Lord when lamenting over Jerusalem: "O Jerusalem, Jerusalem, thou that killest the prophets, and stonest them that are sent unto thee; how often would I have gathered thy children together, as a hen doth gather her brood under her wings, and ye would not!" The reference is evidently made to the Domesticated Fowl, which in the time of our Lord was largely bred in the Holy Land.

Some writers have taken objection to this statement in consequence of a Rabbinical law which prohibited poultry from being kept within the walls of Jerusalem, lest in their search for food they should scratch up any impurity which had been buried, and so defile the holy city. But it must be remembered that in the time of Christ Jerusalem belonged practically to the Romans, who held it with a garrison, and who, together with other foreigners, would not trouble themselves about any such prohibition, which would seem to them, as it does to us, exceedingly puerile, not to say unjustifiable.

That the bird was common in the days of our Lord is evident from the reference to the "cock-crowing" as a measure of time.

THE PEACOCK.

The foreign curiosities imported by Solomon—The word *Tucciyim* and its various interpretations—Identity of the word with the Cingalese name of the Peacock—Reasons why the Peacock should have been brought to Solomon—Its subsequent neglect and extirpation.

AMONG the many foreign objects which were imported by Solomon into Palestine, we find that the Peacock is specially mentioned. (See a passage which has already been mentioned in connexion with ivory and apes.) The sacred historian, after mentioning the ivory throne, the golden shields and targets, that all the vessels in Solomon's house were of gold, and that silver was so common as to be of no account, proceeds to give the reason for this profuse magnificence. "For the king had at sea a navy of Tharshish with the navy of Hiram: once in three years came the navy of Tharshish, bringing gold, and silver, ivory, and apes, and peacocks" (1 Kings x. 22).

That this magnificent bird should have been one of those creatures that were imported by Solomon is almost certain. It would be imported for the same reason as the apes; namely, for the purpose of adding to the glories of Solomon's house, and no bird could have been selected which would have a more magnificent effect than the Peacock. Moreover, although unknown in Palestine, it is extremely plentiful in India and Ceylon, inhabiting the jungle by thousands, and, by a curious coincidence, being invariably most plentiful in those spots which are most frequented by tigers. In many parts of the country, great numbers of Peacocks frequent the temples, and live amicably with the sacred monkeys, passing their lives in absolute security, protected by the sanctity of the place.

Their numbers, therefore, would render them easily accessible to Solomon's envoys, who would purchase them at a cheap rate from the native dealers, while their surpassing beauty would render them sure of a sale on their arrival in Jerusalem. Indeed, their beauty made so great an impression that they are separately mentioned by the sacred chronicler, the Peacock and the ape being the only two animals that are thought worthy of enumeration.

The Peacock may safely be termed one of the most beautiful of the feathered tribe, and may even lay a well-founded claim to the chief rank among birds, in splendour of plumage and effulgence of colouring.

We are so familiar with the Peacock that we think little of its real splendour; but if one of these birds was brought to this country for the first time, it would create a greater sensation than many animals which are now viewed in menageries with the greatest curiosity and interest.

The train of the male Peacock is the most remarkable feature of this beautiful bird; the feathers composing it are very long, and are coloured with green, purple, bronze, gold, and blue in such a manner as to form distinct "eyes."

On the head is a tuft of upright feathers, blackish upon their shafts, and rich golden green, shot with blue, on their expanded tips. The top of the head, the throat, and neck are the most refulgent blue, changing in different lights to gold and green. The wings are darker than the rest of the plumage, the abdomen blackish, and the feathers of the thighs are fawn.

THE PEACOCK.

The female is much smaller than her mate, and not nearly so beautiful, the train being almost wanting, and the colour ashy-brown, with the exception of the throat and neck, which are green.

It seems that after Solomon's death the breed of Peafowl was not kept up, owing in all probability to the troubles which beset the throne after that magnificent monarch died.

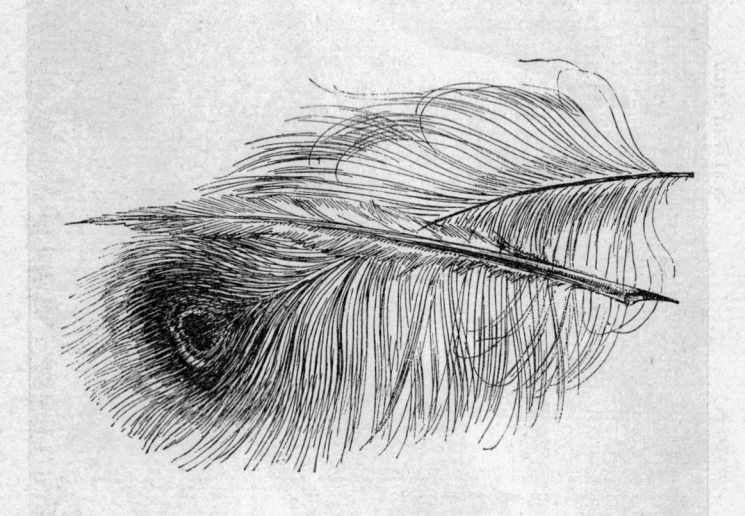

THE PARTRIDGE.

The word *Kore* and its signification—The Partridge upon the mountains—David's simile—The Desert Partridge and its habits—Hunting the Partridge with sticks—Eggs of the Partridge—Egg-hunting in Palestine—The various species of Partridge.

THERE is a bird mentioned in the Old Testament, which, although its name is only given twice, is a very interesting bird to all students of the Scriptures, both passages giving an insight into the manners and customs of the scarcely changing East. This is the bird called in the Hebrew Kore, a word which has been generally accepted as signifying some kind of Partridge. There is no doubt that, like most other Hebrew names of animated beings, the word is a collective one, signifying a considerable number of species.

The first passage occurs in 1 Sam. xxvi. 20. When David was being pursued by Saul, and had been forced to escape from the city and hide himself in the rocky valleys, he compared himself to the Partridge, which frequented exactly the same places: "The king of Israel is come out to seek a flea, as when one doth hunt a partridge upon the mountains."

The appositeness of this simile is perfect. The bird to which David alluded was in all probability the Desert Partridge (*Ammoperdix Heyii*), a species which especially haunts rocky and desert places, and even at the present day is exceedingly plentiful about the Cave of Adullam. The males, when they think themselves unobserved, are fond of challenging, or calling to each other in a loud ringing note, a peculiarity that has earned for the bird the Hebrew name of Kore, or "the caller."

It is a very active bird, not taking to flight if it can escape by means of its legs, and, when pursued or disturbed, running with great swiftness to some rocky cleft in which it may hide itself, taking care to interpose, as it runs, stones or other obstacles between itself and the object of its alarm. Thus, then, it will be seen how close was the parallel between this bird and David, who was forced, like the Partridge, to seek for refuge in the rocky caves.

But the parallel becomes even closer when we come to examine the full meaning of the passage. The Partridge is at the present day hunted on the mountains exactly as was the case in the time of David. The usual hunters are boys, who provide themselves with a supply of stout sticks about eighteen inches in length, and, armed with these, they chase the birds, hurling the sticks one after the other along the ground, so as to strike the Partridge as it runs. Generally, several hunters chase the same bird, some of them throwing the sticks along the ground, while others hurl them just above the bird, so that if it should take to flight, it may be struck as it rises into the air. By pertinaciously chasing an individual bird, the hunters tire it, and contrive to come so close that they are certain to strike it.

THE GREEK PARTRIDGE.

The reader will now see how perfect is the image. Driven from the city, David was forced to wander, together with the Desert Partridge, upon the hill-sides, and, like that bird, his final refuge is the rock. Then came the hunters and pursued him, driving him from place to place, as the boys hunt the Partridge, until he was weary of his life, and exclaimed in his despair, "I shall now perish one day by the hand of Saul."

The Partridges of Palestine are, like those of our own land, exceedingly prolific birds, laying a wonderful number of eggs, more than twenty being sometimes found in a single nest. These eggs are used for food, and the consumption of them is very great, so that many a Partridge has been deprived of her expected family: she has sat upon eggs, and hatched them not.

Just as hunting the Partridge is an acknowledged sport among the inhabitants of the uncultivated parts of Palestine, so is searching for the eggs of the bird a regular business at the proper time of year.

Of these birds several species inhabit Palestine. There is, for example, the Desert Partridge, which has already been

PARTRIDGES AND THEIR YOUNG.

mentioned. It is beautifully, though not brilliantly coloured, and may be known by the white spot behind the eye, the purple and chestnut streaks on the sides, and the orange bill and legs. These, however, soon lose their colour after death.

EASTERN QUAIL.

THE QUAIL.

Migration of the Quail—Modes of catching the Quail in the East—The Quail-hunters of Northern Africa—Quarrelsome nature of the bird—Quail-fighting in the East—How the Quails were brought to the Israelites.

In one or two parts of the Old Testament is found a word which has been translated in the Authorized Version of the Bible as QUAIL.

The word is *selâv*, and in every case where it is mentioned it is used with reference to the same occurrence; namely, the providing of flesh-meat in the wilderness, where the people could find no food. As the passages remarkably bear upon each other it will be advisable to quote them in the order in which they come.

The first mention of the Selâv occurs in Exod. xvi. Only a few days after the Israelites had passed the Red Sea, they began to complain of the desert land into which Moses had led them, and openly said that they wished they had never left the land of their slavery, where they had plenty to eat. According to His custom, pitying their narrow-minded and short-sighted folly, the natural result of the long servitude to which they had been subject, the Lord promised to send both bread and flesh-meat.

"And the Lord spake unto Moses, saying,

"I have heard the murmurings of the children of Israel: speak unto them, saying, At even ye shall eat flesh, and in the

THE QUAIL.

morning ye shall be filled with bread; and ye shall know that I am the Lord your God.

"And it came to pass, that at even the quails came up, and covered the camp" (ver. 11–13).

The next passage records a similar circumstance, which occurred about a year afterwards, when the Israelites were tired of eating nothing but the manna, and again wished themselves back in Egypt. "And there went forth a wind from the Lord, and brought quails from the sea, and let them fall by the camp as it were a day's journey on this side, and as it were a day's journey on the other side, round about the camp, and as it were two cubits high upon the face of the earth.

"And the people stood up all that day, and all that night, and all the next day, and they gathered the quails: he that gathered least gathered ten homers; and they spread them all abroad for themselves round about the camp" (Numb. xi. 31, 32).

The last passage in which Quails are mentioned occurs in the Psalms. In Ps. cv. are enumerated the various wonders done on behalf of the Israelites, and among them is specially mentioned this gift of the Quails and manna. "The people asked, and He brought quails, and satisfied them with the bread of heaven" (ver. 40).

"He had commanded the clouds from above, and opened the doors of heaven,

"And had rained down manna upon them to eat, and had given them of the corn of heaven.

"Man did eat angels' food: He sent them meat to the full.

"He caused an east wind to blow in the heaven; and by His power He brought in the south wind.

"He rained flesh also upon them as dust, and feathered fowls like as the sand of the sea" (Ps. lxxviii. 23—27).

If the ordinary interpretation of *selâv* by "Quail" be accepted, the description is exactly correct. The Quails fly in vast flocks, and, being weak-winged birds, never fly against the direction of the wind. They will wait for days until the wind blows in the required direction, and will then take wing in countless multitudes; so that in an hour or two a spot on which not a Quail could be seen is covered with them.

On account of their short wings, they never rise to any great height, even when crossing the sea, while on land they fly at a very low elevation, merely skimming over the ground, barely a yard or "two cubits high upon the face of the earth."

Moreover, the flesh of the Quail is peculiarly excellent, and would be a great temptation to men who had passed so long a time without eating animal food. Another corroboration of the identity of the Quail and the Selâv is to be found in the mode in which the flesh is prepared at the present day. As soon as the birds have arrived, they are captured in vast multitudes, on account of their weariness. Many are consumed at once, but great numbers are preserved for future use by being split and laid out to dry in the sun, precisely as the Israelites are said to have spread out the Selavim "all abroad for themselves round about the camp."

Accepting, therefore, the Selâv and Quail to be identical, we may proceed to the description of the bird.

It is small, plump, and round-bodied, with the head set closely on the shoulders. Owing to this peculiarity of form, it has its Arab name, which signifies plumpness or fatness. The wings are pressed closely to the body, and the tail is pointed, very short, and directed downwards, so that it almost appears to be absent, and the bird seems to be even more plump than really is the case.

Several modes of capturing these birds are still practised in the East, and were probably employed, not only on the two occasions mentioned in Exodus and Numbers, but on many others of which the Scriptural narrative takes no notice. One very simple plan is, for the hunters to select a spot on which the birds are assembled, and to ride or walk round them in a large circle, or rather in a constantly diminishing spiral. The birds are by this process driven closer and closer together, until at the last they are packed in such masses that a net can be thrown over them, and a great number captured in it.

Sometimes a party of hunters unite to take the Quails, and employ a similar manœuvre, except that, instead of merely walking round the Quails, they approach simultaneously from opposite points, and then circle round them until the birds are supposed to be sufficiently packed. At a given signal they all converge upon the terrified birds, and take them by thousands at a time.

In Northern Africa these birds are captured in a very similar fashion. As soon as notice is given that a flight of Quails has settled, all the men of the village turn out with their great burnouses or cloaks. Making choice of some spot as a centre, where a quantity of brushwood grows or is laid down, the men surround it on all sides, and move slowly towards it, spreading their cloaks in their outstretched hands, and flapping them like the wings of huge birds. Indeed, when a man is seen from a little distance performing this act, he looks more like a huge bat than a human being.

As the men gradually converge upon the brushwood, the Quails naturally run towards it for shelter, and at last they all creep under the treacherous shade. Still holding their outspread cloaks in their extended hands, the hunters suddenly run to the brushwood, fling their cloaks over it, and so enclose the birds in a trap from which they cannot escape. Much care is required in this method of hunting, lest the birds should take to flight, and so escape. The circle is therefore made of very great size, and the men who compose it advance so slowly that the Quails prefer to use their legs rather than their wings, and do not think of flight until their enemies are so close upon them that their safest course appears to be to take refuge in the brushwood.

Boys catch the Quails in various traps and springes, the most ingenious of which is a kind of trap, the door of which overbalances itself by the weight of the bird.

By reason of the colour of the Quail, and its inveterate habit of keeping close to the ground, it easily escapes observation, and even the most practised eye can scarcely distinguish a single bird, though there may be hundreds within a very small compass. Fortunately for the hunters, and unfortunately for itself, it betrays itself by its shrill whistling note, which it frequently emits, and which is so peculiar that it will at once direct the hunter to his prey.

This note is at the same time the call of the male to the female and a challenge to its own sex. Like all the birds of its group, the Quail is very combative, and generally fights a battle for the possession of each of its many mates. It is not gifted with such weapons of offence as some of its kinsfolk, but it is none the less quarrelsome, and fights in its own way as desperately as the game-cock of our own country.

Indeed, in the East, it is used for exactly the same purpose as the game-cock. Battles between birds and beasts, not to say men, are the common amusement with Oriental potentates, and, when they are tired of watching the combats of the larger animals, they have Quail-fights in their own chambers. The birds are selected for this purpose, and are intentionally furnished with stimulating food, so as to render them even more quarrelsome than they would be by nature. Partridges are employed for the same cruel purpose; and as both these birds are easily obtained, and are very pugnacious, they are especially suited for the sport.

Two passages occur in the Scriptures which exactly explain the mode in which the Quails were sent to the Israelites. The first is in Ps. lxxviii. 26. The Psalmist mentions that the Lord "caused an east wind to blow in the heaven, and by His power He brought in the south wind." Here, on examining the geographical position of the Israelites, we see exactly how the south-east wind would bring the Quails.

The Israelites had just passed the Red Sea, and had begun to experience a foretaste of the privations which they were to expect in the desert through which they had to pass. Passing northwards in their usual migrations, the birds would come to the coast of the Red Sea, and there would wait until a favourable wind enabled them to cross the water. The south-east wind afforded them just the very assistance which they needed, and they would naturally take advantage of it.

It is remarkable how closely the Scriptural narrative agrees with the habits of the Quail, the various passages, when compared together, precisely coinciding with the character of the bird. In Exod. xvi. 13 it is mentioned that "at even the quails came up and covered the camp." Nocturnal flight is one of the characteristics of the Quail. When possible, they invariably fly by night, and in this manner escape many of the foes which would make great havoc among their helpless columns if they were to fly by day.

The identity of the Selâv with the common Quail is now seen to be established. In the first place, we have the name still surviving in the Arabic language. Next, the various details of the Scriptural narrative point so conclusively to the bird, that even if we were to put aside the etymological corroboration, we could have but little doubt on the subject. There is not a detail which is not correct. The gregarious instinct of the bird, which induces it to congregate in vast numbers; its habit of migration; its inability to fly against the wind, and the necessity for it to await a favourable breeze; its practice of flying by night, and its custom of merely skimming over the surface of the ground; the ease with which it is captured; the mode of preserving by drying in the sun, and the proverbial delicacy of its flesh, are characteristics which all unite in the Quail.

Before closing our account of the Quail, it will be as well to devote a short space to the nature of the mode by which the Israelites were twice fed. Commentators who were unacquainted with the natural history of the bird have represented the whole occurrence as a miraculous one, and have classed it with the division of the Red Sea and of the Jordan, with the various plagues by which Pharaoh was induced to release the Israelites, and with many other events which we are accustomed to call miracles.

In reality, there is scarcely anything of a miraculous character about the event, and none seems to have been claimed for it. The Quails were not created at the moment expressly for the purpose of supplying the people with food, nor were they even brought from any great distance. They were merely assisted in the business on which they were engaged—namely, their migration or customary travel from south to north, and waiting on the opposite side of the narrow sea for a south-east wind. That such a wind should blow was no miracle. The Quails expected it to blow, and without it they could not have crossed the sea. That it was made to blow earlier than might have been the case is likely enough, but that is the extent of the miraculous character of the event.

THE RAVEN.

The Raven tribe plentiful in Palestine—The Raven and the Dove—Elijah and the Ravens—Desert-loving habits of the Raven—Notions of the old commentators—Ceremonial use of the Raven—Return of the Ravens—Cunning of the bird—Nesting-places of the Raven—The magpie and its character—The starling—Its introduction into Palestine.

It is more than probable that, while the Hebrew word *oreb* primarily signifies the bird which is so familiar to us under the name of RAVEN, it was also used by the Jews in a much looser sense, and served to designate any of the Corvidæ, or Crow tribe, such as the raven itself, the crow, the rook, the jackdaw, and the like. We will first take the word in its restricted sense, and then devote a brief space to its more extended signification.

As might be expected from the cosmopolitan nature of the Raven, it is very plentiful in Palestine, and even at the present time is apparently as firmly established as it was in the days when the various Scriptural books were written.

There are few birds which are more distinctly mentioned in the Holy Scriptures than the Raven, though the passages in which its name occurs are comparatively few. It is the first bird which is mentioned in the Scriptures, its name occurring in Gen. viii. 7: "And it came to pass at the end of forty days that Noah opened the window of the ark which he had made;

"And he sent forth a raven, which went forth to and fro until the waters were dried up from off the earth."

Here we have, at the very outset, a characteristic account of the bird. It left the ark, and flew to and fro, evidently for the purpose of seeking food. The dove, which immediately followed the Raven, acted in a different manner. She flew from the ark in search of food, and, finding none, was forced to return again.

The Raven, on the contrary, would find plenty of food in the bodies of the various animals that had been drowned, and were floating on the surface of the waters, and, therefore, needed not to enter again into the ark. The context shows that it made the ark a resting-place, and that it "went forth to and fro," or, as

THE RAVEN.

the Hebrew Bible renders the passage, "in going and returning," until the waters had subsided. Here, then, is boldly drawn the distinction between the two birds, the carrion-eater and the feeder on vegetable substances—a distinction to which allusion has already been made in the history of the dove.

Passing over the declaration in Lev. xi. 15 and Deut. xiv. 14, that every Raven (*i.e.* the Raven and all its tribe) is unclean, we come to the next historical mention of the bird. This occurs in 1 Kings xvii. When Elijah had excited the anger of Ahab by prophesying three years of drought, he was divinely ordered to take refuge by the brook Cherith, one of the tributaries of the Jordan. "And it shall be, that thou shalt drink of the brook; and I have commanded the ravens [*orebim*] to feed thee there.

ELIJAH FED BY THE RAVENS.

"So he went and did according unto the word of the Lord for he went and dwelt by the brook Cherith, that is before Jordan.

"And the ravens brought him bread and flesh in the morning, and bread and flesh in the evening, and he drank of the brook."

In this passage we have a history of a purely miraculous

character. It is not one that can be explained away. Some have tried to do so by saying that the banished prophet found the nests of the Ravens, and took from them daily a supply of food for his sustenance. The repetition of the words "bread and flesh" shows that the sacred writer had no intention of signifying a mere casual finding of food which the Ravens brought for their young, but that the prophet was furnished with a constant and regular supply of bread and meat twice in the day. It is a statement which, if it be not accepted as the account of a miracle, must be rejected altogether.

The desert-loving habit of the Raven is noticed in Isa. xxxiv. 11: "The cormorant and the bittern shall possess it; the owl also and the raven shall dwell in it: and He shall stretch out upon it the line of confusion, and the stones of emptiness."

WE will now pass to the notices of the Raven as given by the writers and commentators of the Talmud.

Being an unclean bird, and one of ill omen, it was not permitted to perch on the roof of the Temple. According to some writers, it was kept off by means of scarecrows, and according to others, by long and sharp iron spikes set so closely together that there was no room for the bird to pass between them. The latter is by far the more probable account, as the Raven is much too cunning a bird to be deceived by a scarecrow for any length of time. It might be alarmed at the first sight of a strange object, but in a very short time it would hold all scarecrows in supreme contempt.

Its carrion-eating propensities were well known to the ancient writers, who must have had many opportunities of seeing the Raven unite with the vultures in consuming the bodies, not only of dead animals, but of warriors killed in battle. So fond was the Raven of this food that, according to those writers, the very smell of human blood attracted the bird; and, if a man accidentally cut himself, or if he were bled for some illness, the odour of the blood would bring round the spot all the Ravens of the place.

The punctuality with which the Raven, in common with all its kin, returns to its roosting-place, was also familiar to the Talmudists, who made rather an ingenious use of this habit. The ceremonial law of the Jews required the greatest care in observing certain hours, and it was especially necessary to know the precise time which marked the separation of one day from another. This was ascertained easily enough as long as the day was clear, but in case of a dull, murky day, when the course of the sun could not be traced, some other plan was needed.

In the olden times, no artificial means of measuring time were known, and the devout Jew was consequently fearful lest he might unwittingly break the law by doing on one day an act which ought to have been done on another. A convenient method for ascertaining the time was, however, employed, and, as soon as the Ravens, rooks, and similar birds were seen returning to their homes, the sun was supposed to be setting.

This habit of returning regularly at the same time is mentioned by Mr. Tristram in his "Land of Israel:"—

"Of all the birds of Jerusalem, the raven is decidedly the most characteristic and conspicuous. It is present everywhere to eye and ear, and the odours that float around remind us of its use. On the evening of our arrival we were perplexed by a call-note, quite new to us, mingling with the old familiar croak, and soon ascertained that there must be a second species of raven along with the common *Corvus corax*. This was the African species (*Corvus umbrinus*, Hed.), the ashy-necked raven, a little smaller than the world-wide raven, and here more abundant in individuals.

"Beside these, the rook (*Corvus agricola*, Trist.), the common grey, or hooded crow (*Corvus cornix*, L.), and the jackdaw (*Corvus monedula*, L.), roost by hundreds in the sanctuary. We used to watch them in long lines passing over our tents every morning at daybreak, and returning in the evening, the rooks in solid phalanx leading the way, and the ravens in loose order bringing up the rear, generally far out of shot. Before retiring for the night, popular assemblies of the most uproarious character were held together in the trees of the Kedron and Mount Olivet, and not until sunset did they withdraw in silence, mingled indiscriminately, to their roosting-places on the walls.

"My companions were very anxious to obtain specimens of these Jerusalem birds, which could only be approached as they settled for the night; but we were warned by the Consul that shooting them so close to the mosque might be deemed a sacrilege by the Moslems, and provoke an attack by the guardians of the

THE RAVEN. 521

Haram and the boys of the neighbourhood. They finally determined, nevertheless, to run the risk; and stationing themselves just before sunset in convenient hiding-places near the walls, at a given signal they fired simultaneously, and, hastily gathering up the spoils, had retreated out of reach, and were hurrying to the tents before an alarm could be raised. The discharge of ten barrels had obtained fourteen specimens, comprising five species.

RAVENS' ROOSTING-PLACE.

"The same manœuvre was repeated with equal success on another evening; but on the third occasion the ravens had learned wisdom by experience, and, sweeping round Siloam, chose another route to their dormitory."

Those who have tried to come within gunshot of a Raven,

can appreciate this anecdote, and can understand how the Raven would ever afterwards keep clear of the spot where the flash and smoke of fire-arms had twice appeared. In a large garden in which the sparrows used to congregate, it was a custom of the owner to lay a train of corn for the sparrows to eat, and then to rake the whole line with a discharge from a gun concealed in an outhouse. A tame Raven lived about the premises, and as soon as it saw any one carrying a gun towards the fatal outhouse, it became much alarmed, and hurried off to hide itself. As soon as the gun was fired, out came the Raven from its place of concealment, pounced on one of the dead sparrows, carried it off, and ate it in its private haunt.

The nest to which the Raven returns with such punctuality is placed in some spot where it is safe from ordinary intruders. The tops of lofty trees are favoured localities for the nest, and so are old towers, the interior of caves, and clefts in lofty precipices.

THE OSTRICH.

Hebrew words designating the Ostrich—Description of the bird in the Book of Job—Ancient use of Ostrich plumes—Supposed heedlessness of eggs and young—Mode of depositing the eggs—Hatching them in the sand—Natural enemies of the Ostrich—Anecdote of Ostriches and their young—Alleged stupidity of the Ostrich—Methods of hunting and snaring the bird—The Ostrich in domestication—Speed of the Ostrich—The flesh of the bird prohibited to the Jews—Ostrich eggs and their uses—Food of the Ostrich—Mode of drinking—Cry of the Ostrich, and reference made to it in Micah.

THERE is rather a peculiarity about the manner in which this bird is mentioned in the Authorized Version of the Scriptures, and, unless we go to the original Hebrew, we shall be greatly misled. In that version the Ostrich is mentioned only three times, but in the Hebrew it occurs eight times.

The Hebrew word *bath-haya'nah*, which is translated in the Authorized Version as "owl," ought really to be rendered as "Ostrich." Taking this to be the case, we find that there are several passages in the Scriptures in which the word has been used in the wrong sense.

In those places, instead of rendering the word as "owl," we ought to read it as "Ostrich."

The first mention of this bird occurs in Lev. xi. 16, and the parallel passage of Deut. xiv., in which the Ostrich is reckoned among the unclean birds, without any notice being given of its appearance or habits.

In the Book of Job, however, we have the Ostrich mentioned with that preciseness and fulness of description which is so often the case when the writer of that wonderful poem treats of living creatures.

"Gavest thou the goodly wings unto the peacocks? or wings and feathers unto the ostrich?

"Who leaveth her eggs in the earth, and warmeth them in the dust,

"And forgetteth that the foot may crush them, or that the wild beast may break them.

"She is hardened against her young ones, as though they were not hers: her labour is in vain without fear;

"Because God hath deprived her of wisdom, neither hath He imparted to her understanding.

"What time she lifteth up herself on high, she scorneth the horse and his rider." (Job xxxix. 13—19.)

There is rather a peculiarity in the translation of this passage, wherein the word which has been translated as "peacock" is now allowed to be properly rendered as "Ostrich," while the word which is translated as "Ostrich" ought to have been given as "feathers." The marginal translation gives the last words of ver. 13 in a rather different manner, and renders it thus:—
"Gavest thou the goodly wings unto the peacocks, or the feathers of the stork and ostrich?" The Hebrew Bible renders the next verses as follows:—

"She would yet leave her eggs on the earth, and warm them in dust; and forget that the foot may crush them, or that the beast of the field may break them.

"She is hardened against her young ones, for those not hers; being careless, her labour is in vain."

In the same Book, chap. xxx., is another passage wherein this bird is mentioned. "I went mourning without the sun: I stood up, and I cried in the congregation.

"I am a brother to dragons, and a companion to owls," or Ostriches, in the marginal and correct reading. The Jewish Bible also translates the word as Ostriches, but the word which the Authorized Version renders as "dragons" it translates as "jackals." Of this point we shall have something to say on a future page. A somewhat similar passage occurs in Isa. xliii. 20: "The beast of the field shall honour me, the dragons and the owls" (Ostriches in marginal reading), "because I give waters in the wilderness, and rivers in the desert, to give drink to My people, My chosen." The Jewish Bible retains the same reading, except that the word "dragons" is given with the mark of doubt.

Accepting, therefore, the rendering of the Hebrew as Ostriches, let us see how far the passages of Scripture agree with the appearance and habits of the bird.

Here I may observe that, although in the Scriptures frequent allusions are made to the habits of animals, we are not to look for scientific exactness to the Scriptures. Among much that is strictly and completely true, there are occasional errors, to which a most needless attention has been drawn by a certain school of critics, who point to them as invalidating the truth of Scripture in general. The real fact is, that they have no bearing whatever on the truth or falsehood of the Scriptural teachings.

The Scriptures were written at various times, for instruction in spiritual and not in temporal matters, and were never intended for scientific treatises on astronomy, mathematics, zoology, or any such branch of knowledge. The references which are made to the last-mentioned subject are in no case of a scientific nature, but are always employed by way of metaphor or simile, as the reader must have seen in the previous pages. No point of doctrine is taught by them, and none depends on them.

The Spirit which conveyed religious instruction to the people could only use the means that existed, and could no more employ the scientific knowledge of the present time than use as metaphors the dress, arms, and inventions of the present day. The Scriptures were written in Eastern lands for Orientals by Orientals, and were consequently adapted to Oriental ideas; and it would be as absurd to look for scientific zoology in the writings of an ancient Oriental, as for descriptions of the printing-press, the steam-engine, the photographic camera, or the electric telegraph.

So, when we remember that only a few years ago the real history of the Ostrich was unknown to those who had made zoology the study of their lives, we cannot wonder that it was also unknown to those who lived many centuries ago, and who had not the least idea of zoology, or any kindred science.

Still, even with these drawbacks, it is wonderful how accurate in many instances were the writers of the Scriptures, and the more so when we remember the character of the Oriental mind, with its love of metaphor, its disregard of arithmetical precision, and its poetical style of thought.

We will now take the passage in Job xxxix. In ver. 13 reference is made to the wings and feathers of the Ostrich. If the reader will refer to page 310, he will see that the feathers of the Ostrich were formerly used as the emblem of rank. In this case, they are shown as fastened to the heads of the horses, and also in the form of a plume, fixed to the end of a staff, and appended to a chariot, as emblematical of the princely rank of the occupier. In the ancient Egyptian monuments these Ostrich plumes are repeatedly shown, and in every case denote very high rank. These plumes were therefore held in high estimation at the time in which the Book of Job was written, and it is evidently in allusion to this fact that the sacred writer has mentioned so prominently the white plumes of the Ostrich.

Passing the next portion of the description, we find that the Ostrich is mentioned as a bird that is careless of its eggs, and leaves them "in the earth, and warmeth them in the dust, and forgetteth that the foot may crush them, or that the wild beast may break them."

Now it is true that the Ostrich is often known to take the greatest care of its eggs, the male collecting and sitting on them, and watching them with loving assiduity, and by some persons this fact has been brought forward as a proof that the writer of the Book of Job was mistaken in his statements. A further acquaintance with the habits of the bird tells us, however, that in those parts of the world which were known to the writer of that book the Ostrich does behave in precisely the manner which is described by the sacred writer.

Several females lay their eggs in the same nest, if the title of nest can be rightly applied to a mere hollow scooped in the sand, and, at least during the daytime, when the sun is shining, they simply cover the eggs with sand, so as to conceal them from ordinary enemies, and leave them to be hatched by the warm sunbeams. They are buried to the depth of about a foot, so that they receive the benefit of a tolerably equable warmth. So much, then, for the assertion that the Ostrich leaves her eggs "in the earth, and warmeth them in the dust."

We next come to the statement that she forgets that "the foot may crush them, or that the wild beast may break them." It is evident from the preceding description that eggs which are buried a foot deep in the sand could not be crushed by the foot, even were they of a fragile character, instead of being defended by a shell as thick, and nearly as hard, as an ordinary earthenware plate. Neither would the wild beast be likely to discover much less to break them.

A more intimate acquaintance with the history of the Ostrich shows that, even in this particular, the sacred writer was perfectly correct. Besides the eggs which are intended to be hatched, and which are hidden beneath the sand to be hatched,

OSTRICH AND NEST.

a number of supplementary eggs are laid which are not meant to be hatched, and are evidently intended as food for the young until they are able to forage for themselves. These are left carelessly on the surface of the ground, and may easily be crushed by the hoof of a horse, if not by the foot of man. We meet, however, with another statement,—namely, that they may be broken by the wild beasts. Here we have reference to another fact in the history of the Ostrich. The scattered eggs, to which allusion is made, are often eaten, not only by beasts, but also by birds of prey; the former breaking the shells by knocking them against each other, and the latter by picking up large stones in their claws, rising above the eggs, and dropping the stones on them. The bird would like to seize the egg, rise with it in the air, and drop it on a stone, as mentioned on page 414, but the round, smooth surface of the egg defies the grasp of talons, and, instead of dropping the egg upon a stone, it is obliged to drop a stone upon the egg.

Up to the present point, therefore, the writer of the Book of Job is shown to be perfectly correct in his statements. We will now proceed to verse 16 : "She is hardened against her young ones, as though they were not hers." Now in the Jewish Bible the passage is rendered rather differently : "She is hardened against her young ones, for those not hers;" and, as we shall presently see, the reading perfectly agrees with the character of the Ostrich.

There has long existed a belief that the Ostrich, contrary to the character of all other birds, is careless of her young, neglects them, and is even cruel to them. That this notion was shared by the writer of the Book of Job is evident from the preceding passage. It also prevailed for at least a thousand years after the Book of Job was written. See Lam. iv. 3 : "Even the sea monsters draw out the breast, they give suck to their young ones: the daughter of my people is become cruel, like the ostriches in the wilderness."

It is probable that this idea respecting the cruelty of the Ostrich towards its young is derived from the fact that if a flock of Ostriches be chased, and among them there be some very young birds, the latter are left behind by their parents, and fall a prey to the hunters. But, in reality, the Ostrich has no choice in the matter. The wide sandy desert affords no place of concealment in which it might hide its young. Nature has not furnished it with weapons by means of which it can fight for them; and consequently it is forced to use the only means of escape by which it can avoid sacrificing its own life, as well as the lives of the young.

It does not, however, leave the young until it has tried, by all means in its power, to save them. For example, it sometimes has recourse to the manoeuvre with which we are so familiar in the case of the lapwing, and pretends to be wounded or lamed, in order to draw the attention of its pursuers, while its young escape in another direction. An instance of this practice is given by Mr. Andersson in his "Lake Ngami." "When we had proceeded little more than half the distance, and in a part of the plain entirely destitute of vegetation, we discovered a male and female ostrich, with a brood of young ones, about the size of ordinary barn-yard fowls. We forthwith dismounted from our oxen, and gave chase, which proved of no ordinary interest.

"The moment the parent birds became aware of our intention, they set off at full speed—the female leading the way, and the cock, though at some little distance, bringing up the rear of the family party. It was very touching to observe the anxiety the birds evinced for the safety of their progeny. Finding that we were quickly gaining upon them, the male at once slackened his pace and diverged somewhat from his course; but, seeing that we were not to be diverted from our purpose, he again increased his speed, and, with wings drooping so as almost to touch the ground, he hovered round us, now in wide circles, and then decreasing the circumference until he came almost within pistol-shot, when he abruptly threw himself on the ground, and struggled desperately to regain his legs, as it appeared, like a bird that has been badly wounded.

"Having previously fired at him, I really thought he was disabled, and made quickly towards him. But this was only a ruse on his part, for, on my nearer approach, he slowly rose, and began to run in a different direction to that of the female, who by this time was considerably ahead with her charge." Nor is this a solitary instance of the care which the Ostrich will take of her young. Thunberg mentions that on one occasion, when he happened to ride near a place where an Ostrich was sitting on the eggs, the bird jumped up and pursued him, evidently with the object of distracting his attention from the eggs. When he faced her, she retreated; but as soon as he turned his horse, she pursued him afresh.

The care of the mother for the young is perhaps less needed with the Ostrich than with most birds. The young are able to run with such speed that ordinary animals are not able to overtake them, and, besides, they are protected by their colour as long as they are comparatively helpless. Their downy plumage harmonizes completely with the sandy and stony ground, even when they run, and when they crouch to the earth, as is their manner when alarmed, even the most practised eye can scarcely see them. Mr. Andersson, an experienced hunter, states that when the Ostrich chicks were crouching almost under his feet, he had the greatest difficulty in distinguishing their forms.

Owing to the great number of the eggs that are laid, the young are often very numerous, between thirty and forty chicks sometimes belonging to one brood. In the Ostrich chase which has already been described, the brood were eighteen in number, and so great was their speed that, in spite of their youth and diminutive size, Mr. Andersson only succeeded in capturing nine of them after an hour's severe chase.

We find, therefore, that we must acquit the Ostrich of neglecting its young, much more of cruelty towards them; and we will now turn to the next charge against the bird, that of stupidity.

In one sense, the bird certainly may be considered stupid. Like nearly all wild creatures which live on large plains, it always runs against the wind, so as to perceive by scent if any enemies are approaching. Its nostrils are very sensitive, and can detect a human being at a very great distance. So fastidious is it in this respect, that no hunter who knows his business ever attempts to approach the Ostrich except from leeward. If a nest is found, and the discoverer wishes the birds to continue laying in it, he approaches on the leeward side, and rakes out the eggs with a long stick.

The little Bushman, who kills so many of these birds with his tiny bow and arrow, makes use of this instinct when he goes to shoot the Ostrich, disguised in a skin of one of the birds. Should an Ostrich attack him, as is sometimes the case, he only shifts his position to windward, so as to allow the birds to catch the scent of a human being, when they instantly make off in terror.

When, therefore, the Ostriches are alarmed, they always run to windward, instinctively knowing that, if an enemy should approach in that direction, their powers of scent will inform them of the danger. Being aware of this habit, the hunters manage so that while one of them goes round by a long detour to frighten the game, the others are in waiting at a considerable distance to windward, but well on one side, so that no indication of their presence may reach the sensitive nostrils of the birds As soon as the concealed hunters see the Ostriches fairly settled down to their course, they dash off at right angles to the line which the birds are taking, and in this way come near enough to use their weapons. The antelopes of the same country have a similar instinct, and are hunted in precisely the same manner.

Thus, then, in one sense the Ostrich may be considered as open to the charge of stupidity, inasmuch as it pursues a course which can be anticipated by enemies who would otherwise be unable to overtake it. But it must be remembered that instinct cannot be expected to prove a match for reason, and that, although its human enemies are able to overreach it, no others can do so, the instinct of running against the wind serving to guard it from any foe which it is likely to meet in the desert.

When captured alive and tamed, it certainly displays no particular amount of intellect. The Arabs often keep tame Ostriches about their tents, the birds being as much accustomed to their quarters as the horses. In all probability they did so in ancient times, and the author of the Book of Job was likely to be familiar with tame Ostriches, as well as with the wild bird.

Stupidity is probably attributed to the tame bird in consequence of the habit possessed by the Ostrich of picking up and eating substances which cannot be used as food. For example, it will eat knives, bits of bone or metal, and has even been known to swallow bullets hot from the mould. On dissecting the digestive organs of an Ostrich, I have found a large quantity of stones, pieces of brick, and scraps of wood. These articles are, however, not intended to serve as food, but simply to aid digestion, and the bird eats them just as domestic fowls pick up gravel, and smaller birds grains of sand. In swallowing them, therefore, the Ostrich does not display any stupidity, but merely obeys a natural instinct.

Lastly, we come to the speed of the Ostrich: "What time she lifteth up herself on high, she scorneth the horse and his rider."

This statement is literally true. When the Ostrich puts forth its full speed, there is no horse that can catch it in a fair chase. It may be killed by the ruse which has already been described, but an adult Ostrich can run away from the swiftest horse. When it runs at full speed, it moves its long legs with astonishing rapidity, covering at each stride an average of twenty-four feet, a fact from which its rate of speed may be deduced. In consequence of this width of stride, and the small impression made in the sand by the two-toed foot, the track of a running Ostrich is very obscure. Perhaps no better proof of the swiftness of the bird can be given than the extreme value set upon it by the Arabs. Although they are bred to the desert as much as the Ostrich itself, and are mounted on horses whose swiftness and endurance are proverbial, they set a very high value on the Ostrich, and to have captured one of these birds establishes an Arab's fame as a hunter.

Sometimes the Arabs employ the plan of cutting across the course of the bird, but at others they pursue it in fair chase, training their horses and themselves specially for the occasion. They furnish themselves with a supply of water, and then start in pursuit of the first flock of Ostriches they find. They take care not to alarm the birds, lest they should put out their full speed and run away out of sight, but just keep sufficiently near to force the birds to be continually on the move. They will sometimes continue this chase for several days, not allowing their game time to eat or rest, until at last it is so tired that it yields itself an easy prey.

In Southern Africa, snares are used for taking the Ostrich. They are in fact ordinary springes, but of strength suitable to the size of the bird. The cord is made fast to a sapling, which is bent down by main strength, and the other end is then formed into a noose and fastened down with a trigger. Sometimes the bird is enticed towards the snare by means of a bait, and sometimes it is driven over it by the huntsmen. In either case, as soon as the Ostrich puts its foot within the fatal noose, the trigger is loosed, the sapling is released, and, with a violent jerk, the Ostrich is caught by the leg and suspended in the air.

Why the flesh of the Ostrich should have been prohibited to the Jews is rather a mystery. It is much valued by most natives, though some of the Arab tribes still adhere to the Jewish prohibition, and those Europeans who have tried it pronounce it to be excellent when the bird is young and tender, but to be unpleasantly tough when it is old. Mr. Andersson says that its flesh resembles that of the zebra, and mentions that the fat and blood are in great request, being mixed together by

ARABS HUNTING THE OSTRICH.

cutting the throat of the bird, passing a ligature round the neck just below the incision, and then shaking and dragging the bird about for some time. Nearly twenty pounds of this substance are obtained from a single Ostrich.

The ancient Romans valued exceedingly the flesh of this bird. We are told that Heliogabalus once had a dish served at his table containing six hundred Ostrich brains, and that another emperor ate a whole Ostrich at a meal. As an adult Ostrich weighs some three hundred and fifty pounds, we may presume that the bird in question was a young one.

The eggs are most valuable articles of food, both on account of their excellent flavour and their enormous size. It is calculated that one Ostrich egg contains as much as twenty-five ordinary hen's eggs. Cooking the Ostrich egg is easily performed. A hole is made in the upper part of the egg, and the lower end is set on the fire. A forked stick is then introduced into the egg, and twirled between the hands, so as to beat up the whole of the interior. Europeans usually add pepper and salt, and say that this simple mode of cooking produces an excellent omelette.

The ordinary food of the Ostrich consists of the seeds, buds, and tops of various plants. It seems strange, however, that in the deserts, where there is so little vegetation, the bird should be able to procure sufficient food to maintain its enormous body. Each of the specimens which are kept at the Zoological Gardens eats on an average a pint of barley, the same quantity of oats, four pounds' weight of cabbage, and half a gallon of chaff, beside the buns, bread, and other articles of food which are given to them by visitors.

Although the Ostrich, like many other inhabitants of the desert, can live for a long time without water, yet it is forced to drink, and like the camel, which it resembles in so many of its ways, drinks enormously, taking in the water by a succession of gulps. When the weather has been exceptionally hot, the Ostrich visits the water-springs daily, and is so occupied in quenching its thirst that it will allow the hunter to come within a very short distance. It appears, indeed, to be almost intoxicated with its draught, and, even when it does take the alarm, it only retreats step by step, instead of scudding off with its usually rapid strides.

The camel-like appearance of the Ostrich has already been mentioned. In the Arabic language the Ostrich is called by a name which signifies camel-bird, and many of the people have an idea that it was originally a cross between a bird and a camel.

The cry of the Ostrich is a deep bellow, which, according to travellers in Southern Africa, so resembles the roar of the lion that even the practised ears of the natives can scarcely distinguish the roar of the animal from the cry of the bird. The resemblance is increased by the fact that both the lion and Ostrich utter their cry by night. It is evidently to this cry that the prophet Micah alludes: "Therefore I will wail and howl, I will go stripped and naked: I will make a wailing like the dragons, and mourning as the owls" (Ostriches in marginal reading). The cry of the variety of Ostrich which inhabits Northern Africa is said to bear more resemblance to the lowing of an ox than the roar of the lion; but as the bird is smaller than its southern relative, the difference is probably accounted for.

It has been mentioned that the Ostrich has no weapons wherewith to fight for its young; still, though it be destitute of actual weapons, such as the spur of the gamecock or the beak and talons of the eagle, it is not entirely defenceless. Its long and powerful legs can be employed as weapons, and it can kick with such force that a man would go down before the blow, and probably, if struck on the leg or arm, have the limb broken. The blow is never delivered backward, as is the kick of the horse, but forward, like that of the kangaroo. The natives of the countries where it resides say that it is able to kill by its kick the jackal that comes to steal its eggs, and that even the hyæna and the leopard are repelled by the gigantic bird.

THE BITTERN.

The Bittern and its general appearance—The bird of solitude—Difficulty of detecting the Bittern in its haunts—Mudie's description of the Bittern and its home—Nest of the Bittern—Scarcity of the bird at the present day—Food of the Bittern.

The Bittern belongs to the same family as the herons, the cranes, and the storks, and has many of the habits common to them all. It is, however, essentially a bird of solitude, hating the vicinity of man, and living in the most retired spots of marshy ground. As it sits among the reeds and rushes, though it is a large bird, it is scarcely visible even to a practised eye, its mottled plumage harmonizing with surrounding objects in such a way that the feathers of the bird can scarcely be distinguished from the sticks, stones, and grass tufts among which it sits. The ground colour of the plumage is dark buff, upon which are sprinkled mottlings and streaks of black, chestnut, grey, and brown. These mottled marks harmonize with the stones and tufts of withered grass, while the longitudinal dashes of buff and black on the neck and breast correspond with the sticks and reeds.

In a similar manner the tiger, though so large an animal, can lie in a very small covert of reeds without being detected, its striped fur corresponding with the reeds themselves and the shadows thrown by them; and the leopard can remain hidden among the boughs of a tree, its spotted coat harmonizing with the broken light and shade of the foliage.

The following powerful description of the Bittern's home is given by Mudie: "It is a bird of rude nature, where the land knows no character save that which the untrained working of the elements impresses upon it; so that when any locality is in

THE BITTERN

the course of being won to usefulness, the bittern is the first to depart, and when any one is abandoned, it is the last to return. 'The bittern shall dwell there' is the final curse, and implies that the place is to become uninhabited and uninhabitable. It hears not the whistle of the ploughman, nor the sound of the mattock; and the tinkle of the sheep-bell, or the lowing of the ox (although the latter bears so much resemblance to its own hollow and dismal voice, that it has given foundation to the name), is a signal for it to be gone.

"Extensive and dingy pools—if moderately upland, so much the better—which lie in the hollows, catching, like so many traps, the lighter and more fertile mould which the rains wash and the winds blow from the naked heights around, and converting it into harsh and dingy vegetation, and the pasture of those loathsome things which wriggle in the ooze, or crawl and swim in the putrid and mantling waters, are the habitation of the bittern.

"Places which scatter blight and mildew over every herb which is more delicate than a sedge, a carex, or a rush, and consume every wooded plant that is taller than the sapless and tasteless cranberry or the weeping upland willow; which shed murrain over the quadrupeds, chills which eat the flesh off their bones, and which, if man ventures there, consume him by putrid fever in the hot and dry season, and shake him to pieces with ague when the weather is cold and humid.

"Places from which the heath and the lichen stand aloof, and where even the raven, lover of disease, and battener upon all that expires miserably and exhausted, comes rarely and with more than wonted caution, lest that death which he comes to seal and riot upon in others should unawares come upon himself. The raven loves carrion on the dry and unpoisoning moor, scents it from afar, and hastens to it upon his best and boldest wing; but 'the reek o' the rotten fen' is loathsome to the sense of even the raven, and it is hunger's last pinch ere he come nigh to the chosen habitation, the only loved abode, of the bittern."

Secure in its retreat, the Bittern keeps its place even if a sportsman should pass by the spot on which it crouches. It will not be tempted to leave its retreat by noise, or even by stone throwing, for it knows instinctively that the quaking bogland which it selects as its home is unsafe for the step of man.

The very cry of the Bittern adds to this atmosphere of desolation. By day the bird is silent, but after the sun has gone down it utters its strange wild cry, a sound which exactly suits the localities in which it loves to make its habitation. During part of the year it only emits a sharp, harsh cry as it rises on the wing, but during the breeding season it utters the cry by which it summons its mate, one of the strangest love-calls that

BITTERN. CORMORANT.

can be imagined. It is something between the neighing of a horse, the bellow of a bull, and a shriek of savage laughter. It is very loud and deep, so that it seems to shake the loose and marshy ground. There was formerly an idea that, when the Bittern uttered this booming cry, it thrust its bill into the soft ground, and so caused it to shake. In reality, the cry is uttered on the wing, the bird wheeling in a spiral flight, and modulating its voice in accordance with the curves which it describes in the air. This strange sound is only uttered by the male bird.

Like most of the long-legged wading birds, the Bittern is able to change its shape, and apparently to alter its size, in an astonishing manner. When it is walking over the ground, with head erect and eye glanced vigilantly at surrounding objects, it looks a large, bold, vigorous, and active bird. Next minute it will sink its head in its shoulders, so that the long beak seems to project from them, and the neck totally disappears, the feathers enveloping each other as perfectly and smoothly as if it never had had a neck. In this attitude it will stand for an hour at a time on one leg, with the other drawn close to its body, looking as dull, inert, and sluggish a bird as can well be imagined, and reduced apparently to one half of its former size. The Bittern is represented in one of its extraordinary attitudes on the plate which illustrates the cormorant.

The nest of the Bittern is placed on the ground, and near the water, though the bird always takes care to build it on an elevated spot which will not be flooded if the water should rise by reason of a severe rain. There is, however, but little reason for the Bittern to fear a flood, as at the time of year which is chosen for nest-building the floods are generally out, and the water higher than is likely to be the case for the rest of the year. The materials of the nest are found in marshes, and consist of leaves, reeds, and rushes.

As if to add to the general effect of its character, it is essentially a solitary bird, and in this characteristic entirely unlike its relatives the heron and the stork, which are peculiarly sociable, and love to gather themselves together in multitudes. But the Bittern is never found except alone, or at the most accompanied for a time by its mate and one or two young ones.

The localities in which it resides are sufficient evidence of the nature of its food. Frogs appear to be its favourite diet, but it also feeds on various fish, insects, molluscs, worms, and similar creatures. Dull and apathetic as it appears to be, it can display sufficient energy to capture tolerably large fish. Though the Bittern is only about two feet in total length, one of these birds was killed, in the stomach of which were found one perfect rudd eight inches in length and two in depth, together with the remains of another fish, of a full-grown frog, and of an aquatic insect. In another instance, a Bittern had contrived to swallow an eel as long as itself; while in many cases the remains of five or six full-grown frogs have been found in the interior of the bird, some just swallowed, and others in various stages of digestion.

THE HERON.

THE HERON.

The Heron mentioned as an unclean bird—Nesting of the Heron—The papyrus marshes and their dangers—Description of the papyrus—Vessels of bulrushes.

THE name of the Heron is only mentioned twice in the Scriptures—namely, in the two parallel passages of Lev. xi. 19 and Deut. xiv. 18; in both of which places the Heron is ranked among the unclean birds that might not be eaten.

In some of the cases where beasts or birds are prohibited as food, the prohibition seems scarcely needed. To us of the present day this seems to be the case with the Heron, as it is never brought to table. The reason for this disuse of the Heron as food is not that it is unfit for the table, but that it has become so scarce by the spread of cultivation and housebuilding, that it has been gradually abandoned as a practically unattainable article of diet. The flesh of the Heron, like that of the bittern, is remarkably excellent, and in the former days, when it was comparatively plentiful, and falconry was the ordinary amusement of the rich, the Heron formed a very important dish at every great banquet.

The bird, however, must be eaten when young. A gentleman who liked to try experiments for himself in the matter of food, found that, if young Herons were properly cooked, they formed a most excellent dish, equal, in his opinion, to grouse. Wishing

THE HERON.

to have his own judgment confirmed by that of others, he had several of them trussed and dressed like wild geese, and served up at table under that name. The guests approved greatly of the bird, and compared it to hare, the resemblance being further increased by the dark colour of the flesh. There was not the slighest fishy flavour about the bird. This, however, is apt to be found in the older birds, but can be removed by burying them in the earth for several days, just as is done with the solan goose and one or two other sea-birds.

The abundance of birds belonging to the Heron tribe is well shown by some of the paintings and carvings on Egyptian monuments, in which various species of Herons and other water-birds are depicted as living among the papyrus reeds, exactly the locality in which they are most plentiful at the present day.

Unlike the bittern, the Heron is a most sociable bird, and loves not only to live, but even to feed, in company with others of its own species.

I have watched the Herons feeding in close proximity to each other. The birds were fond of wading stealthily along the edge of the lake until they came to a suitable spot, where they would stand immersed in the water up to the thighs, waiting patiently for their prey. They stood as still as if they were carved out of wood, the ripples of the lake reflected on their plumage as the breeze ruffled the surface of the water. Suddenly there would be a quick dive of the beak, either among the reeds or in the water, and each stroke signified that the Heron had caught its prey.

Frogs and small fishes are the usual food of the Heron, though it often grapples with larger prey, having been seen to capture an eel of considerable size in its beak. Under such circumstances it leaves the water, with the fish in its mouth, and beats it violently against a stone so as to kill it. Now and then the bird is vanquished in the struggle by the fish, several instances being known in which an eel, in its endeavours to escape, has twisted itself so tightly round the neck of the bird that both have been found lying dead on the shore.

In one such case the Heron's beak had struck through the eyes of the eel, so that the bird could not disengage itself. In another the Heron had tried to swallow an eel which was much too large for it, and had been nearly choked by its meal. The eel must necessarily have been a very large one, as the Heron has a wonderful capacity for devouring fish. Even when quite young, it can swallow a fish as large as a herring, and when it is full grown it will eat four or five large herrings at a meal.

Now when we remember that a man of average appetite

THE HOME OF THE HERON.

finds one herring to form a very sufficient breakfast, we can easily imagine what must be the digestive power of a bird which, though very inferior to man in point of bulk, can eat four times as much at a meal. Even though the fish be much larger in diameter than the neck of the bird, the Heron can swallow it as easily as a small snake swallows a large frog. The neck merely seems to expand as if it were made of Indiarubber, the fish slips down, and the bird is ready for another.

Generally the Herons feed after sunset, but I have frequently seen them busily engaged in catching their prey in full daylight, when the sunbeams were playing in the water so as to produce the beautiful rippling effect on the Heron's plumage which has already been mentioned.

The Heron does not restrict itself to fishes or reptiles, but, like the bittern, feeds on almost any kind of aquatic animal which comes within its reach. When it lives near tidal rivers, it feeds largely on the shrimps, prawns, green crabs, and various other crustacea; and when it lives far inland, it still makes prey of the fresh-water shrimps, the water-beetles, and the boat-flies, and similar aquatic creatures. In fact, it acts much after the fashion of the lions, tigers, and leopards, which put up with locusts and beetles when they can find no larger prey.

The long beak of the Heron is not merely an instrument by which it can obtain food, but is also a weapon of considerable power. When attacked, it aims a blow at the eye of its opponent, and makes the stroke with such rapidity that the foe is generally blinded before perceiving the danger. When domesticated, it has been known to keep possession of the enclosure in which it lived, and soon to drive away dogs by the power of its beak. When it is young, it is quite helpless, its very long legs being unable to support its body, which is entirely bare of plumage, and has a very unprepossessing appearance.

The flight of the Heron is very powerful, its wings being very large in proportion to its slender body. Sometimes the bird takes to ascending in a spiral line, and then the flight is as beautiful as it is strong. When chased by the falcon it mostly ascends in this manner, each of the two birds trying to rise above the other.

The nest of the Heron is always made on the top of some lofty tree, whenever the bird builds in places where trees can be found; and as the bird is an eminently sociable one, a single nest is very seldom found, the Heron being as fond of society as the rook. In some parts of Palestine, however, where trees are very scarce, the Heron is obliged to choose some other locality for its nest, and in that case prefers the great thickets of papyrus reeds which are found in the marshes, and which are even more inaccessible than the tops of trees.

One of these marshes is well described by Mr. Tristram in his "Land of Israel." "The whole marsh is marked in the map as impassable; and most truly it is so. I never anywhere have met with a swamp so vast and utterly impenetrable.

"The papyrus extends right across to the east side. A false step off its roots will take the intruder over head in suffocating peat-mud. We spent a long time in attempting to effect an entrance, and at last gave it up, satisfied that the marsh birds were not to be had. In fact, the whole is simply a floating bog of several miles square; a very thin crust of vegetation covers an unknown depth of water; and, if the explorer breaks through this, suffocation is imminent. Some of the Arabs, who were tilling the plain for cotton, assured us that even a wild boar never got through it. We shot two bitterns, but in endeavouring to retrieve them I slipped from the root on which I was standing, and was drawn down in a moment, only saving myself from drowning by my gun, which had providentially caught across a papyrus stem."

It may here be mentioned that the bulrush of Scripture is undoubtedly the papyrus. The ark or basket of bulrushes, lined with slime and pitch, in which Moses was laid, was made of the papyrus, which at the present day is used for the manufacture of baskets, mats, sandals, and for the thatching of houses. Many tribes which inhabit the banks of the Nile make simple boats, or rather rafts, of the papyrus, which they cut and tie in bundles; and it is worthy of notice that the Australian native makes a reed boat in almost exactly the same manner.

Compare Is. xviii. 1, 2: "Woe to the land shadowing with wings, which is beyond the rivers of Ethiopia.

"That sendeth ambassadors by the sea, even in vessels of bulrushes." Did we not know that vessels are actually made of bulrushes at the present day, a custom which has survived from very ancient times, we might find a difficulty in understanding this passage, while the meaning is intelligible enough when it is viewed by the light of the knowledge that the Ethiopian of the present day takes gold, and ivory, and other merchandise down the Nile in his boat of papyrus (or bulrush) reeds tied together.

The papyrus runs from ten to fifteen or sixteen feet in height, so that the Herons are at no loss for suitable spots whereon to place their nests. From the name "papyrus" our word paper is derived. The stems of the plant, after having been split into

THE PAPYRUS PLANT.

thin slices, joined together, and brought to a smooth surface, formed the paper upon which the ancient Egyptians wrote.

THE Egrets, which are probably included under the generic title of Anâphah, are birds of passage, and at the proper season are plentiful in Palestine. These pretty birds much resemble the heron in general form, and in general habits both birds are very much alike, haunting the marshes and edges of lakes and streams, and feeding upon the frogs and other inhabitants of the water. In countries where rice is cultivated, the Egret may generally be seen in the artificial swamps in which that plant is sown. The colour of the Egret is pure white, with the exception of the train. This consists of a great number of long slender feathers of a delicate straw colour. Like those which form the train of the peacock, they fall over the feathers of the tail, and entirely conceal them.

THE CRANE.

Various passages in which the Crane is mentioned—Its migratory habits, and loud voice—Geographical range of the Crane—Its favourite roosting-places—Size of the Crane, and measurement of the wings—The Crane once used as food—Plumes of the Crane and their use—Structure of the vocal organs—Nest and eggs of the Crane.

IN the description of the dove and the swallow two passages have been quoted in which the name of the CRANE is mentioned, one referring to its voice, and the other to its migratory instinct. The first passage occurs in Isa. xxxviii. 14: "Like a crane or swallow, so did I chatter;" and the other in Jer. viii. 7: "The turtle and the crane and the swallow observe the time of their coming."

It is rather remarkable that in both these cases the word "Crane" is used in connexion with the swallow, or rather the swift, and that in both instances the names of the birds should have been interchanged. If we refer to the original of these

THE CRANE.

passages, we shall find that the former of them would run thus, "Like a *sis* or an *agur*," and the latter thus, "The turtle and the *sis* and the *agur*." That in these passages the interpretation of the words *sis* and *agur* have been interchanged has already been mentioned, and, as the former has been described under the name of swallow or swift, we shall now treat of the latter under the title of Crane.

The species here mentioned is the common Crane, a bird which has a very wide range, and which seeks a warm climate on the approach of winter.

The Crane performs its annual migrations in company, vast flocks of many thousand individuals passing like great clouds at an immense height, whence their trumpet-like cry is audible for a great distance round, and attracts the ear if not the eye to them. Thus we have at a glance both the characteristics to which reference is made in the Scriptures, namely, the noisy cry and the habit of migration.

It is a very gregarious bird, associating with its comrades in flocks, just as do the starlings and rooks of our own country, and, like these birds, has favourite roosting-places in which it passes the night. When evening approaches, the Cranes may be seen in large flocks passing to their roosting-places, and, on account of their great size, having a very strange effect. A fair-sized Crane will measure seven feet across the expanded wings, so that even a solitary bird has a very imposing effect when flying, while that of a large flock of Cranes on the wing is simply magnificent.

The spots which the Crane selects for its roosting-places are generally of the same character. Being in some respects a wary bird, though it is curiously indifferent in others, it will not roost in any place near bushes, rocks, or other spots which might serve to conceal an enemy. The locality most favoured by the Crane is a large, smooth, sloping bank, far from any spot wherein an enemy may be concealed. The birds keep a careful watch during the night, and it is impossible for any foe to approach them without being discovered. The Crane is noisy on the wing, and, whether it be soaring high over head on its long migratory journeys, or be merely flying at dusk to its roosting-place, it continually utters its loud, clangorous cry.

The food of the Crane is much like that of the heron, but in addition to the frogs, fish, worms, and insects, it eats vegetable substances. Sometimes it is apt to get into cultivated grounds, and then does much damage to the crops, pecking up the ground with its long beak, partly for the sake of the worms, grubs, and other creatures, and partly for the sake of the sprouting seeds.

Although by reason of its scarcity the Crane has been

abandoned as food, its flesh is really excellent, and in former days was valued very highly.

Like the egret, the Crane is remarkable for the flowing plumes of the back, which fall over the tail feathers, and form a train. These feathers are much used as plumes, both for purposes of dress and as brushes or flappers wherewith to drive off the flies. By reason of this conformation, some systematic zoologists have thought that it has some affinity to the ostrich, the rhœa, and similar birds, and that the resemblance is strengthened by the structure of the digestive organs, which are suited to vegetable as well as animal substances, the stomach being strong and muscular.

The peculiar voice of the Crane, which it is so fond of using, and to which reference is made in the Scriptures, is caused by a peculiar structure of the windpipe, which is exceedingly long, and, instead of going straight to the lungs, undergoes several convolutions about the breast-bone, and then proceeds to the lungs.

The Crane makes its nest on low ground, generally among osiers or reeds, and it lays only two eggs, pale olive in colour, dashed profusely with black and brown streaks.

THE STORK.

Signification of the Hebrew word *Chasidah*—Various passages in which it is mentioned—The Chasidah therefore a large, wide-winged, migratory bird—Its identification with the Stork—The Stork always protected.

In the Old Testament there are several passages wherein is mentioned the word *Chasidah*

The Authorized Version invariably renders the word *Chasidah* as "Stork," and is undoubtedly right.

In Buxtorf's Lexicon there is a curious derivation of the word. He says that the word *Chasidah* is derived from *chesed*, a word that signifies benevolence.

According to some writers, the name was given to the Stork because it was supposed to be a bird remarkable for its filial piety; "for the storks in their turn support their parents in their old age: they allow them to rest their necks on their bodies during migration, and, if the elders are tired, the young ones take them on their backs." According to others, the name is given to the Stork because it exercises kindness towards its companions in bringing them food; but in all cases the derivation of the word is acknowledged to be the same.

Partly in consequence of this idea, which is a very old and almost universal one, and partly on account of the great services rendered by the bird in clearing the ground of snakes, insects, and garbage, the Stork has always been protected through the East, as it is to the present day in several parts of Europe. The slaughter of a Stork, or even the destruction of its eggs, would be punished with a heavy fine; and in consequence of the immunity which it enjoys, it loves to haunt the habitations of mankind.

In many of the Continental towns, where sanitary regulations are not enforced, the Stork serves the purpose of a scavenger, and may be seen walking about the market-place, waiting for the offal of fish, fowls, and the like, which are simply thrown on the ground for the Storks to eat. In Eastern lands the Stork enjoys similar privileges, and we may infer that the bird was perfectly familiar both to the writers of the various Scriptural books in which it was mentioned, and to the people for whom these books were intended.

When they settle upon a tract of ground, the Storks divide it among themselves in a manner that seems to have a sort of system in it, spreading themselves over it with wonderful regularity, each bird appearing to take possession of a definite amount of ground. By this mode of proceeding, the ground is rapidly cleared of all vermin; the Storks examining their allotted space with the keenest scrutiny, and devouring every reptile, mouse, worm, grub, or insect that they can find on it. Sometimes they

STORKS AND THEIR NESTS.

will spread themselves in this manner over a vast extent of country, arriving suddenly, remaining for several months, and departing without giving any sign of their intention to move.

The wings of the Stork, which are mentioned in Holy Writ, are very conspicuous, and are well calculated to strike an imaginative mind. The general colour of the bird is white, while the quill feathers of the wings are black; so that the effect of the spread wings is very striking, an adult bird measuring about seven feet across, when flying. As the body, large though it may be, is comparatively light when compared with the extent of wing, the flight is both lofty and sustained, the bird flying a very great height, and, when migrating, is literally the "stork in the heavens."

Next we come to the migratory habits of the Stork.

Like the swallow, the Stork resorts year after year to the same spots; and when it has once fixed on a locality for its nest, that place will be assuredly taken as regularly as the breeding-season comes round. The same pair are sure to return to their well-known home, notwithstanding the vast distances over which they pass, and the many lands in which they sojourn. Should one of the pair die, the other finds a mate in a very short time, and thus the same home is kept up by successive generations of Storks, much as among men one ancestral mansion is inhabited by a series of members of the same family.

So well is this known, that when a pair of Storks have made their nest in a human habitation their return is always expected, and when they arrive the absentees are welcomed on all sides. In many countries breeding-places are specially provided for the Storks; and when one of them is occupied for the first time, the owner of the house looks upon it as a fortunate omen.

The localities chosen by the Stork for its nest vary according to the surrounding conditions. The foundation which a Stork requires is a firm platform, the more elevated the better, but the bird seems to care little whether this platform be on rocks, buildings, or trees. If, for example, it builds its nest in craggy places, far from the habitations of man, it selects some flat ledge for the purpose, preferring those that are at the extreme tops of the rocks. The summit of a natural pinnacle is a favourite spot with the Stork.

In many cases the Stork breeds among old ruins, and under

such circumstances it is fond of building its nest on the tops of pillars or towers, the summits of arches, and similar localities. When it takes up its abode among mankind, it generally selects the breeding-places which have been built for it by those who know its taste, but it frequently chooses the top of a chimney, or some such locality.

Sometimes, however, it is obliged to build in spots where it can find neither rocks nor buildings, and in such cases it builds on trees, and, like the heron, is sociable in its nesting, a whole community residing in a clump of trees. It is not very particular about the kind of tree, provided that it be tolerably tall, and strong enough to bear the weight of its enormous nest; and the reader will at once see that the fir-trees are peculiarly fitted to be the houses for the Stork.

As may be expected from the localities chosen by the Stork for its breeding-place, its nest is very large and heavy. It is constructed with very little skill, and is scarcely more than a huge quantity of sticks, reeds, and similar substances, heaped together, and having in the middle a slight depression in which the eggs are laid. These eggs are usually three, or perhaps four in number, and now and then a fifth is seen, and are of a very pale buff or cream colour.

As is the case with the heron, the young of the Stork are quite helpless when hatched, and are most ungainly little beings, with their long legs doubled under them, unable to sustain their round and almost naked bodies, while their large beaks are ever gaping for food. Those of my readers who have had young birds of any kind must have noticed the extremely grotesque appearance which they possess when they hold up their heads and cry for food, with their bills open to an almost incredible extent. In such birds as the Stork, the heron, and others of the tribe, the grotesque appearance is exaggerated in proportion to the length and gape of the bill.

The Stork is noted for being a peculiarly kind and loving parent to its young, in that point fully deserving the derivation of its Hebrew name, though its love manifests itself towards the young, and not towards the parent.

The Rev. H. B. Tristram mentions from personal experience an instance of the watchful care exercised by the Stork over its young. "The writer was once in camp near an old ruined tower in the plains of Zana, south of the Atlas, where a pair of storks had their nest. The four young might often be seen from a little distance, surveying the prospect from their lonely height, but whenever any of the human party happened to stroll near the tower, one of the old storks, invisible before, would instantly appear, and, lighting on the nest, put its feet gently on the necks of all the young, so as to hold them down out of sight till the stranger had passed, snapping its bill meanwhile, and assuming a grotesque air of indifference, as if unconscious of there being anything under its charge."

The snapping noise which is here mentioned is the only sound produced by the Stork, which is an absolutely silent bird, as far as voice is concerned.

THERE is another species of Stork found in Palestine, to which the fir-trees are especially a home. This is the Black Stork (*Ciconia nigra*), which in some parts of the country is even more plentiful than its white relative, which it resembles in almost every particular, except that it has a dark head and back, the feathers being glossed with purple and green like those of the magpie. This species, which is undoubtedly included in the Hebrew word *chasidah*, always makes its nest on trees whenever it can find them, and in some of the more densely wooded parts of Palestine is in consequence plentiful, placing its nest in the deepest parts of the forests. When it cannot obtain trees, it will build its nest on rocky ledges. It lays two or three eggs of a greenish white colour.

Like the preceding species, the Black Stork is easily domesticated. Colonel Montague kept one which was very tame, and would follow its keeper like a dog. Its tameness enabled its proceedings to be closely watched, and its mode of feeding was thereby investigated. It was fond of examining the rank grass and mud for food, and while doing so always kept its bill a little open, so as to pounce down at once on any insect or reptile that it might disturb.

Eels were its favourite food, and it was such an adept at catching them that it was never seen to miss one, no matter how small or quick it might be. As soon as it had caught one of these active fish, it went to some dry place, and then disabled its prey by shaking and beating it against the ground before swallowing it, whereas many birds that feed on fish swallow their prey as soon as it is caught. The Stork was never seen to swim as the heron sometimes does, but it would wade as long as it could place its feet on the bed of the stream, and would strain its head and the whole of its neck under water in searching for fish.

It was of a mild and peaceable disposition, and, even if angered, did not attempt to bite or strike with its beak, but only denoted its displeasure by blowing the air sharply from its lungs, and nodding its head repeatedly. After the manner of Storks, it always chose an elevated spot on which to repose,

A NEST OF THE WHITE STORK.

and took its rest standing on one leg, with its head so sunk among the feathers of its shoulders that scarcely any part of it was visible, the hinder part of the head resting on the back, and the bill lying on the fore-part of the neck.

Though the bird is so capable of domestication, it does not of its own accord haunt the dwellings of men, like the White Stork, but avoids the neighbourhood of houses, and lives in the most retired places it can find.

THE SWAN.

Signification of the word *Tinshemeth*—The Gallinule and the Ibis—Appearance and habits of the Hyacinthine Gallinule—A strange use for the bird—The White or Sacred Ibis

In the two parallel chapters of Lev. xi. 18 and Deut. xiv. 16, the Hebrew word *tinshemeth* is found, and evidently signifies some kind of bird which was forbidden as food. After stating (Lev. xi. 13) that "these are they which ye shall have in abomination among the fowls; they shall not be eaten, they are an abomination," the sacred lawgiver proceeds to enumerate a number of birds, nearly all of which have already been described. Among them occurs the name of *tinshemeth*, between the great owl and the pelican.

What was the precise species of bird which was signified by this name it is impossible to say, but there is no doubt that it could not have been the Swan, according to the rendering of the Authorized Version. The Swan is far too rare a bird in Palestine to have been specially mentioned in the law of Moses, and in all probability it was totally unknown to the generality of the Israelites. Even had it been known to them, and tolerably common, there seems to be no reason why it should have been reckoned among the list of unclean birds.

On turning to the Hebrew Bible, we find that the word is left untranslated, and simply given in its Hebrew form, thereby signifying that the translators could form no opinion whatever of the proper rendering of the word. The Septuagint translates the Tinshemeth as the Porphyrio or Ibis, and the Vulgate follows the same rendering. Later naturalists have agreed that the Septuagint and Vulgate have the far more probable reading; and, as two birds are there mentioned, they will be both described.

THE first is the Porphyrio, by which we may understand **the HYACINTHINE GALLINULE** (*Porphyrio veterum*). All the birds of this group are remarkable for the enormous length of their toes, by means of which they are enabled to walk upon the loose

IBIS AND GALLINULE (SWAN OF SCRIPTURE).

herbage that floats on the surface of the water as firmly as if they were treading on land. Their feet are also used, like those of the parrots, in conveying food to the mouth. We have in England a very familiar example of the Gallinules in the common water-hen, or moor-hen, the toes of which are of great proportionate length, though not so long as those of the Purple Gallinule, which almost rivals in this respect the jacanas of South

America and China. The water-rail, and corncrake or land-rail, are also allied to the Gallinules.

The Hyacinthine Gallinule derives its name from its colour, which is a rich and variable blue, taking a turquoise hue on the head, neck, throat, and breast, and deep indigo on the back. The large bill and the legs are red. Like many other birds, however, it varies much in colour according to age.

It has a very wide geographical range, being found in many parts of Europe, Asia, and Africa, and is common in the marshy districts of Palestine, where its rich blue plumage and its large size, equalling that of a duck, render it very conspicuous. The large and powerful bill of this bird betokens the nature of its food, which consists almost entirely of hard vegetable substances, the seeds of aquatic herbage forming a large portion of its diet. When it searches for food on the seashore, it eats the marine vegetation, mixing with this diet other articles of an animal nature, such as molluscs and small reptiles.

Though apparently a clumsy bird, it moves with wonderful speed, running not only swiftly but gracefully, its large feet being no hindrance to the rapidity of its movements. It is mostly found in shallow marshes, where the construction of its feet enables it to traverse both the soft muddy ground and the patches of firm earth with equal ease. Its wings, however, are by no means equal to its legs either in power or activity; and, like most of the rail tribe, it never takes to the air unless absolutely obliged to do so.

The nest of the Hyacinthine Gallinule is made on the sedge-patches which dot the marshes, much like that of the coot. The nest, too, resembles that of the coot, being composed of reeds, sedges, and other aquatic plants. The eggs are three or four in number, white in colour, and nearly spherical in form.

As the Ibis has an equal claim to the title of Tinshemeth, we will devote a few lines to a description of the bird. The particular species which would be signified by the word *tinshemeth* would undoubtedly be the WHITE or SACRED IBIS (*Ibis religiosa*), a bird which derives its name of Sacred from the reverence with which it was held by the ancient Egyptians, and the frequency with which its figure occurs in the monumental sculptures. It was also thought worthy of being embalmed, and many mummies of the Ibis have been found in the old Egyptian burial-places, having been preserved for some three thousand years.

It is about as large as an ordinary hen, and, as its name imports, has the greater part of its plumage white, the ends of the wing-feathers and the coverts being black, with violet reflections. The long neck is black and bare, and has a most curious aspect, looking as if it were made of an old black kid glove, very much crumpled, but still retaining its gloss.

The reason for the extreme veneration with which the bird was regarded by the ancient Egyptians seems rather obscure. It is probable, however, that the partial migration of the bird was connected in their minds with the rise of the Nile, a river as sacred to the old Egyptians as the Ganges to the modern Hindoo. As soon as the water begins to rise, the Ibis makes its appearance, sometimes alone, and sometimes in small troops. It haunts the banks of the river, and marshy places in general, diligently searching for food by the aid of its long bill. It can fly well and strongly, and it utters at intervals a rather loud cry, dipping its head at every utterance.

THE CORMORANT.

The word *Shâlâk* and its signification—Habits of the Cormorant—The bird trained to catch fish—Mode of securing its prey—Nests and eggs of the Cormorant—Nesting in fir-trees—Flesh of the bird.

ALTHOUGH in the Authorized Version of the Scriptures the word Cormorant occurs three times, there is no doubt that in two of the passages the Hebrew word ought to have been rendered as Pelican, as we shall see when we come presently to the description of that bird.

In the two parallel passages, Lev. xi. 17 and Deut. xiv. 17, a creature called the Shâlâk is mentioned in the list of prohibited meats. That the Shâlâk must be a bird is evident from the context, and we are therefore only left to discover what sort of bird it may be. On looking at the etymology of the word we find that it is derived from a root which signifies hurling or casting down, and we may therefore presume that the bird is one which plunges or sweeps down upon its prey.

Weighing, carefully, the opinions of the various Hebraists and naturalists, we may safely determine that the word *shâlâk* has been rightly translated in the Authorized Version. The Hebrew Bible gives the same reading, and does not affix the mark of doubt to the word, though there are very few of the long list of animals in Lev. xi. and Deut. xiv. which are not either distinguished by the mark of doubt, or, like the Tinshemeth, are left untranslated.

The Cormorant belongs to the family of the pelicans, the relationship between them being evident to the most unpractised eye; and the whole structure of the bird shows its admirable adaptation for the life which it leads.

Its long beak enables it to seize even a large fish, while the hook at the end prevents the slippery prey from escaping. The long snake-like neck gives the bird the power of darting its beak with great rapidity, and at the same time allows it to seize prey immediately to the right or left of its course. Its strong, closely-feathered wings enable it to fly with tolerable speed, while at the same time they can be closed so tightly to the body that they do not hinder the progress of the bird through the water; while the tail serves equally when spread to direct its course through the air, and when partially or entirely closed to act as a rudder in the water. Lastly, its short powerful legs, with their broadly-webbed feet, act as paddles, by which the bird urges itself through the water with such wonderful speed that it can overtake and secure the fishes even in their own element. Besides these outward characteristics, we find that the bird is able to make a very long stay under water, the lungs being adapted so as to contain a wonderful amount of air.

The Cormorant has been trained to play the same part in the water as the falcon in the air, and has been taught to catch fish, and bring them ashore for its master. So adroit are they, that if one of them should catch a fish which is too heavy for it, another bird will come to its assistance, and the two together will bring the struggling prey to land. Trained birds of this description have been employed in China from time immemorial.

In order to prevent it from swallowing the fish which it takes, each bird has a ring or ligature passed round its neck.

The Cormorant is a most voracious bird, swallowing a considerable weight of fish at a meal, and digesting them so rapidly that it is soon ready for another supply. Although it is essentially a marine bird, hunger often takes it inland, especially to places where there are lakes or large rivers.

While the ducks and teal and widgeons may be stationary on the pool, the cormorant is seen swimming to and fro, as if in quest of something. First raising his body nearly perpendicular, down he plunges into the deep, and, after staying there a considerable time, he is sure to bring up a fish, which he invariably swallows head foremost. Sometimes half an hour elapses before he can manage to accommodate a large eel quietly in his stomach.

You see him straining violently with repeated efforts to gulp it; and when you fancy that the slippery mouthful is successfully disposed of, all on a sudden the eel retrogrades upwards from its dismal sepulchre, struggling violently to escape. The cormorant swallows it again, and up again it comes, and shows its tail a foot or more out of its destroyer's mouth. At length, worn out with ineffectual writhings and slidings, the eel is gulped down into the cormorant's stomach for the last time, there to meet its dreaded and inevitable fate.

Mr. Fortune gives a very interesting account of the feeding of tame Cormorants in China. The birds preferred eels to all other food, and, in spite of the difficulty in swallowing the slippery and active creature, would not touch another fish as long as an eel was left. The bird is so completely at home in the water that it does not need, like the heron and other aquatic birds, to bring its prey ashore in order to swallow it, but can eat fish in the water as well as catch them. It always seizes the fish crosswise, and is therefore obliged to turn it before it can swallow the prey with the head downwards. Sometimes it contrives to turn the fish while still under water, but, if it should fail in so doing, it brings its prey to the surface, and shifts it about in its bill, making a series of little snatches at it until the head is in the right direction. When it seizes a very large fish, the bird shakes its prey just as a dog shakes a rat, and so disables it. It is said to eat its own weight of fish in a single day.

Sometimes, when it has been very successful or exceptionally hungry, it loads itself with food to such an extent that it becomes almost insensible during the process of digestion, and, although naturally a keen-eyed and wary bird, allows itself to be captured by hand.

The nest of the Cormorant is always upon a rocky ledge, and generally on a spot which is inaccessible except by practised climbers furnished with ropes, poles, hooks, and other appurtenances. Mr. Waterton mentions that when he descended the Raincliff, a precipice some four hundred feet in height, he saw numbers of the nests and eggs, but could not get at them except by swinging himself boldly off the face of the cliff, so as to be brought by the return swing into the recesses chosen by the birds.

The nests are mostly placed in close proximity to each other, and are made of sticks and seaweeds, and, as is usual with such nests, are very inartificially constructed. The eggs are of a greenish white on the outside, and green on the inside. When found in the nest, they are covered with a sort of chalky crust, so that the true colour is not perceptible until the crust is scraped off. Two to four eggs are generally laid in, or rather on, each nest. As may be imagined from the character of the birds' food, the odour of the nesting-place is most horrible.

Sometimes, when rocks cannot be found, the Cormorant is obliged to select other spots for its nest. It is mentioned in the "Proceedings of the Zoological Society," that upon an island in the midst of a large lake there were a number of Scotch fir-trees, upon the branches of which were about eighty nests of the Cormorant.

The flesh of the Cormorant is very seldom eaten, as it has a fishy flavour which is far from agreeable. To eat an old Cormorant is indeed almost impossible, but the young birds may be rendered edible by taking them as soon as killed, skinning them, removing the whole of the interior, wrapping them in cloths, and burying them for some time in the ground.

THE PELICAN.

The Pelican of the wilderness—Attitudes of the bird—Its love of solitude—Mode of feeding the young—Fables regarding the Pelican—Breeding-places of the bird—The object of its wide wings and large pouch—Colour of the Pelican.

It has been mentioned that in two passages of Scripture, the word which is translated in the Authorized Version as Cormorant, ought to have been rendered as Pelican. These, however, are not the first passages in which we meet with the word *kaath*. The name occurs in the two parallel passages of Lev. xi. and Deut. xiv. among the list of birds which are proscribed as food. Passing over them, we next come to Ps. cii. 6. In this passage, the sacred writer is lamenting his misery: "By reason of the voice of my groaning my bones cleave to my skin.

"I am like a pelican of the wilderness: I am like an owl of the desert."

In these sentences, we see that the Kaath was a bird of solitude that was to be found in the "wilderness," *i.e.* far from the habitations of man. This is one of the characteristics of the Pelican, which loves not the neighbourhood of human beings, and is fond of resorting to broad, uncultivated lands, where it will not be disturbed.

In them it makes its nest and hatches its young, and to them it retires after feeding, in order to digest in quiet the ample meal which it has made. Mr. Tristram well suggests that the metaphor of the Psalmist may allude to the habit common to the Pelican and its kin, of sitting motionless for hours after it has gorged itself with food, its head sunk on its shoulders, and its bill resting on its breast.

This is but one of the singular, and often grotesque, attitudes in which the Pelican is in the habit of indulging.

There are before me a number of sketches made of the Pelicans at the Zoological Gardens, and in no two cases does one attitude in the least resemble another. In one sketch the

THE PELICAN.

bird is sitting in the attitude which has just been described. In another it is walking, or rather staggering, along, with its head on one side, and its beak so closed that hardly a vestige of its enormous pouch can be seen. Another sketch shows the same bird as it appeared when angry with a companion, and scolding its foe in impotent rage; while another shows it basking in the sun, with its magnificent wings spread and shaking in the warm beams, and its pouch hanging in folds from its chin.

One of the most curious of these sketches shows the bird squatting on the ground, with its head drawn back as far as possible, and sunk so far among the feathers of the back and shoulders that only a portion of the head itself can be seen, while the long beak is hidden, except an inch or two of the end. In this attitude it might easily be mistaken at a little distance for an oval white stone.

The derivation of the Hebrew word *kaath* is a very curious one. It is taken from a verb signifying "to vomit," and this derivation has been explained in different ways.

The early writers, who were comparatively ignorant of natural history, thought that the Pelican lived chiefly on molluscs, and that, after digesting the animals, it rejected their shells, just as the owl and the hawk reject the bones, fur, and feathers of their prey.

They thought that the Pelican was a bird of a hot temperament, and that the molluscs were quickly digested by the heat of the stomach.

At the present day, however, knowing as we do the habits of the Pelican, we find that, although the reasons just given are faulty, and that the Pelican lives essentially on fish, and not on molluscs, the derivation of the word is really a good one, and that those who gave the bird the name of Kaath, or the vomiter, were well acquainted with its habits.

The bird certainly does eat molluscs, but the principal part of its diet is composed of fish, which it catches dexterously by a sort of sidelong snatch of its enormous bill. The skin under the lower part of the beak is so modified that it can form, when distended, an enormous pouch, capable of holding a great quantity of fish, though, as long as it is not wanted, the pouch is so contracted into longitudinal folds as to be scarcely perceptible. When it has filled the pouch, it usually retires from the water, and flies to a retired spot, often many miles inland, where it can sit and digest at its ease the enormous meal which it has made.

As it often chooses its breeding-places in similar spots, far from the water, it has to carry the food with which it nourishes its young for many miles. For this purpose it is furnished, not only with the pouch which has been just mentioned, but with long, wide, and very powerful wings, often measuring from twelve to thirteen feet from tip to tip. No one, on looking at a Pelican as it waddles about or sits at rest, would imagine the gigantic dimensions of the wings, which seem, as the bird spreads them, to have almost as unlimited a power of expansion as the pouch.

In these two points the true Pelicans present a strong contrast to the cormorants, though birds closely allied. The cormorant has its home close by the sea, and therefore needs not to carry its food for any distance. Consequently, it needs no pouch, and has none. Neither does it require the great expanse of wing which is needful for the Pelican, that has to carry such a weight of fish through the air. Accordingly, the wings, though strong enough to enable the bird to carry for a short distance a single fish of somewhat large size, are comparatively short and closely feathered, and the flight of the cormorant possesses neither the grace nor the power which distinguishes that of the Pelican.

When the Pelican feeds its young, it does so by pressing its beak against its breast, so as to force out of it the enclosed fish. Now the tip of the beak is armed, like that of the cormorant, with a sharply-curved hook, only, in the case of the Pelican, the hook is of a bright scarlet colour, looking, when the bird presses the beak against the white feathers of the breast, like a large drop of blood. Hence arose the curious legend respecting the Pelican, which represented it as feeding its young with its own blood, and tearing open its breast with its hooked bill. We find that this legend is exemplified by the oft-recurring symbol of the " Pelican feeding its young " in ecclesiastical art, as an emblem of Divine love.

This is one of the many instances in which the inventive, poetical, inaccurate Oriental mind has seized some peculiarity of form, and based upon it a whole series of fabulous legends. As long as they restricted themselves to the appearance and habits of the animals with which they were familiarly acquainted, the old writers were curiously full, exact, and precise in their details. But as soon as they came to any creature of whose mode of life they were entirely or partially ignorant, they allowed their inventive faculties full scope, and put forward as zoological facts statements which were the mere creation of their own fancy.

We have already seen several examples of this propensity, and shall find more as we proceed with the zoology of the Scriptures.

The fabulous legends of the Pelican are too numerous to be even mentioned, but there is one which deserves notice, because it is made the basis of an old Persian fable.

The writer of the legend evidently had some partial knowledge of the bird. He knew that it had a large pouch which could hold fish and water; that it had large and powerful wings ; and that it was in the habit of flying far inland, either for the purpose of digesting its food or nourishing its young. Knowing that the Pelican is in the habit of choosing solitary spots in which it may bring up its young in safety, but not knowing the precise mode of its nesting, the writer in question has trusted to his imagination, and put forward his theories as facts.

Knowing that the bird dwells in "the wilderness," he has assumed that the wilderness in question is a sandy, arid desert, far from water, and consequently from vegetation. Such being the case, the nurture of the Pelican's young is evidently a difficult question. Being aquatic birds, the young must needs require water for drink and bathing, as well as fish for food ; and, though a supply of both these necessaries could be brought in the ample pouches of the parents, they would be wasted unless some mode of storing were employed.

Accordingly, the parent birds were said to make their nest in a hollow tree, and to line it with clay, or to build it altogether of clay, so as to leave a deep basin. This basin the parent birds were said to use as a sort of store-pond, bringing home supplies of fish and water in their pouches, and pouring them into the pond. The wild beasts who lived in the desert were said to be acquainted with these nests, and to resort to them daily in order to quench their thirst, repaying their entertainers by protecting their homes.

In real fact, the Pelican mostly breeds near water, and is fond of selecting little rocky islands where it cannot be approached without danger. The nest is made on the ground, and is formed in a most inartificial manner of reeds and grass, the general mass of the nest being made of the reeds, and the lining being formed of grass. The eggs are white, of nearly the same shape at both ends, and are from two to five in number. On an average, however, each nest will contain about two eggs.

The parent birds are very energetic in defence of their eggs or young, and, according to Le Vaillant, when approached they are "like furious harpies let loose against us, and their cries rendered us almost deaf. They often flew so near us that they flapped their wings in our faces, and, though we fired our pieces repeatedly, we were not able to frighten them." When the well-known naturalist Sonnerat tried to drive a female Pelican from her nest, she appeared not to be frightened, but angry. She would not move from her nest, and when he tried to push her off, she struck at him with her long bill and uttered cries of rage.

In order to aid the bird in carrying the heavy weights with which it loads itself, the whole skeleton is permeated with air, and is exceedingly light. Beside this, the whole cellular system of the bird is honeycombed with air-cells, so that the bulk of the bird can be greatly increased, while its weight remains practically unaltered, and the Pelican becomes a sort of living balloon.

The habit of conveying its food inland before eating it is so characteristic of the Pelican that other birds take advantage of it. In some countries there is a large hawk which robs the Pelican, just as the bald-headed eagle of America robs the osprey. Knowing instinctively that when a Pelican is flying inland slowly and heavily and with a distended pouch it is carrying a supply of food to its home, the hawk dashes at it, and frightens it so that the poor bird opens its beak, and gives up to the assailant the fish which it was bearing homewards.

It is evident that the wings which are needed for supporting such weights, and which, as we have seen, exceed twelve feet in length from tip to tip, would be useless in the water, and would hinder rather than aid the bird if it attempted to dive as the close-winged cormorant does. Accordingly, we find that the Pelican is not a diver, and, instead of chasing its finny prey under water, after the manner of the cormorant, it contents itself with scooping up in its beak the fishes which come to the surface of the water. The very buoyancy of its body would prevent it from diving as does the cormorant, and, although it often plunges into the water so fairly as to be for a moment submerged, it almost immediately rises, and pursues its course on the surface of the water, and not beneath it. Like the cormorant, the Pelican can perch on trees, though it does not select such spots for its roosting-places, and prefers rocks to branches. In one case, however, when some young Pelicans had been captured and tied to a stake, their mother used to bring them food during the day, and at night was accustomed to roost in the branches of a tree above them.

Though under some circumstances a thoroughly social bird, it is yet fond of retiring to the most solitary spots in order to consume at peace the prey that it has captured; and, as it sits motionless and alone for hours, more like a white stone than a bird, it may well be accepted as a type of solitude and desolation.

The colour of the common Pelican is white, with a very slight pinky tinge, which is most conspicuous in the breeding season. The feathers of the crest are yellow, and the quill feathers of the wings are jetty black, contrasting well with the white plumage of the body. The pouch is yellow, and the upper part of the beak bluish grey, with a red line running across the middle, and a bright red hook at the tip. This plumage belongs only to the adult bird, that of the young being ashen grey, and four or five years are required before the bird puts on its full beauty. There is no difference in the appearance of the sexes. The illustration represents a fine old male Crested Pelican. The general colour is a greyish white, with a slight yellowish tint on the breast. The pouch is bright orange, and the crest is formed of curling feathers.

REPTILES.

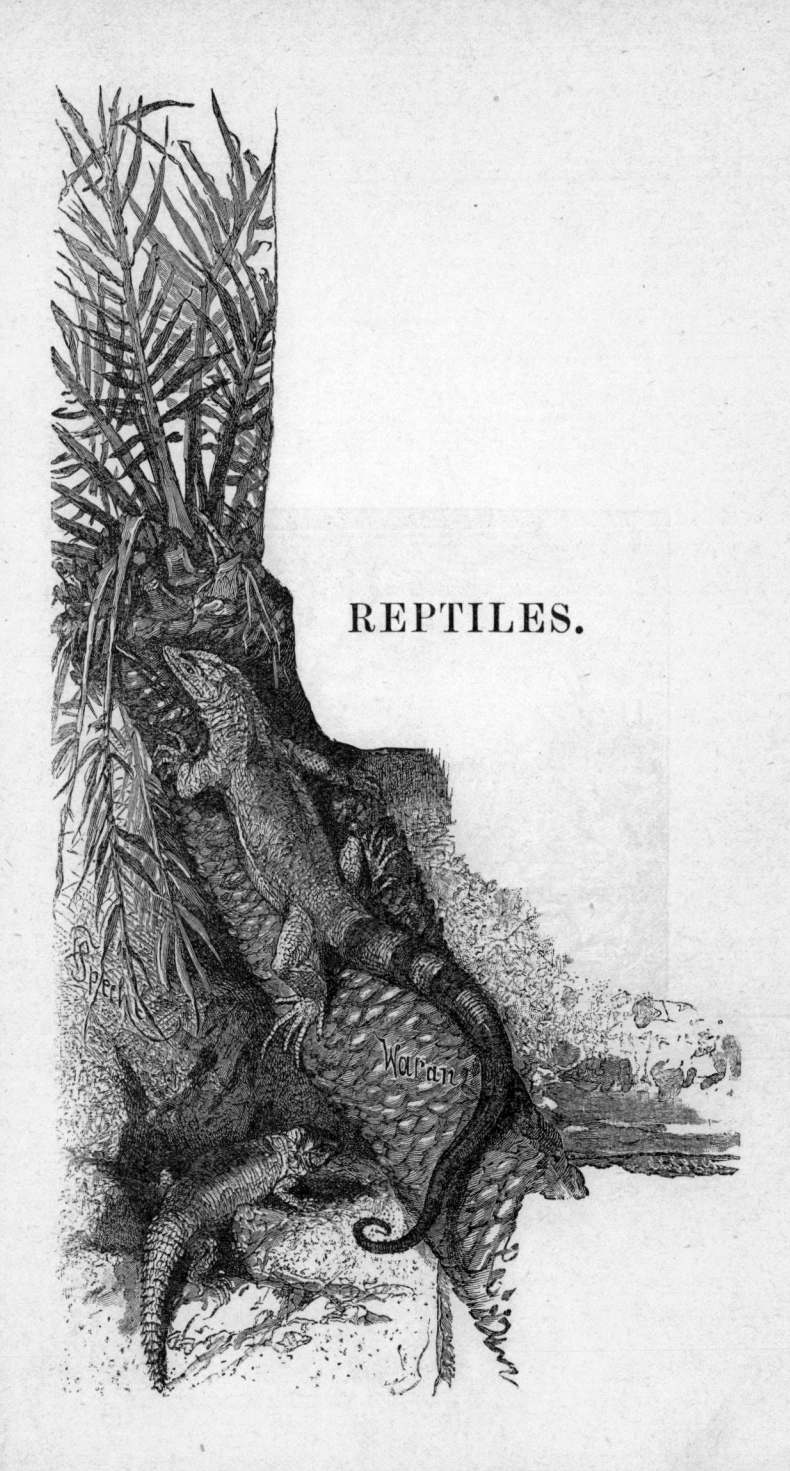

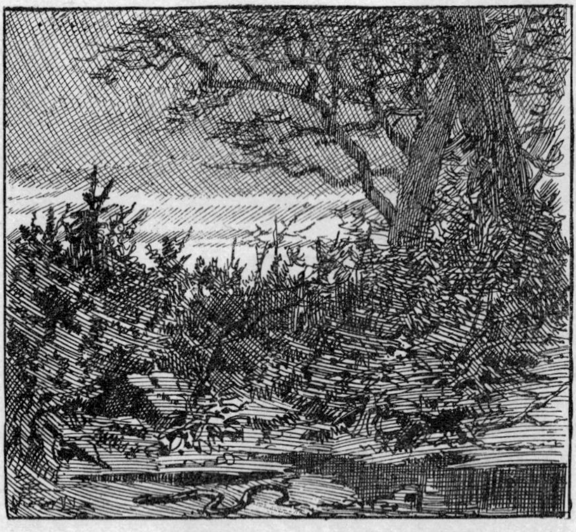

THE TORTOISE.

The Tzab of the Scriptures, translated as Tortoise—Flesh and eggs of the Tortoise—Its slow movements—Hibernation dependent on temperature—The Water-Tortoises—Their food and voracity—Their eggs—Their odour terrifying the horses—The Dhubb lizard and its legends—Its food, and localities which it prefers.

We now come to a different class of animated beings. In Levit. xi. 29, there occurs among the list of unclean beasts a word which is translated in the Authorized Version as "tortoise." The word is *Tzab*, and is rendered in the Hebrew Bible as "lizard," but with the mark of doubt affixed to it. As the correct translation of the word is very dubious, we shall examine it in both these senses.

The common Tortoise is very common in Palestine, and is so plentiful that it would certainly have been used by the Israelites as food, had it not been prohibited by law. At the present day it is cooked and eaten by the inhabitants of the country who are not Jews, and its eggs are in as great request as those of the fowl.

These eggs are hard, nearly spherical, thick-shelled, and covered with minute punctures, giving them a roughness like that of a file. In captivity the Tortoise is very careless about the mode in which they are deposited, and I have seen a large yard almost covered with eggs laid by Tortoises and abandoned. The white or albumen of the egg is so stiff and gelatinous that to empty one of them without breaking the shell is a difficult task, and the yolk is very dark, and covered with minute spots of black. When fresh the eggs are as good as those of the fowl, and many persons even think them better; the only drawback being that their small size and thick shell cause considerable trouble in eating them.

THE DHUBB OR LIZARD AND THE TORTOISE.

The flesh of the Tortoise is eaten, not only by human beings, but by birds, such as the lämmergeier. In order to get at the flesh of the Tortoise, they carry it high in the air and drop it on the ground so as to break the shell to pieces, should the reptile fall on a stone or rock. If, as is not often the case in such a rocky land as that of Palestine, it should fall on a soft spot, the bird picks it up, soars aloft, and drops it again.

The Tortoises have no teeth, but yet are able to crop the herbage with perfect ease. In lieu of teeth the edges of the jaws are sharp-edged and very hard, so that they cut anything that comes between them like a pair of shears. Leaves that are pulpy and crisp are bitten through at once, but those that are thin, tough, and fibrous are rather torn than bitten, the Tortoise placing its feet upon them, and dragging them to pieces with its jaws. The carnivorous Tortoises have a similar habit, as we shall presently see.

This is the species from whose deliberate and slow movements the familiar metaphor of "slow as a Tortoise" was derived, and it is this species which is the hero of the popular fable of the

WATER TORTOISE.

"Hare and the Tortoise." Many of the reptiles are very slow in some things and astonishingly quick in others. Some of the lizards, for example, will at one time remain motionless for many hours together, or creep about with a slow and snail-like progress, while at others they dart from spot to spot with such rapidity that the eye can scarcely follow their movements. This however is not the case with the Tortoise, which is always slow, and, but for the defensive armour in which it is encased, would long ago have been extirpated.

During the whole of the summer months it may be seen crawling deliberately among the herbage, eating in the same deliberate style which characterises all its movements, and occasionally resting in the same spot for many hours together, apparently enjoying the warm beams of the sunshine.

As winter approaches, it slowly scrapes a deep hole in the ground, and buries itself until the following spring awakes it once more to active life. The depth of its burrow depends on the severity of the winter, for, as the cold increases, the Tortoise sinks itself more deeply into the earth.

MENTION has been made of a species of Tortoise that inhabits the water. This is the CASPIAN EMYS (*Emys caspica*), a small species, measuring about six inches in length. It belongs to the large family of the Terrapins, several of which are so well known in America, and has a long, retractile neck, very sharp jaws, and webbed feet, and a well-developed tail.

The body is flattish, and the colour is olive, with lines of yellow edged with black, and the head is marked with longitudinal streaks of bright yellow. After the death of the creature these yellow streaks fade away gradually, and at last become nearly black. The skin of the head is thin, but very hard. In general appearance it is not unlike the chicken Tortoise of America, a species which is often brought to England and kept in captivity, on account of its hardy nature and the little trouble which is needed for keeping it in health.

I have kept specimens of the Caspian Emys for some time, and found them to be more interesting animals than they at first promised to be. They were active, swimming with considerable speed, and snatching quickly at anything which they fancied might be food.

They were exceedingly voracious, consuming daily a quantity of meat apparently disproportioned to their size, and eating it in a manner that strongly reminded me of the mole when engaged on a piece of meat or the body of a bird or mouse. The Tortoise would plant its fore-paws firmly at each side of the meat, seize a mouthful in its jaws, and, by retracting its head violently, would tear away the piece which it had grasped.

They are most destructive among fish, and are apt to rise quietly underneath a fish as it basks near the surface of the water, grasp it beneath with its sharp-edged jaws, and tear away the piece, leaving the fish to die. It is rather remarkable that the Lepidosiren, or mud-fish of the Gambia, destroys fish in a precisely similar manner, though, as its jaws are much sharper than those of the Emys, it does not need the aid of fore-paws in biting out its mouthful of flesh.

Like the land Tortoise, it is one of the hibernators, and during the winter months buries itself deeply in the earth, choosing for this purpose the soft, muddy bed or bank of the pond in which it lives.

Its eggs are white, and hard-shelled, but are more oval than those of the land Tortoise, and both ends are nearly alike. In fact, its egg might well be mistaken for that of a small pigeon. The shell has a porcelain-like look, and is very liable to crack, so that the resemblance is increased.

There is one drawback to these reptiles when kept as pets. They give out a very unpleasant odour, which is disagreeable to human nostrils, but is absolutely terrifying to many animals. The monkey tribe have the strongest objection to these aquatic Tortoises. I once held one of them towards a very tame chimpanzee, much to his discomfiture. He muttered and remonstrated, and retreated as far as he could, pushing out his lips in a funnel-like form, and showing his repugnance to the reptile in a manner that could not be mistaken.

Horses seem to be driven almost frantic with terror, not only by the sight, but by the odour of these Tortoises. In Southern Africa there are Tortoises closely allied to the Caspian Emys, and having the same power of frightening horses.

I have read an account of an adventure there with one of those Tortoises, which I will give. This variety is described as being of an olive colour. When adult, there is a slight depression on either side of the vertebral line.

"Some very awkward accidents have occurred to parties from the terror caused by the fresh-water turtle (*Pelamedusa subrufa*). Carts have been smashed to fragments, riders thrown, and the utmost confusion caused by them. It is their smell, and it is certainly very disagreeable.

"My first acquaintance with the fact was in this wise. I was out shooting with two young ladies who had volunteered as markers; and, as you know, all our shooting is done from horseback. I had jumped off for a shot at some francolins near a knill, or water-hole, and, after picking up my birds, was coming round the knoll to windward of the horses. In my path scrambled a turtle. I called out to my young friends, and told them of my find, on which one of them, in a hasty voice, said, 'Oh, please, Mr. L., don't touch it; you will frighten the horses!'

"Of course I laughed at the idea, and picked up the reptile, which instantly emitted its pungent odour—its means of defence. Though a long way off, the moment the horses caught the scent, away they flew, showing terror in every action. The girls, luckily splendid riders, tugged in vain at the reins; away they went over the Veldt, leaving me in mortal fear that the yawning 'aard-vark' holes (*Orycteropus capensis*) would break their necks. My own horse, which I had hitched to a bush, tore away his bridle, and with the ends streaming in the wind and the stirrups clashing about him, sped off home at full gallop, and was only recovered after a severe chase by my gallant young Amazons, who, after a race of some miles, succeeded in checking their affrighted steeds and in securing my runaway. But for some hours after, if I ventured to windward, there were wild-looking eyes and cocked ears—the smell of the reptile clung to me."

Should any of my readers keep any of those water Tortoises, they will do well to supply them plentifully with food, to give them an elevated rocky perch on which they can scramble, and on which they will sit for hours so motionless that at a little distance they can scarcely be distinguished from the stone on which they rest. They should also be weighed at regular intervals, as decrease of weight is a sure sign that something is wrong, and, as a general rule, is an almost certain precursor of death.

This little reptile is not without its legends. According to the old writers on natural history, it is of exceeding use to vine-growers in the season when there is excess of rain or hail. Whenever the owner of a vineyard sees a black cloud approaching, all he has to do is, to take one of these Tortoises, lay it on its back, and carry it round the vineyard. He must then go into the middle of the ground and lay the reptile on the earth, still on its back; and the effect of this proceeding would be that the cloud would pass aside from a place so well protected.

"But," proceeds the narrator, not wishing to be responsible

for the statement, "such diabolical and foolish observations were not so muche to be remembered in this place, were it not for their sillinesse, that by knowing them men might learn the weaknesse of human wisdom when it erreth from the fountain of all science and true knowledge (which is Divinity), and the most approved assertions of nature. And so I will say no more in this place of the sweet-water tortoise."

THE DHUBB.

WE now come to the second animal, which may probably be the Tzab of the Old Testament.

This creature is one of the lizards, and is a very odd-looking creature. It is certainly not so attractive in appearance that the Jews might be supposed to desire it as food; but it often happens that, as is the case with the turtle and iguana, from the most ungainly, in the latter animal even repulsive, forms are produced the most delicate meats.

The DHUBB, or EGYPTIAN MASTIGURE, as the lizard is indifferently called, grows to a considerable size, measuring when adult three feet in length. Its colour is green, variegated with brown, and is slightly changeable, though not to the extent that distinguishes the chameleon. The chief peculiarity of this lizard consists in its tail, which is covered with a series of whorls or circles of long, sharply-pointed, hard-edged scales. The very appearance of this tail suggests its use as a weapon of defence, and it is said that even the dreaded cerastes is conquered by it, when the lizard and the snake happen to find themselves occupants of the same hole.

The ancients had a very amusing notion respecting the use of the spiny tail possessed by the Dhubb and its kin. They had an idea that, comparatively small though it was, it fed upon cattle, and that it was able to take them from the herd and drive them to its home. For this purpose, when it had selected an ox, it jumped on its back, and by the pricking of its sharp claws drove the animal to gallop in hope of ridding himself of his tormentor. In order to guide him in the direction of its home, it made use of its tail, lashing the ox "to make him go with his rider to the place of his most fit execution, free from all rescue of his herdsman, or pastor, or the annoyance of passengers, where, in most cruel and savage manner, he teareth the limbs and parts one from another till he be devoured."

This very absurd account is headed by an illustration, which, though bad in drawing and rude in execution, is yet so bold and truthful that there is no doubt that it was sketched from the living animal.

As it haunts sandy downs, rocky spots, and similar localities, it is well adapted for the Holy Land, which is the home of a vast number of reptiles, especially of those belonging to the lizards. In the summer time they have the full enjoyment of the hot sunbeams, in which they delight, and which seem to rouse these cold-blooded creatures to action, while they deprive the higher animals of all spirit and energy. In the winter time these very spots afford localities wherein the lizards can hibernate until the following spring, and in such a case they furnish the reptiles with secure hiding-places.

Although the Dhubb does not destroy and tear to pieces oxen and other cattle, it is yet a rather bloodthirsty reptile, and will kill and devour birds as large as the domestic fowl. Usually, however, its food consists of beetles and other insects, which it takes deliberately.

THE LEVIATHAN OR CROCODILE.

Signification of the word *Leviathan*—Description in the Book of Job—Structure and general habits of the Crocodile—The throat-valve and its use—Position of the nostrils—Worship of the Crocodile—The reptile known in the Holy Land—Two legends respecting its presence there—Mode of taking prey—Cunning of the Crocodile—The baboons and the Crocodile—Speed of the reptile—Eggs and young of the Crocodile, and their enemies—Curious story of the ichneumon and ibis—Modes of capturing the Crocodile—Analysis of Job's description—The Crocodile also signified by the word *Tannin*. Aaron's rod changed into a Tannin—Various passages in which the word occurs—Use of the word by the prophet Jeremiah.

THE word *Leviathan* is used in a rather loose manner in the Old Testament, in some places representing a mammalian of the sea, and in others signifying a reptile inhabiting the rivers. As in the most important of these passages the Crocodile is evidently signified, we will accept that rendering, and consider the Crocodile as being the Leviathan of Scripture. The Jewish Bible accepts the word Crocodile, and does not add the mark of doubt.

The fullest account of the Leviathan occurs in Job xli., the whole of which chapter is given to the description of the terrible reptile. As the translation of the Jewish Bible differs in some points from that of the Authorized Version, I shall here give the former, so that the reader may be able to compare them with each other.

" Canst thou draw out a crocodile with a hook, or his tongue with a cord which thou lettest down?

" Canst thou put a reed into his nose, or bore his jaw through with a thorn?

" Will he make many supplications unto thee? will he speak soft words unto thee?

" Will he make a covenant with thee? wilt thou take him as a servant for ever?

" Wilt thou play with him as with a bird, or wilt thou bind him for thy maidens?

" Shall the companions make a banquet of him? shall they part him among the merchants?

"Canst thou fill his skin with barbed irons, or his head with fish-spears?

"Lay thine hand upon him, thou wilt no more remember the battle.

"Behold, the hope of him is in vain; shall not one be cast down at the sight of him?

"None is so fierce that dare stir him up; who then is able to stand before Me?

"Who hath forestalled Me that I should repay him? whatsoever is under the whole heaven is Mine.

"I will not be silent of his parts, nor of the matter of his power, nor of his comely proportion.

"Who can uncover the face of his garment? who would enter the double row in his jaw?

"Who can open the doors of his face? his teeth are terrible round about.

"The strength of his shields are his pride, shut up together as with a close seal.

"One is so near to another that no air can come between them.

"They are joined one to another, they stick together that they cannot be sundered.

"His snortings make light to shine, and his eyes are like the eyelids of the morning dawn.

"Out of his nostrils goeth smoke, as out of a seething pot or caldron.

"His breath kindleth live coals, and a flame goeth out of his mouth.

"In his neck abideth strength, and before him danceth terror.

"The flakes of his flesh are joined together, they are firm in themselves; yea, as hard as nether millstone.

"When he raiseth himself up, the mighty are afraid; by reason of breakings they lose themselves.

"The sword of him that layeth at him cannot hold: the spear, the dart, nor the habergeon.

"He esteemeth iron as straw, and copper as rotten wood.

"The arrow cannot make him flee: sling-stones are turned with him into stubble.

"Clubs are counted as stubble; he laugheth at the shaking of a spear.

CROCODILE ATTACKING HORSES.

"His under parts are like sharp points of potsherd; he speaketh sharp points upon the mire.

"He maketh the deep to boil like a pot; he maketh the sea like a pot of ointment.

"He maketh a path to shine after him; one would think the deep to be hoary.

"Upon earth there is not his like, who is made without fear.

"He beholdeth all high things; he is a king over all the children of pride."

This splendid description points as clearly to the Crocodile as the description of the Behemoth which immediately precedes it does to the hippopotamus, and it is tolerably evident that the sacred poet who wrote these passages must have been personally acquainted with both the Crocodile and the hippopotamus. In both descriptions there are a few exaggerations, or rather, poetical licences. For example, the bones of the hippopotamus are said to be iron and copper, and the Crocodile is said to kindle live coals with his breath. These, however, are but the natural imagery of an Oriental poet, and, considering the subject, we may rather wonder that the writer has not introduced even more fanciful metaphors.

Description of the Crocodile.

There are several species of Crocodile in different parts of the world, ten species at least being known to science.

Some inhabit India, some tropical America, some Asia, and some Africa, so that the genus is represented in nearly all the warmer parts of the world.

They are all known by the formation of the teeth, the lower canines fitting each into a notch on the side of the upper jaw. The feet are webbed to the tips, and though the reptile mostly propels itself through the water by means of its tail, it can also paddle itself gently along by means of its feet.

The teeth are all made for snatching and tearing, but not for masticating, the Crocodile swallowing its prey entire when possible; and when the animal is too large to be eaten entire, the reptile tears it to pieces, and swallows the fragments without attempting to masticate them.

In order to enable it to open its mouth under water, the back of its throat is furnished with a very simple but beautiful contrivance, whereby the water is received on a membranous valve, and, in proportion to its pressure, closes the orifice of the throat. As the Crocodiles mostly seize their prey in their open jaws and hold it under water until drowned, it is evident that without such a structure as has been described the Crocodile would be as likely to drown itself as its prey. But the throat-valve enables it to keep its mouth open while the water is effectually prevented from running down its throat, and the nostrils, placed at the end of the snout, enable it to breathe at its ease, while the unfortunate animal which it has captured is being drowned beneath the surface of the water.

This position of the nostrils serves another purpose, and enables the Crocodile to breathe while the whole of its body is under the water, and only an inch or two of the very end of the snout is above the surface. As, moreover, the Crocodile, as is the case with most reptiles, is able to exist for a considerable time without breathing, it only needs to protrude its nostrils for a few moments, and can then sink entirely beneath the water. In this way the reptile is able to conceal itself in case it should suspect danger; and as, in such instances, it dives under the herbage of the river, and merely thrusts its nose into the air among the reeds and rushes, it is evident that, in spite of its enormous size, it baffles the observation of almost every foe.

Among reptiles, the mailed Crocodiles may be mentioned as most formidable foes to man. Vast in bulk, yet grovelling with the belly on the earth; clad in bony plates with sharp ridges; green eyes with a peculiar fiery stare, gleaming out from below projecting orbits; lips altogether wanting, displaying the long rows of interlocking teeth even when the mouth is closed, so that, even when quiet, the monster seems to be grinning with rage,—it is no wonder that the Crocodile should be, in all the countries which it inhabits, viewed with dread.

Nor is this terror groundless. The Crocodiles, both of the Nile and of the Indian rivers, are well known to make man their victim, and scarcely can a more terrible fate be imagined than that of falling into the jaws of this gigantic reptile. Strange as it may appear, the Crocodile is one of the many animals to which divine honours were paid by the ancient Egyptians. This we learn from several sources. Herodotus, for example, in "Euterpe," chapter 69, writes as follows: " Those who dwell about Thebes and Lake Mœris, consider them to be very sacred; and they each of

A CROCODILE POOL OF ANCIENT EGYPT.

them train up a Crocodile, which is taught to be quite tame; and they put crystal and gold ear-rings into their ears, and bracelets on their fore-paws; and they give them appointed and sacred food, and treat them as well as possible while alive, and when dead, they embalm them, and bury them in sacred vaults."

The reasons for this worship are several. At the root of them all lies the tendency of man to respect that which he fears rather than that which he loves; and the nearer the man approaches the savage state, the more is this feeling developed. By this tendency his worship is regulated, and it will be found that when man is sufficiently advanced to be capable of worship at all, his reverence is invariably paid to the object which has the greatest terrors for him. The Crocodile, therefore, being the animal that was most dreaded by the ancient Egyptians, was accepted as the natural type of divinity.

CROCODILES OF THE UPPER NILE.

Owing to the accuracy of the description in the Book of Job, which is evidently written by one who was personally acquainted with the Crocodile, it is thought by many commentators that the writer must have been acquainted with the Nile, in which river both the Crocodile and hippopotamus are found at the present day.

It is possible, however, that the hippopotamus and the Crocodile have had at one time a much wider range than they at present enjoy. Even within the memory of man the hippopotamus has been driven further and further up the Nile by the encroachments of man. It has long been said that even at the present day the Crocodile exists in Palestine in the river which is called "Nhar Zurka," which flows from Samaria through the plains of Sharon. Several of the older writers have mentioned its existence in this river, and, since this work was commenced, the long-vexed question has been set at rest; a Crocodile, eight feet in length, having been captured in the Nhar Zurka.

No description of the Crocodile would be complete without allusion to the mode in which it seizes its prey. It does not attack it openly, neither, as some have said, does it go on shore for that purpose. It watches to see whether any animal comes to drink, and then, sinking beneath the surface of the water, dives rapidly, rises unexpectedly beneath the unsuspecting victim, seizes it with a sudden snap of its huge jaws, and drags it beneath the water. Should the intended prey be too far from the water to be reached by the mouth, or so large that it may offer a successful resistance, the Crocodile strikes it a tremendous blow with its tail, and knocks it into the water. The dwellers on the Nile bank say that a large Crocodile will with a single blow of its tail break all the four legs of an ox or a horse.

These cunning reptiles even contrive to catch birds as they come for water. On the banks of the Nile the smaller birds drink in a very peculiar manner. They settle in numbers on the flexible branches that overhang the stream, and when, by their weight, the branch bends downwards, they dip their beaks in the water. The Crocodile sees afar off a branch thus loaded, swims as near as possible, and then dives until it can see the birds immediately above it, when it rises suddenly, and with a snap of its jaws secures a whole mouthful of the unsuspecting birds.

Sir S. Baker, in his travels on the Nile, gave much attention to the Crocodile, and has collected a great amount of interesting information about the reptile, much of which is peculiarly valuable, inasmuch as it illustrates the Scriptural notices of the creature. He states that it is a very crafty animal, and that its usual mode of attack is by first showing itself, then swimming slowly away to a considerable distance, so as to make its intended victim think that danger is over, and then returning under water. It is by means of this manœuvre that it captures the little birds. It first makes a dash at them, open-mouthed, causing them to take to flight in terror. It then sails slowly away as if it were so baffled that it did not intend to renew the attack. When it is at a considerable distance, the birds think that their enemy has departed, and return to the branch, which they crowd more than ever, and in a minute or two several dozen of them are engulfed in the mouth of the Crocodile, which has swiftly dived under them.

On one occasion, Sir S. Baker was walking near the edge of the river, when he heard a great shrieking of women on the opposite bank. It turned out that a number of women had been filling their "gerbas" (water-skins), when one of them was suddenly attacked by a large Crocodile. She sprang back, and the reptile, mistaking the filled gerba for a woman, seized it, and gave the owner time to escape. It then dashed at the rest of the women, but only succeeded in seizing another gerba.

A short time previously a Crocodile, thought by the natives to be the same individual, had seized a woman and carried her off; and another had made an attack on a man in a very curious manner. A number of men were swimming across the river, supported, after their custom, on gerbas inflated with air, when one of them felt himself seized by the leg by a Crocodile, which tried to drag him under water. He, however, retained his hold on the skin, and his companions also grasped his arms and hair with one hand, while with the other they struck with their spears at the Crocodile. At last they succeeded in driving the reptile away, and got their unfortunate companion to land, where they found that the whole of the flesh was stripped from the leg from the knee downwards. The poor man died shortly afterwards.

Another traveller relates that three young men who were obliged to cross a branch of a river in their route, being unable to procure a boat, endeavoured to swim their horses to the opposite shore. Two of them had reached the bank in safety, but the third loitered so long on the brink as only to have just entered the water at the moment his comrades had reached the opposite side. When he was nearly half-way across, they saw a large Crocodile, which was known to infest this pass, issuing from under the reeds. They instantly warned their companion of his danger; but it was too late for him to turn back. When the Crocodile was so close as to be on the point of seizing him, he threw his saddle-bag to it. The ravenous animal immediately caught the whole bundle in its jaws, and disappeared for a few moments, but soon discovered its mistake, and rose in front of the horse, which, then seeing it for the first time, reared and threw its rider. He was an excellent swimmer, and had nearly escaped by diving towards the bank; but, on rising for breath, his pursuer also rose, and seized him by the middle. This dreadful scene, which passed before the eyes of his companions, without the least possibility of their rendering any assistance, was terminated by the Crocodile, having previously drowned the unfortunate man, appearing on an opposite sand-bank with the body, and there devouring it.

The crafty Crocodile tries to catch the baboons by lying in wait for them at their drinking places; but the baboons are generally more than a match for the Crocodile in point of cunning and quickness of sight. Sir S. Baker witnessed an amusing example of such an attempt and its failure.

"The large tamarind-trees on the opposite bank are generally full of the dog-faced baboons (*Cynocephalus*) at their drinking hour. I watched a large Crocodile creep slily out of the water and lie in waiting among the rocks at the usual drinking place before they arrived, but the baboons were too wide awake to be taken in so easily.

"A young fellow was the first to discover the enemy. He had accompanied several wise and experienced old hands to the extremity of a bough that at a considerable height overhung the river; from this post they had a bird's eye view, and reconnoitred before one of the numerous party descended to drink. The sharp eyes of the young one at once detected the Crocodile, who matched in colour so well with the rocks that most probably a man would not have noticed it until too late.

"At once the young one commenced shaking the bough and screaming with all his might, to attract the attention of the Crocodile and to induce it to move. In this he was immediately joined by the whole party, who yelled in chorus, while the large old males bellowed defiance, and descended to the lowest branches within eight or ten feet of the Crocodile. It was of no use— the pretender never stirred, and I watched it until dark. It remained still in the same place, waiting for some unfortunate baboon whose thirst might provoke his fate, but not one was sufficiently foolish, although the perpendicular bank prevented them from drinking except at that particular spot."

It may be imagined that if the Crocodile were to depend entirely for its food upon the animals that it catches on the bank or in the river, it would run a risk of starving. The fact is, that its principal food consists of fish, which it can chase in the water. The great speed at which the Crocodile darts through the water is not owing to its webbed feet, but to its powerful tail, which is swept from side to side, and thus propels the reptile after the manner of a man "sculling" a boat with a single oar in the stern. The whales and the fishes have a similar mode of propulsion.

On land, the tail is the Crocodile's most formidable weapon. It is one mass of muscle and sinew, and the force of its lateral stroke is terrible, sweeping away every living thing that it may meet. Fortunately for its antagonists, the Crocodile can turn but very slowly, so that, although it can scramble along at a much faster pace than its appearance indicates, there is no great difficulty in escaping, provided that the sweep of its tail be avoided. As the Crocodile of the Nile attains when adult a length of thirty feet, one moiety of which is taken up by the tail, it may easily be imagined that the power of this weapon can scarcely be exaggerated.

As if to add to the terrors of the animal, its head, back, and tail are shielded by a series of horny scales, which are set so closely together that the sharpest spear can seldom find its way through them, and even the rifle ball glances off, if it strikes them obliquely. Like many other reptiles, the Crocodile is hatched from eggs which are laid on shore and vivified by the warmth of the sun.

These eggs are exceedingly small when compared with the gigantic lizard which deposited them, scarcely equalling in dimensions those of the goose. There is now before me an egg of the cayman of South America, a fresh-water lizard but little smaller than the Crocodile of the Nile, and this is barely equal in size to an ordinary hen's egg. It is longer in proportion to its width, but the contents of the two eggs would be as nearly as possible of the same bulk. On the exterior it is very rough, having a granulated appearance, not unlike that of dried sharkskin, and the shell is exceedingly thin and brittle. The lining membrane, however, is singularly thick and tough, so that the egg is tolerably well defended against fracture.

When first hatched, the young Crocodile is scarcely larger than a common newt, but it attains most formidable dimensions in a very short time. Twenty or thirty eggs are laid in one spot, and, were they not destroyed by sundry enemies, the Crocodiles would destroy every living creature in the rivers. Fortunately, the eggs and young have many enemies, chiefly among which is the well-known ichneumon, which discovers the place where the eggs are laid and destroys them, and eats any young Crocodiles that it can catch before they succeed in making their way to the water.

The old writers were aware of the services rendered by the ichneumon, but, after their wont, exaggerated them by additions of their own, saying that the ichneumon enters into the mouth of the Crocodile as it lies asleep, and eats its way through the body, "putting the Crocodile to exquisite and intolerable torment, while the Crocodile tumbleth to and fro, sighing and weeping, now in the depth of water, now on the land, never resting till strength of nature faileth. For the incessant gnawing of the ichneumon so provoketh her to seek her rest in the unrest of every part, herb, element, throws, throbs, rollings, but all in vain, for the enemy within her breatheth through her breath, and sporteth herself in the consumption of those vital parts which waste and wear away by yielding to unpacificable teeth, one after another, till she that crept in by stealth at the mouth, like a puny thief, comes out at the belly like a conqueror, through a passage opened by her own labour and industry."

The author has in the long passage, a part of which is here quoted, mentioned that the ichneumon takes its opportunity of entering the jaws of the Crocodile as it lies with its mouth open against the beams of the sun. It is very true that the Crocodile does sleep with its mouth open; and, in all probability, the older observers, knowing that the ichneumon did really destroy the eggs and young of the Crocodile, only added a little amplification, and made up their minds that it also destroyed the parents. The same writer who has lately been quoted ranks the ibis among the enemies of the Crocodile, and says that the bird affects the reptile with such terror that, if but an ibis's feather be laid on its back, the Crocodile becomes rigid and unable to

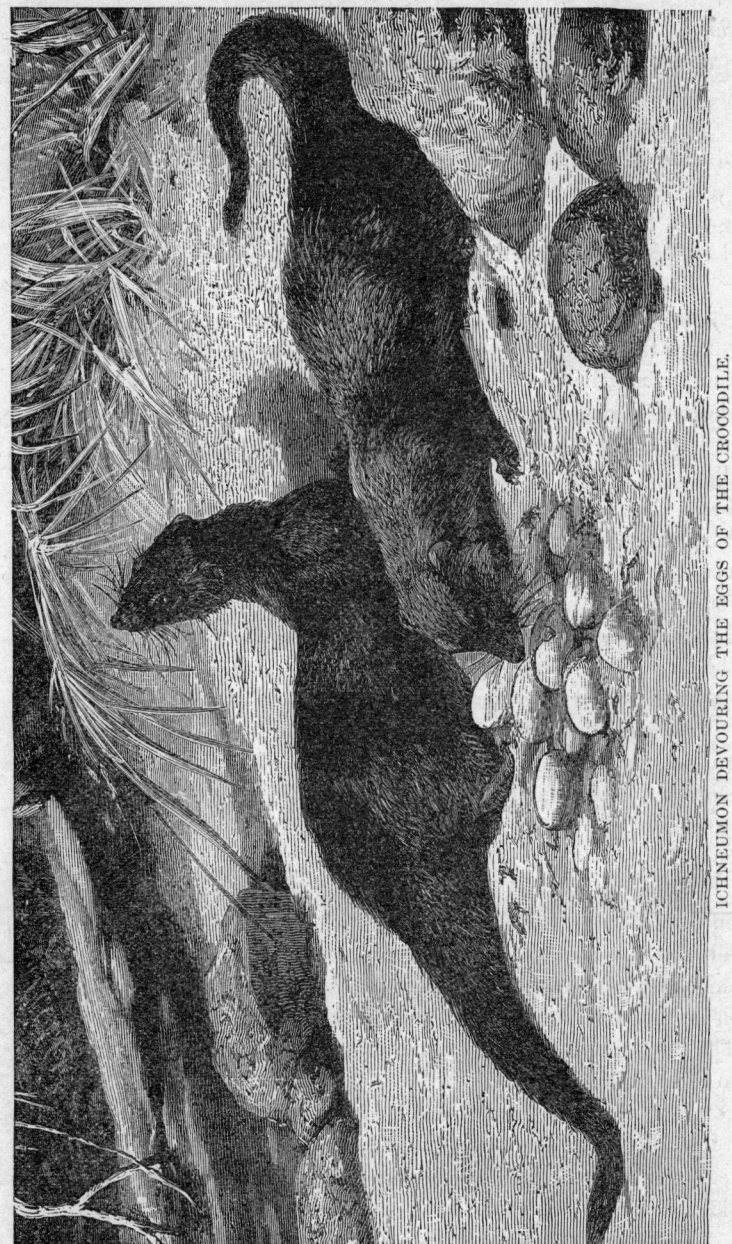

ICHNEUMON DEVOURING THE EGGS OF THE CROCODILE.

move. The Arabs of the present time say that the water-tortoises are enemies to the eggs, scratching them out of the sand and eating them.

As this reptile is so dangerous a neighbour to the inhabitants of the river-banks, many means have been adopted for its destruction.

One such method, where a kind of harpoon is employed, is described by a traveller in the East as follows:—

"The most favourable season for thus hunting the Crocodile is either the winter, when the animal usually sleeps on sand-banks, luxuriating in the rays of the sun, or the spring, after the pairing time, when the female regularly watches the sand islands where she has buried her eggs.

"The native hunter finds out the place and conceals himself by digging a hole in the sand near the spot where the animal usually lies. On its arrival at the accustomed spot the hunter darts his harpoon or spear with all his force, for, in order that its stroke may be successful, the iron should penetrate to a depth of at least four inches, in order that the barb may be fixed firmly in the flesh.

"The Crocodile, on being wounded, rushes into the water, and the huntsman retreats into a canoe, with which a companion has hastened to his assistance.

"A piece of wood attached to the harpoon by a long cord swims on the water and shows the direction in which the Crocodile is moving. The hunters pull on this rope and drag the beast to the surface of the water, where it is again pierced by a second harpoon.

"When the animal is struck it by no means remains inactive; on the contrary, it lashes instantly with its tail, and endeavours to bite the rope asunder. To prevent this, the rope is made of about thirty separate slender lines, not twisted together, but merely placed in juxtaposition, and bound around at intervals of every two feet. The thin strands get between the Crocodile's teeth, and it is unable to sever them.

"In spite of the great strength of the reptile, two men can drag a tolerably large one out of the water, tie up his mouth, twist his legs over his back, and kill him by driving a sharp steel spike into the spinal cord just at the back of the skull.

"There are many other modes of capturing the Crocodile, one of which is the snare portrayed in the illustration.

A CROCODILE TRAP

"Two elastic saplings are bent down and kept in position by stout cords, one of which bears a baited hook, while the other is fashioned into a noose. These cords are so arranged as to release the bent saplings as soon as the Crocodile pulls upon the baited hook. If all works properly, the animal suddenly finds himself suspended in the air, where he remains helpless and at the mercy of the hunter, who soon arrives and despatches him.

"The extreme tenacity of life possessed by the Crocodile is well exemplified by an incident which occurred in Ceylon. A fine specimen had been caught, and to all appearance killed, its interior parts removed, and the aperture kept open by a stick placed across it. A few hours afterwards the captors returned to their victim with the intention of cutting off the head, but were surprised to find the spot vacant. On examining the locality it was evident that the creature had retained sufficient life to crawl back into the water. From this it may be imagined that it is no easy matter to drive the breath out of a Crocodile. Its life seems to take a separate hold of every fibre in the creature's body, and though pierced through and through with bullets, crushed by heavy blows, and its body converted into a very pincushion for spears, it writhes and twists and struggles with wondrous strength, snapping savagely with its huge jaws, and lashing its muscular tail from side to side with such vigour that it requires a bold man to venture within range of that terrible weapon."

Sometimes combats occur between this creature and the tiger, one of the fiercest and most terrible of all quadrupeds. Tigers frequently go down to the rivers to drink, and, upon these occasions, the Crocodile, if near, may attempt to seize them. The ferocious beast, however, seldom falls unrevenged; for the instant he finds himself seized, he turns with great agility and fierceness on his enemy, and endeavours to strike his claws into the Crocodile's eyes, while the latter drags him into the water, where they continue to struggle until the tiger be drowned, and his triumphant antagonist feasts upon his carcass. Such a combat is depicted in the illustration which appears on an accompanying page.

A FIGHT FOR LIFE.

THE CYPRIUS, OR LIZARD OF SCRIPTURE.

THE LETÂÂH OR LIZARD.

Difficulty of identifying the Letââh—Probability that it is a collective and not a specific term—Various Lizards of Palestine—The Green or Jersey Lizard—The Cyprius, its appearance and habits—The Glass Snake or Scheltopusic—Translation of the word *chomet*—Probability that it signifies the Skink—Medicinal uses of the Lizard—The Seps tribe—The common Cicigna, and the popular belief concerning its habits—The Sphænops and its shallow tunnel.

IN Leviticus xi. 30, the word LIZARD is used as the rendering of the Hebrew word *letââh* (pronounced as L'tâh-âh). There are one or two difficulties about the word, but, without going into the question of etymology, which is beside the object of this work, it will be sufficient to state that the best authorities accept the rendering, and that in the Jewish Bible the word Lizard is retained, but with the mark of doubt appended to it.

A VERY common species of Lizard, and therefore likely to be one of those which are grouped under the common name of Letââh, is the CYPRIUS (*Plestiodon auratum*). This handsome Lizard is golden-yellow in colour, beautifully spotted with orange and scarlet, and may be distinguished, even when the colours have fled after death, by the curiously formed ears, which are strongly toothed in front. It is very plentiful in Palestine, and, like others of its kin, avoids cultivated tracts, and is generally found on rocky and sandy soil which cannot be tilled. It is active, and, if alarmed, hides itself quickly in the sand or under stones.

It belongs to the great family of the Skinks, many of which, like the familiar blind-worm of our own country, are without external legs, and, though true Lizards, progress in a snake-like manner, and are generally mistaken for snakes. One of these is the GLASS SNAKE or SCHELTOPUSIC (*Pseudopus pallasii*), which has two very tiny hind legs, but which is altogether so snake-like that it is considered by the natives to be really a serpent. They may well be excused for their error, as the only external indications of limbs are a pair of slightly-projecting scales at the place where the hind legs would be in a fully-developed Lizard.

Though tolerably plentiful, the Scheltopusic is not very often seen, as it is timid and wary, and, when it suspects danger, glides away silently into some place of safety. When adult, the colour of this Lizard is usually chestnut, profusely mottled with black or deep brown, the edge of each scale being of the darker colour. It feeds upon insects and small reptiles, and has been known to devour a nest full of young birds.

IN Levit. xi. 30 is a Hebrew word, *chomet*, which is given in the Authorized Version as SNAIL. There is, however, no doubt that the word is wrongly translated, and that by it some species of Lizard is signified. The Jewish Bible follows the Authorized Version, but affixes the mark of doubt to the word. There is another word, *shablul*, which undoubtedly does signify the snail, and will be mentioned in its proper place.

It is most probable that the word *chomet* includes, among other Lizards, many of the smaller Skinks which inhabit Palestine. Among them we may take as an example the COMMON SKINK (*Scincus officinalis*), a reptile which derives its specific name from the fact that it was formerly used in medicine, together with mummy, and the other disgusting ingredients which formed the greater part of the old Pharmacopœia.

Even at the present day, it is used for similar purposes in the East, and is in consequence captured for the use of physicians, the body being simply dried in the sun, and then sent to market for sale. It is principally employed for the cure of sunstroke, nettle-rash, sand-blindness, or fever, and both patient and physician have the greatest confidence in its powers. It is said by some European physicians that the flesh of the Skink really does possess medicinal powers, and that it has fallen into disrepute chiefly because those powers have been exaggerated. In former days, the head and feet were thought to possess the greatest efficacy, and were valued accordingly.

Like all its tribe, the Skink loves sandy localities, the soil exactly suiting its peculiar habits. Although tolerably active, it does not run so fast or so far as many other Lizards, and, when alarmed, it has a peculiar faculty for sinking itself almost instantaneously under the sand, much after the fashion of the shore-crabs of our own country. Indeed, it is even more expeditious than the crab, which occupies some little time in burrowing under the wet and yielding sand, whereas the Skink slips beneath the dry and comparatively hard sand with such rapidity that it seems rather to be diving into a nearly excavated burrow than to be scooping a hollow for itself.

The sand is therefore a place of safety to the Skink, which does not, like the crab, content itself with merely burying its body just below the surface, but continues to burrow, sinking itself in a few seconds to the depth of nearly a yard.

The length of the Skink is about eight inches, and its very variable colour is generally yellowish brown, crossed with several dark bands. Several specimens, however, are spotted instead of banded with brown, while some are banded with white, and others are spotted with white. In all, however, the under-surface is silver grey.

THE CHAMELEON.

THE CHAMELEON, MONITOR, AND GECKO.

Demeanour of the Chameleon on the ground—The independent eyes—Its frequent change of colour—The Nilotic Monitor.

IN Levit. xi. 30 there occurs a word which has caused great trouble to commentators. The word is *koach*.

There are two lizards to which the term may possibly be applied—namely, the Chameleon and the Monitor; and, as the Authorized Version of the Scriptures accepts the former interpretation, we will first describe the Chameleon.

THIS reptile is very plentiful in the Holy Land, as well as in Egypt, so that the Israelites would be perfectly familiar with it, both during their captivity and after their escape. It is but a small reptile, and the reader may well ask why a name denoting strength should be given to it. I think that we may find the reason for its name in the extraordinary power of its grasp, as it is able, by means of its peculiarly-formed feet and prehensile tail, to grasp the branches so tightly that it can scarcely be removed without damage.

I once saw six or seven Chameleons huddled up together, all having clasped each other's legs and tails so firmly that they formed a bundle that might be rolled along the ground without being broken up. In order to show the extraordinary power of the Chameleon's grasp, I have had a figure drawn from a sketch

GECKO AND CHAMELEON

taken by myself from a specimen which I kept for several months.

When the Chameleon wished to pass from one branch to another, it used to hold firmly to the branch by the tail and one hind-foot, and stretch out its body nearly horizontally, feeling about with the other three feet, as if in search of a convenient resting-place. In this curious attitude it would remain for a considerable time, apparently suffering no inconvenience, though even the spider-monkey would have been unable to maintain such an attitude for half the length of time.

The strength of the grasp is really astonishing when contrasted with the size of the reptile, as any one will find who allows the Chameleon to grasp his finger, or who tries to detach it from the branch to which it is clinging. The feet are most curiously made. They are furnished with five toes, which are arranged like those of parrots and other climbing birds, so as to close upon each other like the thumb and finger of a human hand. They are armed with little yellow claws, slightly curved and very sharp, and when they grasp the skin of the hand they give it an unpleasantly sharp pinch.

The tail is as prehensile as that of the spider-monkey, to which the Chameleon bears a curious resemblance in some of its attitudes, though nothing can be more different than the volatile, inquisitive, restless disposition of the spider-monkey and the staid, sober demeanour of the Chameleon. The reptile has the power of guiding the tail to any object as correctly as if there were an eye at the end of the tail. When it has been travelling over the branches of trees, I have often seen it direct its tail to a projecting bud, and grasp it as firmly as if the bud had been before and not behind it.

Sometimes, when it rests on a branch, it allows the tail to hang down as a sort of balance, the tip coiling and uncoiling unceasingly. But, as soon as the reptile wishes to move, the tail is tightened to the branch, and at once coiled round it. There really seems to be almost a separate vitality and consciousness on the part of the tail, which glides round an object as if it were acting with entire independence of its owner.

On the ground the Chameleon fares but poorly. Its walk is absolutely ludicrous, and an experienced person might easily fail to identify a Chameleon when walking with the same animal on a branch. It certainly scrambles along at a tolerable rate, but it is absurdly awkward, its legs sprawling widely on either side, and its feet grasping futilely at every step The tail, which is usually so lithe and nimble, is then held stiffly from the body, with a slight curve upwards.

The eyes are strange objects, projecting far from the head, and each acting quite independently of the other, so that one eye may often be directed forwards, and the other backwards. The eyeballs are covered with a thick wrinkled skin, except a small aperture at the tip, which can be opened and closed like our own eyelids.

The changing colour of the Chameleon has been long known, though there are many mistaken ideas concerning it.

The reptile does not necessarily assume the colour of any object on which it is placed, but sometimes takes a totally different colour. Thus, if my Chameleon happened to come upon any scarlet substance, the colour immediately became black, covered with innumerable circular spots of light yellow. The change was so instantaneous that, as it crawled on the scarlet cloth, the colour would alter, and the fore-part of the body would be covered with yellow spots, while the hinder parts retained their dull black. Scarlet always annoyed the Chameleon, and it tried to escape whenever it found itself near any substance of the obnoxious hue.

The normal colour was undoubtedly black, with a slight tinge of grey. But in a short time the whole creature would become a vivid verdigris green, and, while the spectator was watching it, the legs would become banded with rings of bright yellow, and spots and streaks of the same colour would appear on the head and body.

When it was excited either by anger or by expectation—as, for example, when it heard a large fly buzzing near it—the colours were singularly beautiful, almost exactly resembling in hue and arrangement those of the jaguar. Of all the colours, green seemed generally to predominate, but the creature would pass so rapidly from one colour to another that it was scarcely possible to follow the various gradations of hue.

Some persons have imagined that the variation of colour depends on the wants and passions of the animal. This is not the case. The change is often caused by mental emotion, but is not dependent on it; and I believe that the animal has no control whatever over its colour. The best proof of this assertion may be found in the fact that my own Chameleon changed colour several times after its death; and, indeed, as long as I had the dead body before me, changes of hue were taking place.

The food of the Chameleon consists of insects, mostly flies, which it catches by means of its tongue, which can be protruded to an astonishing distance. The tongue is nearly cylindrical, and is furnished at the tip with a slight cavity, which is filled with a very glutinous secretion. When the Chameleon sees a

THE CHAMELEON. 609

THE GECKO.

FOOT OF THE GECKO—UNDER SIDE.

fly or other insect, it gently protrudes the tongue once or twice, as if taking aim, like a billiard-player with his cue, and then, with a moderately smart stroke, carries off the insect on the glutinous tip of the tongue. The force with which the Chameleon strikes is really wonderful. My own specimen used to look for flies from my hand, and at first I was as much surprised with the force of the blow struck by the tongue as I was with the grasping power of the feet.

So much for the Chameleon. We will now take the NILOTIC MONITOR and the LAND MONITOR, the other reptiles which have been conjectured to be the real representatives of the Koach.

These lizards attain to some size, the former sometimes measuring six feet in length, and the latter but a foot or so less. Of the two, the Land Monitor, being the more common, both in Palestine and Egypt, has perhaps the best claim to be considered as the Koach of Scripture. It is sometimes called the Land Crocodile. It is a carnivorous animal, feeding upon other reptiles and the smaller mammalia, and is very fond of the eggs of the crocodile, which it destroys in great numbers, and is in consequence much venerated by the inhabitants of the country about the Nile.

The theory that this reptile may be the Koach of Leviticus is strengthened by the fact that even at the present day it is cooked and eaten by the natives, whereas the chameleon is so small and bony that scarcely any one would take the trouble of cooking it.

The Gecko takes its name from the sound which it utters, resembling the word "geck-o." It is exceedingly plentiful, and inhabits the interior of houses, where it can find the flies and other insects on which it lives. On account of the structure of the toes, each of which is flattened into a disk-like form, and furnished on the under surface with a series of plates like those on the back of the sucking-fish, it can walk up a smooth, perpendicular wall with perfect ease, and can even cling to the ceiling like the flies on which it feeds.

In the illustration the reader will observe the flat, fan-like expansions at the ends of the toes, by which the Gecko is able to adhere to flat surfaces, and to dart with silent rapidity from place to place.

SERPENTS

SERPENTS.

Serpents in general—The fiery Serpents of the wilderness—Explanation of the words "flying" and "fiery" as applied to Serpents—Haunts of the Serpent—The Cobra, or Asp of Scripture—The Cerastes, or Horned Serpent—Appearance and habits of the reptile—The "Adder in the path."

As we have seen that so much looseness of nomenclature prevailed among the Hebrews even with regard to the mammalia, birds, and lizards, we can but expect that the names of the Serpents will be equally difficult to identify.

No less than seven names are employed in the Old Testament to denote some species of Serpent; but there are only two which can be identified with any certainty, four others being left to mere conjecture, and one being clearly a word which, like our snake or serpent, is a word not restricted to any particular species, but signifying Serpents in general. This word is *nâchâsh* (pronounced nah-kahsh). It is unfortunate that the word is so variously translated in different passages of Scripture, and we cannot do better than to follow it through the Old Testament, so as to bring all the passages under our glance.

The first mention of the Nâchâsh occurs in Gen. iii., in the well-known passage where the Serpent is said to be more subtle than all the beasts of the field, the wisdom or subtlety of the Serpent having evidently an allegorical and not a categorical signification. We find the same symbolism employed in the New Testament, the disciples of our Lord being told to be "wise as serpents, and harmless as doves."

Allusion is made to the gliding movement of the Serpent tribe in Prov. xxx. 19. On this part of the subject little need be said, except that the movements of the Serpent are owing to the mobility of the ribs, which are pushed forward in succession and drawn back again, so as to catch against any inequality of the ground. This power is increased by the structure of the scales. Those of the upper part of the body, which are not used for locomotion, are shaped something like the scales of a fish; but those of the lower part of the body, which come in contact with the ground, are broad belts, each overlapping the other, and each connected with one pair of ribs.

When, therefore, the Serpent pushes forward the ribs, the edges of the scaly belts will catch against the slightest projection, and are able to give a very powerful impetus to the body. It is scarcely possible to drag a snake backwards over rough ground; while on a smooth surface, such as glass, the Serpent would be totally unable to proceed. This, however, was not likely to have been studied by the ancient Hebrews, who were among the most unobservant of mankind with regard to details of natural history: it is, therefore, no wonder that the gliding of the Serpent should strike the writer of the proverb in question as a mystery which he could not explain.

The poisonous nature of some of the Serpents is mentioned in several passages of Scripture; and it will be seen that the ancient Hebrews, like many modern Europeans, believed that the poison lay in the forked tongue. See, for example, Ps. lviii. 4: "Their poison is like the poison of a serpent" (*náchásh*). Also Prov. xxiii. 32, in which the sacred writer says of wine that it brings woe, sorrow, contentions, wounds without cause, redness of eyes, and that "at the last it biteth like a serpent, and stingeth like an adder."

COBRA AND CERASTES, THE ASP AND ADDER OF SCRIPTURE.

The idea that the poison of the Serpent lies in the tongue is seen in several passages of Scripture. "They have sharpened their tongues like a serpent; adders' poison is under their lips" (Ps. cxl. 3). Also in Job xx. 16, the sacred writer says of the hypocrite, that "he shall suck the poison of asps: the viper's tongue shall slay him."

As to the fiery Serpents of the wilderness, it is scarcely needful to mention that the epithet of "fiery" does not signify that the Serpents in question produced real fire from their mouths, but that allusion is made to the power and virulence of their poison, and to the pain caused by their bite. We ourselves naturally employ a similar metaphor, and speak of a "burning pain," of a "fiery trial," of "hot anger," and the like.

THE ISRAELITES ARE BITTEN BY SERPENTS IN THE WILDERNESS, AND MOSES LIFTS UP THE SERPENT OF BRASS.

The epithet of "flying" which is applied to these Serpents is explained by the earlier commentators as having reference to a Serpent which they called the Dart Snake, and which they believed to lie in wait for men and to spring at them from a distance. They thought that this snake hid itself either in hollows of the ground or in trees, and sprang through the air for thirty feet upon any man or beast that happened to pass by.

WE will now take the various species of Serpents mentioned in the Bible, as nearly as they can be identified.

Of one species there is no doubt whatever. This is the Cobra di Capello, a serpent which is evidently signified by the Hebrew word *pethen*.

This celebrated Serpent has long been famous, not only for the deadly power of its venom, but for the singular performances in which it takes part. The Cobra inhabits many parts of Asia, and in almost every place where it is found, certain daring men take upon themselves the profession of serpent-charmers, and handle these fearful reptiles with impunity, cause them to move in time to certain musical sounds, and assert that they bear a life charmed against the bite of these deadly playmates.

One of these men will take a Cobra in his bare hands, toss it about with perfect indifference, allow it to twine about his naked breast, tie it around his neck, and treat it with as little ceremony as if it were an earth-worm. He will then take the same Serpent— or apparently the same—make it bite a fowl, which soon dies from the poison, and will then renew his performance.

Some persons say that the whole affair is but an exhibition of that jugglery in which the natives of the East Indies are such wondrous adepts; that the Serpents with which the man plays are harmless, having been deprived of their fangs, and that a really venomous specimen is adroitly substituted for the purpose of killing the fowl. It is, moreover, said, and truly, that a snake thought to have been rendered harmless by the deprivation of its fangs, has bitten one of its masters and killed him, thus proving the imposture.

Still, neither of these explanations will entirely disprove the mastery of man over a venomous Serpent.

In the first instance, it is surely as perilous an action to substitute a venomous Serpent as to play with it. Where was it hidden, why did it not bite the man instead of the fowl, and how did the juggler prevent it from using its teeth while he was conveying it away?

And, in the second instance, the detection of one impostor is by no means a proof that all who pretend to the same powers are likewise impostors.

The following narrative by a traveller in the East seems to prove that the serpent-charmer possessed sufficient power to induce a truly poisonous Serpent to leave its hole, and to perform certain antics at his command:

"A snake-charmer came to my bungalow, requesting me to allow him to show his snakes. As I had frequently seen his performance, I declined to witness a repetition of it, but told him that if he would accompany me to the jungle and catch a

Cobra, that I knew frequented the place, I would give him a present of money. He was quite willing, and as I was anxious to test the truth of the charm he claimed to possess, I carefully counted his tame snakes, and put a guard over them until we should return.

"Before starting I also examined his clothing, and satisfied myself that he had no snake about his person. When we arrived at the spot, he commenced playing upon a small pipe, and, after persevering for some time, out crawled a large Cobra from an ant-hill which I knew it occupied.

On seeing the man it tried to escape, but he quickly caught it by the tail and kept swinging it round until we reached the bungalow. He then laid it upon the ground and made it raise and lower its head to the sound of his pipe.

Before long, however, it bit him above the knee. He immediately bandaged the leg tightly above the wound, and applied a piece of porous stone, called a snake-stone, to extract the poison. He was in great pain for a few minutes, but afterwards it gradually subsided, the stone falling from the wound just before he was relieved.

When he recovered he held up a cloth, at which the snake flew and hung by its fangs. While in this position the man passed his hand up its back, and having seized it tightly by the throat, he pulled out the fangs and gave them to me. He then squeezed out the poison, from the glands in the Serpent's mouth, upon a leaf. It was a clear, oily substance, which when rubbed with the hand produced a fine lather.

"The whole operation was carefully watched by me, and was also witnessed by several other persons."

How the serpent-charmers perform their teats is not very intelligible. That they handle the most venomous Serpents with perfect impunity is evident enough, and it is also clear that they are able to produce certain effects upon the Serpents by means of musical (or unmusical) sounds. But these two items are entirely distinct, and one does not depend upon the other.

In the first place, the handling of venomous snakes has been performed by ordinary men without the least recourse to any arts except that of acquaintance with the habits of Serpents. The late Mr. Waterton, for example, would take up a rattlesnake in his bare hand without feeling the least uneasy as to the behaviour of his prisoner. He once took twenty-seven rattle-

THE SERPENT-CHARMER.

snakes out of a box, carried them into another room, put them into a large glass case, and afterwards replaced them in the box. He described to me the manner in which he did it, using my wrist as the representative of the Serpent.

The nature of all Serpents is rather peculiar, and is probably owing to the mode in which the blood circulates. They are extremely unwilling to move, except when urged by the wants of nature, and will lie coiled up for many hours together when not pressed by hunger. Consequently, when touched, their feeling is evidently like that of a drowsy man, who only tries to shake off the object which may rouse him, and composes himself afresh to sleep.

A quick and sudden movement would, however, alarm the reptile, which would strike in self-defence, and, sluggish as are its general movements, its stroke is delivered with such lightning rapidity that it would be sure to inflict its fatal wound before it was seized.

If, therefore, Mr. Waterton saw a Serpent which he desired to catch, he would creep very quietly up to it, and with a gentle, slow movement place his fingers round its neck just behind the head. If it happened to be coiled up in such a manner that he could not get at its neck, he had only to touch it gently until it moved sufficiently for his purpose.

When he had once placed his hand on the Serpent, it was in his power. He would then grasp it very lightly indeed, and raise it gently from the ground, trusting that the reptile would be more inclined to be carried quietly than to summon up sufficient energy to bite. Even if it had tried to use its fangs, it could not have done so as long as its captor's fingers were round its neck.

As a rule, a great amount of provocation is needed before a venomous Serpent will use its teeth. One of my friends, when a boy, caught a viper, mistaking it for a common snake. He tied it round his neck, coiled it on his wrist by way of a bracelet, and so took it home, playing many similar tricks with it as he went. After arrival in the house, he produced the viper for the amusement of his brothers and sisters, and, after repeating his performances, tried to tie the snake in a double knot. This, however, was enough to provoke the most pacific of creatures, and in consequence he received a bite on his finger.

The poison was not slow to take effect; first, the wound looked and felt like a nettle sting, then like a wasp sting, and in the course of a few minutes the whole finger was swollen. At this juncture his father, a medical man, fortunately arrived, and set the approved antidotes, ammonia, oil, and lunar caustic, to the wound, having previously made incisions about the punctured spot, and with paternal affection attempted to suck out the poison. In spite of these remedies a serious illness was the result of the bite, from which the boy did not recover for several weeks

There is no doubt that the snake-charmers trust chiefly to this sluggish nature of the reptile, but they certainly go through some ceremonies by which they believe themselves to be rendered impervious to snake-bites. They will coil the cobra round their naked bodies, they will irritate the reptile until it is in a state of fury; they will even allow it to bite them, and yet be none the worse for the wound. Then, as if to show that the venomous teeth have not been abstracted, as is possibly supposed to be the case, they will make the cobra bite a fowl, which speedily dies from the effects of the poison.

Even if the fangs were extracted, the Serpents would lose little of their venomous power. These reptiles are furnished with a whole series of fangs in different stages of development, so that when the one in use is broken or shed in the course of nature, another comes forward and fills its place. There is now before me a row of four fangs, which I took from the right upper jawbone of a viper which I recently caught.

In her interesting "Letters from Egypt," Lady Duff-Gordon gives an amusing account of the manner in which she was formally initiated into the mysteries of snake-charming, and made ever afterwards impervious to the bite of venomous Serpents:—

"At Kóm Omboo, we met with a Rifáee darweesh with his basket of tame snakes. After a little talk, he proposed to initiate me: and so we sat down and held hands like people marrying. Omar [her attendant] sat behind me, and repeated the words as my 'wakeel.' Then the Rifáee twisted a cobra round our joined hands, and requested me to spit on it; he did the same, and I was pronounced safe and enveloped in snakes. My sailors groaned, and Omar shuddered as the snakes put out their tongues; the darweesh and I smiled at each other like Roman augurs."

She believed that the snakes were toothless; and perhaps on this occasion they may have been so. Extracting the teeth of the Serpent is an easy business in experienced hands, and is conducted in two ways. Those snake-charmers who are confident of their own powers merely grasp the reptile by the neck, force open its jaws with a piece of stick, and break off the fangs, which are but loosely attached to the jaw. Those who are not so sure of themselves irritate the snake, and offer it a piece of cloth, generally the corner of their mantle, to bite. The snake darts at it, and, as it seizes the garment, the man gives the cloth a sudden jerk, and so tears away the fangs.

Still, although some of the performers employ mutilated snakes, there is no doubt that others do not trouble themselves to remove the fangs of the Serpents, but handle with impunity the cobra or the cerastes with all its venomous apparatus in good order.

We now come to the second branch of the subject, namely, the influence of sound upon the cobra and other Serpents. The charmers are always provided with musical instruments, of which a sort of flute with a loud shrill sound is the one which is mostly used in the performances. Having ascertained, from slight marks which their practised eyes easily discover, that a Serpent is hidden in some crevice, the charmer plays upon his flute, and in a short time the snake is sure to make its appearance.

As soon as it is fairly out, the man seizes it by the end of the tail, and holds it up in the air at arm's length. In this position it is helpless, having no leverage, and merely wriggles about in fruitless struggles to escape. Having allowed it to exhaust its strength by its efforts, the man lowers it into a basket, where it is only too glad to find a refuge, and closes the lid. After a while, he raises the lid and begins to play the flute.

The Serpent tries to glide out of the basket, but, as soon as it does so, the lid is shut down again, and in a very short time the reptile finds that escape is impossible, and, as long as it hears

TEACHING COBRAS TO DANCE.

the sound of the flute, only raises its head in the air, supporting itself on the lower portion of its tail, and continues to wave its head from side to side as long as it hears the sound of the music.

The rapidity with which a cobra learns this lesson is extraordinary, the charmers being as willing to show their mastery over newly-caught Serpents as over those which have been long in their possession.

The colour of the Cobra is in most cases a brownish olive. The most noted peculiarity is the expansion of the neck, popularly called the hood. This phenomenon is attributable not only to the skin and muscles, but to the skeleton. About twenty pairs of the ribs of the neck and fore part of the back are flat instead of curved, and increase gradually from the head to the eleventh or twelfth pair, from which they decrease until they are merged into the ordinary curved ribs of the body. When the snake is excited, it brings these ribs forward so as to spread the skin, and then displays the oval hood to best advantage.

In the Cobra di Capello the back of the hood is ornamented by two large eye-like spots, united by a curved black stripe, so formed that the whole mark bears a singular resemblance to a pair of spectacles.

THE CERASTES, OR SHEPHIPHON OF SCRIPTURE.

THE word *shephiphon*, which evidently signifies some species of snake, only occurs once in the Scriptures, but fortunately that single passage contains an allusion to the habits of the serpent which makes identification nearly certain. The passage in question occurs in Gen. xlix. 17, and forms part of the prophecy of Jacob respecting his children : " Dan shall be a serpent by the way, an adder in the path, that biteth the horse's heels, so that his rider shall fall backward."

Putting aside the deeper meaning of this prophecy, there is here an evident allusion to the habits of the CERASTES, or HORNED VIPER, a species of venomous serpent, which is plentiful in Northern Africa, and is found also in Palestine and Syria. It is a very conspicuous reptile, and is easily recognised by the two horn-like projections over the eyes. The name Cerastes, or horned, has been given to it on account of these projections.

This snake has a custom of lying half buried in the sand, awaiting the approach of some animal on which it can feed. Its usual diet consists of the jerboas and other small mammalia, and as they are exceedingly active, while the Cerastes is slow and sluggish, its only chance of obtaining food is to lie in wait. It will always take advantage of any small depression, such as the print of a camel's foot, and, as it finds many of these

HORNED VIPER.

depressions in the line of the caravans, it is literally "a serpent by the way, an adder in the path."

According to the accounts of travellers, the Cerastes is much more irritable than the cobra, and is very apt to strike at any object which may disturb it. Therefore, whenever a horseman passes along the usual route, his steed is very likely to disturb a Cerastes lying in the path, and to be liable to the attack of the irritated reptile. Horses are instinctively aware of the presence of the snake, and mostly perceive it in time to avoid its stroke.

Its small dimensions, the snake rarely exceeding two feet in length, enable it to conceal itself in a very small hollow, and its brownish-white colour, diversified with darker spots, causes it to harmonize so thoroughly with the loose sand in which it lies buried, that, even when it is pointed out, an unpractised eye does not readily perceive it.

Even the cobra is scarcely so dreaded as this little snake, whose bite is so deadly, and whose habits are such as to cause travellers considerable risk of being bitten.

The head of the Viper affords a very good example of the venomous apparatus of the poisonous serpents, and is well worthy of description. The poison fangs or teeth lie on the sides of the upper jaw, folded back, and almost undistinguishable until lifted with a needle. They are singularly fine and delicate, hardly larger than a lady's needle, and are covered almost to their tips with a muscular envelope, through which the points just peer.

The poison bags or glands, and the reservoir in which the venom is stored, are found at the back and sides of the head, and give to the venomous serpents that peculiar width of head which is so unfailing a characteristic.

On examining carefully the poison fangs, the structure by which the venom is injected into the wound will be easily understood. Under a magnifying glass they will be seen to be hollow, thus affording a passage for the poison.

When the creature draws back its head and opens its mouth to strike, the deadly fangs spring up with their points ready for action, and fully charged with their poisonous distillment.

THE VIPER, OR EPHEH.

The Sand-Viper, or Toxicoa—Its appearance and habits—Adder's poison—The Cockatrice, or Tsepha—The Yellow Viper—Ancient ideas concerning the Cockatrice—Power of its venom.

WE now come to the species of snake which cannot be identified with any certainty, and will first take the word *epheh*.

Mr. Tristram believes that he has identified the Epheh of the Old Testament with the Sand-Viper, or Toxicoa. This reptile, though very small, and scarcely exceeding a foot in length, is a dangerous one, but its bite is not so deadly as that of the cobra or cerastes. It is variable in colour, and has angular white streaks on its body, with a row of whitish spots along the back. The top of the head is dark, and variegated with arrow-shaped white marks.

The Toxicoa is very plentiful in Northern Africa, Palestine, Syria, and the neighbouring countries, and, as it is exceedingly active, is held in some dread by the natives.

ANOTHER name of a poisonous snake occurs several times in the Old Testament. The word is *tsepha*, or *tsiphôni*, and it is sometimes translated as Adder, and sometimes as Cockatrice. The word is rendered as Adder in Prov. xxiii. 32, where it is said that wine "biteth like a serpent, and stingeth like an adder." Even

THE TOXICOA. (Supposed to be the viper of Scripture.)

in this case, however, the word is rendered as Cockatrice in the marginal translation.

It is found three times in the Book of Isaiah. Ch. xi. 8: "The weaned child shall put his hand on the cockatrice' den." Also, ch. xiv. 29: "Rejoice not thou, whole Palestina, because the rod of him that smote thee is broken: for out of the serpent's (*nachash*) nest shall come forth a cockatrice (*tsepha*), and his fruit shall be a fiery flying serpent." The same word occurs again in ch. lix. 5: "They hatch cockatrice' eggs." In the prophet Jeremiah we again find the word: "For, behold, I will send serpents, cockatrices among you, which will not be charmed, and they shall bite you, saith the Lord."

Around this reptile a wonderful variety of legends have been accumulated. The Cockatrice was said to kill by its very look, "because the beams of the Cockatrice's eyes do corrupt the visible spirit of a man, which visible spirit corrupted all the other spirits coming from the brain and life of the heart, are thereby corrupted, and so the man dyeth."

The subtle poison of the Cockatrice infected everything near it, so that a man who killed a Cockatrice with a spear fell dead himself, by reason of the poison darting up the shaft of the spear and passing into his hand. Any living thing near which the Cockatrice passed was instantly slain by the fiery heat of its venom, which was exhaled not only from its mouth, but its sides. For the old writers, whose statements are here summarized, contrived to jumble together a number of miscellaneous facts in natural history, and so to produce a most extraordinary series of legends.

I should not have given even this limited space to such puerile legends, but for the fact that such stories as these were fully believed in the days when the Authorized Version of the Bible was translated. The translators of the Bible believed most heartily in the mysterious and baleful reptile, and, as they saw that the Tsepha of Scripture was an exceptionally venomous serpent, they naturally rendered it by the word Cockatrice.

THE FROG.

The Frog only mentioned in the Old Testament as connected with the plagues of Egypt—The severity of this plague explained—The Frog detestable to the Egyptians—The Edible Frog and its numbers—Description of the species.

PLENTIFUL as is the FROG throughout Egypt, Palestine, and Syria, it is very remarkable that in the whole of the canonical books of the Old Testament the word is only mentioned thrice, and each case in connexion with the same event.

In Exod. viii. we find that the second of the plagues which visited Egypt came out of the Nile, the sacred river, in the form of innumerable Frogs. The reader will probably remark, on perusing the consecutive account of these plagues, that the two first plagues were connected with that river, and that they were foreshadowed by the transformation of Aaron's rod.

When Moses and Aaron appeared before Pharaoh to ask him to let the people go, Pharaoh demanded a miracle from them, as had been foretold. Following the divine command, Aaron threw down his rod, which was changed into a serpent.

Next, as was most appropriate, came a transformation wrought on the river by means of the same rod which had been transformed into a Serpent, the whole of the fresh-water throughout the land being turned into blood, and the fish dying and polluting the venerated river with their putrefying bodies. In Egypt, a partially rainless country, such a calamity as this was doubly terrible, as it at the same time desecrated the object of their worship, and menaced them with perishing by thirst.

The next plague had also its origin in the river, but extended far beyond the limits of its banks. The frogs, being unable to return to the contaminated stream wherein they had lived, spread themselves in all directions, so as to fulfil the words of the prediction: "If thou refuse to let them go, behold, I will smite all thy borders with frogs:

"And the river shall bring forth frogs abundantly, which shall go up and come into thine house, and into thy bed-chamber, and upon thy bed, and into the house of thy servants, and upon thy people, and into thine ovens, and into thy kneading-troughs" (or dough).

Supposing that such a plague was to come upon us at the present day, we should consider it to be a terrible annoyance, yet scarcely worthy of the name of plague, and certainly not to be classed with the turning of a river into blood, with the hail and lightning that destroyed the crops and cattle, and with the simultaneous death of the first-born. But the Egyptians suffered most keenly from the infliction. They were a singularly fastidious people, and abhorred the contact of anything that they held to be unclean. We may well realize, therefore, the effect of a visitation of Frogs, which rendered their houses unclean by entering them, and themselves unclean by leaping upon them; which deprived them of rest by getting on their beds, and of food by crawling into their ovens and upon the dough in the kneading-troughs.

And, as if to make the visitation still worse, when the plague was removed, the Frogs died in the places into which they had intruded, so that the Egyptians were obliged to clear their houses of the dead carcases, and to pile them up in heaps, to be dried by the sun or eaten by birds and other scavengers of the East.

As to the species of Frog which thus invaded the houses of the Egyptians, there is no doubt whatever. It can be but the

GREEN, or EDIBLE FROG (*Rana esculenta*), which is so well known for the delicacy of its flesh. This is believed to be the only aquatic Frog of Egypt, and therefore must be the species which came out of the river into the houses.

Both in Egypt and Palestine it exists in very great numbers, swarming in every marshy place, and inhabiting the pools in such numbers that the water can scarcely be seen for the Frogs. Thus the multitudes of the Frogs which invaded the Egyptians was no matter of wonder, the only miraculous element being that the reptiles were simultaneously directed to the houses, and their simultaneous death when the plague was taken away.

Frogs are also mentioned in Rev. xvi. 13: "And I saw three unclean spirits like frogs come out of the mouth of the dragon, and out of the mouth of the beast, and out of the mouth of the false prophet." With the exception of this passage, which is a purely symbolical one, there is no mention of Frogs in the New Testament. It is rather remarkable that the Toad, which might be thought to afford an excellent symbol for various forms of evil, is entirely ignored, both in the Old and New Testaments. Probably the Frogs and Toads were all classed together under the same title.

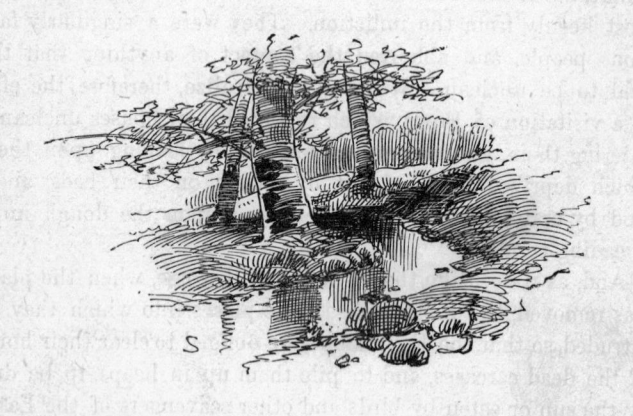

FISHES.

FISHES.

Impossibility of distinguishing the different species of Fishes—The fishermen Apostles—Fish used for food—The miracle of the loaves and Fishes—The Fish broiled on the coals—Clean and unclean Fishes—The Sheat-fish, or Silurus—The Eel and the Muræna—The Long-headed Barbel—Fish-ponds and preserves—The Fish-ponds of Heshbon—The Sucking-fish—The Lump-sucker—The Tunny—The Coryphene.

WE now come to the FISHES, a class of animals which are repeatedly mentioned both in the Old and New Testaments, but only in general terms, no one species being described so as to give the slightest indication of its identity.

This is the more remarkable because, although the Jews were, like all Orientals, utterly unobservant of those characteristics by which the various species are distinguished from each other, we might expect that St. Peter and other of the fisher Apostles would have given the names of some of the Fish which they were in the habit of catching, and by the sale of which they gained their living.

It is true that the Jews, as a nation, would not distinguish between the various species of Fishes, except, perhaps, by comparative size. But professional fishermen would be sure to distinguish one species from another, if only for the fact that they would sell the best-flavoured Fish at the highest price.

We might have expected, for example, that the Apostles and disciples who were present when the miraculous draught of Fishes took place would have mentioned the technical names by which they were accustomed to distinguish the different degrees of the saleable and unsaleable kinds.

PETER CATCHES THE FISH.

Or we might have expected that on the occasion when St. Peter cast his line and hook into the sea, and drew out a Fish holding the tribute-money in his mouth, we might have learned the particular species of Fish which was thus captured. We ourselves would assuredly have done so. It would not have been thought sufficient merely to say that a Fish was caught with money in its mouth, but it would have been considered necessary to mention the particular fish as well as the particular coin.

But it must be remembered that the whole tone of thought differs in Orientals and Europeans, and that the exactness required by the one has no place in the mind of the other. The whole of the Scriptural narratives are essentially Oriental in their character, bringing out the salient points in strong relief, but entirely regardless of minute detail.

WE find from many passages both in the Old and New Testaments that Fish were largely used as food by the Israelites, both when captives in Egypt and after their arrival in the Promised Land. Take, for example, Numb. xi. 4, 5 : " And the children of Israel also wept again, and said, Who shall give us flesh to eat ? " We remember the fish which we did eat in Egypt freely." Then, in the Old Testament, although we do not find many such categorical statements, there are many passages which allude to professional fishermen, showing that there was a demand for the Fish which they caught, sufficient to yield them a maintenance.

In the New Testament, however, there are several passages in which the Fishes are distinctly mentioned as articles of food. Take, for example, the well-known miracle of multiplying the loaves and the Fishes, and the scarcely less familiar passage in John xxi. 9 : " As soon then as they were come to land, they saw a fire of coals there, and fish laid thereon, and bread.

We find in all these examples that bread and Fish were eaten together. Indeed, Fish was eaten with bread just as we eat cheese or butter ; and St. John, in his account of the multiplication of the loaves and Fishes, does not use the word " fish," but another word which rather signifies sauce, and was generally employed to designate the little Fish that were salted down and dried in the sunbeams for future use.

As to the various species which were used for different purposes, we know really nothing, the Jews merely dividing their Fish into clean and unclean.

Some of the species to which the prohibition would extend are evident enough. There are, for example, the Sheat-fishes, which have the body naked, and which are therefore taken out of the list of permitted Fishes. The Sheat-fishes inhabit rivers in many parts of the world, and often grow to a very considerable size. They may be at once recognised by their peculiar shape, and by the long, fleshy tentacles that hang from the mouth. The object of these tentacles is rather dubious, but as the fish have been seen to direct them at will to various objects, it is likely that they may answer as organs of touch.

1. MURÆNA.   2. LONG-HEADED BARBEL.   3. SHEAT-FISH.

As might be conjectured from its general appearance, it is one of the Fishes that love muddy banks, in which it is fond of burrowing so deeply that, although the river may swarm with Sheat-fishes, a practised eye is required to see them.

As far as the Sheat-fishes are concerned, there is little need for the prohibition, inasmuch as the flesh is not at all agreeable in flavour, and is difficult of digestion, being very fat and gelatinous. The swimming-bladder of the Sheat-fish is used in some countries for making a kind of isinglass, similar in character to that of the sturgeon, but of coarser quality.

The lowermost figure in the above illustration represents a species which is exceedingly plentiful in the Sea of Galilee.

On account of the mode in which their body is covered, the whole of the sharks and rays are excluded from the list of permitted Fish, as, although they have fins, they have no scales, their place being taken by shields varying greatly in size. The same rule excludes the whole of the lamprey tribe, although the excellence of their flesh is well known.

Moreover, the Jews almost universally declare that the Muræna and Eel tribe are also unclean, because, although it has been proved that these Fishes really possess scales as well as fins, and are therefore legally permissible, the scales are hidden under a slimy covering, and are so minute as to be practically absent.

The uppermost figure in the illustration represents the celebrated Muræna, one of the fishes of the Mediterranean, in which sea it is tolerably plentiful. In the days of the old Roman empire, the Muræna was very highly valued for the table. The wealthier citizens built ponds in which the Murænæ were kept alive until they were wanted. This Fish sometimes reaches four feet in length.

The rest of the Fishes which are shown in the three illustrations belong to the class of clean Fish, and were permitted as food. The figure of the Fish between the Muræna and Sheat-fish is the Long-headed Barbel, so called from its curious form.

The Barbels are closely allied to the carps, and are easily known by the barbs or beards which hang from their lips. Like the sheat-fishes, the Barbels are fond of grubbing in the mud, for the purpose of getting at the worms, grubs, and larvæ of aquatic insects that are always to be found in such places. The Barbels are rather long in proportion to their depth, a peculiarity which, owing to the length of the head, is rather exaggerated in this species.

The Long-headed Barbel is extremely common in Palestine, and may be taken with the very simplest kind of net. Indeed, in some places, the fish are so numerous that a common sack answers nearly as well as a net.

It has been mentioned that the ancient Romans were in the habit of forming ponds in which the Murænæ were kept, and it is evident, from several passages of Scripture, that the Jews were accustomed to preserve fish in a similar manner, though they would not restrict their tanks or ponds to one species.

The accompanying illustration represents Fishes of the Mediterranean Sea, and it is probable that one of them may be identified, though the passage in which it is mentioned is only an inferential one. In the prophecy against Pharaoh, king of Egypt, the prophet Ezekiel writes as follows : " I will put hooks in thy jaws, and I will cause the fish of thy rivers to stick unto thy scales, and I will bring thee up out of the midst of thy rivers, and all the fish of thy rivers shall stick unto thy scales" (xxix. 4).

FISHES OF THE MEDITERRANEAN.
1. SUCKING-FISH.   2. TUNNY.   3. CORYPHENE.

Some believe that the prophet made allusion to the Sucking-fish, which has the dorsal fins developed into a most curious apparatus of adhesion, by means of which it can fasten itself at will to any smooth object, and hold so tightly to it that it can scarcely be torn away without injury.

The common Sucking-fish is shown in the upper part of the illustration.

There are, however, other fish which have powers of adhesion which, although not so remarkable as those of the Sucking-fish, are yet very strong. There is, for example, the well-known Lump-sucker, or Lump-fish, which has the ventral fins modified into a sucker so powerful that, when one of these fishes has been put into a pail of water, it has attached itself so firmly to the bottom of the vessel that when lifted by the tail it raised the pail, together with several gallons of water.

The Gobies, again, have their ventral fins united and modified into a single sucker, by means of which the fish is able to secure itself to a stone, rock, or indeed any tolerably smooth surface. These fishes are popularly known as Bull-routs.

The centre of the illustration is occupied by another of the Mediterranean fishes. This is the well-known Tunny, which furnishes food to the inhabitants of the coasts of this inland sea, and indeed constitutes one of their principal sources of wealth. This fine fish is on an average four or five feet in length, and sometimes attains the length of six or seven feet.

The flesh of the Tunny is excellent, and the fish is so conspicuous, that the silence of the Scriptures concerning its existence shows the utter indifference to specific accuracy that prevailed among the various writers.

The other figure represents the Coryphene, popularly, though very wrongly, called the Dolphin, and celebrated, under that name, for the beautiful colours which fly over the surface of the body as it dies.

The flesh of the Coryphene is excellent, and in the times of classic Rome the epicures were accustomed to keep these fish alive, and at the beginning of a feast to lay them before the guests, so that they might, in the first place, witness the magnificent colours of the dying fish, and, in the second place, might be assured that when it was cooked it was perfectly fresh. Even during life, the Coryphene is a most lovely fish, and those who have witnessed it playing round a ship, or dashing off in chase of a shoal of flying-fishes, can scarcely find words to express their admiration of its beauty.

THE SEA OF GALILEE

FISHES.

CHAPTER II.

Various modes of capturing Fish—The hook and line—Military use of the hook—
Putting a hook in the jaws—The fishing spear—Different kinds of net—The
casting-net—Prevalence of this form—Technical words among fishermen—
Fishing by night—The draught of Fishes—The real force of the miracle—
Selecting the Fish—The Fish-gate and Fish-market—Fish killed by a draught
—Fishing in the Dead Sea—Dagon, the fish-god of Philistina, Assyria, and
Siam—Various Fishes of Egypt and Palestine.

As to the various methods of capturing Fish, we will first take the simplest plan, that of the hook and line.

Sundry references are made to angling, both in the Old and New Testaments. See, for example, the well-known passage respecting the leviathan, in Job xli. 1, 2: "Canst thou draw out leviathan with an hook? or his tongue with a cord which thou lettest down?

"Canst thou put an hook into his nose? or bore his jaw through with a thorn?"

It is thought that the last clause of this passage refers, not to the actual capture of the Fish, but to the mode in which they were kept in the tanks, each being secured by a ring or hook and line, so that it might be taken when wanted.

On referring to the New Testament, we find that the fisher Apostles used both the hook and the net. See Matt. xvii. 27 : "Go thou to the sea, and cast an hook, and take up the fish that first cometh up." Now this passage explains one or two points.

In the first place, it is one among others which shows that, although the Apostles gave up all to follow Christ, they did not throw away their means of livelihood, as some seem to fancy, nor exist ever afterwards on the earnings of others. On the contrary, they retained their fisher equipment, whether boats, nets, or hooks ; and here we find St. Peter, after the way of fishermen, carrying about with him the more portable implements of his craft.

Next, the phrase "casting" the hook into the sea is exactly expressive of the mode in which angling is conducted in the sea and large pieces of water, such as the Lake of Galilee. The fisherman does not require a rod, but takes his line, which has a weight just above the hook, coils it on his left arm in lasso fashion, baits the hook, and then, with a peculiar swing, throws it into the water as far as it will reach. The hook is allowed to sink for a short time, and is then drawn towards the shore in a series of jerks, in order to attract the Fish, so that, although the fisherman does not employ a rod, he manages his line very much as does an angler of our own day when "spinning" for pike or trout.

Sometimes the fisherman has a number of lines to manage, and in this case he acts in a slightly different manner. After throwing out the loaded hook, as above mentioned, he takes a short stick, notched at one end, and pointed at the other, thrusts the sharp end into the ground at the margin of the water, and hitches the line on the notch.

He then proceeds to do the same with all his lines in succession, and when he has flung the last hook into the water, he sits down on a heap of leaves and grass which he has gathered together, and watches the lines to see if either of them is moved in the peculiar jerking manner which is characteristic of a "bite." After a while, he hauls them in successively, removes the Fish that may have been caught, and throws the lines into the water afresh.

We now come to the practice of catching Fish by the net, a custom to which the various Scriptural writers frequently refer, sometimes in course of historical narrative, and sometimes by way of allegory or metaphor. The reader will remember that the net was also used on land for the purpose of catching wild animals, and that many of the allusions to the net which occur in the Old Testament refer to the land and not to the water.

The commonest kind of net, which was used in the olden times as it is now, was the casting-net. This kind of net is circular, and is loaded all round its edge with weights, and suspended by the middle to a cord. When the fisherman throws this net, he gathers it up in folds in his arms, and, with a peculiar swing of the arms, only to be learned by long practice, flings it so that it spreads out and falls in its circular form upon the surface of the water. It rapidly sinks to the bottom, the loaded circumference causing it to assume a cup-like form, enclosing within its meshes all the Fish that happen to be under it as it falls. When it has reached the bottom, the fisherman cautiously hauls in the rope, so that the loaded edges gradually approach each other, and by their own weight cling together and prevent the Fish from escaping as the net is slowly drawn ashore.

This kind of net is found, with certain modifications, in nearly all parts of the world. The Chinese are perhaps supreme in their management of it. They have a net of extraordinary size, and cast it by flinging it over their backs, the huge circle spreading itself out in the most perfect manner as it falls on the water.

At the present day, when the fishermen use this net they wade into the sea as far as they can, and then cast it. In consequence of this custom, the fishermen are always naked while engaged in their work, wearing nothing but a thick cap in order to save themselves from sun-stroke. It is probable that on the memorable occasion mentioned by St. John, in chap. xxi., all the fishermen were absolutely, and not relatively naked, wearing no clothes at all, not even the ordinary tunic.

That a great variety of nets was used by the ancient Jews is evident from the fact that there are no less than ten words to signify different kinds of net. At the present day we have very great difficulty in deciding upon the exact interpretation of these technical terms, especially as in very few cases are we assisted either by the context or by the etymology of the words. It is the same in all trades or pursuits, and we can easily understand how our own names of drag-net, seine, trawl, and keer-drag would perplex any commentator who happened to live some two thousand years after English had ceased to be a living language.

MODE OF DRAGGING THE SEINE-NET.

The Sagene, or seine-net, was made in lengths, any number of which could be joined together, so as to enclose a large space of water. The upper edge was kept at the surface of the water by floats, and the lower edge sunk by weights.

This net was always taken to sea in vessels, and when "shot" the various lengths were joined together, and the net extended in a line, with a boat at each end. The boats then gradually approached each other, so as to bring the net into a semicircle, and finally met, enclosing thereby a vast number of Fishes in their meshen walls. The water was then beaten, so as to frighten the Fishes and drive them into the meshes, and the net was then either taken ashore, or lifted by degrees on board the boats, and the Fish removed from it.

As in a net of this kind Fishes of all sorts are enclosed, the contents are carefully examined, and those which are unfit for eating are thrown away. Even at the present day much care is taken in the selection, but in the ancient times the fishermen were still more cautious, every Fish having to be separately examined in order that the presence both of fins and scales might be assured before the captors could send it to the market.

It is to this custom that Christ alludes in the well-known parable of the net: "Again, the kingdom of heaven is like unto a net that was cast into the sea, and gathered of every kind;

"Which, when it was full, they drew to shore, and sat down, and gathered the good into vessels, but cast the bad away"

LASTLY, we come to the religious, or rather superstitious, part played by Fish in the ancient times. That the Egyptians employed Fish as material symbols of Divine attributes we learn from secular writers, such as Herodotus and Strabo.

The Jews, who seem to have had an irrepressible tendency to idolatry, and to have adopted the idols of every people with whom they came in contact, resuscitated the Fish-worship of Egypt as soon as they found themselves among the Philistines. We might naturally imagine that as the Israelites were bitterly opposed to their persistent enemy, who trod them under foot and crushed every attempt at rebellion for more than three hundred years, they would repudiate the worship as well as the rule of their conquerors. But, on the contrary, they adopted the worship of Dagon, the Fish-god, who was the principal deity of the Philistines, and erected temples in his honour.

We find precisely the same worship at the present day in Siam, where Dagon has exactly the same form as among the Philistines of old. There is now before me a photograph of a great temple at Ayutia, the entrance to which is guarded by two huge images of the Fish-god. They are about sixty feet in height, and have both legs and feet like man, but in addition the lower part of the body is modified into the tail of a Fish, which, in common with the whole of the body, is covered with gilded scales.

In order that the reader may see examples of the typical Fish which are to be found in Egypt and Palestine, I have added three more species, which are represented in the following illustration.

The uppermost figure represents the NILE PERCH. This Fish is

FISHES OF EGYPT AND PALESTINE.

1. NILE PERCH.   2. SURMULLET.   3. STAR-GAZER.

plentiful in the Nile, and in the mouths of many Asiatic rivers. It is brown above, silvery white below, and may be distinguished by the armed gill-covers, and the three strong spines of the anal fin. The tongue is smooth.

Immediately below the Nile Perch is the STAR-GAZER.

This Fish is found in the Mediterranean, and derives its name from the singular mode in which the eyes are set in the head, so that it looks upwards instead of sideways. It is one of the mud-lovers, a fact which accounts for the peculiar position of the eyes. It is said to feed after the fashion of the fishing-frog—*i.e.* by burying itself in the mud and attracting other Fishes by a worm-like appendage of its mouth, and pouncing on them before they are aware of their danger.

This is not a pretty Fish, and as it is very spiny, is not pleasant to the grasp, but its flesh is very good, and it is much valued by those who can obtain it.

The last Fish to be noticed is the SURMULLET, a Fish that is equally remarkable for the beauty of its colours and the excellence of its flesh.

MOLLUSCS.

The purple of Scripture—The sac containing the purple dye—Curious change of colour—Mode of obtaining the dye—The Tyrian purple—The king of the Ethiopians and the purple robe—The professional purple dyers—Various words expressive of different shades of purple.

LEAVING the higher forms of animal life, we now pass to the Invertebrated Animals which are mentioned in Scripture.

As may be inferred from the extreme looseness of nomenclature which prevails among the higher animals, the species which can be identified are comparatively few, and of them but a very few details are given in the Scriptures.

Taking them in their zoological order, we will begin with the MOLLUSCS.

WE are all familiar with the value which was set by the ancients upon the peculiar dye which may be called by the name of Imperial Purple. In the first place, it was exceedingly costly, not only for its richness of hue, but from the great difficulty with which a sufficient quantity could be procured for staining a dress. Purple was exclusively a royal colour, which might not be worn by a subject. Among the ancient Romans, during the times of the Cæsars, any one who ventured to appear in a dress of purple would do so at the peril of his life. In the consular days of Rome, the dress of the consuls was white, striped with purple; but the Cæsars advanced another step in luxury, and dyed the whole toga of this costly hue.

The colour of the dye is scarcely what we understand by the term "purple," *i.e.* a mixture of blue and red. It has but very little blue in it, and has been compared by the ancients to the colour of newly-clotted blood. It is obtained from several

Shell Fish belonging to the great Whelk family, the chief of which is the *Murex brandaris*.

The shell is shaped something like that of a whelk, but is very smooth and porcelain-like, and is generally white, ornamented with several coloured bands. It is, however, one of the most variable of shells, differing not only in colour but in form. It always inhabits the belt of the shore between tide-marks, and preys upon other Molluscs, such as the mussel and periwinkle, literally licking them to pieces with its long riband tongue.

This tongue is beset with rows of hooked teeth, exactly like the shark-tooth weapons of the Samoan and Mangaian Islanders, and with it the creature is enabled to bore through the shells of mussels and similar Molluscs, and to eat the enclosed animal. It is very destructive to periwinkles, thrusting its tongue through the mouth of the shell, piercing easily the operculum by which the entrance is closed, and gradually scooping out the unfortunate inmate.

Even the bivalves, which can shut themselves up between two shells, fare no better, the tongue of the Dog-Whelk rasping a hole in the hard shell in eight-and-forty hours.

In order to procure the animal, the shell must be broken with a sharp blow of a small hammer, and the receptacle of the colouring matter can then be seen behind the head, and recognised by its lighter hue.

When it is opened, a creamy sort of matter exudes. It is yellowish, and gives no promise of its future richness of hue. There is only one drop of this matter in each animal, and it is about sufficient in quantity to stain a piece of linen the size of a dime.

The best mode of seeing the full beauty of the purple is to take a number of the Molluscs, and to stain as large a surface as possible. The piece of linen should then be exposed to the rays of the sun, when it will go through a most curious series of colours. The yellow begins to turn green, and, after a while, the stained portions of the linen will be entirely green, the yellow having been vanquished by the blue. By degrees the blue predominates more and more over the yellow, until the linen is no more green, but blue. Then, just as the yellow yielded to the blue, the blue yields to red, and becomes first violet, then purple, and lastly assumes the blood-red hue of royalty.

The colour is very permanent, and, instead of fading by time, seems rather to brighten.

In some cases the ancients appear not to have troubled themselves with the complicated operation of taking the animal out of the shell, opening the receptacle, and squeezing the contents on the fabric to be dyed, but simply crushed the whole of the Mollusc, so as to set the colouring matter free, and steeped the cloth in the pulp. Tyre was one of the most celebrated spots for this manufacture, the "Tyrian dye" being celebrated for its richness. Heaps of broken shells remain to the present day as memorials of the long-perished manufacture.

The value which the ancients set upon this dye is shown by many passages in various books. Among others we may refer to Herodotus.

Cambyses, it appears, had a design to make war upon three nations, the Ammonians, the Carthaginians, and the Ethiopians. He determined to invade the first by land, and the second by sea; but, being ignorant of the best method of reaching the Ethiopians, he dispatched messengers to them, nominally as ambassadors, but practically as spies. He sent to the King of Ethiopia valuable presents—namely, a purple mantle, a golden necklace and bracelet, an elaborate box of perfumed ointment, and a cask of palm-wine, these evidently being considered a proof of imperial magnificence.

The Ethiopian king ridiculed the jewels, praised the wine, and asked curiously concerning the dye with which the purple mantle was stained. On being told the mode of preparation, he refused to believe the visitors, and, referring to the changing hues of the mantle and to the perfume of the ointment, he showed his appreciation of their real character by saying that the goods were deceptive, and so were the bearers.

The Hebrew word *argaman*, which signifies the regal purple, occurs several times in Scripture, and takes a slightly different form according to the Chaldaic or Hebraic idiom.

For example, we find it in Exod. xxv. 4: "This is the offering which ye shall take of them: gold, and silver, and brass,

"And blue, and purple, and scarlet, and fine linen," &c. &c.

It occurs again in 2 Chron. ii. 7: "Send me now therefore a man cunning to work in gold, and in silver, and in brass, and in iron, and in purple, and crimson, and blue."

THE SNAIL.

The Snail which melteth—Rendering of the Jewish Bible—Theory respecting the track of the Snail—The Hebrew word *Shablul*—Various Snails of Palestine.

THERE is a very remarkable and not very intelligible passage in Ps. lviii. 8: "As a snail which melteth, let every one of them pass away." The Jewish Bible renders the passage in a way which explains the idea which evidently prevailed at the time when the Psalms were composed: "As a snail let him melt as he passeth on."

The ancients had an idea that the slimy track made by a Snail as it crawled along was subtracted from the substance of its body, and that in consequence the farther it crept, the smaller it became, until at last it wasted entirely away. The commentators on the Talmud took this view of the case. The Hebrew word *shablul*, which undoubtedly does signify a Snail of some kind, is thus explained: "The Shablul is a creeping thing: when it comes out of its shell, saliva pours from itself, until it becomes liquid, and so dies."

Other explanations of this passage have been offered, but there is no doubt that the view taken by these commentators is the correct one, and that the Psalmist, when he wrote the terrible series of denunciations in which the passage in question occurs, had in his mind the popular belief regarding the gradual wasting away of the Snail as it "passeth on."

It is needless to say that no particular species of Snail is mentioned, and almost as needless to state that in Palestine there are many species of Snails, to any or all of which these words are equally applicable.

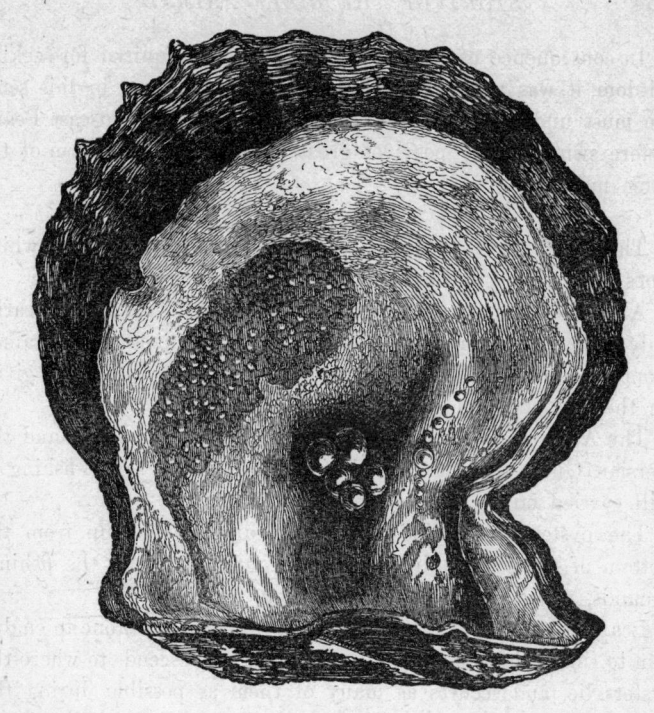

PEARL OYSTER.

THE PEARL.

The Pearl of Scripture—Wisdom compared to Pearl—Metaphorical uses of the Pearl—The Pearl of great price—Casting Pearls before swine.

THERE is only one passage in the Old Testament in which can be found the word which is translated as PEARL, and it is certain that the word in question may have another interpretation.

The word in question is *gabish*, and occurs in Job xxviii. 18. Treating of wisdom, in that magnificent passage beginning, "But where shall Wisdom be found, and where is the place of understanding?" the sacred writer uses these words, "No mention shall be made of coral, or of pearls: for the price of wisdom is above rubies."

653

In consequence of the labour and research required for seeking wisdom, it was proverbially likened to a Pearl, and in this sense we must understand the warning of our Lord, not to cast Pearls before swine. The "pearl of great price" is another form of the same metaphor.

The substance of Pearls is essentially the same as that which lines many shells, and is known as "mother of pearl."

Although a large number of shell-fish secrete "mother of pearl," only a few of them yield true Pearls. The finest are obtained from the so-called Pearl oyster, an illustration of which is given on the preceding page.

The Ancients obtained their Pearls chiefly from India and the Persian Gulf, where to this day the industry of Pearl-fishing is still carried on by the natives.

The oysters containing the Pearls are brought up from the bottom of the sea by divers, who go out in boats to the fishing-grounds, which are some distance from the shore.

Leaping naked into the water, carrying a heavy stone to enable him to sink quickly to the bottom, the diver descends to where the oysters lie, and secures as many of them as possible during the limited time that his breath lasts. On an average the divers remain under water from fifty to eighty seconds, though some can endure a much longer period.

Sharks are the special dread of Pearl-divers, and many are carried off by this fierce monster of the deep. To arm himself against their attack the diver carries a sharp knife, and instances are known of his having attacked and fairly defeated the dread destroyer in its own element.

Not only is the diver exposed to the danger of attack from sharks, but his hazardous calling is necessarily exhausting, and, as a rule, he is a short-lived man.

There are some kinds of fresh-water mussels which contain Pearls of an inferior quality; perhaps the most celebrated of these is the Pearl Mussel of the Chinese, who make a singular use of it. They string a number of globular pellets, and introduce them between the valves of the mussel, so that in course of time the creature deposits a coating of pearly substance upon them, and forms a very good imitation of real Pearls.

INSECTS.

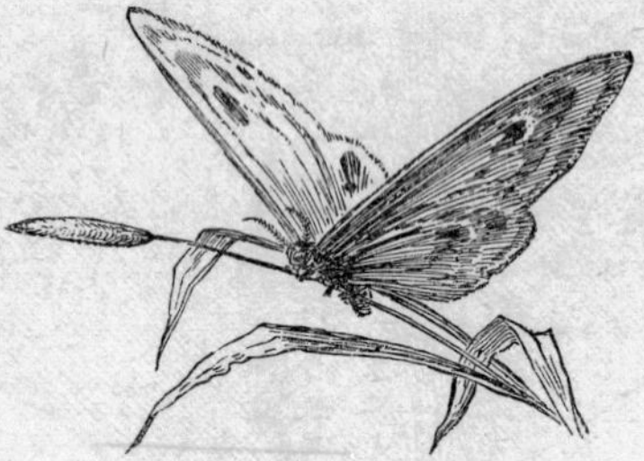

INSECTS.

THE LOCUST.

Insects—The Locust—The two migratory Locusts at rest and on the wing—The Locust swarms—Gordon Cumming's account—Progress of the insect hosts—Vain attempts to check them—Tossed up and down as a Locust—Effect of the winds on the insect—The east and the west winds—Locusts used for food—Ancient and modern travellers—The food of John the Baptist.

OF the LOCUSTS there are several species in Palestine, two of which are represented in the accompanying plate. Those on the ground are the common Migratory Locusts, while those on the wing, which have long heads, are a species of *Truxalis*.

The Locust belongs to the great order of Orthoptera, or straight-winged insects. They have, when fully developed, four wings, the two front being thick and membraneous, while the two hinder wings are large, delicate, translucent, and folded longitudinally under the front pair of wings when the insect is at rest. In the Locusts these characteristics are admirably shown. The appearance of a Locust when at rest and when flying is so different that the creature is at first sight scarcely recognisable as the same creature. When at rest, it is a compact and tolerably stout insect, with a dull though delicately coloured body; but when it takes flight it appears to attain twice its previous dimensions.

The front pair of wings, which alone were seen before they were expanded, became comparatively insignificant, while the hinder pair, which were before invisible, became the most prominent part of the insect, their translucent folds being coloured with the most brilliant hues, according to the species. The body seems to have shrunk as the wings have increased, and to have diminished to half its previous size, while the long legs that previously were so conspicuous are stretched out like the legs of a flying heron.

All the Locusts are vegetable-feeders, and do great harm wherever they happen to be plentiful, their powerful jaws severing even the thick grass stems as if cut by scissors. But it is only when they invade a country that their real power is felt. They come flying with the wind in such vast multitudes that the sky is darkened as if by thunder-clouds; and when they settle, every vestige of green disappears off the face of the earth.

Mr. Gordon Cumming once saw a flight of these Locusts. They flew about three hundred feet from the ground, and came on in thick, solid masses, forming one unbroken cloud. On all sides nothing was to be seen but Locusts. The air was full of them, and the plain was covered with them, and for more than an hour the insect army flew past him. When the Locusts settle, they eat with such voracity that the sound caused by their jaws cutting the leaves and grass can be heard at a great distance; and even the young Locusts, which have no wings, and are graphically termed by the Dutch colonists of Southern Africa "voet-gangers," or foot-goers, are little inferior in power of jaw to the fully-developed insect.

As long as they have a favourable wind, nothing stops the progress of the Locusts. They press forward just like the vast herds of antelopes that cover the plains of Africa, or the bisons that once blackened the prairies of America, and the progress of even the wingless young is as irresistible as that of the adult insects. Regiments of soldiers have in vain attempted to stop them. Trenches have been dug across their path, only to be filled up in a few minutes with the advancing hosts, over whose bodies the millions of survivors continued their march. When the trenches were filled with water, the result was the same; and even when fire was substituted for water, the flames were quenched by the masses of Locusts that fell into them. When they come to a tree, they climb up it in swarms, and devour every particle of foliage, not even sparing the bark of the smaller branches. They ascend the walls of houses that come in the line of their march, swarming in at the windows, and gnawing in their hunger the very woodwork of the furniture.

We shall now see how true to nature is the terrible prophecy

LOCUSTS.

of Joel. "A day of darkness and of gloominess, a day of clouds and of thick darkness, as the morning spread upon the mountains: a great people and a strong; there hath not been ever the like, neither shall be any more after it, even to the years of many generations.

"A fire devoureth before them; and behind them a flame burneth: the land is as the garden of Eden before them, and behind them a desolate wilderness; yea, and nothing shall escape them.

"And the Lord shall utter His voice before His army: for His camp is very great" (Joel ii. 2—11).

Nothing can be more vividly accurate than this splendid description of the Locust armies. First we have the darkness caused by them as they fly like black clouds between the sun and the earth. Then comes the contrast between the blooming and fertile aspect of the land before they settle on it, and its utter desolation when they leave it.

There is one passage in the Scriptures which at first sight seems rather obscure, but is clear enough when we understand the character of the insect to which it refers: "I am gone like the shadow when it declineth: I am tossed up and down as the locust" (Ps. cix. 23).

Although the Locusts have sufficient strength of flight to remain on the wing for a considerable period, and to pass over great distances, they have little or no command over the direction of their flight, and always travel with the wind, just as has been mentioned regarding the quail. So entirely are they at the mercy of the wind, that if a sudden gust arises the Locusts are tossed about in the most helpless manner; and if they should happen to come across one of the circular air-currents that are so frequently found in the countries which they inhabit, they are whirled round and round without the least power of extricating themselves.

In the account of the great plague of Locusts, the wind is mentioned as the proximate cause both of their arrival and their departure. See, for example, Exod. x. 12, 13:

"And the Lord said unto Moses, Stretch out thine hand over the land of Egypt for the locusts, that they may come up upon the land of Egypt, and eat every herb of the land, even all that the hail hath left.

" And Moses stretched forth his rod over the land of Egypt, and the Lord brought an east wind upon the land all that day, and all that night; and when it was morning, the east wind brought the locusts."

Afterwards, when Moses was brought before Pharaoh, and entreated to remove the plague which had been brought upon the land, the west wind was employed to take the Locusts away, just as the east wind had brought them.

" He went out from Pharaoh, and entreated the Lord.

" And the Lord turned a mighty strong west wind, which took away the locusts, and cast them into the Red Sea ; there remained not one locust in all the coasts of Egypt" (Exod. x. 18, 19).

Modern travellers have given accounts of these Locust armies, which exactly correspond with the sacred narrative. One traveller mentions that, after a severe storm, the Locusts were destroyed in such multitudes, that they were heaped in a sort of wall, varying from three to four feet in height, fifty miles in length, and almost unapproachable, on account of the odour of their decomposing bodies.

We now come to the use of Locusts as food.

Very few insects have been recognised as fit for human food, even among uncivilized nations, and it is rather singular that the Israelites, whose dietary was so scrupulously limited, should have been permitted the use of the Locust. These insects are, however, eaten in all parts of the world which they frequent, and in some places form an important article of diet, thus compensating in some way for the amount of vegetable food which they consume.

When their captors have roasted and eaten as many as they can manage to devour, they dry the rest over the fires, pulverize them between two stones, and keep the meal for future use, mixing it with water, or, if they can get it, with milk.

We will now take a few accounts given by travellers of the present day, selecting one or two from many. Mr. W. G. Palgrave, in his "Central and Eastern Arabia," gives a description of the custom of eating Locusts. "On a sloping bank, at a short distance in front, we discerned certain large black patches, in strong contrast with the white glisten of the soil around, and at the same time our attention was attracted by a strange whizzing, like that of a flight of hornets, close along the ground, while our dromedaries capered and started as though struck with sudden insanity.

"The cause of all this was a vast swarm of locusts, here alighted in their northerly wanderings from their birthplace in the Dahna; their camp extended far and wide, and we had already disturbed their outposts. These insects are wont to settle on the ground after sunset, and there, half-stupified by the night chill, await the morning rays, which warm them once more into life and movement.

"This time, the dromedaries did the work of the sun, and it would be hard to say which of the two were the most frightened, they or the locusts. It was truly laughable to see so huge a beast lose his wits for fear at the flight of a harmless, stingless insect, for, of all timid creatures, none equal this 'ship of the desert' for cowardice.

"But, if the beasts were frightened, not so their masters. I really thought they would have gone mad for joy. Locusts are here an article of food, nay, a dainty, and a good swarm of them is begged of Heaven in Arabia. . . .

"The locust, when boiled or fried, is said to be delicious, and boiled and fried accordingly they are to an incredible extent. However, I never could persuade myself to taste them, whatever invitations the inhabitants of the land, smacking their lips over large dishes full of entomological 'delicatesses,' would make me to join them. Barakàt ventured on one for a trial. He pronounced it oily and disgusting, nor added a second to the first: it is caviare to unaccustomed palates.

"The swarm now before us was a thorough godsend for our Arabs, on no account to be neglected. Thirst, weariness, all were forgotten, and down the riders leaped from their starting camels. This one spread out a cloak, that one a saddle-bag, a third his shirt, over the unlucky creatures, destined for the morning meal. Some flew away, whizzing across our feet; others were caught, and tied up in sacks."

Mr. Mansfield Parkyns, in his "Life in Abyssinia," mentions that the true Abyssinian will not eat the Locust, but that the negroes and Arabs do so. He describes the flavour as being something between the burnt end of a quill and a crumb of linseed cake. The flavour, however, depends much on the mode of cooking, and, as some say, on the nature of the Locusts' food.

Signor Pierotti states, in his "Customs and Traditions of Palestine," that Locusts are really excellent food, and that he was accustomed to eat them, not from necessity, but from choice, and compares their flavour to that of shrimps.

Dr. Livingstone makes a similar comparison. In Palestine, Locusts are eaten either roasted or boiled in salt and water, but, when preserved for future use, they are dried in the sun, their heads, wings, and legs picked off, and their bodies ground into dust. This dust has naturally a rather bitter flavour, which is corrected by mixing it with camel's milk or honey, the latter being the favourite substance.

We may now see that the food of John the Baptist was, like his dress, that of a people who lived at a distance from towns, and that there was no more hardship in the one than in the other. Some commentators have tried to prove that he fed on the fruit of the locust or carob tree—the same that is used in some countries for feeding cattle; but there is not the least ground for such an explanation. The account of his life, indeed, requires no explanation; Locust-dust, mixed with honey, being an ordinary article of food even at the present day.

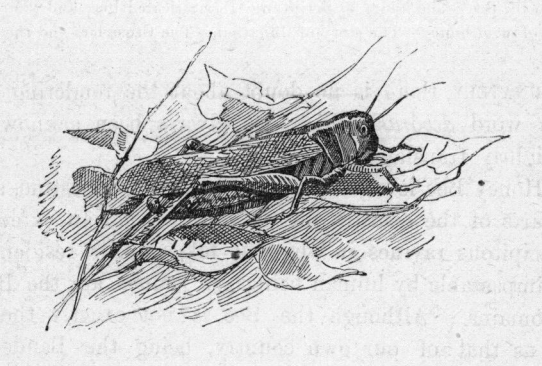

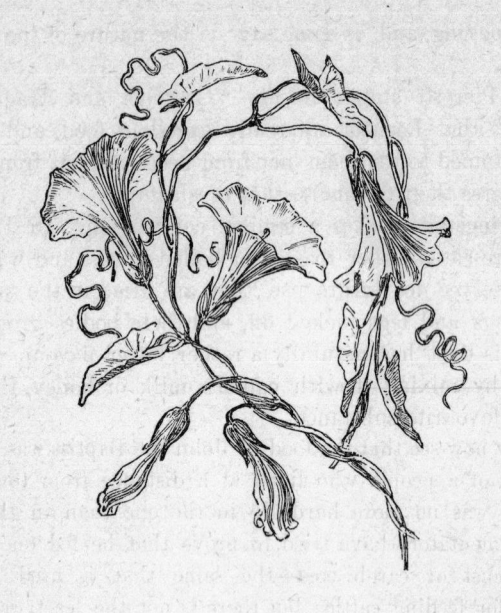

THE BEE.

The Honey Bee of Palestine—Abundance of Bees in the Holy Land—Habitations of the wild Bee—The honey of Scripture—Domesticated Bees and their hives—Stores of wild honey—The story of Jonathan—The Crusaders and the honey.

FORTUNATELY, there is no doubt about the rendering of the Hebrew word *debôrah*, which has always been acknowledged to be rightly translated as "Bee."

The Honey Bee is exceedingly plentiful in Palestine, and in some parts of the country multiplying to such an extent that the precipitous ravines in which it takes up its residence are almost impassable by human beings, so jealous are the Bees of their domains. Although the Bee is not exactly the same species as that of our own country, being the Banded Bee (*Apis fasciata*), and not the *Apis mellifica*, the two insects very much resemble each other in shape, colour, and habits. Both of them share the instinctive dislike of strangers and jealousy of intrusion, and the Banded Bee of Palestine has as great an objection to intrusion as its congener in this country.

Several allusions are made in the Scriptures to this trait in the character of the Bee. See, for example, Deut. i 44: "And the Amorites, which dwelt in that mountain, came out against you, and chased you, as bees do, and destroyed you in Seir, even unto Hormah." All those who have had the misfortune to offend Bees will recognise the truth of this metaphor, the

THE BEE.

Amorites swarming out of the mountain like wild Bees out of the rocky clefts which serve them as hives, and chasing the intruder fairly out of their domains.

A similar metaphor is employed in the Psalms: "They compassed me about; yea, they compassed me about; but in the name of the Lord I will destroy them.

"They compassed me about like bees, they are quick as the fire of thorns, but in the name of the Lord I will destroy them."

The custom of swarming is mentioned in one of the earlier books of Scripture. The reader will remember that, after Samson had killed the lion which met him on the way, he left the carcase alone. The various carnivorous beasts and birds at once discover such a banquet, and in a very short time the body of a dead animal is reduced to a hollow skeleton, partially or entirely covered with skin, the rays of the sun drying and hardening the skin until it is like horn.

In exceptionally hot weather, the same result occurs even in this country. Some years before this account was written there was a very hot and dry summer, and a great mortality took place among the sheep. So many indeed died that at last their owners merely flayed them, and left their bodies to perish. One of the dead sheep had been thrown into a rather thick copse, and had fallen in a spot where it was sheltered from the wind, and yet exposed to the fierce heat of the summer's sun. The consequence was that in a few days it was reduced to a mere shell. The heat hardened and dried the external layer of flesh so that not even the carnivorous beetles could penetrate it, while the whole of the interior dissolved into a semi-putrescent state, and was rapidly devoured by myriads of blue-bottles and other larvæ.

It was so thoroughly dried that scarcely any evil odour clung to it, and as soon as I came across it the story of Samson received a simple elucidation. In the hotter Eastern lands, the whole process would have been more rapid and more complete, and the skeleton of the lion, with the hard and horny skin strained over it, would afford exactly the habitation of which a wandering swarm of Bees would take advantage. At the present day swarms of wild Bees often make their habitations within the desiccated bodies of dead camels that have perished on the way.

As to the expression "hissing" for the Bee, the reader must bear in mind that a sharp, short hiss is the ordinary call in Palestine, when one person desires to attract the attention of another. A similar sound, which may perhaps be expressed by the letters *tst*, prevails on the Continent at the present day.

Signor Pierotti remarks that the inhabitants of Palestine are even now accustomed to summon Bees by a sort of hissing sound.

Whether the honey spoken of in the Scriptures was obtained from wild or domesticated Bees is not very certain, but, as the manners of the East are much the same now as they were three thousand years ago, it is probable that Bees were kept then as they are now. The hives are not in the least like ours, but are cylindrical vases of coarse earthenware, laid horizontally, much like the bark hives employed in many parts of Southern Africa.

In some places the hives are actually built into the walls of the houses, the closed end of the cylinder projecting into the interior, while an entrance is made for the Bees in the other end, so that the insects have no business in the house. When the inhabitants wish to take the honey, they resort to the operation which is technically termed "driving" by bee-masters.

They gently tap the end within the house, and continue the tapping until the Bees, annoyed by the sound, have left the hive. They then take out the circular door that closes the end of the hive, remove as much comb as they want, carefully put back those portions which contain grubs and bee-bread, and replace the door, when the Bees soon return and fill up the gaps in the combs. As to the wasteful, cruel, and foolish custom of "burning" the Bees, the Orientals never think of practising it.

In many places the culture of Bees is carried out to a very great extent, numbers of the earthenware cylinders being piled on one another, and a quantity of mud thrown over them in order to defend them from the rays of the sun, which would soon melt the wax of the combs.

In consequence of the geographical characteristics of the Holy Land, which supplies not only convenient receptacles for the Bees in the rocks, but abundance of thyme and similar plants, vast stores of bee-comb are to be found in the cliffs, and form no small part of the wealth of the people.

The abundance of wild honey is shown by the memorable events recorded in 1 Sam. xiv. Saul had prohibited all the people from eating until the evening. Jonathan, who had not heard the prohibition, was faint and weary, and, seeing honey dripping on the ground from the abundance and weight of the comb, he took it up on the end of his staff, and ate sufficient to restore his strength.

Thus, if we refer again to the history of John the Baptist and his food, we shall find that he was in no danger of starving for want of nourishment, the Bees breeding abundantly in the desert places he frequented, and affording him a plentiful supply of the very material which was needed to correct the deficiencies of the dried locusts which he used instead of bread.

The expression "a land flowing with milk and honey" has become proverbial as a metaphor expressive of plenty. Those to whom the words were spoken understood it as something more than a metaphor. In the work to which reference has already been made Signor Pierotti writes as follows:—"Let us now see how far the land could be said to flow with milk and honey during the latter part of its history and at the present day.

"We find that honey was abundant in the time of the Crusades, for the English, who followed Edward I. to Palestine, died in great numbers from the excessive heat, and from eating too much fruit and honey.

"At the present day, after traversing the country in every direction, I am able to affirm that in the south-east and north-east, where the ancient customs of the patriarchs are most fully preserved, and the effects of civilization have been felt least, milk and honey may still be said to flow, as they form a portion of every meal, and may even be more abundant than water, which fails occasionally in the heat of summer. . . . I have often eaten of the comb, which I found very good and of delicious fragrance."

The Bee represented in the illustration is the common Bee of Palestine, *Apis fasciata*. The lowest figure in the corner, with a long body and shut wings, is the queen. The central figure represents the drone, conspicuous by means of his large eyes, that almost join each other at the top of the head, and for his thicker and stouter body, while the third figure represents the worker Bee. Near them is shown the entrance to one of the natural hives which are so plentiful in the Holy Land, and are made in the "clefts of the rocks." A number of Bees are shown issuing from the hole.

THE HORNET AND ITS NEST.

THE HORNET.

The Tzirah or Hornet of Scripture—Travellers driven away by Hornets—The Hornet used as a metaphor—Oriental symbolism—Sting of the Hornet.

STILL keeping to the hymenopterous insects, we come to the Hornet. There are three passages in which occurs the word *tzirah*, which has been translated as Hornet. In every case when the word is mentioned the insect is employed in a metaphorical sense. See, for example, Exod. xxiii. 27, 28: "I will send my fear before thee, and will destroy all the people to whom thou shalt come; and I will make all thine enemies turn their backs unto thee.

"And I will send hornets before thee, which shall drive out the Hivite, the Canaanite, and the Hittite, from before thee."

The Hornet affords a most appropriate image for such a promise as was made to the Israelites, and was one which they must have thoroughly comprehended. The Hornets of Palestine and the neighbouring countries are far more common than our own Hornets here, and they evidently infested some parts to such an extent that they gave their name to those spots. Thus the word *Zoreah*, which is mentioned in Josh. xv. 33, signifies the "place of Hornets."

They make their nests in various ways; some species placing them underground, and others disposing them as shown in the illustration, and merely sheltering them from the elements by a paper cover. Such nests as these would easily be disturbed by the animals which accompanied the Israelites on their journeys, even if the people were careful to avoid them. In such a case, the irritated insects rush out at the intruders; and so great is the terror of their stings, that men and beasts fly promiscuously in every direction, each only anxious to escape from the winged foes.

The recollection of such scenes would necessarily dwell in the memory of those who had taken part in them, and cause the metaphor to impress itself strongly upon them.

It is needless to say that the passages in question might be literal statements of facts, and that the various nations were actually driven out of their countries by Hornets. Let the insects be brought upon the land in sufficient numbers, and neither man nor beast could stay in it. It is not likely, however, that such a series of miracles, far exceeding the insect-plagues of Egypt, would have been worked without frequent references to them in the subsequent books of the Scriptures; and, moreover, the quick, short, and headlong flight of the attack of Hornets is a very different thing from the emigration which is mentioned in the Scriptures, and the long journeys which such a proceeding involved.

ANTS ON THE MARCH.

THE ANT.

The Ant of Scripture—Habit of laying up stores of food—The Ants of Palestine, and their habits—The Agricultural or Mound-making Ant—Preparing ground, sowing, tending, reaping, and storing the crop—Different habits of Ants—The winged Ants.

ONE of the best-known and most frequently quoted passages of Scripture is found in Proverbs, chap. vi. 6–8: "Go to the ant, thou sluggard; consider her ways, and be wise:

"Which, having no guide, overseer, or ruler,

"Provideth her meat in the summer, and gathereth her food in the harvest."

In Palestine Ants abound, and the species are tolerably numerous. Among them are found some species which do convey seeds into their subterranean home; and if their stores should be wetted by the heavy rains which sometimes prevail in that country, bring them to the outer air, as soon as the weather clears up, and dry them in the sun.

The writer of the Proverbs was therefore perfectly right when he alluded to the vegetable stores within the nest, and only spoke the truth when he wrote of the Ant that it was exceeding wise. Any one who wishes to test the truth of his words can easily do so by watching the first Ants' nest which he finds, the species of the Ant not being of much consequence. The nests of the Wood-Ant are perhaps the best suited for investigation, partly because the insect and its habitation are comparatively large, and, secondly, because so much of the work is done above-ground.

The most wonderful Ant in the world is one which hitherto is only known in some parts of America. Its scientific name is *Atta malefaciens*, and it has been called by various popular names, such as the Mound-making Ant and the Agricultural Ant on account of its habits, and the Stinging Ant on account of the pungency of its venom. This characteristic has gained for it the scientific name of *malefaciens*, or villanous.

The habits of this Ant were studied in Texas by Dr. Lincecum for the space of twelve years, and the result of his investigations was communicated to the Linnæan Society by C. Darwin, Esq. It is so extraordinary an account that it must be given in the narrator's own words:—

"The species which I have named 'Agricultural' is a large brownish ant. It dwells in what may be termed paved cities, and, like a thrifty, diligent, provident farmer, makes suitable and timely arrangements for the changing seasons. It is, in short, endowed with skill, ingenuity, and untiring patience sufficient to enable it successfully to contend with the varying exigencies which it may have to encounter in the life-conflict.

"When it has selected a situation for its habitation, if on ordinary dry ground, it bores a hole, around which it raises the surface three and sometimes six inches, forming a low circular mound having a very gentle inclination from the centre to the outer border, which on an average is three or four feet from the entrance. But if the location is chosen on low, flat, wet land liable to inundation, though the ground may be perfectly dry at the time the ant sets to work, it nevertheless elevates the mound, in the form of a pretty sharp cone, to the height of fifteen to twenty inches or more, and makes the entrance near the summit. Around the mound in either case the ant clears the ground of all obstructions, levels and smooths the surface to the distance of three or four feet from the gate of the city, giving the space the appearance of a handsome pavement, as it really is.

"Within this paved area not a blade of any green thing is allowed to grow, except a single species of grain-bearing grass. Having planted this crop in a circle around, and two or three feet from, the centre of the mound, the insect tends and cultivates it with constant care, cutting away all other grasses and weeds that may spring up amongst it and all around outside of the farm-circle to the extent of one or two feet more.

"The cultivated grass grows luxuriantly, and produces a heavy crop of small, white, flinty seeds, which under the microscope very closely resemble ordinary rice. When ripe, it is carefully harvested, and carried by the workers, chaff and all, into the granary cells, where it is divested of the chaff and packed away. The chaff is taken out and thrown beyond the limits of the paved area.

"During protracted wet weather, it sometimes happens that the provision stores become damp, and are liable to sprout and spoil. In this case, on the first fine day the ants bring out the damp and damaged grain, and expose it to the sun till it is dry, when they carry it back and pack away all the sound seeds, leaving those that had sprouted to waste.

"In a peach-orchard not far from my house is a considerable elevation, on which is an extensive bed of rock. In the sand-beds overlying portions of this rock are fine cities of the Agricultural ants, evidently very ancient. My observations on their manners and customs have been limited to the last twelve years, during which time the enclosure surrounding the orchard has prevented the approach of cattle to the ant-farms. The cities which are outside of the enclosure as well as those protected in it are, at the proper season, invariably planted with the ant-rice. The crop may accordingly always be seen springing up within the circle about the 1st of November every year.

"Of late years, however, since the number of farms and cattle has greatly increased, and the latter are eating off the grass much closer than formerly, thus preventing the ripening of the seeds, I notice that the Agricultural ant is placing its cities along the turn-rows in the fields, walks in gardens, inside about the gates,

&c., where they can cultivate their farms without molestation from the cattle.

"There can be no doubt of the fact, that the particular species of grain-bearing grass mentioned above is intentionally planted. In farmer-like manner the ground upon which it stands is carefully divested of all other grasses and weeds during the time it is growing. When it is ripe the grain is taken care of, the dry stubble cut away and carried off, the paved area being left unencumbered until the ensuing autumn, when the same 'ant-rice' reappears within the same circle, and receives the same agricultural attention as was bestowed upon the previous crop; and so on year after year, as I *know* to be the case, in all situations where the ants' settlements are protected from graminivorous animals."

In a second letter, Dr. Lincecum, in reply to an inquiry from Mr. Darwin, whether he supposed that the Ants plant seeds for the ensuing crop, says, "I have not the slightest doubt of it. And my conclusions have not been arrived at from hasty or careless observation, nor from seeing the ants do something that looked a little like it, and then guessing at the results. I have at all seasons watched the same ant-cities during the last twelve years, and I know that what I stated in my former letter is true. I visited the same cities yesterday, and found the crop of ant-rice growing finely, and exhibiting also the signs of high cultivation, and not a blade of any other kind of grass or weed was to be seen within twelve inches of the circular row of ant-rice."

The economical habits of this wonderful insect far surpass anything that Solomon has written of the Ant, and it is not too much to say that if any of the Scriptural writers had ventured to speak of an Ant that not only laid up stores of grain, but actually prepared the soil for the crop, planted the seed, kept the ground free from weeds, and finally reaped the harvest, the statement would have been utterly disbelieved, and the credibility not only of that particular writer but of the rest of Scripture severely endangered.

As may be inferred from the above description, the habits of Ants vary greatly according to their species and the climate in which they live. All, however, are wonderful creatures; and whether we look at their varied architecture, their mode of procuring food, the system of slave-catching adopted by some, the "milking" of aphides practised by others, their astonishing mode of communicating thought to each other, and their perfect system of discipline, we feel how true were the words of the royal naturalist, that the Ants are "little upon earth, but are exceeding wise."

There is one point of their economy in which all known

ANT OF PALESTINE.

species agree. Only those which are destined to become perfectly developed males and females attain the winged state. Before they assume the transitional or pupal condition, each spins around itself a slight but tough silken cocoon, in which it lies secure during the time which is consumed in developing its full perfection of form.

When it is ready to emerge, the labourer Ants aid in freeing it from the cocoon, and in a short time it is ready to fly. Millions of these winged ants rise into the air, seeking their mates, and, as they are not strong on the wing, and are liable to be tossed about by every gust of wind, vast numbers of them perish. Whole armies of them fall into the water and are drowned or devoured by fish, while the insectivorous birds hold great festival on so abundant a supply of food. As soon as they are mated they bend their wings forward, snap them off, and pass the rest of their lives on the ground.

In consequence of the destruction that takes place among the winged Ants, the Arabs have a proverb which is applied to those who are over-ambitious: " If God purposes the destruction of an ant, He permits wings to grow upon her."

THE CRIMSON WORM.

The scarlet or crimson of Scripture—The Coccus or Cochineal of Palestine compared with that of Mexico—Difference between the sexes—Mode of preparing the insect.

We now come to another order of insects.

Just as the purple dye was obtained from a shell-fish, the scarcely less valuable crimson or scarlet was obtained from an insect. This is an insect popularly known as the Crimson Worm. It is closely allied to the cochineal insect of Mexico, which gives a more brilliant dye, and has at the present day nearly superseded the native insect. It is, however, still employed as a dye in some parts of the country.

Like the cochineal insect of Mexico, the female is very much larger than her mate, and it is only from her that the dye is procured. At the proper season of year the females are gathered off the trees and carefully dried, the mode of drying having some effect upon the quality of the dye. During the process of drying the insect alters greatly, both in colour and size, shrinking to less than half its original dimensions, and assuming a greyish brown hue instead of a deep red. When placed in water it soon gives out its colouring matter, and communicates to the water

THE CRIMSON WORM.

the rich colour with which we are familiar under the name of carmine, or crimson. This latter name, by the way, is only a corruption of the Arabic *kermes*, which is the name of the insect.

The reader will remember that this was one of the three sacred colours—scarlet, purple, and blue—used in the vestments of the priests and the hangings of the tabernacle, the white not taking rank as a colour.

THE CLOTHES MOTH.

The Moth of Scripture evidently the Clothes Moth—Moths and garments—Accumulation of clothes in the East—Various uses of the hoarded robes—The Moths, the rust, and the thief.

ONE of the insects mentioned by name in the Scriptures is the MOTH, by which we must always understand some species of Clothes Moth. These are as plentiful and destructive in Palestine as in this country.

Several references are made to the Moth in the Scriptures, and nearly all have reference to its destructive habits. The solitary exceptions occur in the Book of Job, "Behold, He put no trust in His servants; and His angels He charged with folly: how much less in them that dwell in houses of clay, whose foundation is in the dust, which are crushed before the moth?"

In the New Testament reference is made several times to the Moth. "Lay not up for yourselves treasures upon earth, where moth and rust doth corrupt, and where thieves break through and steal" (Matt. vi. 19).

Even to ourselves these passages are significant enough, but to the Jews and the inhabitants of Palestine they possessed a force which we can hardly realize in this country. In the East large stores of clothing are kept by the wealthy, not only for their own use, but as presents to others. At a marriage feast, for example, the host presents each of the guests with a wedding garment. Clothes are also given as marks of favour, and a present of "changes of raiment," *i.e.* suits of clothing, is one of the most common gifts. As at the present day, there was anciently no greater mark of favour than for the giver to present the very robe which he was wearing, and when that robe happened to be an official one, the gift included the rank which it symbolized. Thus Joseph was invested with royal robes, as well as with the royal ring (Gen. xli. 42). Mordecai was clothed in the king's robes: "Let the royal apparel be brought which the king useth to wear, and the horse the king rideth upon, and the crown royal which is set upon his head.

MORDECAI IS LED THROUGH THE CITY UPON THE KING'S HORSE.

"And let this apparel and horse be delivered to the hand of one of the king's most noble princes, that they may array the man withal whom the king delighteth to honour, and bring him on horseback through the street of the city, and proclaim before him, Thus shall it be done to the man whom the king delighteth to honour." (Esther vi. 8, 9.)

The loose clothing of the East requires no fitting, as is the case with the tight garments of the West; any garment fits any man: so that the powerful and wealthy could lay up great stores of clothing, knowing that they would fit any person to whom they were given. An allusion to this practice of keeping great stores of clothing is made in Job xxvii. 26: "Though he heap up silver as the dust, and prepare raiment as the clay;

"He may prepare it, but the just shall put it on, and the innocent shall divide the silver."

So large was the supply of clothing in a wealthy man's house, that special chambers were set apart for it, and a special officer, called the "keeper of the garments" (2 Chron. xxxiv. 22), was appointed to take charge of them.

Thus, when a man was said to have clothing, the expression was a synonym for wealth and power. See Isa. iii. 6 : "When a man shall take hold of his brother of the house of his father, saying, Thou hast clothing, be thou our ruler."

The reader will now see how forcible was the image of the Moth and the garments, that is used so freely in the Scriptures. The Moth would not meddle with garments actually in use, so that a poor man would not be troubled with it. Only those who were rich enough to keep stores of clothing in their houses need fear the Moth.

THE SILKWORM MOTH.

Probability that the Hebrews were acquainted with Silk—Present cultivation of the Silkworm—The Silk-farms of the Lebanon—Silkworms and thunder.

IN the Authorized Version there are several passages wherein silk is mentioned, but it is rather doubtful whether the translation be correct or not, except in one passage of the Revelation : "And the merchants of the earth shall weep and mourn over her ; for no man buyeth their merchandise any more :

"The merchandise of gold, and silver, and precious stones, and of pearls, and fine linen, and purple, and silk." (xviii. 11, 12.)

That the Hebrews were acquainted with silk from very early times is nearly certain, but it is probable that until comparatively late years they only knew the manufactured material, and were ignorant of the source whence it was derived. As to the date at which silk was introduced into Palestine, nothing certain is known ; but it is most likely that Solomon's fleets brought silk from India, together with the other valuables which are mentioned in the history of that monarch.

At the present day silk is largely cultivated, and the silk-farmers of the Lebanon are noted for the abundance of the crop which is annually produced. The greatest care is taken in rearing the worms. An excellent account of these farms is given by Mr. G. W. Chasseaud in his "Druses of the Lebanon:"—

"Proceeding onward, and protected from the fierce heat of the sun's rays by the pleasant shade of mountain pines, we were continually encountering horseloads of cocoons, the fruit of the industry of the Druse silk-rearer. The whole process, from hatching the silkworms' eggs till the moment that the worm becomes a cocoon, is one series of anxiety and labour to the peasant. The worms are so delicate that the smallest change of temperature exposes them to destruction, and the peasant can never confidently count upon reaping a harvest until the cocoon is fairly set."

After a long and interesting description of the multiplied and ceaseless labours of the silk-grower in providing food for the armies of caterpillars and sheltering them from the elements, the writer proceeds as follows:—

"The peasant is unwilling to permit of our remaining and watching operations. Traditional superstition has inculcated in him a dread of the evil eye. If we stop and admire the wisdom displayed by the worm, it will, in his opinion, be productive of evil results; either the cocoon will be badly formed, or the silk will be worthless. So, first clearing the place of all intruders, he puts a huge padlock on the door, and, locking the *khlook* (room in which the silkworms are kept), deposits the key in his *zinnar*, or waistband.

"Next week he will come and take out the cocoons, and, separating them from the briars, choose out a sufficiency for breeding purposes, and all the rest are handed over to the women of his family. These first of all disentangle the cocoon from the rich and fibrous web with which it is enveloped, and which constitutes an article of trade by itself. The cocoons are then either reeled off by the peasant himself or else sold to some of the silk factories of the neighbourhood, where they are immediately reeled off, or are suffocated in an oven, and afterwards, being well aired and dried, piled up in the magazines of the factory.

"Such is a brief account or history of these cocoons, of which we were continually encountering horseload after horseload.

"As you will perceive, unless suffering from a severe cold in the head, the odour arising from these cocoons is not the most agreeable; but this arises partly from the neglect and want of care of the peasants themselves, who, reeling off basketful after basketful of cocoons, suffer the dead insects within to be thrown

BUTTERFLIES OF PALESTINE.

SYRIAN GRAYLING.   SYRIAN ORANGE-TIP.
SYRIAN SWALLOW-TAIL.

about and accumulate round the house, where they putrefy and emit noxious vapours."

Although our limits will not permit the cultivation of the Silkworm to be described more fully, it may here be added that all silk-growers are full of superstition regarding the welfare of the caterpillars, and imagine that they are so sensitive that they will die of fear. The noise of a thunderclap is, in their estimation, fatal to Silkworms; and the breeders were therefore accustomed to beat drums within the hearing of the Silkworms, increasing the loudness of the sound, and imitating as nearly as possible the crash and roll of thunder, so that the caterpillars might be familiar with the sound if the thunderstorm should happen to break near them.

FLIES.

Flies of Scripture—Annoyance caused by the House-fly—Flies and ophthalmia—Signor Pierotti's account of the Flies—The sovereign remedy against Flies—Causes of their prevalence.

THERE are two Hebrew words which are translated as "fly." One is *zebub,* and the other is *arob,* the latter being applied to the flies which were brought upon Egypt in the great plague. It is probable that some different species is here signified, but there is no certainty in the matter. Any species, however, would be a sufficient plague if they exceeded the usual number which infest Egypt, and which at first make the life of a foreigner a burden to him. They swarm in such myriads, that he eats flies, drinks flies, and breathes flies.

Not the least part of the nuisance is, that they cluster in the eyes of those who are affected with the prevalent ophthalmia, which is so fertile a cause of blindness, and so convey the infection with them. A stranger is always struck with the appearance of the children, who have quantities of these pests upon and about their eyes, and yet seem perfectly unaffected by a visitation which would wellnigh drive a European mad.

Signor Pierotti writes feelingly on the subject:—

" These insects sometimes cause no slight suffering in Palestine, as I can vouch from my own experience. However large or however small they may be, a rabid and restless foe, they attack alike, and make themselves insufferable in a thousand ways, in every season and place, in the house and in the field, by day and by night.

While I was encamped near the tents of the Bedawîn, in the neighbourhood of the Jordan, and to the south of Hebron, flies were brought in such numbers by the east wind that all, beasts and men, were in danger of being choked by them, as they crept into our ears, noses, and mouths, and all over our bodies. My servant and I were the first to fly from the pest, as we were spotted all over like lepers with the eruption caused by their bites: the Bedawîn themselves were not slow to follow our example.

"The flies, therefore, still infest Palestine as they did of old, except that they are not now so numerous as to compel the chiefs of the villages or tribes (answering to the kings of the Pentateuch and Joshua) to evacuate the country before them.

"The Philistines had a special deity whom they invoked against these pests, Baalzebub, the God of Flies, whose temple was at Ekron. The reason of this is evident at the present day, for the ancient country of the Philistines is infested with insect plagues, as I experienced to my cost.

"As, however, we had no faith in Baalzebub, we were obliged to arm ourselves with fly-traps and stoical patience. Many travellers bring with them a perfect druggist's shop from Europe as a protection against these nuisances, and leave behind them this only efficacious remedy, patience. This I strongly recommend; it is very portable, very cheap, and equally useful in all climates.

"It is especially valuable in the case of the insects, as they are found everywhere in greater or less numbers; especially in the dwellings, where they are nourished by the carrion that lies about, the heaps of rubbish, the filth of the streets, the leakage of cesspools and sewers, the dirt in the houses, the filthy clothing worn by the people, and the kind of food they eat. Though the country of Baalzebub is deserted and enslaved, the flies are still abundant and free, self-invited guests at the table, unasked assistants in the kitchen, tasting everything, immolating themselves in their gastronomic ardour, and forming an undesired seasoning in every dish."

GNATS.

The Gnat of Scripture—Straining out the Gnat and swallowing the camel, a typographical error—Probable identity of the Gnat and the mosquito.

It has already been stated that only one species of fly is mentioned by name in the Scriptures. This is the Gnat, the name of which occurs in the familiar passage, "Ye blind guides, which strain at a gnat and swallow a camel" (Matt. xxiii. 24).

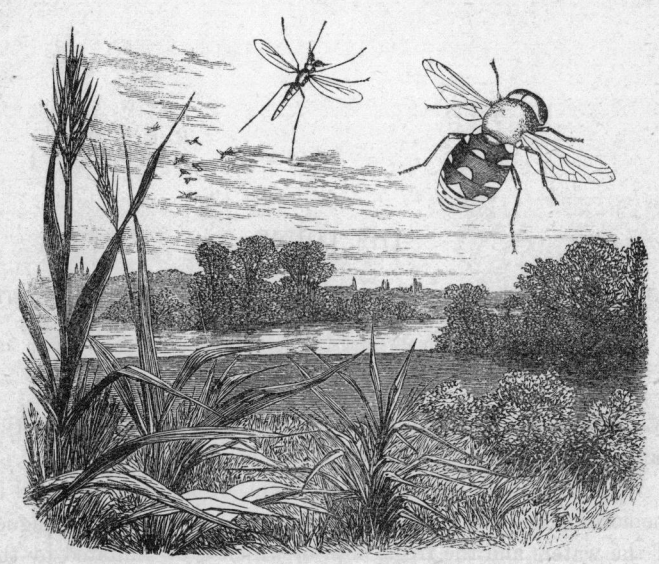

NOXIOUS FLIES OF PALESTINE.

MOSQUITO.   CAMEL FLY.

I may again mention here that the words "strain at" ought to have been printed "strain out," the substitution of one for the other being only a typographical error. The allusion is made to a custom which is explained by reference to the preceding article on the fly. In order to avoid taking flies and other insects into the mouth while drinking, a piece of thin linen stuff was placed over the cup, so that if any insects, as was usually the case, had got into the liquid, they would be "strained out" by the linen.

Whether or not any particular species of insect was signified by the word "gnat" is very doubtful, and in all probability the word is only used to express the contrast between the smallest known insects and the largest known beasts. Gnats, especially those species which are popularly known by the word "mosquito," are very plentiful in many parts of Palestine, especially those which are near water, and are as annoying there as in other lands which they inhabit.

THE LOUSE.

Insect parasites—The plague of Lice—Its effect on the magicians or priests—The Hebrew word *Chinnim*—Probability that it may be represented by "tick"—Habits of the ticks, their dwellings in dust, and their effects on man and beast.

WE close the history of insects mentioned in Scripture with two parasites of a singularly disagreeable character.

With respect to the former of them, we find it mentioned in the account of the great plagues of Egypt. After the two plagues of the waters and the frogs, both of which were imitated by the magicians, *i.e.* the priests, a third was brought upon Egypt, which affected the magicians even more than the people, for a reason which we shall presently see :—

" And the Lord said unto Moses, Say unto Aaron, Stretch out thy rod, and smite the dust of the land, that it may become lice, throughout all the land of Egypt.

" And they did so; for Aaron stretched out his hand with his rod, and smote the dust of the earth, and it became lice in man and in beast; all the dust of the land became lice throughout all the land of Egypt.

"And the magicians did so with their enchantments to bring forth lice, but they could not: so there were lice upon man and upon beast."

Now it is hardly possible to conceive a calamity which would have told with greater effect upon the magicians, by whose advice Pharoah had resisted the requests of Moses and Aaron.

Living in a land where all, from the highest to the lowest, were infested with parasites, the priests were so much in advance of the laity that they were held polluted if they harboured one single noxious insect upon their persons, or in their clothing. The clothing, being linen, could be kept clean by frequent washing, while the possibility of the body being infested by parasites was prevented by the custom of shaving the whole of the body, from the crown of the head to the sole of the foot, at least once in every three days.

It may easily be imagined, therefore, how terrible this visitation must have been to such men. As swine to the Pharisee, as the flesh of cattle to the Brahmin, so was the touch of a parasite to the Egyptian priest. He was degraded in his own estimation and in that of his fellows. He could perform no sacred offices: so that, in fact, all the idolatrous worship of Egypt ceased until this particular plague had been withdrawn.

We now come to a consideration of the insect which is signified by the Hebrew word *chinnim*. Sir Samuel Baker is of opinion that the word ought to have been translated as "ticks," and for the following reasons:—

After quoting the passage which relates to the stretching of Aaron's rod over the dust, and the consequence of that action, he proceeds as follows: "Now the louse that infests the human body and hair has no connexion whatever with dust, and, if subjected to a few hours' exposure to the dry heat of the burning sand, it would shrivel and die. But a tick is an inhabitant of the dust, a dry horny insect, without any apparent moisture in its composition. It lives in hot sand and dust, where it cannot possibly obtain nourishment until some wretched animal should lie down upon the spot, and become covered with these horrible vermin.

"I have frequently seen dry desert places so infested with

ticks that the ground was perfectly alive with them, and it would have been impossible to have rested upon the earth. In such spots, the passage in Exodus has frequently seemed to me as bearing reference to these vermin, which are the greatest enemy to man and beast. It is well known that from the size of a grain of sand, in their natural state, they will distend to the size of a hazel nut after having preyed for some days on the body of an animal."

Granting that this suggestion be the correct one, as it certainly is the most consistent both with actual facts and with the words of Holy Writ, the plague would lose none of its intensity, but would, if anything, be more horrible. Only those who have suffered from them can appreciate the miseries caused by the attack of these ticks, which cling so tightly that they can scarcely be removed without being torn in pieces, and without leaving some portion of their head beneath the skin of their victim. Man and beast suffer equally from them, as is implied in the words of Scripture, and, unless they are very cautiously removed, painful and obstinate is the result of their bites.

THE FLEA.

Prevalence of the Flea in the East, and the annoyance caused by them to travellers—Fleas of the Lebanon—The Bey's bedfellows—The Pasha at the bath—Use of the word in Scripture.

THIS active little pest absolutely swarms in the East. The inhabitants are so used to the Fleas that either the insects do not touch them, or by long custom they become so inured to their attack that the bites are not felt.

But every traveller in Eastern lands has a tale to tell about the Fleas, which seem to be accepted as one of the institutions of the country, and to be contemplated with perfect equanimity. Miss Rogers, for example, in her "Domestic Life in Palestine," mentions how she was obliged to stand upon a box in order to be out of the reach of a large company of Fleas that were hopping about on the floor!

Mr. Urquhart, experienced Orientalist as he was, found on one occasion that the Fleas were too strong for him. He had forgotten his curtain, and was invaded by armies of Fleas, that marched steadily up the bed and took possession of their prey. The people were quite amused at his complaints, and said that their Bey could not sleep without a couple of hundred of them in his bosom. Mr. Urquhart suggests that these little creatures act as a wholesome irritant to the skin, and says that the last two mouthfuls of every meal are for the benefit of the Fleas.

In order to show the perfect indifference with which the presence of these little pests is regarded, I quote a passage from Mr. Farley's "Druses of the Lebanon." He was in a Turkish bath, and was much amused at a scene which presented itself.

"A man, whose skin resembled old discoloured vellum, was occupying himself with the somewhat undignified pursuit of pursuing with great eagerness something that, from the movement of his hands, seemed continually to elude him, jumping about and taking refuge in the creases and folds of his shirt, that was spread out over his lap as he sat cross-legged on his bedstead like a tailor on his board. This oddity was no less a dignitary than a Pasha."

SCORPION.

THE SCORPION.

The Scorpions of Palestine—Habits of the Scorpion—Dangers of mud walls—Venom of the Scorpion—Scorpions at sea—The Scorpion whip, and its use—The Scorpion Pass.

SCORPIONS are exceedingly common in Palestine, and to a novice are a constant source of terror until he learns to be accustomed to them. The appearance of the Scorpion is too well known to need description, every one being aware that it is in reality a kind of spider that has the venom claw at the end of its body, and not in its jaw. As to the rendering of the word *akrabbim* as "Scorpions," there has never been any doubt.

These unpleasant creatures always manage to insinuate themselves in some crevice, and an experienced traveller is cautious where the Scorpions are plentiful, and will never seat himself in the country until he has ascertained that no Scorpions are beneath the stones on or near which he is sitting. Holes in walls are favourite places of refuge for the Scorpion, and are very plentiful, the mud walls always tumbling down in parts, and affording homes for Scorpions, spiders, snakes, and other visitors.

The venom of the Scorpion varies much in potency according to the species and size of the creature, some of the larger Scorpions being able to render a man ill for a considerable time, and even to kill him if he should be a sensitive subject. So much feared were the Scorpions that one of the chief privileges of the Apostles and their immediate followers was their immunity from the stings of Scorpions and the bite of venomous serpents.

It is said, however, that after a person has been stung once by a Scorpion, he suffers comparatively little the second time, and that if he be stung three or four times, the only pain that he suffers arises from the puncture. Sailors also say that after a week at sea the poison of the Scorpion loses its power, and that they care nothing for the Scorpions which are sure to come on board inside the bundles of firewood.

Those passages which mention the venom of the Scorpion are numerous, though most, if not all, of them occur in the New Testament. See Rev. ix. 5: "And to them it was given that they should not kill them, but that they should be tormented five months, and their torment was as the torment of a scorpion, when he striketh a man." Also ver. 10 of the same chapter: "And they had tails like unto scorpions: and there were stings in their tails: and their power was to hurt men five months."

There is, also, the well-known saying of our Lord, "If a son shall ask an egg, will he offer him a scorpion?" (Luke xi. 12.) And in the preceding chapter of the same Evangelist Scorpions are classed with serpents in their power of injury: "Behold, I give unto you power to tread on serpents and scorpions, and over all the power of the enemy; and nothing shall by any means hurt you."

THERE is another reference to the Scorpion in the Old Testament, which requires an explanation. It forms part of the rash counsel given to Rehoboam by his friends: "My father made your yoke heavy, and I will add to your yoke; my father also chastised you with whips, but I will chastise you with scorpions."

The general tenor of this passage is evident enough, namely, that he intended to be far more severe than his father had been. But his words assume a new force when we remember that there was a kind of whip called a Scorpion. This terrible instrument was made for the express purpose of punishing slaves, so that the mere mention of it was an insult. It consisted of several thongs, each of which was loaded with knobs of metal, and tipped with a metal hook, so that it resembled the jointed and hooked tail of the Scorpion. This dreadful instrument of torture could kill a man by a few blows, and it was even used in combats in the amphitheatre, a gladiator armed with a Scorpion being matched against one armed with a spear.

THE SPIDER.

Spiders of Palestine.

THERE are very many species of Spider in Palestine; some which spin webs, like the common Garden Spider, some which dig subterranean cells and make doors in them, like the well-known Trap-door Spider of Southern Europe, and some which have no webs, but chase their prey upon the ground, like the Wolf and Hunting Spiders.

THE HORSE LEECH.

Signification of the word Alukah—Leeches in Palestine—The horse and the Leech.

In Prov. xxx. 15 there is a word which only occurs once in the Scriptures. This is *alukah*, which is translated as horse-leech. "The horseleech hath two daughters, crying, Give, give."

The Leeches are very common in Palestine, and infest the rivers to such an extent that they enter the nostrils of animals who come to drink, and cause great annoyance and even danger. The following anecdote, related by Mr. H. Dixon in his "Holy Land," gives us a good idea of the prevalence of the Leeches, and the tenacity with which they retain their hold :—

"At Beit-Dejan, on a slight twist in the road, we find the wheel and well, and hear a delicious plash and rustle in the troughs. To slip from my seat to dip Sabeah's nose into the fluid is the work of a second; but no sooner has she lapped up a mouthful of water, than one sees that the refuse falling back from her lips into the tank is dabbled and red. Opening her mouth, I find a gorged leech dangling from her gum. But the reptile being swept off, and the mare's nose dipt into the cooling stream, the blood still flows from between her teeth, and, forcing them open, I find two other leeches lodged in the roof of her mouth.

"Poor little beast! how grateful and relieved she seems, how gay, how gentle, when I have torn these suckers from her flesh, and soused the water about her wounds; and how my hunting-whip yearns to descend upon the shoulders of that laughing and careless Nubian slave!"

Persons passing through the river are also attacked by them, and, if they have a delicate skin, suffer greatly.

CORAL.

SPONGE AND CORAL.

Use of the Sponge in Scripture—Probability that the ancient Jews were acquainted with it—Sponges of the Mediterranean—The Coral, and its value—Signification of the word *Ramoth*.

THERE is little to be said on either of these subjects.

Sponge is only mentioned with reference to the events of the Crucifixion, where it is related that a soldier placed a sponge upon hyssop, dipped it in vinegar (*i.e.* the acid wine issued to the Roman soldiers), and held it to the Lord's lips. There is little doubt that the ancient Hebrews were fully aware of the value of the Sponge, which they could obtain from the Mediterranean which skirted all their western coasts.

The Coral is mentioned in two passages of Scripture: "No mention shall be made of coral, or of pearls" (Job xxviii. 18). The second occurrence of the word is in Ezek. xxvii. 16: "They occupied in thy fairs with emeralds, purple, and broidered work, and fine linen, and coral, and agate."

This Coral, which is described as being brought from Syria, was probably that of the Red Sea, where the Coral abounds, and where it attains the greatest perfection.

THE END.

INDEX.

A.

	PAGE
Addax	171–173
Adder	628
Ant	671
agricultural	672
habits of	674
cocoon	675
Aoudad	212–215
Ape	387
brought by Solomon	389
worshipped in India	390–395
Apis	145
Ass	315
domesticated	315
royal	316
treatment of	319
saddle	321
in Cairo	323
uses of	326
wild	328

B.

	PAGE
Badger	96
skins for tabernacle	96–112
Badger skins for robes and sandals	97
nocturnal in habits	100
Barbel, long-headed	639
Bat	401
Bear, Syrian	103
omnivorous	106
a dangerous enemy	108
robbed of whelps	110
mode of fighting	110
Beden	233–237
Bee	664
banded	664
hives	667
honey	667
Behemoth	372
food	376
hunted	380
Bison	160
Bittern	536
haunts waste places	538
cry	538
nest	540
Blue thrush	481
Boer hunting the lion	36–41

INDEX.

	PAGE
Bottles, skin	221–225
Bubale	173–175
Buffalo	149
Bull	142
wild	152
hunted with nets	153

C.

	PAGE
Calf	134
fatted	135
worshipped	146, 148
Camel	248
Arabian	248
Bactrian	248, 286–290
milk of	251
power of carrying water	252
flesh	254
as beast of burden	255–258
riding	259–268
speed	269
malice of	273
food	277–280
foot	280
hair and skin	283
needle's eye	284
Caspian emys	580
hibernates	581
terror to horses	581
legends	582
Cat	52
Cattle	132
Cerastes	624
Chameleon	602
strength of grasp	607
Chameleon, eyes	607
change of color	608
Chamois	211
Chariots	300–311
Chetah	42
Cobra di capello	616
Cockatrice	628
Coney	366
ruminant	368
watchful	370
Coral	695
Cormorant	563
fishing	564
voracious	565
in China	565
nests	566
Coryphene	641
Crane	549
Crocodile	585
description in Job	586
worshipped by Egyptians	589
seizing its prey	592
eggs	595
hunting	598
Cuckoo	487
great spotted	488
Cyprius	602

D.

	PAGE
Deer	238
hunted	244
watchfulness of	244–246
Deloul	268

	PAGE
Dhubb	583
Dishon	171
Dog	55
Dove	489
turtle	489, 496
Noah's	490
in sacrifice	491
carrier	493
blue rock	495
collared turtle	497
palm	497
Barbary	497

E.

	PAGE
Eagle	430
golden	433
short-toed	434
Egret	548
Egyptian mastigure	583
Elephant	349
ivory	349
in war	352
in hunting	362

F.

	PAGE
Falcon, peregrine	445
lanner	445
Fallow deer	173–175
Field-mouse	121–124
Fishes	635–648
apostolic fishermen	635
as food	637

	PAGE
Fishes, manner of catching	643
as symbols	646
Flea	688
Flies	683
god of	684
Frogs	630
plague of	631
green	632
edible	632
Fox	76
plentiful in Palestine	77
feeds upon the slain	78
Samson's foxes	78–85

G.

	PAGE
Gazelle	163
mode of defence	165
manner of capture	166
chase of	166–170
Gecko	605
Gier-eagle	419
Gnats	685
Goad	137
Goat	217
as food	217–219
milking-scene	220
hair for clothing	220
skin bottles	221–225
kneading-troughs	225
scape-goat	226
intractable	227
separated from sheep	227–229

H.

Hamster	124
Hare	126
not a ruminant	127
two species in Palestine	131
Hart	255
Hawk	447
sparrow	448
harrier	451
white	453
dove	453
blue	453
ring-tailed	453
night	462
Herdsmen	144
Arab	177
Heron	542
as food	542
sociable	544
flight	546
nest	547
Hind	255
Hippopotamus	374
Honey	667
Hoopoe	476
legend of	477
Hornet	669
Horse	291
Arab	291
hoofs	295
sale of Arab	296–300
chariots	300
Horse-leech	693
House-top	480

Hyacinthine gallinule	560
Hyæna	85
as scavenger	86–88
haunting graves	88
odour of	89
superstitions concerning	90
Hyrax	366

I.

Ibex	233–236
Ibis, white or sacred	562
Ichneumon	596
Insects	657
Ivory	349–352

J.

Jackal	76
Jerboa	125

K.

Kestrel	449
Kite	440
red	441
black	442
Kneading-troughs	225

L.

Lammergeier	411
food	414

INDEX.

	PAGE
Lammergeier, bone-breaker	414
Lapwing	476
Leopard	42
Leviathan	585
Lion	19
Lizard	602
Locust	657
swarms	658
plague of	660
as food	661
Louse	686
Lump-fish	641

M.

	PAGE
Mole	114
hard to capture	116
frequents ruins	117
food	118
Molluscs	648
Monitor	605
Nilotic	610
land	610
Monkey	387
Mosquito	686
Mouflon	215
Mouse	119
voracity	119
Mule	333
ridden by kings	335
perverse	336
Muræna	639
Moth, clothes	678
silkworm	680

N.

	PAGE
Night-hawk	462
Night-jar	462
cry	464
Nile-perch	647
Nineveh, sculptures of	34

O.

	PAGE
Oryx	154–156
Osprey	436
fishing	436
flight	438
Ossifrage	411
Ostrich	523
neglect of young	526–528
nest in sand	526
chase	529
scent	530
speed	531
as food	532
eggs	534
cry	531
Ounce	42
Owl	454
use in bird-catching	455
little	455
barn	455
screech	456
great	456
Egyptian eagle	458
European eagle	458
Virginian eared	458
Ox	133

INDEX.

	PAGE
Ox, stalled	133
yoke	136
plough	136
goad	137
threshing	138
cart	139
pasturage	141
worshipped	148

P.

	PAGE
Palestine	470
Partridge	505
desert	507
Passover	204
Samaritan	205–210
Peacock	501
Pearl	653
Pelican	567
pouch	569
feeding young	570
legends	570
flight	572
crested	573
Pigeon	489
Plough	136
Porcupine	113
Poultry	498
Purple dye	649
Pygarg	171

Q.

	PAGE
Quail	509
Quail, sent to Israelites	510
flight	511
as food	511
mode of capture	512

R.

	PAGE
Rams' horns	201–203
Raven	516
in ark	516
sent to Elijah	518
notices of, in Talmud	519
ashy-necked	520
in Jerusalem	520

S.

	PAGE
Scheltopusic	603
Scorpion	690
Serpents	613
motion	614
poison	615
sluggish	620
anecdotes of	620
Sheat-fishes	637
Sheep	177
pasturage	177
watering	180
names	186
folds	189–191
dogs	191
broad-tailed	194
uses of	197

INDEX.

	PAGE
Sheep, in sacrifice	203
Shepherds	185
sling	185
care of flock	188
Shephiphon	624
Silkworm	681
Skink	603
Snail	652
Snake, glass	603
dart	616
charmer	617
Sparrow	479
on house-tops	480
value of	483
caught with nets	484
nests	485
tree	486
Spider	692
Sponge	694
Star-gazer	647
Stork	553
sacred	554
migratory	556
care of young	557
black	558
Sucking-fish	640
Surmullet	648
Swallow	466
swift	470, 474
Swan	560
Swine	337
prohibited to Jews	337
hated	338
wild	334

T.

	PAGE
Threshing	138
Tortoise	577
as food	577
slow-motioned	579
Toxicoa	627
Tunny	641

U.

Unicorn	158
a real animal	159

V.

Viper, horned	624
sand	627
Vulture, Egyptian	419
scavengers	421
griffon	423

W.

Wanderoo	395–400
Weasel	92
fond of eggs	94
story of owl and weasel	94
Wild bull	152
goat	233
ass	328
boar	344
Wind-hover	449
Wolf	69

	PAGE		PAGE
Wolf, only mentioned symbolically	69	Wool	199
hunting in packs	71	Worm, crimson	676
fierceness of	71		
special enemy of sheep	72	**Y.**	
tamed by a monk	75	Yoke	136

WITHDRAWN
from
Funderburg Library